EXPANSE

Unbound Book Six

NICOLI GONNELLA

MOUNTAINDALE
PRESS

Dedicated to my patrons, who have supported me since the early days, and without whom none of this would have ever happened quite the same. You folks rock.

CHAPTER ONE

*"The truth of Fire is that it is never satisfied. There is always
more to burn, more to purify. That is why we pair it with Light.
The Light reveals, and the Fire burns the dross away."*
  -Rahven Haim, Master Justiciar,
  Paladin of the Pathless

The yellow-orange grit cut at him as he ran, razors on the wind that split
open the gash at his side again and again. Clouds of it pummeled him,
almost tearing the tattered crimson cloak off his wide, chitin-covered
shoulders. The sands rattled off his armor, blasting thin chunks free with
each new gust, and only his weary use of Chitin Forging kept any of it
whole. The wind shifted, and the cloak at his back twisted and snapped,
flaring open wide enough to display its emblem. A clenched white
gauntlet atop a black shield, all of it superimposed above a golden
sunburst on blood-red cloth. He tossed his horns and snorted, expelling
jets of sand before tucking his head against the wind and pressing on.

Health: 2817/4639

His Health wasn't getting better, and they had almost found him
twice. The sandstorm—furious and loud in a way he felt in his *bones*—
would rage for hours yet, at least. It was cover only a crazy person would
take advantage of; luckily, he'd gone nuts months ago.

"Monster! Unbound!"

A form materialized out of the storm, a tall figure wearing crimson
plate and an identical cloak. A heavy, two-handed sword lifted, ignited,
and golden-orange flame lit the sands. The figure didn't shout anything

else, only charged in a flash of Agility that his Perception couldn't track. Still, he'd fought the Paladins enough to recognize their opening move—it was always the same. A charge and overhand strike.

He dropped his head and took the blow straight to his curved horns. The Paladin gasped.

"You noobs never expect that," he growled.

Then *twisted*.

The Paladin screamed as the greatsword was wrenched from their grasp, its still-flaming blade hurled with a casual jerk of the neck. His hand snapped out, clamping onto the Paladin's helmet and palming it. Yanking them off balance, he slammed them into the shifting dune beneath their feet.

"UAGH!"

The Paladin hit and flared with golden light, flipping themselves to the side even as his mighty stomp collapsed the sands. The over-armored idiot pulled a side sword, a toothpick compared to their usual blades, and charged again. This time, they screamed.

Black-green Mana rolled out of his channels, spearing into the sands. Despite the Paladin's Agility, they never made it into melee range.

Hallow! Now!

A tail made of bone and chitin shot upward from beneath the sands, flashing directly through the Paladin's breastplate. A needle-like tip—as long as a shortsword—stabbed behind the warrior, covered in blood.

"Sick," he said with a queasy swallow. Blood drenched the sands, and the Paladin's Health dropped to nothing.

He winced, his own wounds bleeding again. There wasn't time. *If one found me, then the rest aren't far behind.* Hurriedly, he spread his large hands and let more of that black-green Mana gather from his palms. It coiled, tensing with a purpose he hadn't given it yet. He'd learned this trick through a lot of trial and error, but it worked. Usually.

"Hallowed Rise!" The Mana shot out and down, injecting itself into the Paladin's wounds. Filling them. With agonizing slowness, the corpse twitched and jerked, rising unsteadily to its feet. From within its dented helmet, its once-Human eyes blazed with necrotic energy.

Hallowed Rise is level 34!

"Over here! The creature runs!"

Adrenaline pumped into his veins, and he pivoted on the spot. The sound had come from close by, but directions were hard to judge in the storms. Terror overwhelmed his anger, and he fled.

"With me, you two!" he hissed. Behind him, the ex-Paladin lumbered after with surprising speed, while beneath their feet, a small wave disturbed the sand, following in his wake.

Safety. He knew it was nearby. He only had to make it there alive.

Health: 2343/4639

Dad, he whispered to himself. *Dad, I—I don't want to die.*

————

A discordant yowl tore through his senses, and Felix jerked awake. Through the haze of sleep, he could still hear a faint, thrumming melody on the wind. It was gone in a moment, but not before Felix's Affinity caught impressions of towering sand dunes and a terrible storm.

"Was I a Minotaur?" Felix muttered to himself. It had felt real—extremely so—enough that he checked his own Health.

Health: 7378/7378

He sat up completely, rising from the rock-hard bed, silently praising his Body for its lack of aches and pains. Sleeping on stone like this would have twisted his spine to hell back on Earth. It was dark, the room around him lacking windows, and the one door closed so cleverly it hardly made a seam in the stone. He'd found the chamber after a day of exhausting talking and exploration, the former with his friends and new allies and the latter concerning what remained of the Temple itself. The room he had found was a bedchamber, judging by the empty bed slab that dominated it, though no other furniture survived the Ages. It had been enough.

The bed slab dwarfed him, but Pit slumbered deeply at his side, sized more like a smallish elephant than any dog he'd ever had. Felix scrubbed his face with his hands and smoothed down his wild mane of hair as he swung his feet to the ground.

*That Paladin said "Unbound." And a Minotaur...*A Minotaur was among the seven other Unbound he knew of, the ones he had been shown in his Omen Path. Felix doubted very much it was a coincidence. *Not the way my life is going.*

"Felix. Good morning."

Unfettered Volition!

Corrosive Strike!

Adamant Discord!

All three Skills surged within him, bringing him to his feet while Mana swirled about his fists in clouds of acid and lightning, lighting up his crude bedchamber. A tall, golden-hued figure raised its mismatched hands in a gesture of peace. Even before it spoke again, Felix let his Skills fade.

"Karys. It's early." As he said it, Felix flared his Perception and let it spread beyond his enclosed room and into the Temple itself. His Authority hummed, pushing his awareness even farther so that it swept beyond the Temple and into the forest and river and mountains and—he cut it off. Felix blinked. Nothing seemed much changed from the night before.

Karys stood before him on new legs—a new Body entirely. Felix still hadn't gotten used to the ancient Paragon walking around in the Archon's old armor, but the ten-foot tall body was modified now with pieces of dark iron they'd salvaged from the battlefield. His entire right arm was a smaller version of the left, darker and thinner, but seemed functional enough. The construct had a self-repair function, but it had been gutted when Felix had cleansed the Profane Sigaldry from its chassis. Karys' expertise with Eidolons was all that kept the thing running. He jerked himself into a stilted bow, though the golden helmet that passed for his head never took its eyes off Felix.

"Yes, I apologize for the hour. I know you have exhausted your Stamina and attention since claiming this Territory." Karys took a step closer, clattering only slightly. "But you asked that I awaken you before the day had lapsed."

"Oh," Felix said. "Right. I did."

A day ago, Felix had...acquired, he supposed, the Territory of Nagast. Claiming Authority through a strange array beneath the Temple, he'd taken on a new set of responsibilities as well. Seeing to them, his people as well as his enemies, had taken much of the night and following day. All the while, he was holding off Tempering his Skills, too worried, too concerned that the shadows would contain yet more enemies for him to face.

"If you wait much longer, your Skills will begin to Tier up whether you are ready or not," Karys said.

"I know," Felix said. He brought up his Status.

Name: Felix Nevarre
Level: 56
Race: Primordial of the Unseen Tide (Greater)*
Omen: Magician
Path: Cardinal Fiend
Born Trait: Keen Mind

_____

Health: 7378/7378
Stamina: 6512/6512
Mana: 4909/4909

_____

STR: 1424
PER: 1240
VIT: 1445
END: 1176
INT: 1257
WIL: 1860
AGL: 1142
DEX: 1235

_____

BODY - Calamitous Dawn (Journeyman)
Resistances: The Song of Absolution (L), Level 85

Combat Skills: Dodge (C), Level 63; Heavy Armor Mastery (C), Level 1; Blind Fighting (R), Level 45; Corrosive Strike (R), Level 58; Wild Threnody (E), Level 61

Physical Enhancements: Armored Skin (R), Level 75; Unfettered Volition (E), Level 64

MIND - Fatebreaker (Journeyman)
Mental Enhancements: Deception (C), Level 30; Meditation (U), Level 63; Negotiation (U), Level 26; Bastion of Will (E), Level 74; Deep Mind (E), Level 74; Manifestation of the Coronach (E), Level 63; Ravenous Tithe (E), Level 77

Information Skills: Alchemy (C), Level 32; Tracking (C), Level 30; Exploration (U), Level 53; Voracious Eye (E), Level 73; Aria of the Green Wilds (L), Level 81

SPIRIT - Rising Sovereign (Journeyman)
Spiritual Enhancements: Dual Casting (U), Level 50; Manasight (U), Level 63; Manaship Pilot (R), Level 22; Etheric Concordance (L), Level 74; Sovereign of Flesh (T), Level 74; Unite the Lost (T), Level 49; Fiendforge (Un), Level 1

Spells: Abyssal Skein (R), Level 49; Cloudstep (R), Level 35; Invocation (R), Level 42; Oathbinding (R), Level 35; Shadow Whip (R), Level 46; Stone Shaping (R), Level 68; Mantle of the Infinite Revolution (E), Level 49; Arrow of Perdition (L), Level 40; Cardinal Flame (L), Level 76; Rain of Cataclysm (L), Level 50; Theurgist of the Rise (L), Level 71; Adamant Discord (T), Level 79

Unused Stat Points: 15

Harmonic Stats
RES: 484
INE: 660
AFI: 1446
REI: 732
EVA: 600
MIG: 513
ALA: 845
FEL: 1165

His resource pools had grown tremendously, as had his stats thanks to his new Race and Path. The Skill levels didn't reflect *all* of his gains, however, as his Bastion of Will was currently clamped tight around a handful that were primed to Tier up to Adept.

"Watch over me, please."

"Of course," Karys replied.

Clenching his jaw against the pain, Felix dove down into his core space. He plunged into a sea of darkness punctuated by points of brilliant light. His dual cores—a rarity, apparently—were shaped like two rings made of liquid flame and lightning, stacked atop one another like a sandwich. The red-gold [Cardinal Beast Core] sat atop the blue-white [Thunderflame Core], each spinning in an opposing direction so that they ground against one another, each revolution producing arcs of potent, multi-colored energy.

Between them, where the hole of a ring would be, there was instead an abyss that was darker than the shadows that surrounded them all. It echoed with a hunger that had changed over the months, a willful desire to consume and grow, but one that listened, in a way. *It can be bargained with, at least. That's a lot better than the Maw.*

Pushing through both cores and, somehow, through the abyss, was a branching shape that looked like a tree or veins, depending on the viewer's perspective. It was colored crimson-black and spread both upward and downward, weaving its way into the two Pillars that supported his cores, strengthening them with its power. A Vein of Divinity, the System had called it.

Surrounding all of this was a field of lights that revolved around the center. Like stars, they shone brightly all on their own, convoluted patterns of light and vibration that represented each Skill Felix had learned. Since his defeat of the Archon, they had attained a heft that was not present before, as if the light and sound had gained mass. According to Karys and his friend Harn, it was due to the addition of significance to his core space. It was a solidity of being that came with great power and time, a feature he had stolen outright from the Urges beneath the Temple.

And not the only thing he'd taken.

Above his cores and Skills, a stormy cloud of Essence boiled and flashed. It resembled nothing so much as those nebulas he'd see in colorized space photos or sci-fi movies: a tempest of light and shadow, solar winds and crackling, cosmic energy. That, above all else, was what would help him Temper his Skills.

Below, another painful pulse of sound and pressure swept through him, originating from one of the closest Skills. His Bastion of Will, which resembled an orb of greens and blues while its pattern shifted and thrummed, barely contained the Skill it held back.

Felix stepped back into his body, awareness returning, and let himself stretch. Pit snorted once before falling quiet again, and Felix was careful not to wake his Companion. The guy's day hadn't been any better than his. While his new, bigger form needed less sleep most of the time, eventually they all had to pay the piper. Pit could use a few more hours.

So could I, he thought, before banishing the notion. *No time to sleep. Too much to do.*

"If I do this, I'll be out for hours. What's tomorrow look like?" Felix asked.

"You have a delegation from the Henaari here to see you."

"Really? That was fast. Wyvora only left...six hours ago."

"Mhm. A'zek has remained closed-lipped on the issue, but I believe there are some internal politics at hand."

Felix rolled his eyes. Last thing he wanted to deal with was the politics of the Henaari. "I'm sure they'll love that we imprisoned three of their Dawnguard."

Since Felix had saved them from the Mana well, Ifre and her underlings had been held in a stone-shaped chamber just inside the waterfall Temple, where his people could keep an eye on them. After they had found the wicked dagger in the Archon's chest, it had only taken his Voracious Eye and two seconds of thought to connect them to the Raven and Henaari. They'd attempted to take over his Temple and claim it for the Raven. He was half convinced they'd been told to kill him, too. Ifre, however, wasn't talking.

"Well, that's a problem that can wait. Nothing else?" he asked. After his dream, Felix felt a sense of danger looming over him. A threat he'd forgotten. "Have we heard from Zara?"

"No, and I see no way for her to contact us in such a short amount of time. She was headed in the opposite direction the same time you left, yes?" Felix nodded. "If you had retained the Mark she had placed on you, then perhaps. But the Spirit Tree cleansed that and all the others, too." Karys tilted his golden head. "You are stalling."

"I can't help but feel there's something we missed. Something important. Zara was securing Haarwatch from the Inquisition, and when I enacted the Mirk Enclosure, it *should* have sealed off access to any Territories outside my...my own." Felix licked his lips and began pacing. He had felt the barrier lock into place, similar to the fog that had once given the Foglands their name, but more powerful by far.

Whether that was because of the ancient Nymean array he'd used or because of his Authority, Felix had no idea. What he *did* know was that it wasn't just a smoke screen. The Mirk Enclosure physically prevented people from entering his Territory. "It feels like something is watching me over my shoulder. Waiting for my defenses to drop."

"There are no threats, none that you or your team has not already defeated. Even your former enemies are recovering, and the Haarguard watch them night and day." Karys heaved a metallic-tinged sigh. "You are strained in Mind and Spirit. You need rest, true rest."

"Yeah, well I'll get rest when I'm dead, apparently," Felix said. He blew a short, powerful blast of air through his nostrils. It was forceful enough that it kicked up dust in his chamber. "Fine. Then I'll begin. You will...still watch over me?"

"Of course." He was kind enough not to mention that Felix was repeating himself.

Felix took another deep breath, flaring Meditation, and attempted to steady his thudding heart. He sat down cross-legged on the floor and dove into his core space once more.

CHAPTER TWO

Felix seized his Bastion within the prongs of his Intent, an intangible limb that was exactly what it sounded like: a tool to enact his desires. He loosened his hold on the Skill, and it spasmed, a muscle contracted for too long and a thousand times as painful. Energy burst and flared from within, giving him glimpses of a citadel and landscape inundated in multi-colored light.

He received his notifications.

Invocation is level 43!
...
Invocation is level 58!
Journeyman Tier!
You Gain:
+7 INT
+7 WIL
+7 FEL

Caught up in the general press of his Bastion, Invocation had been held back from his recent advancements. It burned a bit as System energy fed into his core space, but nothing greater than usual. A Journeyman Skill was the least of his worries.

The bundle of blaring sound and skittering lightning, however, had his attention.

Aria of the Green Wilds is level 81!
Adept Tier!
You Gain:

+15 PER
+15 AFI
+15 FEL

Adamant Discord is level 79!
Adept Tier!
You Gain:
+15 AFI
+15 INE
+...

Cardinal Flame is level 76!
Adept Tier!
You Gain:
+15 INT
+15 PER
+...

Ravenous Tithe is level 82!
Adept Tier!
You Gain:
+10 STR
+10 END
+...

Bastion of Will is level 84!
Adept Tier!
You Gain:
+10 WIL
+10 ALA
+...

Theurgist of the Rise is level 72!
...
Theurgist of the Rise is level 79!
Adept Tier!
You Gain:
+50 INT
+50 INE
...
The Song of Absolution is level 85!
Adept Tier!
You Gain:
+50 EVA
+50 FEL
+...

He'd already seen the last, but not the Adept Tier bonuses for the Song of Absolution, nor all the rest. Felix let the surge of System energy hit his cores again, consumed by the flames of his dual rings and expelled once more as red-gold and blue-white light. The energy shook at him, but it wasn't enough to interrupt his concentration. His Will was laser-focused on the next step.

Multiple Essence Sources Detected During Formation!
Choose An Essence Mote!

From above, in his flashing cloud of Essence, brilliant lights dropped out like hailstones. One-by-one, they dropped before him, stopping in his eyesight with claps of thunder, and he knew them.

[Essence of Iterated Annihilation]
[Essence of Corrosion's Touch]
[Essence of Glorious Bounty]
[Essence of the Sheltering Hand]
[Essence of Consonant Influence]
[Essence of Malediction]
[Essence of the Forbidden Elderscript]
[Essence of the Relinquished Heart]
[Essence of Spirit's Bulwark]
[Essence of Earthen Panoply]

Felix goggled at them all. Their number was a touch surprising, but that wasn't it: each one of the Essence Motes were Legendary Ranked. He sensed that many were stolen from the Urges, but a few had the feel of other sources. Specifically, his Spirit Tree...and the Archon himself.

Visions of the Archon's defeat flashed through his Mind, replayed with perfect fidelity thanks to his Keen Mind Born Trait. His use of Unite the Lost and Karys' aid had kicked him out of his armored shell and regrown his mortal Body. He had shoved a Spirit Seed into his gullet and germinated it with stolen power. The man had detonated, rendered into paste by the explosive growth of root and trunk, fertilizer for his new Spirit Tree.

He had thought he'd spent a good chunk of the significance and Essence he'd stolen from the six monstrous Urges and the Mana well. Yet, each sacrifice in that battle had netted him a greater store, a reward perhaps for doing what the System had long desired.

Maybe. Either way, this is more than I expected. He smiled. It was more than enough to Temper his available Skills to Adept Tier. At Journeyman Tier, the Essence Motes chosen had an impact upon the Skills they were used upon, often influencing their growth in subtle or overt ways. It was supposedly even more pronounced at Adept Tier. Felix had to be careful about his choices, as they could affect him for months or years to come.

Taking a calming breath, he started with the last—The Song Of Absolution—feeling at the Essences for one that sang to him and his Skill. *There!*

Legendary Essence Detected During Formation!
[Essence of Iterated Annihilation]

Broken Path and Fatebreaker Titles Found!
Adept Tier Bonus Added!
Calculating Effects...

Choose A Feature:
Persevere - Persist Beyond
Extirpate - The Root Of It
Advance - Step Toward It

Felix was surprised at the connection between his Song of Absolution and the Essence Mote, and more so by the features unveiled by the System. The Mote felt so...violent and relentless; it was clearly from one of the Urges. His Intelligence flared at the same time his Perception did, increasing his cognition while the world—even his core space—slowed down by a good margin. Felix felt at the threads of thrumming Harmony that stretched taut between his Skill and the Essence Mote. Then it came to him, a swirl of thought among a hundred others: his Song of Absolution was also relentless, a metaphysical wall between Felix and harm. Perhaps he did understand it.

Selecting the right feature was simply a matter of relying upon his senses and instincts. He had owned the Song for a long time, and the Skill was not attuned to the root of annihilation. It was about resistance, forging a way past the threats in his way. Likewise, as foolhardy as he'd been before, Felix wasn't one to step toward annihilation willingly—yet when it came for him, he would continue.

Congratulations!
You Have Absorbed The Essence Of [Persevere]!

Harmony and Dissonance warred through him, castoff sparks between the grinding surfaces of his two core rings. Felix gritted his teeth against the assault, but held as the convoluted pattern of the Song of Absolution lit with brilliant, carmine flame and crackling lightning. It swelled, growing beyond itself as threads of those same energies anchored it to his dual cores. Felix felt a thrum through his entire being as the ribbons secured themselves: the first of his Adept Tempers.

One down, five to go. He grimaced and chose the next Essence Mote, this one for Theurgist of the Rise.

Legendary Essence Detected During Formation!
[Essence of Forbidden Elderscript]

Broken Path and Fatebreaker Titles Found!
Adept Tier Bonus Added!
Calculating Effects...

Choose A Feature:
Proscribe - Ineffable Cipher
Atavistic - Untold Precursor
Calligraphy - Illicit Beauty

The resonance between the [Essence of Forbidden Elderscript] and his sigaldry Skill was too obvious to be wrong, though Felix double-checked anyway. He could tell this wasn't from an Urge, but the Archon instead; one of two, he sensed. That made him pause for only a moment before forging ahead regardless. The Archon—Merodach—had been driven insane by isolation and his Mind and Spirit being shattered and splintered. However, the Essence Motes derived from his form bore power, echoes of the invention of a twisted sigaldry the man had invented in Ages past. The first and last features spoke to that Skill—Profane Sigaldry—and Felix shied away from them without pause. He had no desire to tread upon that path.

Congratulations!
You Have Absorbed The Essence Of [Atavistic]!

Again, his Skill shone bright with powerful energies, and the opposing forces of Harmony and Dissonance warred against one another. Threads of fire and lightning leaped across the dark to supplant those cast by his Journeyman Formation. Those that remained seemed dim and wan in contrast. The Adept Tier threads were brilliant beams of sparking power trembling with unspent potential.

Felix felt a rising urgency push through his limbs and core. It was nameless and apparently sourceless, and he shrugged it off with a flare of his Willpower.

Next was his Bastion of Will.

Legendary Essence Detected During Formation!
[Essence of Consonant Influence]

Broken Path and Fatebreaker Titles Found!
Adept Tier Bonus Added!
Calculating Effects...

Choose A Feature:

Solo - Sing For One
Harmony - Sing Together
Polyphony - Sing As One

Knowing his Bastion, the literal fortress within his Mind, Felix was a touch surprised again that it was *this* Essence Mote that harmonized so completely with the Skill. He had anticipated using the [Essence of Spirit's Bulwark], but perhaps that was too obvious. As it stood, the options for features with this Mote couldn't be more clear.

Consonance, from what he recalled, meant a combination of notes that sounded pleasant. While that could be played Solo, it was Harmony that Felix was after. Yet...the last called to him. Sing Together and Sing As One seemed close enough as to be indistinguishable, but the last feature suggested not just harmony...but unity. If Solo was for a singular being, then Polyphony was for multiple beings working as one.

My tower, he recalled. In the center of his Bastion, there was a fortress of dark stone. In the middle of *that*, there was a five-sided tower. At its top was a silver spire tangled with nigh-invisible threads. On three of its five sides, the patterns of other Skills were etched: Unfettered Volition, Deep Mind, and Meditation. Working together, those four Skills had proven to safeguard his Mind and Spirit, for all that Unfettered Volition was a Body Skill. Regardless, if he were to have them work better as one, then all of his Skills would benefit. Right?

Certainty flooded Felix's Mind, though he couldn't be sure why. More instincts, perhaps.

Congratulations!
You Have Absorbed The Essence Of [Polyphony]!

His Bastion quaked, shook by the energies it was subsumed within. It grew, larger than ever before, the shape of it deepening in a way that Felix could feel but couldn't quantify. Unlike his previous two Skills, the growth of his Bastion was stark—it expanded until it was twice the size of its nearest neighbor. Almost as large as his Transcendent Skills, though it was only Epic. Lightning and fire coursed across its pattern, sounding the vibrations of it as more cacophony was cast off from his cores.

And yet...Felix paused, expecting pain and finding less than before. The fight between Dissonance and Harmony—a key feature of his core space—had barely ruffled his feathers, so to speak. The grinding sparks of his two cores meeting were still casting off those sounds, but now they seemed fuller, more complete. Dissonance wasn't an atonal burr, and Harmony wasn't a gorgeous parade of chords. As his Bastion had expanded, the...influence of his [Essence of Consonant Influence] appeared to affect more of his core space.

That's encouraging...is it because my Bastion is linked to more than one Skill? They, too, had grown as Bastion had, though not as much. Deep Mind,

Meditation, and Unfettered Volition, none were ready to Tier up yet, but they also appeared more powerfully present than before. He would find out when the time came, he decided, and pushed forward.

Ravenous Tithe next. He braced himself, followed his senses, and chose.

Legendary Essence Detected During Formation!
[Essence of Glorious Bounty]

Broken Path and Fatebreaker Titles Found!
Adept Tier Bonus Added!
Calculating Effects...

Choose A Feature:
Endow - Gift Of Life
Wergild - Price Of Life
Meed - Just Rewards

Options curled through Felix's Mind, assessing and comparing. Just Rewards felt odd and compulsory, while the Price of Life was darker than Felix liked. The Gift of Life, however, seemed promising. Coupled with the normal effects of his Ravenous Tithe, that one seemed to offer the most benefit.

Life, he mused. *Life would be a nice change of pace from all the death I've brought about.*

Congratulations!
You Have Absorbed The Essence Of [Endow]!

Cacophony and euphony warred briefly around his cores, then fire and lightning slammed into Ravenous Tithe, securing a tether of power around its pattern. Despite the new changes to his core space, his Skill bucked and shook, seized in a paroxysm of vibrations. Pain lanced across Felix's Aspects, enough to overwhelm his Song of Absolution for the briefest of moments.

Followed by a triumphant trilling and a series of blue boxes.

Based On Your Experiences And Achievements, Ravenous Tithe is Evolving!
Calculating...

System energy poured from beyond his core space, flooding like waves at midnight, crashing into his cores and immediately redirecting toward his Ravenous Tithe. The humming increased in volume and pitch, accompanied by an agony that stabbed through Felix's throat and jaw. He screamed, or tried to, but no sound emerged, only pained wheezing.

And then, without fanfare, it was over.

Ravenous Tithe (Epic) Has Become Chthonic Tribute (Legendary)!
Skill Has Retained Its Level!

Chthonic Tribute (Legendary), Level 82!
In the darkest depths, you shall find the brightest glories. Consume completely any object or creature you have claimed, gaining greater rewards from them. Uses Mana to power conversion. Greater chance of gaining Skills and/or Memories from target if applicable.

That's...fuck, that hurt. He looked over his new Skill, now twice the size of its last iteration. *It doesn't even look like it changed? Wait. The bit about physically touching is gone. That's...good, I guess.* Felix had skirted around that requirement anyway, using his Adamant Discord to count as contact, and it had been working fine. What this meant, however, he was unsure. *Greater rewards sound good, though. That, paired with my new Path, means I might be seeing a lot more Skills and Memories coming my way.*

Felix couldn't let himself get bogged down on the details yet. There would be time enough for that later. He kept moving. *Two more to go. Cardinal Flame.*

Legendary Essence Detected During Formation!
[Essence of Corrosion's Touch]

Broken Path and Fatebreaker Titles Found!
Adept Tier Bonus Added!
Calculating Effects...

Choose A Feature:
Dissolution - End It
Fragment - Break It
Consume - Take It

This Essence, at least, made sense to him. Cardinal Flame was still a bit of a mystery to Felix, having only recently evolved, but it had proven exceptionally useful. Moreover, it was clearly tied to his [Cardinal Beast Core], so Tempering it would likely gain him more benefits down the road.

The Skill had dual uses: Mana control (both internal and external) and as an attack. As an offensive feature, Dissolution or Fragment seemed ideal, but for its controlling aspects, it was concerning. The last thing he wanted was to have an array he was constructing break apart or end. Felix knew the definitions of these Essences weren't always so literal, but he'd done this enough to get a feel for their Intent.

Cardinal Beast, Cardinal Flame, all of it connected to the Primordials. To the Maw. Felix took a steadying breath. *Consume it is.*

Congratulations!
You Have Absorbed The Essence Of [Consume]!

Same as before, light and sound and threads of connection forged between his cores and the Skill. The red-gold flames latched on perhaps a touch brighter than the lightning, but it was all so smooth and seamless that Felix barely blinked and it was done. Tempered.

Trying not to look a gift horse in the mouth, Felix moved to his last. *Adamant Discord.*

Legendary Essence Detected During Formation!
[Essence of the Relinquished Heart]

Broken Path and Fatebreaker Titles Found!
Adept Tier Bonus Added!
Calculating Effects...

Choose A Feature:
Forswear - Repudiate Mercy
Passion - Fervor Diverted
Pith - Vital Burden

This *is what my Skill resonates with?* Felix could hardly believe it. At a glance, he knew who this Essence had come from, and he would have rather had the Urge of Spite's influence over the Archon's. But Felix couldn't deny that his Affinity identified the [Essence of the Relinquished Heart] as the best option. *Why?*

As far as features went, the first was immediately out. Forswearing or repudiating mercy were not things Felix was comfortable interring as part of his being. Passion was an option, but "fervor diverted" felt proscriptive, as if the feature were extolling the opposite of passion. Or maybe that was only a redirection of passions; either way, it was not a choice Felix felt happy about taking. The last was better, as pith was the essence or core of something. That was a detail he could work with, though the addition of a vital burden was heavier than he liked.

However, as soon as he read the option, he knew it to be the right one. What was his Adamant Discord, if not a burden he had to bear? All those connections he could feel, even now, weighed on him. And burden was both what he carried as well as his capacity. Felix was strong, and his Skills were powerful, but that unease ate at him still. A threat loomed over him still, nameless and faceless, and Felix would be ready.

Congratulations!

You Have Absorbed The Essence Of [Pith]!

Light and sound inundated him. Blue-white lightning dominated, lashing against his Adamant Discord and followed shortly after by red-gold flames. The Essence sank within Felix's Skill, merging with it instantly as all the others, a concussive blast shaking his entire core space.

3 of 3 Spirit Essences Formed!
Tempering Has Begun!

No matter the newfound changes to the sounds in his core space, pain lashed against him, and Felix fought back screams. The pain was a distraction he had been expecting at this point, and it was one he couldn't afford to indulge. He focused instead on spinning his cores and letting the System power wash through him. And it did, as a tsunami of colorless energy swelled out of the black from all directions. Skills after Skills were subsumed, until the wall of water hit his spinning cores with a hiss and scream that burst blood vessels all around Felix's Body. His Mind quaked, his senses whitened, and his Spirit felt as if it were being torn apart.

Torn apart and remade.

As ineffable as his Spirit Aspect was, the transcendent anguish was very much not. It burned and froze him as pieces were reforged into...something. Something greater, he hoped in moments of lucidity.

Something—

———

Some time later, Felix woke up on the cold stone of his dusty room. He blinked gritty eyes up at the looming form of Karys.

"Good morning, Felix."

Everything hurt, from his toes to his hair, and Felix didn't bother getting up. "How long was I out?" His voice was hoarse, as if he'd torn it screaming. He likely had.

"It has been six hours since you began your Tempering. Remarkably quick, I must say."

"Quick? My other Temperings only took a few minutes, maybe an hour?" Felix worked his jaw. It felt like it had been shattered and put back together, and when he quested around his mouth, Felix found two molars that he'd broken apart. He spat them out, new ones already regrowing in their place. They'd be good as new in a couple hours, he figured.

"That is for the lower Formations. It gets harder with each advancement, though it isn't a smooth progression. Master Tier is far, far harder than this." Karys reached his dull iron arm out and helped Felix to his feet. "But then, you are an exception to most rules, Unbound."

Felix grunted noncommittally. "I don't envy the others for their advancements, then." As he centered himself, the aches and pains faded from Felix's awareness while his Song of Absolution rose. He sighed in relief and focused on his notifications.

There was only one.

Congratulations!
You Have Tempered Your Spirit!

You Have Formed: the Eldercrowned Spirit
+50 WIL
+100 INT
+50 RES
+40 INE
+40 ALA

"Hell. Yes." Felix took a sharp breath through his nose, feeling the System empower his stats once more. He grinned. "Now *that's* how you start a new day."

"Indeed. There are tasks I must accomplish before the others wake. If you will excuse me, Autarch?"

"Karys, no. Don't...the title is weird. It's just Felix."

The metal man hesitated before he nodded. "Very well, if only in private."

Felix sighed as the former Paragon left his room. *Just a few more tasks, myself,* he thought as he settled back onto the slab of a bed. Quests, Titles, there were some things he'd had to put on the back burner while the chaos of battle had settled.

First up, my Champion of the Halcyon Title, and its bonuses....

CHAPTER THREE

Felix took the steps six at a time, and thankfully, the reinforced stone held. He'd found the stairs shortly before finding the chambers he'd spent the night in, deep in the sundered cliff. Access to them was warded, much as the stairs leading down into the Mana well had been, but that meant little to him. The sword at his side saw to that.

"The array is quiet," Karys was saying, his voice buzzing through the same sword. "But that is where I believe you must go."

"That makes sense," Felix said, speeding up the long flights with only some of his massive Agility with his prize tucked beneath an arm. He could have moved faster but feared that pressing his Agility to its limit would break something or someone. As it was, the intricate lacework stone flashed past him in a blur, and a gust fairly howled behind him. "That array is...weird."

"It is just as I remember them, Felix," Karys said. "Perhaps it is not the array that is odd."

He couldn't agree. The array, which was at the center of his Temple, was entirely too helpful to be normal. When he'd accepted System Authority over the Territory of Nagast, it hadn't obfuscated or denied him information. Instead, it had been relatively transparent. Felix swept through empty room after empty room, chambers that were bare of any decoration or furniture that might have hinted at their prior use. He suspected the cliff, itself quite huge, was honeycombed with similar spaces that had once been part of the Temple. Now, it was his.

It was all very strange.

Twenty minutes prior, Felix had made use of his Champion of the Halcyon Title, reaping the rewards he had forgotten to claim in all the hubbub after the Archon's death.

Champion of the Halcyon (Epic)!
By fist and fury, you have defeated multiple enemies of the ancient Halcyon Empire, so thoroughly that not even their Essence remains to taint the Continent. For this, you are to be commended and rewarded.
+5 Levels To One Body Skill Of Your Choice (Below Adept)
+Evolution Of One Body Skill Of Your Choice (Below Adept)

As much as he had wished to see if there was a rarity above Transcendent, the Title wouldn't let him use the bonus on Sovereign of Flesh, as that would put it into Adept Tier. His choices were limited, but not necessarily worse. His Body, which was remarkably sturdy as it was, lagged behind the power of his Spirit and even Mind. Felix was planning to correct that and focused on his next best choice.

Unfettered Volition is level 65!
...
Unfettered Volition is level 69!

The Title bonus had sunk into his core space, a strange feeling that Felix hadn't had the dubious pleasure of experiencing before. It slipped through the dark and right into his Unfettered Volition, setting it spinning wildly with a direct influx of colorless System energy.

Based On Your Experiences And Achievements, Unfettered Volition is Evolving!
Calculating...

The Skill swelled, its pattern of etched light rotating more and more rapidly. Its song, which Felix had grown quite used to changed pitch and timbre, deepening and filling out in a way that sent tingles across his scalp. Power from his own core responded, sparking from his grinding rings and shooting straight at the Skill, soaking it in sound and light.

Unfettered Volition (Epic) Has Become Relentless Resolution (Legendary)!
Skill Has Retained Its Level!

Relentless Resolution (L), Level 69!
You have learned to harness the power of Dissonance and Harmony both. Now you move those chords in a dance of your own reckoning. Consumes Mana and Stamina when activated.

Speed is increased by a moderate amount per level. Consumption of mental strength is reduced a small amount per level.

The Skill roared, an unstoppable train barreling toward anything that opposed it. Snatches of its song, its pattern, took root in his Body, and it made him want to run and dance. To *move*.

Instead, he focused on his completed Quest, the rewards for which he'd put off during the chaos of the last day.

Quest Completed!
Home Sweet Home!
You have secured your ancestors' Temple from all threats, internal and external!
5 of 5 Threats Eliminated
Rewards:
+Title
+Stronghold
+1 Platinum Chest

First, the Title.

New Title!
Sheltered (Rare)!
You have established a Home upon the Continent! A 5% bonus to all regenerations while resting for at least two glasses within your Home, and you will grow less hungry or thirsty while within the bounds of it. Title will increase proportionally with the strength of your Home.

That would've been useful about fifty levels and several mega monsters ago, Felix groused, though he couldn't have completed the Quest any faster. *What did that last bit mean about the "strength of your Home?"*

His musings were cut short, however, by a sudden growl and chime. The sound shook his core space, sending ripples that almost threw Felix out of the place entirely.

What the hell?

Stretching up from between the double-stacked rings of his cores was a trunk half again as thick as those cores, textured as true bark but colored a crimson-black that shone wetly in the light of his core space. It was the Vein of Divinity, the one that had poked from the depths of his cores and abyss both. The piece of the divine that Felix had stolen from a goddess…and it was bigger than ever.

What is it doing?

The trunk extended both ways, above his cores and below. Underneath, it spread out into fine roots that tangled further with the Pillars he had been developing, a fine net that enmeshed the two extant Pillars in a way that he hoped strengthened them. Above the dual rings, the trunk extended for a good distance before branching out once more...directly into the clouds of Essence that hovered above his core space.

It reminded him of a tree with cloud-like, nebula leaves and festooned with flashing, multicolored lights. Those bright lights were the Essence Motes and Memories he'd taken from various entities like Vvim and Karys, all of which were fixed in place by a portion of Felix's Will. He wasn't willing to part with any of them until he had to, but luckily his Will and core space was refined enough to allow him such luxuries. It would make Tempering very useful in the near future.

There were dozens of others, hanging like fruit on the new growth, but many were...rotten. Felix didn't much care how he knew that, only that it was true. Most were Memories taken from the Urges he'd consumed, and even letting his gaze roll across them filled him with revulsion and a distinct need to bathe.

Below him, the abyss—the darkness at the center of his two spinning core rings—gnawed ineffectually at the crimson bark of the Vein of Divinity—Tree of Divinity now, he supposed. Its hunger was constant and frankly somewhat annoying, but Felix had promised it a meal of a monster in exchange for its good behavior. It felt like a monstrous, unseen pet...one he could not trust not to eat everything if it were let loose. If it even could be. Felix believed it to be the Hunger he had inherited from the Maw and had since conquered...but even a Primordial's Hunger was too strong to truly die.

The Memories were vile things he had no interest in seeing or experiencing, and it was almost a relief to hurl them down into the black. The abyss devoured them gleefully, though it had no face with which to emote. Felix just felt it in a way that wasn't dissimilar to his bond with Pit.

Shaking his head, Felix had emerged from his core space to find the tenku in question staring at him curiously.

"Hey bud, you sleep well?"

Pit warbled in the positive, but ended it with a questioning trill. The tenku could speak into his mind with words when he wanted to, but he preferred to send flashes of sense-images to convey his meaning.

"I was Tempering myself and taking care of some...undesirables," Felix said. Pit's large, golden eyes flicked to a portion of the room that was entirely empty. "What is it?"

An approach, he sent back.

Before Felix could ask what that meant, the air around that portion of the room *twisted*. A chest of shimmering silver and blue appeared out of nothing, plonking to the floor with a thud that Felix could feel through his legs. It was huge, easily four feet across and two feet deep and made entirely of smooth metal, without rivets or fasteners of any kind. Exactly like the other chests he'd seen, though those were different colors.

"The Platinum Chest," he murmured. "Right."

He'd received a Silver Chest before, had almost gotten Gold, too, but

Cal took that when she became the Lady Haarwatch. She never did tell him what was inside it. In fact, the Quest "Enemy of the State," the one Cal had issued to all of them, had promised a Gold Chest at its end. Felix and his team didn't see any benefit from it, but it *had* disappeared, indicating it had been resolved. Hopefully by Zara.

Pit put his beak right in Felix's ear, making him jump. Felix laughed. He was letting himself get distracted. He had loot to check. Pit trilled in agreement.

Felix crossed the room in a blink, stirring the dust in the far corners, and threw open the lid. It had no latch or seam, but it opened easily at his touch, revealing a plush, velvet-lined interior. Three objects were nestled within.

"A...jumpsuit?" Felix asked as he pulled a length of shimmering cloth from the Chest. It featured a top and bottom fashioned into a single, gaudy outfit, but the cut and styling was strange and asymmetrical. Beside it, however, were more promising finds. "A jewel and...Wow. No, *that* is a jewel."

A jewel the size of Felix's thumbnail was set next to a faceted, purple stone that looked like amethyst. While the smaller, teardrop jewel had sharp, clear facets, the amethyst had so many it was basically a sphere. Felix lifted all three items from the Chest, and it vanished with the same twist of reality as before.

"What am I looking at here?" he asked as Pit nosed the items. Felix set them down on the floor, and lifted the shiny jumpsuit.

Voracious Eye!

Name: Garment of Many
Type: Clothing (Enchanted)
Lore: An article of clothing in the ancient style, a Garment of Many is an all-purpose covering that will suit your every need. Inscribed with complicated arrays, it is able to change its shape, color, and texture into anything the wearer may imagine. Must be bound to a single wearer.
Self-Repair X - Uses ambient Mana to repair rips and tears in the garment.
Self-Clean X - Uses ambient Mana to clean the garment.
Harmonic Shift XI - Utilizing properties of the Grand Harmony, this garment will change to suit the wearer, but must be provided a steady stream of Mana to do so.

"I take it back; this is really cool." More than that, it would solve a problem Felix had encountered more and more. The enchanted clothing he'd received back in Haarwatch couldn't keep up with the punishment he put it through, often remaining torn or stained for long periods of time. This Garment of Many was leagues better, *and* it could shift into anything he wanted?

He quickly put the clothing on, shedding his old tunic and pants without regret. It took a moment, but flaring his Cardinal Flame quickly revealed the way of things. He was to manipulate his Mana into the cloth, which would then take the form of clothing he desired. He had to keep a continuous trickle of Mana feeding into the Garment, but it was negligible compared to his rate of regeneration.

Seconds later, Felix stood in his room wearing a pair of dark jeans, a comfortable t-shirt, and a light blue hoodie. The changes felt liquid and easy, translating his thoughts into completed clothing with barely any delay. Felix smiled down at Pit, but the tenku clearly didn't appreciate the magnitude of the item. He instead was nosing the smaller of the two jewels.

"Trust me, it's super cool," Felix muttered, before crouching once more. He held up the thumbnail-sized jewel.

Voracious Eye!

Name: Stone of Forte
Type: Gem (Enchanted)
Lore: This polished piece of cobalt spinel has been shaped to catch the refrain of the Grand Harmony so that it might funnel it into the armor upon which it is placed. Said armor will advance by a single Tier, providing increased protection. It is consumable and, upon use, will be rendered the same as any other gemstone. It must be bonded by blood after being placed upon the desired armor.

Felix transmitted it all to Pit, and the tenku's eyes shone. His barding had begun to look a bit ragged around the edges, but perhaps this Stone would prove to be a better addition to it. Felix didn't once think of using it himself. His armor was his skin, much as that annoyed him. Felix would have loved to own a cool suit of armor. Pit pressed at it in excitement, clearly assuming such a treasure would be his—he wasn't wrong, but Felix wasn't gonna worry about that yet.

There was still one last treasure to go.

Voracious Eye!

Name: Dwelling Stone
Type: Upgrade (Tier IV)
Lore: A piece of Belais Crystal imbued with the ancient magic of the System's Residential sequence. Place within your Home for further details.

"Belais Crystal," Felix murmured. He thought it looked familiar. "But what's all this about a Dwelling Stone?"

"A *Dwelling Stone*?!" The sword at Felix's waist had buzzed in surprise and a distinct amount of delight. "You have received a Dwelling Stone?"

"Yeah, I—" Felix began, before a ringing sound interrupted him.

A Stronghold Is Available To You!
Please Visit The Control Node To Access Your Options.

"Right. The last reward for Home Sweet Home. But where's the Control Node?" Felix asked the air.

Karys' voice shook from the sword, shaky in excitement. "I believe I know, Felix. Hurry, and bring the Dwelling Stone."

CHAPTER FOUR

So Felix hurried, moving through the last of the rooms he'd unlocked as Karys urged him onward toward the Control Node. The Garment flowed around his limbs like a cloud, a whisper of weight that allowed for complete range of motion even though his pants were mimicking jeans. As he ran, he tried different materials, cycling through cotton, silk, even corduroy...though the last was a mistake. No matter how free-flowing and loose it felt, the speeds at which he ran produced a godawful noise that would have awakened the dead.

He had tried a couple times to make it into armor, but whatever restrictions were in its arrays prevented it from mimicking steel and thick, boiled leather. Perhaps if he tinkered with it, but that would require him to study the tiny glyphs he sensed all along its design, hidden in seams and along individual threads. Felix wasn't sure he had the time, but he added it to his list of tasks.

He was holding the Dwelling Stone in his arms as he ran, its glowing depths casting wild shadows all around him. It was far heavier than he expected, and it grew heavier the closer he came to his destination. Luckily for him, Felix's Strength was more than up to the task. Pit had caught up with him soon enough as well, the enhancements he'd under-gone doing wonders for his Agility. It was nearly at a thousand points, lagging only behind the tenku's Willpower. Felix wouldn't have been surprised if Pit could match any number of standard Journeyman combatants.

"Race you?" he offered with a grin.

Pit only chuffed an annoyed laugh. *Let us wait. I would test you in the wilds.*

"You're on."

The Control Node turned out to be the center of the odd array at the roots of his Spirit Tree. Seven chambers were interconnected by star-shaped archways and filled—utterly filled—with the most complicated sigiladry Felix had ever seen. Only the first room was lit, however, ever since he'd claimed the Territorial Authority over Nagast. Ever since he'd become the Autarch.

He wasn't a fan of the title.

Karys was waiting for him, standing just outside the array. It wasn't that the constructed man couldn't enter it, but was a sign of respect—another detail from the ancient Nymean culture that Karys trotted out every once in a while. The array was a sign of Felix's Authority, and to trod upon it was a personal insult in addition to being potentially deadly. Ancient sigaldry such as this might have done any number of things to an unauthorized person walking atop it.

"In the center, Felix," Karys pointed. "That is the Control Node. Or it will be, once you step upon it."

Felix chewed at his lip, hefting the Dwelling Stone in his arms. Pit chirruped cautiously, poking a curious beak at the nearest lines of light, lit up with gold and silver. They looped around the first chamber in dizzying patterns that Felix still couldn't make heads or tails of, but he knew all too well what he'd find at the center. A glyph, one that was shaped like an eye of fire and lightning, surmounted by a nine-pronged crown.

His *personal* glyph.

"Felix!"

Before he could walk out into the array, the sound of shouting and clattering fall of metal and booted feet announced the arrival of Evie. She sped into the room, her own high Agility burning at full. As such, she barely caught herself before she ran right over the glowing lines.

"Noctis' tits, what's this?" she asked before shaking her head. "Wait, no, not important. Felix—what are you wearing? Gah! No—there's trouble."

Felix gripped the Dwelling Stone and Pit perked up. "What kind of trouble?"

"Giant kind."

He groaned and pushed the Dwelling Stone into Kary's sturdy arms. The damaged construct barely held onto it, and joints in his newly fashioned arm creaked ominously. "Felix! You should use this immediately—"

"Does it have a time limit, its potency?" Felix asked. When Karys shook his head, Felix shrugged. "I'll play house after I resolve this. Just—just keep an eye on it, yeah?"

Karys glanced between the stone and Felix, the former already slipping to the floor. "I-I shall give it my all, then."

Felix patted him on a tarnished golden pauldron. "Thanks. And I'm serious. I'll be back as soon as this is settled."

"Of course. Your people come first. Just know that this might have solutions all its own."

Felix nodded and followed Evie out of the first chamber, back toward the thickest piece of the Spirit Tree's lowest roots. The room was mostly rubble, but Felix had fallen down here a day ago, and his body had punched a series of holes from the upper levels. After securing the Territory, he had made sure to fashion some half-decent hand holds to climb back up. He couldn't get Stone Shaping to work on the Temple rock, even this far down. So, he had to settle for shoving his fingers into the walls and creating a crude ladder. It was this that Evie quickly grabbed and started climbing.

"Quickly! When I left them, they had that Witch glaring daggers at Vess and Harn."

Felix frowned. *Pit?*

His Companion nodded, and in a flash of light, leaped into Felix's Spirit and vanished from the physical world. He was a noticeable weight, but Felix was made of heartier stuff these days. He eyed the ceiling and the holes that led up into the open air, some six hundred feet above. He reached out, feeling along the threads that connected Felix to his friends and the Spirit Tree itself. Other threads were there, of course, less potent connections to the air and the earth, as well as a set of vibrantly thrumming ones. Threads that were very familiar. Felix frowned.

Adamant Discord!

Lightning surged around his body before he hauled back with the force of his Aspects. All of him was sent flying straight up through the holes at such a speed that thunder followed in his wake.

"Oh, come on!" Evie shouted in annoyance.

Felix laughed, and lightning danced across his teeth. He *pulled.*

A bar of lightning burst from the topmost level of the Temple, flashing through stone and dark and falling water. The waterfall that once careened off the cliff nearby was now filtering into the Temple and flowing ceaselessly into the lower levels. Luckily, none of that reached the array chambers, but it was something he had to address at some point, probably.

There was no one around the opening, thankfully, something Felix had checked on, but it was still nice to confirm with his actual eyes. He shot into the sky, cresting almost seven hundred feet from the bottom of the roots to a space several hundred feet shy of the lowest branches of his Spirit Tree. Hovering there for a moment, Felix took in the Foglands.

All around was forest, mountains, or lake. The sun barely rose above the eastern horizon, filling the sky with pinks and oranges that mingled among the scudding clouds. Birds wheeled through them, huge things far away, and the branches of his Spirit Tree were wreathed in the lowest of the clouds.

Below, at the base of his Temple, where the Archon had ruined the land with massive reservoirs for some unknown purpose, his people had made camp. The reservoirs had been destroyed and the sigaldry running them ruined, though not before Atar and Alister made copies. Finding out what the Archon had planned was one of their top priorities; the last thing Felix needed was for a defeated enemy to bite them in the ass.

Crude stone homes covered that open space, enough to create the idea of a small village. All of the homes were relatively large, around two thousand square feet. In part, this was because it gave his team room to move inside, but also because their other occupants needed the space. Those other occupants were now all congregating around a larger home—one that Felix had designated as his own before he'd found the rooms in the Temple.

Felix scowled as he fell, letting gravity take hold of him. The ground sped upward, wind roaring in his ears, as Felix fell faster and faster. Just a hundred feet shy of the top of his cliff, he flared Adamant Discord once more. A bolt of lightning shot downward as force pushed back up at Felix's feet, slowing his descent with a single, potent pulse. He landed with barely a whisper of his boots.

Showoff, Pit sent.

Felix's scowl threatened to turn into a smirk, but the situation below the cliff kept it in place. Around his dwelling, dozens of blue forms stood arrayed behind two huge women with flowing locks of white hair. Frost Giants, the lot of them, headed by two who called themselves Witches. They were hundreds of feet below him, but Felix's powerful Perception picked out their words easily.

"—doesn't he show himself?" one Witch asked.

"The Autarch does not answer to you, Frost Giant. No matter the rank you hold within your tribe." Vess said. He winced at her use of the title, but the woman was a stickler for proper etiquette. "He will emerge from the Temple when he is ready and no sooner. You may return to your quarters until he does—the same ones the Autarch saw fit to build for you."

The Witch's snort turned to a sneer. "I do not answer to you, *Human*. I shall wait here until the...Autarch graces us with his presence."

Felix hadn't heard quite so good a cue before, and he took a standing leap off the cliff. He flared Adamant Discord, except this time it was behind him, adding to his considerable speed.

Etheric Concordance!

Sovereign of Flesh!

Huge wings of leather, scale, and feathers burst from his back, pulled from Pit's features and grown more powerful with his mastery over his own flesh. The cupped appendages caught the wind like twin parachutes, each of them thirty feet long. But they only slowed him enough that Felix hit the earth with a rumble, rather than snapping his legs in two.

Etheric Concordance is level 75!
Adept Tier!
You Gain:
+15 AGL

+15 DEX
+15 EVA
Etheric Concordance Has Grown! Allows For Reverse Convergence! You May Rest Within Your Companion's Spirit Now! Manifestation of the Coronach is level 64!
...
Manifestation of the Coronach is level 67!

Dirt and dust kicked up in a wild circle around him, and Felix tried to ignore the notifications that flickered past his sight—though the change in his Etheric Concordance was enough to break his stern countenance. He grinned. *You see that Pit? My turn to take a break!*

In response, Felix's wings vanished abruptly, withering off his body as the huge tenku manifested beside him. Pit squawked at Felix and nudged him with a massive shoulder, though it did little to move him. Felix laughed.

"Felix—er, Lord Autarch, sir?"

Vyne and Nevia were the closest to him, and both had been sheltering behind the warrior's tower shield. Felix felt touches of fear and relief humming across their Spirits, fear of his entrance and relief that it was only him. Vyne nodded to the assembled Frost Giants, all of whom were watching with stern faces and clenched fists. *Their* Spirits were a jumbled mess; a mixture of surprise, fear, awe, and...a touch of—*what is that?*

Felix cleared his throat and addressed them, nodding to Vess and Harn among the others. "My people tell me that you want to see me."

The Frost Giant in the lead, a rare female, tossed her hair back like a recalcitrant horse. Another stood behind her, just ahead of a crowd of four dozen Risi—Frost Giants—and all of them stared at Felix like he was a monster.

"Yes. We have...concerns." She drew herself up, emphasizing her almost nine feet height. "Why did you save us?"

Felix's eyebrows lifted. When he had used his Unite the Lost at the end of his confrontation with the Archon, he had cleansed the Marks from all within range of his Spirit Tree. Marks were like spiritual tags that let a greater power track, influence, or even outright control someone of lesser advancement. Felix himself had been afflicted with several, as had the twisted servants of the Archon: the Arcids and the Reforged. When Felix had cleansed them, his Unite the Lost also reverted their bodies to what they once were, restoring lost flesh and bone and blood, restoring Minds and Spirits in addition to their Bodies. All of the giants before him were once raving slaves to the Archon's hate. Now they were free.

"Did you not want to be saved?" Felix asked carefully. There had been a tentative peace over the last twenty four hours, but he wasn't so naive to think it would continue forever. The Frost Giants had been his enemy since the first time he arrived in Shelim. The Witches, moreover, were the power behind Grimmar, former chieftain of the Risi and unwitting pawn of the Maw. He had no idea how much these Witches knew about that situation, or the fate of the Maw, whol they worshiped as a goddess.

"We—You have put us in a difficult position, Felix Nevarre. You, who faced down our High Chieftain in single combat, who survived the Mother's ire, and now come and deliver us from the vile thrall of the Archon." She shook her head, and that strange melody skipped across her Spirit. It was reluctant, almost wayward, but the emotion flitted across all those before him. "It is too much. I must know. What are your intentions for us?"

"Intentions?" Felix asked. He longed to meet Vess' gaze, but the Witch hadn't blinked. He felt certain that looking away would lose him something in the exchange, like running from a predator. Regardless, he thought honestly on her question. Why had he saved them? "To have you be free. That is the gist of it. The Archon took the choice from you all when he turned you into those...things, and I'm just giving it back." Felix made a vague gesture northward. "You can go whenever you like. I won't stop you."

The Witch watched him warily, skepticism clear on her face. "You have embarrassed us time and again and expect us to be grateful. Our honor cannot take the strain of being saved by one so...small." She tossed her hair again. "We demand recompense! A fight to the death to assuage our honor! Our greatest warriors against your own. What do you say to this?"

Felix heard Vess' sharp intake of breath and Harn's low growl in addition to a myriad of sounds from his people. Only Pit seemed unworried. "This will resolve your problems, going forward? Set us square?" Felix asked.

"It will," she promised, and Felix sensed no deceit in her Spirit. He decided to roll the dice.

"Then let's do this. Pick your warriors. We'll do this here and now." Felix said, releasing a pulse of Stone Shaping that firmed up the ground between crude houses. It was a decent size, approximately the length and width of a football field. It only seemed like less because of all the literal giants.

"Agreed. It is better to end things quickly," the Witch said, before barking orders in the Risi tongue.

Vess sidled up to Felix, as did Harn. Alister, Atar, and all the Haarguard lingered further back, all of them frowning at the giants. "Felix, you thinkin' this through? You're strong, but those Risi are half again stronger than they were as Reforged or Arcids."

"I disagree, Harn," Vess said. "Sometimes, we must put force behind our words, as otherwise our actions have no weight or substance. Diplomacy does not only occur in palaces and salons."

Harn laughed. "I do know that. I ain't sayin' he should back down. We can take 'em, but it'll be rough, and I don't know what'll happen after.

Where's Evie? With you, me, and Felix here, we can wipe out whatever they toss at us, but I'd feel better with a fourth."

"She's up there," Felix said, gesturing to the top of the Temple. "But it doesn't matter. Neither of you are helping."

"What?" Harn and Vess both said, equally surprised and annoyed.

"We are ready, Felix Nevarre," the Witch interrupted. Three others flanked her: the other Witch and two warriors that stood twice as tall at around twenty feet.

"Good. So am I," Felix said, and he strode out into the field. Alone.

"Just yourself?" The Witch did not seem surprised, but she grinned widely. Perhaps she had counted on Felix doing this, or maybe she just saw it as an easy win. "You do us no honor if you cannot bring out your best warriors."

"My warriors are resting. You'll have to settle for me," Felix said, then gave her a grin of his own. "Besides, I needed a good warmup, anyway."

The Risi beside her growled, a sound so deep Felix felt it faintly in his chest, even forty feet away. The Witch's smile faded, and she nodded once. "Then let us begin."

Felix glanced at Vess and Harn, both of whom looked ready to attack him themselves. "Let's—"

The Frost Giants exploded forward, massive axes of ice manifesting in their uplifted fists. A rain of blurring yellow-purple light fell from the sky, soaking into Felix's Body even before the warriors crossed the distance.

Status Condition: Hex of Hand. Effective Dexterity Reduced by 5%!
Status Condition: Hex of Thew. Effective Strength Reduced by 10%!

The axes came down. Felix's bare fists, void of Skills, rose to meet them both. A sound like shearing icebergs cracked the air, and a plume of stone dust and ice chips flew in all directions.

The axes, both of them, were hurled back along with the Risi Warriors' arms. They grunted in surprise, but had little time beyond that. Felix, unharmed and unarmed, came for them.

He shot forward, through the smoke and debris and swept both of the warriors' legs. They fell, careening backward, hard enough to make the nearest houses shudder. Felix flared his Agility, moving so fast the Risi had barely touched down when he hefted one of their discarded ice axes.

The axe, easily ten feet long and heavy as a team of avum, was light as a feather in his hands as he lifted and spun it. The bearded blade slammed into the earth just inches from the first warrior's skull, and he looked at Felix with wide, terrified eyes.

"You're dead," Felix said. He blurred away, leaping over the fallen Risi to deliver a single, solid kick to the other warrior's jaw. His bald and bearded skull snapped back, his entire, enormous body going limp. Unconscious, but alive. "You're dead, too."

Felix pivoted toward the Witches.

Waves of ice tore across the field, attempting to bury him under the layers of their spell, but Felix simply pushed himself to his limit. Strength, Endurance, Vitality, Agility, he plowed through wave after wave of ice relying entirely on his stats alone. New Hexes shot out, more comets of yellow and purple Mana—Hexes of Despair—but Felix shrugged these off with a casual flex of his Willpower. Both of the Witches flinched back as their spells rebounded against them, but one recovered fast enough to hurl a thick stalactite of ice at him.

Felix slapped it aside directly into the crowd of Frost Giants. It bowled over several of their warriors, and the Witch gasped. Felix was already airborne, however, his right knee leading the way into the Witch's gut. She crumpled like a house of cards, and Felix's sheer weight and momentum threw both of them ten feet back. Felix rolled from the impact, coming to his feet without losing a beat, and came at their leader.

"Enough!" she cried out, bowing low. "We are defeated." He blinked. The Witch dropped to her knees and prostrated herself on the ground, pressing her forehead to the dirty stone. "We surrender to your strength, Felix Nevarre. We are yours, Autarch, bound by Oath and Power. Upon our honor shall we serve, or else upon our honor shall we die."

All at once, every single Frost Giant did the same. They sank to their knees and pressed their foreheads to the dirt, all of them repeating that same Oath. And it was an Oath, because the silvery threads of them coiled about his Spirit with gossamer chains that were heavier than their ephemeral nature would suggest. He winced at the weight, but the sensation faded almost instantly.

Felix traded shocked glances with Vess and Harn. He hadn't expected this.

"Uh. Okay. Accepted."

A trumpeting fanfare accosted his ears immediately, and a notification box appeared bracketed with gold and silver.

Congratulations, Autarch!
You Have Vanquished A Threat!
The Risi (Frost Giants) Have Joined Your Fledgling Nation!
+25% To All Positive Relations With Giantfolk!
See Your Control Node For Further Options!

CHAPTER FIVE

I'm sorry, what? Felix stared at the notification before him. *Joined my what now?*

Congratulations, Autarch!
You Have Vanquished A Threat!
The Risi (Frost Giants) Have Joined Your Fledgling Nation!
+25% To All Positive Relations With Giantfolk!
See Your Control Node For Further Options!

Oh, you bet your ass I'll be seeing my Control Node. He swiped the notification closed and clenched his jaw. He wasn't sure how much he trusted the Frost Giants' Oath, but he felt out of his depth. Felix scowled at the Witch as she lifted her head from prostration. She flinched, ever so slightly.

"What's your name?" he asked.

"My name has been cast aside. I am a Witch of the Rock, born among the swirling winds of the Hoarfrost and given unto the cold upon my seventh year, I—"

Voracious Eye!

Name: Kimaris, Witch of the Rock
Type: Giantfolk
Level: 45
...

Felix waved away the rest of the information, not needing it. "Kimaris, then."

The Witch flinched again, this time far more noticeably. "How do you know that name?"

He ignored her. "Kimaris, what are your plans now? Will you return home?"

The Witch visibly gathered herself, rising to her knees and making her just as tall as Felix. "We...can no longer return to the Hoarfrost. When the High Chieftain was selected, we cut ties with our land in the hopes of forming a new home here. That—it did not turn out as we were promised. The Mother...lied to us." There was some whispering among the prostrated giants, but Kimaris' glare silenced them. "I would ask you for sanctuary, Autarch. For my people."

Felix kept his face carefully blank. "Let me think on it. For now, you can stay at the southern edge of the encampment. Please move your people in that direction."

"As you wish," Kimaris said before returning to her full height. All around the giants did the same, most of them taller than the houses he'd Shaped. Without another word, the Frost Giants left.

Once they'd left earshot, Felix breathed a heavy sigh of relief.

"That was entirely unexpected," Vess said. She walked up to his side and stared after the giants, many of whom were easily visible as they began to set up their own sort of camp.

"Yeah. I didn't expect them to swear an Oath then stick around," Felix said.

"Not that. You." Vess poked him in the shoulder before giving his clothes a once-over. "What are you wearing?"

"Oh, I got a cool new magic outfit." Felix let himself be distracted focusing on his Garment again. A tiny, barely noticeable piece of Mana fled his channels and the shirt and pants became a pale green tunic and dark blue cloth pants. The tunic was wrapped around his torso, set with an asymmetrical collar that Felix had seen once or twice around Haar-watch. "See?"

"Fascinating," said a light voice, and Atar pushed between Harn and Vess to grab the hem of his newly fashioned tunic. His own battlerobes were dirty and singed, and it looked like he'd tried his best to scrub blood from the hardened fabrics across the chest. "It's all controlled with your Mana Manipulation?"

Felix grinned at the mage. "Basically. There's arrays on the threads that respond to my Intent, apparently. Because I'm certainly not envisioning this whole outfit top to bottom."

"What...what Skill did you use?" Kylar asked. The swordsman had sidled closer and was watching the giants in the distance. "To parry those huge axes."

"Oh. I didn't use any," Felix said.

"I-I'm sorry, what?" Kylar stuttered. Shock played over all of their Spirits, and Felix dimmed his awareness of them all. It felt like cheating, reading his allies' emotions.

"That was Strength alone?" Harn said with a bright look in his eye.

"Strength and Endurance. Tanked a lot of Stamina to take a hit like that," he said before pivoting the conversation. "Did everyone rest up?"

"Not much else to do," Kylar groused, but Vyne shoved him.

"Everyone's healing, or on the path," Vyne said. "Davum's still got a gash across his chest, but whatever was in that poultice the Henaari gave him has been helping."

Felix nodded, happy to hear it, but that same unease gnawed at him.

His people had nearly died fighting the hordes of the Archon. When Felix and his Spirit Tree had stopped the fighting and cured the Frost Giants, it had driven off the various monsters that the Archon had bound to his will. The area wasn't safe around them, not with Prismatic Wretches and Ghostfire Simians and other things creeping about, but none had approached since that night.

Felix was pretty sure it had something to do with the Spirit Tree above them. The Atlantes Anima.

Vess pulled him aside. "Do you trust these Giants? They are Oath-bound, but I cannot help but be skeptical of their allegiance."

"I'm not about to blindly trust someone who tried to kill me—multiple times now. Maybe the Oathbinding is in good faith, or maybe they can work around it, like I can." Felix took a kelaar fruit Nevia offered him in passing. "Thanks. The problem with being an exception is that you see all the weird, contradictory shit the System gets up to."

Vess nodded slowly, concern flickering through her dark gaze as she surveyed the stone houses and retreating Giantfolk. "It feels like the ground turned to sand underneath us. Oathbinding is the tried and true method of governance. My father uses it to enact trade agreements, to extract the truth in civil judgements, even as an oath of service for his military." Vess licked her lips and gave Felix a lopsided grin, cheek dimpling. "I'm only consoled by the fact that your Tyrant of Choice Title was hard-earned. I doubt many could achieve the same."

"Yeah, I'm all sorts of special," Felix said distractedly. Vess and Harn were frowning at him. "What?"

"How'd you get so strong, kid?" Harn asked. His helmet was off, displaying the man's wide, crooked nose and scarred face. "You played with those giants like they were Tier I beasts."

"What happened in the Temple?" Vess asked in a softer voice. "You never said, after..."

True, Felix hadn't said much about what occurred in the Temple. Instead he'd emerged from the ruins to help his friends and scare off the monsters that still lingered in confusion. Patching each other up and erecting the few houses with Stone Shaping to keep them out of the rain had been as active as he'd felt capable of, considering the roiling pain that had been consuming his core space. One thing after another had kept him from advancing to Adept, then he'd retired to sleep off the exhaustion that was still dogging at his heels. Felix tried to smile in a disarming fashion, but knew it was more of a grimace.

"It got dicey. But I advanced, and I forged my Path," Felix said. Harn sucked a breath, while Vess' eyes widened.

"Siva's Grace, Felix. Your Path added so much? I have never seen you move as you did against the giants. It was over almost before it began."

"A Path," Harn said as he shook his head. "You keep surprisin' me, kid. Next you'll tell me you're Master Tier now."

"Not yet," Felix said with a grin. Harn clapped him on the back, hard, but Felix didn't budge. The man grunted, impressed.

"Wait wait, what has your Intelligence and Willpower reached?" Atar asked. He licked his lips, nervously. "Your Mana?"

Felix just grinned and jerked his thumb back at the giants. "We should keep an eye on them for now. Pit? You mind watching them for a bit?" His Companion warbled an affirmative and trotted off. Felix sighed. "According to the System, they're allies. More than that, maybe."

"More than that?" Harn asked. Atar frowned, though Felix wasn't sure if it was directed at his words or that Felix hadn't answered him. "What's that mean?"

Felix shrugged. "I'll know more in a bit. Gotta...consult with the Temple."

Vess raised an eyebrow. "That should not be how it works."

"What?" Felix asked.

"Authority. You gained a Territory, but you should be able to access its options wherever you are." She glanced at the Temple hidden within the cliff. He'd told his original team—plus Alister—all about the odd array. "And that array is strange, from what you have explained to me. Too complex by half, and with all those unused portions? I do not understand it."

"Perhaps the nature of Authority has changed since my time, Your Grace," Karys buzzed aloud. The hooked sword at Felix's waist puffed with green-gold light in time with each syllable. "You are correct in some ways, but not in others. Please, when Felix returns to the Control Node, I would ask that you come with him, if you do not mind."

If Vess was taken aback, she didn't show it, but only nodded to the sword. "It would be my pleasure."

Authority. Felix's attempt had no effect. "Is it blocked until I finish with our project?"

"It is, yes. I can explain within."

"What project?" Atar asked. He stepped closer and lowered his voice, excluding the Haarguard and addressing only Felix, Vess, and Harn. "And don't think I didn't notice you avoiding the question before. I know it's rude to ask for stats, but we're in the middle of some nasty monsters. We —I could use some reassurance, Felix."

Felix's head rocked back in surprise. He hadn't thought of things from their point of view. While he had been fighting monsters and advancing down his Omen Path for great rewards, they had all fought for their lives. Those scuffs and stains on the mage's battlerobes were cast into a different light, for all that Felix had known their origin before. He nodded and brought up his stats before flicking them at Atar, Harn, and Vess.

"Vess? I want to resolve this Authority thing now, if you don't mind. Please meet me at the top of the Temple," he said gently. She nodded, not even looking at the blue screen before her.

Adamant Discord!

Lightning surged down Felix's limbs, and he pulled, launching himself hundreds of feet in a single bound.

"Willpower is over two thou—FELIX! What is this?" Atar shouted behind him.

Felix just grinned into the sky.

He landed atop the Temple to find Evie sitting atop a crumbling ledge, looking down at the encampment.

No, he realized. *Staring at the giants.*

"Shit," he muttered to himself.

"Yeah. It's shit," Evie agreed. She didn't look over at Felix, but he could see the tension in her shoulders. "I heard their Oath. You can't believe 'em, Felix."

"Not sure I do, Evie." He walked closer but stopped when Evie took a deep, quaking breath. "You okay?"

"Thought I was over this, ya know?" Evie looked at him, and her eyes were a touch too bright. "Been months since I even cried about Mags."

Felix spread his hands. "You want me to get rid of them?"

Evie tucked her knees up, wrapping her arm around them. "Dunno. Yes. No. All of it. Just seems unfair that they'd get off consequence-free after murdering my sister." Her chain clinked and somehow managed to sound menacing. "At least when they were Reforged, I could call it fair punishment."

"They're here for now, but honestly I don't know what I'll do with them." Felix didn't have to look over the edge to sense them, moving around far below and casting some form of ice magic on the ground. "Harn'll be watching them. If they step out of line, I'll be the first to drive them out. I can promise you that."

"Thanks, I suppose," Evie said with a shrug. Felix watched her a while longer before releasing a quiet, tired sigh.

"I'll be down in the Temple, if you need me. All right?"

"All right."

And that was that, for now. Felix made a mental note to come back to it when they both had time to rest. The last thing he wanted was to ostracize his friends. Suppressing a sigh, he descended the levels of his aerated Temple, following the path of the Atlantes Anima's trunk until he reached bottom. It was mostly sliding along the bark and dropping through the holes he'd made, but his stats let him achieve it fluidly, without relying on a single Skill.

He entered the first chamber to find Karys standing over the very edge of the array, gold and silver light bouncing brightly off his tarnished armor. Vaporous light coiled about his arm as he let it drift above the sigaldry, like steam off a hot meal. It was Mana, visible to Felix due to his Manasight, but typically invisible to most. From what Felix had gathered, Mana was weakest in its vaporous state and grew steadily more potent as it transitioned to a liquid then a solid; but the sheer amount that crowded the huge chamber made Felix reflexively swallow. The abyss in his core growled.

"Shut up."

Karys turned. "Ah you're back. Is Vess...?"

"She's on the way," Felix said and stepped close to the array himself. He knelt by one of the array lines, flaring his Perception. The line was not a line at all, but thousands of tiny sigils strung together in complicated formations that together gave the appearance of a solid whole. *Like pointillism*, he thought. He had some decent knowledge of sigaldry from his experiences and work on the Wall in Haarwatch, but even the tiny section before him blew him away with its complexity.

The lines spread outward from the Control Node where his personal glyph was etched in light, spiraling around it in a dizzying knotwork of loops and whorls. Each of those tiny sigils was built around other tiny sigils, called the primary, with each row of secondary or tertiary symbols modifying the effects of the central piece. Yet, tens of thousands of primary sigil arrays comprised the lines he saw, and more lingered—inert—in the connected chambers.

"I had only taken a minor glance before." Vess walked in behind him, staring in awe at the silver and gold lines of light. "Far more complicated than my father's Seat. This makes Pax'Vrell look positively provincial."

Felix stood and needlessly dusted off his knees. Nothing shook off, the Garment having discarded any dirt well before he bothered. "Why did you ask Vess to come down as well, Karys?"

The armored construct tilted his head. "She is well-versed in Authority as it stands, and it will be easier to explain this once. Do you have any questions before we begin, Felix?"

He eyed the Dwelling Stone, sitting just behind Karys' feet. "Yeah. I'm still not entirely clear on how this array conveyed Authority over the Territory to me. Can you explain that?"

"As well, please tell me why it requested him to define his motivations," Vess added. "It asked him, directly, why he sought Authority." Felix had relayed that much to her already. It clearly still baffled her. "That is not how Authority works, not to my knowledge."

Karys tapped his helmet right where his mouth would be, had he still possessed one. "To answer your question, I must ask a few of my own. Your father's Seat, you have seen it?"

"Yes, of course."

"May I read the image from your Mind?" he asked gently. Felix frowned. "As a mobile Spirit, I've found parsing proffered thoughts to be a simple enough task, but only if they are willing. The unwilling Mind is far harder to crack, even an Untempered one. Choice affirms their defenses. It is why the System so hated what the Archon did to the Frost Giants, why Felix was able to revert them at all."

"It is just a reading?" Vess asked, clearly as uncomfortable with the idea as Felix.

"A skimming, at best. Simply hold the memory of your father's Seat of Authority in your Mind, and I shall glimpse it."

Vess looked to Felix, who nodded, slowly. Karys had proven to be worthy of trust. "Very well," she said.

There was a moment of silence between the three of them, where all Felix could hear was the subaudible thrum of the array. Then Karys made his own humming noise.

"Ah, I see. That is...strange."

"What is?" Felix asked.

"Do you allow me to share it with the both of you?"

"Go ahead," Felix said at the same time Vess gave a curt nod.

An image of a fancy room drifted into Felix's Mind, swirling into crystal clear clarity. A large, ornate chair made of gold dominated the room. It was studded with gemstones, and its back was fashioned into a roaring drake, wings outspread. Below it, inlaid in the polished stone flooring, were sixteen rings of sigaldry that contained a faint silver luminescence. It was clearly an array made of concentric rings of sigils with a large glyph in the center below the chair. As all glyphs, it was a combination of sigils fashioned into an aesthetic whole; this looked like a raised spear with bat-like wings. Dragon wings.

"My family's Seal," Vess affirmed.

Karys made a light rumbling sound in his patched over chest. "Correct me if I am wrong—my memory is not what it used to be—but it appears that the array in Pax'Vrell is entirely mortal-made. Yes?"

"Well, yes. Our Authority is given to us by the Hierocracy," she agreed.

"Contingent on their approval, I'd imagine," Karys said with a disgusted tone. "Temporary Authority."

Vess nodded, brows furrowed. "Yes. They could, conceivably, take away my family's Authority whenever they wished. It would cause chaos in many ways, but if they wanted to, they could." Vess looked at Felix. "System Authority is rarely granted. Lady Cal and now you are the first two I've ever heard of outside legends."

Karys' disgust rolled off him, waves of it mingled with a cold anger. "That is not how it used to be. In my day, only the System could bless one with Authority enough to rule. Not even the gods had such power." Karys gestured, and the image in Felix's mind flashed around the concentric rings, showing complicated but intelligible glyphs and sigils. He could even pick out the meaning of a couple. "You have created a patchwork atop an ancient rite, gleaning just the barest hints of Authority from the Continent. And missing the point entirely."

"The point?" Felix asked. "What's the point of Authority, then? I had thought it was just to...you know, rule."

"The path of a tyrant is to rule without concern over the governed. Authority is a burden that only the most worthy should ever bear. Long ago, that is how it was done." The metal man looked at Felix with a hint of pride. "It is how it shall be done again."

"So, this is my Seat of Authority, then?" Felix asked, a bit uncomfortable. There were...*expectations* in Karys' eye-fires, and Felix didn't know if he measured up. He forced a bit of a laugh. "Where's my fancy chair?"

Vess smiled. "An old tradition. A seat for a Seat, if you will."

"Yes, the throne is not necessary. Your Seat and Seal are the true indicators of the mantle now upon your shoulders, Felix."

"Been meaning to ask about that. Autarch of Nagast. A Lost Territory that, by the map I saw, extends all the way north to the Hoarfrost, west and south to the Bitter Sea, and east to just beyond the Verdant Pass. That's...that's a lot of area to cover," Felix said.

"Most of it monster-strewn wilderness, as well," Vess added.

"Autarch is an ancient title, one rarely given, even in the glory days of the Golden Empire. It is a mantle, as I said, one of responsibility to the people who inhabit the land you hold Authority over," Karys said.

"And what are those responsibilities?" he asked.

"The same as any with enough power. To protect and defend your people, to raise them up so that they may raise you in turn," Karys said. By his cadence, it sounded like something he'd learned by rote a long time ago.

"My people include a few Humans and a bunch of Frost Giants now," Felix said. He took a breath. "Shouldn't be too hard, right?"

Vess patted him on the shoulder. "Best to start small. My tutors have been schooling me in governance and diplomacy for my entire life. I shall be here to help you whenever you need it."

Felix smiled widely at her, and she lightly squeezed his shoulder.

"Indeed, and this Dwelling Stone will aid you further, Felix," Karys said.

Vess let her hand drop, and she blushed, looking back at the ex-Paragon. "What is a Dwelling Stone?"

"Time to find out," Karys said with a pleased note. "Felix?"

"I got it." Repressing the urge to touch the spot on his shoulder where Vess had grabbed him, Felix walked over to the Dwelling Stone and easily hefted it into his arms. "Just bring this to the Seal, then?"

"Yes. The Seal and your Control Node are one and the same."

Felix stepped out onto the array and let the Mana vapor envelop him. It was almost blinding with his Manasight flared, so Felix kept it at a low burn, only enough to see the power at work around him. The moment he reached his Seat, the floor rumbled. A piece of the stone beneath him lifted up, twenty or so finger-thin hexagonal columns rose to create a slanting platform before him. The top of it depressed, the columns moving so that a pocket was created, one exactly the size of the Dwelling Stone he held.

"Hoo boy. Okay. Here goes nothing," he said. He placed the Dwelling Stone on the platform, and it was immediately lit up with brilliant purple light. Traceries of gold and silver formed atop the hexagonal pillars, climbing up and over the Stone in a lace-like lattice. The designs almost looked fractal to him, but squinting past the bright light showed him they were, in fact tiny, tiny sigils.

You Have Established A Home!
Home's Grade Has Been Increased To Stronghold!
Defensive Fortifications Gained!
Offensive Fortifications Gained!
See Stronghold Menu For More!

A Dwelling Stone (Legendary) Has Been Detected Within Your Stronghold!
Assessing Stored Options...
Options Expanded Due To Increased Grade Of Dwelling...
Options Expanded Due To Threats Eliminated...
Complete!
A Dwelling Stone (Legendary) Contains The Following Patterns:
Tier III Forge
Tier III Alchemical Lab
Tier III Storage Facility
Tier III Glyphworks

Do You Wish To Install Them All?

CHAPTER SIX

Install them all? Felix mouthed. "Uh, Yes?"

Please Stand By...
Mapping Home.
Stronghold Detected.

A sudden holographic display appeared before him, a scale model of the Temple, the cliff, and a sizable portion of the river, lake, and forest around him. At the same time, Felix's sense of the actual physical area swept through him, far more detailed than it had been with his Perception alone. It was a ton of information, but his powerful Mind shifted and sorted it all almost automatically, his Intelligence and Willpower handling the influx with little issue. At most, it made him blink in surprise as a kernel of wonder bloomed within him. *Wow.* The display trilled softly as he ran his fingers through it, like a song made of light.

"This is...?"

"The totality of your Stronghold, yes," Karys said from the side. The room was large, but everyone had Perception enough to hear one another from such short distances.

Please Select Placement Of Your Patterns!

The holographic map flashed at him again, indicating hundreds of places for each of the "patterns" he'd just been notified of. Felix glanced between them all, a little overwhelmed. Beside the map, the patterns appeared again, and he focused on them one-by-one.

Tier III Forge
A Forge with the basic equipment required to create, reforge, and Temper arms, armor, and more. At Tier III, the Forge contains a variety of arrays. Please see the Forge Menu for more.
Basic Requirements: Raw Materials (Varied), Journeyman Tier Or Greater Smith

Tier III Alchemical Lab
An Alchemical Lab with the basic equipment required to create, distill, form, and manufacture a variety of alchemical concoctions. At Tier III, the Alchemical Lab contains a variety of arrays. Please see the Alchemical Menu for more.
Basic Requirements: Tier I Or Greater Raw Materials (Varied), Journeyman Tier Or Greater Alchemist

Tier III Storage Facility
A Storage Facility with Tier III bindings and 10,000 SQ/FT of modular space. Please see the Storage Menu for more.
Basic Requirements: Tier III Stone, Tier III Wood, Tier II Monster Cores, Tier III Monster Cores

Tier III Glyphworks
A Glyphworks contains the basic tools necessary to create arrays that can be used defensively, offensively, or for utility purposes. Please see the Glyphworks Menu for more.
Basic Requirements: Monster Cores (Tier Varies), Tier I Or Greater Raw Materials (Varied)

"Okay, nothing too surprising there," Felix muttered before raising his voice. "But where do I put them all?"

"You can put them anywhere on that map," Karys buzzed through the sword and his armored body at the same time. "However, taking advantage of your natural resources and the design of your Stronghold will be the most optimal."

"My Stronghold currently consists of a half-broken cliff, an even more broken Temple, and several acres of river, lake, and forest. It's not exactly prime real estate," Felix said.

"I disagree, Felix," Vess interjected. "A Stronghold of such size is powerfully advantageous. You can defend yourself here, given a little work. With your Stone Shaping Skill, you could rebuild this place yourself in a day, I bet."

"The cliff, certainly. But not the Temple. It resists my magic," Felix said. "Karys. Where should I put the Forge?"

"A Forge requires running water, an easy-to-reach source of materials, and air flow. All of which are available in the topmost sections of your

Stronghold." Karys gestured across the chamber, and a section of his map pulsed. It was above the Temple proper but still contained within the stone.

Felix mentally grabbed the pattern for the Tier III Forge and nudged it in the direction he desired. With a faint chime, the pattern sank into his map right where he had indicated, and the entire display rippled. A vision of stone grew and morphed in real-time, excavating a series of rooms filled with buckets, troughs, and a huge, cylindrical forge that dominated it all. Several ornate but sturdy exits and entrances sprang up around it, and stone, lattice-work stairs led down into the Temple.

Tier III Forge Will Be Installed.
Confirm?
Y/N

Yes.

Rumbling sounded far above him, and while Felix may have been able to flare his Perception enough to hear it, his sense of his Stronghold provided information far faster. Hundreds of feet up, exactly where it appeared on his illusory map, stone softened and flowed, shaping itself to match the preview appearance he saw. It was over in seconds, and a soft, triumphant note filled the air. Like a hammer against a bell.

Tier III Forge Is Installed!
Please View The Forge Menu For More Details!

"It is over already?" Vess asked. She sounded even more impressed than before.

"Does it usually take longer?" Felix asked.

"I was once allowed to witness my father place a new facility within his City, but it took hours to craft and implement into the array." She shook her head and bent low, inspecting the gold-and-silver sigaldry again. "You were right, Karys. This is truly *vastly* different than my family's Seat."

Karys inclined his head to the woman. "Thank you for the acknowledgement. I do not know what has happened in the Ages of my sleep, but it is clear even the influence of my Empire has long vanished."

"Nym made these arrays?" Felix asked.

"Who else? This is, after all, a Nymean Temple," Karys said. "The System is a natural force, one that the Nym were dedicated to living in tune with. It provided many benefits that I fear are Lost."

"Maybe. But that just means we have to find them again, right?" Felix asked.

Karys perked up, his golden eye-fires flaring. "You are right, Felix. Thank you." He took a deep breath, the sound like air over a deep, metallic jug. Unnecessary, obviously, but Felix supposed the habit was hard to shake. "I suggest you place the other patterns around your Stronghold as well."

"Right." Felix turned back to the map. "Alchemical Lab, Storage Facility, and Glyphworks. Any advice, Karys? Vess?"

"Any sort of storage should be centrally located but also secured. If you are able, I would choose somewhere deep within the Temple itself, where someone couldn't access it without authorization," Vess said.

"Yeah, that's smart. But we'd need to get back and forth from it, right?" Felix asked. "So centrally located, too?"

"That will be less of an issue than you may think," Karys said. "Simply place it deep within the Temple. Somewhere secure. As to the others: an Alchemical Lab also needs to be separated from any living quarters, somewhere with plenty of air flow and access to running water. I would suggest near your Forge, but not too near."

"All right."

"The Glyphworks, you can place anywhere, but I would choose somewhere near the others. It is wise to keep your crafters within a single district, unless there is a good reason not to," Vess said. She was looking at the map from the edge of the array. "Considering that we have no guards or infrastructure in place, I would suggest all of them be heavily fortified."

Karys nodded. "A reasoned approach, and one I have little qualms with. But let us place the patterns before all else, yes?"

Vess nodded, and Felix watched them both with a touch of amusement. He selected the remaining three patterns and mentally placed them around his Stronghold. Beside the Forge, forming an equilateral triangle far above his current position, the Alchemical Lab and Glyphworks came into being.

Much like the Forge, the map displayed shifting stone and excavating spaces in the undisturbed rock above the Temple, but this time he caught flashes of metal forming objects within. Too soon, the spaces were shaped and in place, with more lattice-strewn stairwells, all leading to a central area between the crafting halls. Farther below and near Felix's chambers, the Storage Facility came into being. It was supposedly large, but it barely puckered the stone of the map, only forming a shallow alcove and a huge, twenty-foot tall door in the wall.

Tier III Alchemical Lab, Tier III Glyphworks, and Tier III Storage Facility Will Be Installed.
Confirm?
Y/N

Yes.

Tier III Alchemical Lab Is Installed!
Please View The Alchemy Menu For More Details!
Tier III Glyphworks Is Installed!

Please View The Glyphworks Menu For More Details!
Tier III Storage Facility Is Installed!
Please View The Storage Menu For More Details!

With far less fanfare than the Forge, all three patterns integrated into physical space. Stone shifted, and metal rang out, and it was all done in a handful of seconds. That same bell rang, something Felix could now recognize as a sort of excess vibration from the System doing its thing, but it sounded joyful. His Affinity wasn't picking up real emotions, but there was a strange calm over the array around him, as if tension had been released that he hadn't realized was there.

Congratulations, Autarch of Nagast!
Your Stronghold Has Been Established!
Authority Increased!
See Your Authority Menu For More Details.

A gold and silver button appeared in Felix's vision. His heads-up display was almost invisible, fading in the background like the nose on his face, but with a negligent effort, it all came into focus. He had his resource bars—Health, Stamina, and Mana—along the top, and on the right side were buttons for his Status, Pit's Status, Quests, and now Authority. It had the design of a nine-pronged crown on it, just as his personal Seal did. *Interesting.*
He opened it up.

Authority Accessed.
Welcome, Autarch Felix Nevarre.
What Song Do You Wish To Sing?

A translucent screen appeared, still golden but different than before. Tabs for Territory, Stronghold, Forge, Alchemy, Glyphworks, and Storage were all present and accessible, but a few more existed along the left-hand side. They were grayed out and illegible, so Felix put them out of his mind for the moment. He opened his Territory tab first.

The Song of Territory
Current Residence: **Nagast**
Residence Rank: **Stronghold, Rank I**
Allied Population: **245 Henaari, 59 Risi (Frost Giants), 32 Hoarhounds, 2 Chimera, 7 Humans, 1 Half-Orc, 1 Elf, 1 Dwarf**

"Ugh, I forgot about their frost wolves," he said. Further subsections showed for Factions, Resources, Map, Defensive Arrays, Offensive Arrays, and to his surprise, Threats. Felix navigated to that one first.

Threats:
The Dread

"Shit, that's right," Felix murmured. The Dread was a sea monster he'd met the first few minutes of his arrival on the Continent. Moreover, it was a Blood Beast created by the Endless Maw, and it was certainly dangerous...but it was also trapped in the Bitter Sea, as far as he was aware. "Something to keep an eye on, at least."

Resources:
Syncing With Aria Of The Green Wilds...
Sync Complete.

A list of all the herbs, fungi, fruits, vines, everything he'd ever Analyzed across the Foglands appeared on his screen. There were estimated numbers for quantities as well, which was really cool. Felix resolved to go out and do some reconnaissance to find more natural resources out in his Territory. He was positive they'd come in handy for alchemy, forging, or even just as food sources.

Under Map, he found what he expected: a literal map, much like the display of his Stronghold, that he could display over his outstretched hand. It showed the limits of his current Territory, but not many details. Shelim was there and well-depicted, as was Haarwatch, which was interesting. All the places Felix and his team had passed through recently were clear, but the rest was vague terrain that might have been forests, hills, swamps—anything. He had a feeling he needed to explore his new Territory, and sooner rather than later.

Defensive Arrays had only a single listing: the already-cast Mirk Enclosure, which was an ongoing effect.

Mirk Enclosure - Ritual, Defensive Array, Tier IV
Effect: Encase your Territory in an impenetrable fog, invisible to your people within, but a physical and sensory barrier to all those without.
Initial Cost: 10,000 Mana/5,000 Essence
Ongoing Cost: 5,000 Mana/2,500 Essence Per 12 Hours

A timer was next to the Enclosure, coming close to the end of its twelve-hour run. Karys had warned him about this before, and Felix had upped it the night before, but it was a hungry little spell. Since he hadn't had a chance to up his Essence stores, Felix dumped a healthy chunk of his Mana reserves into it. The timer reset, and Felix fought off the very slight dizziness he felt after using up nearly all his Mana. He shook it off and moved onto the Offensive Array tab. It contained two arrays, but both were lower Tiers than he had hoped.

Earthen Riot - Ritual, Offensive Array, Tier II
Effect: Disrupt the earth, one hundred yards in diameter from
a point you choose within your Territory.
Cost: 3,000 Mana/1,500 Essence

Flame Geyser - Ritual, Offensive Array, Tier II
Effect: Create an area of spouting flames, one hundred yards
in diameter from a point you choose within your Territory.
Cost: 2,500 Mana/1,250 Essence

"Huh," Felix said. They didn't sound extremely impressive, but the area of effect was large, and it sounded like Felix could cast it *wherever* he wanted, as long as it was within his Territory. "That...that might be useful. Karys, is there a way to upgrade Offensive or Defensive Arrays?"

"Absolutely. But you must research the one you have to discover any improvements to its structure. Arrays are not the same as Skills, which grow as you use them and gain greater understanding. It is good that you have a Glyphworks, for it will be instrumental in adding and altering any arrays for your Stronghold or Territory."

This is so cool. Wait. "Do I have to keep standing in here?" Felix gestured to the glowing array all around him and his own Seal burning beneath his feet.

"Oh, of course not. You've established your Stronghold and taken a firmer grip of your Authority. You can access any of these menus now from wherever you find yourself," Karys said.

"Really? I can use my Authority in my Territory while *outside* my Territory?" Felix asked.

"Ah, well, no. Not unless you've established an alliance with the Territory you are within. Otherwise, you can access your menus, but affect no change."

"That, at least, is the same for us as well," Vess said. She waved Felix closer. "What else is?"

Felix walked from the Seal, and as he did so, the entire array dimmed slightly. He could still feel it working, still see the constant stream of Mana in the air, but it banked itself. "Huh, sleep mode."

"What was that?" Vess asked.

"A dumb joke. C'mon, both of you. Let's go check out our new facilities. I want to get on top of our situation before anything else comes barging in." Felix pulled them both down the hall, moving swiftly toward his chambers and the Storage Facility nearby. Yet before he could travel far, a shape resolved from the shadows.

"Felix Nevarre."

Felix pulled up short, annoyed that he hadn't sensed the chimera at all. "A'zek. Why are you down here?"

"My apologies, Autarch. I was sent to request an audience with the new lord of this land." A'zek, a panther-lizard the size of a small horse, bowed. "The Farwalker has need of your judgment."

"My judgment?" He traded a concerned look with Vess. "I'm not in charge of your people, A'zek."

"In this, you are." A'zek pulled himself up and met Felix's gaze with his own, two liquid pools of shadow. "The Synod seeks your judgment over the fate of the Matriarch."

CHAPTER SEVEN

Zara Cyrene, Master Tier, Sorcerer of the Fallen Halls, and Chanter of Cantus Sodalus was very close to killing someone.

"You wish me to beg for aid from Haarwatch? That backward hovel? What good will they do us, when their streets are likely as overrun as our own?" A rounded man with a drooping mustache and a gold chain of office leaned back, his gaze resolutely upon his desk. He refused to look at her.

"We are not begging for aid, Lord Governor. We are demanding passage, and perhaps—*perhaps*—we may send aid to help your citizens," Zara said through clenched teeth.

The Governor of Setoria sat, seemingly unconcerned behind his huge, tarwood desk. Eyes downcast, he sorted through stacks of paper as if hard at work. Nevermind that the man's hair was greasy, his eyes blood-shot, and his Spirit in screaming disarray. Had Zara been in a kinder mood, she would have felt a twinge of pity for the man. He was a petty bureaucrat who'd been delivered an impossible situation: more than half of his city was engulfed in a mystical bank of clouds. None could enter, and none could leave.

"Lady Cyrene, what you ask is most irregular, and had this been a normal day, I would have you dragged off in chains for bursting into my offices as you have." The governor gave a quick, nervous glance around the room. Six other men and women were there, all armed and armored in Haarwatch's guard uniform, and he only had a single Iron Rank Guilder at his elbow for defense. He paled at the sight of Kelgan casually sharpening his spear, flinching at the open aggression in every single one of their faces. "I've only three Manaships under my purview, two of which were on loan to the Inviolate Inquisition. The other is my personal craft for matters of the Territory. Not to be used by any...stranger who enters my offices."

"The Inviolate Inquisition is not a concern any longer," Zara stated. "Most of them are dead."

"You fools," he whispered. His Spirit clenched up like a tattered rag, used and wrung out. "What have you done?"

"They did it to themselves, summoning a construct of solid light into the midst of their own men," Zara said with contempt. "Their Inquisitor doomed them all."

"And would they have done so, had they not been opposed?" the governor demanded. "Would I find my city broken apart by this fog had you not struck at them?"

Zara wrestled with her own anger and frustration and found it upsettingly difficult. In an effort to remain unobtrusive, they had followed "proper" channels and put in a case for transit. For an entire day and night they had waited while the city had gone insane.

With the rising of the fog, panic gripped the streets. Visibility was impossible, the air as thick as it ever was in the Foglands, turning that panic quickly into riots. The governor had united the Setoria branch of the Protector's Guild into action, but in addition to being generally weaker than those in Haarwatch, the Guilders' barracks was almost entirely outside the barrier. Only a few dozen Tin and Iron Ranks were left fog-side of things, more than enough to stop a few Untempered instigators, but woefully ill-equipped to stop mobs the size of entire districts.

Blood flowed through the following day as people grew more desperate and afraid. Cries of a rising dark power, this Autarch, were on the lips of everyone from High Street to Beggar's Way. Fires soon followed, engulfing an entire district, which sent people running from the fog toward the lighter half of Setoria. Unfortunately, they found the barrier utterly impassable. Thousands died before the mob stopped, many crushed and others forced to turn back toward the raging flames.

Zara was forced to rest and recover for much of that time, unable to help those who cried out in the streets. She had not many abilities that could heal, but the Chant was versatile, and had she been able to wield it, Zara would have expended herself twice over to stop the needless bloodshed. Yet, after confronting the Howlers at the city gates, then the Inquisitors and their powerful magic, it was all she could do to master herself. Her soul cried out for the anguished people around her, but she had a duty that she could not set down, not if the entire city were burning down around her.

The Hand and Haarguard protected them while they recovered, which proved fortuitous when roving gangs assaulted the shopfront they'd claimed as shelter. Drifting in and out of consciousness, she witnessed three times when the mob beyond their doors had attempted to force entry. Reed had avoided killing anyone, at the least.

"They're Untempered." He'd scowled at a Haarguard that had gotten too exuberant. "Would you murder a child? No. You teach them a lesson and let them walk away." He grinned. "Maybe bloody 'em up a bit."

She woke for good a bit after that. As soon as she was able to walk, Zara had begun pestering the Governor's office.

"—Inquisition is one of the holy Orders, for Trackless' sake! Why would you interfere?" he demanded.

"Better than curling beneath them like a dog!" one of the Haarguard snapped. Kelgan, part of her Mind recognized.

They had been forced to wade through a mob on their way to the governor's mansion. The people were balancing on the razor's edge of chaos, and a single spark would ignite them into even greater bloodshed. She could feel it, even hurt as she was. Considering her convalescing state, the weight of their terrified regard sent fissures of pain skittering down Zara's Aspects, all of them strained by her use of Harmonics. Wielding the fundamental powers of Creation had a cost, and she was paying it tenfold.

Now she gritted her sharp, shark-like teeth and shoved down her anger and urgency. She hadn't the time to educate the man on the particulars of how he was a wrong-headed ass. Her Mark was missing. She could no longer sense Felix, not his general direction nor moods. The Mark was being suppressed by a greater power. *Or erased...but that, at least, is impossible at his advancement. Even for an Unbound.*

At least she knew he wasn't dead. The System wouldn't have elevated a dead man, no matter his deeds. *An Autarch. Avet's blackened teeth, I need to find out what happened before it is too late.*

The Governor had continued to talk while she mastered herself. "—as you see. I'm up to my ears in blood and murder, and I'll not budge even for an Adept Tier such as yourself. The entirety of Setoria is in an uproar, a wild chaos! If I let you take my ships, then what defense have I against the mob at the gates? Eh? You'll have me dead, woman!"

"You think we care about your Redcloak-aiding life? You're not worth more than the dirt it'd take to bury you. I—"

"Kelgan," Zara said sharply, and the spearman snapped his jaws shut and stepped back, the haft of his spear creaking in his powerful grip. "I am not asking to take your ship, Lord Governor. I am telling you. There is far more at stake here than Setoria. If you or the goons cowering behind your office wall try to stop us, then I'll tear this entire building to the ground."

The governor flinched with every word, his soft features turning tremulous with Zara's rising intensity. When her power flared, the force of her wounded Spirit rounded his eyes in terror. The Iron Rank behind him stiffened in alarm, shooting a wild glance at the leftmost wall. A secret door opened, and ten Iron Ranks charged into the room, swords and daggers bared. They made it no farther than two strides within before they were felled, knocked unconscious by nothing more than Zara's anger.

For her part, she ignored them all, bearing down on the soft, quivering chin of her prey. By the end of her words, the lord governor was half-sunk into his chair and sweating enough for two men. He reached for his badge of office, fumbling with its linkage.

An aquamarine tendril of liquid light tore it from his neck.

"The right decision."

———

Zara marched from the room, meeting up with the rest of the Haarguard in the halls. She managed to pass through three chambers before her legs gave out. Reed, for all his faults, was there to catch her.

"You pressed too hard, Sorcerer," the Hand of Pax'Vrell muttered. "What will you do when I'm no longer here?"

She felt jittery and weak in his arms, but her Will was not inconsiderable. Zara pushed out of his arms and stood, unaided. She could make it to the roof, she hoped. "I have lasted this long without you, Reed. I imagine I survived somehow. Had I pressed any lighter, he'd have wasted those Iron Ranks on a foolish attack. Better to have stopped it cold and saved their lives."

"You leave behind enemies." He snorted, drawing himself to his full height, towering over her by half a stride. "Not capable ones, but we could have moved more quietly."

"And taken who-knows-how-many weeks. We've important business to be about, Darius Reed, and I'll not be held back." Zara prowled down the hall, heading for the stairs.

They made it to the roof quickly, where a special dock had been erected for the governor's private use. The Manaship of the Territory was an emergency vessel provided to only those Territories that proved themselves worthy under the Hierocracy. Despite that lauded distinction, it was small, no bigger than a sloop. Fitting for the low concentration of Mana in the area, it was designed to function on considerably less than standard for the Interior.

"Pathetic," Reed scoffed.

He wasn't wrong. The governor's sloop would likely carry only half of them, and at no faster pace than a steady mount. Luckily, it was not the only ship at dock. Two others were at anchor, both of them slightly larger than the sloop, but no more than Iron Rank craft at best. Each was fitted with three masts and a sleek hull, clearly built for speed and to a far higher standard of Mana than the governor's. They were clearly not property of Setoria but of the Inquisition, as they were built in a style that Zara hadn't seen since she last visited the capital. Zara frowned. Operating it would cost her far more Mana than she could afford, especially if she wished to maintain the speed they needed.

As the Haarguard piled aboard one of the ships, Zara unlocked the moorings that secured the vessel to the dock. The governor's badge of office flared each time with a distinct vibrational signature, releasing the wards with a whisper of her power. A whisper she could just barely afford.

"You're spent," Reed said and she eyed him with exhausted resolve. "You'll never make it to the Foglands. Not loaded up on one ship like that."

"We will because we must. Perhaps among the Haarguard I can find enough pilots to fuel the ship. Thangle is a sturdy fellow, and quite capable with Mana Manipulation. You've your own ship now, free to try the barrier and report back to your Duke. I shall continue on." Zara grinned at Reed and heard the slight squirm in his Spirit at sight of her sharp teeth. "Duty weighs on us all, Reed."

The Hand was silent as Zara finished releasing both boats from their warded lines. Zara managed it all, even keeping her feet when all she wanted was to rest. Yet, when she attempted to mount the gangplank, a hand landed on her shoulder, halting her steps.

"The Lady Dayne is in the Foglands, yes?" Reed asked. "That is where she...fled to, is it not?"

"Indeed. She travels with Felix." Last she knew, anyway, before both of their Marks had gone silent.

"I can feel warriors gathering beyond the barrier," he said. "Even from here. They aren't strong, nothing compared to an Adept, but that'll change soon. The powers will come to challenge this place, to see this fool who declared himself king. And my Duke's daughter is caught up in all of it." The big warrior grimaced at his new Manaship with a sigh of consternation. As if a great deal of tension drained out of him, his shoulders slumped before firming once more.

"You there!" he shouted, and one of the Haarguard froze in instinctual fear. Reed hurled a bundle of enchanted rope up to him, taken from the moorings at their feet. "Bind that ship to the other! Keep it loose, but secure it!"

The Haarguard gave a halting affirmation before gathering up a few others and setting to work. Reed nodded and started up the gangplank.

"What're you waiting for? We've got places to be." He drew himself up and met her gaze. "One threat may be ended, but this is the Chimera's mouth, and I'll have her out of it before it snaps shut."

"As you say," Zara said, grin bright and sharp. "Let us be on our way."

CHAPTER EIGHT

"My first order of business should be more reliable stairs, I think," Felix mused. Even abstaining from Adamant Discord, his own Strength, Dexterity, and Agility let him leap up through the holes in the Temple with relative ease. Vess was right behind him, landing with no less grace despite her lesser stats; no doubt due to her high-level Grace and Born Trait that let her leap extraordinarily high.

"Personally, I like the express path," Vess said with a grin that dimpled her cheek. "Trudging up stairs, even at high speeds, grows tiresome."

"I'll keep that in mind," Felix said. He tapped his lips, thinking on the power at his fingertips. Questions boiled up and over in his Mind, too many to count. He focused on only a few while they ascended the levels toward the outside. Toward this...judgment he was to perform.

Felix frowned. A'zek had gone on ahead, intending to inform the Farwalker of the "Autarch's approach." He had leaped upward at an impressive pace, but not fast enough that Felix's eyes couldn't track him. Yet he still vanished from his Perception, even that extra awareness his Authority afforded him. *Likely a Blessing from the Raven. The Urge's power is better than mine by a long shot.*

That fact made him a little uncomfortable. He had invoked the Raven during his fight against the Urges imprisoned in the Mana well—an action that had no doubt strengthened the Urge of Findings In The Dark but one that was necessary to weaken and dazzle the far more vile Urges he had faced. It had helped Felix beat the dangerous monstrosities, but the Raven's motives felt inscrutable. It loved shiny things, new things, old things that folks had lost or buried, but what did it *want* with it all? Was there a plan to the avarice he'd glimpsed in those huge, black eyes?

"What is a Residential sequence?" Felix asked, pushing his Mind away from the issue. "The Dwelling Stone was imbued with it, according to its Lore." The terminology sounded like it was some sort of packaged code, waiting for use. But everything Felix knew about coding was from movies, which typically showed a person flailing on a keyboard while lights flashed on the screen. Small terms and words flitted by his Keen Mind, enough to convince him that he didn't have the understanding to properly convey what he meant, so he changed tack. "Is it like a...pre-built array in the crystal?"

"Of a sort, I—" Karys said from Felix's waist. The sword puffed a heaving sigh of green-gold vapor. His Body was still below, investigating more of the array in the hopes that it might trigger old memories. "No details come to Mind, and I do not know if that is because I do not know them, or if there are more holes in my memory. Suffice it to say, the Belais Crystal held a pattern that the System extrapolated into your Seat and Seal, and thus into your Stronghold."

"Mhm," Felix said. That much had been obvious. He'd grown used to the specific weirdness of the System and its vibrational underpinnings. Skills were patterns of sound and light, why not a whole Forge, too? "So it's a Stronghold, then. Where are my big walls and towers?"

Vess laughed.

"I would suggest you continue to explore your Authority," Karys said.

"Do you mind sharing while we move?" Vess asked. She looked at him with a touch of hesitation, but ploughed on through her next sentence. "I would very much like to see how your Stronghold functions."

"I don't mind at all," Felix said as he brought up his new menus and flicked them in Vess' direction. A copy of what he was viewing rotating into her view, visible to his sight as well.

The Song of Stronghold
Stronghold Defensive Strength: 20%
Stronghold Offensive Strength: 5%
Chancellor: None Selected
Master of Glyph: None Selected
Master of Forge: None Selected
Master of Treasury: None Selected
Master of Alchemy: None Selected

Two other tabs lined the side, Map and Improvements, but before he could investigate them, a secondary box popped into view.

You Have Established A Stronghold!
Do You Wish To Name It At This Time?

Ugh, I'm bad at names, Felix groaned. *No.* The box vanished, but not for good, he feared. *What do I name a half-broken Temple and some forest?*

He moved on. Under Improvements were subsections for Fortifications, Living Spaces, Professional Spaces, Garden, and, surprisingly, Spirit Tree. When he selected it, he got a warning message.

**Spirit Tree Is Still Attuning To Its Surroundings
Do Not Attempt To Harvest Until Attunement Is Complete.**

Okay, leaving that alone, then.

"Stronghold Defensive and Offensive Strength are both pretty low," Felix said. "I'm guessing that's based on the general...disarray, huh?"

"Precisely," Karys buzzed from the hooked sword. "It counts only the condition of the Stronghold itself, not the people who may or may not defend it. It does not, for instance, factor you into either calculation."

"If you build defensive structures and construct weaponry at your Forge, then those percentages should rise," Vess said. "My family's castle has quite a few such structures and is well-defended against outside attack."

"Do you know how to make those things?" Felix asked.

"..Not as such, no," Vess admitted, a tad sheepishly. "My education was always on governance, diplomacy, and combat. The Path of the Ruler, Father calls it."

Path, eh? Felix thought. *Interesting.* "Well, I've got a few other tabs here under Stronghold. Improvements. Oh, cool. Yeah. Fortifications and Offensive Weaponry have their own sub sections." Felix shook his head. "This Authority thing gets really granular on some of this stuff, huh?"

"It can. Your Authority menus are definitely different than the ones I have seen, and that should only increase your options." Vess easily leaped to the next level, Felix following effortlessly. "Have you selected a Chancellor yet?"

"No, not really sure what that is," Felix admitted.

"A representative to act in your absence. So, you would want to choose someone that will stay here, generally speaking, and who you trust." Vess grimaced. "A challenging selection at the best of times."

They reached the top of the cliff, slipping through a rent in the roof of the Temple—a hole the Atlantes Anima had created when it grew, diverting an entire river and splitting the cliff top in two. The river had at first poured down into his Temple, but Felix had done a little Stone Shaping on the surface to divert it to the west, so that it cascaded down a separate part of the clifftop.

It was a temporary solution, but at least his new home wasn't going to flood anytime soon. The dark brown trunk of his Spirit Tree stretched high above them, and in his Manasight, it pulsed with every color of the rainbow and a few more besides. Leaves, far, far above them hung fat and green and glossy in the mid-morning sunlight—what little of it that could penetrate the thick canopy, that is.

"And the other positions I see? Master of Glyphs and stuff?" Felix asked Vess and Karys, the two of them walking to the edge. "What's that about?"

"A Master of one of your Crafting Halls is responsible for the production within said Hall and lends their own level of mastery toward completed works. So, it behooves a Forge to have a high-ranking Smith as the Forgemaster, you see," Karys said.

"All right, makes sense," Felix said. "Not exactly a going concern yet, though. I don't even have the place set up."

"Felix...do you truly wish to do this?"

Felix stopped feet from the edge and glanced back at Vess. She was looking up at the Spirit Tree, brows down, worry and wonder flitting across her Spirit. Felix clamped down his Affinity again, dulling his sense of her. "Do what?"

"The Authority. Establishing yourself as a power upon the Continent." Vess shifted her gaze, and Felix could only see concern in her dark brown eyes. "You have grown powerful, I cannot deny that. But this is beyond the physical strength of one person. When people find out...when the Hierocracy finds out—"

"When Felix took the Authority upon himself, he was announced to all the world," Karys said.

A flash of icy dread pierced Felix's gut.

"Why would it do that?" Vess asked, outraged.

"It is as it always was," Karys said, confused. "It may invite challenge, but—"

"It will do more than that!" Vess ran her fingers through her hair. Strands already hung loose from the braids she had plaited earlier, but now they stuck out wildly. "You took over a portion of the Hierocracy. They will not take that without challenging you...and that means war at your—our—doorstep."

There it was, the threat he'd been feeling. Still unformed, but looming over him like a dark cloud. Felix licked his lips and took a breath. "I enacted a defensive array in order to help Zara and stop the Inquisition from reaching out. Will that prevent *everyone* from coming into my Territory, Karys?"

"It will. How long depends on how fast they can muster the power sufficient to overcome its defenses. As it stands, your Mirk Enclosure has not been breached, though...thousands have tried." Karys was quiet a moment, almost as if he were reading something. The pause lingered.

"Karys?"

"It...it is not important yet. I shall tell you after your meeting. The Enclosure will hold even against Master Tiers."

"And Grandmasters? Paragons?" Felix asked.

"A true Paragon would walk through it as if it did not exist. A Grandmaster could break it, however, given enough time."

That made his decision for him. "Then we prepare as best we can, and we need to send word to Cal in Haarwatch. They'd face any enemies far before we would. Is there a way to do that?"

"There once was. You must advance your Stronghold to Rank II, however, before communication between locations becomes viable," Karys said.

"Then that's the focus for now. Improve the Stronghold, and," he took a deep, steadying breath again. "And prepare for war. Fuck me."

He looked over the ledge at the stone dwellings far below. A group sat near the water's edge, as far away from the Risi as they could manage. No houses stood, though a few fabric tents had been set up, and what he knew to be two hundred and forty-five Henaari gathered in a loose semi-circle.

"First, we deal with them," he said.

He stepped off the ledge.

Felix took in his target as he fell. The Henaari semi-circle was mostly non-combatants. Men and women who were too old to fight or too valuable as crafters or some other arcane profession, along with a bevy of children, waited below. At the fore were a gathering of women, all robed the same and wearing a broach atop their well-made garb, and a single man in the fantasy version of a wheelchair.

A woman knelt bound and masked between them.

Lightning crackled around Felix's form as he landed among them, briefly pulling him back upward and slowing his descent while also unleashing a wave of half-dried mud. Henaari stumbled back, mainly Dawnguard in their distinctive leather and horn armor. They had formed a protective ring around their people, with the majority of their force facing the direction of the Frost Giants. As Felix straightened, Vess landed just a few paces back, her own Skills blunting the impact.

"Autarch," the Farwalker said in a cautious tone. The man was paralyzed, as far as Felix could tell, and wore a heavy, hooded cloak that completely obscured his face in shadow. He inclined his head to Felix then Vess. "And the Lady Dayne. Thank you for allowing us to rest within the haven of your Stronghold."

"You're welcome to rest, though you're here sooner than I had expected," Felix said. A'zek or Wyvora had clearly given the Farwalker an update on his situation. "Wyvora had left to find you, and I hear you arrived barely hours after she left. I thought you were heading to the Hoarfrost?"

"Circumstances within the Foglands—Pardon me. Within Nagast. They have changed since last we met." The Farwalker moved forward, pushed from behind by Wyvora herself, his sort-of apprentice. "The lands abound with that same thickened mist as once plagued these forests and mountains. It has proven difficult to travel within."

"A spell of mine," Felix said by way of explanation. "A defensive one. I'm sorry if it caused you problems." Though he was surprised it was so thick as to limit the Henaari's movement within the Territory. Felix couldn't even see it around him, and none of his people had mentioned it as bothering them. *Is there like a white list? People it doesn't affect?*

The Farwalker waved a hand, as if uncaring about it. "No matter. We were already coming to you to seek your judgment." He waved a wizened hand at the masked figure between them. "The Matriarch's crimes have come to light, as all things must."

Felix's Eye had confirmed it was the Matriarch as he'd fallen, and he stared curiously at her bindings. It was all a simple, braided rope, but the mask on her face was wooden and shaped into the visage of a hooded serpent. His Manasight picked up threads of power flaring along its rim and likely beneath the wood itself. The Mana seemed to be a combination of purple augmentation Mana, dusty brown earth Mana, and an oily sepia tone that he hadn't encountered much before. "What is with the mask?"

"It is a precaution and a dishonor," one of the Synod said. She was a slight woman for a Henaari, which meant she topped Felix by two inches and had iron-grey hair cut into a practical bob at her jawline. She inclined her head at Felix a touch deeper than the Farwalker had done. "It disrupts the connection to her core space, to her Blessings, and silences her deceiving tongue."

"The Leviathan, the Treacherous One, is the Endless Raven's greatest enemy, a serpent that dwells in the deepest dark and thrives upon secrets and lies," the Farwalker explained. "To be clad in its visage is to be given the greatest insult." He lifted a tattered book, the journal of a former Matriarch Felix had found months back.

"The journal of our blessed leader—Ociala—shed much light upon the dark actions of this traitor. It was she who laced Ociala's food with subtle poison, who sabotaged her gear, and who hid a monster lure within her belongings. The clues of it all, and Ociala's suspicions, are all tidily written within this journal. When the extent of the Matriarch's deeds were discovered, she tried to run." The Farwalker shook his cowled head. "In your fog, she made it less than a mile before our scouts caught up with her."

"I see." Felix clenched his jaw. The treachery of the Matriarch didn't surprise him. The fact that she had something to do with the former Matriarch's fall? It made sense, if only based on how the woman had acted around Felix and his team when they'd first met.

"That is when her...newer actions came to light. The Dawnguard that she sent to follow you carried with them a dagger. An artifact of the Raven called a Dire Talon, a weapon that could end a life with no more than a scratch, or could be expended to claim a hidden space for the Raven. She has confessed that they were to claim your Temple and kill you in the process." That same Synod member spoke again.

She bowed at the waist, far lower than any so far. To Felix's surprise, all of the Synod and the crowd beyond did the same. Even Wyvora and the Farwalker. "We ask your forgiveness, Autarch. Though the Raven seeks out hidden things to claim them for her own, She is not a creature of treachery. This...wretch's actions have marred all of us."

"We offer her up to you, for recompense and justice as you see fit, Autarch," the Farwalker continued. "This has moved beyond the purview of our people and even the Raven. As the wronged party and lord of these lands, you are the arbiter of her fate."

Felix regarded them all, calming his inner turmoil all the while. It sounded like they expected him to have her killed or something. While he was disgusted that she had tried to snake the Temple out from under him, he didn't plan on murdering someone. Besides, he had a better idea.

He stepped forward six paces, feeling the anxiety in the Spirits of the Henaari watching. The fear. None of them wanted murder either, he could tell, but at the same time, they were utterly committed to letting him choose. The Farwalker, of course, was a blank spot in his senses, but Felix was fairly certain he knew how the man felt toward the Matriarch. The bound woman's Spirit flared and shook, somehow aware that Felix approached, and she quietly began to fidget in her bonds.

She went deathly still as Felix laid a hand on her masked face right between the bulging eyes of the wooden snake.

"You have hurt your people far more than you've hurt me," Felix said to her, not caring who heard him. "I will not kill you." A soft set of indrawn breaths came from the crowd, and the Matriarch trembled beneath his hand. "You will not thank me at the end, I don't think."

Chthonic Tribute!

Unite the Lost!

Acting on a hunch, Felix reached into the Matriarch with his newly evolved hunger and grabbed at her core space. He didn't seek to break her into Essence or drain her dry, but to instead seize a portion of her significance. It was like catching smoke, but Felix was able to claim a portion of it—then he burned it, letting Unite the Lost consume its potency. Fuel it.

A brilliant light burst from above, like a spear from the heavens but emanating from the Spirit Tree above them. The Matriarch screamed, her body wrenching backward as the light stabbed through her body and into the earth. Her scream transformed, mingled with the screeching crow of a thousand birds as a massive flock streamed from the light just above her chest. The Henaari cowered, and Vess drew her spear, but the flock merely spiraled around the beam of light before vanishing into the distance. The light winked out.

The Matriarch's scream cut off, and she fell bonelessly to the ground.

Target has been cleansed of all Marks!

Felix stood over the woman's whimpering form before glaring at the rest of them. "I've removed her Mark. Her connection to the Raven is gone."

More murmurs slithered through the crowd, now far more upset and disquieted. Even the Synod were exchanging furtive, terrified looks. Then the air above them all shook.

CAW!
THE RAVEN IS PLEASED!
ALL BLESSINGS HAVE BEEN REMOVED FROM THE LEAST DAUGHTER!
CAW!
FOLLOW! ATTEND THE AUTARCH!
HE IS ANOINTED. HE IS UNBOUND.
HE WILL UNVEIL THE DARK.

Those murmurs turned to frantic rustlings and whispers, and the cry of "Unbound?" became a staccato punctuation upon everyone's lips. Felix, meanwhile, gritted his teeth. He figured he couldn't keep that a secret forever, but the Raven had shit timing. *Or she isn't as pleased as she claims,* he thought.

"So you are Unbound," the Farwalker said with relief. "That explains a great deal, yet reassures me not at all."

"Join the club," Felix said wryly. He frowned at the Raven's message. "Does that mean what I think it means?"

The Farwalker lifted his hands and pulled back his hood. The veil of shadows parted and revealed a lean but heavily wrinkled face with wide-set eyes and a large forehead. He grinned. "The Raven does not command us in all things, but She is our guiding light." The Synod had gathered close, talking among themselves. "I do believe your Stronghold has grown today, Felix Nevarre. Autarch."

Felix shot a glance at Vess, who smirked at him. He suppressed the urge to sigh. "That's what I thought you'd say."

As one, the Synod turned and dropped to a single knee.

CHAPTER NINE

Congratulations, Autarch!
You Have Recruited A Faction!
The Henaari (Night Talons Tribe) Have Joined Your Fledgling
Nation!
+25% To All Positive Relations With Henaari!
+25% To All Positive Relations With The Endless Raven!

The Henaari gave an Oath, similar to the Frost Giants', but unique to their people. It didn't reference the Raven directly, but Felix knew what "swear to find light in the dark" meant in context.

"You really want to hitch your wagon to mine?" Felix asked. The Farwalker chuckled, his lean face still smiling. He hadn't put his cowl on again for some reason, and Felix found it refreshing to be able to look in his eyes.

"Your star is rising, Felix, of that I have no doubt. But that is not my only interest in aligning with your Territory. My people are nomadic by nature, but it was not always that way. Once we had a home, a permanent one among the mountains to the far east. Our Farwalkers and Farhunters would still push into the wilds, looking for hidden places and secrets, but they could return to a place of safety." The man's face took on a wistful tinge.

"What happened?" Felix asked.

"Strife. We collect secrets, after all. Eventually, we became a fruit too ripe not to pick." He surveyed his people, now dispersing back toward the lakeshore. The bound Matriarch had been dragged off somewhere while they had sworn their Oath. The Farwalker read his gaze easily. "As the wronged party, you had the right of judgment. We will take care of her from here."

Part of Felix wanted to ask what the old man meant, but he didn't doubt it would be what the woman deserved. "As long as she doesn't interfere."

"That will not be an issue," the Farwalker said. "Now, I should go oversee the Dawnguard. Without the Matriarch, they are a touch aimless."

Aimless, huh? Felix thought on his menus, and an idea sparked to life. "If you're in need of a task, I could use some aid in scouting these forests. I spent my fair share of time here, but there are countless miles that I know nothing about. I'd like to get a catalog going of useful plants and dangerous monsters. Would that be something your people would be interested in?"

As the final syllable left his mouth, power coalesced with a sudden trill. A blue window appeared before the Farwalker, visible to everyone.

A Quest Has Been Offered!
Hunting For Opportunities!
The Autarch has need of an accurate accounting of his lands.
He has asked that you and your people begin to scout the area
directly around his Stronghold. Battle with dangerous beasts
may be necessary, but it is not required. Information and
samples of both flora and fauna are requested.
Rewards: XP, Varies

"Now that is something I've not seen in a long, long time," the Farwalker said. Wyvora read the window just over his shoulder and looked up at Felix in awe. "Proper Quests."

Felix was a bit surprised at their appearance, though Vess seemed unfazed. *Probably something she saw all the time, her father giving out Quests and stuff. Authority things.* "I had meant to just ask you, but this is better. I'd rather you be rewarded for the aid."

The Farwalker grinned. "We will, of course, accept. This applies to all my people?"

Felix hesitated, but Vess nodded. "Everyone who wishes to join the Quest may do so."

"Excellent. Not all of our people are of a martial tilt, nor even walking the Wilds. If you do not mind, I will have our craftsmen build our homes here, nearest the water." His eyes flicked to the rough, Stone Shaped dwellings Felix had made the day prior. "We can also work on your homes, as well."

"Feel free," Felix said with a chuckle. He knew his attempts were utilitarian at best. "I plan to make this place far more secure shortly. I don't see why it can't look nice, too."

The Farwalker clasped Felix's hand in his. He squeezed with a surprising strength, though it was only a faint pressure on Felix's skin. "It will be nice to have a home again."

The Farwalker moved off, pushed along by Wyvora. She gave him a strange look as they passed, but Felix brushed it off. The Henaari were settled, for now.

"That Farwalker is entirely too clever," Vess said. "He may not have orchestrated the Matriarch's deceit, but he played her as well as any Court Noble."

"A formidable ally," Felix said. "But yeah. I hear the warning."

Vess only nodded. Then she bit her lip. "I should go see Evie. She'll be excited to hear about these hunting Quests you're handing out. It might keep her mind off...certain things." She added the last with a glance at the modest structure of Manawrought ice nearby. The Giants were making themselves at home.

"That'd be for the best, I think. It'll give me time to really dive into these menus. There's—" Felix sighed. "There's a lot. Oh, that reminds me. The Quest I just gave...where does the XP come from?"

"The rewards? Those should be System generated. As a Territory Lord, you can generate Quests, but the System has control over what it will give," Vess explained. "You may put in an additional reward, such as a physical object or service, but the core of it is from the System."

"Oh. Good. I had a weird thought that the XP would come from my own total," he said in relief. "But what stops a Lord from issuing enough Quests to power level everyone up?"

Vess tilted her head, just slightly, and squinted in brief confusion. "Power level—? Oh, you mean assisted growth. While that is possible to accomplish with a team of individuals, Quests feature safeguards that prevent that sort of thing. You will find that you cannot issue Quests for simple or trivial tasks, and the XP rewards are always commensurate with the task itself."

"I'm learning all sorts of things today," Felix said with a smile. "What would I do without you?"

"You would always have me, Felix," his sword chimed in.

"Yes, thank you, Karys," Felix deadpanned.

Vess fought back a laugh, but failed—it was a throaty sort of chuckle that prompted his own grin. "I will see you soon, Felix," she said, gathering herself for a leap.

"Soon enough," he agreed.

Vess leaped away, soaring back up the cliff face in a series of impressive jumps.

"What were you two laughing at, Felix?" Karys asked through his sword. "You two seem quite close."

"Don't go getting ideas, Paragon," Felix said. He realized he was still smiling and let it drop. "She's next in line to be a Duchess."

"And you are an Autarch."

Felix stopped mid-stride. He...hadn't really thought of it that way.

Felix shook his head. "That's not important right now. We have to get this place fixed up, and quickly." He looked at the Henaari, standing close together and discussing something. Likely the Quest he'd offered. The way they were squinting at one another though, made Felix almost slap his head in realization. "Ah, right! Before I forget."

He brought up his Territory menu and selected his Defensive Array tab. Under the active column, where Mirk Enclosure was shown, he poked around until he found a piece just below it listed as "Exemptions." His name, Pit's, and everyone on his team were on that list. Not only that, but Haarwatch was listed. Just the city name. *That explains why I couldn't see the fog as it spread out, or why none of my friends were complaining about it. Did I exempt them automatically? All of Haarwatch, too?*

"Karys?" Felix inquired before explaining his question.

"Ah, yes. The array would have picked up on those directly subordinate to you and given them exemptions to the array," his sword explained.

"Then why not the giants or the Henaari, once they've sworn their Oath?"

"New Factions must be manually exempted from large-scale defensive arrays, due to the nature of fledgling alliances. It is a protective measure built into the process. I feel I have seen it...go wrong, in the past. Though I am unsure."

It made sense, as most things the System did, once he'd worked it out. Felix decided to test it, however, to see if he could take people from the Exemption list at will. He chose himself, and when he was taken off the Exemption list, the area around him was immediately inundated with a fog so thick not even his Perception could pierce more than ten feet of it. Another effort of Will had his name back on the Exemption list, and the fog blipped out of existence like a poorly loaded video game animation.

Dang, I should totally add Zara and the others to this list, too.

So, with a quirk of Willpower, he added Zara and her away team as well as the Night Talons Tribe to the Exemptions list. Distantly, he heard sudden sounds of wonder from their people, but Felix was focusing on holding two separate thoughts in his head. Not *everyone* in those groups should be able to walk free. *Exempt my allies and the tribe...but restrict the Matriarch.*

He didn't even know her proper name, but something rang softly, a tuning fork just barely humming away. It had worked.

"Great." Felix slapped his hands together. "Next step: Fortifications."

———

It turned out his options were relatively limited. Under Improvements, there was a tab for Fortifications, but it only contained two patterns.

Fortifications

Bulwark - Defensive Fortification, Tier II

- **Effect: +0.01% Defensive Strength Per Unit Installed**

Square Tower - Defensive Fortification, Tier II

- **Effect: +0.02% Defensive Strength Per Unit Installed**
- **Limit: 1 Tower Unit Per Every 2 Bulwark Units**

According to Karys, the Tier was determined by the level of dwelling —in this case, a Stronghold—and if it were a simple Home, he would be able to access only Tier 0 patterns, if there were any. Tier II, by contrast, were fairly complex structures. They weren't just stone piled on top of each other, but imbued with sigiladry in elaborate arrays throughout their construction.

He had considered just throwing Stone Shaping together and making walls himself, but the pre-set options had benefits. Felix doubted he could match the boost the Bulwark and Square Towers could afford by themselves. What was most interesting, however, was the Stronghold Map allowed him to plan out the structure before committing to any design. Each wall section was about thirty feet long by ten feet thick by forty feet tall. A solid design, as far as his amateur eyes could tell. It was no orichalcum wall of Haarwatch, but he figured that was a bit above his Stronghold's paygrade.

For now.

Using the Map, Felix envisioned a continuous wall extending around the base of the cliff to the south, into the eastern forests where it would curve north and finally terminate against the banks of the lake. The squared towers would fit between every two sections of wall, adding places for future guards to watch the surrounding areas or even launch Skills from on high. The towers were fifteen feet taller than the top of the wall and had crenelated tops. If he had siege weaponry, he could place them atop the towers, too. Felix's Mind raced, thinking of possibilities, but he refocused himself back on his current task.

The patterns.

Wait a second.

He could hear them, just as any Skill or System construct. Placing them all out on his Stronghold Map had created enough resonance that it became an obvious song. They hummed through his Affinity, a mesh of light he could almost see. If Felix's Perception and Affinity stats weren't so high, he might have missed it entirely, but now a new world opened up.

With his Keen Mind—a Born Trait that allowed him to have perfect recall for thirty days prior, and a higher chance of recall after thirty days —and Journeyman Temper, Felix could memorize the shape of the patterns with extreme accuracy. It took him several minutes to get it down, due to all the detail, but he did it.

"Karys, if I used my Stone Shaping and Cardinal Flame to make these defensive fortifications, could I get the same amount of Defensive Strength?" Felix asked.

"Perhaps. Most likely not. Even with your Skill set, replicating the complexity of System patterns would require more than simple stone and a few sigils. I do not have the senses to parse their construction—not anymore—but I know even Tier II fortifications are complicated works of art." Karys hesitated. "But if you were somehow able to match the System's patterns exactly, then your personal power would certainly boost their effective strength."

That was good enough for him.

Felix had an idea. If Stone Shaping wasn't enough, then what about other Shaping Skills? He knew of a few people in his camp that had such Skills, and his new Path made him far more efficient at earning new Memories and Skills.

His steps took him to the Frost Giants' side of his Stronghold. The Risi had constructed an ice wall easily as large as his prospective Bulwark, and likely as sturdy, too. Felix had been feeling them building *something* all this time, so it wasn't a surprise; yet the construction of it left much to be desired. It was a jagged wall of crystalline shards so cold they steamed in the summer air, likely adding to the fog the giants still perceived. Indeed, when Felix walked up, he surprised the two Risi Warriors standing guard at the gate.

"Step back, stranger, you—" one began, but was soon interrupted.

"Geir, hold your tongue. You speak to the Autarch," the other warrior said. He looked at Felix with a stoic face, though his Spirit trembled with equal parts anger and fear. "How might we help you, my Lord?"

Felix simply walked up to a section to their left, where the jagged pieces of their ice wall protruded just slightly. "How would you prevent someone from climbing this wall?" he asked.

"It is...a working of our people. The Witches have ensorcelled it to repel those who wish to harm us," the second guard said—Holger, according to his Voracious Eye. "Those who test it will find themselves in dire troub—hey!"

Felix snapped off a piece of the wall, a chunk bigger than his torso and dripping with ice Mana. Workings flared along its length, but Felix batted them away without looking, sending blunted blocks and razor-sharp claws of ice smashing back into the wall. His true attention was on the piece he'd broken off, and the...sounds he heard from it.

He blinked after a moment, realizing where he was, and smiled sheep-ishly at the Risi Warriors. "My apologies. I should have warned you. I'll be taking this piece with me, all right?"

The Warriors only stared at him as he walked away, their blue skin turned almost grey. "O-of course."

Chthonic Tribute!

Only bothering to step a few dozen yards away, Felix consumed the chunk of ice wall with no little impatience. Immediately, he could hear more of those same sounds as when the wall's defenses had discharged. They were like...flavors, but texture and noise. The abyss within him rumbled, hungry for whatever he held above his core space, but it was always hungry. He ignored it.

The flavors were more like rhythms. Patterns of vibration. *Of Mana?* He'd long ago learned everything was made of Mana, then he'd learned that had been not quite true. Mana made things up, but vibrations were what constituted Mana itself. The Grand Harmony. Even Dissonance seemed to have a role to play, annoying as it had been in his life.

So Felix felt at and listened to the different vibrations of the ice he consumed, while the dross of the physical structure melted away. The black smoke that Felix took in with his Tithe—and now Tribute—always held secrets buried within them, as long as you had the eyes to see and the ears to hear.

And Felix had both in spades.

Buried within the Essence that had been the ice shard, Felix found light. He gripped that stuff between his Will and Intent and let the rest filter down. Half fed into his abyss and the other half into his cores. Power pulsed, but it was a faint wisp quickly absorbed by his Skills nearest his cores.

Left in his grasp were a collection of patterns and lights. Skills and Memories. The lights were dim and unfocused, and the vibrating patterns were small and faint, but it was precisely what he'd been searching for.

Chthonic Tribute and his stats could sift the wheat from the chaff, now.

Felix grinned.

The Skills and Memories were thrown to his topmost core—the [Cardinal Beast Core]—and quickly consumed and experienced in a way he'd never done before. The Memories themselves were brief and vague. More sensory impressions and emotions than anything else, they didn't even take him to that strange liminal space he often experienced.

Those impressions flitted against his Mind, containing a certain amount of rage from whomever built the wall. Rage at being subservient to a Human, even if he was the strongest Human they had ever seen, coupled with a keen desire to kill and conquer that was being stymied by the Witches. The Memories soon guttered out like candles in the wind.

The Skills, however, were more interesting.

Ice Breath (Common), Level 1!
Cold Resistance (Uncommon), Level 1!
Frost Claws (Rare), Level 1!
Hoar Hammer (Uncommon), Level 1!

All four were useful—though he already had a version of Cold Resistance—and were clearly part of the defenses that had just activated against Felix. But they weren't what he was looking for...thankfully, he found something that almost fit the bill.

Frost Touch (Common), Level 1!

It wasn't quite a Shaping Skill, as he had with Stone Shaping or Kikri had with her Green Shaping. But it was a way to directly manipulate ice Mana. Felix was looking for a way to work with more materials on a base level, and if this worked, he'd ask to sample some of Kikri's Mana as well. So, while it wasn't exactly what he'd searched for, Felix was interested. Even more so when he felt a familiarity with its pattern. Its edge looked quite similar to Cold Resistance, the rhythm and thrum of it repeating a comparable pattern.

One that he could, perhaps, combine.

Felix had more than a little experience with combining Skills. His earliest attempts had required arrays and monster cores and quite a good deal of pain. But, as he was now, he didn't need all of that. He'd proven that in the Path. He just needed energy. And if there was one thing Felix had, it was an excess of energy.

Thief of Fate Title Engaged!
Forge Of Cardinal Thunderflame Title Engaged!

Synergy Detected!
Ice Breath (C), Frost Touch (C), Cold Resistance (U), Hoar Hammer (U) and Frost Claws (R) Are Compatible!
Do You Wish To Combine And Evolve?
Y/N

Yes.

The System blipped as the five Skills surged with light and power taken from Felix's core. Essence dwindled a bit, and his Mana dropped by hundreds of points, but he barely felt the pain anymore. He'd had far worse.

Instead, Felix focused on the pattern of his Stone Shaping. Fixing his attention on its loops and whorls and clutching tightly to the System's process. He had a Shaping Skill. *Follow* this *pattern, System!*

A trill of sound accosted him, far sooner than Felix expected, and notifications streamed past his eyes.

You Have Combined Ice Breath (C), Frost Touch (C), Cold Resistance (U), Hoar Hammer (U), and Frost Claws (R) Together!

New Skill!
Rime Shaping (Rare), Level 1!

Ice bends to your Will! Seize direct control of ice Mana in your environment or your core and perform wonders. Precision, strength, and speed of manipulation increases slightly with Skill level.

Felix grinned and got moving. He had an Elf to see.

CHAPTER TEN

Felix's conversation with Kikri was short and to the point. While his original Title would have required him to eat her blood or something, it was far easier now. "Just hit me with some Green Shaping, all right?"

"If you're sure?" the Elf asked. She traded glances with the Dwarven mage, Nevia, who shrugged.

"He's strong, right? That means you can go all-out," the mage suggested. Felix pointed at Nevia and nodded.

"She's got the right idea. Give me your best shot, full blast." Felix walked a distance away, perhaps a hundred feet or so down the row of stone dwellings. The sounds of Mana and discharging Skills nearby pricked at his attention, but it was simple to tell that it was the Henaari setting up their own houses. Felix spread his arms wide. "Fire at will."

Kikri's face firmed as some sort of resolve settled over her, and she lifted her gorgeously carved longbow in one hand while reaching out with the other. One of the few trees in the space shuddered beside her, suddenly disgorging forth a mass of green-gold energy and pale wood. In a smooth motion, the wood formed into a large arrow—more like a tiny spear—and the Elf let loose. It screamed through the air, leaving visible trails of smoke as the tip heated up into a brilliant orange that warped his vision. Like a miniature train, it bore down on him.

Chthonic Tribute!

Felix caught it and consumed it in a single motion.

The arrow and its green-gold light vanished, and Felix let it flow through his channels and into his core space. There, it tangled among the crimson-black branches of his Divine tree-thing, greenery upon the boughs. The bright lights of Essence Motes and Memories fixed among the Essence clouds at the top of his weird tree, held in place by his own

Will and Intent as well as the crimson-black structure. He wondered, briefly, how long they would hold there...and suspected the answer was as long as he wished. Felix's Will was not to be denied, not anymore. Not for this.

The Mana and Essence of the arrow, however, slipped from his fingers and into his cores. A short spark and tiny bump of power was all he found. Felix returned to the world, frowning. "Again."

"I'm sorry?" Kikri asked.

"Again. Do it again," Felix said. "And this time, don't hold back."

"I don't think that I—"

"Are you afraid to hurt me?" he asked. "Don't be. I've survived...a lot, actually."

Kikri stopped and Nevia sucked in a tight breath. The Elf swallowed nervously. "No, it's not that. I just cannot in good conscience try to hurt you, sir. You're a Lord, for Noctis' sake!"

"Hm," Felix grunted. That was annoying and unexpected. "It's a matter of motivation. Okay. Then just try to kill me before I kill you."

"What—?"

Felix exploded forward, arms swept to the side, and Kikri screamed.

———

Vess found Evie in the wooded hills to the east, sitting atop a high branch close enough to camp to see it, but far enough away for some privacy. She hesitated before broaching that solitude, but Vess knew Evie well enough to know when she'd prefer company.

Plus, she came bearing gifts.

"Evie?" Vess said, announcing herself as she neared. The tree she sat within was quite large, a lethan fruit tree, according to her Analyze. It had small, brilliantly colored berries, each one a slightly different shade than the next. They were meant to be restorative, and a handful would bring a healing boost to one's Aspects for a short period of time. "Strange. There are so many plants in the Foglands that have healing properties."

"Ain't so strange," Evie said from ahead. Vess could sense her but not see her through the thick greenery. "Place used to be Nymean, yeah? Those folks seem prone to helpin', from all that Felix tells us. Could be they just planted it all, Ages past."

"That..." Vess looked around them, at the forest that spread wild in all directions. "That makes a remarkable amount of sense."

"Well, I ain't an idiot all the time," Evie said.

Vess sniffed. "Please. You have more sense in your head than any dozen courtiers I have had the displeasure of entertaining." Vess took a small hop through the leaves, and landed on a wide branch next to her friend. Evie was leaning against the trunk, one leg dangling over the edge. "Unrefined and unintelligent are not the same thing."

That, at least, made Evie laugh, amusement crowding out the blunted pang of anger and grief. Vess was getting better at using her Harmonic Stats, specifically her Affinity, but subtleties still tended to evade her. "On brighter news, Felix has discovered how to give out Quests."

"Hm," Evie said. "He's turnin' into a proper lord, isn't he?"

"He is growing into it, I believe. The Quest is a scouting mission. Hunt the wilds for plants and beasts that are useful or threats. Do you—do you want to join in?" Vess asked, smiling hesitantly. "You and me, together? We can hunt all we want and earn some bonus experience as well."

Eager amusement played across Evie's Spirit, and Vess' halting smile was matched. "Damn, if you don't know how to talk to a girl's heart." She snorted and stood. "Hope there's plenty of monsters to go around, cuz I ain't plannin' on doin' this half-assed."

A sudden, ear-piercing boom shook the air, and both of them turned back toward the encampment.

"What's all that about?" Evie asked.

Vess clucked her tongue. Through hundreds of strides of tree and branch, she could see Felix's broad, athletic back looming over someone on the ground. "He was testing his newfound Authority," Vess said slowly. "...And apparently beating up our resident archer."

"Rude of him," Evie snorted.

"And unusual. He's not the type to pick a fight," Vess said.

"Are we talkin' about the same guy? Big muscles, scales sometimes? Likes to fight gods and Primordials and maybe a few ancient constructs before lunch?" Evie stretched her back and re-slung her chain about her waist. "I'm pretty sure Felix has some aggression issues he keeps bottled up. Ain't no reason for him being as good at fighting as he is, otherwise."

Vess's mouth quirked to the side. She saw him helping the Elf back to her feet and saying something too low for even her Perception to pick out. Kikri was shaking with fear, but looked astonished. *What is he doing?*

"Is this progress I see?" Evie asked in a sly voice.

Vess blinked and looked up at her. Evie was looking between the distant Felix and Vess with a growing smirk. "You've been spending more time together."

"He has...questions. About Authority," Vess said. She straightened her leathers, a needless task. They were enchanted to fit her as comfortably as possible. "We simply compared the details of our Seat and Seals."

"Ah. 'You show me yours, I show you mine' type situation. I see."

Vess' face lit up, and she feared at how fiercely she blushed. "Nothing of the sort, Evie. Get your Mind out of the gutter."

"Gutter born and raised, I'm afraid." Evie stretched and laughed. "You'll have better luck breakin' *him* in than me."

Vess shook herself and summoned her silver Spears. "Enough talk. Come. We will take the Quest and do some exploring."

"You know, that'd be nice," Evie said. "First monster we see is mine, though, Duchess."

"Only if you're fast enough, guttersnipe."

Both women blurred into motion, leaving only wind and scuffed bark behind.

———

Some time later, after the screaming had stopped, and Kikri had finally fired at him in earnest, Felix walked away happily. A new Skill was sitting in his grasp.

New Skill!
Green Shaping (Rare), Level 1!
The Green Wilds are varied and deep. You have touched upon a mastery that delves those mysteries. Where life Mana is imparted upon flora, you hold sway. Precision, strength, and speed of manipulation increases slightly with Skill level.

Felix had in no way intended to hurt the woman, but he could see that Kikri was blunting her edge both consciously and subconsciously. He'd had to put her into a life and death situation to truly get her to attack, and it had worked out wonderfully for both of them. Felix had consumed her attack at a far higher concentration, and she had earned six entire Skill levels. By the time she had gotten over the worst of the shakes, he swore the Elf was going to ask him to do it again.

Might be a good idea, in fact, he thought. *Some training for everyone.*

But first, fortifications. He rolled up the sleeves of his tunic, now a rich brown accented with gold thread. He'd changed it a handful of times already, still delighted by its extremely responsive array. The sleeves, instead of simply folding back, literally shortened until they were just below his elbows. *Man, this thing is cool.*

Expanding his senses, aided by both his connection to the Spirit Tree above him and his Authority, Felix felt at the edges of what the System called his Stronghold. He'd already had the Haarguard go around and ensure no one was in the construction zone, but he felt compelled to make one last check.

Everyone was either well within the boundaries or beyond them. A number of Henaari had taken up his Quest, and he could even sense the fading presences of Evie and Vess to the north. *Good. Nothing Evie likes more than fighting. Good job, Vess.*

He was ready. Once more, Felix lined up the patterns for Bulwarks and Square Towers as provided by his interface and took a single, steadying breath.

"Here goes nothing."

The patterns burst alight in his senses, becoming suddenly real. Visible only to him, a strange set of vibrating cords erupted from the earth, almost like wire-frame models made of light; System Mana poured into them, and the dirt and stone beneath slowly rose.

"No no, not that," he said. Felix reached out and fixed his Willpower and Intent upon the fortification patterns, all of them at once. The energy from the System squealed.

WARNING!
System Construction In Progress!
Do You Wish To Take Manual Control?
Y/N

Felix grinned. *Yes.*

The squealing stopped, and the earth quieted beneath the still-visible patterns of walls and towers. Fearful of losing a moment, Felix sounded his own Skills.

Stone Shaping!
Rime Shaping!
Green Shaping!
Cardinal Flame!

Mana drained from Felix like a sieve, thousands of points in seconds, as stone turned to liquid before crawling upward all along the edge of his Stronghold. At the same time, a variety of seeds beneath the earth, inert or hibernating, suddenly burst into frenetic life. Flowing trunks, vines, and branches all sprang upward, tangling among the liquefied stone as dusty brown and green-gold Mana met and intertwined. Through it all, he laced the crystalline formation of ice, laying it out in accordance with the patterns he'd memorized and burning sharp-edged sigils and glyphs within each distinct coating.

Felix began to sweat almost immediately, and his Body quaked as if he were physically lifting every inch of the growing wall himself. It was maddeningly difficult, far more so than he had expected. Felix's powerful Intelligence sped up his thoughts while his Perception flared in order to keep all of it in view at all times. It was a powerful burden, and had he known how much, perhaps he would have started with just a single wall at first. *Too late now,* he thought with a grimace.

But his stats were well above the Third Threshold now, and his Mind and Spirit worked in smooth concert with one another. Standing stock still, Felix directed power to the edge of his nascent Stronghold, and the world around him changed.

Congratulations!
You Have Built Your First Fortification!
XP Earned!

Your Stronghold Has Improved!
Continue Improving It To Increase Its Rank!

Stone Shaping is level 69!
Green Shaping is level 2!
...
Green Shaping is level 19!
Rime Shaping is level 2!
...
Rime Shaping is level 22!

It was done.

Felix hissed a breath through his teeth and wiped sweat from his brow with a shaky arm. He felt like he'd been doing hard labor all day, and his muscles quivered with sympathetic strain. Looking up, Felix considered it well worth the aches and pains. In what felt like hours, but was likely only five minutes, a huge wall had risen from the depths of the earth. A dull roar of amazement, wonder, and a dash of fear sounded in Felix's ears, both physical and not; but he paid them all little mind. He was far more interested in the wall itself.

Just as the pattern had indicated, the wall was forty feet tall and thick. It all appeared to be made of a glassy, dark blue-black stone veined with a faintly luminescent red-gold. The towers were fifteen feet taller than the top of the wall, and both featured those same crenelations along the edge, as well as a parapet where guards could walk the length of it.

At the base of each tower was a door made of a darker stone, and arrow slits were formed into the walls. Unadorned steps were interspersed along the wall to provide access to the tops, and all of it was seamless. There were no visible blocks or joins, no mortar or clever junctions. It had been raised as a single, monolithic fortification.

Felix opened his Stronghold menu and checked the overview again.

Stronghold Defensive Strength: 40%
Stronghold Offensive Strength: 5%

The offense rating of his Stronghold was unchanged, but seeing the huge jump in defense made Felix's heart soar. "Karys, you seeing this?"

"I am. It appears your efforts have been rewarded. The effects of your manual control were overwhelmingly positive. Hm," his sword buzzed. "Likely because you fused it all into one piece. Was that intentional?"

"If I say no, does that make it less impressive?" Felix asked with a tired grin.

Karys laughed. "No. But please keep in mind that efforts like this put you at risk. If this were a proper settlement, you would have engineers to worry about construction like this."

"We have the Henaari now, so perhaps engineers aren't quite so far off," Felix mused. That largely depended on how well the Henaari integrated with his people, and what exactly Felix's plans were, going forward. "What's next on the agenda, then?"

"You wish to make your Stronghold safer, yes?"

"Of course."

"Then next must come the Forge."

CHAPTER ELEVEN

Harn wasn't sure why he'd climbed the tumbled scaffolding alongside the cliffs, except that something inside felt...different. His core space had trembled for the smallest of moments, a hammer the size of the Guild tower smashing into an anvil built from the heart of a mountain. The warrior had felt the lurch in his channels, a surge of power that made him dizzy.

What caused it? he wondered for the fifth time. He was standing at the broken open entrance to the Nymean Temple, gazing into its sundered depths. The majority of the space was dominated by the gargantuan trunk of the Spirit Tree, though a number of gaping holes in the flooring led to far deeper levels. The tree itself was smooth and, for lack of a better word, muscular with a twisting bole that felt powerful for all its fixed rigidity. It was a darker shade of cool brown with large horizontal bulges cut across it like huge, healed-over scars. Harn could feel a distinct pressure from it, as if from a combatant leveraging their Spirit. But that hadn't been what he felt.

Other than the Spirit Tree, the first floor of the Temple was filled mostly with rocky debris. Yet in the far corner, near the once-locked green-metal doors, were a set of stairs that had not been there before. They, too, were covered in broken rock and loosened stone, but they were dressed stone, and his Perception caught angles that hadn't ever been worn down by tread or time. They were new.

And he felt something...humming from above.

Harn took the steps quickly, but cautiously, one of his axes in hand. The flight was relatively short, and it led onto a landing that spread outward for twenty strides. A six-sided lamppost had been erected in the center of the landing, more grown than constructed, and the floor detailed with those same star-shaped tiles. Within the hexagonal crystal casing was a flickering flame—it alternated between blue-white and red-gold.

Three more staircases—each as newly constructed as the first—extended upward to his left, right, and ahead. The paths bore into the stone above the Temple, and the tunnel walls were carved into intricate patterns of vines, stars, and various animals, all tangled together like knotwork.

The staircases weren't the same, though the dizzying patterns were a bit hard to follow, even with his Perception. Only one path still called to him. Harn followed the instinct slower than before, his senses extended as far as he could manage. As he approached a door atop the right-most flight of stairs, the air had a slight char to it, and the distinct tang of hot metal. The door was heavy and a handspan thick, made of gleaming steel and stamped with the symbol of a burning eye surmounted by a crown.

He pushed it open, and the door swung easily on silent hinges.

"Blind gods," Harn whispered.

The chamber before him—one of several, he could tell—was huge, measuring at least sixty strides across and twice that in length. The walls were studded with large stone and iron furnaces, half built into more knotlike patterns of stars and vines. Row after row of tables and counters flanked the furnaces, as well as racks of basic forging tools he recognized from long ago.

Dominating the center of the room was a large and impressively complex-seeming forge, shaped to look like the yawning mouth of some great, whiskered beast. A faint, yellowish flame flickered in its basin, enough to glow brightly in the dim hall. That is, until Harn stepped fully into the room, whereupon Manalamps lit up the walls with a steady, white illumination.

Beautiful. Harn walked through the crafting hall, his hands gently caressing the tools laid out in neat rows atop a nearby table. A hammer found its way into his hands, a thing with a head the size of a large melon, and the warrior hefted it with appreciation. *Solid tools. Was this always here?*

The hall felt familiar to Harn in a way all forges did; he'd grown up beside one after all. His core space was something he called the Armory, where his Skills were weapons forged by the power of his core, that massive hammer and anvil constantly striking against one another. Skills lined the walls of his Armory, much like the tools here were presented, each one with a use and function.

"Oh Harn, hey."

The warrior froze, having become so distracted he hadn't even noticed the presence of another. Felix stepped out of a cleverly worked door featuring realistic-seeming vines, his face wide and smiling.

"I didn't expect anyone would come up here. Do you need something?" he asked.

Harn let out a breath. "No. I was just... What is this place? I know it's a forge, but where'd it come from? You never mentioned it before."

"Oh, that's because it's new." Felix waggled his hand. "Sorta. Got it from the System when I completed a Quest, then my Stronghold just sorta...built it."

Harn grunted, not exactly understanding, but knowing enough not to ask any dumb questions. If the kid said it was a System reward, then it was; Harn had seen stranger things than a self-building room.

"In fact, I came up here because Karys said I needed to inspect the place. It's pretty interesting, to be honest. Lotta arrays in these walls."

"Oh?" Harn raised an eyebrow. *Arrays in the walls?* "What're they doin'?"

Felix pointed at the lamps then the furnaces in the walls. "Ignition scripts for the furnaces and illumination ones for the lamps, as well as a big ambient siphon in the floor." He tapped his foot, his armored greaves ringing lightly against the smooth and polished stone. "I think it's a heat sink. Seems to pull from those tub things over there as well as generally from all over the Forge."

Harn glanced at where Felix pointed and nodded. "Quenching basins." He walked closer and noticed that all of them save the one for water were empty. "You use different liquids on metal to cool and harden a piece after workin' it. Water, oil, even heard of monster blood bein' effective."

"Interesting," Felix said, and Harn was surprised to find that he was; the kid seemed to be fascinated by everything. "The rest of the arrays all seem centered around the forge and this anvil."

Harn believed it. The forge was an impressive-looking beast in itself, while the anvil Felix had pointed out was made of a dark metal that he'd almost missed, despite its size. And it *was* big, at least as wide as Harn's shoulders and standing on a hexagonal plinth. The thing looked to weigh as much as Pit.

"That anvil and the forge beside it are the focal points of this Hall's pattern," said a new, grand-sorta voice from behind him. Harn didn't bother to look, as he'd already seen the faint wisps of green-gold Mana hanging about Felix's waist, but it was awfully strange that he had a talking sword. "I am positive you will find some unique formations centered around this place."

Harn felt pang as he looked at the anvil, at the tools all around him. Felix noticed. Sharp kid.

"Harn? You okay?"

"Fine. Just rememberin'," he said. "My uncle had an inn—I told you about him before, yeah?" The kid nodded, and Harn ran a hand over the dark anvil. It felt harder than normal metal, the metal Mana within it slightly different than steel. Harn felt it resonate within him, as his core slammed faster for a brief moment. "Well, out back there was a smithy.

Little thing, barely enough to shoe those exotic horses when they came into town, but the Smith had real skill. A craftin' Adept, he was."

"Those are pretty rare, I understand," Felix said.

"They are, but not as much to the east as out here. Most master craftsmen are Adepts at best. The true Masters run their guilds or live in seclusion." Harn grinned. "Why an Adept was out in my uncle's shack, I never knew. But I took every chance I could to watch him work. Eventually, he put me to work, too. Spent a lotta time at the bellows. Workin' with pig iron. Sweeping and haulin'. Gave me a fighter's body, well before I earned my Brawler's Physique."

"You're a Smith?" Felix asked, a little surprised.

"Nah, nothin' so fancy, though I once thought maybe." Harn shook his head. "Another life, that. But it stuck with me, you know? Even affected my core space, somethin' I call the Armory." He slapped the anvil. "My core looks like this, a big ol' anvil, shapin' Mana and Stamina and all that into fuel for my Skills."

"Each Skill is a weapon, honed and Tempered by your core," Felix said.

"Er, yeah. Good guess," Harn said, a little confused. "Did I tell you this before?"

"Oh no, I was just making connections." Felix waved the issue away. "Sorry, that was rude, interrupting like that. Those sound like some good memories."

"Aye. They are." Harn looked around the Forge. "Comin' back extra strong in this place. Feels like it squeezes it outta me, you know?"

"I know exactly what you mean," Felix said. He walked around Harn and up to the anvil, resting one of his hands on it. Immediately, the thing bloomed with light, releasing a tight cloud of purple and silver. A series of illusory circles formed from the cloud, each one showing a web of symbols that hovered above the anvil like smoke above a fire.

Harn wasn't all that versed in sigaldry, but he knew his basics. The circles all showed primary glyphs surrounded by secondary and tertiary sigils, each smaller and more exacting than the last. All of them modified the function of the controlling glyph, giving it strength and flexibility at the expense of power efficiency. Harn grunted. It'd take a good chunk of Mana and Stamina to operate the Forge, it seemed.

Felix hummed to himself before spinning a blue window into Harn's view. It rotated into place, and Harn whistled as he read it.

Forge Of The Stronghold!
At Rank I, The Following Array Is Available!

- **Tempering Array - Tier I - All materials placed upon this anvil can be Tempered, their structures enforced up to one (1) Tier above its current state. Only**

applicable once. A secondary attempt will have no effect.

Requires: Suitable Material/Item, Monster Core(s), Elementally Attuned Mana

"That's a damn sight better'n most forges, I'll tell you that," Harn said. "Most Smiths don't even use arrays. Too expensive, too complex. This is a noble's Forge." He shook his head and amended that statement. "A king's Forge."

"An autarch's Forge," Karys corrected, his refined accent sounding offended.

"Aye. Sure." Harn shrugged. "Don't see much difference between a king and an autarch, though."

"I'm no king," Felix protested, his attention still grabbed by the array before him. "Whatever an autarch is, though, it's full of responsibilities. Duties that I don't really understand yet, but are already eating up all my time. I've got three Crafting Halls, you know." He laughed. "There's a part of me that wants to run them all, becoming a master Smith, Inscriptionist, and Alchemist...but time is against me. Against all of us. I told you about the Enclosure, but apparently that message we all saw? Declaring me Autarch? *Everyone* saw that."

"Everyone?"

"Everyone on the Continent, according to Karys."

Harn's gut dropped. "That's...that ain't good, no matter how you shake it out. They'll be coming for you."

"I'm aware," Felix said wryly, but Harn noticed the wrinkle in his brow, the tension across his shoulders. The kid was more worried than he wanted to show. Felix tapped his sword. "Karys and I have been discussing our approach, and first up is making this place defensible. I earned a Stronghold from my Quest, and I plan to fortify the hell out of this place for when folks come knocking."

"We need to send messengers out to Haarwatch. Cal's gotta be made aware, as she's in the path of whoever is comin' your way," Harn insisted.

"You're right." Felix ran his fingers through his dark black hair. It was getting entirely too long, though some folk liked it that way. "Maybe we can get some Henaari to make the trip. They're fast, but it's still a few weeks."

"Your Enclosure is strong as I hear it, so we've got some time. Let's have a meetin' with that Farwalker and consider our options tonight, yeah?" Harn gripped Felix by the shoulders. The kid felt like a rock and twice as heavy, but Harn squeezed. "We can make our way through this. Just gotta take it one step at a time."

Felix took a breath and nodded. Harn let him go and grinned. "If you're tryin' to get your new house up to snuff, then why come here? You gonna forge some tools or weapons?"

"I had considered it. But like I said, I've no time to be the Master of the Forge here." Felix hesitated, then his eyes flashed a bright sapphire as a wide smile crept across his face. "What about you?"

Harn scowled. "What about me?"

"How would you like to be the Forgemaster?"

"Me?" Harn was thunderstruck. His hands clenched atop the anvil. "I'm just an old soldier, kid. I'm good at killin', not makin'."

Felix leaned close, and Harn swore those eyes of his just about *crackled* with lightning. "Would you like to try?"

———

Felix felt good.

It had felt right to give Harn the Forge, in a way he couldn't exactly quantify. There seemed to be an affinity between the special room and Harn. A...syncopation between his core and the Forge. Felix had heard it several times during his conversation with the grizzled warrior, but it wasn't until the man had waxed nostalgic about his childhood. The connection thrived in that moment, impossible to miss.

Felix's first thought had been to somehow get the Coldfires to his Stronghold, even though that would have left Haarwatch with fewer craftsmen. He hadn't seen Harn make anything yet, but this was a far better solution. And it gave the man something more to do than babysit the Haarguard, a bonus benefit Felix wasn't sure he'd realized yet.

Making him the Master of the Forge was as simple as deciding and Harn accepting it. A System message had trumpeted, celebrating the choice and announcing it to everyone within his Stronghold, then Harn's eyes had truly widened. Felix's Authority and ownership of everything around them afforded him an extra layer of awareness, something his Mind and Intelligence easily handled.

Harn's own Mind wasn't weak, but Intelligence wasn't his focus, either. When the sudden awareness flooded him, he fell to his knees. A Mana construct wrapped around him, a net of invisible lines that tied into the man's Aspects.

That had been scary. Felix was close to severing the construct when Harn stumbled back to his feet. His eyes were a bit wild, and he flinched as he moved a bit too fast, but he claimed he was fine. More than fine, apparently, as a giddiness overwhelmed Harn's Spirit, so bright and loud that even Felix's banked Affinity could sense it from him. Harn had run his hands over the anvil, over a set of tongs and hammers and specialized tools like he'd never seen them before.

"What was he feeling?" Felix asked.

"Likely a link to the tools and equipment within the space," Karys answered. "A Hall Master is connected to their Hall in a way that others cannot replicate; there's an intimacy to it. Once he settles in, I doubt even you could walk into the Forge without Harn knowing it."

In addition to that bond, Harn suddenly had access to a series of Quests. They had been waiting for him or whoever became the Forgemaster. There had been three.

The Hand Which Tempers
Temper 100 pieces of weaponry and/or armor, bringing out the latent potential within them.
Reward: Title, XP, Varied

Kindle The Forgeflame
The Forge comes with a furnace of standard flame, if quite magical. A true Forgeflame, however, is something found and sourced by a Smith. Kindle the Forgeflame and earn access to a second Tier I array.
Reward: Title, XP, Tier I Forging Array

Reforging I
All items carry within them multiple lives. It is up to the Smith to transform them, changing their purpose and bringing forth hidden potency. Reforge an item of Tier I or greater and begin your path.
Reward: XP, Varied

It had proven to Felix, once and for all, that crafting gave its own rewards. Previously, he had gathered that it was the work with difficult materials and such that garnered them XP, as the case with Elle and Rafny. But his "old-style" Authority allowed crafters to advance far more directly.

Karys explained that quests like these could come from a Lord of a Territory or their representatives, but would rarely be given to every crafter around. It was a benefit of having relatively few crafters, and the fact that Harn would be the Master of the Forge.

The first Quest seemed to be a matter of using the Tempering Array on as many items as possible. The second was...harder to conceptualize. Neither Harn nor Felix knew what a Forgeflame was, which was annoying as its reward was another forging array. Karys hadn't been able to explain it, though, not because of holes in his memories—he had just never really gotten into smithing while he was alive. The man could whip up sigils and slowly repair his own metal Body, but the specifics of smithing weren't in his purview.

Regarding the last Quest, Felix had his club, which had been damaged ever since he had cleansed the Profane Sigaldry from everything during his fight with the Archon. His club had suffered, becoming nothing more than a big metal bone, not even able to take on Essence any longer. Thankfully, his Fang of the Blade was untouched. Felix was sure that was by virtue of it being tucked into his

Spirit along with Pit, sheathed into his Companion's barding during the climax of that fight.

"I still think your Inscribed Femur of the Envoy is too advanced for Harn to affect," Karys said. "The Quest said Tier I or greater, but the sliding scale of difficulty must increase significantly Tier to Tier. Your Femur is Tier III, easily. Journeyman or Adept, were it a sapient being."

"With it wiped clean, I can't use it as a weapon any longer. So, I might as well let him do what he can with it." Felix wasn't particularly worried. He'd used his oversized weaponry less and less as the weeks went on; returning to his roots, he thought of it, as he looked at his broad fists. "I've still got my Fang and the Inheritor's Will, anyhow. And if he manages to make something of it? That's just extra XP and probably better rewards."

Felix crossed the landing, which now featured that lamppost. It was a neat little feature, looking more like a half-stone, half-crystal pillar containing the light of his two cores. Red-gold and blue-white. His Voracious Eye called it a Beacon, and Karys had explained that they were like tiny relays, siphoning power back to his Seat and Seal while also spreading his influence wherever they were constructed. When Felix had asked Karys what that meant—spreading his influence—Karys hadn't been able to answer, except to say that eventually he would gain the ability to make them throughout his Territory.

They were cool light sources, at least.

"Felix, pardon the intrusion, but why have you not combined your new Shaping abilities?" Karys asked as Felix mounted the steps toward the Glyphworks. "You were quick to do so with the ice-type Skills you had garnered."

He climbed the last few steps and walked slowly to the white stone door leading to the Glyphworks. It was marked with hundreds of script circles, each radiating off another in a wild, almost organic pattern. He paused before he touched it. "I thought about it. But they feel...incomplete. The patterns of them weren't resonating, not like how those ice Skills had." Felix shook his head. "I don't *really* understand how it's done— other than Willing it to be so—but I know that if I am going to successfully combine Skills together, they need that connection. I'm missing something, and until I figure out what that is, I'll level them separately."

He had briefly considered asking Harn about his weird armor, as it could shape itself in strange ways. But that was clearly an inscription of some kind, not a Skill Harn possessed. Felix was positive he couldn't consume an item and learn from an array; he'd eaten enough magical items to know.

"I'll keep an eye out for more Shaping Skills, but for now, we've got other work ahead of us," Felix said. He pushed open the door to the Glyphworks, and the sigils lit up in a brilliant fountain of red-gold sparks. When they cleared, Felix grinned into the chamber beyond. "Oh, now that's cool."

CHAPTER TWELVE

Atar stood at the top of the steps, staring nervously at a white stone door before him.

"Atar! Did you see that lantern? Analyze calls it a Beacon, but can't give me any lore entry on it." Alister came up the steps behind the fire mage, still looking backward. "Strangest design, too. I wonder what it does—Oh." He stopped, Atar in his way. "What's going on?"

"Look at this door, Alister. It's...gorgeous," Atar said softly. He walked forward slowly, reverently, as the many script circles gleamed atop the perfectly polished planes of the door. "*Echo, force, structure*, all of it called out, reinforcing itself against entry. If it were locked, this room would hold out against any number of Journeyman Tiers. Even an Adept for a span of time."

"It is certainly impressive. The exacting demarcations are finer than most I've seen," Alister agreed. "But you're scared—and don't lie to me. I know you too well. A force ward, no matter how well-made, is not enough to scare you, Atar."

The fire mage blew out a shaky breath. It had been a rough stretch of days. Battle and mayhem had ruled over all their lives, all in an effort to access this Temple. Atar looked around, noting the details of the short hallway that he'd overlooked. Overlapping stars and vines were carved into and out of the stone in wide bands that arced overhead, while along the floor there were panels of small creatures running and...frolicking? They were strange, furred things, with too many legs and bushy tails; nothing he had seen back in the Expanse where he'd been born.

In the end, Atar was worn and tired and stretched too thin from Mana drain. He'd recovered all of his Mana pool by that point, but the fatigue remained, as the two of them had been spending long hours studying the remains of the Archon's foul reservoirs. The disgusting pits had been sundered by their attacks then Felix's cleansing of the area, but enough remained that the two mages were piecing together their purpose.

The Archon had been capturing monsters and sacrificing them to the reservoirs, until the interiors were slurry pits of flesh and fluids, all of it bound by stones inscribed with the madman's Profane Sigaldry. They both found it fascinating: a new type of sigaldry invented by a singular being. Yet it was awful. Even looking at the few remaining scraps hurt their eyes.

"I'm just tired. And Felix called us up here for something. You think he's mad we're looking into the Archon's sigaldry?" Atar looked to his lover, but Alister only shrugged and walked closer to the door.

"You've known him longer than me, but Felix seems fair-minded. We've been advancing the knowledge of our arts; nothing wrong with that." Alister raised an eyebrow at Atar. "You think he'd truly punish us for it?"

"I don't know. Felix is...he is more than he appears. Every time I think I have him pegged, I find something else, some other impossible side to him. It's infuriating." Atar walked up quickly, lifting his arm. "But it's easier to just get this over with."

They opened the wide door together.

Beyond was a pristine chamber in the shape of a nine-pointed star. Each pointed alcove contained slabs of stone and a selection of silver and gold implements, mimicking the materials in the center of the room, which featured a similar set of slab stone in the shape of another, smaller star.

Basins and covered bins dotted the central area, all of it in stainless white stone that had been polished to a mirror shine. Above them all were hanging orbs of thick glass, each filled with red-gold flames. Strangely, the flames were steady and not flickering at all, bright enough and numerous enough that the entire chamber was evenly illuminated.

"Avet's own, it looks like a sea of stars," Alister whispered.

"It's beautiful, isn't it?"

Atar jolted. In the center of the room, at the crux of everything, Felix stood. He was smiling and also gazing around the chamber, as if proud.

How'd I not see him?

"The Forge was a lot more utilitarian, but this is just," Felix groped for words.

"It's art," Alister said. He ran his fingers across the smoothed top of the central formation. "I can sense the interplay of sigaldry through everything. It's like arrays were used to make all of this."

"It was. A pattern from a Dwelling Stone, reward for earning my Stronghold. Gave me a few crafting halls and some storage. Still haven't checked the Alchemy Lab or Storage, though." Felix sighed.

Atar looked closer at the so-called autarch. The man looked tired, which made no sense to the mage. If he had the Endurance and Vitality that Felix possessed, Atar would have felt practically immortal. "You called us here? That spirit of yours made it sound urgent. How'd it reach us, by the way?"

Felix wagged his hand. "My Seal is strongest in my Stronghold. Pushing his voice around is becoming easier, so long as he does it from the center. But that's not why I asked you both up here."

Atar wanted to protest; he wanted to hear everything Felix could tell him about his Seat and Seal. The bits he'd heard of the massive array beneath the Temple were enticing in the extreme. But it was Felix's secret to dole out, if he wished. Atar let his protests die out and nodded. "Then why?"

"So, it turns out Strongholds have ranks. Levels, of a sort, that determines what features it can access," Felix said.

"Of course," Alister nodded. "You established a Home. I've heard the stories."

"Right. Well, the second rank of my Stronghold, coupled with my Authority as a Territorial Lord, opens up some options. Most important of those is a line of communication between us and Haarwatch."

"Haarwatch?" Atar asked. "Why? How?"

"Since Felix was ensconced as the Autarch of Nagast, his Authority has engulfed and superseded Lady Boscal's," said the sword at Felix's waist. It pulsed and flared, and in Atar's limited senses, it had a faint haze of green-gold. More than faint, actually. "She is a vassal of Nagast now."

"Oh she'll love that," Atar chuckled.

"That's exactly what Harn said," Felix sighed. "Hopefully, she's not too mad. Not much I can do about what the System does—" Felix cut himself off and bit the inside of his cheek.

"Felix?"

"Hm? Oh, I was thinking of—nevermind. It's not important." Felix waved his hands, and one of the countertops began emitting a strident light. Mana vapor, white and undifferentiated, began to swirl atop it. "We have a store of undifferentiated Mana, apparently. Not sure how, but it'll refill itself once it's depleted. Takes a few days, though, from what I can tell. This'll let you utilize more than one or two types of Mana, giving the arrays a little more flexibility."

"Highest Flame, that's amazing," Atar said. Alister ran his hands through the vapor, easily visible in the environment. "I can even see it all. The sheer *detail*..."

"Mm, yes. Apparently, these rooms enhance your sense of Mana. I noticed it earlier in the Forge. Frankly, that alone is worth a ton; without my Manasight, I'd have been in the dark in too many situations to count." Felix smiled, as if to himself. "Anyway. I called you up here because I need to reach Rank II, and the best way to do that is to improve the Stronghold. Harn's already taken over as the Master of the Forge, but I have need of a Master of the Glyph."

Atar and Alister traded stunned looks. Alister even stuttered. "F-felix. That's...an honor. Truly."

"Less of an honor than you might think. I don't have enough resources yet to do any truly interesting work." Felix gestured to bins and covered receptacles cleverly placed around the chamber. "We need more monster cores, Tier I wood and stone and a number of other things in order to even make the two arrays I have on file."

"On file?" Atar asked, and Felix simply gestured to the center counter. The top deformed, rising up to create a finger-high plinth, and on top of that plinth was a book. It was large enough to need two hands to hold it, but it was thin, anemic really. Felix casually flipped it open.

"These," he said. A rush of undifferentiated Mana poured into the book and up into the air, transformed into purple and gold vapor. Augmentation and light. A System screen appeared before them all.

Glyphtome Of The Stronghold!
At Rank I, The Following Arrays Are Available:

None

The Following Arrays Have Been Inscribed:

Earthen Riot - Ritual, Offensive Array, Tier I

- **Effect: Disrupt the earth, ten yards in diameter from a point you choose within twenty feet.**
- **Activation Cost: 482 Mana**
- **Materials Cost: 15 Monster Cores (Tier I), Stone (Tier I) Markers**

Flame Geyser - Ritual, Offensive Array, Tier I

- **Effect: Create an area of spouting flames, ten yards in diameter from a point you choose within twenty feet.**
- **Activation Cost: 356 Mana**
- **Materials Cost: 9 Monster Cores (Tier I), Wood (Tier I) Markers**

"These are copies of a Territorial array I have access to...but transcribing them into the Glyphtome rendered them an entire Tier lower. They're not *bad*, I guess, just a lot less than before." Felix shrugged.

"A Glyphtome," Atar said in reverence. Elder Teine had possessed such a treasure, but he'd never let his apprentices so much as touch it. "The beating heart of a Glyphworks. A master record of arrays."

"Well, the beginnings of one, at least," Alister said. "Those arrays are impressive, though, and the material costs aren't too terrible. Not out here."

"Why—" Atar couldn't believe he was about to say this, but it had to be said. "Why aren't you taking the role of Glyphmaster? Your Sigaldry Skill is higher than both of ours." Alister looked up from the Glyphtome, curiosity plain on his face.

"I'm interested, don't get me wrong. But I can't be...everything. No matter how much I might want to be." Felix smiled ruefully. "The Master is not only what sort of bonuses are conveyed to the Stronghold and to the works produced, but they're to handle the day-to-day and Quests that arise from the process. I've no time, not for these and the rest that are coming my way." He tapped the book again. "Turns out, however, it doesn't stop me from using the rooms. So I'll be coming to bug you plenty."

He clapped his hands. "So! Which one of you is it gonna be?"

"Atar."

The fire mage looked in surprise at Alister, who only grinned. "Don't look at me like that. You're leagues better at this stuff than I am. You built an untested battle array *in the field*. So no false modesty."

Atar flushed with pride and affection and a touch of embarrassment. "Well, my Sigaldry Skill is nearing the Adept level. I'm sure some practice in here will truly push it to Temper."

"Good. It is quite beneficial for the Glyphworks if the Master Tiers up. It adds a touch extra when calculating the bonuses the Hall provides." Karys' voice was pleased. "An excellent choice, Felix."

"Thanks, Karys. Okay, Atar. You ready?" Felix stepped closer to the mage, who felt an instinctive desire to back up.

"Ready for what?"

"Your promotion." Felix reached out and tapped Atar on the forehead.

Suddenly, Atar's Mind was filled with a flurry of sensations, from the smooth feel of cold stone to the blazing hot vibrations contained within the reservoirs around the Glyphworks. He felt almost one with the chamber, exalted above simple flesh. That faded quickly, however, and Atar suddenly became just Atar again. A notification window popped before his eyes.

Congratulations!
You Have Been Made Master of the Nagast Glyphworks!
Glyphworks, Tier III!

Journeyman Tier Advancement Detected!
The Following Bonuses Now Apply:
3% Increase in Production Speed
-1% Resource Loss
3% Increase in XP Generation By Completing Craft Quests

0.01% Increase in Stronghold Offense and Defense per array added to the *Glyphtome*

Complete Quests to Advance The Glyphworks!
Advance Yourself To Increase Bonuses!

The Following Quests Are Available:

Compile Your Legacy I
Create 10 new arrays and add them to the *Glyphtome* for future use.
Reward: Title, XP, Varied

Many Hands Make Light Work I
Recruit more inscriptionists to your Hall. Production Speed will increase by a small amount per new recruit, dependent on their Tier.
0/10 Inscriptionists Recruited
Reward: Title, XP, Increased Production Speed

Gather Resources I
A Glyphworks needs fuel to power its arrays and formations. Secure the following resources to satisfy your Hall's requirements.
Resources: x50 Monster Cores (Tier I and above), x500 lbs of Wood (Tier I and above), x1000 lbs of Stone (Tier I and above)
Reward: New Hall Function, XP

"By all that burns," Atar whispered. "This is...it's amazing."

Felix laughed. "That's what Harn said. You got about the same bonuses he did, too. Good. It seems it's about level across the Tier."

Atar shared the details of what he saw with Alister. If he were being honest, he enjoyed the way the man's eyes popped at all the details.

"You have some Quests, too, which is great. I'd say let's get started on those as soon as you can. I'll handle the resources; I have the Henaari scouting out the land around us. My resource list has already started filling in."

"Ah yes. That's...perfect." Atar was a bit dazed. He walked around the central, star-shaped counter and slipped through a gap to reach the Glyphtome. "I have...so many ideas already. Alister! We can formalize the force transfer array we used during the battle!"

"Yes! Of course!" Alister's eyes lit up in excitement and he, too, hurried over to the counter. "But first, make me one of your Inscriptionists."

As if with a limb he hadn't before possessed, Atar reached out and selected Alister, mentally marking him as a "recruit."

Congratulations!
1/10 Inscriptionists Recruited!

Alister saw something appear in his vision, but he simply swiped it away. "Okay. Time to get to work, then."

Atar grinned. "Well past time. Start jotting down the central glyph, and I'll start on the radial modifications."

"Of course, Glyphmaster."

"Shut it," Atar laughed.

He never noticed when Felix left them.

CHAPTER THIRTEEN

Once more across the Beacon landing and up another set of stairs had Felix to the final Crafting Hall. The Alchemical Lab.

"And then there was one," Felix said.

"What?"

"Nothing, Karys."

This door was a plain, dark wood. Age-worn, despite being recently constructed. It opened at his touch, and Felix could feel dozens of wards and locks disengaging the moment he chose to open it. *Intent-sensitive*, he realized. The other doors had opened the same way to his Authority, and likely would to their new Masters as well. *Very cool.*

Inside was just as impressive as the other Halls. Where the Forge was a study in metal and stone, and the Glyphworks was all pristine white, the Alchemical Lab was dark woods and black metal. All three Crafting Halls had a suite of rooms to them, each different in their own way, and the Lab was a long hall, almost sixty feet long and twenty wide. No less than six chambers branched off, three to a side, each marked by a trefoil arch and a dark wooden door banded with iron. Sigils were marked out on the iron, each glowing very slightly with red-gold light—not arrays or enchantments so much as signs. Or they would be. For now, every one read "Undesignated."

Central to the main Hall were a series of stations, much as the other Halls had individual crafting stations. An assortment of hooks and pliers, tweezers and clamps, all made of silver and gold and heavily inscribed. At a casual glance, they were meant to preserve whatever they held or dismembered; likely monsters. Felix even saw a field-dressing knife, much as Magda once owned, likewise enchanted to preserve monster flesh once cut, preventing it from sublimating into that noxious black smoke.

Another station held alembics and vials, those weird tube-things that spiraled about, and other glass oddments. Inscribed points of the counters were meant to heat up to incredible temperatures, and others were meant to cool down, all of it operating on ice and fire Mana stored in reservoirs below the floor. Felix could sense them, the alternating pitch of the Mana itself; it wasn't a huge amount, nothing like what he could hold, but more than most folk, he'd guess.

In the very center of the Hall was a desk larger than all the rest. Black and dark brown, iron and wood, filled with little planters and already budding plants. Not many, just a few local samples that Felix had seen growing atop the cliff, but plenty of room for more. For a whole little garden. Felix recalled the entry on his Authority menus, the one for his Garden, but a casual perusal of that showed him nothing in the sub-menu. It was clearly separate from what his Alchemical Lab contained.

Beyond the plants—among them, really—was a series of tables, basins, and the most elaborate set of alchemical paraphernalia he'd ever seen. Scales, alembics, aludels, odd pots and jars that looked to be woven of vines but were in fact a type of bronze. A large oven or furnace sat in the center, with inscribed circles atop it in a series of stone rings mounted with black iron. The mountings were attached to a central frame and could rotate, so that the stack of enchanted rings could spread out like a tree. His Eye called it a Ladder of Ascension, which was interesting.

Name: Ladder of Ascension
Type: Alchemical Equipment (enchanted)
Lore: The name comes from a persistent belief that alchemy was the path to the peak. The rotating rungs of the Ladder are individual heating or cooling surfaces, depending on how their inscriptions are activated. The arrays, however, are flawed and require more Mana than usual to operate.

It was, in essence, a far better-equipped space than Aenea's was back during their fight against the Revenants. Better than it was now, even. Felix didn't know the purpose of half of the bits and baubles around him, but his Voracious Eye would solve that, in some regards. He'd received some small instruction in Alchemy weeks prior, but there was no one else to take control of this Crafting Hall. Just him.

Congratulations!
You Have Chosen To Become The Master of the Nagast Alchemical Lab!

Alchemical Lab, Tier III!
Journeyman Tier Advancement Detected!
Primary And Harmonic Stats Exceed Minimum Values!
Primary And Harmonic Stats Exceed Average Values!

The Following Bonuses Now Apply:

- **15% Increase in Production Speed**
- **-5% Resource Loss**
- **5% Increase in XP Generation By Completing Craft Quests**
- **0.5% Increase To Final Product Quality**

Complete Quests to Advance The Alchemical Lab!
Advance Yourself To Increase Bonuses!

Before that window resolved, another followed, trilling across his senses.

Titles/Skills Meet Minimum Requirements!
The Following Special Bonuses Now Apply:

Title - Savant of the Green Wilds

- **+15% Effects And Harvests From All Flora**

Title - Natural Scholar II

- **+1% Chance To Properly Harvest Uncommon And Lower Rarity Flora And Fauna**

Skill - Aria of the Green Wilds

- **+50% Chance To Properly Harvest Rare And Lower Rarity Flora**
- **+25% Chance To Properly Harvest Rare And Lower Rarity Fauna**

All Titles And Skill Special Bonuses Apply To Those Working Under You.
As Autarch, That Includes All Sworn To Your Banner.

The windows flickered and faded, but a rising thrumming came upon Felix like a wave. A bright gold notification lettered in silver appeared.

You Are Connected To A Spirit Tree - Atlantes Anima!
Due to your connection to the Spirit Tree in your Stronghold, all beneficial effects of your Alchemical creations are enhanced. All detrimental effects are diminished.

The Following Quests Are Available:

Harvest I
Dissect 25 monsters of Tier I or greater potency. Extract their
cores and any usable materials.
Reward: XP, Monster Cores, Varied

Distillation Is the Key
Distill an Essence Draught
0/1 Essence Draught
Reward: Title, XP, Essence Draught

Alchemical Talent
Recruit ten new alchemists.
0/10 Alchemist Recruited
Reward: Title, XP, Increased Production Speed

Spirit Tree's Bounty
Harvest Spirit Fruits when the Atlantes Anima is ready.
0/??? Spirit Fruits
Reward: Spirit Fruits, Varied

"Wow," Felix breathed. His head rang with the volume of Harmonies that shook through him, more potent than the ones he'd felt course through Atar and Harn. Perhaps it was because he was Autarch as well as Unbound and any number of things Felix had come to be saddled with; it was hard to keep track after a while. "Intense, but these bonuses are great. What'll they be when I Tier up to Adept?"

That moment was a way off, still. He had to level up his Body and Mind Skills...while somehow also doing this leader thing.

One step at a time. "Karys? It's done. All Crafting Halls have been assigned a Master."

"Very good. I can already sense the Stronghold nearing the edge of its current Rank."

"What else can we do? I don't want to be in the dark any longer than necessary, and if Cal is going to face some army because of me, she needs to know." Felix looked around at the vials and tubes all around him. "Would it help if I made...something?"

"Creations in service of the Stronghold work toward its Rank, yes, but only to an extent. There is only so much benefit from creating a vial of Twice-Distilled Acid versus a tank-full; a definite increase, but limited in scope," Karys said.

"So it's better to develop wide-ranging changes, things that can and will alter the Defensive or Offensive structure of the Stronghold?" Felix tapped his lips in thought. "What about a ballista that shot acid bolts?"

"Um, certainly. That does seem a bit far off of your current capabilities in crafting, Felix," Karys said.

"Gotta have goals. But I suppose I'll start with an old project of mine."

Felix looked around, noting a distinct lack of materials. "First though, we need more resources." He pulled up the Resources Menu for his Territory, noting dozens of new entries.

"The Quest you assigned the Henaari is working well, I see."

Felix nodded and swiped through the list. "Yeah. Now we just have to harvest them. These bonuses are going to come in handy, I think. Ooh," he said, jabbing a finger at a point on the list. "Tier I and II Stone, found at the base of the eastern mountains. That's just what I need."

Felix walked back out of the Lab and hopped down the stairs. He could feel the other two hard at work, but if they were to properly prepare then they needed more crafters. And that meant more resource gatherers, too. *Hunters and miners and loggers.* Felix stopped next to his Beacon, watching the interplay of dual lights within its crystalline shape. *I need more help.*

"Karys? Send a message to Kimaris. I need to speak with her."

"As you wish."

There was a lot to do.

———

The winds high above the forest were wild and untamed, filled with white-green flows and sprinkled with playful Sprites. Pit wheeled among them. Air Mana uplifted his immense bulk, allowing his Agility and Dexterity to shine as he corkscrewed across the lowest level of clouds, pinions brushing through them with every spin.

He cried out, unrestrained glee in his throat. He dove.

The Sprites were little things, spun of white-green glass into jagged angles that only vaguely resembled mortals, with long trailing bits that streamed behind them like ribbons of solid light. They were rare creatures and were exceedingly hard to spot. Just not for him. They frolicked about Pit's wings and tail, spiraling around him in joyful movements that spurred him to even greater speeds. He aborted his dive, banking into a wide, sweeping turn above the craggy top of Felix's cliff.

Pit tried not to stray too far from the air above the Stronghold. *His* Stronghold. His and Felix's.

There was a faint rumble in the air, and the Sprites scattered. Even the air Mana faltered, dropping Pit tens of feet in an instant. Pit squawked in alarm before the wind returned, buoying him back up. He eyed the Tree, whose branches extended far above the tenku's flight.

Fine. Your *Stronghold, too, I suppose.*

Again, a faint noise, but this time it sounded of creaking branches and fluttering leaves. A pleased murmur. Pit rolled his eyes.

The Spirit Tree was still technically asleep—*attuning* itself, whatever that meant—but that didn't stop it from occasionally reaching out to Pit across the strange connection it had established. One that enveloped Pit and his Companion equally. Even the Sword-Armor—though to a far lesser extent. At best, that one could feel the slow awakening of the Tree as a nagging itch. To Pit, it was a worm in his Mind, wriggling after a long, restless sleep.

So far, it had only communicated four times. Twice just now and twice more after Felix had done something below. A quick inquiry with his Companion had revealed he'd added dens of some sort to the rock, and it confused Pit as to how that affected the Tree in any way. Regardless, the Tree had been rustling and creaking away, conveying a sense of contentment. None of it made sense to Pit. Perhaps when he was done watching the Frost Giants, he would speak with Felix about it all.

The Cold Children were another issue entirely.

Pit had been sent to keep an eye on them, and the past day had seen him tracing long patrols over their encampment, watching for suspicious activity. The Chimera trusted them less than Felix did, and their Oath even less; they had proven themselves villains and would again. Pit simply had to spot it before it put anyone in danger. So, as the Pretty Killer and Dangerous One had gone off into the forest along with those Wanderers, Pit had kept watch. And as the Axe, Firebrand, and the Stabby One retreated into the mountain to speak with Felix, Pit had continued.

For all his diligence, he saw the Cold Children do nothing more than construct their lodges then a jagged wall around themselves. They grumbled and complained, and too few ever thought to look up, so Pit was able to hear some of their words. But most of them spoke their own tongue, and those words were gibberish. Angry gibberish, but without meaning or meaningful action, Pit could only continue to watch.

It was boring. And he was hungry.

So, when the day stretched into evening, and Felix landed among the Cold Children, Pit decided he'd watched long enough. He strayed from the Stronghold skies and the overarching branches of the Spirit Tree, heading north along the small western mountains. Along the river.

The sun was beginning to dip below the horizon, though high as Pit flew, he'd have light for hours yet. The sky turned fiery red and orange and gold, while pinks and greens played along the scudding clouds that floated higher still. To the east, darkness began to roll along the firmament, a dark purple bruising that spread incrementally with every moment. The fading light was no bar to Pit's Perception, however, nor to his burgeoning hunger. He scanned the forests below, looking for a half-remembered memory.

There.

He dove once more, dropping from the skies like a dark boulder, his russet and black plumage stark against the sunset. The emerald forest rose up, swallowing him.

Wingblade!

First one, then dozens of blades burst from Pit's form—condensed and shaped air Mana, spun out from his channels along each wing. They slashed downward, cutting through branches as thick as he was. Clearing the way. He bounded off of trunks, talons tearing deep gouges into bark and branch, until he leaped fully into a deep clearing. He spread his wings, allowing the dissipating air Mana from his Wingblades to lift him up just enough to counteract his immense downward velocity. With a resounding *thud*, Pit landed among fifty or sixty toppled trees.

So many?

It was a field of fallen giants, as the smallest tree was easily three hundred feet tall. Most of the trunks bisected the entire clearing, leaning drunkenly upon their still-standing brothers and sisters and draped with moss and mushrooms the size of Pit's head.

Pit sniffed the air, tasting something tantalizing upon the breeze. Underfoot, he found hundreds of fruit, most of them smashed to pieces. The fruit were a bright yellow interspersed with blue vertical striations, and from their scent, they were delicious. A memory tingled at the back of Pit's mind—of eating such fruit in the distant past—a memory that was nearly as enticing as the scent of its pungent flesh.

Pit gorged himself. He had remembered correctly—they were so very good. He ate and ate, cleaning the undergrowth of the sweet fruit before his large body bumped into one of the fallen trees.

"*Hissss!*"

The tenku warbled questioningly, lifting his beak with juices still dripping, and beheld a fat little...thing. It wriggled at him, snapping sharp pincers the size of the Pretty Killer's throwing daggers. Pit nosed forward, sniffing.

"*Hisss! Sklurb!*"

A jet of bright green Mana spewed outward; it was that which was hissing, not the wriggle-thing. The liquid splashed against Pit's face and beak, smelling of familiar things before it started to tingle. Pit drew back and shook his face, casting much of it out and against the undergrowth. Plants and weeds sizzled, burning away as the liquid touched them.

You...attacked me?

The wriggle-thing undulated forward, a small hop but aggressive, and Pit growled low in his throat. It was a basso rumble, quaking through his wide chest and out into the air. Yet the wriggle-thing only reared back, displaying its nubby, clawed appendages and clashing its mouth daggers.

Pit killed it instantly with a Frost Spear.

You Have Killed A Copse Grub!
XP Earned!

Oooh. New food. He lunged forward and bit into it, finding it rubbery but delicious. Spicy, too. He devoured the grub's corpse in a few bites, before his Perception caught the wriggle-hiss of more, each of them boring through the fallen trees. He let out a warbling cry before sending out a storm of Wingblades, each one severing a fallen trunk in two. From within, countless grubs spilled out of carved tunnels and acid-worn abscesses.

Mm. Dinner.

Some time later, when evening's dark had finally caught up with him, Pit lazed upon a tangle of split trunks. His tummy was full and his mood much improved. He barely minded it when a shadow appeared atop a wind-sheared stump and chortled at him.

"Pleased with yourself?" A'zek asked.

The harnoq was sleek and deadly looking, his black fur and dark scales almost melding with the yawning purple shadows of late evening. Pit tilted his head questioningly at his fellow Chimera.

A'zek snorted. "You've gorged on fallen fruit and harmless bugs. Is this what a Guardian Beast amounts to?"

Pit trilled and settled himself further atop his makeshift nest. *Sleepy. I* —his head snapped up. *Guardian Beast?*

"Do you know what it means, Pit? What a Guardian Beast truly is?"

They...guard? he asked. He was a protector for his Companion, for his friends. His wings rustled along his back, suddenly restless. *What else?*

"That isn't the half of it, little one." A'zek hopped down off the stump, barbed tail lashing. "There are deeper mysteries, if you know how to listen." Without another word, the harnoq vanished into the gathering gloom, leaving Pit to stare after him.

Little one? I'm big. Pit stood. *And you'll not be rid of me so easily, A'zek. Tell me what you know!*

Kicking off his trees, Pit followed the harnoq into the dark.

CHAPTER FOURTEEN

It was the morning of the fifteenth day since they had departed from Setoria that Zara heard the cry.

"Haarwatch! Quarter-glass out!"

The shout was one of glee, unmistakable to anyone who heard it. The Haarguard around her cheered, the fog of sleep burned away in their contagious excitement. Not even Zara could keep a fierce smile from slipping across her lips. It was good to see the city again. The Verdant Pass had been filled with countless monster hordes that had come down from the mountains and through the mines, attacking villagers and clogging the Gates that spanned the Pass.

They had even spent precious days combating them in efforts to secure the monster lures that had drawn the hordes together. Lures the Redcloaks had left scattered across the Pass and which drew in beasts by the hundred.

"I'll admit, I cannot wait for a bath," Reed said from beside her. "Close quarters living with this many soldiers is bringing back unpleasant memories. Unpleasant smells."

"You should have attuned to water Mana," Zara said. She let small waves manifest above her left palm, swirling with aquamarine light. "It is quite good at cleansing."

"I've had to settle on redirecting the air flows around me," Reed said with a frown. "Air Mana attunement is a tradition among the Daynes."

"And you're a member of their House, are you?" Zara asked.

"Adopted, yes. Ever since I made Captain of the Duke's strike team." Reed sighed as he leaned forward, his overly large hands gripping the Manaship's railing as if he could wring more speed out of the craft. "A House I'll find myself without if something has befallen my ward."

Zara kept her Spirit carefully veiled and only nodded slowly. Sagely, perhaps. "I trust she is safe from harm. Felix will have protected her."

"I fear the Fiend's intentions more than some monster," Reed growled. "Something is...off about that boy."

The Chanter hummed in contemplation. "Your fear is misplaced, Darius."

Reed narrowed his eyes at her, and this time she heard the railing crack beneath his grip. "I fear no child, Sorcerer. Autarch or not." He spun away from her and onto the deck, calling out for more speed from the helmsman.

The Manaship thrummed beneath her, processing more power through its complex arrays. It was a feat of etheric engineering that Zara had no solid grasp of—aside from the basics—but which impressed her to no end. Perhaps this was how the ancients traveled, rushing across leagues on a transport hewed from the earth and flung into the heavens. It would have been a divine miracle were one of these crafts invented when she was a child. Zara grimaced; those had been dark times. The Continent she had walked across these many centuries had changed much. Too much, if her mentor were to be asked.

It will change far more in the coming years, she thought. *If we have that long.*

With their extra speed, the walls and buildings of Haarwatch soon came into clearer view. Now even those with minimal Perception could make out the sprawling remains of the Sunrise Quarter, filled with the early morning bustle of market and industry. Zara could make out smoke and raised voices from the river and the Dust Quarter, men and women of all Races waking to begin their days.

The mines must have been recovered, she mused. They had been lost due to lack of wards, filling quickly with monsters from the deep. That she could spot the nearest mines active again meant they were once more safe. *An impressive feat.*

Almost as impressive as the newly rebuilt Haarwatch Manor at the elevated center of the city. It was twice as high as it had been only a few months ago, evidence of the industrious population, and it resembled nothing so much as a fortified castle. Cal had intended for it to be a place of safety in the city, somewhere everyone from all Quarters would be welcome. It now exuded a sense of stout defense, a shelled beast huddling over the city skyline. At its top, however, three cylindrical towers stuck up into the sky. Each one was a third as wide as the Manor itself and equipped with ringed platforms around their topmost levels.

Air docks. That they had built them already was surprising. Yet, when she glanced about at the city, she changed her mind. The destruction left in the wake of the Ravager King, Revenants, and the "Battle of Haarwatch" had been largely repaired. She felt at the air with her Affinity, and a rousing melody sprang up from below, bracing and strident but calm for all of that. A stark difference from the chaos unfolding in Setoria. *That's a relief, at least.*

Their convoy of Manaships passed over the walls of Haarwatch, and the hustle of the guards increased as packs were fetched and armor buckled. Kelgan shouted crisp commands as the Haarguard assembled atop decks, a few still rubbing sleep out of their eyes as they gazed out at their home.

"It's been a long journey," the spearman lieutenant said. His left arm was in a sling, one of many injuries that they hadn't time to heal. His right arm clung tightly to his well-worn spear, covered in scratches and dings, but newly polished for the day. "All of you have proven yourselves twenty times over, gaining levels and Tier Formations. You've become strong. Defenders of Haarwatch by any measure of the word."

Kelgan paused, his eyes searching among them. "Yet not all of us have returned. Before we land upon our city once more, let's think on that. On the Skill and Strength of arm that saw us through; on the sheer dumb luck. Mostly, though, on all of you. Without every one of you, living or dead, we would not have made it to this point. To home."

Silence hung thick in the rushing winds, and more than one Haarguard shed a quiet tear. They'd all lost someone, friends and more, all to stop the Redcloaks from dropping on their city in a wave of light and fire. Zara beheld them and was surprised to find none sang the discordant burr of hate she had expected. Her Affinity only sensed pride and the stirrings of grief, by waves stronger and lesser through the crowd.

"And now we return! Victorious!" A cheer went up, a scream into the wind, and Kelgan grinned at them all. "Once that gangplank hits the dock, you're all on leave for a full week. Enjoy it."

That elicited a far more boisterous cry, and Zara had to pinch her Affinity so as to not be overwhelmed. She still smiled, though. *Enthusiastic idiots.*

They approached the air docks, which looked like nothing so much as an unfolding claw, curling outward from the tower at its center. Ridges along the flat stone claw were lined with anchors for mooring lines, where a clutch of attendants stood in robes and...armor.

No. Not attendants. Zara realized. Her eyes picked out a sewn patch on their chests. *Legionnaires.*

The ship rocked as the Hand piloted it in close, banking the varied streams of Mana around its shell. Moor lines were cast out, only to be secured by those same armored soldiers. Soldiers who watched their two ships with hooded, almost hostile eyes.

This should prove interesting.

———

The Hand took the lead down the gangplank, his great slab of a sword secured against his back. His tunic was torn and a little stained after the long weeks behind them, but the gleam of his armored shoulders more than made up for it. Behind him came the regimented lines of the Haar-guard, spilling out onto the docks in an orderly sprawl.

All the while, the legionnaires watched them. Zara studied them in return, noting the unease in their Spirits and the crackling lightning Mana churning in several of their cores. Their leader was a Hobgoblin, his dusky red skin stark against his blue-gray robes and golden eyes. Her Analyze named him Kev'al Slene, a level 32 combatant with a hefty Mana pool. All of the mages had significant investments in their Mana, and as such their Willpower. They, at least, did not flinch when Reed planted himself before them, his boots stomping hard enough to send a slight shiver through the dock.

The warriors beside them, however, almost drew their weapons then and there. None of these legionnaires were a threat to them, but Zara was curious exactly how things would play out.

"Who bars my way?" Reed all but snarled. Kev'al inclined his head, his composure unchanged before the Hand's clear wrath.

"I am the First of Arclight, and they are of the Blade. You have arrived in the Autarch's vassal state of Haarwatch, and we are one of its protectors. Do you see the mist?"

The Hobgoblin's voice was steady and calm, as was his Spirit. Void of the anger or aggression Zara felt from the Blades. At his question, the Naiad tilted her head while Reed clenched his gauntleted fists tight.

"No, we haven't seen that blasted mist for weeks now. What is the meaning of this?" he demanded. "I am the Hand of the Duke of Pax'Vrell, *she* is the Sorcerer Zara Cyrene, and these are members of the Haarguard that set out with us—from this very city, mind—less than two months prior."

"I understand, Lord Hand," Kev'al said with a slight incline to his head. The other mages stood down, the tension in their shoulders and tumult of their channels relaxing to Zara's senses. "Our duty comes first. We cannot allow those who are not welcomed by the mists within our walls."

"I see," Reed said slowly. His eyes swept across the Legionnaires, noting their almost-uniform. "And is the Fiend here?"

"No, my Lord. The Autarch has taken up a city in the west, we are told. If we are lucky, perhaps one day he will send for us." Kev'al inclined his head, a touch deeper this time. "If you would follow me, I shall lead you below."

"Our people need healing," Kelgan said with a grimace at his own arm. "More than a few."

"Of course, Lieutenant," the mage said again before gesturing to one of the sword-wielding Legionnaires. "Mervin? If you would, please."

A tow-headed youth saluted, fist to heart. "As you wish, First. Sir? If your injured would come with me?"

At Zara's nod, Kelgan and a large contingent of the Haarguard filed after the legionnaire, quickly entering the tower through a wide set of double doors. "The rest of our people have earned a rest, please have one of your legionnaires bring them to the lower levels."

"My pleasure, Lady Cyrene." Kev'al nodded to a mage at his side, and they led the rest of the Haarguard down the docks. "If you would not mind, please follow me. The Lady Haarwatch wishes to speak with both of you."

Reed looked to Zara, a question in his gaze, but the Naiad merely inclined her head. "Lead the way."

The First of Arclight, his remaining mages, and no fewer than ten warriors fell in beside them as they walked. They were led through the same double doors as their soldiers, and Zara noted that they were freshly made and had yet to be painted or stained. As they traversed the halls and winding staircase, she found much of the same—places where the Manor had been hastily constructed. Or rather, where function had taken precedence over form. Walls were unpainted and undecorated, more doors unstained, but everything felt solid to her senses. No wobbling floors or misaligned joins showed themselves, despite whatever haste had possessed them.

"They sure finished this in a hurry," Reed said in a low tone. "Why, do you think?"

"I am unsure," Zara admitted. "Perhaps the Lady Haarwatch will be able to enlighten us."

The Hand grunted.

Their escort shed the farther they walked, the Blades leaving soon after they had exited the tower, and the Arclight dwindling to half by the time they reached another set of double doors. These were in far better condition, stained dark, and decorated with silver accents. Two armored Half-Orcs wearing the blue tunics of the Haarguard had stiffened the moment their group exited an adjoining hall, their hands flexing on the hilts at their waists. Zara felt the staccato rhythm of nervous fear from the guards—and not directed at them, but at the legionnaires.

Kev'al stopped several strides short of the guards and gestured behind him. "I bring the Lord Hand and Lady Cyrene to meet with the Lady Haarwatch. If you would please let her know."

The shorter of the two slipped between the great double doors, letting them close with a soft boom. Zara delved into the Spirits around her, Affinity plucking at the ripples in the air in an effort to understand. *Why do they fear them?* She could feel the tension even without her Affinity, for all that the guard and Kev'al tried to pretend it didn't exist. Yet she was only given a few moments before the door opened once more.

"The Lady Haarwatch will see you now," the guard said. Zara and Reed started forward, as did Kev'al. "*Just* the Lord and Lady."

Displeasure scudded across the Hobgoblin's face and Spirit before vanishing entirely from the former. "Very well. My Lady, my Lord, this is where we leave you." He bowed deeper to Zara than the Hand, a fact which deepened the frown on Reed's face. "May the skies smile down on you."

"Thank you, First," Zara said lightly. "Perhaps you and I can speak again later."

Kev'al's face broke into a smile. "I would like that, my Lady."

She smiled, keeping her sharp teeth hidden behind her full lips, and swept into the room before Reed could barge in himself.

Zara had visited Cal's offices before, but it had always been a sparsely decorated chamber with little more than a desk piled high with missives and paperwork. The large desk and paperwork remained—the latter seeming greater than ever—but now the room was filled with a bevy of items Zara could only describe as junk. Baskets of bread and fruits sat atop crates of pig iron, even a few extra chairs in a number of styles.

Weapons hung on the walls, the only thing placed with any reverence, each of them polished and maintained. In the center of it all was a woman with tawny hair cut short about her ears, wrapped in leather armor. A collection of knives were strapped to her chest and waist, with two foot-long blades at either hip. She was leaning casually against the large desk, eating a kelaar fruit and reading a scroll.

"You've been busy, Cal," Zara said as she walked in. Lady Calesca Boscal—Lady Haarwatch—gave Zara a sour look over the top of her scroll.

"That's a way of seein' it," she agreed, nodding at the both of them. Zara noticed the scroll she was reading was marked with a burning eye surmounted by a crown. "If you're both here, then I assume the Redcloaks have been squared away?"

"For the moment. We were able to neutralize all the Order members who had run off, but not before they engaged the Waystone." Zara gestured, and a wave of aquamarine light moved a crate of more kelaar fruit out of one of the armchairs. She sat down, arranging her skirts about her knees. "Thankfully, Felix's fog barrier activated, shutting down the Waystone and sealing us off."

"Sealing us off? As in, none can leave?" Cal asked, brow furrowed.

"And none can enter, including any agents of the Inquisition." Zara sighed. "Though that presents its own set of problems." She briefly explained how Felix's claim of Authority had been broadcast to the entire Continent.

Cal rubbed her temples. "That fog just about started a riot here in town, for all that it disappeared shortly after arriving. Plenty of folks out there were convinced the monsters were coming for a second try. It got...ugly, and would've gotten worse had the Haarguard and Legion not stepped in as they did. Took a while, but we calmed everyone down."

"Setoria was not so lucky," Reed grumbled. "The governor there is less than useless, and they could not see through the fog. I am still unsure as to why we can."

"I already explained that to you, Darius. Felix would have had to manually exempt us from the array. From the sounds of it, he had exempted all of Haarwatch from the start." Zara pursed her lips thoughtfully. "Is that why you have the Legion questioning travelers before allowing them to disembark? To prove that Felix is allowing them into the Territory?"

"They're *what*?" Cal asked, anger warring with exhaustion on her face. "No. No, I didn't ask them to do that. Gods, they cause me so much stress. You're the first and only visitors to come by Manaship, but they've been pulling the same stunt at the Sunrise Gate as well. I had to put a stop to it before, and I'll do it again." She let out an aggrieved sigh. "Which one was it?"

"The First of Arclight, I believe," Zara said. "They seem quite...competent."

"Oh they are. The Legion train themselves constantly, pushing their stats and Skills higher by the day. Emulating their lord, they say," Cal scoffed. "As if they could keep up with—" She coughed, and Zara could tell the woman was distinctly *not* looking at the Hand. "Anyway. They're a pain, but useful. Haven't had to worry about monster surges in quite a while, but those few that come have been stopped every time by the Legion."

"How many are there?" the Hand asked.

"Around a thousand, now. About half the number of my Haarguard. The promise of training and free meals drives my recruits. I dunno what pushes folk after the Legion, however. They're fanatics." Cal took another sloppy bite of her fruit.

"They've been violent?" Reed asked.

"No, nothing like that. The opposite really. After they helped settle things down, they joined in on the efforts to rebuild. Way I see it, once their heads were outta their asses, they realized this city couldn't take much more chaos." Cal shook her head. "We rebuilt, everyone helped. Even finished the Manor quicker than expected, which let us start on the people's homes and even the Wall."

"The Wall? I'm surprised you were able to do that," the Hand said.

Cal shrugged. "It's only a patch. Won't handle nearly as much strain as before. It's only Tier II steel. Orichalcum's still too precious. Ain't found much yet."

"I'm surprised that any would be left to mine in these mountains any longer. That is not a metal often found in areas of such low Mana density," Reed said.

"True enough. But the mines've been busy lately, too. We'd been stockpiling Tier I and II ores to sell before the fog fell, but hearing now about being cut off...I'm not sure what we should do with all of it."

A knock sounded at the door moment before a green-skinned face poked through. The guard adjusted his helmet nervously under their gazes. "My Lady, I apologize for the interruption." His eyes were wide. "There are Henaari at the Haargate."

"What?" Cal asked. "What do they want?"

"They said they wish to speak with you." The Half-Orc licked his lips, and his Spirit sang with wonder. "They say they were sent by the Autarch."

CHAPTER FIFTEEN

He dreamed of flames.

There were figures in them. Faces, though he couldn't make them out. They flickered and bloomed before Felix, a wildfire consuming countless rolling hills beneath a blackened sky. The figures were beckoning to him. They wanted him to join them in the inferno. Felix backed away, but the fire followed.

Faces wept. A pale woman with sharp cheekbones and colorful feathers. An ashen-faced man with a bulbous nose and hands weaving silken threads. Two small creatures screeching, running from the jaws of a colossal serpent. A Minotaur, standing tall among the dead. He beckoned, and the corpses rose on strings of light. Sunken cheeks and hollow eyes stared at him through the flames that now surrounded a city. A floating mountain that burned forever.

And below...below something screamed.

———

Felix snapped awake, his cores spinning wildly as waves of fear screamed through him. His bedchamber flashed blue-white, lightning surging off his reclining form, but Felix held tight to his Willpower and shoved the panic back down. With a single, powerful tremble, Felix took possession of himself and his power.

Just a dream, he told himself. *Just another dream.*

They had become an increasingly common occurrence over the past two weeks. Usually, he remembered nothing from them, just flashes and impressions despite his Born Trait, but this one stuck with him. Felix could recall every detail, reconstructing it with such fidelity that he could almost feel the phantom heat of the flames. His limbs tingled with pain, unreal nerve endings scorched from temperatures enough to melt some metals. The dreams always felt the same, despite the hazy details: desperate, pained, and full of fear.

He'd spotted several of the other Unbound in those flames—the ones he saw in his Omen Path visions—and a terrible sense of danger and grief surrounded all of them. This was one of the only times he saw anything like that, aside from that realistic dream from his first night, when he'd *been* the Minotaur. Nothing like that had happened again, however.

Felix shook himself and stood up, letting his coarse blankets fall from his body. He was wearing a pair of gym shorts and a t-shirt, courtesy of his Garment, which was still one of the coolest things he owned. He padded to the far side, opposite the door to the hallway, and pushed open the thick wooden door to his bathroom. Manalamps bloomed within, reacting to his entrance with a soft glow along the walls, revealing the bathroom's modest contents.

There was a chamberpot (gross), a washbasin, and an actual, for-real tub. What's more, the Nymean Temple contained a magical version of plumbing that transported water from the river far above. The downside, of course, was that it was freezing cold at all times, but that was less of a problem for his advanced Body. He pulled the lever, opening the sluice and letting water cascade into the tub.

With an effort of Will and Mana, his Garment flowed off his limbs and folded itself neatly in his hands. He set it down and focused. While his Body could deal with the cold, to the point where he'd barely even feel it, Felix would rather be comfortable.

Mantle of the Infinite Revolution!

Mana spun tightly about his body, swirling faster and faster as it generated more heat and flame. Soon, he was a brilliant light in the dimly lit room, and when he stepped into the tub, the water *steamed.*

Oh yeah, this is much better.

Felix let himself relax, pushing away thoughts of other Unbound too far away for him to do anything about. He frowned. Instead, his Mind focused on the issues his people were dealing with locally.

Today's to-do list, he thought, cataloging the tasks ahead of him.

Over the past two weeks, his team and those people sworn to him had settled in comfortably. For the most part. Flora and fauna were being collected and categorized, and every Quest that was completed was more resources for his Stronghold to access. Having so many varied parts at his disposal had done wonders for his understanding of Alchemy, pushing the Skill up several levels just from studying the ways various reagents combined.

Even better, they had found and begun harvesting a Domain nearby. *That* had been a surprise. Apparently the Archon's wasn't the only one in the area, as six miles south there was a cavern filled with metal Mana type monsters and a Domain dominated by the same theme. It was here that the Frost Giants had proven their worth.

After his discussion with Kimaris, they had agreed to gather resources for the Stronghold, but the results were...lackluster, at first. While some had involved themselves in the collection of timber, most had either lazed about or hunted for their own entertainment. When the Domain was found, however, they had been the first to volunteer to delve it. It had proven to be a surprisingly powerful place, averaging levels in the forties and fifties and boasting Tier II monsters.

The Frost Giants, however, were crafty and resourceful. They had established a beachhead just inside the entrance, creating a veritable ice fortress and slowly whittling away at the Domain's inhabitants. So far, it had proven to be a great source of metal ore of various rarities, all of which were stockpiled in his Storage Facility.

Felix leaned back into the now-hot water, letting it cover all of him as he thought on the last of his special rooms. And the strangest. While the others had been Crafting Halls and benefited by multiple users—Alchemists, Smiths, and Inscriptionists respectively—the Storage Facility had no such functionality. Instead, it was a huge space that had at first been entirely empty, but did not stay that way for long.

Thanks to Felix's Savant of the Green Wilds Title, and because he was Master of Alchemy and Autarch *and* Lord of the Stronghold, every single person sworn to him was granted a 15% boost to quantity when harvesting plants and herbs. Add on top of that bonuses to successfully harvest both beasts and plants with greater fidelity, and soon the resources had flooded his Storage.

Like the Crafting Halls, the Storage Facility also had an advanced set of arrays that helped to sort and catalog resources the moment they were placed within. Stone shelving, jars, and boxes were all formed as needed by the arrays, fashioned from the floor and walls. Now it was a quarter full with piles of Tier 0, Tier I, and even some Tier II Stone, Wood, and a variety of harvested plants. Monster parts too, which the facility typically stored in stoneware urns and the like.

The most interesting thing, of course, had been how the materials got there in the first place. Karys had been right, as he usually was, when he'd said not to worry about the Storage Facility's placement. While it physically was only a hundred feet from Felix's own bedchamber, others could deposit items into it from all over the Stronghold. Anything placed beside a Beacon could be sent to the Storage Facility with a small Mana cost, and the Stronghold had grown enough that he now had a total of three of the crystalline lampposts.

One was between the Crafting Halls, and the other two had sprouted at either end of his Stronghold. They had appeared after his Glyphmaster and Forgemaster had started to make headway on their crafting Quests.

People, unfortunately, couldn't be transported in that way. At least not living ones. A monster corpse would transport, but not even a small insect would go along for the ride. Which was good, in a way, as Felix didn't want just anyone accessing his Storage. It had a lot of neat things in it now. Most materials were Tier 0 or Tier I, but he had a few Tier II materials and a single Tier III monster core from that metal Domain. All of it was necessary if they were to advance his Stronghold. And his crafters.

Which reminds me. Time to finish Pit's armor today.

Felix grinned and let himself relax for a moment longer, willing the unease of his dreams to dissipate. His own perfect recall fought against him, but Felix was undeterred. It was an exciting day, and there was much to do.

We'll make it to Stronghold Rank II today, I can feel it.

———

"Carefully now," Felix cautioned. Nevia lifted the vial and passed it to him with steady hands, though sweat beaded at her temples. "Okay. Pour it over the Stone."

Nevia slowly tilted the small vial into the retort, located at the bottom of his Ladder of Ascension. The solution within pooled around a faceted green malachite gemstone. When clear liquid hit the gem, it hissed and bubbled furiously, as if rising to a boil in an instant but Nevia kept pouring until it was completely submerged.

Air bubbles rose from it in violent streams as Nevia, Vyne, Kikri, and the other apprentice alchemists backed up. Felix stepped closer, hands fiddling with several array controls. He'd boosted his Perception with his bonus stat points, putting in the majority of them while dividing the rest among Endurance and Agility. It was an effort to stay balanced, truly, but Perception was of the most use to him.

STR: 1464
PER: 1351
VIT: 1445
END: 1202
INT: 1687
WIL: 2027
AGL: 1182
DEX: 1272

It made spotting the changes in solutions a touch easier and handling fine measurements easier still. As such, the moment the clear liquid began to leach the malachite of its green hue, he moved.

Cardinal Flame!

Red-gold flames lit beneath the retort, heating the solution as sigils formed around the base of it. Felix crafted each of them with careful precision, having practiced this type of distillation for days. In an instant, the Stone of Wild Echoes liquified within the solution, forming a compound of swirling potentiality. He focused his Intent, funneling even more Mana into the formations beneath the retort, and those wild bubbles increased exponentially.

"It's working!" Kikri said.

"Shh!"

Felix ignored them all, carefully tending the outpouring of his Mana and the level of heat in the array. His Cardinal Flame was Mana control and fire all in one, a useful tool in alchemy he had found, especially when distilling. The now-green solution steamed, releasing vapors of Mana that swirled up through the retort's spout and into another bulbous container at the next level-up. The Tempered and enchanted glass funneled the vapors onward, pooling within a cooling alembic. Felix engaged that array as well, wasting Mana on the inefficient array but not caring as the vapor was once again rendered to liquid.

Cardinal Flame!

The cold switched to heat, and the alembic vaporized the green mixture, sending it rising another level up his Ladder. On and on, cooling and heating by turns while an array of his own design worked at it all. Felix all but held his breath at each transfer until it finally reached the final vessel, where a square-cut piece of cobalt spinel sat suspended in a second solution of clear liquid.

The green vapor dropped into the vessel, and Felix flared the cold array around it, super-cooling it and layering the vapor and gemstone with his Intent and Will. They sang against one another, a chorus of voices within the sublimated stone and solid gem. The green sank into the small layer of liquid, staining it just as the blue of the spinel began to leach outward as well.

Now.

Felix seized all of it with his Intent, those layers of his Will sinking deep into the matrices of the cobalt spinel. The Harmony roared, a refrain he had heard many times before, one he'd studied for days before attempting this. Felix found the edges of its vibrations, matching green to blue as seamlessly as he could sense. Power poured from the Mana Gates in his palms, swirling around and through the mingling compound until it all burst in a flash of green-blue light.

You Have Successfully Distilled A Compound!
You Have Created A New Item!
A Stone Of Alloyed Refrain Has Been Created!
XP Earned!

Alchemy is level 33!
...
Alchemy is level 43!

"I was right. Undifferentiated Mana was required to form a solid bond," Felix muttered to himself. But not *just* undifferentiated Mana, hard as that was to acquire for most, but liquified Mana. That meant condensing enough power to form the liquid, which was again very difficult for most alchemists to manage in teams, let alone mostly by themselves.

Felix, however, had both the Skills to render objects into Mana and the reserves to waste, pooling his Mana and wasting it to form drop after drop of liquid power. It was terribly inefficient and took *hours*, but it had worked. He hoped. Suspended by a tiny platform inside the vessel, a faceted gemstone of green-blue color flashed at him. It was glowing with an internal light that was steady and flickering by turns.

Voracious Eye!

Name: Stone of Alloyed Refrain
Type: Gem (Enchanted)
Lore: Two stones, each enchanted with the power of the Grand Harmony, condensed and combined together by a mighty Intent and Will. Placing this stone upon a piece of weaponry or armor will advance it by a single Tier, providing increased protection. The armor or weapon will also gain the ability to alter in size to fit its wearer, as well as masking the physical form of the one to which it is bonded. The armor or weapon must be bound by blood to a single user.
Chosen Form: Unknown
Mask of Echoes IV - Once bound by blood, the Stone will allow the wearer to appear as a [Chosen Form].
Chanter's Intent I - The Harmonic Song of a Chanter was used to enchant this item, and it bears their Intent. +10% Effectiveness of Mask of Echoes.
Chanter's Inversion I - Addition of Dissonance to invert the item's properties, hiding them.

Felix blew a ragged breath and slumped back onto his bench. The wood groaned beneath his weight.

"I did it."

"Congratulations, sir," Vyne said, and Kikri nodded vigorously.

"I'm not even sure what you did," the Elf said. She peered at the Ladder of Ascension as the arrays finally winked out. "You melted the other Stone? And...merged it together?"

"Something like that," Felix said. He stood, groaning, and carefully recovered the blue-green stone from the glass vessel. It had doubled in size and was surprisingly heavy—not to his physical touch, but to his Perception. *It's like it's being..pulled inward.* He pocketed it.

The others tried to ask more questions, but Nevia shooed them all away, and soon they returned to their various tasks. Felix smiled at the

Dwarven woman, but she waggled a finger at him. "I expect a lesson on this at some point...sir."

Felix's smile widened. "When you're ready, I'd be more than happy to give one."

Nevia nodded, more to herself than him, and moved out of the central station. Each of his alchemists had their own counter and equipment where they were attempting to produce as many tinctures and poultices, things Felix remembered from his brief work in Aenea's shop. His Keen Mind Trait was handy for recalling those procedures, even if they were months ago at that point. So far his alchemists couldn't handle the more complicated formulae he'd glimpsed, but as their Skill levels rose and methods improved, he hoped that would change. A hundred or a thousand Healing Potions to hand was an intoxicating possibility, especially since he didn't have to worry about them losing potency for a long time.

A distinctly amazing feature of his Storage Facility meant that anything stored within it was kept fresher and more potent for longer periods of time. He could feasibly have gallons upon gallons of Health Potions in there, and they'd take a dozen years to fade away. Stockpiling was his first idea as a way to keep his people safer.

Felix had found five people among the denizens of his Stronghold who had an interest and talent for alchemy. Nevia and Kikri, of course, but also two Henaari named Oswyk and Palyn. Dwarf and Elf were diligent, and the Henaari were quietly capable, following his every instruction, often to the letter. Surprisingly, Vyne the shield warrior had also found an interest in the craft, and he'd proven to be one of the more diligent crafters. His experience in patience, carefully waiting out the blows of the enemy, had translated well to the lab.

"What's the plan now?" Atar asked. The two mages had remained fairly unobtrusive during the whole process, but their eyes gleamed at the sight of his completed Stone.

"Yes. You've combined the two Stones, but what about making more? Another two dozen Stones of Forte would be a serious boon to our equipment efforts, considering Harn's anvil array," Alister pointed out. "I noticed a series of glyphs that flashed above the Stone as they merged, but the pattern was too fast to follow."

"I saw something, too," Felix admitted. It had happened fast, but he'd been focused entirely elsewhere. He shrugged. "My Mind was occupied at the moment, however. It's...muddled. I'll have to think on it, see if I can reconstruct what I saw." He walked as he talked, and the mages followed out of the Alchemical Lab and down to the Beacon. "Have you figured out any more about those Mana Relays around the Foglands?"

Alister shook his head. "We've made very little headway. The glyphs on them are too sophisticated. Master Tier at the very least."

"I thought you had devised your Force Redirection array from them?" Felix asked, mounting the steps to the Forge.

"It's called Kinetic Reflection, and no. We used an idea gleaned from those Relays, but that was it. The core of it is too advanced by half," Alister admitted, sounding a bit sour.

"We're attempting to decode the smallest of glyphs, but we've yet to divine its true purpose," Atar said. His voice firmed, and a measure of certainty filled the cracks of failure. "We're close."

"Good. Keep at it," Felix said. Atar had recruited two other burgeoning Inscriptionists from among the Henaari, though Felix hadn't had much time to meet them.

Too many things to do, he thought as he pushed open the gleaming steel door.

And never enough time.

CHAPTER SIXTEEN

The Forge was even more bustling than Felix's Alchemy Lab, though it had far less folks. Only Davum had been suited to smithing from among their many inhabitants; neither the Risi nor the Henaari had any interest in the application of heat and metal, preferring ice and wood, respectively. In fact, there were a few Green Shapers down in the Henaari village, though their main focus was on architecture and ornamentation. Here, in the Forge, they were focused on the inevitable advent of violence.

"Quench it!" Harn bellowed, and his Half-Orc apprentice rushed to obey. Davum took a huge slab of metal—at least four feet in length—and plunged the length of it into a viscous basin, releasing a great gout of steam and fetid stink. Harn walked over, pulling the weapon from the quench with his bare hands. Dark red liquid oozed from the hunk of shaped metal and over Harn's fingers as he hefted it from side-to-side. "Good. The ichor is working. Quickly, to the Forge."

Harn carried the length of metal in his hands while Davum rushed to the central bellows. He began to steadily pump them, driving not air but air Mana into the Forgeflame and brightening its glow. Felix pursed his lips as he watched it unfold, eyes devouring the process to try himself some day.

Forging was fascinating on the Continent, involving more arcane steps in much the same way alchemy and sigaldry did, and the end products could be exceptionally useful. His vambraces and greaves, for instance, were forged by accomplished Smiths so that they could collapse and contained a few spells in their construction. Not particularly powerful spells, but it was proof of concept to him.

If I could layer something like Arrow of Perdition into a blade, or better yet, an arrowhead? That *would be an impressive weapon.* And it'd undoubtedly shoot his Stronghold past Rank I, finally. Felix was beginning to chafe at the wait and had spent much of his time chasing that ever-distant horizon. The...was delegation the right word? The messages with the Henaari he had sent to Haarwatch were likely there already, which was good, but being able to communicate with Cal directly would be far better.

Atar caught Davum's eye. "What's he doing? What's in that basin?"

"It's—haah, hahh—it's monster blood," Davum panted. He was working the bellows, but the Mana of its operation partially came from him. A flaw in the array, Felix assumed. One of many flaws he had no idea how to fix. "A Skalg. Toxic venom."

"And you're layering the poison Mana in its blood into your weapon," Alister realized. "Clever."

"Standard technique," Harn said, banging a bright silver hammer against the blazing hot metal. Flakes of impurities and sparks shot off, sandwiched between his hammer and the anvil. "Foldin' Mana into the base material was the third thing I learned, all those years ago."

"What was the first?" Atar asked.

"When to shut up," Harn grunted. Atar snorted.

"Bit beyond my knowledge," Felix admitted. "Though I see the how of it, now that you explained it." His Manasight traced the lingering elements of the monster blood as each strike of Harn's hammer pounded into the metal. "I think it's working, too."

"Oh, Yyero's blighted backside," Davum said. His arms were quivering, but never once stopped moving. "Finally."

"Been at it a while?" Atar asked.

Harn grunted, but didn't stop his hammer. "Fifth try."

Alister whistled. "You running on dregs of Mana then, Davum?"

"Less than that," the Half-Orc panted.

"Shove over then, let me take over," Felix said as he walked to his side. "I've got Mana to spare."

"No, you can't! It has to be my Mana, or else I don't get credit!" Davum protested, never once slacking on the bellows. "I gotta finish this."

"Tch. All right, that's fair. Guess there isn't any harm in waiting a bit longer," Felix said before sitting on a nearby bench. "And here I'd thought I'd do a little smithing."

"You can always help us refine this design, Felix," Alister said. He held the Glyphtome in his hands, showing a page of the book featuring a complex, multi-layered formation. "Been meaning to adapt this to your wall defenses."

"Oh. *Ooh*," Felix said, catching the gist of the formation, even in pieces. His Mind worked at a fast clip as he flipped through the pages. "You're putting this on a siege weapon?"

"That's the idea. Dunno if it'll work, though," Atar said. "It's Alister's adapted design."

"Kinetic Reflection, I remember," Felix murmured. He pointed to a sub-section. "You can fit this on a ballista bolt?"

"Nah, too complicated. But we can place it on the weapon itself. With enough Mana, it'd generate its own bolts," Alister explained. "In theory."

"That's expensive on the caster. Unless—" Felix snapped his fingers. "Unless you tie it into the defenses."

"Specifically, *your* defenses. I doubt most other Lords have the Mana pool of a Tier V monster." Atar's voice was dry as the desert he came from, but it had little heat. "It's a badly inefficient design, otherwise. No offense, Al."

Alister shrugged. "None taken. It's barely usable, but it has promise."

"You're not wrong," Felix said. His Mind whirled through several possibilities. "Give me a minute."

A minute turned out to be entirely too optimistic. Minutes turned to hours as Felix studied the Glyphtome, and Harn sweated away at his Forge. Felix had other things he could be doing, but working on an array as intriguing as the one before him was worth every second of his attention.

It described a formation—a collection of arrays, though the terms were used a bit interchangeably—that took Mana and forged a missile of force Mana before hurling it at a very high speed. Or that was the idea, at least. Like Alister had said, there were problems with the arrays, mostly in the conversion of one Mana type to another. That alone would waste even a dedicated mage's Mana pool in only a few shots.

Well, unless they were Felix. He could probably operate it for hours before it'd overcome his unnatural regeneration. That is, if the rest of the arrays worked like they should. And it was clear that they didn't.

But why?

Eventually, the hammer stopped and a sharp explosion of steam tore into the air. Harn gasped a ragged breath.

"Finished." Felix and the mages looked up, their low conversation interrupted to find Harn wearily holding a battleaxe. Double-headed, it was made of darkened steel that was all one piece. It squirmed with a stormcloud of poison Mana, the vapors of it practically weeping from its shape. "Still has to be sharpened and all, but it's done. Davum can take care of the rest, eh?"

The weapon was given to the Half-Orc apprentice, and his arms trembled. Felix could see the man's Stamina was about to bottom out, but the warrior only clutched the battleaxe like it was his lifeline. "Thank you, sir."

Harn grunted and waved him off. Davum half-slunk, half-fell toward his own work station, careful not to let his prize fall to the ground.

"His personal weapon?" Felix asked. He remembered the warrior using a big axe previously.

"Yeah. Kid's been good help, so this is his reward." Harn shrugged and grinned. "Provided me with practice, too. Got my Smithing Skill up to level 39 and Mana Folding to level 45."

"Ah, apprentices. It's nice, isn't it?" Atar said, stretching himself. His skinny shoulders quivered with released tension before he started massaging his back. "My three Inscriptionists are all right so far, but the language barrier is a bit rough."

"My apologies, Professor. I have trouble speaking 'desert brat'," Alister said with a broad smile.

"Shush, you."

"Anyway, the kid's got some poison Skills, so I figured folding some monster blood into it would work well," Harn continued. "We'll test it once he's got it sharpened up some."

"And takes a nap, no doubt," Felix said. "Have you been able to touch the Femur yet?"

Harn laughed, throwing a rag wet with grease and sweat onto his table. "Not a chance. I'll need Smithing to at least Adept Tier before anything I do can dent it. Can't even get the Forgeflame hot enough to warm it, let alone shape the metal—bone—whatever. Gonna have to follow that Quest and source my own sometime soon."

"Anyone know anything about Forgeflames? Might speed things up," Felix asked. He looked to their resident fire mage. "Atar?"

The blonde mage was fiddling with the straps that held the Glyphtome at his waist. He looked at them in surprise. "How would I know? I'm no crafter."

"You're the Glyphmaster," Harn pointed out.

"Sigaldry is an art form, not a craft." Atar gestured to a stack of metal plates on the far side of Harn's anvil. "Is that what we're here for, Felix?"

"Hm? Oh! Yes, of course. Pit's barding," Felix said. He took two steps toward it before his Eye activated, and he faltered. "Aw, Harn. You used the Tempering Array without me?"

For once, the axe-wielding warrior looked abashed. "It was only an attempt. It fails more often than not. Worked on that, though."

"Well, I guess that's good at least," Felix said, more than a little disappointed. He had wanted to see it in action. "You'll have to show me the process later."

"Sure. For now, help me lift it up to the table. It's damn heavy."

Before Harn could approach the barding, Felix reached down and easily hefted it up and onto the table. Plates clattered, and buckled straps jangled, and Felix shifted it until it sat fully on the crafting table. "Simple enough."

"Right. Simple," Harn grumbled. "Remind me to call you next time I need a wagon and team lifted, yeah?"

Felix grinned. "Too strong for my own good, I guess." He patted the barding. "Let's get on with it, though. Right here?"

"Yeah, at the junction, just under the gorget."

Felix shifted the barding, the armor that Elle had made for Pit back in Haarwatch. It had served its purpose, and the last time Felix had seen it, the armor was scorched and dented from a hundred different impacts. It had been made from the Scales of a Ravager Queen, powerful stuff, and

Spiritbound, so it and whatever was stored in it could travel with Pit when he converged with Felix's Spirit. But it had only ever been Journeyman Tier. The Tempering Array had changed that, forcing the equipment to Adept Tier by way of magic that Felix had no understanding of; it had been why he wanted to see it in action.

Regardless, now the armor was all shiny and new, a helm, gorget, chest, and foreleg armor all connected by clever strapping and joins. Under the gorget was a crest, one carved by Rafny and Elle that had seemed at least somewhat prophetic. His "personal crest" they called it, basing it off the crude design the Fiend's Legion sported. It was a glyph, a pairing of several sigils to form a new symbol. This one was a combination of *fire*, *eye*, and *lightning*, just as it was on the Legion's cloaks...or it had been.

"Great," Felix muttered. The crest had changed, taking on the glyph at the center of his Seat and Seal. Still an eye, still composed of those same sigils, but now surmounted by a nine-pronged crown. "Did you do that?"

"No. Just changed on its own, same as the rest of it." Harn shook his head and patted the anvil next to him. "I really have no clue how this array works."

"Mm," Felix grunted. He fished the Stone of Alloyed Refrain from his pocket. The green-blue gemstone flashed with an internal light, easily the size of his thumbnail.

"That's a damn fine rock," Harn said.

"Let's hope it works as good as it looks," Felix muttered. He pressed it into the center of the crest. Into the eye.

A wash of complex sigils spread into and through the armor, visible only in flashes as a song rose in volume. Felix winced, the melody too loud and strident to bear, but he was rooted to the spot. His fingers were stuck to the alchemically altered Stone as if glued, and his Mana was being sucked up in huge gulps. It didn't hurt, per se, but the loss of almost a thousand Mana in seconds was a little worrying. When it started taking Essence, too, Felix swallowed nervously.

TRING!

Moments before it would have drained Felix entirely, it finished. Felix stifled a groan as his vision swam, but it passed quickly as his regeneration caught up. For his Mana, at least. His Essence store was two scoops shy of empty, and his core space shook slightly with strain. He couldn't let his Essence drop too much, or else the Harmony would overwhelm the Dissonant parts of his core space. It felt like burning eels squirming within him. Burning eels with bodies of razor blades.

A notification popped into his vision.

You Have Successfully Installed Stone Of Alloyed Refrain Onto A Set Of Spiritbound Barding.
Tier Increased!

The scales of the barding had taken on a more red-gold hue than before, shining with a strange new luster. Moreover, the entire piece had *changed*, extending back and over the haunches and rear legs. It appeared far more sleek and almost dangerous, the feel of it a touch overwhelming to everyone nearby, save Felix.

"The Stone worked," Alister said in a hoarse whisper.

"Master Tier armor," Atar said. "And it's for a Chimera, of all things."

Voracious Eye!

Please Bloodbind Barding To See Further Details.

Felix grunted, annoyed he couldn't see its details yet. He'd need his Companion to make sure. He felt at their bond, feeling a great distance between them.

"Has anyone seen Pit?"

———

In the forest to the north, battle raged.

Icicles festooned the forest, piercing trees and loam and stone with equal savagery. However, none were more targeted than the smoking corpses of some sort of bear-sized beasts. A lot of bear-sized beasts, enough that the undergrowth was trampled for a mile out, and little of it was uncovered by fetid smoke or hulking corpses.

The ground rumbled, the icicles wobbling, before a tree at least ten feet thick burst apart. A flurry of russet and black feathers and fur blasted through it, launched through the air. Smaller trees toppled, a consequence of his immense speed and size, but wings the size of a small plane snapped out and air Mana marshalled beneath Pit's tumbling body. He reoriented, ruff standing up and golden eyes blazing in anger as he landed.

A creature stepped out of the origin of wreckage, a beast with six clawed legs that looked like a cross between a wolf and a badger. It was three times the size of the bear-sized beast corpses, bigger even than Pit. It roared in challenge, so loud and deep that it shook the leaves around them.

Pit screeched right back.

Wingblade!

A massive crescent of dense air Mana shot forward, but two white, prehensile tentacles rose from its back. They batted the Wingblade away, green, venomous Mana flashing against white-green air. Another tree fell, bisected.

"A Guardian Beast does not simply *react*," A'zek said from a nearby stone outcropping. He lounged, his cat-like face devoid of concern. "A Guardian Beast seeks a harmonious exchange."

Pit sent aggravated confusion at the harnoq but was already charging at the monster. The badger-wolf advanced with a roar, its bulk moving almost as fast as Pit's.

Frost Spear!

A cluster of icy spears manifested above Pit's back before flitting forward, each one hitting with the force of one of Felix's grenades. The beast's tentacles wove a dense defense, slashing back and forth to intercept and redirect each one. The two met, talons and claws slashing. The beast fastened its wide jaws onto Pit's feathered ruff and shook, attempting to rip into his throat, but Pit's Vitality and Endurance was too much for it. Pit raked at the beast's chest, his own talons finding bare purchase in its own powerful hide.

"You cannot move from conflict to conflict and hope to attain your goal, Pit," A'zek said over the din.

Pit shut out the harnoq's words. The beast couldn't tear into his throat, but it had him held in place; its Strength was seriously impressive. The real danger, then, were the tentacles on its back—the tips of which were spiked with venomous barbs. Pit knew that well from their last exchange. The white appendages flashed downward, aiming for his eyes.

Wingblade!

Wingblade!

Dual cast Wingblades shot out from Pit's pinions, not at the beast but at the earth beneath it. The loam fountained upward, a geyser of dirt and redirected force that tossed the beast aside. For a precious second, it lost grip on Pit's neck. He moved.

Poisonfire!

Cry!

Pit's Body burst into green-colored flame, while he screeched directly into the badger-wolf's ears. Already disrupted by the explosion, his Cry caught hold. It fell, helplessly on its back, trapping its now-limp tentacles.

Your Cry Has Stunned A Badger-Wolf For 2 Seconds!

What followed was not nice or pretty, as Wingblade and Frost Spear followed Pit's claws and beak as he tore into the beast below. Without its agile tentacles, Pit's Agility and Strength overcame it in short, bloody order.

You Have Killed A Badger-Wolf!
XP Earned!

A'zek sighed from atop his rocks. "You must Choose, Pit. And act to bring that Choice to harmonious fruition."

Poisonfire is level 69!
Cry is level 64!

Wingblade is level 72!
Frost Spear is level 73!
Bite is level 64!
Rake is level 66!

Feels harmonious to me, Pit sent. He was pleased with his advancement. Slowly, he was catching up to his Companion.

"You have so far to go, tenku," A'zek shook his great, black head. "The mysteries hidden within your Path, *our* Path, are so many they cannot be counted. But you must *Choose.*"

Pit shrugged. He had been enthused when the other Chimera had indicated he knew how to take advantage of his new Path, one that A'zek claimed to share, but he had been evasive on actual answers. Mostly, they had sought out challenges in the forest and surmounted them, usually involving Pit getting bloody.

Choose what? he sent back.

"Your destiny."

Pit opened his beak, ready to screech annoyance at the harnoq, when he felt it. The air shook, and the earth quivered, both tremors too faint to feel with base senses. It transmitted across the thickened cord of intangible connection, between him and Felix...and the Spirit Tree.

Pit! Where are you? Wait, no, nevermind! Do you feel that? It's the Tree! Felix's voice burst with excitement across their bond. *It's finally attuned! And more!*

The tenku felt the quiver turn to a triumphant shout—a strange sensation from a plant.

The Spirit Tree has made fruit!

CHAPTER SEVENTEEN

"Spirit Fruit?" Alister panted from behind, only just clearing the steps down from the Crafting Halls. He had to shout at Felix's back, who was already at the base of the Spirit Tree, staring upward. "I thought it was still attuning? Isn't that what he said?"

"It's—what I heard," Atar said from beside him.

High above them, hundreds of strides, the Atlantes Anima rose upon a gracefully turning trunk. Higher still, its branches swept outward in a woven net of wooden limbs and massive emerald leaves so thick it blocked much of the morning sky. The sun was only a touch above the horizon, and it lit up a significant portion of the Tree with a buttery light. But those branches seemed to conjure their own shadows. Alister could almost feel something from it, a presence that he half-thought was a trick of his Mind. He felt...observed.

"Spirit Trees are more complicated by far than any mortal plant," the sword at Felix's waist buzzed. "Felix."

"Yeah, I know," he muttered, low enough that Alister had to strain to hear it. "I'm going ahead. Wait here."

"Wait? Can't you—?" Alister started, but Felix had already gone. An explosive wave of air and fine dust rolled into them, knocking the two mages back into the armored chest of Harn. Alister looked up, catching only the faintest blur of Felix's form as he ascended on a bolt of azure lightning. "—take us with you...Damn."

Harn pointed up, beyond the blaze of Felix, to the canopy above. "Look."

Atar gasped. "Like stars in the night."

He wasn't wrong as the dark underside of the Spirit Tree's branches bloomed with light. Not just light, but Mana so powerful it was easily visible to all of them—no observation Skill required. That they could practically feel their potency from so far below was astounding, and when Alister switched to his Domineering Eye, he could see a maelstrom of ambient Mana swirling all around the Spirit Tree. Each point of light was a center of its own gathering storm, filled with flashing opalescent colors.

"Could you imagine what it's like to eat one?" Harn asked, hunger in his tone. Alister couldn't stop thinking about exactly that.

"Spirit Fruit are said to be a powerful restorative," Atar said, his voice lightly distracted. "I heard of one that was so potent it forced a slew of Skills to instantly Tier up."

"That's not likely. But if Felix can't make powerful Essence Draughts out of them, I'll eat Harn's anvil." Alister walked closer to the Tree, motioning Atar to join him. "Help me inspect its trunk. All that Mana swirling about, it has to be doing something."

Pit? Are you on the way?

Yes!

Felix reached out and grasped the textured bark of the Spirit Tree. It had a relatively smooth bole, but its sheer size meant the horizontal striations were thick enough to act as hand-holds. His strong fingers found easy purchase. *Find Evie and Vess and bring them along, please.*

Frustration roiled along their bond, and Felix's senses were swept into Pit's for a few seconds. The tenku was flying fast above the northern forest, tracing his way back down the river, and he warbled in clear reluctance. *Fine.* The world tilted as his Companion banked hard to the left, cutting deeper into the forest, toward the eastern mountains. *But I get the first Fruit.*

Slipping back into his own senses, Felix laughed. *Absolutely.*

Pit trilled, pleased.

As their connection muted slightly, he looked up, taking in the distance still to travel to the base of the lowest branches. His eyes could easily take in the details from this distance, but the blazing points of Mana defied casual observation, even for him. He needed to be closer, and soon.

Relentless Resolution!

The evolved form of Unfettered Volition, his movement Skill, was not much different, at first blush. He had made use of it a couple times since its change, and had felt much the same fluidity of movement and near-instant translation of thought to physical action. Now, however, Felix felt something different. A brilliant cord of energy sang to him, a connection as large as the one between him and the Archon, thrumming with the same swelling harmonies. It pulled at him, like how he manipulated connections with Adamant Discord, but subtler.

Felix lifted his hand, placing it on the smoother surface of the trunk, and his confidence soared. He almost felt glued to the bole, his body moving freely but almost tethered by the pull of his connection. Felix's Agility and Strength flared, each handhold catapulting him upward at speeds no car could match. No lightning coursed along his limbs, just his own easy ascension up the vertical trunk.

Relentless Resolution is level 70!

This is so cool, he thought with a giddy rush.

The wind tore through his hair and Garment, rippling the coat he'd formed about his shoulders like a cape. For all his speed, he was careful not to slam his hands and feet down too hard, a task he had found difficult after his recent stat increases, but which weeks of practice had made easier to manage. Thankfully, the Spirit Tree was also extremely hardy, and his metal-shod feet barely scraped the bark as he reached the lowest tangle of branches and stepped into the crook between trunk and limb.

The branch was ten feet wide, as were all the rest that spread outward in a cage that trapped the sky. They were interwoven like a living puzzle, a knotwork design filled with huge, emerald leaves the size of cars. It was still early, the sun only an hour into the sky, but from up there, it blazed. Warm, summery air fluttered through the leaves, a little chillier this high than lower to the earth. Animals, birds mostly, flitted among the branches and their calls were another layer of music upon his senses.

Exploration is level 54!
...
Exploration is level 61!

Then there were the fruit. They hung from the branches, lush and ripe and speckled with dew. Mana vapor curled about them like steam, while more gathered in from the environment around them. Called ambient Mana, it was simply the diffuse remnants of Mana exuded by all things, and when there was a particularly powerful object or creature those remnants would react. He had seen it before with some formidable Essence Draughts in the past, and again with beings like the Maw, the Ravager King, and others. Now that storm of energy gathered around each individual fruit, at turns pulled in and seeped back out.

Voracious Eye!

Name: Atlantes Anima
Type: Spirit Tree
Lore: Spirit Trees are a rare and powerful organism imbued with elemental Mana dependent on their growth cycle. Due to your strong connection and the circumstances of its origin, the Spirit Tree has taken on a measure of Unbound nature. The Atlantes Anima is attuned to all and none.

What? Attuned to all and none? What does that mean?

"Felix? Felix are you up there now? What do you see?" Karys asked.

"I uh, I'm not sure," Felix said before repeating the Spirit Tree's lore entry. "What does that mean?"

"Fascinating! You're aware of course that Spirit Trees attune to the Mana around them," Karys began.

"Yeah, we talked about it."

"I had expected this to be the same. It is not an abnormal Spirit Tree, despite its immense size. But it appears it has taken more from you than we had assumed...and more from the Archon."

"The Archon?" Felix asked. "Is that what it means by 'origin?' He fertilized its original growth, so it took something from him?"

"And you. You sacrificed a sizable portion of significance to its branches. Now it passes that generosity back onto you." Felix could tell Karys was shaking his golden head. "The rate at which you produce the miraculous is somewhat dizzying, Felix."

They had spoken of Spirit Fruit before, right after Felix had unlocked the Alchemical Lab Quest to harvest them. Karys had explained a bit about them, mostly that they were excellent resources for developing one's core space. Advancement in this world was hinged on two separate but interconnected features: gaining personal levels and Skill levels, and advancing the stage of your core and core space.

Felix had done well in all of the above, so far, but he'd still yet to reach Adept Tier. His Adept Mind and Body were still incomplete, in part for lacking more Essence Motes but also due to the fact that leveling his Skills was proving challenging. Ironically, it was that things weren't challenging enough that he'd made so little progress: his Skills, stats, and Aspects were too powerful by far than any creatures around him. Felix had resolved himself to the fact that Tiering up into Adept might take him longer than his usual breakneck pace, so the Spirit Fruit were not for him.

They were for everyone else.

"Will these help my friends Temper themselves?" Felix asked.

"That and more. From what I've gleaned, most have not yet reached the Compression Stage of advancement, save for Harn. He is also the closest to Adept Tier, except yourself, and clearly has been for a long while," Kary said.

"Compression Stage? I don't know that one," Felix said. "There's Mote, Visualization, Actualization, Ring, Weaving...where does Compression fall in?"

"An...older name for what you call the Ring Stage. The compression of Mana is required to reach it, a lot of it. It is the reason so many Humans do not reach the higher Stages of advancement." Karys sighed. "Would that I still recalled all the methods to push your teammates higher...but they elude me still."

Felix could feel Karys' uncertainty through the sword. He was still having trouble with his memory, though being around the Seat and Seal seemed to help. It was one of the reasons the metal man rarely left the lower levels of the Temple.

Karys cleared his throat. "Spirit Fruit can provide a number of benefits, wholly depending on the Tree from which they are harvested and the Skill of the harvester. Considering the...Unbound nature of your Tree, they may prove to be more of a boon than we anticipated."

"Then let's stop wasting time," Felix said. He padded down a wide branch, completely at ease despite being higher than most skyscrapers back on Earth. His Dexterity combined with his Relentless Resolution made it feel like he was walking on sturdy grass and loam, and he quickly reached the first swirling point of light and Mana.

He blinked away his Manasight, focusing on the swirled golden texture of the Fruit; it looked a lot like a peach, were it to have grown to the size of a watermelon. Carefully, Felix reached out and grasped it in both hands, his Skill-borne instincts telling him where to place his fingers and how to squeeze it at the top of the Fruit. It came free instantly...but immediately blackened and withered in his hands.

"What?" He tossed it down, the rind splatting against the branch beneath him. It released a disgusting scent, like rotting meat and cantaloupe somehow. "What did I do wrong?"

"I—I am unsure," Karys said.

Felix tried again, another Fruit only feet away from the first. This time, he reactivated his Manasight and watched those swirls of power enter and exit the Fruit as he approached. Again, he gripped the flesh of it and at the top of its vine, not squeezing but instead sending a blue-red streamer of his own Mana through his right palm Gate. It was unshaped, possessed only of his Intent to harvest the Spirit Fruit. It sank into the joint between Tree and Fruit, before it weeped back out through the Fruit's dewy skin. The Mana tingled, now colored distinctly golden, and plunged into his left palm.

He sucked in a shocked breath, the power coursing through him like ice in his veins. When it reached his core space, it burst, swirling above his Essence and cores like an aurora. Felix could feel another Intent within it, layered into his own desire to harvest the Fruit. It felt like...words, almost. A whispered request.

"Uh, may I have this Fruit?" he asked.

Immediately, the Spirit Fruit dropped into his hands, whole and unharmed.

Aria of the Green Wilds is level 82!

"Awesome," he whispered.

———

Aria of the Green Wilds is level 85!

Green Shaping is level 22!

By the time Pit arrived, bearing two wind-tousled women on his back, Felix had amassed several huge piles of Spirit Fruit beside himself. He'd had to lash them together with a series of makeshift boxes and rope, the materials for which were Shaped from the greenery all around them. To be safe, Felix had asked permission for that as well; and to his surprise, he'd received rustling wind in leaves and creaking wood in answer. Even more surprising was that Felix almost understood it.

A talking tree, he mused as Pit touched down. *Not the weirdest thing I've seen, but one of the coolest at least.*

"Felix? Are these...?" Vess didn't complete the question, as her own observation Skill had her covering her eyes from the pile of Spirit Fruit. "They are so bright!"

Evie crouched next to the pile and poked the side of one. "Picked a lot of these, huh?"

"Benefit of my Titles and Skill, apparently," Felix explained. "Each time I grabbed one, I found another close by...except I'm pretty sure it wasn't there before." They might have been, but Felix's Perception was high enough that missing details like that was extremely unlikely.

The only explanation he or Karys could offer were the benefits from his being the Alchemist Master of his Crafting Hall. All those bonuses were working together to increase the bounty of what he was harvesting, and it wasn't the first time. Felix had heard murmurs from the scouts a few times, but he figured they were being hyperbolic. The forests were chock full of herbs and resources—couldn't they have been mistaken? But clearly they hadn't been, and Felix felt a bit silly to have not considered the stories factual.

Still, seeing a Fruit just...appear was wild. And beneficial. It had allowed him to collect a surprising amount in a short time, progressing along one of his Quests.

Spirit Tree's Bounty
Harvest Spirit Fruits when the Atlantes Anima is ready.
62/??? Spirit Fruits
Reward: Spirit Fruits, Varied

Evie lifted one of the Fruits and hefted it in her hands. She grunted, surprised. "Oof. Heavier than I expected. But they don't seem so impressive. We supposed to eat these?"

"No! Not like this, at least," Karys said. Felix had placed the sword and scabbard down near the pile itself. Green-gold life Mana swirled up from it, almost caressing the Fruit. "They must be rendered into a...more appropriate form. A Draught, most likely."

"Like an Essence Draught?" Vess asked.

"Precisely."

"We can Temper with these?" Evie asked with an uptick of interest. Still, she eyed the pile with some annoyance. "Why do we have to wait? I have a few Skills that are right on the cusp of Adept Tier myself."

"As do I," Vess said. "I have heard stories that Spirit Fruit could be consumed raw and immediately, often greatly benefiting one's power and Skills all at once. Why are these different?"

"Felix made 'em, of course they're different," Evie quipped. "We're not gonna sprout scales and glowy eyes if we eat them, are we?"

"Funny," Felix said dryly. Evie grinned at him. "No, Karys and I have been over them a few times now. They take after the attunement of the Tree itself which is...complicated. Technically, I think that means anyone can use the Fruit to Temper themselves, but the process of it would be bad."

"Bad how?" Evie asked.

"It would likely tear apart your channels from the inside out," Karys stated.

Ever so carefully, Evie placed the Spirit Fruit back onto its pile.

"Hm, if you are able to make Essence Draughts from a stable source, able to be used by anyone..." Vess' cheeks dimpled and her eyes flashed. "You would stand to make quite a lot selling these to other nations."

"Or he'll have folks comin' to tear it away from him," Evie pointed out.

"I cannot gainsay that. But the greatest advantage of the Protector's Guild is that it holds the secret of their universal Draughts. Iron, Bronze, Silver, and Gold Essence Draughts are not flashy or as powerful as more specific blends such as the ones you and I took to advance into Apprentice Tier, Felix. Yet they can be used by anyone, and that is a treasure worth fighting a war over." Vess ran her hand carefully over the still dewy surface of a Fruit. "Only the vast size of the Guild and the Draughts' relatively weak mixture has kept them safe from the greater powers on the Continent. If it had not one or the other, then the wolves would have come for them long since."

"Great," Felix sighed. "Another thing to worry about."

Evie slapped him on the back. "Look at it this way. Maybe you'll botch it and won't be able to make any Draughts at all."

"Ah, there it is, the silver lining," Felix said. For all her rough edges, Evie could always get him to smile. All of his friends could, in their own ways, and his time with them in the Foglands only strengthened his resolve to keep them safe. "I'll be taking this batch down soon. Gonna get to work on a recipe as soon as I can—"

"Pit!" Vess shouted.

Too late, they all saw Pit eat a Fruit with a single, giant bite.

Light and sound exploded from the tenku, his throat suddenly blazing with energy to Felix's Manasight. Multi-hued Mana coursed through him, surging down into the Chimera's belly before bursting into every corner of his Body, Mind, and Spirit. It swelled, music and furious brilliance blinding them all and—

Then it stopped. Pit stood there, unharmed and nonplussed by all their worried gazes.

He burped. *What?*

"Felix?"

Feeling shaky, Felix diverted his attention away from his greedy Companion. "What is it, Karys?"

"Have you looked at your Stronghold notifications recently?"

"No, why?" Felix asked, already toggling them open.

"Because something you did has pushed us over the edge," Karys explained.

Congratulations!
Your Stronghold Has Reached Rank II!

"The array has changed. We have a connection with your vassal state now," Karys said. "With Haarwatch. The line is already alight."

"What? What does that mean?" Felix asked. He looked to Vess, but she only shrugged.

"Someone is trying to reach you. I can only sense impressions, but a name is transmitting." Karys paused. "Do you know a Zara? She seems quite rude."

CHAPTER EIGHTEEN

I'm fine, Pit sent as Felix ran his hands across his fur and feathers.

"I'll believe that when I see it," he muttered. The call with Zara was important, but Felix needed to know if his friend was hurt. That Spirit Fruit was dangerous. He sent his senses questing into Pit's flesh, trying to see...something. Anything. But other than a strong heart beat and the gurgle of his internal organs, his mundane Perception couldn't pick up much.

"Shouldn't we get to your Seal thingy?" Evie asked.

"I agree. I'm concerned about Pit as well, but if Lady Zara is asking to speak with you..." Vess trailed off at the look Felix gave them both. She raised her hands in defeat. "Ah. I suppose she can wait, after all.

Felix nodded gratefully at them both. "Hold still, bud. I have to try something else."

Pit warbled agreement before Felix engaged his manipulation Skill.

Cardinal Flame.

Mana rose through his channels and pooled in his right palm, a crackling blue and red liquid. More light than liquid, it swirled up from Felix's palm and flowed down and into Pit's channels. Cardinal Flame, while usable offensively, was mainly a control and shaping Skill—for Mana specifically. He hadn't tried this particular technique before, but Karys had said it was possible if hard. And without a Skill to guide him, it was going to waste a *lot* of Mana. Felix pressed on regardless.

His Mana probe—for lack of a better word—delved into Pit's channels, following their twisting concourse. Wherever it went, a sort of feedback was felt in his Spirit, like a blind man's touch. It was electric and icy cold and burning hot; strange sensations, any way you could describe them. Combined with their bond, it provided Felix with a tactile map of Pit's channels wherever his Mana spread.

They felt very different from Felix's, less looping and more diverging lines, as if each pathway was connected to a dozen others. He wasn't sure if it was because Pit was a Chimera as he had no frame of reference for others, but it was a maze within his Companion. A far cry from Felix's relatively straightforward pathways, and his Mana was dropping fast as he searched, hunting through Pit for any sign of damage.

That feels...not good, Pit sent.

"I'm sorry, man. I'm trying to be gentle." Felix looked at Pit's Status. "You're not losing any Health or gaining a Status Condition. Let me check a little longer."

Pit huffed a breath through his nostrils, but nodded.

Felix switched his attention back to the wisps of Mana that washed through his Companion. There were flecks of...he hesitated to call them anything. Anti-sensation, maybe. His Mana fed nothing back to his Spirit, like they were tiny dead spots. Worriedly, Felix marshaled even more Mana—dropping his reserves by nearly half—and pushed through the tenku's entire system, sweeping it like a wave down narrow passages that all led to his core.

He blinked.

Upon entering the core space, it felt like falling into a vast cavern, utterly unmoored from sensation, save for what blasted out of the core itself. A brilliant, gem-like stone sat within his friend, black and streaked with crimson. It was arcing with energies, pulsing waves of brilliant Mana that formed a shifting cage of wild power around it. That net or cage was like static across his Mana, interrupting the smooth flow of things as it spat and flared chaotically. It felt a lot like the aura of power around the Spirit Fruit, he realized, and the flecks of nothing were present here as well.

And in far greater number.

Felix knew little of monsters and how they advanced, other than it was a natural process that resulted in them growing larger than usual, in most cases. That was why he'd so often fought apes and insects and bison far larger than anything on Earth, though some of those had likely started big in the first place. Pit wasn't a monster, though. He had a Race, not a Type—the latter being a designation by the System for those that weren't what it considered sentient, or so it had been explained to him.

Felix had some issue with that piece of information, as the Frost Giants had a Type, yet were as intelligent as most folks he'd met on the Continent. So it wasn't clear-cut, that was obvious, and Chimeras made it stranger still. From what he'd gathered in Shelim, the Chimera were made or evolved from other creatures entirely. The how and why was, again, a mystery, but it ultimately meant he had no clue whether Pit's core was abnormal or not.

The power is unnerving, and those flecks worry me, he sent to Pit. *Affinity isn't hearing anything jarring about it, but you and I both know that ability isn't as reliable as we could hope.*

Pit trilled in reluctant agreement. Felix pulled the big bird-dog's beak down and pressed their foreheads together. "I just don't know what it could do to you. Don't eat any more—"

A trilling noise filled both of their ears, and a blue box flashed before them.

Atlantes Anima Spirit Fruit Has Been Fully Digested!
+20 STR
+20 END

Felix met Pit's gaze, and he grabbed the Chimera by the beak before he could lunge for another Fruit. "No. Bad Pit."

They're good!

"No, they're strange, and I need to figure them out. No more until I can figure out what they're doing to you, okay?" Felix asked. Pit sat back on his haunches in the biggest sulk he'd ever seen.

Fine.

When he was sure his Companion was behaving himself, Felix looked at the others. "We need to move these down to my Lab."

"All right," Evie drawled, eyeing the large Green Shaped crates. Each one weighed at least twice what she did, and there were three of them. "How do you figure we'll do that?"

Green Shaping is level 24!

It had taken almost all of his Mana, but Felix was able to use Green Shaping to rig an impromptu harness system for the crates. With Evie's aid to lighten the load with her Born Trait, and the assistance of Vess' Spears, they managed to lower all three of the large boxes in short order. Felix could have, perhaps, hefted the lot of them with Adamant Discord, but he had no idea how the crackling lightning of his Skill would have affected the Fruit. Cooked them, most likely.

"I'll be back for the rest of them as soon as possible," Felix promised. He patted the tree trunk awkwardly, not quite sure if it could hear him. "Uhm. Thank you."

The sedan-sized leaves rustled in a sudden breeze, and Felix felt the faintest pressure against his Spirit and Mind. It was unfocused and diluted —as if it were a Mind spread out over miles of terrain—but definitely there. With a wondering final look around him, he dropped from the branches.

The fall was only a little faster than his ascent, and Felix only accessed his Adamant Discord in a final pulse upward, slowing himself so that he landed in his Temple with only a muffled boom. The others were all looking in the crates, Harn and the mages peering at them with wonder and no little hunger. None had grabbed any, so Felix was assured Vess and Evie had warned them off.

"How soon before you can make something useful out of them?" Atar asked. "I'm pushing closer to Adept every day, especially in Sigaldry."

"Aye, and the same here. I've been hoverin' around Adept for years," Harn said, engrossed in the power wafting off the Fruit. "Be nice to cross that threshold."

"I'll work on figuring that out soon. First I have to go talk to Zara, apparently," Felix said.

"She's here?" Alister asked in confusion. "How?"

"I'll explain later. If you all could get these to the Lab, I'd appreciate it. And keep my assistants from touching them. I don't want anyone tempted until we can figure out a way to make them safe." The others quickly agreed, and Felix and Pit left them, dropping once more through the crevasse in the Temple floor.

Soon enough, they found their way to the Seat and Seal, where Karys was fiddling with a collection of hexagonal pillars. Each one was covered in a fine mesh of interconnecting sigils, gold and silver light flashing with his every gesture.

"Oh, Felix. Thank the ancestors," Karys said with a sigh. "She is getting quite impatient."

"This is the communication array?" Felix asked, pointing at the chest-high pillars. Chest-high on Karys, that is; for Felix, it was well over his head.

"It is the mouthpiece of it, yes. The array is built into the formation of this Temple on a level that I cannot quite parse." Karys nodded to several swirling lines of sigladry that disappeared into the thrumming complexity of the main formation. "This is all you need to access, however. Come, step to it."

Trading a look with Pit, Felix moved forward as Karys backed away from the pillars. As they switched places the hexagonal pillars lowered until they were chest height to him, rotating as they did so and revealing more scrolling sigaldry down every single stone plane. A glyph beneath his feet lit up, humming with power fed into it by the pillars and responding to Felix's presence.

Autarch, A Transmission Is Pending.
Vassal State Of Kesra, New Designation: Haarwatch
Identification Marker: Zara Cyrene
Warning. Transmission Origin Is Suspect.
Do You Wish To Receive?

Suspect? That's...what does that mean?
"Yes." He'd find out, one way or another.

Transmitting...

"—know if he'll even answer. I—Felix? Felix are you there?"

Felix grinned. It was definitely the voice of the Chanter he knew, whatever his array suspected. "Zara. Glad to hear you're still alive."

"I should be the one saying that. What happened? Did you...How did you claim Authority?" Though he couldn't feel it over the transmission, Felix imagined her Spirit to be a crowded mess of emotions.

"That's a long story. You're in Haarwatch?" he asked.

"Yes. We arrived just a day ago on a pair of Manaships we acquired for the task." Zara's voice paused, and the sigils around him dimmed. They were pulsing with each word she spoke, each of the pillars vibrating at a specific pitch in order to replicate her voice. "We were stopping only to drop off the Haarguard, then we were coming to you. Did you secure the Temple? Did the Archon claim the power within?"

"Are you alone?" Felix asked.

"No, Cal is here, as is the Hand," Zara said.

"The Hand?" Felix choked out.

"Indeed. He is quite concerned about his ward."

"She's fine. Upstairs, actually, when she isn't hunting for materials," Felix said, hoping that his voice sounded casual. "If it is just the three of you, then I'll explain."

Felix went into a truncated story about the events leading up to and surrounding the claiming of his Authority. He left out Vvim, anything to do with being Unbound, and any and all details about his Omen Path, leaving a bare-bones story that he could tell was raising more questions than it answered. But he did reveal that he now had Authority over the Territory and his own personal Stronghold that he was currently trying to bring up to snuff.

"—and there's where we stand, at least for now," he finished.

"A Spirit Tree, in this barren wilderness?" Zara murmured. "Has it borne fruit yet?"

"We can talk about that when you get here, I think," Felix said, diverting the subject. "I'm more interested in who else you can bring with you."

"Bring with us?" she asked.

"Yeah, there's aspects of the work here that I need help with, and not enough people to do it with. Zara can you ask Cal who might—wait, no, lemme try something." Felix ran his finger across a series of glyphs at the top of the central-most pillar. Each symbol let out a different tone as they activated.

Vassal State Representative Detected.
Do You Wish To Expand Transmission?

"Yes."

Connection Established.

"Whoa that feels odd," said a new voice.

"Hi Cal," Felix said brightly. "Welcome to the group chat."

"The what?" Zara asked. Felix ignored the question.

"Next time a little warning would be nice," Cal continued. "Seeing a glowing glyph form under my feet doesn't bring back the most pleasant of memories."

"Oh, sorry. I actually have no idea how this works on your end. I'm in a big chamber designed for it. Guess I thought it'd be similar for you," Felix explained.

"No, Zara just started talkin' about the 'music of the spheres' and it 'shifting' but we didn't know what she meant. At least, not until that array burst outta the floor. Burned right through my carpet, too."

"My apologies, again, for not clearing the space properly beforehand," Zara said. Her voice didn't sound the least bit contrite. "But let us return to the matter at hand. You wish to have more residents at your Stronghold?"

"Wait, do I need to repeat myself for the others?" Felix asked.

"No, they can hear you, they just could not communicate with you until you did...whatever it was you did," Zara explained.

"Ah good. Cal, do you have people you can spare? Anyone who wants to move out into the Foglands can, at least, anyone that can fit on Zara's Manaships," Felix said. "We may have stopped the Inquisition this time, but I doubt we'll be left alone for long."

"You are right there," Zara said. "The notification of your ascension to Autarch was blared out to all the Continent, and that is bound to draw challengers. Your Enclosure is powerful, but not against the gathered might of the Hierocracy. If the Hierophant chooses to intervene, she would tear it apart like tissue paper."

Felix swallowed. He knew the defensive array wasn't a perfect solution —more of a stopgap, really—but to hear again how it could be trounced so easily and by the person he least wished to face...if he hadn't already been worried, that would have done it.

"My Stronghold is Rank II now, which has afforded me some new options, as well as a few other unique features." He briefly mentioned the Forge, Glyphworks, and Alchemical Lab. "I could use help advancing them, as well as increasing my fortifications here."

"The Legion will want to come," Cal stated. "Gods know they've been begging me to chase after you for weeks now. The Orders will leap at any chance to follow in your footsteps, Felix."

"Oh," he murmured. He'd made it a point to not think about the Fiend's Legion, but he still remembered every face he'd met back in Haar-watch. "Right. Well, I suppose they can come, too. But only if you don't need them—"

"I definitely don't," Cal said quickly. Too quickly, perhaps. "My Haarguard are enough to protect us, and now that you are within the Foglands, I don't think we'll have nearly as many issues with monster hordes."

"Well, I can't control monsters, but the one who was sending them at you is gone." He glanced at Karys and his golden Body. "More or less."

"If you are speaking of who to send from your Vassal State, I would like to make a request," Karys said. "Someone to act as a proxy representative of your Vassal State, empowered to make agreements between our two settlements."

"Can't any agreements be over this?" Felix asked, gesturing to the pillars.

"What?" Zara asked. "Who are you speaking with?"

"My giant robot adviser is telling me you need to send a representative," Felix explained. "Someone you trust, Cal, to make decisions on your behalf. It has to be in-person, I guess."

"Hm. All right. I can do that," Cal said.

"Robot?" Zara asked.

"Yeah. I'll explain that later, too."

The conversation wound down after that, each of them hammering out what might be needed and what Felix could possibly do to help Haarwatch in turn. Pit, meanwhile, fell asleep by the entrance. It was decided that the two Manaships would leave in a day, after they'd been loaded up with volunteers, and would likely reach Felix in a week or so. Provided they had enough Mana to burn, that is. Felix remembered well how fast a Manaship could fly, if you gave it the right sort of fuel.

All in all, he felt positively optimistic when the line darkened and the hexagonal pillars lowered into the floor once more. The array around them dimmed until it was a bare glimmer of silver on the stone, the tips of the pillars utterly indistinguishable from the floor over the chamber.

"Amazing," Felix muttered to himself. "I have a landline."

"Felix."

Karys stood at the edge of his Seal, staring further into the rooms beyond. There were seven chambers, including the one they were in, all of them connected in a ring. But all of them were darkened. Except...

"Is that—?"

"Yes." One of the six chambers was burgeoning with light. It went straight backward, a single silver line pulsing with traceries of gold as power moved between the Seal and this new array formation. "I had not noticed it when the Stronghold ranked up, but it must have opened at that point."

"What's in there?" Felix asked.

"I do not know. It will not allow me close, not without your authorization," Karys said. "But it feels...significant."

Felix stood, glancing at his sleeping Companion. "Well, let's go find out."

CHAPTER NINETEEN

Felix stepped over the glimmering lines of his Seal, trailing wisps of swirling Mana vapor as he approached the smoldering second chamber. It didn't feel like anything, though Karys acted as if a solid wall prevented him from advancing. He flexed his Will and Intent, and the armored Paragon took a surprised step forward before regaining his equilibrium. They stepped into the dark together.

It wasn't completely dark, though aside from the faint Mana vapor wafting from the array beneath his feet, it was as dark as he'd ever seen it on the Continent. His Manasight could pick out the ambient Mana in the air and earth with relative ease. Only in the Temple had he encountered places that seemed utterly devoid of it. *Or warded against my sight,* he thought. *The stones are too advanced to be touched by my Stone Shaping, why wouldn't the Mana be affected, too? The question is, why? To keep others from seeing details of the workings?* It was a conscious choice, he had to assume. There was too much artistry in the Temple for it to be anything else.

So, they followed the glimmering lines of sigaldry into the room, his Perception gleaning what it could from the limited light source. The chamber was just as large as the last one, and he walked for about thirty feet before encountering a complicated glyph in a radial arrangement of sigils. More lines of inscription extended outward, like the spokes of a wheel, pushing toward the unseen edges of the room. Each line described concepts Felix was starting to grasp. Simple, elemental markings for *fire, ice, air, light, shadow,* and so on all tangled with sigils he still could not identify. All of the work he'd done with Hector and the books he'd read and the intrinsic knowledge granted by the Skill itself, none of it gave him even a hint at what the array was doing.

Bracing himself, Felix stepped into the central glyph. Immediately a window appeared.

Greetings, Autarch.
The Second Chamber Is Available.
Do You Wish To Activate?

Felix shared the window with Karys, who simply shrugged. "I do not see the harm. It will consume some of the power your Seat and Seal have been gathering, but there appears to be plenty at the moment."

"Hm," Felix said as he looked around, squinting into the dark.

Hesitation Detected.
Do You Wish To Activate Auxiliary Power Only?

"Karys? How smart is this array supposed to be?" Felix asked, unnerved. He showed the new notification to him.

"A measure of intelligence to the System is expected. It—" Karys halted, his eye-fires narrowing. "The holes in my memory still plague me...your Seat and Seal are simply predicting options for you. I...I do not recall more. But as you gain more Authority, you will find yourself with greater options. That I know. And this seems like the more cautious option. I would suggest accepting its suggestion."

Yes. Activate Auxiliary Power.

Beneath him, the glyph pulsed and ignited, sending out waves of power in all directions at once. The faint glimmers of Mana brightened to a steady stream, liquid and gaseous light pouring outward toward the walls, where they crested and splashed like breaking tides. Beneath, sigils sparked into gleaming life, describing more of the same overly-complex workings that raced along the ground, the walls, the ceiling. Intricate arrays bloomed, illuminating the chamber around them better than a dozen lamps, and revealed the true reason for the room.

"Blessed ancestors," Karys whispered.

There were nine of them, set into the walls but taking up enough space to encroach on fully half the square-footage of the chamber. Each one was forty feet tall and circular, though the similarities between them ended there. They were filled with carvings—made of them, even—sculptures made of glittering metal and polished precious stones. The star and vines motif continued, as in much of the Temple, but also water. Mountains. Lapis-lazuli skies, cold iron peaks, serpentine and silver trees, all of it done in exquisite detail and alluring composition. The sculptures were layered atop one another, building depth within the circular formations, even as they depicted breath-taking detail.

He walked toward the nearest one, which looked like a tropical jungle formed around the towering, split peak of an iron mountain. Each step revealed a glimmer of brilliant ruby hidden in the clever crevasses of the iron, like streams of molten lava. The great, gaping center of it—the empty hole in the circular artifact—was filled with a darkness that the chamber's illumination did not touch. It...called to him, like an old friend.

"What are they?" Felix asked.

"I never knew a Heart lay within these lands," Karys said, as if he hadn't heard Felix.

Felix drew his hand back, wresting control of his impulses. He realized his hand was only inches away from the shadow cast by the layered structure, and he could feel a bone-deep chill emanating from it. He shuddered. That it had affected his Willpower was...terrifying. "What—what's a Heart?"

Karys spread his golden and iron arms, turning slightly to include all of the chamber. "This. A Heart of Darkness it was called, once upon a time. I—I remember pieces of it." He took a step toward the circular artifact before Felix, then another. "Shadowgates. All of them are Shadowgates."

Felix swung back toward the split peak and dark beneath. *Voracious Eye!*

There was a sense of heavy resistance, like the object was fighting back against him. He hadn't had anything push back like that in a long while. Felix doubled up his efforts, throwing his Will against the resistance —it crumbled.

Name: Shadowgate
Type: Artifact (enchanted)
Lore: Built by the Conclave, a united league of nations, the Shadowgates were built as stabilized Passages between the members of the Conclave.

"Passages?" Felix said dully. He blinked. "Fast travel? Like a portal?"

"I do not know what you mean by the last, but yes, the Shadowgates were ways in which our people would quickly travel between points in the Empire." Karys carefully touched a stream of carved ruby. "These took artisans decades to craft, requiring the greatest talents in alchemy, sigaldry, and smithing to come together for a project of such vast scope it beggared some nations." Sparks trailed from Karys' fingers, drawn from within the rubies. "So finely tuned, it still holds a latent charge to this day."

"Wait, so we can jump across the Continent with these?" Felix asked. His heart started hammering and he licked his lips. "Anywhere?"

"Not anywhere. Each Shadowgate is paired with one other permanently. Some places act as hubs such as this—the Hearts of Darkness." Karys took a shaky breath, sounding like a bellows.

Felix walked around the sculpted mountain, looking it up and down. "How do they work?"

"I—I do not know. Or recall, if I ever knew. I do know they pierce the Realms, riding along ancient roads in the Everdark. How they do so is beyond my understanding," Karys said.

"Wait, wait," Felix said, his head popped back around the frame of the artifact. "Everdark. Don't tell me that's—"

"You may know it as the Cognitive Realm," Karys provided.

"The Void," Felix said, his voice going sour despite himself. He walked back around the gate until he could look into the shadows that gathered in the center of it. "Those aren't just shadows, are they?"

"Indeed not, though they do not carry the potency required to access the Passages as they are. These Shadowgates are inactive and need to be reconnected to their ancient pairings before they could be of use to us." Karys pointed at several dull inscription lines, just as wildly complex as all the rest. "Your choice to provide only auxiliary power keeps them banked, but it would require far more than Mana to bring these to full function."

Felix swallowed as he stared into the dark, realizing why this portal hub was called a Heart of Darkness. Why they were called Shadowgates. *The Void.* The abyss inside him roused just as his one Void Skill spun a tad faster. *I can't escape you, can I?*

He hadn't had the greatest of experiences in the Void. He'd been trapped there, in fact, accosted by pirates and monsters both. The Whalemaw was still there, a creature that had taken a great deal of the Maw's Primordial Essence into itself. So were the Korvaa of Echo's Reach, though he assumed they had all fled that place after it had been burned and gutted. His thoughts lingered on Estrid and her kids, on whether they had survived. *Could I...could I bring them out with a Shadowgate?*

"Does this transport you through the Void directly?" he asked.

"Yes and no. It was not my field of expertise, but it relied upon what the ancients called Dark Passages, which are naturally forming tunnels between points in space. They exist all over the Continent, but all are short. It is hard to use a liminal space for a lengthy period of time, else you draw...unwanted attention." Karys shuddered. "There are some truly terrifying beasts within the Everdark."

"Tell me about it," Felix said dryly. "Liminal space, though. The same as Domain sheaths and the Omen Paths. Which means it's not truly the Void, just Void-adjacent." Which meant he couldn't reach his friends; that hurt. Hope coming and going in a flash, like he was leaving them all over again. "We couldn't reach the Void directly, right?"

"That would be unwise," Karys said. "That would require greatly damaging a Shadowgate. And...the Void is not a place for the living. Not for long, anyway."

"Mm," Felix said, studying the Shadowgate even closer. "What was the Conclave?"

"Ah. Yes," Karys backed away from the Shadowgate and folded his dinner plate-sized hands before him. "When the War was in its infancy, the greatest nations united to defend themselves and those lesser Territories that would be crushed in the conflict. The Conclave was a tool of sanctuary for countless millions."

"The Nymean Empire and who else?"

"The Prismatic Towers. The Orrestry. Ahkestria. Many more," Karys said. "Most I fear are no longer extant upon this modern landscape."

Felix had never heard of any of those places, but he filed them away to ask Vess about later. It was past time he learned more about the world outside of the Foglands. If the Hierocracy wanted to destroy him—or would soon, as he feared—then maybe having nine different escape options would come in handy.

"How do we reconnect them?"

"Well, these seem to be in relatively good repair—likely preserved by the enchantments in the Temple. So the first step would be to fully activate this chamber, as the Seal suggested. Then..." Karys drifted off, looking around once more. Felix followed his gaze across gates resembling forests and strange cities and even a series of clouds. They were all done so realistically that in the flickering light of the silver-gold array lines they seemed alive. Real. "I cannot remember the how of it. I would need to inspect them far more closely."

Felix nodded. "Do it. Just be careful."

"Very well. Do you wish to assist? I believe you would be of great use, for many reasons."

He wanted to, but shook his head anyway. "No, I have to figure out how to use these Spirit Fruits." He quickly told Karys what he'd sensed in Pit's monster core.

"Those sound like impurities from the Spirit Fruit's digestion. Pit was able to absorb a direct stat gain due to his deep connection to you, garnering him an Unbound advantage. But not enough. They must be driven out and cleansed from your Companion's system, or else they could weaken him permanently," Karys said. "I seem to recall elixirs that could do such a thing in an instant."

"Do you remember how to make them?" Felix asked, hopeful. Hopes that were dashed when the golden giant shook his metal head. "Damn. Well, that doesn't change my plan, I suppose." He snapped his fingers as something occurred to him. "Thresholds. Do you know if they apply to beasts and monsters?"

"Not as such. Those creatures with a Type as opposed to a Race will typically experience Evolutions, rather than Tempering themselves with Essences. Thresholds are thus also relatively meaningless to them. That is where the Tier designation came from; Tier 0 beasts have never evolved, while Tier I beasts have evolved once." Karys ran a hand gently over a tree worked in silver and golden bronze. "Pit is an anomaly, but no more so than any Chimera. He has not evolved at all, right?"

"Uh, not that I know of," Felix said. "Not unless you count all the growing he's been doing."

"I do not. Monster cores will strengthen and grow until they are ready to change, typically into a form that their Type determines. Chimeras are different, but..." Karys growled, a sound like a lawnmower engine failing to catch. "The holes...they sneak up on me when I least expect it. I know nothing of Chimeras, other than that they are different than any standard beast."

"I'll have to see if I can strengthen his core any further, then. Perhaps push it toward an evolution, or whatever is next for him." Felix stepped away from the Shadowgates, back to the central glyph.

"If you seek more, I recall that there once were Beast Masters who devoted their advancement to the nurture of many Companions. If you can find information on them, then you might be able to glean a better path forward," Karys said.

"Thanks," Felix said. His thoughts drifted to the Farwalker, the only person he'd ever met with a Companion besides himself. "Do you want me to fully activate the chamber?"

"No, not yet." Karys leaned over, his eye-fires like flashlights in the darker portions of the gates. "Let me study this while it is still mostly quiescent. Besides, if they have been damaged by the passing of Ages, then activating this chamber could likely ruin them completely."

Visions of an easy escape hatch crashed and burned in Felix's Mind, and he stepped away from the central glyph. "Yeah, I don't want that. Keep me updated, though."

"As you wish, Felix."

CHAPTER TWENTY

"Drink this, Pit."

Felix tilted a blue-stone carafe into his Companion's open beak. The tenku choked on it, warbling in agony.

"It doesn't taste that bad," Felix chided. He stroked the Chimera's feathered throat, encouraging him to swallow the mixture and grimaced as the smell wafted back up at him. "Okay, it's...not the best. But it's good for you."

Pit drank it all while his tail lashed angrily into a stack of half-empty barrels to the staccato tattoo of furious displeasure. Felix watched his friend struggle with the mixture, thick as it was, but he finished it all. Carefully, he lowered the carafe and backed up.

"All right?" he asked.

In response, Pit cautiously shrugged. Golden eyes widened. Feathers lifted and his tail bristled like a chimney brush.

"Again?" Felix groaned.

Pit retched, neck and chest undulating as clouds of noxious, black fumes roiled from his gullet, followed closely by a thin stream of fetid fluid. The clouds boiled upward, slipping into the grated vents located in the ceiling while the liquid pooled thickly on the polished floors. A smell like rotting meat and vegetation filled the air, making everyone in the Lab gag in disgust. It was not the first time they had smelled such, and much as Felix wished it were otherwise, he did not think it would be the last.

Felix carefully stroked his friend's back as he tried to empty himself of all the impurities his Cleansing Tonic had isolated, until only bile was coming up. By that point, the liquid had itself sublimated into a far thinner smoke, leaving only a stain upon the pitted, wooden floor.

"At least it wasn't as much this time," Felix said, giving Pit an extra pat between his shoulder blades. "I think we're getting closer to getting all of it."

Really? he sent.

"...No. This is barely scratching the surface," Felix admitted before rubbing his hands across his tired face. He'd been up for an entire day distilling that tonic, and still it had only grasped the most superficial of impurities in Pit's channels. With a quick flex of Cardinal Flame, a tendril of Felix's Mana delved Pit's pathways. "We haven't even touched your core space yet."

Pit wilted, his triangular ear tufts drooping.

"But, uh, have hope, we'll figure this out," Felix said. "These impurities aren't impeding you yet. Karys says you could most likely evolve and suffer no diminished capacity at all."

Sword-Armor? Pit snorted. *The one with holes in his Mind?*

Felix opened his mouth before letting it shut with a snap. "Fair point."

They had tried this mixture three times now, and over the past week, Felix had put the majority of his attention into solving the mystery of a Cleansing Potion. There were no records of how to make one, and none among the Stronghold's residents had been of any help, not even the Farwalker—though the man had been a font of knowledge regarding Companion Pacts.

In the end, Felix had been forced to improvise his Cleansing Tonic, though he'd been given good general instruction by Karys' faulty memory. Alchemy was as much about the physical process of mixing and distilling as it was about the crafter's Intent. One could, in fact, skip much of the basics and simply impress Mana and one's Intent upon a mixture and make a passable Healing Tonic. Not a *great* one, mind, but passable. Enough to cure a few scratches and bruises. Coupled with Felix's impressive Intent and near bottomless Mana, and they had, at the very least, a place to start.

"I'll mark this variation as 'needs improvement,'" Felix said as he set the blue-stone carafe upon his workstation.

Also "tastes like krem butt," Pit offered.

"I'll make a note," Felix said, grinning. If Pit's sense of humor had returned, then it wasn't as awful a process as he'd feared. "We still have variation number four brewing in the cold storage. Hopefully, the lack of heat will—"

"Sir!"

Felix whirled toward the voice and saw Vyne urgently waving at him. The man was standing near Felix's Ladder of Ascension, where a series of tubes, alembics, and retorts fed into a vial at the very top...a vial that was supposed to be holding his newest attempt at distilling the Spirit Fruit. Instead, the vial was producing a large quantity of prismatic steam, all of it so heavy it was pooling around the base. It sparked, like fireworks going off, popping and snapping.

"Get back!" he shouted, while driving his Intent and Affinity through his core space. His Stone Shaping responded, manifesting a foot-thick dome of gray stone around the entire Ladder, which slammed in place just as an explosion rocked the Lab. It was so powerful Felix could feel it through his feet, numbing his toes while it sent his alchemist falling to their knees in pained shock.

Vyne, meanwhile, had slammed a massive shield made of blued steel into the wooden floors. The dome cracked, releasing a rainbow-hued spray of Essence in a sharp-bladed arc that neatly bisected his very impressive shield and threw the warrior back a dozen paces. Felix sent Mana hurtling across space, while his core rang out the pattern of Stone Shaping once again. Another slab of stone burst upward, shattering floorboards as it turned aside the explosion's deadly edge.

"Vyne!" Nevia said, rushing to his side. She held a pair of Healing Tonics in her hands, but the young guy sat up all on his own.

"I'm, *ouf,*" he winced and held his chest. Blood welled up, but it was a shallow cut. "I'm fine. Barely scratched me."

"You stupid oaf," Nevia cursed. She poured one of her Tonics onto his chest, letting the solution bubble and fizz against his opened flesh before pulling out a roll of bandages. "You're supposed to run from a failed experiment!"

Vyne gave a pained chuckle. "I didn't know you cared. Ow!"

Nevia smiled smugly, deftly tying the knot she'd just tightened. "Hold still."

"Gonna need a new shield," Kikri mused, running a finger across the sundered edge of his former armor. She hissed and recoiled, her finger bloodied. "It's sliced clean through."

"That's why I brought the granite in here," Felix said as he walked by. "Nevia's right. Next time, run."

"A-aye, sir," Vyne said with a swallow. He traded glances with the Dwarf.

Felix left them to it and inspected the dome of granite. It had been cracked all along a side, and within he could only see swirls of chaotic Mana. With a flex of his Will and expenditure of Mana, he tore the thickened dome apart into chunks of swirling liquid stone. They spun about him for a second before returning to the block of Tier II Granite that he had kept nearby for exactly these situations, reconstituting it seamlessly.

Stone Shaping is level 74!

Beneath the dome was absolute wreckage. Felix let out a heavy breath, annoyance and resignation both, and inspected the remains of his Ladder of Ascension. The alembic and nearly every retort had been shattered, while the frame and circular inscriptions were all twisted beyond remedy. Perhaps, if Felix had managed to figure out Metal Shaping, he'd have been able to reconstitute it in some form, but that Skill had been elusive.

He was sure it existed, but again, his Shaping Skills were missing something. He'd yet to find out what.

At the top of the broken Ladder, the vial holding his latest attempt at an Essence Draught was split in half. It contained nothing more than an oily foam, like bubbles in an oil slick.

"Failure. Again." Felix had tried distilling an Essence Draught an entire sixteen times while working on the Cleansing mixture, but where he'd found limited success with the latter, the former had proven a stubborn obstacle to his alchemic advancement. He massaged his temples, fighting back the stress headache that was taking up more and more of his mental space each day. He wasn't getting much sleep as it was, and the strain of his friends being held back by this was maddening. "How many Spirit Fruit do we have left?"

"Over two hundred," Kikri said.

Felix nodded. He hadn't harvested an eighth of what the Spirit Tree had to offer, but squandering even one of them felt like a colossal waste. "Get me another."

Need sleep, Pit said from across the Lab.

"I need to figure this out," Felix insisted. The others went about their tasks, ignoring him talking to the air. Half-conversations between Felix and Pit had become commonplace. "Sleeping can wait."

Dreams are worse, he said. *I hear them.*

Felix looked up at his Companion. The tenku was looking at him with concern in his big gold eyes. The headache behind his eyes redoubled, a pain sharp enough to push beyond his Song of Absolution. His Body, Mind, and Spirit all felt like taut strings, stretched over the rim of a hollow abyss. The dreams were still there, worsening by the day. "I know. I'm sorry."

No sorry, Pit snorted. *Fix. Action. Confront your dreams.*

"What—?"

BEWARE.

Felix stumbled, the words shoved into his brain rather than a blue-box notification. It almost felt like the System was talking to him, except that it came from the very earth around him. He looked around, unable to shake away the impression of enormous footsteps headed in his direction.

What is it? Pit asked, leaping to his feet. His wings rustled.

"Someone's here," Felix said. No matter how he pushed his Perception however, he sensed nothing amiss in the Crafting Halls or beyond. "Come on."

They tore out of his Lab, down the steps and across the Beacon's landing and into the Temple proper. He leaped, bouncing off the steps he'd constructed around the base of his Spirit Tree, out of the crevasse and into the early autumn air above. There, he and Pit skidded to a stop, the waterfall thundering to their left, and the cliff dropping toward his Stronghold on their right.

I see it!

A speck hovered in the distance, just beyond the jagged peaks of the eastern mountains folks were starting to call the Teeth. It flashed once, twice, before splitting into two specks. Felix focused, his Perception tightening upon their shapes until they took up most of his vision. It was a feature of high Perception that he rarely utilized, but what amounted to telescopic vision was handy as hell. Now, it allowed him to see that the two specks were, in fact, two Manaships.

A woman stood on deck, her long sea-green hair tied back in a series of braids. She raised her hand in greeting, the midday sun glinting off a smile that put sharks to shame.

"Zara," Felix whispered. Then, more fiercely, "They're here!"

What followed was a mad scramble to clear space among the houses and impromptu market that had sprung up in the past weeks. They had kept the football field-sized area clear where Felix had fought the Giants, at first simply because they had the housing they needed, then because it made for a good place to trade the resources found within the Foglands.

When Felix and the Henaari had set about creating more residences within the walls, they had intentionally set aside a number of open spaces. This was due to the Henaari's understanding of civic engineering more than any decision on Felix's part. He simply chose to listen to the more experienced voices among them, devising the start of roads among all the stone and wooden homes. The Frost Giants, meanwhile, had remained staunch isolationists beyond their frozen wall, venturing out only to hunt, train, and trade within the market.

Relations between the Henaari and Frost Giants, while tense, were not overtly hostile. Yet when Felix had landed among them, shouting for the area to be cleared, they had both responded the same way.

They scattered in fear.

Felix wasn't exactly happy that people feared him, but it had proven useful on more than one occasion. He'd take the advantage while he could. Drawing from his memory of airship docks back in the Void, Felix hastily constructed a sort of dry dock out of the stone beneath them. It was barely more than a deep V supported by rocky framework, but based on what he'd seen of the ship's general shape, it'd do the trick.

The Manaships soon cleared the distance between the Teeth and his Stronghold, and by that time, everyone had noticed them. Crowds gathered, the Henaari pointing in excitement and curiosity while Giants fingered the hilts of weapons and cast nervous looks into the skies, as if more were coming.

His team trickled down from the Temple too, gathering behind Felix as he stood near the makeshift dry docks, waiting with him as the ships slowly landed. Jets of powerful air Mana shot off from beneath them, massive downward drafts that normally swirled about their hulls in a complex whirl of power. Unlike the ships in the Void, these Manaships seemed to operate on entirely different premises, weaving dizzying strains of power within and without their hull to harness the winds.

"Blind gods, those're big!" Evie shouted over the roaring wind. "How'd they get them?"

"Stole them from a Governor, I'm told," Felix said.

Evie laughed and nudged Vess in the ribs. "Your minder finally lose that stick up his ass?"

Vess smiled primly. "Doubtful."

Evie snorted even harder.

The Manaships settled into the docks with a groaning of stone, and Felix quickly shaped a few more supports for the structure. The whole thing was eyeballed, so that it worked at all was enough for him, and when the swirling Mana finally cut off, he made sure to cast his Perception and Affinity across the whole structure. He grunted in approval. It'd hold.

The gangplanks on the first ship dropped to the earth with a crash, and the first off the boat was a hulking figure in freshly pressed robes of green and yellow and gleaming silver armor. A sword the size of a small tree was on his back, the man more than large enough to wield it, and even beneath his impressive armor, Felix could see his muscles bunch and flex during his stolid descent.

"He's lookin' healthy," Evie said, admiration clear in her tone. Atar gave her a sideways look. "What? He might be a dick, but I can appreciate a good Body when I see it."

Alister barely stifled his laughter as members of the Haarguard filed off the ship behind the Hand. Felix hadn't expected that, especially not thirty of them. The Haarguard seemed intent on staying in Haarwatch, which had been fine with Felix. Anyone was welcome, so long as they were willing to listen to him. The ones who had traveled with him for so long had been indoctrinated into the team at that point, but thirty more, and all of them looking like they were following the Hand?

"The Blade Overcomes!"

An Apprentice Tier shout shook the air as first one then dozens more men and women of various Races marched off the Manaship. All of them carried a sword of some sort, whether slung over their back or at their hips, and their dark blue uniforms were accented with bronze-colored armor across their chest and leading arms. Their long coats extended in flaps that hung to their knees, where greaves and boots of the same bronze color stomped the ground in a rhythmic march. The lead was a bald Human named Fenwick Cole, nearly as burly as the Hand, if still only an Apprentice Tier. He marched to the fore and saluted to Felix, hand to heart. "We serve."

Suppressing a grimace, Felix only nodded.

"The Fist Prevails!"

"The Bone Remains!"

"The Arc Ascends!"

One after another, the legionnaires stepped off the Manaships, the first and then the second. Damn near fifteen hundred men and women marched out in surprisingly solid formation, divided neatly by their orders or divisions or whatever they called it. *Blade, Fist, Bone, and Arc. The last one is new.* He'd spotted each of their insignias, one of which was the same glyph for fire, lightning, and eye. The other depended on their affiliation, and they looked increasingly professional. All of them wore jackets and pants with armor laid atop them, save for the Arc, who were kitted out in much the same as any Guild mage might have been. He was so preoccupied by the ranks saluting him, Felix almost missed the black and gold robes of his mentor until she was right in front of him.

"Zara," Felix said, repressing the urge to step back from her; she was standing entirely too close. Then he looked again, noticing her surprisingly gaunt face. "You're tired. What happened?"

"What happened is that I burned most of my Mana fueling these ships," the Naiad said. She begrudgingly tilted her head toward the Legion behind her. "The mages of your little army here did provide some aid. It is why we were able to reach you so fast."

"About half a week before schedule," Vess stated. She seemed distracted by the presence of the Hand, still some yards away, and for good reason. They hadn't left on the best of terms. "I am impressed."

Zara inclined her head. "Thank you, your Grace." Her eyes danced across the faces of the Henaari and Frost Giants. He hadn't told her of them before, but if she were shocked, none of it showed upon her face or Spirit. "It has been a long week. If the grandstanding portion is over with, I'd greatly appreciate a bed."

"Of course. We prepared for your arrival, though we're all living a little rough out here, so I can't promise all the amenities you'd find in a city," Felix said. He motioned to his team, and they split up as they had discussed, each of them going to address a different portion of the group. "We'll lead you to your rooms now, and later… Later, we can talk."

Zara met his eyes, her ice blues meeting his own darker set, and neither of them so much as blinked. She inclined her head, in much the same way she had for Vess. "As you wish, Autarch."

"Felix Nevarre."

Sound and activity stopped among the crowd, the words not so much as bellowed as they were spoken with such utter authority. Adept-Tier lungs shook the air as a Body of a small giant strode toward Felix—the Hand approached.

"You have given question to my honor and my duty. By endangering my ward, you have endangered the House she represents and the Territory for which I am a representative. By Oath and Blood I challenge you, Fiend of the Fog. *Autarch.*"

CHAPTER TWENTY-ONE

"You cannot be serious!" Vess hissed at the man, trying and failing to keep her voice down. The silence was so leaden even an Untempered could have heard a pin drop down the street. "Here? Now?"

"When else?" the Hand replied, his gaze never once leaving Felix's. "What say you, Fiend?"

Felix only frowned, but his eyes were unblinking as well. "And this will solve it? Put all our grievances to rest?"

"It will satisfy my honor, *Autarch*," the big man said in his smooth baritone voice.

That's...really stupid. But what else did I expect? "Yeah. Okay." Felix rolled his shoulders. "Duel it up, then."

"*Men*," Vess hissed in frustration.

The crowd burst into frenzied whispers, quiet enough but not to someone with a few Tempers under their belt. It was more like a tide of sibilant susurrations; distracting at best. The Spirit of the crowd, however, was an entirely different beast. It blared, a great horn for those with the proper ears to listen, and that clawed at his balance like nothing else. He could feel the Legion watching, along with the Giants and Henaari, and among them Zara. She pursed her lips in annoyance, but didn't interfere. For that, he was thankful.

Felix shut it all off as his friends cleared the market-turned-air dock, returning it to its first use: an arena of battle. He stretched his arms, always a good choice even when you have supernatural Agility and Endurance, and took to the center of the cleared space. The Hand followed after. He was still wearing his fancy armor and cape, and the massive sword hung in its sheath along his back.

"You accepted far faster than I expected, Fiend."

Felix shrugged. "You said this would end our beef. That's good enough for me. You sure you want to go through with this, though?" Felix let his eyes flick to either side of them. "Last chance to back out. We can talk this over if you really want to resolve the whole Vess abandoning you thing—"

"Enough," the Hand growled. He pulled free his giant greatsword, and the thing just about pealed like a bell in his hand, high and clear. "I'll only be satisfied with your blood on my blade, boy. *That* will end our *beef.*"

"Fine," Felix said, before raising his fists in a defensive position. "Let's get it over with."

Zara and Harn followed them out into the center. She raised her hands to the crowd, and the whispers fell silent. "A duel under the auspices of Oath and Blood has been proposed and accepted! These two will fight until one can no longer continue or until surrender. Killing is forbidden, but all else is acceptable." She fixed them both with her ice blue gaze. "Do you understand the terms?"

"I understand and welcome them," the Hand intoned.

"Yeah," Felix said. "Harn? What're you doing here?"

"I'm here to interfere in case things get heated," he grunted. "Keep the strikes clean, and we won't have a problem."

"You question my honor, Onslaught?" The Hand gripped his heavy blade so tightly it groaned. "You dare think I'll kill your little protégé?"

"I'm not here to stop *you*," Harn shot back. The Hand frowned.

"Gentlemen. Let us get this over with," Zara said. "Begin!"

The Hand lashed out with a big, booted foot, hitting Felix square in his chest. He took the blow head-on without flinching, sliding back thirty feet before halting himself, which was more than enough time for the Hand to unsheathe his immense sword and imbue it with a brilliant flow of white-green Mana.

"Windblade!"

Similar to Pit's attack, a crescent of compressed air Mana tore through the intervening space. It tore up the earth, leaving a trail of dust in its wake, and while it was too slow to hit Felix, it did obscure the Hand's location. Only for a moment, but that was all he needed.

"Wind Drake's Fall!"

The crowd screamed. From above, a mesh of white-green Mana lashed downward at lightning-fast speeds. It hit the earth, slicing straight through stone and hurling even more dust into the sky, coiling it together into a dust devil beneath the mid-morning light. Felix grunted, enmeshed in it all; he funneled his power and Intent through his core.

Sovereign of Flesh!

Felix's body grew, muscles snapping across his frame as he grew to twice his former size. He slammed his clawed hands together with all of his monstrous strength, and the storm of dust and wind was ripped apart. He glared upward, directly into the startled face of the Hand, standing atop a platform of swirling wind.

"Monster," he whispered.

Felix only grinned, bearing his fangs. He *exploded* upward, shattering the lacerated earth beneath him. The Hand flinched backward, lifting his slab of steel in a low guard, clearly designed to fight against a rising enemy.

Cardinal Flame!

Red-gold flame exploded from the Mana Gate at the base of his skull...and through his open mouth. The Hand howled, his sword turned white-hot in the instant before Felix impacted him like a runaway train. The sword bent, but it took the brunt of Felix's charge and instead sent the Hand flying up into the air even farther. He careened, grasping at his odd movement Skill until he came to a stuttering halt near the ground once again.

Adamant Discord.

Lightning lashed about himself as Felix *pulled* toward in two directions at once; the sky and the earth. The result was a slow descent to the ground while blue-white electricity coursed about his chest and limbs.

"Very flashy," the Hand said with a sneer. "But you've not managed to harm me in the slightest, yet."

Felix noticed that the man had to look up at him now, which was more than a little satisfying, if petty. "Do you see any scratches on me?"

The Hand growled and sent a wave of white-green Mana coursing into his blade, straightening it and cooling it at the same time. "I've given you pause. I can feel the fear in you, Fiend. At best, you've dented my weapon. Surely, this isn't all the vaunted Fiend is capable of...is it?"

Felix only grinned and waited.

"I'll start with skinning that ebon hide from your back!" The Hand burst forward, pushed along by a clever use of air Mana and his own powerful Strength. He closed the distance in a blink and his slab of sword came up, a flickering slash meant to split him in two.

Relentless Resolution!

Felix danced away, just barely avoiding the slashing storm of Reed's attack. The blade's reach was enormous, keeping him at bay without offering any opening to slip into the Hand's guard, but Felix didn't care. His Agility and the movement offered to him by his evolved Relentless Resolution were more than enough to keep ahead of his opponent's attacks. The Hand's substantial Endurance would flag eventually, and when it did...

"Why? Why are you so angry?" Felix asked.

"Hold still!" Reed gasped, brandishing his blade ever faster. "This is combat to prove our honor! Both of us! Take! This! Seriously!"

"Fine." Felix was dodging strike after strike, but suddenly stopped and ducked low. "As you wish."

Mantle of the Infinite Revolution!

Rime Shaping!

Felix surged upward from beneath the man's guard, while ice and cold spun off his form like fog and hail, impacting Reed with the force of a blizzard held in Felix's grasp. The Hand blocked the blow with his sword, as Felix had expected him to do, and the intense cold hit the tortured metal instead. Frost formed across its surface as it was supercooled, just as Felix followed through with a secondary blow.

The sword shattered.

And the Hand was thrown bodily into the sky.

Felix watched the man soar upward, limp with unconsciousness, and felt only annoyance. He wasn't hurt after facing the Adept-Tier warrior, not even slightly winded from the exertion. It had felt like beating up a child, almost. He disliked the feeling. It was only saved by the fact that the Hand *had* been able to fight back...it just hadn't amounted to much at all.

Reed's body fell, rocketing back to the earth like a meteorite. Shaking off his annoyance and slight guilt, Felix raised his left hand to catch him in a net of Adamant Discord but was preempted. Aquamarine Mana vapor coiled about his falling form, slowing down his descent until the Hand was floating leisurely to the ground. Yet Zara did not even glance at the representative from Pax'Vrell. Instead, her eyes never left Felix.

He nodded at her. <Later,> he signed.

She only blinked before walking off, Reed's floating body in tow.

Silence seized the crowd, and Felix leveled his gaze all around him. He could feel it blaze, crackling with blue lightning. "This is over. Go."

None protested. In seconds, the marketplace-turned-arena had transmogrified back into a silent field of dusty stone.

———

Later, Felix watched the sun sink closer and closer to the western mountains, small as they were. As early as it was in autumn, the light was still warm and plentiful, though he'd felt an occasional chill in the breeze. A harbinger of things to come.

He had let his friends do their jobs, leading the various groups to their assigned housing. Felix had made sure to build enough housing, crude as his workings often were; the Henaari were good with making things more homey, at least. With Vess and the Synod's help, he'd even done some rudimentary city-planning. All the stone and wooden houses now made proper streets and pathways throughout his Stronghold.

Now everyone was settling in or doing one of the myriad jobs their settlement required, from hunting to gathering and planting in his underground Garden, a facet of his Stronghold he had not spent much time within. Quests were still being accomplished, the standing order of materials and information feeding back into his Resource menus. Aside from his repeated failures with alchemy, things were looking good. Not "stand up to a foreign invasion" good, but decent enough.

Meanwhile, Felix had retreated from everyone else. After that little showing, he had felt the fear spinning untamed in the people's Spirits.

Fear of him. It wasn't a new sensation, but it made him uncomfortable every time, even if it was well-deserved. He looked at his hands—fully human ones now—and at his unmarked Garment. It had torn when the Hand had attacked him with those blades of air Mana, but the thing had repaired itself quickly.

Now he wore a long-sleeved tunic with an asymmetrical collar he could prop up against the wind. He might not be affected by the cold, but he could still feel it in a sense, and he was a Florida boy. Cold wasn't his favorite. But the Garment and his skin beneath, they were leagues above where he had been only a few short months before...he'd beaten the Hand! That felt a little unreal, considering how long he'd worried about that guy gutting him for giving Vess the wrong sorta look.

But now what? Would the man be fine after he woke? Or would he rage about the loss? Felix hadn't a firm enough grasp on the Hand's personality to tell, and Vess had disappeared with all the newcomers, so he hadn't been able to ask. He knew he should go and track Zara down, confront her about the Mark she'd left on him, or ask what the Cantus Sodalus was, or any number of responsible, leader-type things.

Instead, he sat silent atop the Temple cliff—close enough to the waterfall to feel its light spray and far enough to not be entirely embroiled in its thundering cacophony. Curiously, as his Perception advanced, it grew not only more sensitive but more exacting and malleable. He could, if he wished, block out the noise of the waterfall entirely and focus on the other sounds around himself. Felix had played with that aspect of his stats in the past, but as the hours passed into late afternoon, he simply sat there. Taking it all in.

He still heard the footsteps behind him, of course. He wasn't deaf.

"You're lookin' right sad," said a sharp, familiar voice. Felix turned, truly surprised.

"Rafny? I didn't know you were coming, too."

A dark-haired Dwarf stood several strides away, arms akimbo. "One of us had to, you big lug. Establishing a Stronghold and a Forge, and you didn't tell us? Elle was in fits, I can tell you." She peered at his face. "You don't look much like a monster."

Felix laughed. "That's just my....battleform. No, I'm not calling it that." He waved his hand. "Uh, my transformation. I don't keep it going too long. Burns up a lot of energy."

"Naw, not what I mean. Though that bulk is somethin' impressive, for sure," she said, walking closer and peering uncomfortably at the cliff's edge. "Everyone down there is hootin' and hollerin' about the Fiend. The Fiend and the Night Of A Thousand Lights. The Fiend and the Endless Fog. The Fiend and the Ice Witch. The stories they tell..." she chuckled nervously before backing from the drop. "They paint you up a great deal. The Ferocious Fiend."

Felix hadn't heard any of those stories before, but he could probably guess the contents of most of them. He shook his head. "I'm just me. Been through a bit, but—"

"You're more than that to them, I'd say," Rafny jerked her chin toward the ledge. "They're afraid of you."

Felix sighed. "I know. I try to counteract it, but everything I do just feeds the flames."

"Oh, you misjudge me," the Smith said. She tested her weight against a small boulder nearby, half-grown over by tufts of stringy weeds. "It's good. It's a solid thing, fear. Keeps 'em in line, especially those Frost Giants. That was a bit of a surprise." She laughed. "But the way they looked at you. Like a Primordial come alive."

"Hm," he said. "If I'm going to lead them in any capacity, I'd rather they respect me than fear me."

"Bah, respect is fear given time enough to hew off the edges. Let 'em sit in the fire a bit, soften 'em up before you take the hammer and shape 'em. Yeah?"

Felix laughed. "You've got a way with words. Anyone ever tell you that?"

Rafny grinned. "Not ever. So!" She clapped her hands loudly together. "You gonna show me that Forge, or what?"

"All this, so you could angle for access to my Forge?" Felix stood. "Shameless Dwarf."

"Fool Human," she shot back, eyeing the cliff uncertainly. "Stop playing on the edge of things. You make me nervous. I came up to see the Forge, and you. Figured I'd need your permission before I could get near the thing. The Alchemist is probably mustering the guts to do the same thing."

"Oh, nope. I mean, yes, but you can also ask Harn. He's the Forge-master now," Felix said. "Wait, Alchemist? Aenea is here, too?

"She and her husband took ship the moment Cal put out the word. Somethin' about a 'treasure trove of alchemical reagents' in the Foglands." Rafny raised an eyebrow. "And Harn's your Forgemaster? He and I should have words, then."

Felix closed his mouth and quelled the rising excitement in his guts before gesturing ahead of himself. "I'll lead the way, then."

CHAPTER TWENTY-TWO

"He is still unconscious, your Grace. The Autarch struck him quite powerfully. I'm...surprised we found so little harm done," the Henaari woman said to Vess as she led her deeper within the single-story healer's ward. They hadn't any dedicated healers yet, not unless those mages in the Legion had such talents, but a few Henaari herbalists manned the halls in order to better care for their scouts and hunters. The woman leading Vess was tall, with the signature high forehead of her people and large, wide-set eyes that made them look a touch too different from a Human. They hadn't the same fragile beauty of an Elf, but the grace was there, she could admit that much.

"The Autarch would never have struck to kill, Miss...?"

"Pylyk. Gatherer Pylyk."

"Gatherer Pylyk. Their duel was a formality, to...settle an old debate." She managed not to grind her teeth at the words, though her blood all but boiled at both of them. To think, fighting over her like she was some...some object. *Honor, pfah!*

"Well, begging your pardon, your Grace. Remind me never to argue with the Autarch."

The hallways they traversed were all made of a uniformly featureless granite, the bedrock of the area she was told. However, the austere design had been softened by the addition of wooden panels and floors, as well as borders and lintels all carved with a hundred tiny figures and birds. Ravens, she had no doubt. The Henaari were remarkable crafts-men, another point in their favor. Truly, Vess would have been a great fan of them, had they worshiped a proper god instead of one of those creatures.

"Here we are," Gatherer Pylyk said before unlatching a wide wooden portal, carved with a dizzying design of leaves over a sleek hunting drake. Vess' fingers lingered on the door as she passed.

"Did you carve this for him?" she asked.

Gatherer Pylyk inclined her head. "The room was too bare to be without, so we drew inspiration from your guardian. He follows the Path of the Drake, does he not?"

Vess narrowed her eyes. "How do you know that?"

The woman smiled gently. "We have eyes to see and ears to hear, your Grace. Few things stay secret for long, even in a land as large as ours."

Instead of addressing that, Vess swept past her and into the anteroom beyond. "Please see that we are not disturbed."

"...As you wish, your Grace."

Pylyk retreated, that same gentle smile on her face as the door closed with a soft, muted *thunk*. Vess was left alone in a dark antechamber with no furniture of any kind, only the carved detail of a chair rail depicting more ravens in flight. A single doorway sat opposite the entrance, and it lacked any sort of door at all, instead opening into a slightly larger room with an oversized bed and a simple chest of drawers. Courtesy of the Henaari's odd Blessings, no doubt. A bulk of blankets sat atop the bed, breathing deeply.

Vess walked closer.

"You have been practicing your Steps. I barely heard you," Darius said. He groaned as he sat up, letting blankets fall from his chest. "I'm impressed."

"Darius."

"Vessilia. I am happy to see you alive."

"You doubted it?" she said with a furrowing of her brows.

"I doubt everything, most of all your safety. That is my job," he said, far more calmly than she had expected.

"You came here for me," she said before planting herself on the smooth stone floor. "I intend to stay here. With my allies and friends. If you try, I—"

"As you wish."

"What?" Vess was poleaxed. The furrow of her brows deepened. "What...what is this?"

"An...admission." Darius' face creased with a frown of his own. His gaze drifted to the sole window, shuttered against the gathering chill. Not that it would have affected either of them overmuch. "Events have outpaced me. My sense of honor, of duty to your Father, it has been tested time and again these past months. The Guild, the Revenants, the Inquisition.

"I was to be a bulwark against danger, especially after the Foglands. Your Father...when he received that missive that said you were missing, he was in a rage. I was to find you, protect you, and train you in the Guild's stead." He sighed, and it was like the big man was deflating. "I have only succeeded in pushing you further away."

Vess said nothing, only watched as Darius wrestled with something. She could hear the edges of it—his Spirit, usually guarded, seemed tired. "I have decided to stop pushing. I was appointed your guardian, but I cannot be there for you if I am discarded. So, I will follow your lead."

"If you truly felt this, then why the duel? What possible purpose could that have served?" Vess clenched her jaw against her urge to accept the man's contrite words. Darius was stone stubborn, a mirror of her Father, and she didn't trust his about-face. "If you had won, you would have accosted the System-anointed Lord of the Territory within his own Stronghold. My friend. You think I would have simply gone with you?"

"No. But it was necessary," Darius rumbled. He lifted his hands, clenching and unclenching them as if literally grasping for words. "If I am to place myself in the...Autarch's chain of command, then I had to test his mettle. I had to know, for *certain*, what he could do. I have his measure now."

"No, you really do not," Vess said. She shook her head. "Did you not see it? He was holding back."

"What? That's..." Darius' eyes flashed back to Vess'. "Explain." He gritted his teeth. "Please."

"No. I am more interested in what you meant before," Vess said, snagging a chair from the corner. It was carved all over with trees and ravens. "You said my father was sent a missive. From whom? When?"

"It was...from a concerned House. A minor one in Haarwatch. We received it approximately a week after you had left. Why does it matter? All of that was months ago and hardly pertinent any longer."

"Humor me. It was sent via Manaship? Waystone?" she asked, leaning forward.

"It was ciphered along the Waystone network, yes," he said.

"An official missive, sent along channels that would have taken months to reach on foot, and would have cost them a significant fee in gold," Vess murmured, half to herself. "And you never questioned its provenance?"

"I searched for the House when I arrived in Haarwatch, but they had—"

"Fallen mysteriously, no doubt," Vess finished for him.

Darius nodded, worry blooming in his face. "Yes. The last of their line had died beyond the Haargate a month before I arrived. Their manse in the Sunrise Quarter was bought by another party. What are you doing?"

Yet Vess was already leaving, her skirts swishing furiously.

———

After Felix brought Rafny to see Harn, he discovered that she had not come alone. Thirteen apprentices were in tow, most of which he recognized from the Dwarf's smithy back in Haarwatch, but a few that seemed to be fresh recruits. When he asked her about it, he learned that was exactly what happened. Before they had left Haarwatch, the Coldfires had put out a call for new apprentices. All of them had promise, he was assured, and were more than willing to relocate to the Foglands.

Felix hadn't been sure what to expect from Rafny, but she had fallen in beside Harn with little issue, only providing him with assistance when he requested it. For his part, Harn wasn't shy about asking questions, and soon the two of them were thick as thieves. He had left them to it, loudly talking about the right sort of weapons for their growing forces.

The Legion, right, Felix thought as he left the Crafting Hall. He lingered around the Beacon upon the landing, an area now fitted with Henaari-crafted benches for some reason. *I should go visit them sometime, shouldn't I?* There was no answer from within him, as Pit had gone off with A'zek again, but he didn't need one. He'd provided the Legion with a type of priority housing against the base of the cliff, though each were relegated to one of several long, barracks-style structures. Some Stone Shaping had carved them from the cliff itself, and he'd reinforced them with more of that blue-black stone he'd conjured to create the wall and towers. *I'll give them a bit to settle in before visiting.*

Yeah. That was for the best. He definitely wasn't putting off dealing with them.

"Felix!"

A familiar man with dark hair and a closely-cropped beard was coming up onto the Beacon's landing. He had a young girl riding on his shoulders, and his smile was wide as anything.

"Hector!" Felix closed the distance and took the Inscriptionist's hand. "Been a while. How are things back home?"

"Good enough," the man said, fumbling to get his daughter off his shoulders. She was bigger than before, two or so inches talle,r if his memory served—and it usually did. "We finished up the Wall. Had to patch it with steel, but we scrubbed the Archon's inscriptions from it and rerouted the city's defensive power back into the structure. It's not pretty, but it'll serve."

"That's great to hear," Felix said in genuine relief. "I was worried that a monster horde would tear into the city sooner or later."

"Oh, they tried. Legion helped a lot with that," Hector said before bending toward his daughter. "Amaya, my light, do you remember Felix?"

The little girl nodded, her dark brown eyes wide and assessing. "You're the Monster my Mommy complains about."

Felix grinned, and Hector tutted. "Amaya, don't be rude." He looked back up at him and shrugged helplessly. "Sorry, Felix. I don't know where she gets these things."

"I heard you and Mommy arguing on the ship," she said quite calmly. "It was very loud."

"Ah," Hector said, his face heating up. "Well, ah, I didn't know you were awake, dearest. I hope we didn't wake you."

"No. I—" Amaya shrugged and leaned into her father's leg. Not shy but...hiding something. "It's hard to sleep, up so high."

"Oh, little light, it's okay to be frightened," Hector began, but his daughter shook her head and clung tighter to his leg. "Oh dear."

Felix knelt so he could look in her eyes. She did appear tired, now that he was looking for it. But he felt something else from her small Spirit, and it wasn't fear or timidity. "You weren't afraid."

Hector raised an eyebrow, but Amaya cautiously peeked her head out. She shook it, once.

"You were..." Felix let his Affinity expand, skimming across the timbre of their Spirits and others nearby. He grinned. "Curious. You wanted to see the Mana engine."

What else was there to be curious about on a Manaship? Felix had been eager to see one himself, the first time he'd piloted a ship.

"It's not fair that only Daddy's apprentices could see it! I'm big now," Amaya said with surprising force. She looked up at her father, and there was steel in her gaze. "Please? I want to know how it works, Daddy."

Felix couldn't keep the smile off his face as he stood and watched Hector melt. "The engines are dangerous, little light. Perhaps—"

"Perhaps she could take a look at my Glyphworks," Felix suggested. The girl's eyes lit up, and Hector shook his head, a grin plastered on his own face. "I know you want to anyway, right?"

"You've caught me. We climbed into your Temple when we heard where the Crafting Halls were located." He looked at the three sets of stairs, leading upward. "Up there?"

"Middle one. Big white door covered in sigils," Felix said. "I would've shown you eventually, but I foolishly thought everyone would want to settle in a bit." He laughed. "You're the second group to find their way up here."

"Oh? I suppose Coldfire stomped her way into the Forge, did she?" said another voice. Felix had sensed her and those with her when he'd stretched his Affinity. "Typical. She never had any patience."

A woman with cold eyes and a severe face mounted the steps. She wore a woven gown over pants and a long-sleeved shirt, while at her waist was a thick, girdle-like belt absolutely *filled* with pockets and straps. Her long, dark hair was done up in a series of complicated braids to keep it out of her face, and a small pair of spectacles sat across her nose. Behind her were a score of young men and women of various Races—mostly Human—and a few he even recognized. Alchemy and inscription apprentices, the lot of them.

"Aenea. Welcome to my Crafting Halls," Felix said. "I see you've come looking for my Lab."

"Indeed. I was informed that you were in the Temple, somewhere." She sniffed. "When your...assistant warned us away from the deeper tunnels, it informed us of your location."

"Oh, right, forgot to mention that," Hector said, sheepishly. "The Golem you have pointed us in your direction. Said we weren't allowed deeper into the Temple." He huffed a breath. "Must say, it gave me a fright. Never seen a talking Golem before. How'd you manage that?"

"I didn't," Felix said. "And he's right. You're not allowed." He had a hard time not sounding like he was apologizing, but weeks of leading had given him practice. "Perhaps someday, but for now, access to the Temple is restricted to myself and Karys."

"The...Golem? Of course," Hector said, mustering his good nature again. "It is your Stronghold, after all. Right, dearest?"

Aenea waved away the concern in Hector's voice. "Naturally. You are the Autarch, after all."

Indeed. A cold woman, Aenea; she had never really liked him. Thankfully, his ability to learn quickly and his advanced version of Analyze had earned him some favor in the past. *At least she's playing nice. She wants to see the Alchemical Lab as much as anyone.* Felix smiled and felt everyone except Amaya shift, fear and eagerness warring against one another. *Lucky for her, I need the help.*

"How about I show you just what this place can do?" he said.

Zara leaned against the wall of her new home, willing the cool stone to drive the fatigue from her bones. That boy, Atar, had guided her to this particular house up against the cliff. Far from the elaborately carved stairs leading up toward the Temple proper. Isolated, one might say, with only the Frost Giants to one side and a bevy of Legion barracks on the other. The little fire mage had nothing to say to that point, but his Spirit had swayed more than a Zurian veildancer when she mentioned it.

He doesn't trust me, she realized. She hummed, drawing some of vibration from the dark granite behind her, pushing away a portion of her aches. *Felix's grown guarded, and the feeling has spread among his team.* Her skin felt feverish, but no Status Condition blinked in her personal display. Instead, it was her Aspects that plagued her; they were still recovering, Spirit most of all, and the push into the Foglands had not done the Sorcerer any favors.

Damned boy, making me chase him across the Continent. She took three measured breaths, letting her Skills and Chant work their magic. The Grand Harmony sang through her, soothing her fevered flesh with a hymn of solid stones, frozen winds, and water-attuned Mana. Aquamarine power flooded her channels, cycling slowly. *And he neglected to mention a blasted Spirit Tree.*

Seated on her simple bed and hay-stuffed mattress, Zara could see its branches overhead. They blocked the sky, darkening an otherwise bright afternoon, filling it with a false night. *And false stars.* She could see the Spirit Fruit, dangling hundreds of feet up, unguarded and utterly packed with potency. *What changed? I need him to talk to me.*

The sound of hollow knocking shook through her home's barren interior. Zara flexed her Perception and frowned. It was not who she expected. Not at all.

She stood and walked silently down the solid, shaped-stone stairs and paused at the front door. Gathered herself and waited. Just before the knocks sounded again, she pulled open the door, leaving Evie Aren with her fist upraised. Atar was next to her, his olive complexion ashen at her appearance. She simply let an arch smile tilt her mouth before walking away, toward what she assumed was a sitting room.

"Zara, we're here to—"

"Come in, if you're staying. And help me find a kettle in this place," she said. "I'd kill for some tea."

With a minor hum, she yanked the doors closed behind them.

CHAPTER TWENTY-THREE

Felix had a great time introducing the crafters to the two remaining Halls. Hector and his people—five Humans, a Half-Elf, a Gnome, and three Hobgoblins—had stared wide-eyed at the smooth white stone and gleaming gold and silver arrays that traced about each workstation. Alister was there, along with his Henaari apprentices, and the lot of them were almost as flummoxed as the new arrivals. Felix introduced them all, and soon Hector was talking animatedly with the force mage about the work they had accomplished while his apprentices lingered uncertainly around the various tools and implements. The Henaari, however, stayed aloof and cautious regarding the newcomers. Only Felix's presence seemed to put them at ease.

He hadn't stayed there long, leaving Alister to entertain Hector and his inquisitive daughter while he took Aenea and her apprentices to see his Alchemical Lab. She had been quite self-possessed while watching her husband exclaim at various features of the Hall, but she couldn't hide the apprehension jittering across her Spirit. When he had finally thrown open the black iron door to the Lab, she had gasped audibly.

"Yeah, that's what I did, too," Felix had said.

What followed after that was a lot of poking and prodding around the various workstations, even peering over the shoulders of his apprentice alchemists still hard at work on Healing Tonics. That had given him an idea, and soon he had—with his Authority's help—crafted a Quest.

A Quest Is Available!

Skill And Talent!
The Master of the Alchemical Lab and Autarch of Nagast

desires to see the potency of your alchemy! Craft at least ten compounds each to recover Health, Stamina, and Mana! All materials will be provided. Quality and quantity will affect the ranking in this Quest.
Reward: XP, Title: Inner Apprentice, +1 Free Stat Point

The bustle of the Lab died instantly as blue windows bloomed before them. Almost as one, they looked to him.

"The materials needed are to the left of each workstation, and there are more than enough for all of you," Felix said, before grinning. "Who wants it the most?"

Madness ensued.

"What else were you expecting?" Aenea asked him when he'd expressed his dismay at the racing apprentices. They were all Tempered at least once, so their movements weren't ungainly, and there were no collisions that couldn't be walked off, but it was chaotic. And surprisingly loud. "That reward is quite generous."

"Well, I don't really control the rewards. I'm just the...translation point for the System to filter through." Felix sighed. "At least it's worth their while."

Aenea shook her head, but her expression was amused. "It certainly is, at that. I'm tempted to try *my* hand at it, just for that free stat point."

The chaos died away as the prospective Inner Apprentices got to work. The least experienced among them simply aided the others, fetching and carrying water and herbs that were now stored in sorted containers throughout the lab. Herbs were powdered and saturated, solutions distilled, and mixtures sieved as the clink and clatter of apparatuses filled the air. It was the white noise of industrious undertaking, and Felix began to feel more confident in his plan. Already, he spotted several Stamina Tonics completed, and one of the more experienced alchemists had made a Mana Potion from spotted chelk fungus.

In fact, it was working so well that Felix made a quick stop at the Glyphworks and Forge to issue similar Quests. For the Glyphworks, it was to inscribe elemental arrays on the weapons Harn had been making (and it was a lot), with the prize going to those that made the most and the most functional enchantments. Hector and his people set to the task with gusto, Alister functioning as the lead and judge. Atar was apparently off doing something "important, don't bother me" according to his partner, but he'd be roped into the endeavor soon enough. In the Forge, Harn and Rafny had organized their underlings to begin working on strong weaponry to be inscribed by the Glyphworks, the prize going to those who —again—produced quantity and quality.

It was a frenzy of activity as Felix returned to the Alchemical Lab, and in the center of it all, he found Aenea calmly inspecting his workstation. She was pouring over the bent and charred Ladder of Ascension, tracing its stressed frame. He'd cleared it of the broken retorts and tubes, and it sat like a sad, wilting potted plant over his alchemical furnace.

"Flawed design, but impressive nonetheless," she said. "The System provided it?"

"Part of the hall package," Felix said. "Only the reagents and other resources were brought in by my people."

"Your people," she said, looking back at him over the rim of a twisted iron circle. "Urge-worshippers and giants."

"Yes." Felix would offer no apology for people who had sworn to him. Why should he? The Frost Giants hadn't even caused much trouble. "Regarding this particular piece of equipment...I ruined it trying to refine a particularly difficult item."

"Oh?" Aenea's eyes flashed and her Spirit sang with anticipation. "This item would not have come from the thousand-foot tall Spirit Tree you have, would it?"

"How'd you guess?" Felix asked with a smile. He activated an embedded inscription, and a stone container slid from beneath the iron and wooden counter. Within shone six Spirit Fruit, swirling with potency.

"Great heavens, blessed be my eyes," Aenea whispered. "Spirit Fruit. And—wait. How is this possible? They have no attunement?" She looked at Felix with dawning horror. "They're useless if they've no attunement, Felix!"

"Oh, no. It's not that," Felix said before explaining the basics of their nature. "So being able to touch upon all things at once means they're supposedly perfect for everyone...provided they could eat one without exploding."

Aenea was flabbergasted, one of the few times he had seen her as such. "I had heard the Urge-worshippers muttering things when we were guided to our residence, but it felt..." She shook her head. "Who can trust words from such backwards people?"

Felix had a feeling he knew what they had been muttering. "I find them to be quite trustworthy. At least, just as much as anyone else."

"They call you Unbound, Felix Nevarre. But that would be impossible," she said. Her gray eyes searched his, hunting for confirmation perhaps. "It would mean I'm in the company of a demon. A childhood nightmare made real."

"Boo," he said, half-heartedly. Still, she flinched, and he regretted it instantly. "Sorry. They're telling the truth, though I'd like to believe myself nicer than a demon."

Aenea swallowed, but to her credit she did not back up, nor did her Spirit contain anything like anger or violence. There was fear there, but curiosity overpowered it. "An Unbound. So much of what you've done makes sense now. All your unthinkable achievements and the Titles by which you provide benefits to this place." She accessed a formation on his counter, a sort of mini Control Node for the Lab. Others couldn't affect anything, but the details on the Lab's bonuses were available to all. "It is too much for a mortal man. Far too much."

"Mm," he said, still gauging the woman's reaction. "And still I've been unable to refine one of these Spirit Fruit into an appropriate Essence Draught. Worse, I need a Cleansing Elixir to remove the impurities from my Companion's core space and channels...and the best I've managed has been a scratch on the surface." He gestured to the Master workstation around them. "Would you be willing to help me? Even after knowing what I am?"

The woman licked her lips and regarded Felix with her cold, gray eyes. "Pass up a chance at working in this fantastic environment? Lend me your gaze, Felix, and we'll see what we can accomplish."

She rolled up her sleeves, and the two of them got to work.

———

A final, soaring leap brought Vess down to the sparse square near the cliff face. The long, low barracks of the Legion sprawled around her, stacked atop one another in tiers built into the stone's craggy exterior. Effort that would have taken dozens of laborers weeks had taken Felix only an hour to shape, though his talents at architecture left something to be desired. Still, Vess could envision the utilitarian shapes of the barracks in just about any military camp in her father's Territory. Legionnaires were walking about them, their armor polished and coats buttoned up as they seemed to vacillate between stolid duty and jittery excitement. The Haar-guard, those that came with her minder, were stashed close by as well, and for all that their gear looked similar, they seemed ill at ease with one another.

Nevermind all that, she chastised herself. *Zara. I'm here for Zara.*

After speaking with Darius, a series of events in her past had come to a startling clarity. Her Mind worked at the issue, turning it over for cause and concern, wondering at it. What was the purpose? What, exactly, was Zara's goal?

She found Zara's new residence in rapid order, situated at the extreme end of the Stronghold, between the barracks and the jagged ice wall. Mist breathed off that construction, its awful chill making the autumnal air seem a balmy summer breeze. It coated the ground in a thick carpet for approximately forty spans outside its bulk, fading just as it reached the carved door of Zara's home. It depicted a swooping bird of prey diving from the stars and into a stormy sea. The artistry of the Henaari tended to be dramatically on point, but this felt more symbolic. Vess traced her hand across its raised surface. *Was Zara the bird...or the storm?*

The door opened, much as it had those months ago when they'd found Zara at her home. A home she was increasingly certain had belonged to a minor noble House, lost tragically in the Foglands. No one was at the door, much as last time, though she spotted the fluttering shape of small, jewel-colored wings. Zara's familiar, no doubt. Vess stepped across the threshold, entering the spacious, unadorned interior. She set her partisan down by the door, leaving it as a sign of peace; she wanted no fight with the Sorcerer, just answers. Two arches were on either side of her as she entered, and a staircase went up to the second level, while the hall ahead squeezed past the stairs and into another arch. Based on her knowledge of the layouts, it was a kitchen in the back, a sitting room on the right, and to the left...

She opened that door as well, only to find it empty. Vess backtracked to the sitting room and that was empty as well, so she headed back to the kitchen. A rudimentary counter and stone-lined chimney were here, large enough to fit a pot over though little other accommodations of modern living was in evidence. It was also bare and cold, without even ashes in the fire to suggest anything had been put to use. But there were sounds beyond the stout stone door in the rear, sounds that Vess could tell were from her friends.

"Evie? Atar?" she called out as she opened the rear door. "What are you two doing here?"

Zara's residence, much like the barracks, was fitted against and into the mountainous cliff face. Anything behind it had to have been excavated to be of any use. Felix hadn't bothered with digging into the stone much, other than to ensure folks had housing. He had expressed some concern at allowing folks access to the roots of his Temple, even though the temper of its stone was impossible to break into...at least for anyone below Master Tier.

But the Sorcerer hadn't been satisfied with her living arrangements and excavated a cavernous expanse, easily a hundred strides deep by fifty wide. It was more space than any one person really needed. Evie and Atar were currently forming translucent balls of ice and flame respectively, though both burst into fading shards as Vess broke their concentration.

"Oh, hey Vess," Evie said with an easy wave. "Been gettin' more lessons on this Chant stuff."

"Burning ash, Dayne. I was *this* close to mastering my Sparkbolt unaided!" Atar groused. He stood and wiped dust from his dark robes. "Now, I'll have to start again."

"If your Intent is so weak it can be shaken by a simple greeting, then you still have a long way to go," Zara said. That kingfisher alighted on her shoulder, murmuring something Vess couldn't make out, and the corner of the Naiad's mouth twitched. "Welcome, your Grace. Do you wish to resume lessons as well? It has been a long while since I've taught any of you on the mysteries of the Grand Harmony."

"I—Atar, you've unlocked Harmonic Stats?" Vess asked. The fire mage looked pleased as the cat who got the cream as he resettled his robes against his shoulders.

"The study of glyphs had surprising benefits. I was able to unlock Intent after dissecting part of an ancient Relay glyph. I came to seek an understanding of my new capabilities. After seeing what Felix can accomplish, I would be remiss to not seek any avenue of improvement." Atar frowned at his hands as a flickering, ghostly spark spat from his channels. "It has proven...harder than I had anticipated, however."

"Damn annoying, is more like it," Evie said. She massaged the palms of her hands.

"They are seeking to expand their potency," Zara said. "Felix's surprising growth is a lash which spurs on their need for growth. I applaud their drive. It is why I opened up this section of the mountain. Here, training in the Chant will not put others in harm's way and should remain quite secret." The woman fixed Vess with a knowing gaze. "Do you wish to join us, your Grace?"

Vess regarded her, from the ochre luster of her slightly lined skin to the tips of her sea-green tresses. Everything about Zara screamed "beautiful and authoritative," a combination that put many on edge. She would know; her mother had used similar tactics when governing Pax'Vrell.

Power was more than the Temper of your Aspects; it was also the illusion of power that allowed proper governance to occur. As any proper illusionist would tell you, the first step was never to lie to your opponent. It was to let them fear the truth, then to provide a convenient alternative. Zara claimed to wear masks; she had never lied about that, but Vess was certain she wanted more than to teach them her heretical brand of magic.

"Why did you contact my father, Zara?" Vess asked.

Evie's head snapped up as Atar's working collapsed again. They both craned their necks at the Sorcerer, a woman who held Vess' steady gaze with not a stitch of repentance.

"It was you, was it not, who contacted my father? That had the Hand dispatched to Haarwatch when we were all still within the Foglands? I had always wondered at the reasoning; Darius would have had to leave months in advance to reach Haarwatch when he did. Which meant someone had warned my father in advance, far before I ever set foot in the Foglands with Magda and Harn." Vess stepped down from the rear door, gracefully crossing the smooth stone field. "Why? What is your game, Zara?"

The Naiad's expression had gone carefully blank, and Vess could feel nothing at all from her Spirit. It was as if she was not there at all. "You, all of you, are important. Evie and Atar have found themselves with access to Harmonic talents now, but I had not anticipated them. However, with your mother's talent for the Chant, it was likely you would also manifest such ability. I was not willing to lose you to the Foglands, or whatever the Guild Elders were planning.

"Yes," she held up a hand, forestalling Vess' half-spoken words. "I was aware of the turmoil within the Elder Council. The specifics were hidden from me, but their disdain for Magda and Harn was not a particularly well-held secret. After Magda's death, had Darius not come, their use of you would likely have grown more...bold."

"That is it?" Vess said. She wished she hadn't left her partisan by the door; the feel of its cool haft would have given her annoyance an outlet. She settled for clenching her fists. "Because we have accessed the Harmonic Stats and can learn your Sorcery? What value does that have in this world, when knowledge of it is enough for the Hierocracy to execute us? There is more you are not telling us, Zara."

"You've summed up my feelings exactly, Vess," a new voice said from behind them. Zara's eyes widened, and her closely held Spirit seemed to spasm in surprise. Felix stood in the doorway, filling it with his wide shoulders. His face was serious, blue eyes glowing among his wind-blown hair. "We've a lot to talk about. All of us."

CHAPTER TWENTY-FOUR

"Where—how did you approach without my noticing, Felix?" Zara asked.

Felix only shrugged. "My Agility and Dexterity are pretty good now."

"That shouldn't matter; it's your Aspects that resonate with the Grand Harmony," Zara said, her own Spirit still doing that shuddering spasm. Felix frowned. "I can see you, but you feel..." she blinked. "Everywhere." She looked up, directly at where the Tree was soaring above them. "Spreading around us like the branches of a tree."

"Ah," Felix said. "Yes, well. My Spirit Tree and I have more in common than I had figured, I guess."

Zara stared then laughed. It felt as tired as it sounded, and it unnerved Felix. *She's more worn out than I realized.*

He had been working with Aenea, attempting to fashion a Cleansing Potion. It was the best she could manage, but said it would be possible with the materials on hand and System-provided equipment. Unfortunately, it was not a swift endeavor. Aenea said it would take at least a day to properly make, and even that was pushing it. Which was when Karys made Felix aware of strange vibrations emanating from near the Temple. With no reason to linger in the Alchemical Lab, Felix stepped out to look at it and found the rarefied vibrations coming from Zara's residence. It was no less surprising that his friends were there, practicing.

"Wait, Felix is a Tree now?" Evie asked. "How many things can you pack into those muscles before you burst? Maybe make yourself into a Manaship next. It'd make travel a lot easier."

"Shut up," Felix said, smiling.

"Since you're all here, I won't have to repeat myself," Zara interjected and gestured for them all to follow deeper into the bore she'd made in his mountain. Twenty strides in, she paused and looked around herself; Felix could almost feel her feather-light touch testing the boundaries of her crafted room. Wards of aquamarine light were sunk deep in the walls of the place, wards that Felix guessed prevented sound and light from exiting this mostly sealed cavern. "Please. Conjure a chair. You may wish to sit for this."

Taking cue from the others, Felix drew on his Affinity and Intent, sounding his Skill and shaping its effect. Four armchairs rose from the striated stone floor, as if injection molded from the earth itself, with nothing more than the faintest whisper of sound. Zara looked impressed.

"You have come a long way, Felix," she said.

Felix disregarded her words, though he didn't miss the disgruntled look from Evie and Atar as they all sat. Zara ignored them all, contemplating her folded hands as if secrets were written there. "I belong to an...organization. Called the Cantus Sodalus."

"I'm aware," Felix said, surprised at the anger in his own voice. He had hoped for a flash of emotion from the woman, but she had mastered her Spirit once again, and only silence met his senses. "I saw the evidence of that in the Mark you left on me."

Zara clenched her jaw. "That was only to keep track of you, Felix. When you left the city, I could not risk you falling beyond my reach."

"So you Marked me? Without my consent?" Felix asked. "I thought we were to trust one another?"

"We are. But there is more that you do not know. Could not, until it was time. I—" Zara ran a hand through her sea-green locks. "My order—"

"Chanters, I assume," Vess said.

"Indeed. All of us are well-versed in the mysteries, dedicated to preserving the ancient histories and uncovering the secrets of Lost Ages. To keeping the world alive, no matter the cost." She met Felix's gaze. "Four years ago, the Divine Oracles of the Hierocracy all saw the same thing, echoed across the fabric of the future. A silence stalking the far-flung higher realms, expanding as it came. It left every one of them broken in Mind and Spirit, sundered by the experience, unable to utter anything but a single word."

"Ruin," Felix breathed. The others stilled, their attention sharpened.

"Exactly so. Most passed the warning off as a false cry. After all, the Ruin is a myth. The Hierophant, however, believed. She sent the Orders out to find any scrap of information on the Ruin and sought anything that would stem its advance."

"But the Ruin destroys everything in its path, even evidence of its passing," Atar pointed out. "That seems to be its primary function."

"Which is why they found it so hard to find reliable information," Zara said. "Until they stumbled upon a record that had long evaded even our grasp: the ritual to summon the Unbound."

Felix could feel everyone staring at him, but he couldn't spare them any mind. He leaned forward. "Are you saying I was brought here by the Hierophant? To do...what? Fight off the Ruin?"

"That was the intention, yes," Zara admitted. "But not as you may be thinking. The Hierophant believed with enough Unbound under her banner, she could muster defense enough to save a chosen few. Not the entire Continent, or even the entire capitol. Just the elite."

"Typical," Atar muttered, and Evie nodded along with him. Even their scowls were similar.

"How would they know the Unbound—*we* would work for them?" Felix asked. "What would have stopped us from turning on them as we grew stronger?"

"There is a great deal you still have not experienced, Felix. If the Hierophant were to hold sway over you from the start? When you were at your weakest? There would be no defending, no future revolt," Zara snapped, her sharpened teeth more growl and grimace. "They would own you, Body and soul."

"Oathbinding," Vess stated, dread in her voice.

"Among other techniques, yes," Zara affirmed. "The prevailing order in this nation rules for a reason. Their strength cannot be contested, not alone. If the Hierophant's plan had come to fruition, they would have held the reins of nine Unbound soldiers, beings of incalculable potential. Imagine what nine of you could do, Felix."

He couldn't begin to think of it; the idea was too massive. Alone, he'd bested Master Tier existences and fought back ancient godlings. What, then, were the other Unbound doing now? What impossibilities had they achieved?

"My order opposed the Hierophant's plan. Not that the Unbound shouldn't be summoned; we need you, for good or ill," Zara said. "Instead, we wished you all to be free of the Hierocracy's control, so we infiltrated the summoning ritual with one of our own. He...sacrificed himself to keep you free, Felix. Your arrival was cast to the four winds, with no one able to tell where you'd land. Because the Oracles had gone mad, the Hierophant also had no way to find you. We hoped—still hope—it would be enough to let us find you all first."

"And apart from tracking my every movement, what is the Cantus Sodalus' goal?" Felix asked.

"My order has dedicated itself to search for you all, to gather you and keep you safe from the powers of the Hierocracy. Because none of you are invincible."

"Dunno. Have you seen him punch a Frost Giant?" Evie asked. "Pretty powerful, if you ask me."

Zara shook her head. "No matter how strong you have become in the last few months, you cannot hope to stand up to an entire nation."

"Then what do you propose?" Felix asked. "The Hierophant wants us as a personal protection squad against the Ruin, and likely against anyone else they dislike in the meantime. But what do the Chanters want?"

"We...we want to save the world, Felix. Or as much of it as we can manage," Zara said. Her cheeks seemed hollower than before, her eyes baggier. "All of us were sent hunting for signs of your arrivals. To all corners of the Continent. Only I have had any true success, though hints of the others trickle through rumors and far-flung reports."

"So, you want me to fight, too?" Felix asked. "Against a...force that obliterated entire civilizations? How? I've seen the coming of Ruin, and it is not something I can punch into submission." Felix's Mind flickered with dark violet flame, of being pinned by the innumerable hands of the divine. Of being utterly unmade...

"The ancient legends speak of the many miraculous things once done by the Unbound. You are greater than you know, Felix." Zara included everyone in her gaze. "All of you are important in the struggle to come. Especially since we've no clear idea where any of the other Unbound might have landed."

"I do."

Zara stopped, and it was a measure of her fatigue that her Spirit was audible to Vess and Felix both; he could see the heiress wince at its intensity. Her Spirit flip-flopped, a fish floundering in consternation and astonishment. "How?"

Felix frowned, his eyes feeling dim as embers. "Dreams."

———

The next thirty minutes were spent explaining his recurring dreams to Zara and the rest. He hadn't really shared them with anyone outside Pit and Karys, the latter only because he'd been there for one of Felix's many rude awakenings. When he briefly touched on his Omen Path and the vision of seven Unbound all being held by Paladins...that had piqued Zara's interest immensely. Yet, when she inquired deeper on his Path, he shut her down. Felix had no interest in sharing the details of his Omen Path and only gave the bare minimum of what she required.

"You have built a connection to the other Unbound, one that I'm assuming exists due to your all being summoned together," Zara mused as she walked. "Your Affinity has grown, and your power... Whatever happened to you during your Omen Path must have strengthened the link enough for these visions to interfere with your dreams."

"Why dreams, though?" Atar asked. "Seers and oracles operate on the whimsy of dreams, but Felix is neither of those."

"Dreams, all dreams, touch upon the Cognitive and Ethereal Realms. Thoughts drift along connections, skirting the vast expanse of the Void, intermingling and diving into the confluence of all things...There is much that even the dreams of mortals can unveil," Zara said.

Felix frowned at the thought. "So my Affinity has snagged onto these strengthened connections and is...transmitting events around them? How does that work?"

"You are not seeing events exactly the moment they unfold, but echoes upon the fabric of the Continent," Zara explained. "Seers function similarly, though they call it by different terms. None would admit that what they do is closer to Sorcery than their limited understanding of magic. The Masters and Grandmasters know, but true Seeing as done by an Oracle is too powerful to be tossed aside. Bah."

She waved her hand, dismissing the lot of it. "They are finding resonance with your own nature, and the echoes follow after. If we can establish a stronger link, we might even be able to locate them before the Hierophant or any other nation can."

"And what makes your group better than the rest?" Felix demanded. "All I am hearing is justifications and excuses. How would *you* use us, Zara?"

The room went quiet as Felix and Zara matched stares. It was not so much a battle of Wills as it was an effort of sincerity; Felix *wanted* her to offer him a reason, an idea, *something*. Yet in the end, the Naiad let her eyes drop.

"We would ask that you fight the Ruin," she said.

"That is precisely what you are admonishing the Hierophant for attempting," Vess accused.

Zara held out her hands. "No. No, I am asking. We are asking. To fight against this is not something one can be coerced or tricked into attempting. It must be a decision made with the fullness of the truth. A Choice." Zara looked again to Felix. "That is what my order is offering you. A Choice to fight...or to flee."

"Flee?" he asked.

"Where there is a summons, there must also be the inverse," she explained. "If you wished it—if you Chose—we would give whatever aid we could to send you home."

Home. What?

Before Felix could even begin to process that, Zara knelt upon the ground. She lowered her head but kept her vivid eyes on his own. "Please. Eight others such as yourself in the hands of those madmen; free for them to shape, to influence. It would be almost as bad as the Ruin itself. Please help me find them."

Felix's jaw worked, Mind awhirl with the implications of all she had revealed. In the end, however, he found his resolve. "...What do you need me to do?"

CHAPTER TWENTY-FIVE

A ritual was needed.

Felix sat amid a wash of sigils and glyphs, all of them radiating around him in a spiraling array of confusing concepts. Sigils for Mind, Body, and Spirit were circled by *dream, air, fire, water,* and *lightning,* those circled by yet more in a formation of at least six different arrays.

"Wh—where did you learn this?" Atar asked the Naiad. Zara only grunted, scraping a strand of aquamarine Mana across the final section. "I don't even see how it functions...where is the input? The output?"

"I've learned many Skills in my years." Zara straightened with some effort. "To explain everything you do not know would take several lifetimes, child."

"Are you up for this?" Felix asked, cutting off Atar's angry retort. He was concerned for the woman, despite everything Zara had hidden. "I can tell you've strained your Spirit, and your Body—"

"You look like ten leagues of bad road," Evie said, hands on her hips.

Vess' face was serious, but Felix spotted a faint twitch on her lips. "I echo her concern, Zara. Should we not wait until you are in greater health?"

"We cannot. Perhaps his link will persist, or perhaps it is degraded by the day. I have no way of knowing which." Zara wiped her brow, but her face was steady, resolved beyond any effort to dissuade. "We begin."

As instructed, Felix let himself drift down into his own core space, letting sound his Meditation, Deep Mind, and Bastion of Will. Zara had given him some bare directions for this process; he was to let his senses drift, searching his core space for the thread of connection that was the cause of his spate of unsettling dreams. For him, that meant utilizing his Bastion of Will, the fortress within him that was a world of its own and contained the impressions of several other Skills. Meditation, Deep Mind, and Relentless Resolution were each inscribed upon the five-sided tower in his Bastion, and as the fortress hummed to life, each of them pulsed in sympathetic vibration.

Most important, however, was the silver lightning rod that stuck from the very top of that tower. It was looped with countless, colorful strands that arced down from the sky before returning again into that clear blue. Each of those strands was a connection that Felix had established in the world, one for every person, creature, and thing he had influenced in some way...and those who influenced him.

Felix strummed those threads, the mental projection of his fingers combing across them even as his Affinity sought out the one he needed. There were so many, it would take him an entire lifetime to even count half of them...and this was the amount after only a half year on the Continent. How much would this swell in the years to come? How would Felix be required to change by then?

Or...or could he actually go home? Could Zara truly send him back to Earth? To his family?

To see Mom? Or Gabby?

A strident call came from beneath his fingers as a dozen strands vibrated to raucous life, and Felix was scalded. He hissed, the pain overcoming his impressive resistances. He beheld nine threads flush with opalescent hues, each singing at a pitch only slightly different from one another.

What was it? The thought of home? Of Earth?

The threads blazed with life again, though some far more than others. One, a light that was predominantly ebon-gold all but drowned out the others; its thread felt the thickest of all. The strongest. Yet when he reached for it, the light turned his hand away, like a wall separated them. Beside it, a thread of black-green and sandy-brown illumination threw wild shadows over the rest, and was the second-most robust of the connections.

Why—?

Unwilling to waste time, Felix gripped the second thread. He found no resistance, and the moment he made contact, he was ripped off into the distance. His Bastion faded into streaks of blues and greens, until he felt like he was bridging a vast divide between the here...and a place impossibly distant. Barriers of light came and went, shattering as he traversed them, breaking into tiny, razor-edged stars that sliced at his Will. Felix screamed, but he would not relent. He would hold!

All the world became a hurricane of light.

Until it stopped.

With a floundering quake, forward movement became a relentless quiescence, and Felix was abruptly aware of fine, red sand beneath his feet. Heat packed in around him, like a jar half-again too full with insufferable temperature, made all the worse by brilliant flare-ups strong enough to melt sand into smears of thin glass. Sound came soon after touch, and Felix immediately recognized the roar of chaotic battle.

Sandstorms swirled around his position at the edge of a silken dune, and vivid displays of light and fire Mana streaked into the skies and down again onto the earth. All the land was rolling dunes, with the barest hint of red-orange mountains to the southeast, but most of it was blotted out by the whirling tornadoes of sand and flame. Among the dunes and storms, figures in bulky red armor wielded golden weapons against a shambling horde that seemed to...emerge from the whirlwinds themselves.

"Hallow! I can't control them!"

Felix spun. Whatever this was, his senses were weirdly blunted—so much so that he hadn't noticed the hulking Minotaur only three feet behind him. He was staring not at the clashing forces, but at a charging contingent of more shambling forms. *Undead*, he realized with a sickening lurch. He could see threads of writhing colors stretching between the walking dead and strange sand-twisters. *The whirlwinds are full of undead.*

"Hallow!" the Minotaur bellowed again, his tone fully panicked now. He was dressed in worn, chitinous armor, much as before. "Why can't I take control?"

A voice, cool and calm and distinctly feminine came from beneath them. "They are still bound to the Tomb, Michael. You cannot take possession of them until you take the Tomb as well."

The sands parted as a horse-sized scorpion rose from beneath, its barbed tail lashing and massive claws clacking. Blackened green light shone between the cracks in its carapace and from its eight beady eyes, but the calm, feminine voice was absolutely coming from its form. Behind it, three more shapes rose, a segmented Multipede and two humanoid figures in broken crimson platemail. As with the undead and the whirlwinds, threads wove among the glowing figures, and all of them led to the Minotaur.

A Skill?

Whatever it was, it meant the Unbound had a powerful connection to his creatures. Summons, perhaps. Summons that could speak and think, somehow. And take action on their own, it seemed, for as the shambling horde reached them, the Multipede and humanoids swept forward to meet them. Their mandibles and swords glowed with that same blackened hue, tinged liberally with green. Necromantic Mana, his Manasight told him, and things made a sudden sense.

It was a zombie fight.

The humanoid warriors hit the undead like speeding trucks, mowing through their ranks with brutal efficiency while the Multipede was more like a bullet train. It tore across the sands, weaving complex, looping pathways that skewered the enemy with every leg and clash of mandibles. Only a few made it so far as the Minotaur, and he ended them with a swing of a massive maul the size of a boulder, crushing all of them at once in a cataclysmic strike.

"Seismic Shatter!"

The ground erupted in a spreading cone, one that neatly diverged around the glowing warriors and hit the final stragglers with a fatal flurry. The enemy undead were splattered across the crimson sands.

"The Paladins," the Minotaur said with a choked-off gasp. Through their connection, Felix felt the guy's Spirit and Mind quiver, telltale signs of Mana exhaustion. "Hallow. How're they doing? Are they in AOE range?"

All four of his necromantic pets froze, facing toward the storms only a couple dunes away. Felix could spot more undead pouring out, but they were met with a constant barrage of golden Mana vapor. Lashes and manifested blades of light cut down columns of the encroaching dead.

"They are. I recommend running. They are sure to overcome this latest defensive measure," the scorpion said. Mana puffed from it, much like Felix's sword when Karys spoke through it. "You are still not strong enough to contend with them directly. I suggest—get back!"

Without warning and surprising even Felix, a rain of liquid light tore from the sky. Golden shafts of radiance formed deadly spears that burst the entire dune they stood upon. He could see the scorpion move almost as fast as himself, throwing itself between the burly Minotaur and a burst of the golden spears.

"Run!" its once-calm voice bellowed, now pained and panicked.

The Minotaur—Michael—stumbled back, too slow to have even seen the strike coming, his bovine face a picture of astonishment that swiftly changed to anguish. "Hallow!"

"I will be fine! You must run!"

From across the other dunes, the whirlwind had all but ceased, and a phalanx of red-armored warriors were marching in double time toward them. Their hands gripped lances and greatswords and huge axes made of liquid, golden light. Felix whipped back, staring at the Minotaur, and his face crumpled with tears.

He ran, and the Paladins overcame the scorpion. It fought bravely, but it was no match for their reach and numbers. In moments, it was taken apart.

The second it died, Felix was yanked forward, appearing at the Minotaur's side like he'd been teleported. The guy was bent over, clutching at his chest and staring in the direction they had left. The ground rumbled, and that huge Multipede reared from the sands, bearing the two humanoids that were clearly former Paladins. Its eyes shone a blackened green.

"You must keep running. They will find you," said the exact same voice as before, now coming from the big bug.

"I felt you die," the Minotaur whimpered. "Ugh. It *hurt*."

"I am sorry, Michael."

"Don't call me that. It's not my name anymore," the Minotaur said. He drew himself up to his full height, likely close to eight feet tall and filled with thick slabs of muscle beneath his rough, chitinous armor. He hefted his boulder-sized maul and trotted down another dune. "Where do we go?"

"Back to the city. Find Naos. We will find a measure of safety there, for a time."

A strange tugging started at Felix's navel, but he held onto the vision, lingering beside this other Unbound. He wanted to see more, to see what the man was planning and how he'd fight back against the Hierocracy. Yet, when the Multipede mentioned a city, the connection between him and the Minotaur thrummed in teeth-buzzing dissonance. In Felix's Mind, the image of a towering storm flashed, two thousand feet high. A sandstorm of red, but also sheets of incandescent yellow-white flame, hot enough to send jagged shards of glass spiraling out all around it. He could glimpse the faintest impression of soaring towers through the storm, but a hailstorm of deadly projectiles drove men in red plate armor back and away from its perimeter.

Something tugged at him, far harder than before, and this time Felix let it take him. The hurricane of light returned, far swifter now, until he slammed into a wall of enduring darkness that swept him away entirely.

––––

Bastion of Will is level 85!
Meditation is level 69!

Deep Mind is level 75!
Adept Tier!
You Gain:
+10 AFI
+10 ALA
+10 EVA

"—is my home! What is the Hierocracy doing there? We're not a part of your union!" Atar was on his feet and shouting when Felix came to his senses. He jabbed a finger at the space above Felix's head, where a projection of his experience was supposed to have been displayed. It had worked, apparently. "Those sands are inviolable!"

"The why is simple. They are hunting an Unbound," Zara said.

"The—the bull...man?" Vess asked. "That was...that is an Unbound? The same as Felix?"

"All Unbound choose the Race as they arrive, as well as a few other advantages," Zara explained. "That is what the old texts say, and Felix's experiences support it."

Felix stood, combating a momentary dizziness before mastering himself. "She's right. He must've chosen a Minotaur during his arrival."

"Minotaur? That's what he was?" Evie asked. "Looked about as tall as Karys. Burlier, too."

"A Lost Race," Zara muttered. There was already a scroll in her hand, and it was half-covered in cramped notations that she added to as she spoke. "Possibly with a Strength and Endurance bonus at each level. Do you know how strong he is? Will he survive those Paladins?"

Felix's Mind flashed back. It had been chaotic, but he'd gotten a fair measure of the guy. "He's tough. Hurt, though. I don't know how long he'll last on his own."

"He had those...bugs with him," Vess said. "A curious Skill. Might they be Companions to him?"

"That looked like a Slayer Scorpion, and the other was a Multipede, both deadly denizens of the Scorched Expanse," Atar explained. "My home."

"I'm more concerned about the hundreds of walking corpses we just saw," Evie pointed out. "Was that your Unbound friend's doin'?"

"That's just the Expanse. Undead are a...recurring problem," Atar said. "But this is beyond their normal activity. Why isn't Ahkestria taking action? Those Paladins, the undead; my Master would never have let things get so bad."

Felix's memory roused again, summoning the last image he'd captured from the Minotaur's Mind. "Ahkestria. Is it covered in a burning sandstorm?"

Atar stilled, his brows furrowing. "Yes, but only when attacked. It keeps the city safe from the undead and a long litany of past invaders...you don't think—? The Paladins would never dare to attack the City of Embers!"

"I got a flash, a memory, from the Minotaur. He'd seen that city, and it was covered up by a storm as nasty as the columns of soldiers trying to enter it." Felix shook his head and carefully extracted himself from the formation. "That's where the guy was headed, at the end there. To the city."

"Then that is where I must send my order," Zara said, tucking her scroll back into a pouch at her waist. "A Chanter by the name of Isla was to be tracking this particular Unbound—that she is not with him makes me quite nervous indeed. Tough or not, this Michael must not be allowed to fall."

"Then we should go there ourselves," Atar said. His Spirit simmered with barely lidded rage. Clearly, what he'd seen had affected him more than he was letting on. "I could speak to my Master—former Master, and find out what is truly happening there."

"You will never make it in time," Zara said. "The trip would take months, if you were lucky, and events would have far outstripped our small glimpse here."

"Then what? Let things fall apart, as they did in Haarwatch?" Atar asked. Evie, much to the fire mage's surprise, spoke up on his side.

"Haarwatch was bad enough. I ain't lettin' that happen to someplace else," she said.

Vess nodded. "If we have a way to help, then we must pursue it. Sure there is some manner of aid we can provide? Zara. How do you reach these other Chanters?"

"An ancient artifact, bound to my order. But it is not foolproof, and messages move slowly," Zara explained. "I'd like nothing more than to throw everything aside and rush after this child. They're like you were Felix, moving blind through the world. That he fights against the Paladins speaks to his character, but few can withstand multiple battalions of the Hierophant's elite soldiers."

"Then there's nothing we can do?" Evie asked. Her hands gripped at the chain wrapped about her waist. "I don't like the idea of leavin' anyone against those odds."

"We...I might have an option," Felix said carefully. "It all depends on our luck, though." He gripped his sword. "Karys? Hope everything's dusted off; I'm bringing some people into the Temple.

"We need to see the Heart of Darkness."

CHAPTER TWENTY-SIX

As a group, they all descended into the bowels of Felix's Temple. Vess had seen the Seat and Seal before, but none of the others had, and their reactions were pretty amusing. Evie stared in slack-jawed amazement, first at the huge Spirit Tree roots then at the gold and silver lines of the inscribed formation. She hadn't a lot of experience with inscriptions, but even a blind man would've been able to feel the power that coursed through that first chamber. Atar practically vibrated with excitement; he'd been pestering to get a look at the array for weeks. The fire mage dashed about, running his hands over the complicated sigaldry and compounded glyphs stamped into the floors and walls, even as his eyes raked over the marked ceiling with naked hunger.

Zara's reaction, however, was the best of them all.

"Wild cries," she whispered. Her ice-blue eyes roved across the interwoven, almost fractal complexities of the formation, gold and silver light dancing across her face. "I've never known a Nymean Temple to harbor such a treasure. This is beyond the scope of any modern Territory that I know of...the *weight* of it all."

"It is adequate, yes," Karys said, and Zara started. Her hand leaped to her throat, but she'd mastered her Spirit again, and weak or not, Felix did not feel the fear that was evident on her face. Karys, ever the gentleman, bowed low to the Naiad. "I apologize for startling you. I...keep forgetting how my appearance affects you all."

"No. No it's fine," Zara said. She straightened, smoothing her blue on black robes before speaking again. "Felix warned me of your current Body, but not..." Karys tilted his head, the golden eye-fires in his empty helmet burning inquisitively. Yet Zara did not elaborate; instead she turned to Felix. "This is your Seat and Seal? How did you claim it? Right of conquest?"

"Sort of," he said and patted the crooked sword at his hip. "After the Archon was put down, well, I stepped into the center and claimed it."

"Just like that," she muttered to herself. The others were poking around at the edges of the formation, giving the three of them space to talk. The chamber was more than large enough. "I cannot imagine it was so clear-cut."

Felix shrugged. "It asked me a question. I gave an answer."

"It did not approve of your answer," Karys reminded him. "Though that did not stop you."

"Yeah, I recall," Felix said, dryly. "What use is two thousand points of Willpower if you don't put them to use every once in a while?"

Zara stared between the two of them. "You...brute forced the System into granting you Authority?"

"When you say it like that, it makes me sound like a jerk." Felix rubbed his chin, thinking back on the events. "It was more like...the System couldn't understand me." He shrugged again. "So I made sure it did."

The Naiad's face rapidly twitched between dismay, astonishment, and something bordering on intimidation. Then it smoothed, caught and mastered again by the woman's training. "What was the question?"

Why Do You Seek Authority, Felix Nevarre?
Why Do You Seek The Crown?

Felix jerked at the blue window's appearance, and Karys' chest rumbled apologetically. "My doing. This is the notification he received."

"How'd you do that?" Felix asked. "Can you access all of my old notifications?"

"Only those connected to this Seat. The tricks I learned Ages past have come in handy these past weeks," the metal man said.

"It spoke to you directly?" Zara asked.

"This is a function of the array," Karys explained. "Not how your...modern Seats handle things, but it is the traditional way. The Call and Answer before Authority can be bestowed."

"And your answer?" she asked.

"To help," Felix said with a laugh. He started walking forward, motioning for the others to follow. "The System thought it was too vague."

"It is not wrong," Karys murmured. Felix ignored him.

"C'mon. I didn't bring you here to show off my monogramed cavern floor." Felix sped up, parting the Mana vapor that was actively pushing the others back. He stopped, just inside the secondary chamber. He gestured and activated the illumination scripts. "Behold—!"

"Whoa what are *these*?" Evie said, rushing forward to inspect one of the massive, circular carvings.

"They're—"

"This is...this is Levantier," Vess said with quiet wonder. "I recognize the Lucent Towers, though none of the rest of it makes any sense. There is no mountain anywhere near Levantier, just the northern sea."

"The sigaldry on these interconnections," Atar said in a rush, not looking at the massive circular portals but at the tiny inscriptions on the smooth floor. "Less complicated than the previous chamber, but no less inspired. I cannot make out more than an eighth of what I'm seeing, but it's truly amazing!" His eyes then caught on the gates. "Burning ashes, what are they?"

"Shadowgates," Zara said.

Felix frowned. "Yeah okay, they're Shadowgates." He glanced at the Naiad; only the woman's broken composure was compensation for his ruined reveal. She looked poleaxed, turning her head to look at all nine of the massive gates, as if she were trying to memorize their details all at once. "Portals between two far-off points on the Continent."

"That's impossible," Atar started saying, but Zara interrupted him.

"No, but it is dangerous," she said. "Felix, do you realize what you've done? Shadowgates are a myth. A legend and a dream of every known power on the Continent, vast as it is. How? How is any of this possible?"

"They were sealed here. If the Archon hadn't tried to kill us, if I hadn't fed him to the Spirit Tree, if the roots of that Tree hadn't burst apart the sealed ceiling...ten thousand things happened." Felix laughed, not without warmth, but the bitterness was hard to hide. "I don't really care about 'how', but if I can use them to save at least one other Unbound, then it'll be worth all the trouble."

Felix ran his hand over the details on one of the Lucent Towers Vess had pointed out. "I'm not entirely clear on how they work, but Karys is confident that they do. It's a place to start, at least."

"Well, only a few are operational at this time," Karys interjected. "I've been attempting to restore and clean what I could, but some are quite marred by the sheer weight of Ages, and others appear to be cut off."

"Cut off?" Ves asked. "How do you mean?"

"They require a paired gate to link to," Zara said, as if understanding had dawned on her. "Just as the Dark Passages do; these are simply more stable."

"Far more than simply stable," Karys scoffed.

Zara ignored the golden giant and stepped toward another Shadowgate, this one shaped as a field of wild, malachite grasses and deep, swirling pools of cool, multi-colored kyanite. Pale, pinkish feldspar hills rose up above, framing the opaque shadows within. "I imagine most of the paired gateways are either blocked or destroyed completely. I was not exaggerating when I said I have never seen these before; thousands across the Ages have hunted such artifacts, following ancient clues and hints left in rotting tomes and blood-soaked Domains. This is why I suggest the paired gates are lost. They would have been found otherwise."

"All right, well, how many does that leave us?" Felix asked.

"There are four that have the potential to be made operational," Karys said.

"That's a lotta 'ifs'," Evie pointed out. "Potential's just a fancy word for maybe."

Zara ran her fingers across pools of tri-color crystal. "Of all the gates, this one is closest to our target. If you're right, and these all reside in Nymean Temples, then it is highly likely this resides within the Ghreldan Hills."

"The Ghreldan Hills are forty leagues from the edge of the Scorched Expanse," Atar protested. "Surely there is somewhere closer?"

"Not that I can identify. But you're right. It is still at least two week's hard journey by foot. Less if we press ourselves, and less still if I press my Body to its limit." Zara clenched her jaw, her face a picture of determination.

"That'd leave you with nothing left in the tank when you found the guy," Felix pointed out. "You're not going alone. A small team, at the very least, one that can cross terrain fast. We head south, get into the desert, retrieve the Minotaur, and come back. Bonus points if we can find your friend, Isla, but the goal would be to pull the Unbound out of danger."

"I...I approve," Zara said. "I can admit that I am far from at my best. And you have grown exceedingly capable these months. We can accomplish this together, I know it."

"Uh, you're missing one major detail," Atar said. "If the Expanse is being overridden by the undead *and* Paladins, then Ahkestria will need aid. Felix," he said, turning to him. "You have an entire army here. Could we not bring them with us? Render assistance to my home?"

"The Dark Passages are not easy to traverse. These Shadowgates might reduce the threat, but nothing can eliminate it. The last time I traversed them, we nearly died as a creature from the Void broke through. A large force would only call more attention than we can afford."

"Wait, what?" Felix asked. "I thought that wasn't possible. The sheath of the Void shouldn't be permeable through liminal space."

"That is how it usually is for Domains, yes. But the Passages are patchwork, gossamer cobwebs between weakened points of the Corporeal. Ancient pathways that require much skill in traversing and more power than is wise when traveling with a large group. Voidbeasts were expected, and they crowded around the periphery like sharks—we should not have drawn such a huge, terrible beast however."

"We can handle a few voidbeasts," Felix assured her. "Hell, not to toot my own horn, but I'm pretty sure I could fight off whatever decided to come for us. Voidbeast or no."

"Not this one. At my strongest, I would not even be able to dent its skin. You know it, Felix. You are the one who told me of it."

"Describe it," Felix demanded as a chill crawled down his spine.

"A mountainous beast with rust-red scales and yellow tendrils. It vaguely resembled what I know of as Narhollows, but it was like them as an emberfly is to a dragon."

"Fuck," he cursed. "Whalemaw."

"That sounds bad," Evie added.

"Bad is an understatement. It's..." Felix sighed. "It's another piece of the Maw. The largest piece, apart from...me, I suppose."

"Another Ravager King?" Vess asked.

"Worse. This thing got the bulk of the Maw's power when we got banished to the Void," Felix explained, giving them a run down of events. "It chased me around the Void for weeks, though I managed to lose it. Twice. But if what you're describing is right, then it's even stronger now."

"Why's it chasing you?" Evie asked.

"His power," Atar said. Felix looked at him and nodded. "It wants his power."

"Yeah. The same reason I was able to rip the Maw's potency from the Ravager King; the Whalemaw wants the relatively tiny piece of Primordial power that's in me." Felix could feel the certainty of that in his bones. "It wishes to be whole. And apparently even knowing me is enough to draw its attention."

"Of course. It could sense our connection," Zara said.

"And it'll do it again, if it's anywhere nearby. Unless..." Felix drummed his fingers on the edge of a carving. "Unless I could make a replica of the array that hid me before, in a village in the Void. Then maybe we could risk it."

"Give me the sigils, and we'll make it happen," Atar said. "If Hector's here, then I'm sure it can be done. And if we garner no attention on this Passage thing, then we can bring the Legion, right?"

"That'd be a sight," Evie chortled. "Imagine the look on those zealots' stupid faces."

"An entire army, though?" Vess asked. "How will they be fed? Billeted? Supplied with healing resources and replacement equipment? The Gheldan Hills might be neutral territory, but if the Paladins are already in the Expanse, then it is a surety they will have a rear camp in the Hills. How do you propose we move an entire army without them noticing?"

"Do we even know if the Shadowgates will hold so many?" Zara asked.

"Sorry to interrupt, but the Shadowgates should be enough to send a sizeable contingent through them. They are far superior to these...remnant walkways you are describing," Karys said with clear disdain for the idea of these Dark Passages. "The Autarch's power alone could make do for several hundred soldiers in his retinue. And you should have a retinue, Felix, especially seeing as you shall be visiting a foreign city."

"We're not visiting, and I don't need a retinue. Besides, it's way better if we move with less than our full force," Felix said. "I wouldn't want to leave Nagast undefended. Let's not forget the challenge I apparently put out into the world. Someone is bound to come knocking eventually."

"Another good reason to move fast," Atar said, but followed it with a defeated huff. "Fine. A *small* army."

Karys cleared his throat, a sound like a metal file on an empty aluminum cylinder. "The Shadowgates still require a considerable donation of Mana and Essence to function. Some of that will be provided by your Seat and Seal, Felix, but the initial spark will have to come from you. And," he paused, eye-fires flickering between Zara and Felix. "The gates' connection to the liminal corridors between the Realms will need to be reestablished."

"Meaning what, exactly?" Evie asked.

Felix met Zara's gaze and found her calmly considering him and the golden giant. He smirked. "It means we have work to do. All of us. And fast."

CHAPTER TWENTY-SEVEN

"Why concern yourself with Isla's charge? Eh? Have you resolved your issues with the...Primordial child?"

A small head hovered above a beaten copper basin filled with aquamarine liquid, connected to its pool by shimmering threads that animated its puppet-like facsimile. The head pivoted and peered up at Zara, its rheumy eyes flexing in a way that a normal face could never have accomplished.

"No, Mauvim, and new challenges await us," Zara said to her teacher. "He has claimed a Territory. A Lost one, at that, establishing himself as an autarch above one of the most complex Seats I have ever witnessed."

"Yes, yes. We saw the notification as much as you did," Mauvim said sourly. "I had hoped you would keep him on a tighter leash, child. Now he's gone and riled up every nation within spitting distance of the Hierarchy's western border."

"We are not collars for the Unbound, we are liberators," she admonished. Her mentor's slack face crumpled with annoyance, but Zara pressed on. "He—Mauvim, he has progressed through his Omen Path, and by all accounts has returned ever more potent than before. The window during which I could force him to do anything has passed us by."

"Hm, an Omen Path for one so young. He is not yet an Adept?" the head asked. "Surely he could not stand against a Master."

"He stands at the cusp of Adept Tier, that much I can sense from his core space. But I personally witnessed him trounce an Adept warrior with little effort. From what I saw, I suspect a Master would provide him with a challenge, at best."

"I find that unlikely, Zara."

"Would that you could feel his power personally. It is a storm he holds within him. I would not envy anyone caught in his path when that storm breaks."

"So strong so quickly," Mauvim muttered. "Do you trust him? In finding this other Unbound, finding Isla, do you trust this Felix to do the right thing? To make the right Choice?"

Zara looked up, as if staring through the stone at the Temple and Spirit Tree sprawling above. She felt him everywhere, in everything beneath that Tree, a mistake that she still couldn't overcome now that she was aware of it. He had successfully surprised her earlier because she could not differentiate between him and the air itself. Had he wished ill on her, Zara would never have seen it coming. Instead, he'd asked for explanations and listened calmly as she'd laid out the truth of their order. He had flinched, but no more than anyone might when faced with the danger that was coming.

"Zara? What say you?" Mauvim's tiny, Mana-wrought face squinted at her intently. "Speak up, girl. If I'm to tell the others of this development, I need the whole of it from you. Will he Choose to fight?"

Zara cleared her throat. "He will."

"He must," Mauvim rasped. "If he can also rescue another Unbound from the grasp of the Hierophant, then all the better." The tiny, withered face pursed its lips, considering. "Can you tell me of how you're reaching the Expanse soon enough for it to matter? I fear Isla and this Minotaur will fall before you reach them."

"I cannot say. Only that there is a way."

"Secrets? From me?" Mauvim cracked a smile at her. "My, but this Mask is a rebellious one."

Zara snorted.

Mauvim sighed. "Very well. Take your charge after Isla. We have not heard from her these past weeks, and that is unusual, even for one of her temperament. Find her or complete her duty yourself, before the Paladins can."

"It will be done, Mauvim."

———

"Perhaps this orbital section can go here," Felix suggested, pointing out a cluster of tertiary sigils that Alister had sketched out in charcoal. "It'd reinforce the edges of the array."

"Too inflexible," Hector pointed out. "Your team would have to remain in rigid formation throughout the entire journey. Do you know how long it's going to take?"

Felix shrugged, and Atar carefully kept his face neutral. The man hadn't spread the word on his Shadowgates, and for good reason; news like that had a tendency to spread far and wide, fast. Atar followed his lead and hadn't even told Alister all the details, other than he was going on a trip.

"What *can* you tell us of this journey?" Alister asked. His eyes flicked to Atar's quickly, and though his face was perfectly composed, the fire mage thought he detected a glimmer of annoyance from somewhere deeper. "Atar has been close-lipped about the whole thing."

"Only that it's urgent, and we will be leaving in a day," Felix said. It was all he'd told anyone so far, aside from the various crafters he had working double-time on various projects. "And there is much work to be done before we go. So I'd appreciate it if we can hammer out this array soon."

"We can do this. You've provided us with most of the pieces, and the few we don't have won't be hard to finalize," Atar said. "The real problem is miniaturizing it. The ward you encountered was leagues wide, no?"

"Bigger, but it also operated on basically zero ambient Mana." Felix pointed out the multiple ciphers for Mana transfer. "This is where they'd have to be manually filled with Mana before operating. Its inclusion led to a lot of wasted space."

"That particular design is fascinating," Hector said. He ran a finger over the sketched designs, tracing the pathways of power the array supposedly depended on. "If I could make these smaller, then the rest would follow suit. We'd have to account for a non-standard ward perimeter, of course."

"What if we..."

The planning and discussion went on for two glasses, long enough that Felix was forced to leave and attend to his other duties. He'd given them all that he claimed to remember of the original ward, the amount of which had surprised all of them. Atar was jealous, frankly; the man's Intelligence was incredible, and paired with his Born Trait, there was little Felix ever truly missed. Why he allowed Atar to be the Glyphmaster, the fire mage would never know. Hector was more qualified as well, a fact which dug at Atar's confidence all the more.

Another six hours passed, their conversation limited to the particulars of the work. But as all things, it ended eventually.

"There, the last inscription is complete," Alister said as he lifted his stylus with a flourish. Sixteen slabs of Tier II basalt were laid out on the table, cut and dressed into rounded rectangles and filled to the brim with their modified warding array. "This should do it, I think."

"Provided no one drops them," Atar noted.

"Any Tier II stone can take a lot of punishment. Anything less than a full out Journeyman Tier attack won't do much to them," Hector assured him.

"Yes. We can all attest to that, I suppose," Atar said, massaging his left hand. They'd worn through two styluses, and none of them were feeling their best. "How many weapons and armor did the apprentices inscribe?"

"Ah, let me check," Hector said. "You two can rest, perhaps go eat."

"Thank you, I think we'll do just that," Alister said. He leaned back and massaged his lower back as the tall Inscriptionist hustled to the nearest apprentices. "A good man. Glad he came with everyone else."

Atar only nodded as he packed up his tools. He had a personal set for traveling, but leaving a mess at his workstation had always driven him a bit mad. As far as Atar was concerned, organization was the key to good sigaldry, second only to an eye for detail, though the two often went hand-in-hand.

"Atar."

He looked up, his blond hair dragging low before his eyes. It curled in the humid air, a feature of the location despite the season, but it was long enough that he'd given thought to a cut several times. Now, however, it meant he didn't have to meet Alister's gaze in its entirety. Atar hadn't been looking forward to the conversation.

Alister stood, arms crossed, and gave the fire mage a once over. "You're very bad at keeping secrets. Even worse at hiding bad news. Come out with it. What is it you and Felix are getting up to?"

"I'm not..." Atar looked around them, but saw none of the apprentices anywhere close by. With a minor effort of Will, he activated the muffling array built into his workstation. It was designed to prevent loud noises from disturbing the others, but it would more than suffice for a private conversation. "We're going south. It's...it's dangerous."

"South," Alister said, teasing at the word. "To Keskin? That's the nearest city I can think of—no?" Alister paused at Atar's head shake. "Where then?"

"Home."

Alister's eyes widened. "The City of Embers? That'll take you months!" His expression darkened, concern overlaid by a touch of anger. "You were going to leave for most of a year and not tell me?"

"I was! I am, right now!" Atar protested.

"Only because I asked," Alister said with heat.

"Look," Atar started, glancing once more at the closed doorway. "I don't know if I should share this, but the trip will take far less time. There's...something below. We can get there and back in just a couple weeks. A month at most, according to Zara."

Alister raised an eyebrow. "How?"

"It's Felix's secret," Atar said. "I'm only telling you because I trust you—"

"And because I asked. Angrily."

"—Maybe. But also so you wouldn't worry." Atar tried to smile, though his worry and guilt made it more sickly than he intended. "Do...do you want to come with me? Us, I mean?"

Alister's scowl softened. "Are you only asking because I'm angry with you?"

"No, I meant to ask when I could, but all of this," Atar gestured around them, to the Glyphworks. "It needs a lead, and I didn't know if you wanted to give them up for a time. Then we started working, and it was too late, and—"

"You're a big idiot, Professor," Alister said, poking him in the chest. "Of course I'll come, no matter how dangerous. And this place'll be here when we get back. Blind gods, Hector will do a better job running all this than I would!"

Atar grinned, catching Alister's hand in his own. "Good. Then it's settled. We leave at noon tomorrow."

The force mage smirked right back, before looking down at the slabs of basalt they'd just finished inscribing. "What exactly is this all for, then?"

Atar paled, slightly. "Ah, yes."

His partner didn't love Atar's explanation, but then, neither did Atar.

———

Felix slunk across his Stronghold, Abyssal Skein active to avoid unnecessary eyes. There was so much to do before they left, and while he had a day before they departed, the last thing he wanted was to get into an awkward conversation with some starstruck legionnaires or aggressively respectful giants. Abyssal Skein was his solution for that, the thin layer of Void-stuff around his Body allowing him to fade from the Corporeal Realm. A step toward the Void itself, and far harder to detect even to those with keen observation Skills.

He hadn't used it much, not since their flight across the Teeth when it had strained his Aspects farther than he had liked. He was stronger than ever now, however, and it was barely a tickle against his core space. Ultimately, he liked walking through with it active, an unseen observer. It reminded him of his first few weeks in Haarwatch, before he started getting recognized.

Sure, Felix could fly over the whole Stronghold, but that ran counter to what he wanted to do now. He kept his eyes on the structures he'd built over the past weeks, residences mostly, as they didn't have anything close to a real economy going yet. The houses were sturdy, and about as good as he could make them with his Stone Shaping and, later, adding Rime and Green Shaping to the mix as well.

Stout and sturdy, they were simple boxes, mostly one story, but the Henaari's added details really made them feel like homes, though. Folks bustled around him, Henaari, giants, and a smattering of Haarguard and legionnaires. Tense looks and quiet conversations were the norm, but there was no violence. Felix had made it exceedingly clear how he felt about that.

Walking through the streets, such as they were, he almost regretted that he was skipping out right as it was starting to really become something. But there was little choice, at least to Felix's mind. Minotaur or not, with a name like Michael, that other Unbound was clearly from Earth, and Felix wasn't going to let him die without trying his damnedest to stop it.

Felix came to a stop just outside the Legion barracks. He'd set this part of town apart from the rest, giving them a parade ground at Vess and Harn's insistence. The grounds separated the barracks from the rest of the Stronghold, a stark division when compared to the slow intermingling of the rest.

Well, except the giants. They were still contained within their spiky ice fortress, though as he had seen, they did come out while attending to their various duties and Quests. As he watched, two Frost Giants dragged fifteen massive logs behind them, not stopping until they were within touching distance of the nearest Beacon. The crystalline pillar flashed once, twice, and on the third flash, the logs were gone. The giant workers grunted in acceptance, both of them swiping away notifications Felix couldn't see, likely an XP reward. Those had been Tier II trees, and worth more than Tier 0 or I. *Still don't have a use for all these materials. I imagine that'll change soon enough.*

Who knew what was on the horizon?

A single group of legionnaires were out on the parade grounds, doing maneuvers or something. Felix walked closer to them, careful to keep his steps quiet and far enough away from the action that no one would trip over him. He was a ghost, though, and not a single one of them noticed him as they sparred in a set of shifting formations.

There were several squads, each of them fighting the others in a shifting sort of chaos that made little sense to Felix, but seemed to work for them. They grappled and kicked, threw each other over hips, and locked limbs in complicated-looking holds. Some of it Felix was familiar with, coming with the levels in Unarmed Mastery he'd earned, but others were foreign. It was...fascinating, and Felix made sure to study each and every useful technique. He never knew when such things would come in handy. He watched for a solid twenty minutes before the combatants began to flag, and their leader clapped his hands, signifying the end of things.

"A good spar. I noticed several of you have leveled your Unarmed Mastery. Keep it up. Next we practice our Meditation, as the Fiend has so generously proscribed," Oskar Akales, the First of Fist said.

Oh. Right. My advice on creating a stronger core, Felix thought, noticing two approaching figures with a start. *They're here already? How long have I been watching? Jeez.*

A group of Blades and Arclight were exiting their barracks, clearly headed to train as well, and they were the first to notice the approach of Harn and Evie. The latter of which wasn't exactly a picture of stealth.

"All right, you Fiend-lovin' jagoffs!" she shouted, her arms akimbo and a wide smile on her face. "The time for restin' is over!"

"Lady Aren?" Bald, red-faced Fenwick Cole said from their left. He stood with a handful of other Blades and spoke loud enough that he might as well have been shouting. "To what do you refer? Has the Lord Fiend called on us?"

There was a significant amount of rustling among the groups as eyes glanced about in excitement. Evie looked flummoxed, suddenly unsure of herself, while Harn just laughed.

"He said he was comin' here a half glass ago," Evie muttered to her friend, softly but not beyond Felix's senses. Harn started to shrug, amusement still clear on his face, and Evie clucked her tongue. "Slackin'! All this hero-worship's gone to his head."

Felix rolled his eyes and let his Abyssal Skin drop. Then, for extra effect, he tightened his grip upon a connection leading straight into the sky and *pulled*. Not hard enough to lift himself, but enough that the Skill discharged a bolt of blue-white lightning up into the clouds. The crack of thunder drew everyone's eyes, and, almost as one, the Legion dropped to a single knee.

"Lord Autarch!"

"Lord Fiend!"

"Good of you to show up," Harn said, crossing the distance between them. Evie eyed him up and down.

"You been there the whole time?" she asked.

Felix only grinned and addressed the growing crowd. The Legion had returned to their feet, but their fists were still over their heart, and more of them were pouring from the barracks. The First of Fist, Blade, and Arclight walked closer, their expressions eager and curious.

"How might we be of assistance, Lord Autarch?" Oskar asked, much to Fenwick's frowning annoyance. The bald man snapped his mouth shut, clearly about to ask the same thing.

"I am mounting an expedition," Felix said, giving them an extremely truncated version of events. "...I will be taking some of the Legion with me, but space is limited. I wish for you to send only your very best, and then only if they wish to volunteer. This is to be an extremely dangerous expedition."

The eyes of all three Firsts gleamed in a way that unsettled Felix, but they quickly and happily called their people to the parade grounds. Messengers were sent out to retrieve those in the other parts of the Stronghold, but the Firsts did not wait long before beginning to discuss things.

"I have plenty of able swordsmen in my society, Lord Fiend," Fenwick said. "You have but to choose any of them, and they will serve you well."

"Aye, the pugilists under my command are ready and willing to join your expedition. But, as you said, I have in mind several who might be the best fit," Oskar said.

"Of course, I do as well. I am simply saying that *all* of my swordsmen are my best, for we do not skimp on proper training," Fenwick said, his Spirit all but bristling at the other First. The First of Arclight, meanwhile, was self-possessed and quiet. He merely digested Felix's words with a calm demeanor that clearly indicated a focus on Willpower.

"Gentlemen, you misunderstand me," Felix said. "I want you to send your very best to us here, now, and we will see who shall come with us." He raked his eyes over the legionnaires, and there wasn't one among them that could meet his gaze. "Your chosen few will have to pass inspection first."

Kev'al, First of Arclight, straightened at that. "Inspection?"

Felix grinned, but it was Harn who spoke up. "Aye. Gather your soldiers." He loosened his axes in their sheaths. "Evie and I will tell ya if they pass muster."

"They won't face you, sir?" Fenwick asked, looking askance at his two friends. "It would mean a lot for them to try their power against your own. Sir."

"You lookin' to get your men trampled?" Evie asked. "You don't send children in to wrestle an auroch, friend. Your people will be fightin' us, and that's already a stacked deck."

Felix let his smile widen at the confidence he felt surge in the Firsts and the other legionnaires. *Good.*

They'll need it.

CHAPTER TWENTY-EIGHT

Evie ducked beneath the glacially slow swing of a mace, tucking up into her opponent's guard and stomping the inside edge of his foot. She flared her Born Trait, enhancing her own mass for emphasis. The Boneman—as they hilariously called themselves—yowled in pain and shifted himself back, choking up on his weapon to strike down at her...but he was ten heartbeats too slow, and Evie already slid through his grasp. She flicked her chain, its blades blunted by her Skills, and caught in the man's legs before yanking him completely off them.

"And that makes twenty-three," she said, the barest edge of a pant in her voice. She tucked a loose strand of midnight hair back behind an ear and grinned at the legionnaires still waiting for their turn. "Who's number twenty-four?"

Their eyes jittered between her slight, unassuming form and the latest in a lengthening line of failures. He was being lifted by Kikri and Nevia, commandeered from the Alchemy Lab to assist the trial, but neither were healers. They gave him a Health Tonic and got him to his feet, allowing him to toddle off to the growing patch of ground that held the twenty-two others she'd fought.

"No one's volunteering?" Evie asked. "Where's that eagerness gone?"

"Don't taunt them, Evie," Harn growled from across the way. He had his own roughed-out ring of stone; a mini arena Felix had fashioned before swanning off into the sky to do...whatever it was that he did. "Test their mettle. That's all."

"Hmph," Evie said, pursing her lips and looking over her challengers. There were several with lightning bolts stitched into their battlerobes. Evie had fought six Blades, five Bones, and twelve Fists, but she hadn't tried her hand against the magic ones yet. "You. You're next."

The lightning boy in question took a tentative step forward. He was a Half-Orc, though on the slender side, despite his Race's bonuses to Strength. Clearly, he devoted his free stats toward the Mind and Spirit side of things, because lightning began crackling across his fingers even as he nervously licked his lips. He bowed. Evie bowed back.

"What's your name?" she asked.

"Loqius," he said. The lightning flickered out once before surging back to life from his palms.

"You ready, Loqius?"

He nodded, and Evie sprang forward, chain in hand. She was met by a wall of crackling lightning, which made her laugh in surprise. She leaped, lightening herself so she all but flew over the Mana construct. Mid-air, she unspooled her chain, letting it whip downward at the mage with just enough speed to hurt but not kill. Yet the Half-Orc surprised her, twisting just enough to only take a portion of the strike, he grabbed at and recast the lightning from his wall...straight up the chain.

Every muscle in her body seized for a brief moment, forcing her to land hard on the packed earth. She couldn't even pull her hand from the chain itself, as if it had been welded to her skin. Loquis rushed forward, his hands now draped with flickering planes of force Mana, clearly ready to hit her while she was down.

S-smart, she thought through the scramble of energies inside her. With a silent scream of effort, she engaged her icy core.

Scorpion's Tail!

Without moving her arm at all, the chain in Evie's hands whipped out and took Loquis' feet from under him. The mage tried to jump free, but moved too late, and his battlerobes limited his mobility. He fell, and the effect of his lightning spell dissipated immediately.

Bindings of the White Waste!

New, phantasmal chains of white ice burst from all around the Half-Orc, grappling with his limbs and securing him to the earth. Ice crackled across his arms and feet, the insular nature of the Mana preventing his magic from manifesting properly. He tried to grab the chains, but hissed as the extreme cold burned him.

"Ah ah," Evie tutted as she climbed back to her feet. She ached all over, but she didn't let it show any more than she had to. She had an image to maintain, after all. "Not normal chains, are they? Gotta be honest, you surprised me with that lightnin' spell. Caught me square. I'm impressed." She stopped, several strides from the mage's sprawled body. "You yield?"

Loquis met her gaze, the fight still blazing in them before he nodded sharply. "I...yield."

The chains dissipated, turning into purple-white vapor, and Evie helped the mage back to his feet. "Good. Go stand over there." When the Half-Orc started walking toward his injured fellows, Evie stopped him. "No. Not with them. There."

She pointed to a far smaller group of legionnaires between the two mini arenas. Loquis' mouth gaped and his eyes widened, clearly flabbergasted.

"Congratulations. You get to risk your life with us," Evie said with a smirk.

"Next!" Harn shouted.

———

Felix desperately wanted to head back to the Lab, but a Henaari messenger had reached him before he could leave Evie and Harn's testing of the Legion. It appeared the Farwalker needed to speak with him, and Felix had an inkling why. Secrets, it appeared, were hard to keep in a place as small as his Stronghold.

Adamant Discord sent him hurtling across the sky in a parabolic arc from the barracks to the edge of the Eire River. Not bothering with his Abyssal Skein, it was far faster and better suited his mood. Speaking to the Legion, bringing some of them along, that was necessary. Especially if they were going up against an entire army. The Henaari, however, had no reason to follow him into the desert to fight Paladins and actual, literal undead. That last bit was still screwing with him; he'd seen a lot of messed up things on the Continent, but real necromancy hadn't been one of them.

Grumbling to himself, Felix swept past the rows of bowing Henaari on the—far nicer—streets of their part of town. They all seemed to regard him with a mixture of awe and quiet approval, far different than the chaotic, buzzing clamor in the Spirits of the Legion. It was easier to ignore, for one thing, and Felid did just that as he made a beeline for the Farwalker's wooden hut.

It looked exactly the same as it had back in their hidden camp, and likely was; Felix had come to learn the Henaari's version of Green Shaping drew on patterns much as a Dwelling Stone did, though in far less complicated ways. Still, they were able to store and rebuild a house with startling fidelity. It was another thing that Felix wished to learn, yet never had the time.

The hut's door was open, and the Farwalker was inside, contemplating the crystalline lattice of Mana that extended from a wooden plinth in the center of his hut. The lattice revolved and shifted, each turn twisting it into a new pattern, yet if he were to touch any part of it, the thing would feel as solid and warm as a glass filled with hot cider.

"Welcome, Autarch, to my humble home," the old man said, lowering his dark hood. "That you came with such speed honors me. I know much is asked of you, and more in the weeks to come."

Felix came to a stop a few feet from him and the Mana lattice. He folded his arms. "What do you know? And how?"

"I know that you will soon be leaving us, at least for a time. And...the

Chain Maiden is fast, but perhaps not as fast as her tongue," he finished with a smile.

Evie. Felix sighed. "It was bound to get out eventually. I assume you called me here to discuss my expedition."

"Yes, I did indeed." The man wheeled his chair around to face Felix directly. "I understand that you are entering into a significant amount of danger. Is this accurate?"

Felix nodded, slowly. "It is."

"We must discuss your Companion, then."

"What?"

"Guardian Beasts," the Farwalker said. "We've spoken on their nature before, but always in the vaguest of terms. I have given you and Pit some advice, and I know that A'zek has been mentoring the young tenku these past weeks so that his first evolution will not take him completely by surprise."

"Pit's told me a bit about it, though it sounded like a lot of Skill training rather than lessons on...whatever he's supposed to be doing," Felix said. "Vaguest of terms is the right way to say it. I still don't have an understanding of what Pit's Path even means."

Unlike with his own Path of the Cardinal Fiend, Felix had not seen nor experienced a vision of potential future with Pit's Path. The Chimera had chosen his own when Felix was...indisposed.

"Generalities and ambiguity, while maddening, is a necessity in this case," the Farwalker explained. "No Guardian Beast walks the same Path, and to speak in absolutes only muddies the waters of understanding. Just know, Pit is long past when his first evolution should have occurred. His latency is curious, but no doubt a function of his bond with you. A Pact that has transcended itself."

The Farwalker shook his head, chagrin and wry amusement on his face. "Etheric Concordance. Such a Skill I've never heard of in any of the ancient tales, but then, the rules do not apply to an Unbound. For an Unbound...his Guardian Beast would be a thing of terrible potential. Terrible temptation."

"Temptation?" Felix asked.

"The Path winds strange, Felix. No two are alike, though they may share a name, and power has a way of corrupting even the most stalwart of us." The last was said sadly and a touch bitterly. Felix's own thoughts touched on the former, ousted Matriarch. "You both must take care. Our Choices define us, you more than most, and by extension, Pit. They may guard us, but we must guard them in return. See that your friend does not lose himself on his journey, whatever its turns may be."

"I will." Of course he would. It was Pit. "But...I don't like that there's so much to...everything. The System itself is just shrouded in mystery, and every time I think I get a handle on it, I run into something like this." He took a deep, controlled breath.

"Explanations are counterproductive at a certain point, Felix. I could describe a sunset to a blind man for years, but he would never truly see it." The Farwalker looked back at the Mana lattice as it shifted between a thousand varied shapes. "I can only gesture at the truth hidden within this world. What little I know, that is."

Felix shrugged it away, suppressing his frustration. A strong Will was useful, now and again. "Mm. Was that it?"

"No. There was one other thing." A smile returned to the Farwalker's aged face. "A'zek wishes to go with you on your journey, but the old cat fears leaving me alone. Instead, I would send some Dawnguard with you, Felix."

"That's not necessary," he started, but the old man waved him down.

"It is. For us. You are the first foreign power we have sworn ourselves to for as long as memory recalls, and our memory is long, Felix. Pride is a...complicated thing. Long has our pride been tied to our independence and competence, our cleverness and guile. These past few weeks have put some of my people to rustling, whispering of 'better times.'" The Farwalker shook his head. "They must find a new sense of pride. The Raven bid us to follow you, but that is only one of the reasons why the Synod chose to kneel. We sense great things in your future, Felix Nevarre. The Unbound Autarch who brings to life Lost things with a wave of his hand. My people must know that you see us as worthy of sharing in that future."

For all his annoyance at the Farwalker's vague words on Guardian Beasts, Felix still felt guilty that he'd lost touch with the Henaari's community; all of this was unknown to him. *Not much of a lord, am I?*

"I can take a few of them. No more than, say, twenty," he said.

"That would do. I'll have the most capable sent with you. The rest shall defend this Stronghold in your absence."

"Shouldn't come to that," Felix said, reaching out and clasping the Farwalker's wrist. "We'll be back long before you've anything to worry about."

"Let us hope."

———

There was a small, rocky area behind the Healer's Ward. It was covered in long grasses and waist high rocks that protruded from them with a quiet majesty. Trees sprouted, tall things that dwarfed the houses around them, but also smaller growths that fenced the area from neighboring eyes. Or would, eventually, when there were neighbors.

The Hand met Vess out here, as she had requested. She hadn't expected him to be fully armored, however.

"You've recovered?" she asked, skeptically. The man had no bandages, but she wouldn't put it above him to have ripped those off the moment he'd had the chance. "Your Body—"

"Is well enough," Darius said, his voice like gravel. "He didn't hit so hard as all that."

Vess simply raised an eyebrow. Darius' frown intensified before it wavered, and then disappeared entirely.

"I..." Darius took a large, almost regretful gulp of air before releasing it. "If you plan to follow the Autarch into battle, I will not stop you."

Vess peered at him, hands gripping the haft of her partisan. She didn't question how he'd learned of it all; the wind carried many things in its embrace, secrets most of all. "I do not believe you."

"Pfah, believe what you must," he said, restrained frustration overflowing. "I am your minder, but you've little need for me. But," he lifted his new, equally massive sword and pointed it at her, hilt first. It halved the distance between their two bodies. "I will follow you."

"No," Vess said, adamant. "I will not have you breathing over every decision I make, nor your disapproving glare. If you want to serve my interests, then you shall remain here and protect the Stronghold."

"Protect it from what?" he asked. "These wilds are dangerous, but he has pet Giants and Henaari at his call, and not one of them is weak. That barrier? The one he summoned with his Authority? It will withstand countless blows." Darius shook his head, but his sword remained between them. "If you must tread into danger, then let me be a bulwark against it. For your father's sake."

She couldn't parse his Spirit with her Affinity, not entirely. Flashes of anger were there, but there was an earnest timbre to it all, and his face was more...vulnerable than she was used to seeing. "What is this? You have never been so... What do you hope to achieve? Is this about getting back at Felix?"

"Nothing more than your safety. The fight between myself and the Fiend was the final nail in our...disagreement. He defeated me fairly, with everything I had pitted against him." For the first time, the sword wavered slightly in his grip. "My honor, my duty is appeased, and the weight of our opposition no longer hangs between us. I know now that, were I to fall, he could protect you."

"I am not a frail creature to be protected by minders," Vess said, her own anger boiling up at Darius' reasonable tone. "I need neither you nor Felix to guard me."

"Prove it," he said, and the greatsword moved. It flipped, once, neatly landing hilt first in his hand. The wind of its revolution threw Vess' hair back. "We fight, here and now. If you can best me, then I will remain behind to care for things in the Stronghold."

Vess gritted her teeth, but eagerly took up her spear. "And if not?"

"Then perhaps I am still of use to you, your Grace," he said, inclining his head. "Begi—"

Before he finished his words, silver Spears descended upon his position, forcing the man to parry them with a wide, horizontal swipe of his blade. Vess detonated them all and moved, air Mana screaming along the edge of her partisan.

She dove into the breach.

CHAPTER TWENTY-NINE

Time flew on leaden wings. Felix, finished with the diplomacy of his position, retreated to the Alchemical Lab and spent the next six hours working at Aenea's side. Four painful failures behind them, Felix and Aenea had finally done it. A Cleansing Potion, the limit of their combined Skills, and shining bright with all the power of a selection of Tier II herbs, distillations, and topped off with a hair of the dog that bit him: the Spirit Fruit.

"Okay, one last go, bud." Felix lifted the bluestone carafe, and Pit regarded it with suspicion.

Will it hurt?

"Uh, probably," Felix admitted.

Most things do, Pit agreed.

Felix hesitated, meeting his friend's golden gaze. He felt only steady trust from him. "Ready?"

Ready.

Pit drank the gleaming potion, a full quart of liquid, and grimaced expectantly. A confused warble slipped from his throat though, and he opened his eyes in surprise.

It tastes good.

Felix grinned, trading looks with an excited Aenea. She rubbed her hands together, a touch anxious. "Do you feel anything?" she asked.

A...wriggling, Pit sent to Felix. He still couldn't communicate effectively to anyone without an unlocked Affinity stat. *It is...a worm in my belly. I—*

Felix dodged back, dragging the Alchemist back with him in the second of warning he had; still, they both only narrowly avoided the *deluge* of brackish liquid that poured from Pit's channels. Shouts of alarm went up in the Lab, but Felix didn't answer their inquiries, only watched with mounting concern.

Pit wretched as if vomiting, and that liquid kept coming out of everywhere like a swarm of ten thousand flies all made of thickened oil. They flowed outward for five entire minutes, a lake of impurities that pooled around him until he lost control of his legs, and Pit splashed down into it all.

"Pit!" Felix dove into the disgusting goop, cradling all that he could of his friend's massive form. "Pit, are you okay?"

There was a surging tide of percussive beats, each one louder and more wild than the last, until the pool around them flashed away into light. Dark was rendered into motes of radiance, impurities washed clean. All of it dissipated, leaving behind a foul, acrid scent as Pit's shudders ceased.

I'm...okay.

Felix helped the tenku stand, the Chimera's massive weight nothing to his Strength, and he didn't let go until he was sure Pit was truly fine. Pit trilled at him, pleased yet annoyed, and finally Felix backed away several steps; close enough to catch him should he fall again.

I feel good. Better than before, Pit sent.

"Before eating the Fruit?" he asked, and Pit nodded his big head. A taloned foreclaw lifted and swiped at something Felix couldn't see...until a blue window rotated into his view.

Chimeric Core Strengthened!
+10 To All Stats!

Pit shook his body like a wet dog, wings still tucked tight, and let out a pleased warble.

"Wow," Felix said, sharing it with Aenea. She let out a low whistle. "That was just from the Spirit Fruit?"

Aenea laid a tentative hand on Pit's side, and when he didn't protest, she peered at his thick fur as if looking through it. Into him. "When Pit ate the Fruit, he should have been hurt badly by its power—burned up from the inside at the very least. What your Companion has done flies in the face of what I understand about attunement and the elemental nature of our souls."

"A habit of ours, I think," Felix said. *Pit, I'm going to check your channels and core now. Okay?* He activated Cardinal Flame when the tenku agreed and sent it questing into his Companion's channels with an effort of Will. Mana drained from him rapidly as his power flowed and filled the pathways, looking for any instance of a stained black. He reached Pit's core without finding anything out of the ordinary, and in fact, the channels felt healthier and thicker than before. Sturdier. When he reached the core, he knew something had definitely changed.

Where he had once felt a vast cavern filled with a cage of wild power, now that same space was almost entirely filled by the gem-like stone. The stone, Pit's core, used to be black with streaks of crimson, matching his fur and plumage. Now it flashed with rainbow hues, cascading with a thousand internal colors and a tactile potency. Of the impurities, there was no sign, not even the barest fleck of darkness on his shining center. Felix withdrew his Mana and let it dissipate back into his own channels.

"You're better than ever. Your core is different, though," he said. "Stronger. Bigger."

Evolution?

"Maybe. The Farwalker said it should have happened already." Is this what happened to monster cores as they progressed? Thinking on it, Felix could recall extracting quite a few of the things, and their core varied depending on the monster's Tier and Type. Coloration, composition, size, all of it fluctuating. "Aenea, does size determine anything about a beast's core?"

The Alchemist was still stroking Pit's side as she answered. "Yes and no. It indicates the creature in question has grown fairly large physically, but the density of the core and the Mana within can still be quite low in quality. I've even seen some relatively small Insect Types that have cores the size of my fingernail so packed with Mana that they'd outshine your furnace there."

Reluctantly, she stopped petting Pit and stepped back, visibly collecting herself. "I do not have a Skill to inspect your Companion's core, but if it has changed as you say, then perhaps a tipping point is being reached. There is a Type of sea-dwelling creature to the east, near the Fury's Chasm, a creature that lives within a shell its entire life. As it grows and advances, the creature abandons its old shell to find a new one that will fit its stronger form. I believe most beasts and monsters function in the same manner, their old selves outgrowing their forms, necessitating a change. Or, so I have theorized," she finished, offhandedly. "It is not my area of expertise."

Felix chewed the inside of his cheek for a moment, thinking. "Whose area of expertise would it be? Do you know of anyone like a Beast Master? Someone who specializes in Companions?"

Aenea shook her head, much to Felix's disappointment. "No. That Title is not familiar, and before your Companion, I was always taught it is folly to tie yourself to a beast." She shrugged at Felix's sour look. "It is what the Guild teaches, at the very least. Aside from that, few study monsters rather than eradicate them. For that, you'd have to travel to the north, to Levantier, and speak to the Scholars of the Lucent Towers."

He nodded, making a mental note. *Levantier. Hm. Vess said one of the Shadowgates had those Lucent Towers carved into it.* He groaned inwardly. *We could go there next, if we didn't have this Unbound to save. We'll make it there after, okay?*

Pit nodded, his Spirit unconcerned. *I feel good. Strong. We will face whatever comes, together.*

Felix grinned, scratching Pit along his neck. "Together."

"What was that?" Aenea asked.

"Don't worry about it. How's the Draught coming?" Felix asked.

This time, Aenea's sigh was heavy. Weary. "I've cracked the how, but it is a certain deficiency in equipment that is causing me problems. I cannot manage to distill even the smallest sample of Spirit Fruit." Felix frowned, but Aenea kept speaking. "It isn't that my lab is much more advanced than this. It's the Spirit Fruit itself. We'd need a Master Tier's instruments to properly separate the useful from the dangerous elements contained within."

An idea wormed into Felix's head, and he almost smacked himself. He'd long since figured out how to separate his foe's Mana and Essence and Memories from the chaff of their power. Why couldn't he do that for the Spirit Fruit, too? He walked past the Alchemist and pulled a new Spirit Fruit from the storage chest, holding it up as the ambient Mana swirled around it like a mini whirlpool. He could consume the Spirit Fruit, but the real question was whether he could bring the separated portions back out of his channels at all.

Only one way to find out, he thought. "Aenea, grab me two flasks. Big ones, I think."

"What are you doing?" she asked, grabbing two stoneware containers and placing them on the counter before Felix.

Felix grinned. "No reward without risk, right?"

Her eyes widened. "Wait—"

Chthonic Tribute!

The Spirit Fruit burst asunder, rendered into a flashbomb of blinding power. It was like he was suddenly holding the *sun*, and as it passed into the Mana Gates in his palms, Felix bit off a scream that tried to well up his throat. The Essence of the Fruit rocketed through him, taking the most direct route toward his cores, until it burst wild and free into the vast semi-physical space within him. Yet, as it tried to crackle and explode as it had done within Pit, Felix's Will and Intent clamped *hard* upon it. All of it.

No, he sent to it, his Intent a blade that cut free the spitting impurities from the Fruit. *Be this. Pure.* He hewed off chunks of it, holding both with the iron grip of his Will as it all dangled above the Divine Vein and the spinning of his dual cores. The power resisted him, but it had no chance, and before long, there hung two writhing, formless shapes in his core space.

Now for the tricky part, he thought.

Cardinal Flame!

Mustering his internal control, his Intent, and his Willpower, Felix hurled the two wriggling masses from his Mana system. They spun off, each down a separate pathway that snaked and looped along his chest and shoulders before traveling directly down his arms. Pieces of it tried to escape, to latch onto his channels, but Felix was relentless and all-encompassing. His Will would not be gainsaid.

One final tug of resistance, twin streams of liquid power poured from his palms. His left was a stinking mass of foul waste and impurities, while his right deposited a gleaming volume of opalescent fluid, both of them so copious that the stoneware containers were filled to the brim.

"By all the moons," Aenea whispered. "How?"

Felix, his Will finally relaxed, took a soft set of breaths. "Trade secret."

Aenea just swept toward the containers, her own powers questing toward them as if to test their potency and composition. She physically recoiled from the waste container, her face a mask of disgust, but the gleaming fluid was little better. It made her tremble to be so close, as if she'd looked for it all her life. "This is...you've created a formless distillation. Attunement-neutral, able to...this could take any attunement we want." She met Felix's eyes, and for once, he saw real admiration in her gaze. "With this...with this, we could make a universal draught. It would work on...anyone. At any Tier. And with a far greater Mana capacity than the Guild's mixtures by several orders of magnitude."

Felix nodded, feeling a bit tired after all that. "Good. We need to make as many as possible."

"Let's run it through once together, then I can handle the rest," she said. "I'll need you to continue doing...whatever it was you did. How often can you perform such a miracle?"

"As often as I have to," he said, fishing out another Fruit while more stoneware clattered atop the counter.

They got to work.

Cardinal Flame is level 77!

...

Cardinal Flame is level 79!
Alchemy is level 44!

...

Alchemy is level 49!

Four more hours swept past in a flurry of activity. Felix sifted and siphoned the power from twenty-seven Spirit Fruit, each one filling a gallon-sized container with useful material. The other gallon-sized containers held waste, which Felix had emptied into an enormous granite urn he'd shaped from his supplies. That cut out most of its stink, thankfully, while they decided what, if anything, could be done with the foul stuff.

The good stuff, however, was quickly used. As things turned out, they couldn't make universal draughts, but they could infuse the distillation with a measure of attuned Mana and make it suitable for specific core types. Felix didn't understand a lot of it; Aenea was operating on another wavelength, and he could only grasp snippets of meaning from her words and movements. In the end, however, she had furnished Felix with eighty-one Essence Draughts. Each Spirit Fruit had been able to make three, all of them more than potent enough to Temper someone into Master Tier, according to the Alchemist.

Name: Essence Draught Of Atlantes (Air/Metal)
Type: Essence Draught
Lore: An alchemical distillation of a powerful Spirit Fruit from the Atlantes Anima! It is a near-universal draught, able to be used by someone of any Tier to advance themselves, so long as it is attuned to their core's element(s).

Simple description, but powerful results, Felix thought as he left the Alchemical Lab. He held one of the draughts in his hand, no more than a tall vial and glittering with potent air and metal Mana. Infusing the draughts had been relatively simple, compared the rest of the process, as it had required someone to pour the requisite Mana type into the distillation, and Felix had just about every kind.

Without his aid, however, making them would be far more complicated. *We've a whole night ahead of us. I think I can handle making a lot more to stock up on. The Storage Facility would keep them fresh, as most of what they require is sufficient ambient Mana.*

Given enough time, Felix would be able to Temper everyone now in his Stronghold. Even if he was gone awhile, when the time came for the Legion, Henaari, or even the Haarguard Reed had brought with him, they could all Tier up properly. He gripped the vial and hopped down the stairs into the first floor of his Temple. *I wonder where Vess is? She'd like to see this, I bet.*

He made it only four steps before he noticed a presence waiting. For him, specifically, or so his Harmonic senses told him; there was a chiming connection between them, taut with anticipation. More than anything else however, Felix was surprised to find out it was Kimaris, the Witch, who had come to see him. She stood at the opened edge of the Temple, where the diverted waterfall only half-covered the gaping hole where a cliff face once stood.

"Autarch," she said, inclining her giant-sized head to him. Silky white hair slipped over her shoulder and swung with the movement, which only drew attention to the swaying of her loose, drapery-style robes. They were a blue, darker than her skin, and detailed with complex fractal patterns along the hem. A wide belt of pale leather and moonstones cinched the whole thing together.

"Kimaris. How can I help you?"

The Witch did not smile, but affixed him with her grave stare and the force of her personality. "You are leaving."

"Jesus, what's the point of saying it's a secret if no one listens to me?" Felix muttered to himself. "I am, for a time."

"You are leaving, and you are not taking a single of my warriors with you," she said. Her thin, white eyebrows drew down. "Yet you offer a spot for those...vermin-worshippers."

The Henaari, he realized. Closer, he also noticed that the patterns on her robes were actually *ice*, shaped to look like embroidery. "Yes, the Henaari are coming with me. A few. I don't plan to be gone long."

"You must allow us representation, Autarch."

"What? It's...we're going to the desert. You're Frost Giants," he said.

"We have charms to prevent extremes of temperature from harming us," she said, waving aside his concern. "We are warriors. As your sworn vassals, allow us to prove our worth."

"You've been doing a great job so far with the Domain."

"Pfah. Child's work. You go to face these armored fools who praise the Trackless One, yes?"

Who is flapping their gums? "I'm not clashing with them if I don't have to," he said. "My hope is to slip in and out. Gone before anyone notices we were there."

Kimaris nodded, firmly. "You will fight them. You've the blood of a Titan, a true warrior. Battle calls to us, whether we ask for it or not. We shall join you."

"...Fine. But only a few, and they will follow the chain of command. You listen to me, then you listen to those I designate over you, got it?"

Kimaris inclined her enormous head, letting her thick white locks sway forward once more. "It will be as you say, Autarch."

Felix doubted it would be so easy.

CHAPTER THIRTY

It was shortly after dawn when they assembled on the first floor of the Nymean Temple. They clustered around the trunk of the Spirit Tree, eyes roving the still-damaged chamber or the oddly smooth bark of the Atlantes Anima. At the head, next to the Tree itself, Felix stood while his team conversed quietly among themselves.

"Almost time. Where's Vess and Harn?" Evie asked.

"They'll be here," Atar said while Alister double checked the straps on his backpack. All of them wore one, filled with basic supplies for a long journey. While none of them required much in the way of food and water, Atar advised them that the Scorched Expanse was not a normal area, and the heat of it would and could drive even Masters to dehydration. "I can't imagine either would be willing to miss this."

"Perhaps he's repairing his armor," suggested Alister. "You two fought every single legionnaire yesterday, did you not?"

Evie groaned, and Felix spied the hint of a bandage peeking from the collar of her gambeson. "Don't remind me. Some of those bastards can hit, so long as they land a clean shot. My legs are so sore," she complained. "Harn tore through those guys, though. Those Bonemen had the best shot against him, but I only saw two that did more than scuff his chestplate. Man's a beast."

"Thank you for that, again," Felix said to her. He looked askance at the gathered crowd. "But did you two have to approve of so many?"

In the gathered crowd were no less than ten members of each legion —society, they called themselves. Blade, Bone, Fist, and Arclight, all of them shined up and standing in neat ranks before Felix. They were a stark comparison to the others who filled the space, and several bore bandages and poultices from their spar, but every single one practically trembled with an eager excitement.

Evie laughed. "Those are the ones who could actually fight. Might be we're thankful they're comin' soon enough."

"So long as the gate can hold them all," Zara said, her bearing regal and eyes shrewd. "But more blades at hand will doubtlessly prove useful."

"Perhaps. They do lend us a sense of unity, at least," Vess said as she landed next to Felix. She looked a touch out of breath, and her left arm was bandaged, but she flashed a dimpled smile at him. "I apologize for being late. I was...unavoidably detained."

In Felix's senses, another presence mounted the steps at the open end of the Temple, a presence he hadn't expected. "You're fine, we're just about to begin. But...why is he here?"

Vess' eyes didn't so much as flicker toward the large figure moving through the crowd, like a stout ship through crowded waters. Irritation and embarrassment warred in her Spirit before Felix again backed away from listening too closely. "We had an agreement. Unfortunately, I...lost."

Abruptly, the sensory information his eyes and ears had been feeding him made sense. "You fought. Over him coming with us?"

Vess nodded, and there was a trace of bitterness in her voice. "I am not yet strong enough to best him, it seems."

Felix only clasped her uninjured arm and smiled at her. "We'll change that soon." With the Essence Draughts in his possession, they'd all be pushing into higher Tiers at a significant advantage. Or so he hoped. "For now, I suppose we'll let Darius help out, so long as he's willing to listen."

"I am," the Hand said as he drew abreast. "Autarch."

Hmm. Felix nodded, once. "All right. You're a man of war, right?"

"I've led and organized over two dozen battles in my Lord's name," Darius attested.

"Good. Then you'll be in charge of the warriors we're bringing." Felix said, gesturing to the assembled masses. There were the Legion societies, of course, but also twenty Henaari Dawnguard and fifteen Risi Warriors. The Frost Giants had even brought their Hoarhounds with them—ice-white,pony-sized wolves—one for each Warrior. "Think you can handle them all?"

Darius pondered, his face serious and his emotions reigned in. Felix could feel a smattering of things from the man—excitement, concern, a touch of fear—but most of all was an icy, analytical consideration. "I shall have no issues."

"Great," Felix said and clapped the man on the back. Startlement rippled through the Hand's Spirit, but it was tamped down quickly. "Just last checks, and we go."

"Where are we—"

Darius' question was cut off by a loud argument and the clanking footsteps of two Smiths.

"No, it'll still be there when you get back, you big lug," Rafny said as she pushed at Harn's impressive bulk. The warrior was clearly allowing himself to be moved, but he didn't seem happy about it.

"Just, the Tempering Array is sensitive to any metal weaker than Tier II. You'll—"

"Have to adjust the output, yes, you've told me six times," Rafny said with an eye-roll. "Now go. They're waiting for you."

Harn growled at the Dwarf and secured his helmet over his head with a sharp snap. "Fine."

Felix grinned, happy to leave the Forge in good hands for a bit. Rafny would take care of things, just as Hector and Aenea would run the other Crafting Halls with deft hands. The Inscriptionist and Alchemist were there, actually, just behind Rafny atop the wide steps leading to the Halls, their daughter hoisted on her father's shoulders. Little Amaya waved at Felix, and he waved back.

Others doubtlessly would have swarmed the Temple had Felix permitted it, but he was pretty clear on who was allowed into this part of his Stronghold. The remaining legionnaires and Dawnguard knew to enforce that as well, so other than the crafters their small army—battalion?—they were alone. That was just as well.

Felix appreciated his crafters being there, especially considering the help they'd all provided in outfitting everyone with some Journeyman Tier armor, all of it enchanted for increased durability and decreased weight. That had been the easiest inscription to create on short notice and would likely offer the most benefits in a prolonged journey, or so others had told him. For weapons, each of them had to make do with what they had brought, but all of them were well-equipped.

Moreover, Aenea and he had managed to create a large number of Essence Draughts over the long night. He personally had enough for himself and his entire team. More were in the saddlebags strapped to Pit's haunches. Felix had also packed a number of Spirit Fruit as well, and the packs were practically bulging. It was a commodity, just as the Essence Draughts were. Vess had insisted he had something to trade with, and that meant Spirit Fruit, monster cores, and a few rare resources that weren't too heavy or unwieldy.

"We are ready?" Zara asked. She had regained her composure after a day of rest, and once again, her Spirit was unreadable to him.

"We are," Felix said. To the rest, he raised his voice—just slightly— and it boomed outward. "We begin now. Follow me."

Felix approached the Spirit Tree, and sounded his Green Shaping through Affinity and Intent. He hummed, letting it build around him like layered echoes as Mana poured through his sounded Skill. Along the smooth, banded trunk, vines grew from the tiniest of crevices, expanding and twisting among themselves until they formed a succession of wide platforms that spiraled down its immense length. It was a difficult task, one that required not only an immense amount of Mana but also a certain mental stamina; the spell resonated through him, through the air, but it was the Tree itself that let him proceed. Their connection was all that allowed it to happen, as the Atlantes Anima gave him the equivalent of an unconcerned shrug and let the vines take root.

The Skill quivered in his core space, on the cusp of Apprentice Tier, and Felix pressed on, fashioning platform after platform as he walked. His team followed, and the small army followed them. Down. Into the dark.

There was a pressure there, one that only skirted the edges of Felix's awareness, emanating from the Tree and pressing down upon everyone else. Vess had commented on it before, that it felt like an enormous down feather mattress attempting to casually crush her to the floor. To Felix, it felt like a tingle in his brain, a susurration, but it was an amiable thing. The Tree was sentient, if not sapient—at least not yet—and some part of Felix knew that because he was there, the Tree would not act out against those who followed him.

What would make it do so, I wonder? he mused as he walked the slow path with his expanded team. His Affinity tangled with their connection, sensing only a few bare glimmers of Intent from the Tree. Growth and protection were key among them, and those who Felix considered allies were allies of the Atlantes Anima. He had little to worry that it would attack his people while he was away. *Though*...he pushed a thought at the Tree, as an experiment. *Do not let anyone except those allowed by Karys down below the first level of the Temple.* The Atlantes took in his Intent without question, releasing back to him a shuddering thrum across their bond. An affirmation. *Huh. That was easy.*

Felix felt lighter, more sure than ever before as they reached the base of the Tree, and the crowd behind him filed into and through his Seat and Seal. Gasps of awe and wonder rippled through them, and even the stoic Risi were silently impressed. Felix kept the whole array dimmed, so as to not blind everyone and keep his secrets...perhaps in the future, they could find a better way to access the portal room. For now, they marched on through to the rear chamber and the Shadowgates.

"Welcome to the Heart of Darkness," Karys intoned, eliciting gasps of alarm from nearly everyone.

Evie snorted. "Can't get over that name. How dramatic can you get?"

"It is a grand name," Karys agreed, his tone sharp. "And more fitting than you know." His golden body gleamed in the light of the banked arrays, save for the dull iron arm, and his eye-fires danced with excitement. "Autarch, we are just about ready."

"Excellent. Pit, Battlelord Ari—if you'd go with Harn and Vess." Felix nodded to his friends, and they, along with the leader of the Frost Giants, moved to the central area of the portal hub. There, supplies had already been set out. Crates of healing supplies—tonics, poultices, salves, and potions of a variety of types—were stacked atop one another. Survival consumables, such as resistance balms, especially for heat and fire, as well as barrels of fresh water and dried, non-perishable foods. There were even smaller packs. Each crafted container was fitted with a specialty harness made of Tier II monster leather and coated in an alchemical oil that increased their resistance to wear and tear. Felix had wanted to inscribe all of the harnesses, but there hadn't been enough time, and there were too many other things to worry about.

Pit, Ari, Harn, and Vess began distributing the casks and crates to the other Risi, each of them more than capable of hoisting their contents, not to mention the Hoarhounds with them. Ari, their Battlelord, had to tough talk a couple of them into carrying it all, but he got the job done. They also passed along smaller packages onto the legionnaires, small survival rations and a sort of primitive med-kit, all of which was put into their packs. Pack mules, all around, and Pit wasn't spared, either. His saddlebags, already loaded up with Spirit Fruit and Essence Draughts, had a couple hundred pounds of supplies added. The weight was hardly noticeable to the increasingly hefty Chimera, though he whined anyway.

You're fine, Felix sent while shouldering his own oversized pack. *And I'll try and shape some sort of cart once we arrive. I've never tried wheels before, but I can manage a bunch of sleds.*

Pit just grumbled. Aside from his bulging saddlebags, the tenku looked like an armored tank. The Master Tier barding he wore was massively impressive. He was already head and shoulders bigger than any of the Hoarhounds, but the extra gleam of metal atop his head, chest, forelegs, and haunches made him seem all the more deadly. Pit, from the way his Spirit roiled and crashed, felt like one of those giant lizard-oxen things they'd seen back in Haarwatch. Or, as Felix would have termed it, a pack mule.

Voracious Eye!

Name: Abjuration Barding
Type: Armor (Enchanted)
Tier: Master
Lore: A set of heavy armor designed exclusively for Pit, Companion of Felix Nevarre. Scales of exotic metal form a powerful barrier against harm, and the sleek design hugs tight to Pit's Chimeric body, covering his legs, neck, back and chest. An attached helm completes the set, and all of it is a unique red-gold coloration thanks to the bond between Companions. An enchanted gem has been placed just below the gorget of the barding, a Stone of Alloyed Refrain, and it confers several bonuses. The armor has gained the ability to alter in size to fit its wearer, as well as masking the physical form of the one to which it is bonded. The armor must be bound by blood to a single user.
Chosen Form: Unknown

Mask of Echoes IV - Once bound by blood, the Stone will allow the wearer to appear as a [Chosen Form].
Chanter's Intent I - The Harmonic Song of a Chanter was used to enchant this item, and it bears their Intent. +10% Effectiveness of Mask of Echoes.
Chanter's Inversion I - Addition of Dissonance to invert the item's properties, hiding them.
Spirit Smithed I - A Unique enhancement, bestowed by a Forge that has been directly influenced by an Elder Spirit Tree. Increased resistance to Spiritual pressure given by those of greater Temper.

Felix patted his metal-clad neck. *Worse comes to worse, I can hold you in my Spirit. The barding should let everything you carry come with you, too...hopefully.*

That had cheered his Companion up considerably, and Felix went about making sure everyone was settled and ready before making his way to Karys...and the Shadowgate.

"The array is functioning and ready to be primed," the metal man said. He leaned back from a set of carved lapis lazuli waves crashing against a squared off structure, located down at the bottom of the circular artifact. "There is little else to be done."

Felix eyed the center of the Shadowgate, where the darkness of the chamber was most evident. It pooled there, cast shadow but also something else. Something more. Not for the first time, it reminded him of the abyss in his center, making him aware that it was once again grasping at the glimmering fruit that hung above his core rings. It wasn't lost on Felix that the Vein of Divinity had grown into a tree of Essence and shining orbs of Memories, so much like the Spirit Tree that rose through his Stronghold. Parallels and signs, or more likely Choices and Consequences.

"Karys, before we go I have something for you," Felix said. The Paragon turned to him, curious and surprised. "A gift of sorts, though maybe more of a burden."

Felix swiped through his Stronghold menu, selecting the subsection under Chancellor. "Karys Taiv, I'd like for you to become Chancellor of my Stronghold and Territory."

A Position Has Been Offered!
Chancellor of Nagast!
Do You Accept?
Y/N

Karys stared, baffled at first and then incredulous. "You cannot—as an Eidolon, I am not allowed such a position!"

Felix shrugged. "You're not an Eidolon Exult anymore. You're...unique, I think. The System doesn't seem to have a problem with the appointment, but if you really feel uncomfortable, then I understand."

Karys' bright eye-fires flared wide. "No! I am only at a loss, Felix. This is an incredible trust you place in me...as Chancellor, I would control your Territory in your absence."

"Yeah, no, I get it," Felix said with a smile. "Dude, you've been helping me all this time, and I wouldn't have been able to manage half the stuff going on here without you. Least I could do is make it official."

A pleased syncopation rippled across Karys' Spirit, and his breath rattled in his cavernous chest. "Then I would be honored...my Lord."

Congratulations!
You Have Chosen Karys Taiv As Your Chancellor!

A bright, brassy blare of horns announced the change, audible only to the two of them. Felix tilted his head. "Is that it? Seems...anticlimactic."

Karys' amusement rumbled through him. "It is complete, however. I have access to all of your Territory and Stronghold menus, my Lord. With this freedom, I can even...I can even access Quests and give them out."

"Oh good, I was hoping you could," Felix said with relief. "Honestly we'll need to keep these folks busy and focused on making this Stronghold as safe as possible. I want you to make that a priority."

"As you will, my Lord."

"Ah, don't. You don't have to do that, man," Felix said. "Just call me Felix."

"It is not proper for a Chancellor to address his liege in such a way," Karys insisted. Felix rolled his eyes.

"Fine." He gripped the energies in his core space tight with his Will. "One final thing, though. Give me your hand."

"My Lord?" Karys asked, but did as he was bid. His large, rough iron hand was easily twice the size of Felix's own. He gripped it, pressing his palm against Karys'.

"A little trick I learned in the Lab," he said, and let loose his Intent. Motes of incandescent light—Memories—tore from the crimson tree within his core space, pulled by his Cardinal Flame and Will combined. All of them surged through his pathways, up and over his chest and down his arm...into his palm. Into Karys. Felix grunted. "I believe these...belonged to you."

"Th-thank you," Karys said in a shaky voice. The golden man bowed so low he put his forehead onto the ground. "Autarch."

"I think that'll help with the memory loss," Felix said. "or so I hope. At the very least, if you can unravel those Memories, you can get that much more out of them."

Karys all but vibrated with gratitude, words choked off in his chassis. Felix patted him on the shoulder—a little awkwardly, he could admit—and turned back to the Shadowgate. "Hopefully, once we get through this,

I can still contact you through the sword," he said, patting Inheritor's Will. "I've no clue what its range might be."

"Neither do I, my Lord," Karys reached out and caressed the Shadowgate. "But we shall find out. Everyone! Please assemble before the gate!"

There was a general rumbling and rustling as folks jostled for position, though the giants stayed in the back with their hounds. Zara, Pit, Harn, Vess, Evie, all of them pushed a bit closer. Felix spared them only a glance before studying the Shadowgate. It was taller than the tallest giants, perfectly circular in the center, and festooned with those ornate carvings. Layers upon layers of them, all of them showing flowing waters, columned structures, and pink rolling hills.

"So I just...activate the chamber fully?" Felix asked Karys.

"It is the first step, but it will require a sacrifice of significance to reestablish the pathways through liminal space," Karys said. He stood a step behind him, out of deference Felix assumed.

Felix took a breath. "Okay."

Greetings Autarch.
The Second Chamber Is Available.
Do You Wish To Activate?

No. Activate this Shadowgate.

Activate Shadowgate, Designation #5W?

Yes.

Power flexed through the floor and walls, the lines of sigaldry flaring to brightness as his Seal redirected energies to the gate. The carvings abruptly flushed with light and color, the gemstone, wood, and mineral materials of its makeup coming to vibrant life. Malachite grasses swayed and tri-tone lakes swirled, not illusory motion but actual movement. Each carving was infinitely more fine than Felix had guessed, and the whole of it working together made it appear as if they were all staring at a window into a strange landscape.

"Blind gods," Vess whispered. "It is beautiful."

"Burnt ashes, that's fancy. How's it work?" Evie asked.

"Damn," Harn grunted.

Within the gate's center that mote of darkness expanded, filling the opening like a liquid, but swirling like a gas. It viscerally reminded Felix of the interior of the Mana well...and the creatures that had dwelled within. He shoved that thought away, his Willpower effective in delaying that particular fear, and focused instead on the faint burr he sensed deep within the Shadowgate's depths.

"I feel the missing connection," Felix said. "A series of dangling threads...I think I can..."

He reached out with his Affinity, clad in the strength of his Will and honed to purpose by his Intent. Awareness of his surroundings faded as the liquid darkness engulfed his senses, until all Felix could feel was the radiant glimmer of the gate itself...and the frayed ends of an ineffable geometry that clashed with wild acoustics.

Felix could tell it existed, but it was distant in the same way a star was, so far it was pointless to reach for it. And yet, without questioning the urge, he tore free a measure of significance within his core space. How much was uncertain, only that Felix felt a distinct dimming within himself before things revved back up, like an electrical circuit close to blowing a breaker. The weight of his existence spiraled outward, flowing along the same connections his Chthonic Tribute took all in, and wove into the complex vibrations of the Shadowgate. A song of clashing rhythms and harmonies became suddenly, brilliantly at peace.

Felix was ejected, shunted back into his bodily senses with all the delicacy of a car crash. He grunted in pain before the Shadowgate ignited once more, and this time it shone like a black sun had descended upon them all. Everyone cried out, shielding their eyes, but Felix stared into it. Beyond the light and the dark and the noise there was a great unending...nothing. It called to him, to the abyss between his cores, and both of them reached out and grasped it.

They *pulled*.

Connection Established!
Shadowgate, Designation #5W Is Active!

Sigils of gold and silver crept along the Shadowgate's frame, blazing into being in a grand arc across the top of the carved portal. In its center shone a liquid darkness, fuller than before, like tar made of shadows and smoke.

"The gate is open," Zara said, breathlessly. "Are you well, Felix?"

Lethargy pushed at him, but he shook it off. "I'm fine. Ready to go."

Zara hesitated, but only an instant before she pointed at the sixteen people—giants, Henaari, Legion all—who were holding the array stones strapped to their chests. "Do not drop those. On your lives."

Nods of conviction were her response as their bearers tightened the leather straps across their shoulders and chests. The array stones were inert at the moment, waiting for Felix to activate them upon entering the passage.

"Felix," Atar said in a low voice. He was fearfully watching the roiling surface of the gate. "You'll help them, won't you? Ahkestria, my home? If it's besieged by the Paladins—"

"I'll do what I can, Atar. If there's a way to stop the Hierocracy from getting what it wants, then I'm all for it," Felix said.

Atar nodded, seeming a bit relieved. He took a shaky breath. "Right. Then let's not waste time."

Felix looked back at the company, making sure to meet as many eyes as he could stomach. Nerves made his guts flip-flop, but he held his expression firm. Strong, he hoped. "Eyes up. I don't know how long this will take, but if we stay close, we will be fine. I'll keep you safe."

Before he could think better of it, Felix jumped through the gate, Pit at his heels.

CHAPTER THIRTY-ONE

There was a terrible, stomach-churning lurch before Felix's leading foot found solid ground. Well. Solid-ish.

He looked around, that lurch having transformed into a nauseating twist. All was a blank darkness, an infinite black in every direction. His feet stood on something, but there was nothing there, just an echo of an echo of what ground may have been. Pit trundled in after him, his armored head pivoting in all directions as he parted the thick, liquid-smoke of the gate. He chirped, the sound deadened.

We return.

"Yeah," Felix said with a grimace. "Back in the Void. Or close enough."

Behind them, the Shadowgate was a patch of darkness over the infinite Void; black on black, invisible to normal eyes. To his Manasight and Affinity, it was a riot of elemental Mana tendrils, each one interwoven into the form of a massive circle. As his friends and team disgorged from the smoky dark, ripples of power spread outward, flashing up and around them like lightning and just as quick. Zara was among the first to stride out, and her carefully controlled expression slackened with wonder.

"Astounding. Do you see this, Felix?" She gestured up around them. "A protective sheathing surrounds us...extending from the gate toward our destination."

Felix could see it, barely. It danced in the Void, hidden from his Manasight by the dark. His Affinity, however, could hear it plain as day, though he had thought it was all coming from the Shadowgate. It was, in a sense, but the threads of power weaving around them were those same connections he'd had to sacrifice a portion of his significance to fuel. A corridor was formed, extending into the distance; toward the other gate, he had to assume.

The others filed out, every one of them stumbling on entry as if the ground were thickened mud. Unlike Zara, Pit, or Felix, everyone else struggled with their footing and gaped at the blank darkness around them. All of which slowed down the procession a great deal, forcing Felix to start pulling folks forward so that the gate wasn't clogged up. Once through, the sixteen ward-bearers hustled to the edges of the group, several falling in their haste, but all of them eager to do their job.

Felix engaged the array just as the last of their company entered the gate. The process tugged a good chunk of Mana from his cores, which was taxing but more than manageable. A bright pattern of sigaldry and glyphs expanded beneath their feet and above their heads, flashing into existence with flares of blue-white and red-gold before subsiding to a smoldering, nigh-invisible silver.

A pressure descended, not unlike the pressure of the Spirit Tree but more intimate. Instead of a heavy mattress atop their shoulders, it was a cloak that hugged their Aspects tightly, pulling everything inward.

Hopefully it's enough to avoid detection by the worst of the voidbeasts.

"What now?" Alister asked. His blue and silver battlerobes were bright against the Void.

"Now we walk," Harn grunted.

"Walk? In this?" Atar said. He could barely lift his legs, exactly as if he were wading through knee-high water or mud. "We'll not make it far, not at any true speed."

"Is it supposed to be like this?" Evie asked. "Seems bad for transportin' anythin' at a reasonable pace."

"The Shadowgate is providing a stream of power, holding the path while we are within and requiring no excess effort on our part," she said. "The footing might not be ideal, but this...this is superior to the Dark Passages scattered around the Continent."

"You made a path, last time we were here," Darius pointed out. "Can't you do that again?"

Zara had explained to Felix her trick, what she had done during their jaunts through liminal space. She shook her head. "I am still not at my strongest, and a journey such as this would beggar me of what little strength remains."

Vess, Atar, Alister, and, surprisingly, Darius looked concerned at that admission. Evie and Harn, however, seemed to hone in on it.

"You're too weak? Why'd you even come?" the chain fighter asked. "Coulda stayed back in your shiny new house."

"I've a duty, Miss Aren. We all do, but I more than most. I'll see it through, to the end."

Felix caught Darius nodding in approval. The Autarch cleared his throat. "Either way, we're here now. And I'll not have us move so slowly."

"Can you do as Zara did?" Vess asked. "Forge a path?"

"Should be able to," Felix said. "Got the Mana for it, but...there's something else about this place." Felix could feel it now that he'd been within the gate for so long. Shapes and colors flashed at the edges of his senses. He focused on them, feeding them his Mana and even a measure of Essence, guiding himself along the strands of connection and significance that threaded the corridor between gates. And then, a result.

Sympathetic Connection Detected!
Skill Extant!
Do You Wish To Proceed?
Y/N

For all that the message made no sense, Felix could *feel* its meaning. Intent, baked into the System message, enough that he answered "yes" without questioning it. Abruptly, the humming darkness transformed itself. Matter erupted from nothing, stones beneath their feet and soil and weeds, then thick trees with roughened bark and wide, grasping branches. It drew on Felix's cores, and on his Intent, but mostly it drew on a particular Skill.

Connections swelled and firmed until the path was worn, ancient stone pavers in a wild wood. Around them, further, an entire world unfolded. Black nothing turned to rolling hills of green grasses and patches of more dark forest, while above the sky lightened to a robin's egg blue. Strands of multicolored light streaked across the heavens, moving from a distant spot on the horizon where a fortress of dark stone sat.

It was his Bastion of Will.

Pit perked up, looking to Felix with an excited glimmer in his eye. *What's this?*

I'm not really sure, bud.

"Noctis' tits," Evie said, staring around her. "Did we arrive already?"

"No, this is just a...reflection," Felix said.

"Of what?" Zara asked.

"Is that a castle?" Atar said, shielding his eyes against the midday sun. "Is that the *sun?*"

"Something like that." Felix gestured down the weed-strewn path. "Let's get moving. We should all be able to keep a quick pace now."

And so they did. Felix was able to avoid too many questions by taking the lead and plunging down the wooded causeway, his Strength and Endurance matched by no one, no matter how they tried. He worried, at first, that his Bastion would make their array meaningless, but he could still feel the effect of the array. The environment-shift seemed almost like it was...meant to happen. The place where his Intent and Skill had slotted into the gate's corridor had felt purposeful. Was this what the ancient Nym did when they traveled? Someone would envision a world for them to race across?

Were they really in his Bastion?

That last bit was something he thought about a lot, though he didn't have a way to test it without stopping everyone and wasting more time. Ultimately, it wasn't important, except to satisfy his curiosity, and Felix let the urge flow over him. Away. He focused instead on keeping everyone going; on getting out.

They ran for hours.

The forest was unending, and though the terrain immediately around them altered, his view of his Bastion fortress never varied. Always, it was just over a hill, the pentagonal tower in its center blazing with strands of light. The forest thickened and thinned, but it never went away completely, not even as they appeared to approach the bitter green sea that abutted his fortress. It made the world feel a bit like a treadmill, and it grated at Felix's nerves. Once or twice, he felt rumbling along his Bastion, like something scratching at a door. Each time, it faded in moments, and holding it all required too much of his focus to pay it much mind. After the sixth hour, that changed.

"Something feels...off," Zara said. She labored beside him, keeping up with his light pace he'd adopted after the first few hours. Felix could have left them behind easily, but that defeated the purpose of bringing them in the first place. Zara gestured to the trees on their right. "There's movement in the trees."

None of them slowed down, but Felix practically heard a dozen pairs of eyes pivot toward the thickened copse as they passed. Observation Skills fired off, some exuding streams of Mana and some only singing in Felix's ears—a new development, that. The scratching he had felt earlier intensified, almost growling against the fabric of his Bastion before it went suddenly slack. Moments later, an Arclight mage shouted.

"Monster!"

Writhing shapes moved through the woods, mostly obscured by the dense trunks and greenery. But Felix didn't need his Voracious Eye or even to see their whole bodies to identify them—the flash of mottled gray tendrils and swooping, squid-like movements told Felix all he needed to know.

"Tenebrils," he said in a hiss. "Swarm hunters, but they're cowards." He raised his voice. "We have nothing to fear from them unless they get you alone. Don't get separated, and we'll be fine. Let's keep going."

"You heard the Autarch! Move, double-time!" Darius bellowed. The company, Henaari, Legion, and Frost Giants startled; Felix was certain most of them didn't realize they'd stopped to stare. They all ran on.

Felix kept the Tenebrils in sight as he ran ahead of the rest, Evie, Vess, and Harn close behind him. The mindless balls of hunger and barbed tentacles wafted through the trees, moving at a remarkable clip but otherwise not doing anything overtly threatening.

"They...they don't seem like much," Evie panted. Her Agility was remarkable, but her Endurance had always been on the low side. "Why don't we clean them up and move on?"

"Because Tenebrils are rarely alone," Felix said. Pit growled. "Worse things follow in their wake. And I'd rather have them as bait than be on the hook myself."

"Smart," Harn grunted. His armor moved soundlessly, the many tiny plates of it gliding across one another as if greased. "Little fish to distract the big ones."

"Big fish..." Vess considered the flitting shapes, still at least a football field length away from them all. "What sort of predators do such creatures have?"

"I'm hoping you don't find out," Felix said with conviction. A clamor shook his Bastion, something he felt in his chest more than around himself. "But I don't think we'll be so lucky."

A scream ripped across the idyllic forest, several tones all jumbled together into one enormous voice. From the left and cutting across their path came a nightmarish serpent clad in dusk-colored scales and festooned with spiny fins that arced like sails. These fins cut through trees and stone alike, beyond razor sharp, as it undulated at the swarm of distant Tenebrils.

"Halt!" Darius shouted, barely stopping the company from marching right into a whipping fin bigger than a Frost Giant. The creature, a Noctnatter, was absolutely massive, and it plowed a terrible furrow through Felix's Bastion.

And more were coming.

"Run!" Felix shouted, just as their right exploded into movement. Six more hundred-foot long serpents burst from the depths of the forest, taking wild passage toward their Company and the Tenebrils beyond. Mouths the size of a mini-van hinged open, revealing teeth like swords and multiple lashing tongues. "No!"

Felix shouted at his team, but it was too late. Fireballs and force pillars, ice chains and air spears all exploded against the voidbeasts, not to mention the crackles of lightning and various weapon Skills that skittered off their hide. All around them, the Bastion quaked, while Felix could hear the music that made it all begin to shudder and fail.

"It's unraveling!" Zara shouted. She sang, full-throated and furious, conjuring walls of green-blue water out of nothing that severed two of the nochnatters' heads. "Felix!"

"I know! I can feel it!" he bellowed back. "Stop fighting! Run!"

The order was taken up, his words echoed frantically, and everyone took off at a manic sprint. The aquamarine walls failed seconds later, those massive void serpents tearing across where the company just stood. Bloodied and apparently smart enough to know why, the nochtnatters chased after.

"They've pierced the sheath," Zara said through her gasping breaths. She held a hand to her side, just under her shortribs, but she ran with the relentless form of an Olympic sprinter. "More will come, and fast."

"What do we do?" Felix asked, casting his senses as wide as he dared.

He could have pushed further, but to do so would have blanked out his present eyesight; what he felt was enough. Hundreds of voidbeasts were pouring in, some from the entry the Tenebrils had made and others from the gaping abscess torn by the nochtnatters. Movement and his own hectic hurry made identifying which kind of voidbeast difficult, but Felix didn't doubt all of them would be deadly under the right circumstances.

"All we can do is reach the end. Any further attacks against them will unravel this place you've constructed for us," she said through her teeth. "And could end up hurling us into the Void itself."

Great. Felix could already feel the strain against the array he was holding, not to mention the Bastion all around him. Right now, he could feel those tears in the sheath like holes in a piece of paper; only his Will was holding them together, keeping them from spreading. More presences ripped through the breaches, drawn as much by their kin as the prospect of sustenance. They attacked one another as often as not, but there were too many for that to matter much. Thousands now, all bearing down on them.

"We're not gonna have much choice!" Alister shouted over the roar of beasts and clatter of armor. The woods were flooding with dark shapes. "Look!"

Ahead of them was an absolute frenzy of void flesh. Scales, rubbery skin, and appendages he'd never before seen roiled through a riotous pile of thrashing limbs and fangs. Felix could feel the Bastion tear even further, weakening ahead of them like water on paper—as if one wrong step would shatter his Bastion entirely.

The company couldn't afford to stop. Monsters chased them from all sides, hemming in their path. Felix growled, and Pit joined him, their bond burning bright.

"Enough!"

Cardinal Flame!

Red-gold fire ignited across the ancient causeway, and ear-piercing screams shook the daylight air. Sigils of *flame*, *earth*, and *force* were inscribed in the air, as crude an array as Felix had ever made. But it worked. Flames speared from them and into the ground, burning so hot, that several trees were turned to charcoal in a blink. Explosions of molten earth followed, rendering Void flesh into brilliant explosions of multi-colored Mana. Darker red flames followed his, ripping into scales and skin, while silver spears chased after them. Bursts of air Mana fueled the flames, enhancing their hungry mouths as it tore a hole in the monstrous horde.

Adamant Discord!

Lines of connection blazed to life in Felix's hands and he hurled them aside. Lightning slithered like twin whips in his hands, and the corpses and thrashing bodies of the voidbeasts were tossed from their path. He felt his Mind and Body strain, though his Spirit felt less of it as he held back monsters and onto his Bastion at the same time. Veins protruded from his neck like steel cables, his arms tensed as if made of steel. Thankfully, they knew what to do.

"Advance!" Darius hollered, just as Harn and Vess and Zara all said the same. The company ran on, bursting anew with desperate speed as two nochtnatters grew ever closer to their rearguard. Too close. Teeth flashed, just barely missing the Frost Giant's packs.

"RAHH! Tua ra falla!" one of the Frost Giants bellowed, turning on the nearest serpent with his huge axes made of ice and stone. He brought it down in a crescent arc, its impact enough to slam the void serpent's body into the earth and its length thrashing behind it. Hundreds of void-beasts fell to its sharpened fins and scales, but the giant was thrown as well...straight into the hungry horde.

No! Felix tried to spare the strength to stop it, but it was too late. The voidbeasts were on him in a blink, splattering the devastated forest with dark blue blood. *Goddamn it!*

Onward, until they approached a cliff. The briny, acidic scent of the sea assaulted their noses, now suddenly ahead of them. Darius didn't stop, merely maneuvered down the cliff face, still following the slab stone path they had been set upon. As Felix ran at the center of the pack, hurling off monstrosities, by the time he came to the cliff, it was clear where they had to go.

"The exit gate," he said. An orb of shadow hovered atop a chain of tiny jagged islands, each one ten to fifteen feet away from each other. The islands were more like exposed roots of stone, and they were no bigger than twenty feet wide, not nearly enough to hold everyone at all times. Darius and the others led folks to the water's edge, where the acid sea hissed against the sands. "Hold on!"

Stone Shaping!

Sand and raw stone ripped up from the water, crude bridges between islands. The moment they came into existence, his people leaped atop them, racing for their lives. Felix followed after while Pit took to the sky.

Wingblades and Frost Spears lanced into the voidbeast horde, as did the attacks of his friends. Their magic was deteriorating the strange connection to his Bastion, but Felix felt that was inevitable at that point. Already, he could see darkness devouring the sky and distant hills, could feel the green leached into nothing, like an ache in his heart. Felix held onto his Bastion with everything he had, but it was sand through his fingers, slipping inexorably into the Void.

Someone shouted, but Felix was too focused on the beasts and his Bastion to know what was said. Pit screeched and dove, heading for the Shadowgate, and Felix realized that almost everyone had made it through. Finally.

The Bastion was awash in monstrosities, so many that the beach was a graveyard of hideous corpses and gnashing teeth.

We're through! Pit sent to him, but his voice was distant and growing further away. *Felix!*

"Then there's no more reason to hold back," he said.

Cardinal Flame!

Adamant Discord!

Rain of Cataclysm!

Fire and lightning shook through the skies as his Bastion truly failed, ripping across hundreds of voidbeasts as they clawed for him and sending them all hurtling backward beneath plumes of incandescent flame. From above, Mana coalesced into a storm, unleashing a deluge of virulently green power onto the beasts. Acid rain tore through them, each sizzling drop a bullet from the sky.

Notifications he'd been suppressing flashed by him. One hundred, three hundred, seven hundred...twenty-five hundred voidbeasts killed. XP surged through his core space, pushing him ever closer to that new level, but Felix didn't care. He laid about himself with power until nothing remained, until only a tiny sand spit existed beneath his feet within the unceasing, infinite Void.

Dead. Everything's dead. He took a strained step backward, more hurt by holding the path than the fight. *Good. I—*

A caterwauling cry shook the Void and sent a thrill of terror through Felix. It was enormous, a mountainous sound that quivered the burning flesh all around him like an earthquake. A primal, furious *Need* assaulted his Mind, and Felix gasped in recognition. He'd lingered too long, used too much power without his protection array.

The Whalemaw had sensed him.

What was worse, that Need he felt was an echo. The Whalemaw desired his power...and the feeling was mutual.

Cutting off the sensation with his Willpower, Felix turned and leaped through the Shadowgate.

CHAPTER THIRTY-TWO

Darkness parted, and Felix fell much farther than he expected. He hit the ground with a muted grunt, unhurt but surprised. Orienting himself, he looked behind him only to find his team huddled together in a dark chamber...but no Shadowgate.

Look up, Pit sent to him. The tenku was pawing at a nearby wall, green and black with strange plants.

Puzzled, Felix saw the glimmering face of a Shadowgate mounted to the ceiling of all places. More important than its stupid placement, though, it flashed and sparked, clearly not in the best repair. The inky darkness at its center bubbled and popped like boiling tar or burning smoke. And from its depths, Felix could still feel a discordant cry of excruciating Need and Fury.

The Whalemaw was drawing closer.

"We need to shut that gate off!" he shouted.

Zara stood rapidly, looking from him to the gate. "Did you see it?"

"No, but I heard it. Can hear it, still," Felix said with a dry swallow. "It's getting closer. Karys? Karys can you hear me?"

The hooked blade at his waist was inert for an upsetting moment before it flickered with green-gold life Mana. "I do. Wonderful! I was—."

"Karys, how do we shut down the gate?" Felix interrupted.

"Shut it down? But then you would have to reinstate the connection, wasting more—"

"We need to shut it down! Your side, too! Now!" Felix felt that Need tear at him from above, an almost physical force.

"I—I, of course, my Lord! Find the *joining* glyph, reminiscent of a loosened knot."

"Found it!" Atar said, clearly picking up on the tension. He pointed at something directly above himself, at least fifty feet away. His hands charged with orange Mana regardless. "What do I do? Split it?"

"What? No! That'll misalign—no! Felix—my Lord!—pull out the power from the gate. Devour it!"

Felix didn't question his friend, but reached out his Intent and latched onto where Atar pointed. A glyph, shimmering with a deep blue light, woven around itself like Celtic knotwork. He seized it with his Will.

Chthonic Tribute!

The *joining* glyph spat fire, enough that Atar howled and leaped aside, and Felix tore it into his channels.

The Shadowgate flickered once and cut out. The dark of the Void turned instantly into mere shadows, while the roar of furious Need vanished like a popping bubble.

"Karys! Did you shut down the gate on your side as well?" Felix asked his sword. There was a faint buzzing and an upsettingly long pause...before it blazed to life once more. Ribbons of green-gold Mana spun about the blade's hilt.

"It is done, my Lord."

Felix trembled, feeling muscles unclench that he'd never known he'd had. He eased himself down against the wet, mossy stone of...wherever they had landed.

"Avet's black teeth, what was that?" Alister asked.

"Your Whalemaw," Zara said. "It sensed you, after the array slipped through."

"Yeah."

"That was not a great deal of time," Vess pointed out. She leaned on her partisan and peered upward at the ceiling-mounted Shadowgate. "How did it sense you *and* reach you in mere fractions of a glass?"

"Time does not flow correctly in the Void," Zara said. "It is...an unmoored Realm."

"Karys," Felix said to his blade. "How long since we left?"

"It has barely been a glass," he said.

Murmurs swept through the group, and Felix did a quick head count. Faces and names flashed through his Mind, and all but one of them accounted for—that was a relief. No one had been left behind by accident, and the voidbeasts had been denied. Mostly.

With that worry off his mind, Felix focused on the tilted room around them. As always, Mana streamed off of every surface, coiling to physical structures like a wireframe of shimmering, colored light. It was confusing and chaotic, but his long practice had made it far easier to use—that, and his exceedingly high Perception.

The room was roughly a hundred feet long and half that across, though it was not boxy by any means. Alcoves and columns, most broken, put divots in the chamber's facade while the floor was a spacious lattice of cut stone, similar to many Nymean architectural features. Beneath its porous surface, Felix could see more water, brackish but not terribly deep.

The water deepened the further out one traveled, until it dropped off into a dark pool at the far end of the chamber. Green and black plants—moss mostly—covered the walls and ceiling, and the smell of ages old must and mold filled Felix's nose.

Exploration is level 62!

"I see a door," Ari rumbled, his head halfway to the ceiling. He pointed a heavily muscled arm, blue as ice. "There."

Felix could see it, too. It was a heavy thing, also made of stone and...unless he missed his guess, heavily warded.

"Anyone else think this place is...odd?" Evie said. "Why's it tilted?"

"I'm more concerned about this...leaking," Atar said, pointing out a few intermittent streams that came from above.

"True. I thought this was supposed to be the desert," Evie said, wrinkling her nose. "Why's it so wet? And smelly."

"The Ghreldan Hills are filled with several thousand lakes," Zara explained. She sniffed. "This Temple was clearly built atop one."

"It ain't atop one now," Harn pointed out.

"No, it is not. And that would account for why no one knew a Temple was here," Zara said. "It must have sank."

"Oh burning ashes," Atar moaned. More whispers rippled through the Legion, and even the Dawnguard traded guarded glances.

"We're fully underwater?" Felix asked. He pushed his Perception outward, but much as the Waterfall Temple had, the stone seemed to actively block his senses. He couldn't even detect anything beyond the warded door.

"Unclear," Zara said. Wavering forms of aquamarine light manifested above her palms and elbows, casting a cool light over the stone lattice. "I can feel my attuned element strongly, but it is being muffled by layer after layer of enchantment. Were it not for the architecture, that alone would confirm that this is another Nymean Temple."

Felix looked up at the Shadowgate on the ceiling, trying to parse details. Much of it was overgrown with the same black and green moss around the chamber, but his Perception wasn't blocked here. It was designed like a set of sweeping mountains, several rows of what he called the Teeth interspersed with malachite forests and thick rivers of sapphire. Along one side, he could even clearly make out a large waterfall. *Would all the gates leading back to my Stronghold feature the same design?* He was fairly certain it would. *The Nym were definitely all about their aesthetics.*

His eyes caught on a feature of the gate, mostly hidden by the fronds of moss that grew from it.

"This Temple is more than just tilted," Felix said, pointing up again at the inert Shadowgate. "Unless it's common to put steps on something in the ceiling."

"Oh," Vess said.

"This whole place is just about flipped," Atar said through a heavy breath. Sweat was beading on his brow. "We're underwater and in a fallen, crumbling ruin. Oh, Highest."

Alister rubbed the mage's back comfortingly, but looked to the others with urgency. "We need to leave here. There's no telling how safe all this is."

"I agree with that," Harn said from across the room. Half-submerged, near where the water met the lattice-floor there was a statue of a woman with a four-pronged star in her upraised hand. Harn knelt down and pressed his fingertips to the statue's wrist and grunted. A trickle of unformed Mana puffed into the star, igniting it with a bright sodium yellow light that quickly raced across the stone-lattice floor, tracing the outline of stars and leaves and leaping, stylized creatures in blazing radiance. Stars of solid stone across the structure, across all the walls, lit up with Mana, forming a constellation of light that all but banished the shadows in the flooded room.

"Magelights, cleverly hidden," Vess said, kneeling to inspect one herself. "I do not see the inscriptions."

"It's inside," Harn said as he stood, shaking water from his hands. "Seen these before, in some ruins Mags and Cal and I raided. Even broke open one of them stars. You could see the little sigils and everthin'."

"You...broke them?" Atar asked, his outrage almost overcoming the panic attack he'd been having. "Why would you do such a thing?"

Harn shrugged. "See how they worked. Sometimes things gotta break before you can fix 'em, ya know?"

The lights revealed the disrepair of the room, cracked pillars and splintering walls, as well as more and more of those hanging fronds. They were black with green edges, as was the thick moss that dominated the less-drenched portions of the chamber. Where the light had traveled, however, the plants were burned away, leaving an acrid stink in the air that wrinkled Felix's nose. Between that, the mold, and the musty water, he almost wished his Perception wasn't so strong.

However, the light also illuminated the water between them and the warded door. They could see fish swimming about in there, silver things about a foot long. The light was agitating them like nobody's business, likely rousing them from their darkened fish homes. In those depths, Felix could see broken statuary and more of the stone lattice, chunked and eroded by long Ages. The pool was deep, the chamber clearly broken at the bottom where swirling mud and darkness once again claimed the waters. It was likely that, were they to swim down, they could find a way out and up to the surface of whatever lake they were in...

Yeah, fuck that, Felix said with a shiver. Dark waters and tight spaces? He'd rather fight the Maw again.

"How're we gonna get across?" Darius asked, only to be met with the crackling snap of ice manifesting. A wide bridge of smoking ice crawled across the waters, sinking pillars into the muck as it expanded, and stopping only when it abutted the warded door. Three Frost Giants stood from the water's edge, all of them trading nods with the large Adept. Darius made a noise in his throat, something between surprise and appreciation. "Huh. Good initiative."

"We are more than axes in battle," Battelord Ari grated. He looked pleased. "Water such as this holds no domain over the Risi."

"Good, because there is a lot of it," Zara said, moving to the bridge.

Felix followed, the ice creaking beneath his massive weight, his eyes lingering over the ice's construction. He felt Rime Shaping within him tingle in sympathy with the display, almost calling out to him to use it and try something new and interesting. It wasn't the Skill, not really, but his own eagerness to play with the power at his disposal. Felix had spent the last month or so doing relatively little fighting, serving instead as a Mana battery for his arrays and building up his Stronghold. He was excited to get out of the Foglands and see something new.

The warded door was thick and stout despite its deceptively fragile appearance. A forest of trees and rolling hills covered its face, a preview of what was to come if Ghreldan was like what Zara said. Curiously, the moss didn't touch the door at all. It didn't even come within a foot of the lintel, and the edges of it were blackened. In his Manasight, the door was simple stone, glowing with earth and hints of metal Mana, but unremarkable for all of that. He put his hand on it, feeling a thrum through his Affinity for all that his fingertips detected only solid stone. *Definitely warded.*

He stepped back. "What do we do? I'm sure we could break it open, but I'd rather not."

Zara sniffed again. "You can try, but from what I'm seeing, these wards would even hold *you* at bay."

Felix shrugged. "Fine. Then we disarm them. How?"

"With some finesse," Atar said. He stepped forward and adjusted the collar on his black and crimson robes. "Step aside, let the Glyphmaster through."

"I regret everything," Felix murmured, drawing a grin from Alister. Atar pretended he didn't hear him.

While the Inscriptionists and Zara were focused on the door, Felix decided he'd try his hand at reinforcing the bridge. He knew from past experience that he couldn't Stone Shape the stone of a Nymean Temple, so anything he made would have to sit precariously atop the uneven ground far below the water. Annoying at best, dangerous at worst. Instead, he focused on his other tools he had to hand.

Rime Shaping!

Mana surged from his channels and out of the bottom of his feet, hitting and spreading across the already formed bridge before snaking down into the water itself. Pillars of ice formed, thick as Ari's torso, and plunged into the sediment far below. As each one formed, Felix expanded the bridge until it would certainly hold everyone's weight without question. It was for him and Pit as much as everyone else, though the giants weren't exactly lightweights. By the end of it, the water level below them had dropped substantially, and more than a few silver fish flopped on outcroppings and statuary as the murky water sank. Pit cooed in delight and, with the help of the Dawnguard, was able to capture a good amount of them; they'd make for a good meal later on.

Or now, he thought as Pit ate almost half of them.

"Ooh, well that's interestin'," Evie commented. Felix followed her gaze to where something yellow-white poked up from the repurposed water. "Skeletons. A lot of em."

Dozens of bones littered the slimed statuary, some fish, some definitely not. A few were even quite large, as if a beast the size of a giant had been devoured. Felix made out jagged scrape-marks on the massive ribs and vertebrae. The water was so low that it only covered a tiny portion of the bottom of the chasm, and there it was dark as night and thick with mud. Whatever had made its home there was clearly not present any longer.

"I do not think I want to meet whatever did that," Vess said. She looked to the Hand once before stiffening her spine. "But we should prepare ourselves. If something that big was in here, there is no telling what the rest of this Temple will hold."

The company checked their weapons and armor, ensuring they were ready for battle, and Darius nodded at his ward. Felix almost rolled his eyes. *Vess knows how to lead, man.*

"Aha!" Atar cried out at the same time a flare of blue-white energy zipped along the large door. "We did it!"

A deluge of water sprayed through the crevices of the door and quickly became a startling flood as they shuddered open. Ages-old hinges protested against the liquid weight, and everyone scrambled backward. The mages shouted in alarm, and the bridge quaked from the impact of the flood, but Zara threw her hand up and into the outpour. Blue-green light flared, and the water split around them, arcing neatly past the edges of the ice bridge and directly into the now-empty chasm below.

"T-thanks," Atar said.

"My pleasure, Atar," Zara said before rubbing the palm of her hand as if it ached. The water had finally leveled out with their own chamber as the chasm below filled up over the level of the ice bridge. She lifted her sandaled feet, immune to the chill of the water but not the rotting stink of it. "This is not freshwater."

"Great," Atar muttered. Alister helped him to his feet, but his black robes were waterlogged. They draped from his spindly form, sloshing with every movement. "Gonna have to waste Mana to dry this out."

"I wouldn't bother," Evie said, slipping to the front and peering into the darkness beyond the heavy doors. "I got a feeling we're all gonna get soaked before this is over."

Felix peered into the gloom, attempting to ignore the fetid fumes of mold and rotting...things. The room was big enough to make the Shadow-gate chamber feel like a coat closet, with huge vaulted ceilings and massive statuary of robed figures within alcoves big enough to park a Manaship inside. More statues lifted from the water, which had gone still after it had leveled off, and Felix could even make out the green line along the walls where the water once rested.

"This seems...pleasant," Vess offered.

Felix grinned at her. "Better than a Domain full of Primordial-Spawn, at least?"

"Most things are," she replied dryly before hefting her spear. "Who shall be vanguard?"

Before Felix could answer, a voice slipped across the still waters—a harsh, sibilant echo.

"Who daresss to walk in my demesne? What mortal filth tries their hand at the secretsssss of the godssss?"

The dark waters bulged and roiled, splitting for a wedge-shaped head the size of a minivan. Rivers cascaded down a face, pebbled with scales. Its flesh was pale as snow, and its eyes burned a vicious, brilliant red.

Name: Jadorak, the Horror of Haestus
Type: Nagafolk
Level: 241
HP: 10495/10495
SP: 14223/15843
MP: 3984/3984
Lore: Nagafolk are extremely agile swimmers and have the Endurance of a creature an entire Tier above them, no matter their level. Aggressive, territorial, and cruel, these monstrosities kill by crushing their foes or by injecting them with a deadly venom. Albino Nagafolk are rare and all the more deadly for it.
Strength: More Data Required
Weakness: More Data Required

"Who are you, to challenge me in my place of worssship?"
Fuck.

CHAPTER THIRTY-THREE

Okay. Okay, not so bad. You can handle one giant snake, Felix reassured himself. *Pit?*

Ready. Always. The tenku's feathers rustled, sounding like a hundred papers being shuffled.

Let's take it easy for a moment. Maybe we can avoid a fight, Felix sent. Pit rolled a dubious eye at his back, which Felix promptly ignored.

"Hi there," he said, voice echoing in the expansive chamber. Water streamed from the pale Naga's face and neck as it jerked its huge head to look at him. "We're just traveling through, not intending to disturb you."

"Yet disssturb me you did," Jadorak hissed. It—he?—swayed slightly, sloshing water in surprisingly large waves. "Here, in the holiest of lakesss. *My* lake."

"Haestus is the name of a lake near the Ghreldan border," Zara whispered out of the corner of her mouth. "We are in the right place."

"Who speaksss, but not at me?" Jadorak shouted. Felix wasn't entirely sure how he was forming words with his snake-mouth, but they were perfectly clear, if overly sibilant. "I alone am chosssen by the Godsss above, chosssen in might and purified by their very touch! NONE SHALL IGNORE ME!"

The Naga's voice ripped into the vaulted ceiling, loud enough that even Darius winced. Light from some ancient source high above lit against Jadorak's scales, illuminating them with a pearlescent brilliance. Felix's eyes fixed on the source, and he realized it was a crystal fixed in the eye of a statue so massive he hadn't noticed its features in the gloom. *Nymean* features. He'd noticed the robed figures around the periphery, but not the three huge faces of stone carved into the apex of the chamber, nor the crystal clear gemstone that sat in one of their faces. *Belais Crystal, but it's emptied of power.*

"Ah, listen man, we're not trying to disrespect you, but you gotta give us a minute. You're coming on hot and heavy here," Felix said without thinking. He snapped his mouth shut, but the damage was done. Jadorak's red eyes flared, and his Spirit roiled with a gleeful rage.

"Give me *one* reason why I sshould not devour your entire party, little whelp," the Naga hissed, dropping his face low enough they could feel his hot breath. It smelled of rotten fish and blood. "Ssspeak one word awry, and I will not hessitate to end you, even before the Ssstone God'sss eye."

Stone God? He thinks that's a god? "We are traveling to the south and had to stop here by necessity. It was not our intention to disturb you or your...gods," Felix said. He wasn't worried about himself, not really, but what of the dozens that followed him? Would they survive an attack from the giant snake monster? He had no clue, and he wasn't interested in finding out. "If you let us pass, we'll gladly go on our way immediately."

"Go? You desssecrate our holy temple, lie to our god'sss chosen, and you wish to ssimply leave?" Jadorak laughed in the back of his throat. Around him, the waters sloshed and rippled as more Nagafolk rose from the dark depths, all of them dark blues and greens. "I do not care about your intentionsss. My people are not onesss to give up a meal, no matter how pretty they talk."

"Don't do this," Felix warned, feeling his two cores spin within him. The branches of his Vein of Divinity rustled and flexed. "It's not gonna go how you think."

"My brothers! To me!" Jadorak screamed, lunging at the same time. *Sovereign of Flesh!*

In a burst of incandescent pain, Felix's fist and arm quadrupled in size, erupting in black scales even as his fist rocketed into the snapping jaws of the albino snake. The impact was an explosion, the force of it sending water hurtling away in a shockwave as Jadorak's entire skull was thrown back and into—through—a set of unattached columns.

"Jadorak! Halt!"

A new voice ripped across the vast chamber, this one far more Human-sounding. Another Naga, but with the torso of a massively muscled humanoid and a face that approached something similar. He was covered in brown and tan scales and slithered atop the water as if it were dry land. "All supplicants are to be brought before the Deepking. You know this, child."

The huge, albino serpent wrenched himself free of the tumbled architecture and fixed Felix with a gimlet eye. The scales along his jaw were broken and bleeding. "This one ssstruck me, Garox. I would have sssatisfaction!"

"You are denied," Garox the snakeman said in a tone that brooked no argument. Jadorak clearly wanted to, however, from the way he undulated toward Felix's team. "Jadorak. I shall not say it again. Leave us."

The white snake's red eyes burned bloody crimson, and hate boiled off him in waves that Felix needed no Affinity to sense. With a frustrated yowl, Jadorak dove back into the dark waters and was gone...as were the dozen or so Nagafolk that had joined him.

"That was new," Vess murmured in surprise. Her eyes tracked the ripples in the water where the Nagafolk had disappeared, hand on her partisan. "I have never witnessed your Body do such a thing."

"Not new, just haven't had the chance to test it yet," Felix said through deep, steady breaths. He'd shredded the sleeve of his Garment, which was now tugging at more of his Mana to repair itself. "And I don't think I'll get a chance here, either. Looks like diplomacy is still on the table."

Vess flashed him a grin, moving her gaze to the new, calmer enemy. "My favorite. He seems...reasonable."

Garox approached them slowly, both of his hands raised away from the curved blades at his waist. His snake body lashed at the water, moving across it in a winding manner that recalled any number of snakes Felix had encountered back home.

Voracious Eye.

Name: Garox, the Bladeless
Type: Spirit Naga
Level: 297
HP: 15495/15495
SP: 18772/19278
MP: 4569/4569
Lore: Nagafolk are extremely agile swimmers and have the Endurance of a creature an entire Tier above them, no matter their level. Aggressive, territorial, and cruel, these monstrosities kill by crushing their foes or by injecting them with a deadly venom. Garox has evolved beyond the base form of the Naga, to its most common secondary evolution: Spirit Naga. It sacrifices sheer mass for proficiency in Mana Skills, among other changes.
Strength: More Data Required
Weakness: More Data Required

Bladeless? Pit asked. *He has two.*

Felix sent back the mental equivalent of a shrug.

"Mortals," he said, halting only ten feet away; close enough that Felix could reach him with the power he'd already demonstrated, but the Naga's weapons wouldn't reach Felix. Curious. "You are to come with me."

"Whoa, wait, why?" Evie asked. She at least had the grace to flush when Zara and Harn both turned frustrated glares on her.

"I have heard your reasons for coming here, and perhaps you speak the truth," Garox said with a calm, measured tone. He sounded nothing like Jadorak, though his face wasn't exactly Human. Enough serpent remained through his jaw and nose that it made more than a few in Felix's company nervous. "But that is not for me to decide. That is the sole domain of my Lord. I shall bring you to him, as guests, to offer you the chance to bow before the Deepking."

"The Fiend don't bow to no one!" someone shouted from behind, and was just as quickly silenced by a whipcrack of air Mana.

Garox looked among them. "The Fiend..." a tongue tested the air and it oriented on Felix. "This is you?"

"Yeah, that's me," Felix admitted. He realized that was the first time he'd ever done so. *How thrilling.* "This Deepking...he's Nagafolk, like you?"

"The Deepking is nothing like me," Garox said, and for the first time Felix felt something from his Spirit. It was pure, unadulterated devotion. It hit him with the same intensity as Jadorak's hate, unvarnished and raw. "He is above all but the Stone Gods themselves."

Felix desperately wanted to trade concerned glances with Zara, but instead held Garox's gaze. He nodded. "Then let us meet your Lord. I would...like to exchange greetings, for ah, intruding." With Vess so close— no matter how he shuttered his Affinity—he would have felt the wave of approval from her Spirit regardless.

"Very good," Garox said, and Felix got the distinct impression that this Spirit Naga would have dragged them to his king no matter their answer. "Fiend. Allow me to escort you to my Liege Lord. If you would all follow me."

The Naga slid over the water, rippling it but otherwise leaving its depths undisturbed. Felix frowned. "Garox, I will need to use magic to get my people across. Is this acceptable?"

Garox looked behind them at the ice bridge still visible. He nodded. "This is allowed. But have a care. I would not have you wake my brethren below."

They all looked down into the black depths, most of them nervously. Felix could distinguish large shapes he'd taken for fallen columns, many of them dozens of feet in length or more. A stressed, mad giggle tried to force its way out of him, but Felix shoved it down. "Of course," he said evenly.

This time, instead of spending a bunch of Mana on a massive pathway, Felix set to work fashioning a set of ships for him and his people. The Mana had barely unfurled from his channels when Zara placed a gentle hand on his wrist.

"What?" he asked.

"You do too much yourself," the Naiad murmured, low enough that few would hear.

"I can handle it. My Mana will regenerate before we get halfway across this chamber," Felix said.

"That's not the point, Felix. You devalue your people," she said. Her ice-blue eyes flicked back toward the company behind them. "If you do everything for them, then what are they to think of their purpose? Why should they grow strong, if you fight their battles for them?"

"What? I'm not, I'm just using my resources as wisely as I can," Felix protested.

"She is right," Vess said from his other side. She looked back at the Legion, Dawnguard, and Frost Giants, all of them watching Felix or the waters or Garox. "Leading is as much about delegation as it is taking responsibility for the welfare of others. They are your resources as well, and providing them a purpose, a task, especially in situations like this? It will hold them together."

"And hold them to you all the more," Zara said, flashing her sharp teeth.

Felix frowned. He could see the sense of it, had even been doing exactly that back in his Stronghold, if only because he literally *couldn't* do everything at once. Not that he hadn't wanted to..."Alright. Point taken. Battlelord Ari," he said.

"Yes, Autarch?"

"I will need your people's help," he said with a smile. The Battlelord's stoic expression never changed, but he nodded and listened as Felix described what he needed. All of them had the passive Mantle of the Long Night, as he once had, which could generate ice in a field around them, but that was entirely too broad for his current needs. However, over half also had access to some form of Rime Shaping. Together, they built a large barge out of shaped ice and some tangled roots Felix grew from the mossy walls. The roots sank through the ice, reinforcing what was basically a big, flat rectangle with a railing around it.

All in all, it took them perhaps five minutes of concerted effort to fashion the barge, likely double the time it would have taken Felix alone. Yet the jangling notes of pleasure and approval from the Frost Giant's Spirits were enough to convince him he had done the right thing. Moreover, Ari himself had shaped the hull, adding far more of a draft to it. When Felix had asked why the shape mattered, the Battlelord had only muttered, "Stability."

He had left it at that.

As his team climbed aboard, the whole thing bobbed a bit but was so wide it accepted their weight easily. When the giants climbed up, it sank considerably, as when Felix and Pit had boarded, but the deep draft kept it from sinking too far. It felt steady and solid as a rock. Felix met Ari's gaze and nodded. "Stability."

The barest flash of white shone through the Battlelord's blue lips, easily mistaken for a grimace, unless you could hear someone's Spirit. Satisfaction and approval thrummed across the giant's emotions...and not just the giant's. Vess and Zara looked on, their Spirits almost a match before the Naiad clamped control over hers.

Felix strode to the prow while the Frost Giants moved to the sides, oars of shaped ice in their hands. Yet, before they began to move forward, the water roiled before them. Two Naga rose from the depths, sending a spasm of fear through literally everyone. They were both giant serpents, though lesser in size than Jadorak. Garox gestured to them, a bit impatiently.

"These two will tow your vessel in our wake. Come." He turned and began winding across the chamber. "We will waste no more time."

Fashioning a set of vine ropes from the bare hints of plant matter in the ship, Felix handed them over to the Nagafolk, both of which took them gently in their mouths before swimming forward. With a lurch, they were off.

"Oh, shit," Felix said, turning. He anchored his feet, even forming a quick Rime Shaping to hold him to the barge.

Adamant Discord!

A flash of blue-white lightning surged across the chamber, hitting the far doors and pulling, hard. The barge and the Naga both jerked to a sudden, hissing halt. Felix flared his Skill and yanked the heavy, warded doors shut with a muffled boom. The wards flared blue, sealing shut automatically. The two Naga looked at him, irritation clear on their snake faces.

"Sorry. Left the front door open. We're good now."

Confusion and annoyance swirled on both of the serpents, but they cast it aside. If they happened to jerk them all a little harder than necessary in their rush to catch up to Garox, then Felix didn't blame them, though one of the legionnaires almost fell off.

"Can't have him touching that Gate," Felix muttered to the others.

"Wise," Atar said, eyeing the water and giant snakes. "I don't trust these things."

"They're big snake people," Evie said, leaning against the railing languidly. "What's not to trust?"

"Don't lean. Unless you want to fall in," Harn warned her. Evie stuck her tongue out at him, but she straightened up.

"So...we're going to meet a king," Alister said. "And none of us are dressed properly."

"A scandal," Evie said, lips quirking up. "We can never show our faces in snake society again."

Alister nodded sagely. "Mhm. Though, in all seriousness, do we know the protocol for meeting a Nagafolk king? I haven't even heard of their monster Type, let alone knew they had royalty."

Felix looked to his Chanter mentor. "Zara?"

She shook her head. "Little is known, other than they claim dominion over many of the deeper bodies of water in the Ghreldan Hills. I did not know their kind were so organized, however, nor their claim of royalty. I can only surmise that one of their kind evolved beyond all the others and took control of this Temple. It would certainly appear attractive as a den, especially to creatures that are not known for building anything for themselves."

"The Deepking is strong, at least stronger than Garox," Felix said, working out what they knew. "Some of those serpents down there are huge, but Garox was smaller. So perhaps this king will be smaller still, more Human?"

"I do not know the evolutionary stages for their Type, and based on Garox's reverence, this Deepking could very well be something far from the norm," Zara said.

"You think you could take 'em?" Evie asked. "If we have to?"

Felix considered a moment, running down the details he knew. He even threw a quick Voracious Eye at their escorts. They proved far weaker than Jadorak, leveled in the high one hundreds. "I think so. My concern is for everyone else."

"They'll be fine," Evie said, waving her hand casually. "Probably."

Vess snorted, then blushed. "Should conflict erupt, we shall prioritize keeping them from harm as long as we can, Felix. You and Zara are by far the strongest individuals here and are better spent focusing on the larger threats."

"Hm," Harn grunted in agreement.

They were led through chamber after chamber, all huge, all twisted and broken as if they had fallen a great distance. Yet, somehow, they endured as whole structures and even exuded a palpable sense of power. Zara commented she could feel the water now, all around them. They had to be several hundred feet below the surface. That made Atar very uncomfortable, but no one was happy about it. Pit least of all. The poor tenku's wings were sagging the longer they remained in the sunken ruins, and there was a steady thread of *yuck, too much water, too wet, too low* from him. Felix extended what comfort he could, if only emotionally.

In each chamber they traversed, Felix could sense more of the Naga. Many were resting on ledges, and more still were below the waters, coiled in great piles of scales and fangs. A nightmare, but one that was quiescent at the moment. He hoped. Felix couldn't feel much from the sleeping Naga, though the ones pulling him were clear as day, their Spirits unguarded and remarkably uncomplicated. Flitting emotions of pride and irritation, mild discomfort, even a thinly veiled hunger sparked when one of them caught sight of Felix's company.

Garox was different. From him came nothing but a calm certainty, his Spirit a placid well of tranquility so utterly unlike the naked hostility of Jadorak that it was like Garox was an entirely different species.

I suppose he is. A Spirit Naga, whatever that might mean.

While his allies spoke quietly among themselves, Felix made a point to study the Nagafolk. How they moved, their bodies, everything he could glean. According to the feel of his Voracious Eye, most they encountered hovered around Tier II, but there were still many, Garox included, who were Tier III. Tier III was the equivalent of a Journeymen combatant, and probably on the stronger side, too. Monsters usually were, according to everyone he'd ever met. They also seemed as agile as their Lore suggested, but their scales weren't as dense on their bellies. If they were to fight, he surmised that he could conjure ice spikes up into their undersides, putting them out of commission in rapid order.

Yet again, Garox was another thing entirely. He may have only been Tier III—and that made him a match for most of his company—but he wasn't just a serpent. With humanoid arms and the weapons sheathed at his waist, he had all the deadly grace of the serpent-form Nagas but with the added versatility of a bipedal warrior. He would require a substantial investment of power to defeat. Felix, Zara, or even Darius maybe could manage it without much issue, but it'd take them from the fight of the literal hundreds around them.

No. Fighting wasn't the way he wanted to get out of the sunken Temple. He could only hope the Deepking actually wanted to talk, and this wasn't a drawn-out ruse to eat them.

At the end of a long, winding passage, they reached a wide set of doors made of an ivory material. Eyeing it, Felix was surprised to find it was bone made far more crudely than anything else they had seen. Garox moved in front of it, still atop the water, and traced his long-fingered hands across its surface. Sigils ignited sepia and dark blue in an array that lifted the bone door straight up into the ceiling, revealing a relatively small chamber fronted by another bone door. Garox gestured for them to follow, and they crammed themselves into it. Once inside, the rear doors closed again and sealed.

"This is...unnerving," Alister said.

"Those sigils are just a sealing ward to prevent entry or exit," Atar said. "But why have us all in here?"

At the far end, the bone doors flashed with light and slid upward, and suddenly the water roared and the barge bucked upward. Everything began moving far faster, and Felix had to clench onto the ice railing to keep his footing. They drifted forward, faster and faster, until they hit the point where the doors had been...and the roaring and drop was made clear.

Below, the river-like passage turned into a spiraling set of cascading rapids, set with fallen stones and roaring spray.

"Brace!" Harn and Darius shouted at once, and the barge dropped into the chaos.

CHAPTER THIRTY-FOUR

The water thundered around them like a windless hurricane, a growl so immediate that it shook Felix's guts while the fall sent them fleeing into his chest cavity. White waters surged all around them as they descended at an insane speed, the ice barge ill-suited to such exploits and smashing into every outcropping and bit of fallen masonry that littered the spiraling river. A river that bore a clear resemblance to an expansive set of stairs.

Men and women screamed as the barge slammed and bucked down the sluiceway, a gauntlet of shattered stone and severed, upthrust statuary. Hands half the size of their ship rose before them, splitting the white, rushing water, and Felix bellowed.

Adamant Discord!

The entire ship lurched to the left, slamming into a metal railing along the edge and missing the ramrod columns of stone by mere inches. Yet the lightning had barely faded when the barge hit a water-smoothed outcropping, lifting the left-most third of the ship into the air.

No!

People flew from the barge, armored bodies careening into one another like pinballs, and Felix's stomach dropped. His feet were still iced to the craft, so he plummeted with it as legionnaires, Dawnguard, and several Risi were thrown free.

Shadow Whip!

"Bindings of the White Waste!"

"Pillars of the Domineering Sentinel!"

"Spear of Tribulation!"

Powers sped outward, chains of ice and pillars of force and spears of solidified air and metal. All of them snagged or dragged falling folk from the air or waters, hauling them back aboard while Vess' Spears formed a shifting wall to keep more from falling out. Even Pit flew up, snagging falling soldiers by their cloaks and armor. Felix's Shadow Whip snagged eight people in every direction, and a simple flex of his arm brought them all crashing back to the barge's icy deck.

"On your feet! I'm locking you all in!" Felix shouted as they navigated a swirl of stones. "Now!"

Rime Shaping!

As he had done to himself, Felix sent ice Mana surging up from beneath everyone's feet, locking them to the deck from their knees downward. He hoped it wouldn't hurt them too much, but Felix had no desire to pluck his company out of the water after every jostling wave...because there were plenty more to come.

Water and stone, foam and spray, the careening tide was chaos incarnate. The Frost Giants used their ice oars to shove them away from some of the rocks and statues, though more than a few oars splintered or shattered completely under the strain. Even the Dawnguard had their hooked polearms out, eager to prevent the barge's capsizing.

Felix sent lightning skittering across the waters more than once, pushing and pulling at the forces around them in a desperate bid for control. The stone was too enchanted for him to shape, and the water too bountiful to freeze. Anything he managed would have been flooded by the deluge coming from above. In fact, Felix caught several glimpses of glyphs deep beneath the water, though it was too fast and too hectic to tell their meaning. He tried to sunder them, but something about the array protected itself, and they were moving too quickly for him to hit the same spot repeatedly.

All they could do was hold on.

"Hold low!" Harn shouted, followed by Darius' voice.

"Brace!"

They hit another statue, this one on its side and serving as a ramp that sent their craft sailing thirty feet. Zara sang a dark melody, and Felix could almost hear the crash of cymbals above the roaring waters. A wave of aquamarine Mana surged up from below, catching their barge in its confines and lowering them back into the rapids. The Mana wrapped around the hull, tinging the purple-white ice Mana with its touch but cushioning every rock and wave that tried to flip or crush them to smithereens.

"Thanks," Felix said over the noise. Zara's ochre skin had paled to a startling degree, but her nod was loose and easy, as if she felt none of the strain holding their entire ship. He doubted that. "That can't be easy. You okay?"

"Fine, Felix," she nodded ahead, sharply. "But that will prove a challenge."

They were nearly to the bottom now, but where the path had been zig-zagged with fallen debris, now it was positively choked. It looked like an entire wall had been dropped onto this former stairwell, and only a few, relatively small cracks broke its bulk. Felix's eyes caught the flash of deep green scales as their Naga helpers slipped through the obstruction with ease. He growled deep in his chest.

"That's definitely gonna be a problem!" Evie shouted.

"We won't fit! We're too wide by half!" Atar's blonde curls were flat against his forehead, as waterlogged as his battlerobes. "We need to abandon ship!"

"No!" Felix shouted back at them. "I got this!"

With a flex of his Will and Mana, the ice around his legs vanished, and Felix leaped forward off the barge's railing, shattering it and sending the entire craft skidding backward a whole foot.

Adamant Discord!

Lightning cracked the air, and Felix pulled himself along a line toward the disappeared Nagafolk. The obstruction, of course, was in his way, and he hit that instead, quickly slamming his fists straight through its surface. Felix had a brief, insane urge to try and smash his way through, but a better plan was to hand.

Chthonic Tribute!

The slab resisted for the briefest of moments, as if the Tier of stone was enough to anchor it, but it could not fight Felix's Willpower and Intent. With a hissing implosion, the entire contiguous surface of the obstruction turned to blackened smoke filled with dusty-brown glimmers of light. Still crackling with lightning, Felix hovered for a brief moment, buoyed by Adamant Discord but also the influx of Essence before he dropped—

Right back into the barge as it sped beneath him.

Felix straightened to find dozens of eyes on him, nearly all of them some variation of awed, impressed, or relieved. All except one. Zara was an unreadable statue, Spirit and face both harder stone than the one he'd just eaten.

What's going on with you?

The barge cleared the final span of rushing water, now flowing in *far* greater quantities than before. The stone wall had acted as a dam of sorts, keeping the water within the staircase and circulating with those glyphs he'd spotted, but now all of it dumped out into the next chamber. They splashed down into a swirling pool at the base of the stair rapids. The barge bobbed once, sloshing dark, foul water onto the deck, before righting itself into a lazy, sideways drift. A metal hand clanged into Felix's back, patting him firmly.

"Well done, kid," Harn grunted. He grinned. "Snakes'll be right confused about their little slide bein' ruined, though. Spoilin' for a fight about it, maybe."

Felix glanced back and snorted. The staircase had all but dried up, with only a few weak streams still pouring down the algae-slicked steps.

"Let's go find this Deepking," he said, his anger on a low simmer. "I'm in a bad mood. I could use a fight."

———

"Loquis, did you see that?" Pava asked, nudging the Half-Orc man in the ribs. "Can *your* lightning do that?"

"I don't think that was the lightning, Pava," the Half-Orc said, somewhat sourly as he rubbed his ribs. The woman had notoriously sharp elbows. "That was something else."

Like everyone around him, Loquis watched as the Fiend—*Lord Autarch*, he reminded himself—talked with members of his team. The others pretended not to, feigning interest in the ice barge the Lord and giants had made, or in the dark waters around them, but Loquis saw no need to hide it. He was fascinated by them all.

The fierce and beautiful Lady Dayne, whose spears had saved many of his friends' lives, just now on the rapids and previously in Haarwatch. The stoic Onslaught, whose reputation among the Guilders was enough for even the most grizzled veteran to give him nods of respect. The mages V'as and Knacht, scorching flame and shattering force, mighty and far more clever than Loquis could ever hope to claim. Loquis was told that they enchanted the weapons the legionnaires all bore and the powerful armor that was provided to them. Not to mention the mysterious Lady Cyrene, a *Master* Tier and personal mentor to the Lord Autarch.

But what kept his eye was the beautiful and deadly Evie Aren. She was laughing at something Lady Dayne told her, showing perfect teeth in a wicked grin. A grin that reminded him of their fight a day ago, of the...respect in her eyes.

"She moved like quicksilver to catch us," Pava said, clearly following his gaze. "Well, me and Nell. Didn't Lord Knacht get you?"

Loquis grimaced, thoughts flashing back to the crunching impact of a pillar of blue force arresting his fall—before tossing him back onto the ice barge. "He did. Dented my battlerobes, too."

"Tch. Just a side panel. You can have the Forgemaster there fix it, no?" Pava said with a shrug. The sword belted at her waist bobbed with the movement.

Loquis laughed, low and mirthlessly. "You suggest I go to Onslaught himself and ask him to repair my equipment?"

"Yeah. Isn't that, like, his thing now? Mervin says he's nice enough."

The Half-Orc stared at Pava, her skin so similar to his, though she was brown to his green. *Skin and bone, just as me, but more different than I can imagine.* "No. I'll not be doing that. The Autarch's team has better things to worry about than me."

Pava shrugged again, as if dismissing the matter entirely, and went back to inspecting her sword. The Blades made it a point to keep their weapons in perfect condition at all times, and sometimes it seemed to border on the edge of obsession. Surely, a piece of metal was meaningless in the greater scheme of things. It wasn't like it was *magic*, after all.

Magic had been Loquis' ticket out of the Dust, just as it had for many others in the Arclight Legion. After the Battle of Haarwatch and the fall of the Eyrie, he'd lost almost everything. Then he saw it; lightning coursing across the sky, shattering rank after rank of hideous monsters. And in the center of it, *him*.

The Fiend.

He was an enigma to all of them, having swept into their lives without warning just as the world turned to shit. Saved them, one and all. Everyone in the Legion had a similar story, of the Fiend dropping from the sky to kill Prismatic Wretches only seconds before they were devoured. Or of him leading his team against wave after wave of Revenants. Or pulling folks from the wreckage of their homes. Time and again, the Fiend was at the center of it all, a powerful figure that...helped. From what Loquis could tell, the man never even expected anything in return. How could he? What could a skinny Half-Orc offer a man even a third as strong as the Fiend?

Then the Legion was announced, in whispers at first. But it had no place for the magic that stirred in his core, the lightning that had so inspired him, not until the First of Arclight had begun recruiting. Loquis joined up immediately. And now he was here, in the midst of an adventure with his heroes.

He hoped he wouldn't screw it all up.

———

Exploration is level 63!

After the wild ride on the stairs, the grand hall they entered seemed almost pedestrian, despite the ninety-foot ceilings studded with pale purple Belais Crystals. Or the massive, stone reliefs carved into the curving walls. The chamber was bigger than the one they had faced Jadorak within, enough so that Felix couldn't make out the far end. A mist rose from the black water, something he mistook for fog before realizing that it was most definitely steam.

When had the water gotten so warm?

After a while, it actually took a fair bit of concentration to keep the ice barge from melting, though he had the good idea to ask the Frost Giants for aid. Their Mantles of the Long Night were more than enough to combat the water's rising temperature and maintain the ship's general shape.

The walls grew closer, the stone reliefs revealing a detailed story, though it was infested with hanging moss and lichen. The carvings depicted ancient peoples of various Races with their hands raised and long tables of food between them. A celebration, he had to assume, right next to the image of those same people raising tall, thin towers around the shores of various lakes. On *top* of lakes, even. And among them all, Felix spotted the robed-and-armored form of the Nym. Stars in hand, they

were casting some sort of benediction on all of the workers and cele-
brants, depicted as beams of light.

It told a far different story than the last Temple he'd been within, but
much of this was hidden by fog, moss, or damage. This Temple had not
fared well with the passing of the Ages.

As they drifted forward, pushed by ice oar and the occasional Shadow
Whip tether onto protruding columns, Felix also searched the waters and
steam-fog for the Nagafolk. He couldn't sense them, not like he could in
the colder waters up above, but he sensed something shifting in the water.
Far, far below. Something enormous.

And below that was something else. Something he'd seen once before.

"You have arrived," Garox said in his sharp accent, as if he were
biting off the words as he said them. "The First Challenge has been
overcome."

"Challenge?" Evie asked, before Vess could stop her. "You're sayin' you
normally throw guests down a gauntlet before smashin' 'em into a rock?"

"It is as it was decreed," Garox said, his voice as emotionless as his
snake-face. "I am pleased that you have succeeded."

"You said First Challenge," Felix pointed out. "There are more?"

"That remains to be seen," rumbled another voice, this one so deep it
sent waves trembling across the waters. Following it came slithering foam
and spray as a gargantuan Naga emerged from the black waters. It was at
least sixty feet in diameter, and the portion that rose above the waves was
a hundred feet long if it was an inch. Moreover, the Naga's immense head
was bigger than both of Zara's Manaships put together. It was covered in
smooth scales colored a deep, waterlogged green, with eyes the size of
their entire barge and just as icy in their burnished regard. They burned
with light, a hum of power Felix could feel without trying, and the copper
in them flashed as it regarded them all.

"Fiend, you are blessed by the Stone and Wave, for before you is the
Deepking, Kar'casitrix of the Abyssal Shores," Garox intoned, his calm
voice once again infused with that zealous fervor. "My Lord, might I
introduce the Fiend and his companions."

Voracious Eye.

Name: Kar'casitrix, the Deepking
Type: Abyssal Serpent
Level: 845
HP: 42399/42399
SP: 28487/30233
MP: 9735/9735
Lore: Abyssal Serpents are an advanced evolution of the Naga,
though their exact nature is not well known. What is known,
however, is that an Abyssal Serpent is a catastrophe when
roused.
Strength: More Data Required

Weakness: More Data Required

Holy shit. His Voracious Eye could easily feel the strength of the huge serpent, and it was beyond any creature he'd encountered outside of Primordials and gods. It shook him, more than a little. Felix had grown used to the idea, if only a bit, that he was stronger than anything he'd encountered. Zara was a poor example, weak as she had been feeling, but it had bolstered his confidence in a way he hadn't truly noticed. Now, faced with the Deepking's power, Felix could only clench his jaw and nod to it, attempting to calm his wildly beating heart.

The Deepking returned the nod with narrowed eyes, in almost the exact same manner. The slightest of tilts, eyes never leaving the other; the greeting of two equals, as Karys had coached him. It was a bit of rebellion on Felix's part, and the Abyssal Serpent knew it.

"Why have you come to my realm, Fiend?" the Deepking asked in a voice like rasping boulders. It was not the voice of a human throat or anything approaching it. Felix sensed several of the Legion sway on their feet. "Why do you trespass here?"

"We are passing through, and only stopped here on our way south," Felix said.

"Passing through," the king rumbled. "Beneath the Haestus Lake? So deep that creatures greater than Garox would have long since hunted you for their dinner?"

"We got lost."

The Deepking blinked once before his copper eyes flashed again. "What chamber did they enter from, Garox?"

"From the sealed one, off the Chapel of the Eye, my Lord."

"Sealed. But no longer," the Deepking rumbled thoughtfully. "Fiend, what lies within that chamber? How did you reach my Temple?"

"That is Nym business," he said. Beside him, Zara and Vess tensed, but that was peanuts compared to the Deepking's reaction.

"Nym!" The shout sent eight-foot waves out from its huge body. "What claim do you have on the business of gods, little Fiend?"

Felix felt a flutter of nerves in his stomach, but forged ahead. "*I* am Nymean."

Silence met his words, one populated by a palpable, murderous Intent. "You lie."

"Why would I bother?" Felix asked, shoving aside his fears and worries. The Abyssal Serpent loomed over them, lower than before, and it would only take a single snap of his jaws to consume them entirely. "I am Nymean, and I plan to claim this Temple."

"Oh shit," Evie said from behind.

"Felix," Zara warned.

The silence stretched only a moment longer before a cataclysmic, earth-shaking tsunami burst into life around them. The air quivered, screamed with vibrations so loud they weren't sounds anymore, just a buzzing against flesh. His people screeched in pain, and Felix winced as he held tight to the railing, riding through the immense waves.

The Deepking was laughing.

"Brave! You are brave, little Fiend! I wish my warriors were half so bold." The Deepking pulled its head back, lifting it from their barge and damn near touching the ceiling. "I shall discard the standard Challenges for this. If you wish to claim Divinity, very well. Prove yourself, little Fiend."

"What do you propose?" Felix asked.

The Deepking smiled, an expression Felix didn't realize snakes could manage. "There is a great danger below us. One that even I cannot face. If you are truly a Nym, a god given flesh, then prove it. Destroy that which lies beneath, or else perish by its jaws...or ours."

CHAPTER THIRTY-FIVE

Below, huh?

Felix looked over the railing of the barge and into the black, steaming water. It was so opaque he couldn't see further than twenty or thirty feet. But, just as before, Felix felt the thick coils of the Deepking and something else at the very bottom of the chamber. If it was what he thought it was, then Felix knew exactly what the crafty snake wanted them to do.

The Abyssal Serpent rumbled, contemplative. "Do you hesitate? Wish to recant, little Fiend?"

"You want us to face what's in the Manawell, right?" he asked.

The Deepking's eyes widened. "Mana...well? Ah, is that its name? Curious. Yes, that is your Challenge. I shall part the waters and open the way below, letting you pass into this well. Eliminate this threat to my realm, and you will have proven your strength and power."

"Couldn't I just show you my Race in my Status screen?" Felix asked, thinking on the Amulet of Veiling around his neck. While his Race said Primordial now, the Chanter amulet could make it seem to say Nym. Yet the Deepking only growled.

"There are ways to twist the eye, Skills that would hide the truth from us. A show of strength is the only way." Felix tried not to let the scowl of annoyance show on his face as the serpent rumbled on. "If you are what you say you are, little Fiend, then it shall not be difficult for you in any case, hm?" The Deepking let out another laugh, this like an avalanche of shale.

"A show of strength. Right." Felix gripped his Inheritor's Will. "Karys?"

The sword buzzed to life, exuding a breath of green-gold Mana vapor. "My Lord?"

"I'm in this Temple's containment chamber. Gonna need access to the Manawell. Can you help?"

The voice of his Chancellor hesitated. "My influence is less comprehensive at such a distance, but I can assist in the initial connection. You will have to negotiate—"

"Yeah, I get it," Felix said. "Do it."

Pit warbled a note of interest as he ambled to the front of the barge. Felix spared him a quick glance.

Danger. I smell it. Urges?

"I uh, I'm not really sure. It feels weaker, but..." Felix looked to Zara and the others. "I need all of you to stay still and do not engage. Alright?"

"What are you—?" Zara tried to ask, but the giant snake king boomed over her.

"They are not allowed to interfere in the Challenge. This is for you alone, little Fiend." The Deepking tilted his huge head at them all. "What are you doing? I sense a power among you...bright and fecund. It is...no. Stop your servant! What you try is not to be done! I shall open the waters, let you within—"

"Let me?" Felix furrowed his brows, feeling Kary's power catch on something. "You want proof of my strength? Fine." He pressed his senses downward, toward the object below, and found Karys' presence holding the tattered edge of a long-worn inscription. Silently, it was pressed into Felix's grasp, and he secured it with a layering of his own Intent and iron Will. A trilling sound brought a blue window flashed into being before him.

Welcome Inheritor.
Internal And External Containment Breach Detected
Do You Wish To Access Containment Unit #609?

"Here's your proof," he said. "Yes. Access Containment Unit."

"No! Not all the way!" the Deepking roared. "You fool!"

The opening to the Manawell below them was all but identical to the one in the Waterfall Temple, and it *shattered* as a darkness flooded into the waters. The Deepking roared, thrashing his insanely huge body and sending the barge bucking high atop twenty-foot waves. Shouts among his company had them brace, hanging tight to railings and bindings of ice. Yet, if the Deepking's response was violent, it was not nearly as frenetic as his Naga servants. The smaller—but still huge—serpents bellowed into the hot air and dove into the black waters in violent tangles.

Something met them. Felix could feel it like the light of the rising sun until it filled everything below them with the acid-bright sensation of blood and rot. Massive hands composed of a thousand tiny bones thrust upward, catching the Nagafolk like they were worms on a hook before pulling them down. They vanished into the storming waters.

"Felix, what did you do?" Vess cried. "A presence...there is a creature below us, and it..." She screamed and fell to her knees as the barge was thrown atop another wave. "It *hates*."

Evie and Zara were also twisting in obvious pain, even Atar to an extent. The rest looked pale, as if someone had dragged a dagger across their soul.

"It's comin'," Harn said, his voice thinner than Felix had ever heard it. "Whatever you're plannin', do it now, kid."

Rising from the black waters came a figure, a small mountain to rival the Deepking himself. It was made of putrefied bones, hundreds, thousands of them all stacked and lashed together by cords of rotting flesh. It rose, black water pouring from its abscesses like cataracts, split by a hundred jagged ribs and three twisting columns of vertebra. Its back was hunched and spread over with paper-thin skin, the full bodies of a hundred different Races stacked atop one another, all of them interwoven by spikes of rusted metal.

It was a horror. Literally.

Name: Shambling Horror
Type: Spirit (Necromantic)
Level: 924
HP: 87258/108932
SP: N/A
MP: 32400/93452
Lore: A denizen of battlefields, a Shambling Horror is thought to form when the deaths of war pile high enough to choke even the greatest of funeral pyres. Spirits of necromantic death seek out these corpses, weaving them together to form bodies of ever-mounting rot. The greatest of these scavenger spirits will form into a Shambling Horror, a monstrosity that will not die so long as a single piece of it still remains whole.
Strength: More Data Required
Weakness: More Data Required

Felix swallowed, feeling the pressure on him from just its presence. The giants and legionnaires had fallen to the deck, overwhelmed by its savage Spirit, and the Henaari were barely braced against the railings. Felix's Eye felt its power and something of its advancement: it laid comfortably beyond any Master Tier he'd ever faced.

And yet...there was a brittleness to it. A hollow of empty bellies and dusty tombs. Felix shook off the images that assaulted his Mind, just in time to get hit in the face with the Horror's vile voice.

<<FREE. TRULY FREE AFTER SO LONG!>>

Its voice was the voice of thousands, man, woman, and child all overlapping and screaming. A skull fashioned of some great beast pushed free of its rotting hunch, and its eyes were pits of black-green radiance that oozed as if more oil than light. Its broken jaw hung open and gaping, fangs the size of swords gleaming with ancient ichor and dripping water.

<<WHO HAS DONE THIS? YOU!>> It snarled at the Deepking, and its immense bulk shifted toward the great serpent. **<<YOU, WHO FED US BY DRIPS AND DRABS FOR HUNDREDS OF YEARS. WHO STRENGTHENED US AFTER AGES OF WASTING. YOU ARE TO BE COMMENDED, FLESH SLAVE!>>**

"You dare speak to the King of the Deep in such a way!" Garox bellowed, and ten more Nagafolk emerged from the steaming depths. They were covered in burns, but they bared their fangs without hesitation. "You will die for the affront!"

The Naga rushed the Shambling Horror, Garox at their fore. They surged over the waves, cutting through them at one point, all deadly fang and unsheathed scimitars. The Horror thrust one of its limbs forward, and blackened green light flowed down...into the water. Bone claws the size of passenger jets ripped from the deep, clasping savagely around four of the advancing Naga and tearing them asunder.

"Noctis' tits," Evie whispered as the fight raged on. She balanced atop the rocking barge with ease, but her face was tinged green at the sight of the Horror. "That is..."

"The biggest undead I have ever seen," Atar finished. "It was held here?"

"Do-do we attack?" A legionnaire asked. She held her sword, still sheathed, in a white-knuckled grip.

"No, this is for the Autarch alone," Zara commanded. "Everyone else, hold tight to the barge, and we shall protect you."

The others rushed to obey, even the recalcitrant Frost Giants bowed their heads to the Sorcerer's words. Harn, meanwhile, looked at Felix with a question in his gaze. "What do we do, kid?"

"I need—" Felix started, but was interrupted by another titanic wave, and the guttural cry of the Abyssal Serpent. The Horror had killed another clutch of Naga, and the Deepking howled.

<<DID YOU THINK THESE PATHETIC CREATURES WERE ENOUGH? WE ARE THE DEAD OF COUNTLESS WARS, OF STRIFE YOUR PEOPLE HAVE NEVER BEFORE SEEN!>> It lifted two Naga corpses and fed them into opening, skeletal jaws all over its Body. Flesh and scales were rendered to crimson mush as it fed and the Deepking growled in outrage again. **<<WE HAVE BEEN HELD TOO LONG AND REQUIRE...SUSTENANCE.>>**

The Shambling Horror lunged for the Deepking just as the Abyssal Serpent dove to strike, his wide maw at least big enough to clamp around the Horror's chest. Their blows cracked against one another, sending each other sprawling–the Horror into the water and the Deepking crashing into the marred walls behind him.

<<WEAK. WEAK WEAK WEAK,>> the Horror chanted, its rippling Spirit filled with frustration and rage. It didn't seem harmed by the Deepking's bite, but it was staggered. **<<KEPT IN A CAGE, LEFT TO ROT. NO DEATH, NO LIFE, ONLY INTERMINABLE SILENCE.>>**

"A silence to which you will return, vile creature!" Garox howled, slashing forth with his twin scimitars. They flashed as they struck, spikes of ice erupted from the Horror's bones where they were struck. The Horror flinched back, looking harmed for the first time, but raged all the more.

<<NEVER TO RETURN! WE HAVE SUNDERED THAT WHICH LIES BELOW! WE ARE FREE!>> The Horror spun, ignoring the Spirit Naga and advancing on the Deepking in a wave. **<<NO GODS. NO NYM. WE ARE WITHOUT EQUAL!>>**

Just as the Horror closed, the Deepking struck, his huge head bashing into the Horror's labyrinth of rib cages. Bones snapped like gunshots, but the Horror's multitudinous claws found purchase on the serpent's back, digging deep trenches as they grappled. A third arm lifted from its hunched back, formed of reshaped bone and ligaments, rearing as if to strike as a scorpion stings. It thrust...and was held fast.

<<WHAT? WHO DARES?>>

Black strands of shadow Mana clung tightly to its bone-forged limb, and the Horror's monstrous skull turned to follow them to their origin.

"Unf, hi there," Felix grunted, holding onto his Shadow Whips with both hands. "As much as I'd like to see the...Deepking there...kick your ass." Felix shifted his grip, moving the strands of shadow into one hand. With his other, he traced a series of sigils in red-gold flame. "You're...kinda my fault and test at the same time."

Cardinal Flame!

The Horror all but froze, its entire Body seized by coursing, red-gold flames. It twitched, trembling with rage.

Felix let go of the Shadow Whips with a sigh and rose on a crackling column of blue-white lightning. Mana poured from his channels, red-gold traceries that clung to the Horror like napalm, dropping his resource pool faster than his regeneration could fill it. The monster was *strong*, taking everything Felix had to hold it in place, inches from tearing into the Deepking's throat.

<<WHO?>> it cried, trembling with everything it had to throw off Felix's dominance. **<<WHO ARE YOU?>>**

"Just a...good Samaritan," Felix grunted. Red-gold flame ignited, limning Felix's form between the bursts of electricity, and he could feel his eyes *burn*. He unsheathed his crooked sword and pointed it at the Horror's chest. The Horror's oily gaze widened, the green fading to a desolate black, and Felix felt its rampaging Spirit convulse. With fear.

<<INHERITOR! NYM!>>

The shout caused the surviving Naga to reel backward, and some of his own people to collapse, but Felix shrugged it off with a minor effort of Will. It truly had been weakened by its long imprisonment, and the force of the Horror's Spirit was dropping by the second, which was great news for his own plan. He was getting low on Mana, fast.

<<YOU CANNOT IMPRISON US! THE WELL IS SHAT-TERED,>> the Horror said with a dark chuckle. The fear masked itself with more anger and now malicious glee. **<<THERE IS NOTHING YOUR KIND CAN DO. YOU CANNOT KILL US! NONE OF THEM EVER COULD! WE ARE ETERNAL AND UNDYING!>>**

"You were," Felix said, just as Pit vanished in a flash of light that rocked the barge below. "Now, you're *mine*."

<<NO!>>

Chthonic Tribute!

Will to Will, Felix fought for only a moment. The Shambling Horror was strong, and perhaps in its prime, it would have destroyed Felix, but that time was long past. Now it was barely holding itself together after years of confinement. The Cardinal Flame ate at its corpse bones, ripping them to charred dust as the rest burst into black smoke. Lights of a thousand hues flashed and pulsed within that column of dark smog, all of it sucked into Felix's channels over the span of thirty seconds.

Nothing remained.

Cardinal Flame is level 80!

Felix dropped back onto the barge, his Body cracking the ice so badly he was forced to spend more of his Mana to patch it, which made his Spirit and head ache all the more. The barge bucked again, and this time it was due to the black water that swirled around them all. Groans from the stone and gurgling roars could be heard, deep below the surface where the Mana well now stood open...and empty.

"The water is draining into the well," Felix said.

Their barge picked up speed, now racing around the massive, cavernous chamber at breakneck speeds. A whirlpool formed within the center of it all, right above the mouth of the Manawell and the water level in the chamber began to drop. Significantly so as more drained into the well than the cascading staircases could replenish.

"Zara?" Felix asked over the roar. "Can you stop this?"

The Naiad was already watching the water and lifted her left hand. Blue-green light flowed from her, arcing out into the dark whirlpool and down. Felix could feel it drop away from them, a mote of power as strong as many of his own Skills. Then it vanished, like a popped bubble. Zara's face contorted, her brow furrowing as a sharp cadence sang out into the air. It was too much, too fast for Felix to follow, but he certainly felt the shift below them. A booming reverberation through the Mana of water and air, then the whirlpool abruptly dissipated.

Zara hissed, holding her hand as if she'd cut herself, but stood up without aid as the barge spun the last few times around the chamber.

"Thank you," he said to the Naiad, and she gave him a nod in return. "Did you close the opening somehow?"

"I forged a plug of woven water, imbued with enough of my power to sustain it a very long time," she said, now flexing her hand. It looked whole and healthy.

Felix eyed the chamber, the steam-fog all the worse since the Horror's defeat. "That sounds complicated."

"It is. And I...appreciate that you know that," she said. "I'd advise you shape a stone lid over it before long, just to be safe."

"That's a good...idea...."

He trailed off, just as the gargantuan form of Kar'casitrix rose once again from the waters all about them. His huge head tilted, regarding their tiny vessel as it lazily drifted in the dissipating currents, and his copper eyes flashed with an emotion Felix had trouble parsing. More Naga rose from the depths—ten, fifteen, fifty, more, until Felix couldn't look anywhere but see one of the enormous snakes. Their colors ranged between deep sea-green, warm brown, and deepest blue decorated them all. Their scales glimmered in the light of the Belais Crystals so far above their heads. Even farther, now that the water had dropped.

Felix felt tiny before the Deepking's regard, though he tried not to let it show. The man squared his shoulders and faced the Abyssal Serpent, noticing for the first time several oozing wounds on the great beast. *No wonder he's pissed. The real question is, did I pass their dumb test? I—*

Without warning, the Deepking...bowed.

And every single Naga followed suit.

"You have proven who you are—*what* you are, and the strength you possess," the Deepking shuddered. "It is mighty. Forgive this one for failing to recognize you, my Lord."

The bow deepened, until the Abyssal Serpent was just below eye level with Felix. His enormous, wedge-shaped head tilted sideways so that their eyes could better meet, though the king's were staring at Felix's feet.

"We acknowledge and surrender to your strength, God of Thunder and Flame. We are yours, bound by Oath and Power. Upon our honor shall we serve, or else upon our honor shall we die." The Deepking's rockslide voice shook the chamber as his copper eyes gleamed with an intense fervor. "This I swear! We shall henceforth serve the Returned God, in all things!"

"In all things!" came the echoed shout from every single Nagafolk present.

"Ah," Felix began to say, more than a little uncomfortable with the god bit. But Zara gave him a sharp look that stopped the words before they could form. Clenching his jaw instead, Felix only nodded. "Sure. That'll do."

Congratulations, Autarch!
You Have Vanquished A Threat!

The Nagafolk (Cold Depths Tribe) Have Joined Your Fledgling Nation!
+25% To All Positive Relations With Nagafolk!

Authority Recognized, Inheritor!
For Defeating A Territorial Threat And Peacefully Subduing The Local Inhabitants
You May Lay Claim To The Haestus Temple!
Do You Wish To Increase Your Authority?
Y/N

Yeah, Felix thought at the System. *Yeah I do.*

CHAPTER THIRTY-SIX

Congratulations!
You Have Extended Your Authority, Autarch!

The notifications trilled at him pleasantly, and Felix felt a weight settle atop his shoulders. It was there only an instant before vanishing, but in that instant, all of him was pressed to its very limit. Mind, Body, and Spirit screamed in pain and subsequent relief, as if he had condensed a week of extreme physical exertion into a single moment. He fought to stay standing, and even the ice beneath him splintered from the metaphysical burden.

Authority...A mountain that will crush us, he thought as he flexed his legs and locked his knees. It was all that kept him standing. *Yet I can't get out from under it, can I?*

A burning hiss drew his attention inward, toward the Essence that roiled within him. The Necromantic Spirit had been a vile thing, as bad as the Urges in its own way, but it had been reduced to its quintessential parts and made...not safe, exactly. Digestible. Essence, motes of Memories, and the shimmering song of more danced in the swirling cloud among his Divine Vein—or Divine Tree, he supposed.

A heaviness sat among those branches, pulling them ever so slightly downward, settling the Tree further into Felix's dual cores far below. *Significance,* he recognized. *The weight of...what?*

Significance was explained to him as a solidity in the core, where everything was firmer and more potent. The why of it had not yet been explained to him, though he planned to change that soon. If Zara would actually tell him the entire truth, for once.

Felix put that thought out of his mind, focusing instead on the prompts that spread around him. The threads of the System wove wide, interfacing with each of the beings in the vast chamber and beyond. A cursory tracing of it suggested it was going out to everyone in the Temple.

The Haestus Temple Has Been Claimed!

His Inheritor's Will flashed, the first and second glyphs on the blade pulsing in time with the faint melody of the notification. Each time his Authority increased by virtue of being the Inheritor, the sword had pulsed. Now it practically strobed with a worrisome insistence.

"Karys?"

"I am unsure, Felix. Perhaps—ah, there we are." A coil of green-gold Mana vapor spun and pointed directly upward, to where a cluster of faintly glimmering crystals hung from the ceiling. Stalactites made of precious minerals. "Belais Crystals, and in the center is the Control Node. The Inheritor's Will is acting as a conduit for the System's re-integration of this Temple. Like all the rest, it was Lost and cut off, but you can change that. Simply thrust the Inheritor's Will into that formation, and the rest of the process should complete itself."

"Why? Nagast didn't work like this," Felix pointed out. "The sword didn't even come into play there."

"The Waterfall Temple was in far better condition than Haestus," Karys said. "I can practically feel the mold all around you. It is quite unpleasant."

"Fair." He eyed the distance. "I think I can make it."

"Make it?"

No sooner had the words echoed from the blade than Felix hurled it straight up. Karys' scream in surprise was cut short as the blade hilted itself between two large growths of crystal.

Around them, a fractal array burst alight, illuminating the dark waters and filling them with wisps of vibrant Mana. The dark opacity fled before the light, rendering the waters crystal clear and exposing the mess of bones and cast-off scales and waving plant life clinging to the far bottom. Yet the process didn't stop there. Silver and gold lights tore up the walls, filling in the outlines of carved peoples and creatures, until the entirety of the containment chamber was blazing with light.

The Deepking flinched from it, as did his brethren, many of whom ducked into the waters in trepidation. But there was no escape from it all. At the apex of the chamber, the Belais Crystal strengthened until its amethyst brilliance shone down on them like a second sun, and the ambient Mana in the vast room doubled. Felix could feel his breath come a touch harder than before, the rising magic pressing at him almost as hard as the Shambling Horror.

Temple Seat Reestablished, Autarch.
Do You Wish To Begin Restoration?

Warning: Stores Of Essence and Significance Are Detected. They Will Be Consumed In The Process.

Felix blinked and used Adamant Discord to yank free his hooked sword. It fell, though Felix had to pull in it to make sure it landed back in his hands. With the connection between him and the sword—and Karys on the other end—it was easier than breathing. Their link was steel solid and twice as strong.

"I-I-I do *not* like that, Felix," Karys said, an edge to his voice. "I actually think I feel sick. I do not even have a stomach!"

He grimaced. "Oh, you could, ah you could feel that? Jeez, sorry man. I didn't think the sword transferred stuff like that to you."

"Standard Perception sensations, though with our bond between you, the sword, and this Body it is no wonder I feel things more strongly. Just," Karys' voice firmed up, that slight note of subservience returning. "Please refrain from doing such things in the future. Or at least warn me, my Lord."

"I will," Felix muttered, tamping down the urge to apologize again. Instead he looked up, meeting the eyes of the Deepking. "The System wishes to restore the Temple. I...have a feeling that restoring it wouldn't be in your best interest."

The Abyssal Serpent hesitated, its dark scales twitching in surprise and then acquiescence. "Whatever you choose to do will be accepted, Returned God. But my people would be easy prey without the protection of our...your Temple. Our home."

"Then how about a limited sort of restoration?" Felix asked, only partially speaking to the Deepking. "Karys, can we break down the restoration function? Like just the exterior walls or something?"

"It should be possible. We would need to look at the array directly, however." The sword vibrated in his hands. "Don't you dare throw me again."

"We'll go up together. Atar, Alister, Zara, I'll need all of your eyes on this one."

It took some doing, but Felix was able to fashion a pillar and crude staircase up to the ceiling of the chamber. There the five of them studied the complicated array, and were able to isolate enough of the sigaldry that Karys and Felix felt out the limited connection to the restoration sequences. They had been packaged among a series of large glyphs, one of the few formations that were still functional after Ages of wear and tear. Tweaking the array and his own access to the Temple Seat, Felix got a flurry of new notifications.

Theurgist of the Rise is level 80! Invocation is level 59!

Limited Restoration In Process!

A solid quarter of the Horror's significance and Essence was pulled from Felix's channels and siphoned into the array, but it was far less than what a full restoration would have required. As it was, he could almost feel shattered masonry and broken walls begin to repair themselves in rapid order, returning to a semblance of what they had been before the Temple had fallen into the lake.

The water remained, as the Deepking had requested; Felix had no issue with the Nagafolk residing in the Temple, so long as he was allowed to use the Shadowgate without complications. In fact, having them there to protect it was to his benefit, or so Zara kept repeating.

As the array engaged, the silver and gold threads of light blazed brighter than ever. The power of it all struck the Naga, even the Deepking, sending fissures of pain skittering across their flesh. The Temple was transforming, fixing itself, and Felix's Spirit was woven into that process. The weight of it, now augmented by the Horror and the Urges and his Spirit Tree, the heft of it slammed into the Temple like thunder. A bell the size of a skyscraper. Not even his own people were spared the feeling as the array hit its crescendo. Legionnaires and Dawnguard and Risi Warriors all buckled and fell to their knees. Only those nearest Darius and Zara still stood, the two of them mitigating the force of it all.

"Perhaps a warning next time Felix," Zara said through her sharp teeth. "It is quite rude to unveil your Spirit in such a way."

"Wasn't exactly on purpose," Felix said. He started down the crude stairway, heading back to the soldiers far below.

"That is another issue entirely then," Zara said. "When we reach dry land, we will begin lessons in such things."

By the time they reached the ice barge again, the progress of the array finished with a flare of gold-silver radiance and a final spike of Spiritual pressure. The waters below roiled as a pale, ghostly serpent rose from the depths, his eyes blazing like burning blood.

"My king!" Jadorak cried out. His wide, snake-mouth hissed in rage. "I came as sssoon as I saw the blasphemousss System message! What have those creaturesss done?" Red eyes swept between the present Nagafolk, many of whom were still reeling from the pain of the Temple's activated arrays. When none of them, the Deepking included, answered Jadorak quickly enough, the serpent's rage boiled over into something far more volatile. "You! What have you done!?"

Jadorak lunged for Felix, the Naga's already unbalanced emotions adding fuel to a bountiful fire. Yet, Felix didn't have to dodge or defend himself at all, as Garox interposed himself between the charging Naga and his new liege lord.

"Enough, Jadorak!"

The albino Naga reared back, stunned. He looked to the Deepking, outraged at the Spirit Naga's actions. "My king! Thisss foul Human has befuddled you! Did you not see the message? This is a trick of the Fathom to sssteal our home!"

"Jadorak. This is no Human you accost, nor is it of the Fathom. He is Nymean," Garox said.

"That...that is imposssible!" Jadorak's great head swept between his king and the humanoid serpent. "It cannot be!"

"Silence your incessant prattle, Jadorak!" The Deepking roared. Water kicked up, thrown into five-foot waves by the force of the king's shout. The albino serpent cringed backward. "Do you doubt my Mind? Do you cast aspersions on my sovereignty?"

"N-no, my Lord. Of coursssse not—"

"Then be silent and accept the truth. The Nym have returned, and the God of Thunder and Flame stands before you!"

Jadorak's crimson eyes turned incredulously to Felix, who did his best to exude a sense of "don't fuck with me, I'm maybe a god, probably." It was, he feared, less than convincing. At the very least, however, Felix maintained eye contact with the albino Naga until the guy turned away with a sneer.

"My Lord," the Deepking intoned, facing Felix once again. "I am relieved that you have chosen to preserve our home and that you allow us to remain. The waters of Haestus and others besides are no longer safe to my kind. Bereft of these walls, we would fall mercy to the Fathom."

"The Fathom?" Vess asked. "I am not familiar with this term."

The Abyssal Serpent's gaze flickered between Felix and Vess, as if assessing how he should respond to this new figure. "They are an old threat come anew. The darkest, deepest places of the ten thousand lakes of these Hills hold things that no sky has ever shined upon. Ruins unseen, treasures untold, and monsters that would chill your soul. The Fathom are among those creatures, and the worst of them. We have fought many long years against its vile children, a war from which all Nagafolk have suffered. Season after season, we dwindle while the Fathom flourish."

There was a vast sadness bowing across the king's Spirit, a descending note that shook the very room they were in—to Felix's Affinity, at least. And he was not alone. Vess, Evie, Zara, and even Atar looked affected by it. The Deepking nodded to Jadorak and the other Naga gathered in the chamber around them, their scales a smattering of greens and browns and blues.

"My people have waged war against them, brought the battle to them, but they are too many. Too...irksome to be vanquished altogether. I mention this only so that you understand the danger that this Temple protects us from, and what you shall have to brave if you are to leave it." The king hesitated, a strange thing to see on a giant snake. "I would beseech your aid, however, should you be willing to offer it."

New Threat Discovered!
The Fathom!

New Quest!

Defend The Depths!
The Deepking has outlined a nascent threat to your Authority:
the Fathom. Find and neutralize the threat, protect your new
people, and seek out the Fathom's purpose.
Purpose 0/1
Reward: Increased Authority, Resources, XP, Varies

Felix blinked at the notifications, a little surprised at the new Quest, before an explosion of movement and sloshing water filled the air. Jadorak, without another word, had dove into the water and surged away, vanishing through some underwater passages that Felix hadn't noticed before. A feeling of frustrated fury left with him, and no less than ten other Naga followed.

"As much as we would like to take on this Quest, we must head south without delay," Zara interjected.

The Deepking rumbled in his throat.

"Are the Fathom an immediate concern?" Felix asked.

"No," the Abyssal Serpent said. "We hold them at bay for now. The power of the Returned God would be a mighty boon to us, but we are still safe."

"Alright. Then I promise, after I settle up with things in the south, I'll be coming back. We can take a look into these Fathom at that point." Felix spread his hands. "That's all I can do at this time."

"Then that is what we shall accept." The Deepking bowed low enough to put his head once more on level with Felix and crew upon the ice barge. "That you have listened to our pleas at all is an honor, my Lord."

Unsure of what else to do, Felix nodded. It seemed to work, as the giant serpent lifted its head once more and called out in a guttural tongue to its people. To him, he said, "I offer you my people as guides to the edge of Haestus. As I said, the waters are not safe beyond these walls."

"That would be most appreciated," Zara accepted on his behalf. "We would like to leave immediately."

"So be it."

CHAPTER THIRTY-SEVEN

The Deepking and Garox led them through a door cleverly hidden in the walls. It was huge, clearly sized for some grand procession or creatures of far greater dimensions than the Nym. The Abyssal Serpent fit quite easily, and the enchanted flows of water along its length had obviously been modified by the Naga to make upward traversal a comfortable prospect for them. The question of who had laid the inscripted arrays was put to rest as Garox altered a sigil on the fly as they moved, increasing the amount of water that poured in from above so that all of them would be able to make use of the tunnel at once.

His people were nervous, but settling to an extent. The Deepking, the Horror, the restoration of the Temple—all of it was enough to inure someone to new surprises. At least to an extent. His friends were no exception, and as their ice barge was pulled up the large tunnel by another pair of Naga, it was like their lips were all unfrozen.

"So. Snakes," Evie said. "You're the snake king now."

"Please, Aren," Atar said in a haughty tone. Alister watched them both with a faint smile on his face. "He's the Naga King."

"My apologies," she said, offering him an elaborate bow. "I hope I have not offended hiss Majesty."

Felix groaned. "You're killing me, Evie."

The woman looked shocked and even placed an outraged hand against her chest. "Me? An assassssssin?"

"Oh my god!"

This passage was far calmer than the tumultuous one that brought them down, and in less than ten minutes, their group exited the water-logged tunnel into another series of long hallways. Garox and the Deepking still led the way, the latter parting the waters with his immense body while they all swept along in his wake.

Now that Felix knew what to look and feel for, he could sense a number of other secret passages throughout the halls. Where they led he was unsure, and the stone of the Temple still kept his Perception confined to the interior, but it was nice to feel more aware of his surroundings.

Finally, they were led into a tilted dome, where the Temple itself had once been shattered. Already the repair function was reconstructing the shattered dome, with traceries of gold and silver building new stone atop old. For now, however, the wall was open to the elements and a curtain of liquid hung across their path, flowing smoothly across the gaping hole but not rushing into the Temple. It was all dark, like an evening sky just before the sun sets.

"Impressive," Zara said. "A major ward is a difficult array to fashion with such fidelity."

Garox bowed to her, accepting the compliment. "It is the work of our ancestors, one which we have maintained for an Age. We have not the Skill to replicate it, sadly, but it protects us here. Beyond this point, the Haestus spreads wide. We must prepare before venturing out into its waters."

The Deepking spoke this time, coiling his huge body around their barge and all but filling the shattered dome. "We are a hundred lengths beneath the lake's surface, far enough that most creatures will die long before they escape. If you will allow me, my Lord, I shall cast a warding on all of your people so that they may survive the depths."

Felix exchanged a quick look with his friends. "I don't see why not. Go ahead."

The Deepking chanted something in his rumbling voice, and the Abyssal Serpent's scales lit up from within as Mana steamed off his body. It was a deep, deep blue and it reached out as the king finished his chant, winding around each and every one of Felix's company. Himself included.

Status Condition: Sunken Ward!
Waterbreathing and protection against the pressure of the depths has been woven around your Body.
Duration: 1 hour.

Very nice. Felix fought off the urge to eat the spell, instead letting it wrap around him like a gossamer cloak. The abyss inside him was still happily munching away at the Horror's Essence, but it was greedy—Felix could feel it stretch out toward the Sunken Ward before he forced it back. Not that it typically did anything without his consent, not for months. In fact, there was a good chunk of his own Mind that wanted Sunken Ward for himself. It could prove useful, were he able to extract a Skill from its Mana pattern. *No. What are you gonna do? Ask if they'd cast it twice on you? That'd be awkward. Just...just let it go.*

Four Nagafolk lined up in the water beside the ice barge, their ridged backs wide enough to accommodate all of his people were they to split up. That was a relief, actually—their swimming speed was doubtless faster than what his people could manage alone, and he wouldn't be required to figure out how to get them to the surface alone.

The Henaari climbed aboard with fascinated expressions, each of them inspecting different parts of the Nagafolks' backs, while the Risi were more stolid about it. They climbed atop them and hunkered down, intent only on keeping their weapons free and easy to draw. The legionnaires were more scattered, ranging from fearful to curious, but the firm hand of Darius had them in place in no time.

A pale green Naga rose up next to Felix, offering its ridged back. "Settle atop my back, if it pleases you, Returned God."

"Ah, thank you..." Voracious Eye flared, and Felix smiled. "Le'lani. I appreciate you offering to help us like this."

The Naga tilted her head, regarding him with eyes the color of cool iron as cautious fear swirled among her Spirit. Like the other three Naga escorts, she was strong but did not hold a candle to Felix's power, and somehow she could tell. The shock in her eyes was enough to tell that. "We serve."

Felix had a few complicated emotions about *that* declaration, but he pushed them aside for the moment. His first responsibility was to get his company out from the bottom of a lake. The ethics of claiming divinity could wait until later. From atop Le'lani, Felix looked up at the Deepking. "Our thanks for this," he said.

"It is the least we can do for you, Returned God. I only wish I myself could escort you...but there is much to be done. The rest of my people must know of your arrival and that you shall lead us against the vile Fathom when next you return." He nodded far below him, where Garox's much smaller shape waited. "Garox will lead you all toward the shoreline, and from there guide you on your divine mission. If you need anything else, you have but to ask."

Felix nodded. Hesitated. "There is one last thing..."

"Name it and I shall do it, Returned God."

Chthonic Tribute!

"Can you cast that warding on me again? Mine seems to have faded."

There was rude and there was stupid. Perhaps he wouldn't get the chance to consume the spell before it faded, or something else unforeseen would happen. Better to cover his bases while he still could.

———

The water of Lake Haestus was really, really cold but none of them could properly feel it. Felix could *tell*, Perception being a weird extension of his literal senses, but the Sunken Ward prevented the cold, pressure, or downright filth in the water from touching them. That said, it did nothing to stop his vision, for which he was extremely grateful.

Atop Le'lani, Felix (and Pit converged within his Spirit) had a wide view of the darkened depths around them. Water Mana swirled with shadow and flickers of other, stranger colors. They passed over his sight so quickly he couldn't identify them, only serving to highlight the sprawling swathe of fallen architecture all around them. Columned porticos and sagging triangular roofs proliferated, smaller structures that were part of a grander whole.

It had been an entire complex at one point, but now individual structures all leaned haphazardly against one another, separated by rocky shelves and maze-like growths of pale coral. Fish and other, more sinuous shapes flickered through the periphery, the smaller creatures driven out by the naked aggression emanating from their Naga escorts.

Garox swam ahead, his swords sheathed but his body primed with swirls of deepest blue Mana. As they passed several tangled fronds of seaweed, each bigger than one of their Naga escorts, those swirls slashed outward. Swords of water Mana severed the plants with precision, cutting free just enough space for the Naga to slip through, under, or over the crumbled arches and tilted passages of the Temple complex.

A few times, they had to dive deeper than before, and Felix caught glimpses of muted light that wasn't just more Mana vapor. Sigils and array lines of gold and silver almost boiled in the dark water, casting shifting shadows through stone and plant matter, and Felix could hear the song of the Temple repairing itself ever so slowly.

<<Why are we swimming so low?>> Felix asked Garox, his voice warbling along the Sunken Ward. All of them were connected in a loose sort of fashion, allowing for a measure of communication so long as they were near one another.

The Spirit Naga did not stop as he inspected the next tilted thoroughfare. <<As the king mentioned, the open waters are not safe, not even for us. We swim low to stay within the reef and to avoid unnecessary detection.>> Garox paused, looking back at Felix uncertainly. <<Unless you wish to swim higher, Returned God. Were you to wish it, we would brave the risk of Fathom attack.>>

<<No,>> Felix sent, firmly. <<I can withstand a lot, but my allies are not so durable. I'll not risk anyone's life without reason...and that includes all of you.>>

Garox shifted, his Spirit tumbling with a confusing mixture of sounds. He bowed deeply at his humanoid waist. <<You honor us.>>

At his back, Vess chuckled. Her Spirit hummed in approval. <<That was well done.>>

Felix shot a look over his shoulder. <<What was?>>

<<That is what I like most about you, Felix,>> Vess sent, flexing her legs around the curve of Le'lani's ridged back. <<You are so very honest with your feelings.>>

Pit snorted within his Spirit, amusement echoing across their bond. *Shut up, you.*

They continued on, until the fallen ruins of the sunken Temple were left behind and only the craggy expanse of deep water trenches lay before them. A massive tangle of seaweed rose all about the area, a veritable forest compared to the solitary copses around the Temple—easy to hide in as they swam for the surface.

<<Easy to get ambushed, too,>> Harn sent, the Naga he rode with Evie and a contingent of Legionnaires. <<Eyes up, everyone.>>

Another serpent rode from the dark ruins, this one bearing Atar, Alister, and the majority of the Arclight Legion. Their artillery snake, Felix mused to himself. The rest of the Legion were on Le'lani with him. None aboard Atar's Naga looked particularly excited to be swimming through the dark waters with barely enough light to see, let alone cast spells. Yet Felix thought he could feel a particular revulsion emanating from the fire mage.

Weird. He really doesn't like the water, huh? Felix thought, and Pit trilled at him. Images came to him of A'zek recoiling from a too-deep river in the Foglands, along with Pit's whistling laughter. *Kindred spirits, I suppose.*

Mm, Pit sent, too amused with himself to answer fully.

<<Dawnguard, spears at the ready. Giants, you too,>> Darius said as his group neared. Dawnguard rode behind him and Zara, their attention split into as many directions as they had members, all of them looking like the picture of battle-ready. Meanwhile the Frost Giants were all latched nervously onto the largest of their Naga escorts. The massive serpents were eerie in the dark waters, their eyes reflecting minute light and seeming to glow—they clearly made the Hand nervous, for all that they bore no aggression or ill will toward Felix or his people.

<<Legionnaires! Keep your weapons sheathed. Do not engage unless ordered.>>

Low mutters of assent met Darius' command, but Felix wasn't paying attention to them. Instead he focused on Garox, who had come swimming steadily back to them after scouting the seaweed forest.

<<We shall proceed. Divine, if you would follow me.>>

Le'lani slithered after the Spirit Naga, keeping close to his whipping tail.

The weeds engulfed them all until everything was shifting shadows and stuttering beams of murky light. Fronds waving in the currents that grew all the more wild the higher they traversed. Where before the Naga moved as slow, sinuous sherpas through the ruins, now they were arrows in flight. All four of them swam and flowed around the swaying fronds, chasing after the rapidly advancing form of Garox. Once or twice, Felix even saw crystalline blue light following their convoy—light that resolved into tiny crystalline figures made *entirely* of dense water Mana. Sprites. They vanished and reappeared without warning, like tiny stars in a sky...filled with seaweed.

Felix shrugged. He'd made worse metaphors before.

Still, it was a heady experience, especially devoid of almost all the discomforts such a dive and ascent would normally inflict on someone. The Sunken Ward was frankly amazing, so far as Felix was concerned, and he decided he'd make it a priority to digest its secrets as soon as they reached dry land.

The light above grew stronger and stronger as they swam, until Felix could make out fluid, rippling sunstreaks that flashed far above. Garox let out a surprising sigh of relief.

<<We will reach the shore without issue, my Lord.>>

Which, of course, was when everything went to shit.

A screaming roar shook the seaweed forest only instants before lithe, fifty-foot long forms attacked. Serpent jaws parted, baring poisonous fangs at their escorts, more Nagafolk but possessed of a hideous, bloody hatred. A dozen emerged from the weeds, circling around them, cutting them off. A familiar white bastard was leading them.

<<Jadorak! What are you doing?!>> Garox screamed, and his warded voice sent shockwaves among the weeds. <<The Deepking has declared safe passage!>>

<<He has been fooled! Not I! Never I!>> Jadorak lashed his tail through the water, stirring a flurry of bubbles. <<Kill them all!>>

His cronies rocketed forward, propelled by fin and movement Skills, straight toward Felix's people. The Naga pulled back, their own fangs bared, but the dozen attackers were too many to fight off.

Felix's team were no slouches, however.

Water boiled and ripped as gouts of crimson flame and pillars of intractable blue force were launched outward. Three Naga were knocked aside with hissing screams, while chains of ice and sweeping metal arcs caught still more in their grasp. Spears of wind, blades of air, and local-ized whirlpools of blue-green water spread outward, ripping gashes and tears in their enemies' hides even as more advanced on Felix's party.

The Spirit Naga leaped forward, a great wave of power emanating from him and hurling into the jaws of their attackers. With a half-second's respite, Garox pressed his advantage and engaged all of them.

<<Ride! To the surface! Ride!>> Garox shouted, his voice throwing the enemy back once again. His blades of water Mana spun around him like shadows of the scimitars he wielded. <<Fulfill your duty!>>

The four Naga under them surged upward, so hard and fast that Felix barely had time to pivot and see the Spirit Naga enveloped in a press of bodies.

<<We are just leaving him?>> Vess shouted, her face torn by indeci-sion as the waters flowed around them. <<Can he survive them all?>>

<<Maybe! But all of us won't!>> Evie hollered back.

Evie was right about that, at least as far as their followers were concerned. Felix's core team would likely have survived, but he didn't just have them to worry about anymore. He—

Felix's Perception screamed at him only instants before another five serpents collided with their party. Fangs sank into scaled flesh, and water bubbled with impacts as serpentine bodies twisted around one another. Men and women screamed in panic, nearly thrown free.

<<No!>> Felix shouted, his voice throwing out waves of pressure. He leaped off Le'lani, flaring Relentless Resolution.

<<Felix!>> Vess shouted in warning. Too late.

A blur of pale scales slammed into him, hard, and fangs the size of greatswords came down on him. Felix brought his hands up in time, catching the teeth around him and preventing their close, but Jadorak's speed brought them careening upward. The rush of water and rotten breath and flexing jaws soon replaced by the blasting relief of air and sun and sky.

"You are not worthy!"

A forked tongue lashed against his body, stabbing at Felix's gut. The *apparently* barbed tongue stabbed straight through his Garment and impacted his torso hard enough that it launched him from Jadorak's mouth entirely.

Felix tumbled into the open air, finding himself high enough that he could see a distant smear of land to the south. *Shit! Pit!*

With a screech, his Companion exited Felix's Spirit and soared up into the air. A quick Shadow Whip snagged onto the tenku's hindleg, letting Felix swing unceremoniously below his ascending friend. Doing so, he saw that Jadorak was arcing above them, flipping back down toward the lake far below them as gravity finally took hold.

Felix twisted his body, leveraging his weight to swing in greater arcs. *When I say, Converge, okay?*

Pit trilled in frustrated confirmation.

I got this one, bud. Felix grunted as his Shadow Whip pulled him into another, wider arc. *I'll let you take the next idiot who attacks us.*

Jadorak, his bloody eyes blazing and white scales glistening in the mid-morning sun, roared as he fell like an arrow. His fanged mouth was agape, ready to swallow them whole. Felix reached the pinnacle of his arc and let go of his Shadow Whip.

Now!

Pit vanished in a flash of light, and Mana *exploded* out of Felix's channels.

Rain of Cataclysm!

The storm of Mana blasted from Felix's channels and took root in the sky as they fell. Clouds appeared, a virulent green streaked with a deadly purple-gray that discharged a deluge of deadly projectiles. Acid fell, punching into Jadorak's scales with relentless impunity. Hot knife, meet butter. The albino Naga howled in pain, his falling form twisting against the rain as they both finally impacted the lake's surface.

Sound and fury overwhelmed Felix's senses for a moment, the bubbles and roar of water and thrashing sea serpent too much to parse. But he reached out blindly and sent his Shadow Whips in all directions. He felt them snag on a writhing bulk and pulled, hard, yanking himself clear of the water and right onto Jadorak's perforated hide. The bastard was ragged as hell, covered in blood and streaks of dissipating acid. He thrashed beneath Felix's grip and took off, speeding atop the surface of the lake. South, toward land.

"You will...never rule...my people...!" the Naga screamed at him. His breath was labored, but his Spirit was firm. "We will kill you!"

Felix could sense more Naga rising from the depths, at least six, all of them converging on Jadorak's path. "What is wrong with you? We were leaving!" Felix shouted back.

Jadorak twisted, slamming Felix into the lake's speeding surface. Water tore at him, ripping his Garment to pieces, but leaving Felix's powerful Body unharmed. That is, until churning blades of water stabbed upward, aiming for his chest and neck. Felix flinched, pulling back on his Shadow Whip just in time to avoid a devastating wound. Instead, his shoulder and right arm were torn bloody as if by a thousand tiny teeth. Jadorak laughed deliriously.

"You're no god!"

"You're right," Felix said. "I never claimed I was! But I am Nymean."

"More lies!" The Naga turned again, pulling them closer to his converging allies. They were running parallel now to the rocky, tree-crowded shoreline. "You will die here, false god!"

Adamant Discord!

Felix grabbed onto the rocks and trees and everything he could manage, finding their connections too weak alone. Instead, he burned his Mana and strained hard against his Aspects, grappling with Jadorak and the land itself. Yowling in surprise, the Naga was turned astray, his parallel path flipped instead into a collision course.

"I'm done with reasoning!" Felix howled, pulling harder. Lightning spat from his hands, shocking him as well as the Naga beneath, and he could almost feel rocks and trees breaking apart. "I'm done!"

With an unwilling bellow, Felix and Jadorak slammed into the shoreline. Jagged, upthrust rocks and tangled marsh trees met their implacable charge, and Felix was hurled bodily from the serpent's back. Stone and tree shattered and snapped beneath his dense Body, a tumble of limbs that furrowed the soaking wet earth.

When he came to a sudden stop, Felix could only groan into a gutter of thick, putrid mud.

"Fuck."

He climbed out, his Body aching and torn, to find the albino head of Jadorak only feet from his own. His neck was stabbed clean through by a tree trunk as wide as a car.

You Have Killed Jadorak, The Horror Of Haestus!
XP Earned!

Two hundred feet back, in the waters of the Haestus, the albino Naga's backup watched him. Anger and disbelief echoed off of all of their Spirits, and Felix gestured. Jadorak's head burst alight with red-gold flame.

"Come and get it, then."

Almost as one, the Naga slunk back into the lake.

CHAPTER THIRTY-EIGHT

Felix rushed to the shoreline, skipping over rocks and trees, all of them overturned, broken apart, and festooned with the gory remains of Jadorak. He was *everywhere*, and he would have thought it pretty gross if he'd have paid it any mind. Instead, Felix landed atop a thirty-foot tall stone split unevenly down the middle. He scanned the choppy surface of Haestus Lake, searching for his friends.

"C'mon," he muttered. "Pit? Can you—?"

A flash of light heralded Pit's emergence from Felix's Spirit, and the tenku soared off into the air above the lake. Felix's eyes could pick out details hundreds of yards away, but all he saw was a whole lot of nothing. Water and torn-up seaweed. Pit, however, cried out almost immediately.

There!

Pit pointed a clawed paw at a place further down the shoreline, and with a stone-shattering leap, Felix was able to see it, too. His friends and their Naga escorts were making landfall.

Adamant Discord!

Lightning burst around him, and Felix took off through the sky, quickly overtaking Pit. The tenku huffed in annoyance and flapped his wings harder, manipulating the air Mana around himself as best as he could. Still, Felix tore past him and landed in a shower of pebbles and outflung muck, just outside the hastily formed perimeter of legionnaires. Muted shouts rang out, far too late, had Felix been a hostile force.

"Shut up! It's the Autarch," Darius shouted, his voice pitched quietly but just as imposing as if he'd shouted at the top of his lungs. "Felix. You're a sight. Is the other one dead?"

"Yeah," he said, frowning at his disheveled Garment. He focused, and the material restored itself into a blue-gray tunic and dark black pants. "He didn't give me much choice."

Pit landed and set a huge spray of swampy water in all directions. The legionnaires cried out, the Sunken Ward had faded and now they were soaked to their skin. Felix shook his head. "Did we lose anyone?"

"No, thank the gods," Zara said, stomping her way toward them. "Our escorts were more than capable of outpacing them once we'd blunted their claws."

"Good." Felix walked past them both, finding the pale green form of Le'lani and mottled brown of Garox. The Naga were still in the water, though their heads all reached at least twenty feet high. Garox was contemplating the rolling waters.

"Jadorak perished, yes?" the Spirit Naga asked.

"He did. I tried to stop him, but—"

Garox nodded in grim acceptance. "He was a...driven warrior. The Fathom have pushed many of our young ones battle-mad, and Jadorak was no exception. His end was only ever to come in violence."

Felix frowned at the snake-man, at his placid Spirit in the face of his people's deaths. "What of the others? I'm told most of them got away."

"Yes. But they cannot go far, not before I find them. I promise you, Returned God, they shall pay for this affront." This time Garox's Spirit flared bright and acidic, a song of wild dissonance and frantically plucked notes. "The others will be brought to you, so that you may pass your judgment."

"No! No," Felix said with a cough. "I'll leave that in the capable...coils of the Deepking."

"As you wish, my Lord." Garox bowed so low his upper, humanoid body ran almost parallel with the ground. "If you head further south, you shall find the town of Bogfeld. It is the nearest to this lake and to the southern Stormeater Peaks."

"Stormeater, huh?"

"I do not know where it is you are going, my Lord. Nor am I questioning it. But," and here Garox looked truly upset, his face matching the unease humming across his Spirit. "The dry lands beyond breed death. Fire and dust are all that lives within. A god does not need my warnings, but still, on behalf of my people: tread carefully."

"Oh, uh, sure," Felix said, unnerved by the Spirit Naga's intensity. "I appreciate it."

"We shall guard your Temple with our lives, and the room within," Garox promised. "None shall enter the sealed chamber while we still breathe."

"Right," Felix said. What better way to keep the Shadowgate safe? "I'll be back as soon as I'm able."

"It is as it must be." Garox bowed low again, pressing his smooth, scaled forehead into the dirt. Then, with a soft, sighing rustle, he slipped back into the water. In moments, all the Naga were gone.

"Giant snakes," Felix muttered to himself. He turned back to his team. "What's next?"

———

It took a half hour to get everyone dried, organized, and sorted out before they took off at a quick march. More of a trot, really, something that Harn and Darius agreed that the majority of the company would be able to maintain for several hours. For the leadership, it was nothing, and Felix it felt like he was walking when he should be running. A half-dozen times had him pushing harder and harder, with only the cautionary words of Vess or Zara to remind him to slow down.

It was difficult. His dreams of the Minotaur Unbound were etched in his brain, and the sense that the other man was riding the ragged edge remained strong in Felix's Mind. Every delay or break or conversation with snake kings meant they were one step closer to losing the guy, or so it felt.

Essence helped distract him. Processing the consumed pieces of the Sunken Ward took more time than Felix cared to admit—sifting through the power for its unique pattern was a challenge while jogging. Eventually, however, he was able to isolate it from the rest of the devoured Essence, which he sent streaming down to his eternally hungry abyss. The pattern, however, he pressed down into the gleaming, spinning rings of his cores.

New Skill!
Sunken Ward (Rare), Level 1!
A warding designed to protect a target from the hostile environment of the deepest of waters. Duration increases per level, Mana cost decreases per level, number of targets increases per level.

Useful, he mused, taking the marshy path at a steady clip. *I'll need to find the time to level this one. Not really sure how often I'll get to use it in the desert, though.*

Felix briefly considered leveling it by diving into one of the *many* pools of swampy water in the surrounding terrain, but the crust of algae and fetid stench put him right off that idea. Sure, maybe the ward would protect him from all that, but at such a low level, did he want to risk it? He'd grown far too used to being clean in the last half year, there was little chance of Felix returning to his earliest grimiest days on the Continent. Indeed, just marching through the Ghreldan Hills was proving to be gross enough. The Hills were forested and wet, the very definition of a swamp between the humps of the hills themselves. Paths existed, but they were narrow things stretched between long-standing pools of slimed trees and mossed-over stones the size of pickup trucks. More than once, Felix had heard folks call it the "boglands," which was admittedly pretty funny.

After the second hour at march, Zara approached him, her steps as steady and sure as any among their party. Felix was surprised in part because he couldn't sense that fragility that had dominated her person in recent days. She seemed to have rallied and healed since her arrival in the Foglands, which was for the better.

"Zara."

"Felix."

They ran on a bit longer, both of their Perceptions sweeping the wet, wooded terrain for evidence of threat or civilization. Eventually, Felix cleared his throat. "You said we Unbound were summoned. Right?"

"...Yes," she answered, her voice lingering as if unsure of where he was going with his question. "The Hierophant in Amaranth performed the ritual summoning."

"How was it done?"

She raised an eyebrow. "You plan to bring more Unbound into the Continent?"

"What? No. I'm just trying to get a sense of things. Were there requirements for the ritual? Most I've seen now needed a bunch of monster cores as fuel, but I would think a summoning from across the...galaxy? Universe? I assume it would take a lot more power."

"It would, and it did." Zara looked up at the sky, contemplating the darkening clouds. Rain was on the way. "It is one of the reasons why the ritual was discarded in Ages past. The cost was too much for any mortal to bear."

"Any...mortal? So you're saying—"

"The Hierophant tapped into her patron god's divine power in order to fuel the ritual," Zara shook her head. "It is not an option for the rest of us. Only the Pathless remains of the divine pantheon, and he does not grace any but his chosen with power."

"Divine power," Felix muttered. He huffed a breath through his nose. "It keeps coming back to the gods. How'd you stop it, then? You said you disrupted the ritual."

"*I* did not. My...colleague did. Another Chanter spent his life to stop the final portion of the array."

Felix glanced at the Naiad from the corner of his eye. Her face was drawn, and her Spirit quiet, but he saw sadness in the cast of her eyes and tilt of her head. It wasn't his Affinity or anything supernatural, just a feeling. "He was a friend?"

"He was," she said, and this time yes her eyes were a touch brighter than normal. "But he knew what he was doing. The summoning wasn't stopped, just diverted so that the Hierophant couldn't get their hands on you all."

"Because you need us," Felix said quietly. "For the Ruin."

Zara watched him; he felt it on the side of his face. "Yes."

They ran in silence after that.

The ground rose and fell frequently, the Hills living up to their name, but mostly the land consisted of the flat valleys between such rises where water pooled and flowed, often playing host to any number of monstrous creatures. Most of such creatures ran at his company's approach, though more than a few decided to attack them.

The legions, Risi warriors, and Dawnguard proved more than a match for any of them, though their organization left something to be desired. The giants were dour, solitary combatants for the most part, while the legions did not work very well among one another, Blade, Fist, Bone, and Arclight all having their own way of doing things. The only exception were the Henaari, who quickly became the company's scouts as the hours turned to days among the Hills.

Moods were souring as their march pushed into its third day, the fighters tiring of the wet, humid air and the wet, muddy ground. The weather was warmer there, presumably because they were closer to the equator of the planet, but Felix had yet to see a map of the Continent that encompassed more than a small section. Buzzing insects hovered around them, at least until Vess and Darius started circulating flows of air Mana around the group, forcing them away.

The bugs and most of the smaller critters around them were lower in level, barely pushing beyond level twenty, but every once in a while, they'd encounter something bigger. A crocodile-thing the size of a minivan slithered through one waterway, and a moss-covered simian as big as a giant swung through the upper branches. Neither bothered to even glance at their group, which was a relief. As much as Felix could handle a giant, magic crocodile, he'd much rather run on uninterrupted.

Eventually, however, the Dawnguard approached him.

"My Lord, there is a town ahead," one murmured, low enough that only he would have heard it.

"Bogfeld?"

"So the signs declare, my Lord," another scout said.

Felix felt a slow tempo thrum from their Spirits. Caution, maybe. "What's wrong?"

"The Paladins, my Lord. They're here."

"Show me."

———

Bogfeld, despite its humble name, was a fairly bustling town. Situated on a hill that had its top chopped off and built all around with tall, wooden walls, the town was a fortress that few monsters could properly assault, though it was clear many had tried. Large ditches surrounded the hill, easily twenty feet deep and filled with water and sharpened logs, and Felix could spot thirty or more monstrous corpses impaled on their defenses. Black smoke rose like a pyre all around the town's edges...and from inside.

"There was a monster attack?" he asked the scout.

"So it appears," the scout said, a woman named Krys. "You can see their guards still standing there and there. The battle was only in the last glass."

Felix followed the scout's finger and saw men in dark, burnished armor standing atop the walls. Knights, according to his Voracious Eye. They held very long spears, designed to stab from the top of the wall, and all of them were smoking as monster blood boiled off of them. "Where are the Paladins?"

"There."

In order to get a good vantage, the two of them had climbed a tall tree at least a mile from Bogfeld, but the scout's sight was good enough to make out basic details. Felix's Perception was a good bit higher, so he could clearly see the men and women in dark red armor, strutting around the town's streets as if they owned the place. His Voracious Eye confirmed their allegiance.

"Forty or fifty have been spotted, and they are quartered near the far gates, where the fortified path leads to the Stormeater Peaks." Krys pointed them out. The wooden walls were built up and around a solitary path up and into the foothills that backed the town. Beyond that, the Stormeater Peaks dominated the southern horizon, so big that it was hard to tell its true size. It just looked like a wall at the edge of the world, miles high and miles wide. Somewhere, among the thick forests and guarded pathways, the Caleph Pass existed.

"Can we get around it? Bypass the town entirely?" he asked.

"It is possible, my Lord. My men have not completed their mapping mission yet, so I can tell you more by midday when they return," Krys said.

"Sounds good. Thank you, Krys."

"Of course, my Lord."

Felix nodded and jumped down out of the tree. He fell, heedless of the distance, until he hit the mossy earth below with a dull *thump*. A slight flex of his knees was all he needed to absorb the impact, and his Health didn't even flicker.

High Endurance and Vitality is so very cool, he thought.

The rest of the company were settled further back, in a hollow between two larger hills where their forces would remain invisible to even the keenest of eyes in Bogfeld. Felix approached them and quickly gathered up Zara and the others, leaving the Legion, giants, and Henaari to finish enjoying their rest. He quickly explained the situation.

"Circumventing the town seems the wisest course of action," Vess agreed. "Though the Pass is likely well-guarded. It is one of the few ways through the Stormeaters, and trade with the desert cities is very profitable."

"Avoiding Paladins. I'm not keen on that idea," Evie said. "How'll I kill 'em if I have to keep hiding?"

"The point isn't to fight them, Aren. We're here to find the...other, and get out," Alister said.

"The Paladins are a plague, but I agree that engaging them here is not the wisest course of action," Zara said. "My main concern, however, is our supplies. The food and fresh water are running low after our trek. It seems Frost Giants require a great deal of both throughout the day."

"Hm. Bogfeld looks prosperous. Should we send someone into town to resupply?" Felix asked.

"That is up to you, Autarch," the Naiad replied with a smirk that quickly faded. "It would be unwise to enter the Scorched Expanse without adequate water, at the very least."

"A death sentence," Atar said. "I also don't like the idea that the Paladins are controlling the Caleph Pass. Those Knights...they would have to work for one of the Princes. Why are they not contesting the Hierocracy's presence?"

"Not sure on the politics, but sounds like there's a mite few more holy idiots than Knights," Harn said.

Felix nodded. "Scouts have counted at least forty Paladins, and I clocked like barely half that of Knights. Could be more in the town, but there's likely more Paladins, too."

"The Thousand Princes of Ghreldan are weak," Vess pointed out as Alister nodded. "If they could actually band together, they could amount to something. As it is, they remain fractious enough that they barely hold onto their capital cities and surrounding farm lands."

"Meaning those Knights are on their own," Alister said. "They'll likely be strong—Journeyman Tier at least—but without the threat of a proper backing, they'll not stand up against the Hierocracy's thugs."

Felix tapped his lips, thinking. "Then we have to go into Bogfeld, a few of us at least."

"Several teams would be best," Zara pointed out. "We cannot be seen collecting too many supplies at once. They will assume we're making for the Pass, but that is easier to pass off if we are a small group."

"Smart lady," Harn grunted. "I'll take a few in, get the water we need. Evie? Can you behave yourself?"

Evie blinked her big, green eyes at the grizzled veteran. "No promises."

Harn grunted.

"Right, then a couple more for food, and...we need information." Felix met Atar's eyes. "I need to know what the Paladins are planning. This many for one person? Something else is up."

"Perhaps. But do not miscount your value, Felix. Or our bullish friend's. Nations would move mountains to secure one such as yourselves," Zara said.

"Your code needs work, Zara," Darius said. He had been there the whole time and was most of the reason they had avoided using the word "Unbound." "Who is it we are chasing? And why would the Hierocracy be interested in them, to this extent?"

"I'll tell you once we're in the desert," Felix said. "I promise." Darius

frowned but nodded anyway. "For now, let's rest and wait on the Dawnguards' return. After that, to Bogfeld."

"I love a shopping trip," Evie said, but her eyes were staring intensely
into the distance, as if she could bore a hole through the hills straight to
the town. Her fingers caressed the edge of her bladed chain.

Felix swallowed. *It'll be fine. Probably.*

CHAPTER THIRTY-NINE

Felix walked down the path, his metal boots crunching against the stone and dirt. His silvered greaves remained the same as always, as did his pants and tunic. But over it all, he shifted his Garment to form into a nondescript brown cloak. It was an easy task for the magical item, even when he added a deep hood to it and altered the cloak's details. He made it a touch threadbare and ragged at the edges—something that had been passed down a couple times, perhaps. It was enough to hide the sword at his waist and divert a little attention. The others donned cloaks and hats of their own, wide-brimmed things designed to shade from the sun.

They had split into discrete teams, with Felix, Vess, Zara, and a Converged Pit all taking the lead. The majority of their forces had begun the slow process of circling around the town, angling through muddy waters for the Pass beyond. The Dawnguard scouts had identified a few paths that led to the break in the Stormeaters, but most were barricaded or had a token smattering of Paladins guarding them.

Only one remained that would serve, and it was in such disrepair that traversing it would be truly foolish had they not several among them who could shape ice, however crudely. Darius had taken charge of that effort, which left Evie and Harn and Atar and Alister to lead two more teams to retrieve food and water for their journey.

At first, Felix was worried that they would stick out like a sore thumb in the swampy Hills and chose to stagger their three teams approach. That turned out to be unnecessary, as stragglers were flooding the main causeway leading to Bogfeld's gate. Felix and his people slipped in among them, careful to keep their heads down and go with the flow. He saw many were sporting grisly wounds, and some of the worst were being pulled along on crude litters.

"Siva's mercy," Vess whispered. "All of these people were stuck outside during the monster attack?"

She was clearly right, as muted conversation among the crowd confirmed. Felix heard more than a few snippets of aggrieved rage, blaming everyone from the blind gods to the Knights of Tevin that supposedly protected the area.

"Who or what's Tevin?" Felix asked the women.

"Prince of Tevin, the supposed leader of this portion of the Ghreldan Hills," Zara explained. "Though he does not control much at all."

"You said that before. Why?"

"The Hills are too big to rule properly, too wild," Vess explained. "The little I know of the Thousand Princes is that they are constantly warring over the tiniest slices of the overall Territory, with none of them ever able to gain a solid upper hand."

"So these Knights are agents of Tevin," Felix said. "Would they be on our side or the Paladins'?"

Zara shook her head. "Their own. The Hierocracy has many enemies, but the Princes would not dare to challenge their authority. Not unless they had a significant advantage."

"So, they're cowards," he said as they shuffled forward.

"Not everyone is so strong that they'd throw themselves at a greater power," Zara said. "Or so foolhardy."

Felix clenched his jaw, ready to retort, but the crowd swelled and pressed closer. The gates were just ahead, fifty foot double doors that were only just barely held open. Two Knights stood at the gate, directing traffic as folks poured into the town.

"In, in! If you need healin', then go to the priory. If you need food, market's open! No violence inside, or else we'll thonk you good and toss you in the undercroft!"

The Knight repeated that, varying the words now and then, but always the same gist. Healing, food, and punishment. The folk around him gave him nods of acceptance before disappearing into the busy streets of Bogfeld.

Felix Eyed them both, noting their levels of 74 and 65 respectively, and that they were both in the late stages of Journeyman Tier. Their armor, burnished and dark, was made of a series of forged strips that overlapped across their chests and shoulders, and appeared to provide a significant amount of protection. It even had a full helm, covering all but a narrow slash by their eyes. Teasing items from a person's being had always been difficult for Felix, but he pressed, forcing Voracious Eye's pattern to sing ever louder.

Name: Chevalier Mail
Type: Armor (enchanted)
Lore: Designed by a Prince of Tevis six hundred years ago, these suits of armor are said to be able to withstand two entire

blows from a Master-Tier opponent. Against creatures of a Tier equal to the user, it is more than remarkably resilient and enhances the Strength of those who wear it.

Voracious Eye is level 74!

It was Journeyman-Tier armor, he could feel, and both Knights exuded a sense of solidity that Felix didn't want to test. He wasn't *always* foolhardy.

They moved forward, finally reaching the gate and the Knights waved them in without fanfare or fuss.

"Alright, we need to find—" Zara began saying, when Felix heard a yelp of surprise.

Behind them, a spear crossed Vess' path, the Knight attached to it peering at her curiously through the slits in his helm. He reached out and grasped a corner of Vess' cloak. "Mighty fine cloak there, little lady. Mighty fine."

Vess looked at the man, shocked and clearly at a loss. Her Spirit smoldered in anger. "Let go of me," she demanded.

The Knight didn't, but instead rubbed the fabric in his fingertips and smacked his lips. "What's a lady like you, with a cloak so fine, doin' in Bogfeld?"

Vess snatched her cloak out of the Knight's hands, much to his surprise. "My own business, thank you very much."

The Knight drew himself up, his burnished armor glinting in the midday sun. "That business involves Bogfeld, and that means it's *my* business. What are you doing here, woman?"

"We're here for healing!" Felix interrupted, drawing the Knight's ire down on himself. He grabbed Zara by the shoulders, and she tensed under his hands. "My mother here is quite ill. So my wife and I are taking her to the priory. To be healed. Of the illness."

There was a beat of silent confusion all around, though Felix silently begged them all to understand. Thankfully, he did not wait in vain.

"I-I need to sit," Zara coughed. A rasping, awful sound came from her chest and throat, so bad that Felix had a pang of worry. "I am feeling faint again, boy."

"Of course, Mother. Please, if you'll excuse us."

Felix took hold of Vess' arm and Zara's shoulder, steering the both of them into the town and out of the queue. He took streets at random, pushing further into the maze of back alleys and side streets, practically dragging the other two along with him. He did not stop until he was sure the Knights had lost sight of them, his Perception telling him that they never once left their post at the gate.

"Okay, I—I think we're good, now," Felix said, peering back the way they'd come. "We—"

"Wife?" Vess asked, sharply. "Bold of you, Lord Nevarre."

"Oh," he chuckled awkwardly. "Yeah, sorry, it was—"

"Mother?" Zara said, even more acerbically.

"It was the first thing I could think of!" Felix said, frowning at the warbling giggle he felt through his bond. "Shut it, you. Everyone's a critic, even my magic bird-dog. We got in, and that's what matters, right?"

Vess and Zara exchanged cryptic looks and, as one, began walking down the alley.

Pit trilled joyfully, high and loud across their bond.

"What? It worked!"

———

"What'll it be?"

Harn looked up from his study of the room and flashed a smile at the bartender as she approached. She was pretty enough, as curvy as he usually liked them, but that didn't hold his attention this time around. He nodded to a large cask behind her, tapped and ready to serve. On its side, it was easily the height of a large Human.

"I'm lookin' for some ale," he said.

"Ah well, we've got ale aplenty," the bartender said, shrugging her shoulders in a way that affected her blouse in...interesting ways. She grinned. "But you look like a man with a real thirst for more than just ale."

"You're right," Harn said, and he reached to his waist and pulled out a pouch of weight coin. The woman's eyes lit up. "How much for the cask?"

"Oh ho, a man after my own heart," she said, pressing a hand against her chest. "The whole cask, eh? You headed into the Expanse?"

"Couldn't say. Employer only told me what we needed. Been tight-lipped about all else, the whoreson," Harn lied glibly. "Just need food and drink, as much as our team can carry." He gestured back toward where the legionnaires were seated around a pair of tables. Evie was at their head, frowning.

"I've got that and more," she said, before extending a hand to him. "I'm Palin. I own this place."

Harn shook her hand. "Harn. A nice setup, this."

He wasn't blowing smoke up her ass, either; Harn could appreciate a good tavern, having grown up in one. The sawdust floors, the older, well-worn furniture, even the bookshelves he spotted along the hearth, all of it pointed at a place used more for joyful entertainment than wild abandon. He'd picked the Lamia's Lament out of a lineup of dozens of others, all of them much the same on the outside, save that the Lament had just received a shipment of exactly what he was looking for; ale enough to last the hot sands of the south.

"Thank you. If you're headed anywhere, you'll likely want more than simple ale," Palin said. Without looking, she filled a glass with a dark, amber drink and slid it down the counter. Someone exclaimed in joy.

Harn grunted, impressed. "What do you have in mind?"

"It's Bread Ale. A Dwarven recipe my mum passed down to me, and it's more filling than water and road rations. No matter where you go, it's the right choice."

"Bread Ale, huh? Beginner Tier?" Harn asked.

Palin scoffed. "What am I? A child? No it's Apprentice Tier—strong enough to give your boys a solid buzz but not enough to impair them. Lest I miss my guess, your men are well above Apprentice." She spread her hands. "What do you think? I've got ten barrels you can have for, say, eighty swords."

"Pricey," Harn grunted.

"You'd be clearing out my stock. Takes two months to get that back," she said. "That's a steal."

Harn tapped the counter. "Let me try a mug."

Palin grinned. "Aye, sir." She ducked into the back of the tavern, behind a heavy door.

Given a moment alone, Harn's smile grew. He had missed talking with normal folk about normal things. Too much of his time lately had been spent fighting monsters in the woods and conversing with adventurers twice as crazy as he was—it was nice to get out, even for a few hours, and just buy some ale.

Now, *technically*, Felix had asked for water. But ale had loads of water in it, and it wasn't going to be particularly strong. Not for anyone beyond Apprentice Tier, at least, and that was everyone in their company.

And if it can feed an empty belly as well as wet our whistles? Well that's a smart deal, far as I'm concerned.

The tavern was getting fairly full, folks drinking the edge off now that the monster attack had died down. A minstrel had started tuning his harp at the far end of the bar, and the common room was awash in the murmurs of a hundred different conversations. A good amount of chatter focused on the attacks–how many died, who was wounded, and how ineffective the battlements at the Pass were proving to be.

Harn found a remarkable amount of peace at the forge, but a tavern had a similar—if different—sense of atmosphere. Had he not been on a mission, it would have been a truly relaxing time.

The door slammed open, silencing the rising voices, and even the minstrel's harp twanged in an off-key spasm. Filling the threshold were a number of towering figures in crimson armor and crested helmets that brushed the lintel as they stepped within.

Paladins. Harn held back a growl of distaste, the sense of them bright and hot and bitter, like burning ashes. His gaze flicked to Evie, but to her credit, she just lounged harder than before, though her eyes kept track of the three burly men.

Palin returned to the bar with a stout mug filled with an appetizing amount of foam and set it hastily down on the countertop. "Sir Noxum. How might I be of service?"

The Paladin in the lead removed his crested helm, revealing a startlingly young-looking man with a sharp chin and two scars across his left eyebrow. He smiled, and Harn didn't need any Affinity or whatever to know it wasn't good tidings on his Mind.

"Palin. Please. I've told you to call me Gregis. A beauty such as yours shouldn't need to use honorifics."

Palin smiled, but her arms crossed in front of her chest. "…Gregis, then. How might I help you?"

"We've come for our standard order," the Paladin said.

"Of course." The tavernkeep nodded to a Dwarven woman near the hearth. She stood, along with six others, and went into the back room. "My workers will load up your wagon."

"Ah, that will not be enough, this time. It's thirsty work, up at the Pass." Gregis spread his hands helplessly, and his smile turned regretful. "We will be requisitioning all of your stock."

Palin frowned, folded arms going to her generous hips. "You'll be doin' no such thing! Yarl, go tell the ladies to stop the loading process!"

The minstrel clutched his harp to his chest and scurried away, following the Dwarven women into the back. Gregis Noxum stepped forward, the mass of him more than capable of looming over the relatively short tavernkeep. "That is an unwise decision, Palin. You know who protects this town from the undead of the Pass. Who *controls* this town."

Palin shook, her rage easy to read as much as her fear. She glanced around, noting that none of her patrons bothered looking up from their mugs and tables. Only Harn stared, but he tried to leash himself, to let things play out. They weren't supposed to get involved in a ruckus, not if they could help it. He cast a glance at his people, most of whom were clenching their fists angrily, chief among them Evie, who was viciously digging her dagger into the table.

Don't be stupid, girl, he thought. Harn wasn't entirely sure who he meant, warrior or tavernkeep, but it didn't matter. If either one acted now, it'd get ugly real fast.

"As you wish, Gregis," Palin finally grated out. Harn felt a knot loosen in his gut. "If that will be all?"

"Ah, see? We could come to an arrangement, couldn't we? Have that all delivered to the battlements by the end of the day, and your little…outburst will be forgotten." Gregis smiled, just as boyishly charming as when he'd arrived, despite the clear threat. "Next time, simply listen, woman. It will be easier for all involved, hmm?"

Without another word, he turned in a flare of cloak and clanking armor, his two cronies following him out.

Palin was shaking when she returned to the bar, having sent another runner after her people. Harn couldn't decide if she was scared or furious, but from their conversation, he was certain this was not the first time something like this had happened. He took a long, slow pull from his mug. It was good, and felt just as filling as she had promised.

"It's good, this ale. Pity that armored twit is takin' all of it," Harn said.

The tavernkeep let out a surprised huff. "Watch how loudly you wag that tongue, stranger. The Paladins don't take kindly to...anything, really."

Harn shrugged. "Dealt with worse than them in my day. But it's a real shame, losin' out on a drink like this." He smacked his lips appreciatively and eyed the dark brew. "Took 'em to the battlements, they said. Why?"

She sighed, frustration draining from her tone, replaced by bitterness. "They've taken over the guard posts once manned by Tevin's Knights. Thought it was good news, at first." She barked a laugh. "Knights could hardly stop those undead from clamberin' over the walls. The Paladins have at least stopped the constant raiding...but instead we get this." She spat onto the floor. "Burning ash, they can go rot before I'll send them my brew."

"Perhaps we could come to an arrangement, then." Harn leaned over his mug and lowered his voice. "Tell me about these battlements."

CHAPTER FORTY

Bogfeld's streets weren't as complicated as they had felt when he was rushing, but still it was a warren of ill-planned byways. They'd taken two wrong turns and leaped over a stone wall before reaching a modest square and a slight crowd. A bunching line of injured folks—Humans, Hobgoblins, and Dwarves mostly—were trotting up a hilly path toward a large stone cathedral. Or something very like it.

"What's that?" Felix asked.

"The priory, I assume," Vess said.

"Like a monastery? Are they priests or something?"

"The Priory of the Blessed Fen," Zara said. She nodded to a banner that hung from a nearby lamppost. It depicted a white stalk of teardrop-shaped leaves on a blue and green background. "Not priests or choristers, but herbalists. They are prevalent in the Hills and a few other places. Good people, generally speaking. Come."

The Naiad started up the hill, and the two of them had little choice but to follow.

The path was easy enough, a gentle grade that was lined with large stones that had clearly been there a long time. Grasses and weeds had overgrown them, and a few blooming flowers stuck up between their cracks. The people around them were limping on crutches and the shoulders of loved ones, all of them walking resolutely up the ridiculously long pathway to the priory. The thing wound up from the side of town and followed a serpentine path atop what seemed like ancient earthworks. Here and there, Felix could spot architecture emerging from the ground, like tiered pillars or archways beneath the path, but it was all so weathered as to be featureless.

"Are these Nymean ruins?" Felix asked.

"Of course not," Zara said from ahead of him. "In Ages past, more than the Nym have made their mark upon the Continent."

"So who made these?"

"It is unknown," Zara admitted. "No records remain of these ruins, and nothing more than what you see lies beneath the dirt. Just weathered stone and a winding path."

"The Ruin?" Felix asked, keeping his voice low. Vess frowned but looked to Zara for the answer.

"It is...likely, yes."

Hmm. Felix regarded the bits he could see with a finer attention to detail. He spotted pitting and strangely smooth edges, as if a great heat had washed against the rock at one point. Images of dark fire flashed in his Mind, of gods with too many limbs and heads of blinding light, all of them pointed at him. Of being consumed.

"Felix."

He started, jerking his arm away from Vess' gentle touch. She looked at him in confusion before curling her fingers back. Hurt flickered across her face, and though he tried to not read her Spirit, he still heard the jagged sounds of dismay.

"Sorry, Vess. I...Sometimes my memory is too good," he said. "Old ghosts come back to haunt me."

"Oh," she said, her Spirit recovering slightly. He still marveled at the effect of simple words, no matter how many times he'd seen changes in peoples' Spirits after a few well-chosen sentences. It wasn't manipulation, but he felt almost dirty for having such a window into her moods. He reined back hard on his Affinity, just as she gathered a clutch of optimism. "So...I am your wife."

Felix grinned, if a bit nervously. He was glad for the subject change, but the phrase "out of the frying pan and into the fire" danced in his head. "Well, it made sense in the moment."

"Did it?" she asked, arching a brow.

"Sure. We appear to be around the same age, while Zara is a good deal older." Felix shrugged, but made sure he lowered his voice on the last part. She didn't *seem* to be paying them any attention, but he doubted she missed much. "I've made worse lies."

"Worse? How low do I rate, Felix?"

He froze, panic slipping down his spine like fire. "Uh, heh, no not worse. It's uh—"

Vess bumped his shoulder with hers. "Relax. It was a jest."

The knot in his belly untwisted, and Felix forced a smile. "Um, good joke."

Vess chuckled, a low sound in the back of her throat. "No it was not."

Felix's smile turned real. They walked a while longer, this time more comfortably. The injured trudged far slower than they, and the three of them quickly left the new arrivals behind as they ascended what was now a series of sagging steps.

"This town..." Vess trailed off, casting her eyes over the rooftops as they climbed. At the steps they were higher than most houses, and the smoke of decaying monsters was more evident than ever in the distance. "I do not like it. Something rots here."

"How do you mean?" Felix asked.

"The monster attacks. The injured Untempereds. Those Knights... My father's men would have never treated anyone that way."

"That's...kind of how everyone in power has acted. Ever since I got here, everyone's always throwing their weight around." Felix shook his head and kept walking. "That Knight was probably the most benign example, all things considered."

Vess breathed sharply through her nose as she followed behind him. "He may have been doing his job, but only those I have faced in combat have ever touched me in such a way. The look in his eyes..."

Felix had noticed that, too. Even before the Knight had deemed her a problem that needed solving, he had been...eyeing her up, for lack of a better word. "Well, if I hadn't moved, we would be fighting all the Knights in town. Even without your partisan, I'd put good money on you walking from that conflict."

Vess' eyes danced, amused. Her dimple puckered her cheek as she made that same low chuckle. "Such a charmer. Do you compliment all of the women like this?"

"Just the ones who can summon magic spears out of the air," Felix said with a laugh.

"I should watch you around the Dragoons, then."

Felix tilted his head. "You've never really spoken about them. What are the Dragoons? A Guild?"

"Of a sort. They were founded in the Second Age to combat the dragons that terrorized the skies above the Continent and were a key reason for Humanity's survival in our darkest days." Vess gripped her spear, running her fingers over the curling dragons on its haft. *Dusk Dragons*, Felix realized. *Rafry carved Dusk Dragons onto her weapon.*

"Are dragons a worry anymore?" Felix asked.

"Yes and no," Vess said and sounded a little annoyed by her answer. "The Continent abounds with drakes and wyverns and basilisks and other draconic beasts, but true dragons have not been seen in centuries. My mother believed them to be dead, though others claim they are merely hibernating in the dark places beneath the earth." She shrugged. "Not even Seers have found any trace of them. So, now the Dragoons protect people from all sorts of monstrosities, though we excel at ground-to-air combat."

"Mhm, I've seen you jump. Even with Evie cheating with her Born Trait, you're far better at it."

Vess laughed. "I would hope so! I have trained all my life in my Skills and stats. Had my tutors not forced statecraft down my throat, I would have been in the training yard with the soldiers from dawn until dusk." They reached the top of the sloping steps and were afforded a sweeping vista of poorly repaired roofs and the now-fading smog of monster corpses. "I miss it sometimes."

"Pax'Vrell?"

"Home, yes. It has been over two years now since I last saw my city. That feels too long."

Ahead of them, the pathway opened up into a circular courtyard at the edge of the steep hill. On the other side, iron-bound double doors of scarred wood were left open, each one twenty feet tall and twice that wide. Men and women of varying Races bustled to and fro, their arms filled with cloth and buckets of water and strange smelling sachets.

Rough cots filled the interior of the priory, a courtyard open to the sky above, and every single one of those cots were filled with beaten and bloodied figures. Low moans and sobbing could be heard among the bustle of activity, with more noises coming from farther within. Those who looked calmest among the mass of bodies were wearing blue and green robes belted over sturdy leather trousers and gloves that went all the way to their elbows. A white branch and leaf was emblazoned on their chest and backs.

Holy shit. So many people. Felix hadn't seen so many injured since the aftermath of the Battle of Haarwatch. Their group stopped just outside the large open doors, unsure how to enter that fray. *Who would we even ask for information?*

A woman with a set of small spectacles on her nose stepped out of the doorway's shadow, a scroll tacked onto a thick board in one hand and quill perched in her other.

"Name, birthplace, and description of symptoms?" she asked in a no-nonsense tone.

"We are not injured, Mender," Zara said, inclining her head. Her locks of sea-green hair bobbed, accentuating the motion.

The Mender tutted and pursed her mouth. "Then please step aside so I might help those who ascend the steps behind you."

"Gladly, of course. But I wished to know if we could be of any service?" Zara asked.

That took the Mender aback, but she recovered fast and peered at the three of them. She did not seem pleased to see Vess' spear and Felix's khopesh strapped to his waist. "And what service would you be able to provide?"

"Healing, of course."

Felix looked at the Naiad, eyebrow raised. Beside him, Vess nodded. "I do not have any Skill in healing, but I have sure hands. I would be honored if you would allow me to aid your people, however you see fit."

The Mender looked to Felix, who only shrugged. "What they said."

She snorted and jerked her head toward the inner courtyard. "Come, then. We've more bodies than hands, and even a set of muscles to carry water pots is needed right now." She pointed to their weapons. "*Those*, however, are to remain bound. If a weapon is drawn within the priory, you will be banned from using our services ever again. Do you understand?"

Vess and Felix nodded, quickly. The lady's voice had that quality all moms developed, one that stiffened the spine almost without you noticing.

The three of them followed her into the throng.

———

"I thought you were getting water?" Atar asked.

Evie rolled her shoulders and thrust a thumb at Harn. "Ask the big man."

Harn finished guiding a team of avum into the alley they had designated as their meet up spot, the wagon meant for their haul trundling behind him. "You got the rations, Atar?"

"...I did." The fire mage gestured to his team, all of whom held a tightly wrapped bundle filled with meat, cheese, and journey loaf. "Place your burdens in the wagon. Quickly."

The legionnaires followed orders, though they jostled a bit in the effort. They had been unruly to handle, even fractious at times—the divide between their little martial societies had firm lines established, that was clear. Atar had been ready to pull his hair out or set fire to them all, he wasn't sure which. Luckily, Alister had accompanied them and his cool temper and head for leadership had prevailed. He'd cajoled the legionnaires into a semblance of cooperation, and they had completed their task to great success. They had more food now than they had when setting out from Nagast, and even accounting for the Frost Giants' enormous appetites, they would make it to the City of Embers with plenty to spare.

But the lack of water concerned the fire mage. He knew the deserts, how harsh they could be and unforgiving. Food was scarce out there, and more as like to be necromantic, even the plants. But water was precious. He sidled up to Harn and lowered his voice. "What happened?"

"A minor...event. Nothing more," the axe warrior said. Atar looked in Evie's direction, and Harn laughed. "No, not her fault, though she was itchin' to punch out the red-shelled bastard."

"Paladins," Atar said, annoyed.

"Aye. They had the brass to commandeer a tavern's entire ale supply —all of it, mind, to be delivered to their little wall up the Pass." Harn spat to the side.

"Alright. That's...unfortunate, but what does it matter to us?" Atar asked. "We've got men and women to keep alive out there, Harn. I'll not be mixing in with the troubles of others without reason."

Harn held up a hand, stemming Atar's outburst. "I've a way to get all the water we need *and* get us through the Pass."

"What's this, then?" Alister asked, wiping his hands against his robes. Streaks of reddish dust marred the darker blues. "A way through the Pass? That's good to hear, considering there's some sort of wall there. Everyone kept rattling on about it in the market."

"To keep the undead threat out of the Hills," Atar explained for the sixth time. "I heard the Paladins are manning it and kicked out the Knights."

"Knights didn't seem happy about that part, least not the ones we spoke to at the market." Alister nodded at Evie's hands, still clasped around her chain. "She cause any trouble?"

"*She* did not," Evie snapped. "Why's everyone always thinkin' I'll do somethin' stupid?"

Alister held up his hands. "My apologies, Evie. You just seem...more on edge than usual."

"Pathless make me mad, is all." Evie huffed a short, controlled breath. "Can't help but wanna lash out a little. But I'm not gonna screw up our mission just to vent, understand?"

"I didn't think you would," Alister said. A lie, but a well-done one. They'd both talked about Evie and her temper before.

"We follow my plan, and you'll get your chance, kid, if you're smart," Harn said.

Evie perked up. "Then let's hear this plan."

"Wait, does this involve attacking their wall at the Pass?" Atar asked. "That wall is keeping this town safe. We can't damage it."

"Ain't gonna. Just some light prunin'."

"The Knights would gladly take it back over, I'm thinking," Alister added. "And the word is the attacks are getting worse. You all saw the corpse fires."

"Either someone is doin' a shit job, or it's all gettin' worse. Either way, I'm not leavin' an enemy at my back when we walk into that desert," Harn said. "Remember, we gotta trek back through here on the return trip home."

Atar couldn't argue that. It would be unwise to leave Paladins at their backs, even if it were only a few dozen. "Alright. What's your solution?"

"Listen close."

The fire mage chewed at his cheek, uncertain, but he leaned in. They all did.

———

The three of them were quickly put to work.

When Felix admitted to having no Skill with medicine, he was told to tote water from the spring at the far side of the priory and given two large clay jugs, each roughly the size of his torso. The width of his shoulders was apparently enough to assume he could carry such things, filled up with water.

They weren't wrong. In fact, it was as easy as anything with his Strength and Dexterity, ensuring he quickly refilled their stores without spilling a drop. He noticed more than a few appreciative glances from the female Menders, quite of few of which were pretty attractive. A particularly lithe Half-Elf woman had lauded his efforts, placing her hand on his bicep and squeezing. He'd almost dropped the jug that time, at least.

Vess was among the patients, set to re-wrapping bandages and working with needle and thread at the instruction of a Mender. Apparently, she knew a scattered bit of battlefield medicine, enough to know when to aid a fallen soldier or when to end their pain. It was one of the many disciplines she had been forced to learn in her father's House.

And here all my mom taught me was long division and how to do my taxes, Felix thought with a snort. The two of them were truly from different worlds.

If Vess was busy, however, Zara was swamped. She had quickly established that she could use her power to heal, and now she was walking among the most direly injured and administering flows of blue-green Mana and subtle song. Wound closed up and broken bones healed in her wake, leaving the Menders to follow in clear awe. They guided her to the worst cases as swiftly as they were able, and though she was a Master Tier with all the depth of Mana and Stamina that suggested, not even she could keep up.

Too many injured poured through the priory's gates as the day wore on, their wounds all oozing and blackened like they'd been rotting for days. The monsters, whatever they were, had done a number on the outlying villages, and Felix had no doubt that dozens if not hundreds of people had died on their way to the priory. Perhaps even on the winding path leading to its gates. That made him mad, but it was a frustrating, target-less anger. Why weren't there more centers for healing? Why weren't the Menders at the town gates, providing aid down there? Why did the attack happen in the first place?

Felix didn't have the answers, but he wanted to figure them out. They felt important for more than the here and now—if he were to be a leader of a town or, *Jesus*, a Territory, then he needed to account for things like hospitals and monster prevention and...and so much. That frustration burned, and coupled with the emotional turbulence in that courtyard, it was enough to make him nauseated. Felix ended up squeezing shut his Affinity as best he was able, numbing himself from the sensations even more tightly than with Vess.

"That is enough water, by the gods," a Mender said to him as he carried his most recent jugs. "You've filled us to the brim, boy." The woman was older, an Orc, and she shooed at him. "Go and speak to Mender Louisa. She will let you know what else you and your strong back can accomplish."

Nonplussed, Felix left, lingering closer to the patients. Vess and Zara were doubtlessly asking questions and investigating the situation in town and in the Pass. They needed to know about the Paladins, and he'd hoped the healers at the priory would be able to provide some answers. No one was talking to the manual labor, however, so Felix tried mimicking Zara's tune near a sleeping patient.

It was a low series of notes, tapping into something beyond himself, so pure he felt the vital vibrations of it all through his center. But...it didn't resonate with anything in his core space. Felix had no healing Skills. Chanting was a way to circumvent the System's processes, but it didn't make something out of nothing. It was a workaround and an augmentation, tapping into a primal source to fuel a boost in power.

No healing Skills, but I do have something related. He fished a vial from the satchel at his waist. It glimmered blood red in the afternoon light. *Alchemy and healing potions.*

He had quite a few on his person, and Pit had even more in his saddlebags, though those were a bit harder to access at the moment. As surreptitiously as possible, Felix popped the cork and fed the Health Potion to the sedated Dwarf before him. He focused, and his Manasight traced the blooming flow of power that traveled down into the Dwarf's channels and burst before fading from his view. People, unlike inanimate objects, were far harder to see through with Manasight. Too complex. However, he watched as the potion restored their skin and muscle, wounds knitting in real time as a healthier blush flooded the man's cheeks.

Felix looked around. No one had noticed, so he got back to it, tipping potions into the worst patients' mouths. His men had more potions back at camp, so he wasn't worried about his supply. After all, he had stored the ones on Pit and in his own satchel for his personal use. Felix hadn't the need for Health Potions, not usually, so using them on these villagers didn't phase him much. He could always make more.

Life bloomed behind him, different than Zara's powerful workings or Vess' diligent effort. All of them saved lives that afternoon, and it felt good. It felt damn good.

"Just *what* are you doing, young man?"

Felix pulled a potion back from a mangled woman's lips, waiting for it to settle into her wounds. Once they started to close up, he turned to the Mender who was staring daggers at him. "Healing."

"With what—? Where did you get those?" Her face paled so fast Felix almost offered her a potion. "Who are you?"

Felix smiled. "A friend, I'd like to think. Do you know who else might need help? Any particularly bad cases? I've got some interesting mixtures on me, but I'm not a doctor. I'm just going to the people who look the bloodiest."

The woman's mouth opened and shut, like a fish on land. "Wha-? You can come with me. I'll show you the worst. You have more potions, you said?"

"Yeah, tons."

"Oh, Siva's grace, thank you," she muttered to herself. "Come with me. Quickly, please."

Felix followed her, but they didn't go to any patients in the courtyard, but through a narrow archway and into the priory proper. "Where are we going?"

"To save a life," the Mender said, breathlessly. "Blind gods, I hope we are not too late."

CHAPTER FORTY-ONE

The Mender fairly flew up the steps ahead of him, robes gathered in her hands. She was older, but spritely, and somewhere around her Journeyman Formation as well, according to his Eye.

"Please, this way."

She led him up another flight of stairs that twisted around the interior of some tower, until it opened up into a narrow hallway stretching back along the length of the priory. Midway across, the hallway opened up into a large vaulted chamber, and Felix could even see rows of small pews arrayed far below. They crossed the distance, soon moving through a large door on the opposite end and into another set of far wider corridors. Eventually, Felix ended up at a large set of double doors made of carefully crafted dark wood, polished to an impressive shine.

The Mender hesitated before them, hands on the latch. "What you will see is to stay between us. Do you understand?"

"Of course," Felix said. His curiosity soared as the woman nodded curtly and opened up the door.

Within was a sparsely furnished chamber containing two simple armchairs, a throw rug, and a large, four-poster bed. Two other Menders, both women and both Human, looked up sharply at the intrusion. Pit warbled, his attention caught by the display and something else.

Danger, he sent.

"Dahria, what is the meaning of this?" one demanded.

"How is she?" his guide asked. "I've brought aid."

The two women looked Felix up and down, but he didn't care about their scrutiny. Every ounce of his attention was fixed on the figure on the bed, currently wrapped in soaked linens. She was a Gnome, four feet tall at most, with long, white hair that was matted to her forehead in a mixture of sweat and blood. Her eyes were closed, brows furrowed and teeth bared against a terrible pain—and for good reason. Her torso was split with ugly, blackened gashes, each weeping blood and pus and filling the room with a fetid stench that struck Felix as familiar.

Pit chirruped in disgust.

"What did this?" he asked. His Manasight traced flows of black-green necromantic Mana unfurling from the wounds, like smoke off of a fire. "This is...a monster?"

"Yes," said one of the attendants stiffly. "Can you help her or not?"

Felix was already pulling out vials from his satchel, sorting through Mana, Stamina, and Health Potions. He had a few other things in there, tinctures and solutions that he figured might come in handy on their journey, but none were immediately applicable. At least not as far as he could tell.

Voracious Eye!

Name: Alessa Kartez, Prioress of the Blessed Fen
Race: Gnome
Level: 63
HP: 322/1268
SP: 22/435
MP: 14/874
--

He cut off the rest of the information. "Her Health has dropped to a quarter of her total, and her Stamina and Mana are all but gone. Does she have a Status Condition?" he asked.

The Menders exchanged looks before answering. "Dustborn."

"What's that? I've never heard of it." He selected one of each major potions he had and uncorked the Mana first.

"Her flesh will lose water until all that remains is dust," Dahria explained.

"Jesus. Okay." He tipped the Mana Potion into the Prioress' mouth. She drank greedily, though her eyes never opened. Felix Eyed her, watching her Mana tick back upward by two hundred points. He uncorked the next, a yellow Stamina Potion, and did the same. Only when both totals were comfortably above two hundred did he try the Health Potion. It went down like all the rest, pushing her Health back up toward five hundred points. He could even see some of the woman's minor cuts and abrasions heal over...but the jagged wounds across her chest remained.

Then she started convulsing.

"Whoa! Hey!" Felix leaned forward, holding the Gnome's body down with a single hand. Her head still snapped around until the Menders reached over and each secured her shoulders and skull. "What's happening?"

"This is worse than any I've seen before!" one of them grated out, straining to hold the Gnome woman still.

"The dust is fighting back!" Dahria half-wailed. "Please! Do you have anything else?"

Felix gaped at them all, thinking as fast as he could. Ideas flashed through his Mind, medical concepts he barely understood from back on Earth and things he'd picked up on the Continent, but nothing made sense enough to try. He licked his lips, almost tasting the foul stench from the woman's wounds, he—

That smell. His cores quivered in realization, and that darkness inside him roared in hunger. *Oh god. I know that smell. That flavor. But it shouldn't...how?*

Pit shrieked in defiance and rage. He knew the feel of that rot all too well.

Felix reached up and placed his hand over the Gnome's weeping wounds, feeling the Mana burn against him just as the blackened rot stabbed up into his flesh.

"What are you doing! You'll become infected by its vile Skill!" someone cried, but he paid them no attention at all.

"This isn't just some monster Skill," he said. The rot crawled up his hand, spreading like a darkness in his veins—Felix gritted his teeth against it.

Chthonic Tribute!

Felix seized the rot crawling up his arm, tearing it from his flesh and following it back along toward its source. It coiled deep within the Prioress, rooted so fully he was almost afraid to rip it free...but his Tribute did not stop. The corruption yanked from her Body and Spirit, a visceral net of putrid blackened-green lines and throbbing brown Mana, clear even to normal eyes. The Menders hissed in terror, and at the crimson blood that followed the corruption's emergence. They hunched forward, trying to stem the tide.

Felix couldn't pay them any mind, however, as the corruption was wrenched forcibly into his channels.

It screamed into his core space, a knot of twisting Essence that lashed out at everything. An ill-Intent seemed baked into it, so similar to one he'd faced before but also distinctly different, like distant, murderous cousins. Felix's Will bore down on it, holding it all in place as he guided it down into the abyss between his spinning cores. That darkness roared in excitement, a vibration of greedy glee that almost made Felix stop...but the alternative was to let the corruption take root in his own core space. He wasn't having that.

He fed it into the abyss, letting the corruption yowl as it was consumed utterly.

A spasm rippled his cores, spreading outward from his abyss. Then a current of potency flooded in all directions, setting his red-gold and blue-white rings ablaze and sending streamers of light up and into the Divine

Tree atop it all. Essence bloomed atop his Tree's branches, filling out the already crowded "foliage" with a thicker and more opalescent display.

You Have Consumed The Essence Of A Primordial!
Primordial Bloodline Detected!
Divinity Detected!
You Are Protected From Its Curse: Dustborn!
You Have Absorbed A Small Amount Of Its Essence And Significance!

Chthonic Tribute is level 83!

Felix hurled himself back to awareness, his Body still perched over the Prioress and the Menders all staring at him in horrified confusion. He blinked, leaning backward, and Eyed the Gnome.

"She's...she's fine now," he said, a small hitch in his breathing. The potency of the Primordial's touch still burned at his core space, like a bad case of acid reflux. He pulled out another Health Potion. "Give her another one of these, and she'll be fine."

Dahria took it from him with shaky hands, as if afraid he'd...what? Attack her? Felix frowned and released his hold on his Affinity, letting his sense spread outward like a swirling wind. Fear was there, but as the Menders looked at the Gnome woman's recovering complexion and now easy breathing, hope wormed its way across it all.

"What...what did you do, boy?" Dahria asked.

"Saved her life," he said. *More than that. The way that corruption was spreading, it reminded me of the Revenants.* Pit made a retching sound in his Spirit at the thought of *them*.

"But how? You tore the sickness from her like...I have never seen such a thing," Dahria continued. "You cleansed her curse."

"I've had practice," Felix said, distractedly. *Where had the Primordial come from? The desert?* "How did she get this way? This is important."

"At the battlements. The Caleph Pass. We Menders came to heal the Knights and Paladins alike after the recent monster surge," she explained. "A second attack occurred while we were still there."

One of the other Menders spoke up. "Knights and Paladins wear armor to protect them from the undead scourge, but we wear none. It inhibits our mobility and...and some of us were not fast enough to escape. The undead swarmed the walls, a larger creature at their head. Man-shaped, too thin to be alive, it was a horror." She looked down at the Prioress. "Our Lady threw herself in front of its dire attack, absorbing the worst of it and driving it off with her power."

"She saved all of us," said another.

"And the creature? This thin man-thing?" Felix asked.

"It fled, back into the wastes. And we retreated back here, focusing on healing the Prioress and the others," Dahria said.

"Wait." Felix's stomach dropped. "Others?"

———

Felix was led down the hall toward a closed off room where those injured at the wall were sent to recover. It was sequestered from the rest of the priory, a place of restorative quiet, Dahria said.

"Not everyone injured at the battlements was so bad as the Prioress," she explained as he hurried down the hall. She fought to keep up, and he lingered only enough for her to give directions. "None of them were as affected as she. Most only had broken bones and suffered blood loss. Why are you in such a hurry?"

Felix didn't answer as they came upon the thick door, noticing an array warding against sound on its wooden surface. He wrenched at the door, feeling it resist him at first. He had to put his full strength behind it, tearing the entire thing from its frame and tossing it behind him. The stench of blood immediately assaulted his senses, a rotten copper tang, equaled only by the screams.

"The door—! Blind gods!" Dahria exclaimed.

Cots were overturned and blood painted almost every surface, along with so many corpses. Ten or so men and women scrambled from the far end, only now noticing the opened exit. They were bloody and limping and ragged with terror. That hit him too in a wave of Affinity, along with a mindless, aggressive Need.

"Help us! They're killing us!"

"The others! They've changed!"

Behind the sparse survivors were six figures, each one of them twisted and skeletally thin. Their faces were half scaled-over with a bone plating, and their hands ended in long, vicious claws.

Voracious Eye!

Name: Dustborn Wraiths
Type: Primordial Spawn (Lesser)
Level: 47
HP: 2344/2344
SP: 3225/3289
MP: 0/5632
**Lore: Having succumbed to the Dustborn curse, this unfortu-
nate person has become the spawn of a Primordial's ancient
Will. They are needlessly violent, filled with the urge to destroy
all living things they encounter.**
Strength: More Data Required
Weakness: More Data Required

His Eye picked the same information from all of them, though their levels, Health and such varied. Beside him, Dahria gasped.

"They look like the creature from the battlements!" she whispered.

Felix stepped into the room, his Eye traveling over the survivors. "Do you see the Dustborn condition on them?"

Dahria shook her head. "They're all fine, but hurt. I have to help them!"

"No," he cut her off. "Stay here."

"There are too many for you to face alone! You will die!"

Relentless Resolution!

Felix burst from his standing position into a full sprint, crossing the distance between him and the survivors in moments. He wove among them, Eye flaring. "All of you! Get to the door! Now!"

He skidded to a stop among tumbled and shattered cots. With a stomp he dismissed his greaves and vambraces, letting them retract into silver rings around his ankles and wrists. His Garment flowed and shifted, dissolving the cloak from his shoulders and the tunic from his chest, until all he wore were a loose pair of trousers.

The Wraiths skittered forward, limbs angled strangely. Behind, he felt the survivors near the door, but not enough had passed through.

Stone Shaping!

Intent and Affinity sounded his Skill, and a wall of stone slammed down a dozen feet in front of the door, cutting off the exit for himself and the Wraiths. The survivors were safe.

"Finally. Some alone time."

Sovereign of Flesh!

Scales rippled across his skin as his muscles bulged and grew, and his bone structure snapped in viscerally unpleasant ways. Fangs grew into his mouth, and Felix spat out his normal, flat teeth onto the ground and flexed his newly-grown talons. The Wraiths were unfazed, except to charge him with greater ferocity.

With a roar, Felix rushed forward.

———

"Felix!" Vess shouted in the open-fronted halls of the priory. She could still see the inner courtyard, but thankfully the groans of the dying had faded into the troubled sleep of the mending. Mostly. More people still poured in, but the Menders had things under control. As under control as one could be, given the circumstances. "Where did he go?"

She had stepped away when the injuries had eclipsed her ability to address them and had decided to go find her friend. He had been hefting water for the Menders, but though she saw a plethora of water, there was no Felix.

"Oh, Zara! Have you found Felix?" she asked, spotting the Naiad.

The woman shook her head, the age lines on her face somehow enhancing her ethereal beauty. "No."

The frustration boiling off the Naiad was almost palpable, and Vess had to fight off a smile. *Not so easy when you cannot just Mark us to keep track, is it?*

Perhaps that thought was unkind, but Vess had been more than a little disgusted when she discovered that Felix *and her* had both been Marked by Zara. It had been a way to keep them safe, or so the Sorcerer had claimed, but it had also been a violation.

As it was, Vess was only slightly concerned at not finding Felix. He was a grown man and had a good amount of common sense. It was not as if he would tear the priory apart or any such thing. "He will be fine on his own, I am sure," Vess said.

Zara's mouth pinched. "I'm sure."

"Hey!"

The two of them turned and stared across the courtyard. Evie ran up, with her leathers and knives and chain slung across her shoulder, moving fast but blowing hard. She skidded to a staggering stop. "Found you. Gods, that was a long run."

"Evie? What's wrong" Zara asked. She waved off a Mender who had come toward them, scroll in hand.

"Been," she swallowed between pants. "Been lookin' all over for your sorry faces."

"Has something happened?" Vess asked, looking beyond her friend through the double doors. The city seemed the same as it had hours ago.

"No no. It's fine. Probably. We're about done, got our food and stuff, and we're gonna do somethin' about the way outta here—" She frowned, stopping her flood of words. "Where's Felix?"

"We were just searching for him, actually," Vess said. "Help us as you tell us more. What do you mean by 'do something'?"

Evie flushed a bit and opened her mouth to explain—and the priory tower exploded.

CHAPTER FORTY-TWO

The Wraiths fought hard, moving like greased shadows in the confines of the sick room. Their emaciated forms looked like they could barely hold their own weight, but they left cracks wherever their feet slammed into the stone flooring. Blackened green Mana spooled off them in waves of vapor as they burned some sort of movement Skill, leaping off floor, walls, and ceiling to attack him from all angles at once.

Adamant Discord!

Lightning blasted off of him in all directions, a direct line to the chests of each Wraith. They were hurled back, hit hard enough by his power that they cratered the stone walls and coffered ceiling.

"You might be fast, but I'm faster," Felix growled. A closer Wraith swiped at his legs, but he kicked their talons away with his scaled foot, his own claws scoring its fleshless arm.

Adamant Discord!

Corrosive Strike!

This time, he focused on a single Wraith, yanking it toward him and driving his fist through its skull. The creature collapsed, red-orange sand leaking from its shattered head in lieu of blood. "And I'm a *lot* stronger."

You Have Killed A Dustborn Wraith!
XP Earned!

Corrosive Strike is level 59!

Pit shrieked, eager to get on the action and frustrated that his size would limit his effectiveness in the relatively small chamber. That Felix could understand that about his Companion just from his screech almost made him mistime a punch.

Etheric Concordance is level 76!

Next time, bud. I have a feeling this isn't the last we'll see of them.

The Wraiths went wild, charging at him. Their claws skittered off his scales, too weak to penetrate his boosted Endurance and Armored Skin *and* Sovereign Flesh. They flashed about, nimble things despite their ungainly movements, but they were not enough.

He struck until sand flowed as water.

You Have Killed A Dustborn Wraith (x4)!
XP Earned!

Four of them fell fast, their heads and chests ruptured, their withered skin no match for his claws or the sheer Strength behind them. Felix paused, scanning the room and letting his Perception flare. He knew there was one more, but it had vanished somehow. The windows were shut and shuttered, their slats letting in horizontal bars of light, all of them undamaged.

Shit. Did it get into the hallway? He could just imagine the damage it would do if it were unleashed. *Pit? Do you sense it?*

His Companion did...something, an inward pull, and sudden Felix was inside a shimmering black and red sky. He was floating, utterly free of gravity and everything else. In a flash of understanding, aided by the melodic thrum of his Etheric Concordance, Felix realized he was inside Pit's Spirit. *Which means....*

A hazy window appeared in the black and red sky, and suddenly Felix was watching the outside world through Pit's golden eyes.

Pit?

A resounding chirrup shook the heavens.

Uh, do you sense the thing?

Nope. There was a pleased note in the tenku's voice, a satisfied one.

You always wanted to try this, huh? A warbling affirmative came back to him, sending the crimson clouds scudding across the skies. *Okay. Well, maybe now isn't the best time for it?*

Then when?

Felix opened his mouth but hesitated. His friend had a good point. *Alright. Find the straggler, then, but switch out for me to kill it. I don't want it to infect you.*

Pit chirruped happily and began to stalk.

It was a strange experience, floating around inside of Pit's Spirit and only vaguely experiencing things on the outside. He didn't like that bit, and he poked at their connection, flaring his Affinity all the while. Pit's point of view snapped into sudden clarity, as if the tenku's eyes were

Felix's own. He was prowling down the length of the room, eyeing the cots and the thickened shadows in the corners, sniffing all the while.

Everything smelled awful, and clearly Pit's sense of smell was greater than Felix's own, despite his increased Perception. Something to do with being a Chimera, perhaps, but unpleasant just the same. Pit didn't notice, and was instead sucking in great lungfuls of the rotting air, seeking any trace of their final enemy.

There was a flicker of shadow at the edge of his peripheral vision, and Pit leaped aside, just barely missing the claws of the last descending Wraith.

Felix tried to seize control again, but their bond stalled halfway. Intuitively, he understood that they had to agree on that particular course of action.

Pit! Switch me back in!

The large tenku was dancing back, his large form surprisingly quick to the Wraith, judging by its frustrated screams. But Pit was bulky, his Body too great for the small confines of the chamber. The Wraith ducked beneath Pit's raking talons and tackled into his chest, throwing him back into the shuttered windows. The shutters splintered, and the stone casement cracked with the impact.

PIT!

A startled trill answered him, and without warning, Felix was back, his legs braced against the window sill behind him. The Wraith was in the midst of flinching, its eyes squeezed shut from the flash of their Convergence.

Shadow Whip!

Tendrils of shadow Mana burst from his palms, each one splitting into four, then eight separate strands with a flick of his Will. They tangled the distracted Wraith, wrapping around limbs and torso and neck and face. With a grunt of exertion, Felix pulled and pivoted, *slamming* the Primordial Spawn into the wall ten feet to his left.

The impact was like a cannon going off. The wall cracked.

And the bastard got back up.

"No," he said, still fuming about Pit. He leaped for the bony bastard. "We're done here!"

Adamant Discord!
Cardinal Flame!
Arrow of Perdition!
Wild Threnody!

Fire and lightning exploded outward from Felix's fist in a straight, devastating line as he shoved with all his might into the chamber wall. And then his fist, glowing golden-azure with a deadly potency, drove into its chest.

The wall didn't just crack. It *exploded* outward.

You Have Killed A Dustborn Wraith!

XP Earned!

Arrow of Perdition is level 41!
Arrow of Perdition is level 42!

Felix leaned out of the hole he'd made, pushing his Perception out far enough to see the Menders far below, scurrying around like angry ants. And to see a lower roof, its tiled surface cracked and fragmented by the Dustborn Wraith corpse that had landed on it. Or what remained of the corpse.

Dead?

"Yeah, all dead Pit," Felix said, retracting his Perception. The room was still as a grave, with only the enormous hole in the wall to break the monotony. "What about you? Are you hurt?"

Fine, he sent, flickering with an undercurrent of...was that embarrassment?

"That thing was fast. Don't beat yourself up over it," Felix said. Pit only whistled dejectedly back, almost matching the wind that caught at Felix's hair. The Menders were going to be mad about the hole, he was positive. "I should fix that."

A quick Stone Shaping, and Felix restored the stone wall, though it was clear where the hole had been. His work left it too smooth and without the layer of plaster that had adorned it previously, but he figured it was fine. Better than no wall at all, right?

Chthonic Tribute!

The bodies in the room—and the one on the lower roof below—burst into black smoke streaked liberally with brown, sepia, bloody red, and surges of blackened green. It was thin, barely anything when compared to the Revenants he'd faced in the past, but it was potent all the same. The Essence flowed through him, and he fed it into his abyss. Wild glee shook that darkness, and a distinct sense of...appreciation rose from its depths.

That's...okay. Weird, but okay.

His Mind and Spirit felt a little strained after the influx of Primordial Essence, but not too bad, all things considered. His Body felt fine, which was a relief. He'd been getting better at Adamant Discord, and it hardly strained his Aspects at all when the targets were light enough. Felix was more than ready to keep fighting, if things called for it; he didn't think it'd come to that, not at the moment, at least.

With a grunt of effort, he released his Sovereign of Flesh and summoned back his shirt and tattered cloak. A third flare of Will and Intent dissolved the wall he had shaped, revealing a number of very surprised Menders. Several stumbled forward, clearly having been leaning against the wall as it dissolved back into the floor and ceiling, and more were standing with satchels of herbs and clenched fists.

"It's done," Felix said.

"The others...?" Dahria asked, her face pale.

Felix's expression softened. "All dead in here. Those that weren't...I need to speak with your Prioress."

"That is impossible," said a Dwarven Mender, one he hadn't seen before. She eyed his spotlessly clean clothing and the bloody mess behind him. "The Prioress is indisposed and not taking visitors."

"She'll take me," Felix said as he brushed past her and the others. He felt hands try to reach for him, to stop him, but ignored them all. A few of them fell over, not expecting to be pulled along in his wake after grabbing hold of his cloak or shoulder.

"Stop!"

"He can't—!"

Felix marched down the hall, back the way he had come. A gaggle of Menders followed for a ways, but most turned back to inspect the sick room he'd destroyed. He felt Dahria hounding his steps, however, and she hustled by him in a flurry of skirts and frizzing hair. She didn't try to stop him physically, at least.

"The Prioress is resting now, sir. We appreciate what you've done, but now is not the time for an audience!"

"It's either now, or you can explain why your entire town is dead," Felix said. The Mender paled and let out a frightened squeak, but she stopped talking. *Good.*

He shoved open the door to the Prioress' room, setting stacked papers flying and gauzy curtains billowing. The two Human Menders were there, along with a Goblin and an Orc in similar garb. All of them exclaimed at his entrance, brows furrowed and Skills singing in the air. But it was the Gnomish woman seated atop the bed that he was focused on.

Manifestation of the Coronach is level 68!

His frown deepened. The secondary effects of the Skill didn't activate —likely because Felix wasn't sure if they were his allies or his enemies.

One of the Human women sputtered. "Now sir, your miraculous aid was appreciated, but if you think that you can simply barge into—!"

"Was anyone else injured in the Pass? Anyone else touched by that skeletal undead you faced?" he demanded. "Prioress."

The Gnomish woman had her white hair loose about her shoulders and still in her dressing gown, but she was as calm and self-possessed as Zara. "You were the one who saved me? Who cleansed the Status Condition?"

"Yeah. I also just had to kill six of your Menders who had been turned by it," Felix said, careless of the gasps that spread around him. "So I need to know if anyone else was injured by the thing that got you. It's a curse, and it'll spread, though I don't know how fast." Felix paused, thinking. "How long since the attack?"

"Two days," Dahria offered.

Felix tried to remember what he knew about diseases back home, but scrapped that line of thought. This was a magical curse—a flesh curse, as Karys had once called it. And he'd seen it before in the Revenants, though that had been more diluted than this Dustborn curse was—it had taken people weeks of exposure to succumb to the remnants of the Maw's curse.

The Prioress stared at him. "Nina. How many were wounded by the Wraith?"

The Human woman beside her swallowed. "Counting yourself, it was seven in total."

Felix nodded, relief sweeping through him and Pit both. "Then it's contained. For now."

"How did you cleanse the affliction from me? I would know this so that we can prevent it in the future," the Prioress asked.

"It's a Skill, and not one I can teach," Felix said. "I'm more concerned about why this happened in the first place."

The Gnome watched him, and he felt as if her eyes were weighing him. "You saved me. Saved my people, it seems." Behind him, he felt Dahria nod firmly to the Prioress. "I would be happy to explain what we know of this creature."

Felix let himself smile a little. "That would be appreciated."

"Is it altruism that drives you, sir...?"

"Silas. Silas Veil." It had been an identity his friends had agreed on, though Felix had picked the name itself. They didn't want to risk people recognizing his real name...there had been a Continent-wide notification, after all. "And...maybe. I've just seen curses like this spread before, and it's never pretty." His dumb memory conjured hauntingly realistic memories, but he shrugged them away. "I've got the power to stop it, so I did."

"Indeed. 'What is the virtue of power, if its only facet is to dominate?'" she said, as if quoting something. "Have you read the *Vicissitudes* by Tern?"

"Uh, no," Felix said. "Never heard of them."

She tilted her head. "You echo his sentiments well. Surprising, from a....you are a mage, are you not? I sense a great deal of Mana from you."

Felix shifted his feet, spreading his Perception around himself. The Prioress seemed wary of him—they all did—but he found no aggression in their Spirits or postures. "I am...a bit of a mix."

"Hm. Uncommon, those. A lack of focus has proven the death of many upon this Continent."

Felix only watched her, taking a page from Harn's playbook.

"In any case, you wish to know of this creature. The Wraith from the desert." Felix nodded and the Prioress continued on, still abed and disheveled, though he could barely tell through her regal bearing. "The undead of the Scorched Expanse are similar in composition, but not in size nor in strength. The Dustborn curse is transmitted by their vile Skills as well, but it...is nothing like this."

Felix recalled. The Mender had said it would drain someone of their moisture until they turned to dust. Not a pleasant way to go.

"It takes many, many weeks for it to claim a life. In the interim, we can defend against it with ample water and rest. That alone is often enough to ward off the Status Condition, even without magical healing." The Prioress picked at the sheets folded over her lap. "The Dustborn Status Condition is resistant to our magic, which is why water and rest are the surest way to recovery. But what you described is a horror. A dreadful change must have come over the Expanse."

"Have you seen these Wraiths before?" he asked.

Nina shook her head, from beside the Prioress. "No. This was the first."

That's probably good, right? Might mean there aren't too many of them. To the others, he said, "Where do the undead come from?"

"No one is sure. The desert is so vast, its reaches have never been truly explored. The undead have roamed the dunes for Ages, riding the winds and hurled hither and yon by unknown forces. It is a danger just as the heat and lack of water are dangers there. But it is not unmanageable." The Prioress looked out the window, which faced the Stormeater Peaks. "Ahkestria usually has patrols through the sands, guides for caravans and travelers. Not now. Not since the Paladins moved into the south in force, not two months prior. That is when their contingent was left here to cause all sorts of trouble."

"And your Knights haven't done anything about it?"

"Not our Knights. And they are only marginally better than their Prince," Nina scoffed. She laughed bitterly. "The Knights are scoundrels —interested mainly in food, women, and wine—but they know their duty. The Hierophant's thugs do not care for what must be done, or what always has been needed. They man the wall as if soldiers were to march upon it, never paying mind that the winds of death do not care for mortal tactics."

"Winds of death...you mean the cyclones that hurl the undead around." She nodded at him, and he continued, looking between the Menders and Prioress. "How does that work?"

The Gnomish woman sighed, barely suppressing a cough. "A mystery unsolved these long Ages. If there is a Mind to the winds, we have never seen it. All we know is that the undead seek life to snuff it out, and they are growing stronger. I wouldn't be surprised to find that the entire expedition of Paladins were already dead."

If only, Felix thought.

"So the Paladins went off into the desert...did they say why? Was it to fight off this undead problem?" Felix asked.

"No, I doubt they much cared about the Threats to our Territory," the Prioress said, and Felix just about heard the capitalization in her words. She must have had some piece of Authority, or at least been educated in its uses. The latter made sense, considering her leadership position. "No, the Paladins were sent to do what they do best: hunt heretics."

Pit bristled within his Spirit. "Heretics?" Felix asked.

"It is a guess only. The Hierocracy keeps counsel with none but itself."

The Unbound, obviously. And the Paladins left behind are simply to secure their way home. Felix frowned. *And Primordial Spawn undead are infesting the desert. This is getting better by the minute.*

"Okay. That's all I needed, I suppose," Felix said with a sigh. The Menders had known a bit, but not as much as he'd hoped.

"Do you intend to traverse the depths of the Scorched Expanse, Sir Veil?" the Gnome asked.

Felix didn't answer, just let his gaze linger on the Prioress and her retinue. The Gnome shook her head, gracing him with a small smile. "I do not mean to pry. But I would warn you: do not travel during the day. That is when they scour the sands, and it is then that the undead will find you unless you stay hidden."

"That's...appreciated," he said.

At that moment, the door opened to admit a small, mousy woman in the blue and green robes of the order. She was wringing her hands and bowing quite low as she entered.

"Mother Kartez, there is a woman, a...a *Master* Tier and a noble Lady insisting on piercing the inner chambers of the priory," the small woman said, her entire posture harried. "They claim to be searching for a man named Silas."

The Prioress gave Felix a look, this one shrewder than the others. "My, you seem to be in high demand, Sir Veil."

Felix forced a laugh. "I've been gone a bit. My friends are likely worried." He stood and walked to the door as the junior Mender scurried out ahead of him. "It was nice meeting you, Prioress, and all the rest of you."

"Sir Veil, the pleasure was mine, I assure you," the Gnomish woman said. Her lips quirked to the side, but she had remarkable control of her Spirit when she wanted. Felix read nothing from her.

Not knowing whether to bow or genuflect or whatever, Felix just turned and walked out.

"The *audacity*...!"

Felix winced. Clearly, he'd chosen wrong.

CHAPTER FORTY-THREE

Primordial in the desert. Undead. Paladins hunting our Unbound friend. Felix huffed a frustrated breath. *Things are getting complicated.*

Felix marched down the hall, Mind turning over with these new facts and threats. The information he'd gotten from the Prioress had been enlightening. While the Paladins hunting down heretics was vague, it jived with his visions: they were definitely hunting the Minotaur. Perhaps more, but that remained to be seen.

"Sir Veil! Please wait!"

He was halfway down the stairs when the voice called out to him. A flex of his Perception identified the Mender, though she was beyond the curve of the staircase, and he waited. Mender Dahria caught up a few moments later, panting.

"You—you are remarkably speedy, Sir Veil," she panted.

Huh. Didn't think I was moving all that fast. "What's wrong?" he asked.

"Nothing. The Prioress," Dahria pulled a thick, rectangular object from her robes. "She wanted you to have this, by way of thanks." She handed it to him.

It was a book. Wooden planks covered in fine leather, and on the front were a series of unfamiliar shapes, followed by a title in the common language. "*The Vicissitudes.* Huh." He cracked the spine and saw it was filled with slightly off-set print. He scratched his head and stowed it away in his satchel. "Thank her for me."

"I shall." He started to turn, but she reached a tentative hand for him. "My pardon, Sir Veil, but the Prioress also asked that I inquire about your potions. They are remarkably potent. Would you be willing to sell your stock to us? They would be of great use to the people of this region."

"Ah, no. I'll be needing what I have, but," Felix clucked his tongue.

"But I represent someone who can make more of them. Maybe, when I return, we can discuss starting some sort of...business agreement?"

Dahria licked her lips, as if hesitating, but her Spirit surged excitedly. "Yes, that would be fine. We will expect you when you return from your journey."

Felix nodded and was gone before she could blink. He heard a soft exclamation from the Mender, which made him smile. High Agility was pretty damn fun sometimes.

Navigating the passages of the priory was as simple as reaching for the memory of his original climb, though he supposed he could have jumped off the bridge and onto the pews far below. That would have drawn attention, though, and Felix figured he'd done quite enough of that. It was time to leave Bogfeld and move into the desert. Time felt like it was running out.

A few chambers from the inner courtyard, Felix found Zara and Evie being kept company by a gaggle of Menders. The women were laughing and smiling, which was a surprise, especially Zara. The woman had a humor about her, but it was usually so reserved, and Vess...her eyes were alight and her gesticulations wild as she told the tail end of some story.

"—I pulled the arrow out, and he gave me his barony, he was so grateful," Vess laughed. "He recanted later, and I did not hold him to the promise. Men will say the strangest things when under pressure."

"Oh not just men, my Lady," tittered one of the Menders. A Goblin, apparently.

"Lady Zara, you must show us the technique you used to reset that clavicle. It is a mending that does not take well, normally."

"Ah, perhaps another time. It seems our time with you is at an end," Zara said, and Felix knew she had spotted him. She smiled gently at the Menders, and their disappointment was like a physical wave. He was surprised it didn't rattle the vases off the nearby mantle. "Felix."

"Zara. Vess." He turned to the Menders and inclined his head. "Menders."

The women eyed Felix—a number of them giving him a once-over—before thanking his friends and leaving.

"You two seem comfortable," he said, before correcting himself. "Oh. Three."

"Us? The Menders told us you were speaking with the Prioress," Evie shot back, raising an eyebrow. She had some sort of pastry in her hands and was leaning against the jamb of an adjoining room. "What happened?"

Felix started walking. "I'll tell you on the way. We have to move. Are you all finished helping?"

"We have reached the limit of the aid I can offer," Vess said, gathering her partisan into her arms. She blushed slightly. "I even gave away a few of my potions to the worst affected."

Zara patted her on the shoulder. "A generous move. I, too, have exhausted those who are worth the expense of my power. The rest will be healed by the Menders."

"Does everyone have the supplies we need?" he asked Evie.

She grinned, and a jaunty tune skipped across her Spirit. "About that...."

––––––

"I hate that I couldn't figure out a better plan," Felix muttered from atop one of many wagons currently rumbling toward the Caleph Pass. His hands loosely held onto a set of reins connected to a team of *very* stout-looking avum. "Over the mountains, or perhaps through them. I feel...exposed."

His people were packed into the train of wagons, the entire company —giants included—stowed away among barrels of ale and liquor strong enough to strip paint. Ale and liquor that were almost all dosed with a little something Aenea had taught Felix to mix. It wasn't all Health and Mana potions in his stores, after all. The real trick, however, was making the Paladins drunk enough to miss the Status Condition when it activated. That part relied heavily on just how potent the Lamia's Lament made their booze.

Though it had taken an effort of time and skill to arrange for the wagons, move the barrels, and hide his people—enough that evening was well on its way—they had left the town gates of Bogfeld in just a few hours. The Paladins stationed there gave them no trouble, thankfully. In fact, the woman at the front, Palin something or other, had barely stopped before being waved through. They moved slowly, a caravan not being the most speedy of conveyances, but the teams took them inexorably up the winding path toward the Pass...and the fortress within.

"We are too many now. Had we remained in our small team, we could have moved past them with ease," Vess pointed out.

"An' I don't like leavin' them at our backs," Harn added, not for the first time. "Your change to the plan isn't gonna save us trouble, Felix."

"For the last time, Harn, I'm not *murdering* people—" Felix began, also not for the first time.

"Ain't murderin' if you'll just be killin' them in battle later, is it?"

"You know what I'm talking about. I'm not doing it, and neither are any of you." Felix focused forward and flicked the reins. The wagon lurched forward slightly as the avum picked up speed. Vess had to pull the reins out of his grip and haul back slightly, slowing the team before they crashed into the wagon ahead of them. Felix grimaced apologetically. "Sorry. If things go to plan, then they'll never know we were here."

"Plan," Harn grumbled. "War or skirmish. Ain't never seen those work out whole."

The approach was relatively narrow, though the forest was cleared away and replaced with sharpened stakes in a complicated palisade around the entirety of the path. His people had scouted ahead and found that, while they could skirt Bogfeld, approaching the fort in the Pass was only possible from a single, armored direction. Moreover, there were perches for archers and pikemen aplenty on that palisade, but all of them were empty. Felix didn't understand why they were there in the first place.

"Isn't this place meant to defend against what comes out of the Expanse?" he asked.

"The Hills are a fractious place," Zara reminded him. She sat behind Felix and Vess, straddling a short keg of ale the same as Harn. Legionnaires were packed in, about ten of them, though more space was reserved for the other casks and barrels. "Many Princes would love to hold the Caleph Pass and the trade that moves through it."

Vess nodded. "Right. Tevin is only the most recent occupant of this region. I believe...Kaldis had claimed the Pass previously?"

Zara smiled. "Your father saw to an impressive education, your Grace. Yes, not thirty years ago, this was all held by the Prince of Kaldis. And Ophale before that. On and on, conflict without end or purpose." The Sorcerer breathed through her nose, slowly, and shook her head. "So much conflict."

"And here we bring more," Felix said. "Your Continent is a rough place to live."

"I'll not argue that," Zara said.

"It can be beautiful, if we but try," Vess said.

Evie snorted from beside the wagon where she kept pace at a light jog. "I once saw a Lure Viper. Looks like shiny jewels until you grab it, which is when it sinks its nasty fang in and pumps you full of venom. Beautiful? Gimme ugly, at least then I ain't fooled when the bad stuff strikes."

Felix spared his friend a glance—she was in a nastier mood than usual. He lowered his voice. "You okay?"

Evie just grunted. "Nothin' a little fightin' won't fix."

Within his Spirit, Pit warbled in concern. Felix agreed, but now wasn't the time.

They had reached the fort.

Huge stone walls, almost black against the dusky orange stone of the mountains to either side of them, it wasn't until they came closer that Felix could tell they were simply an incredibly dark red. Aside from the priory, it was the first proper stone structure they had seen. Everything else had been made from local lumber.

Darkened Duststone. A Tier VI Stone? He blinked in surprise after Eyeing the small fortress. It was as strong as the Temple walls back home. *There goes the option of boring a hole through with Stone Shaping.*

The mountains, however, offered some options. They were sturdy, but the orange rock—called Pale Duststone—was only Tier III. *Except...the fort was likely mined from deeper in these mountains. So the mountains also can't be simply bored through, not by me at least.* Felix's expression firmed. *Not yet.*

The guards at top of the gate were young men in white and crimson tabards and simple leather armor. None of them looked older than fifteen or sixteen, and were all less than level twenty. Squires, his Eye told him, and obviously new recruits given grunt work. It was they who shouted about the wagons' approach and they who cranked open the sally port beside the larger main portcullis—a smaller entrance but still heavy if their sweat and labored breathing meant anything. From within strode a single figure, wrapped with that red platemail he'd seen in his visions. It was tailored to their form, fluted along the torso and pauldrons to resemble waves or perhaps flames, a motif that extended up to their visored great helm.

They strode out and planted themselves before the caravan.

"Who comes to the Purifying Flame?"

The what? Is that...their name? Or the fort's?

"Palin, of the Lamia's Lament, bringing the...requested delivery of ale and spirits," the woman said from the wagon in the front. She had insisted on coming, along with her crew of workers, in order to sell their ruse. Felix hadn't liked it, but it made sense.

"All that is ale and spirits?" the Paladin said, surprise and greed in his voice.

"It is. As requested by Sir Noxum, the entire stock of my tavern brought to the Purifying Flame's gates." *Ah, they named the fort that.* Felix was impressed. Not with the name, that was dumb, but the woman's voice barely shook at all, belying the absolute *ocean* of rage that boiled in her Spirit. "Free of charge."

The Paladin laughed, a short, cruel bark. "Good ol' Captain! Alright! Open the gates!" he shouted to the Squires up top. "On the double!"

Felix let out a small breath of relief. He hadn't been sure if the Paladins would inspect their wagons, but it seemed their eagerness to get drunk outweighed their caution. Just as he'd hoped.

The wagons rumbled through the gates, their covered tops just barely clearing the rising portcullis, and into a wide, dusty parade ground that was more than chock full of the bric-a-brac of an active fort. Men and women hustled by, wearing full crimson armor, while smaller forms in pale tunics brushed and led avum around the periphery. There were several staircases leading up to the walls on the Bogfeld and desert side of the fort, where more Squires scurried to and fro while the larger Paladins only half-watched the sands of the Pass.

All of that came to a standstill as the wagons circled around the flagstone floor, and the Paladin from the gate shouted aloud.

"Tithe from the Lamia's Lament!"

A man, larger than most, stepped out of a balcony on the far end of the courtyard. Felix's Eye hummed to life within him, pulling the man's details immediately.

Name: Captain Gregis Noxum, Paladin of the Pathless
Race: Human

Level: 52
HP: 8413/8413
SP: 9611/9723
MP: 899/899
Strength: Strength and Endurance are high. Has long reach
with Greatswords, and strong armor plating.
Weakness: Agility and Dexterity lag behind Strength,
Greatsword is slow to change direction.

He omitted the Lore entry on Humans, having seen that hundreds of times already, but was interested to note the Strength and Weakness entries were filled in. He hadn't fought the Paladins yet, but he'd seen the Minotaur manage it, and apparently his subconscious was paying attention.

Low Agility and Dexterity, huh? Do all Paladins share similar weaknesses? He let his Eye roam around the battlements as he hopped out of the wagon. Squires and Paladins of varying ranks were closing in on the parade grounds, their eyes eager and curious by turns. Many of the Paladins showed a high Strength and Endurance, but not all had a greatsword, and they showed the usual "More Data Required." None of the Squires had any details on their Strengths or Weaknesses, though they didn't matter as much—if it came down to it, the Squires would not be an obstacle.

"Palin! You've outdone yourself!" Gregis said from the balcony. "You have brought us a true bounty! A worthy reward for those who saved the lives of all of Bogfeld. Jakis! Ioldo! Aid the beautiful tavernkeep and her assistants!" He flung his hands outward as the sun blazed in the sky almost directly behind him through the gap in the mountains. "Let us celebrate!"

A boisterous cheer went up from the Paladins, loud enough that it buffeted the Squires and workers alike with its volume. The Paladins were all Journeyman Tier, after all. Felix mimed a stumble, hoping the others had the presence of mind to do the same. Someone clapped him on the back.

"Oi there! Don't be droppin' that keg, little Hill boy!" a Paladin said with a guffaw. Jakis. "Or else we'll take its worth outta your hide!"

That was met with more raucous laughter and another wave of pressure from their unfettered Spirits. Felix saw a number of Palis' Dwarven laborers fall to their knees under it all, but the Paladins didn't care a whit. A bared edge of someone else's Spirit caught his attention, and he met Evie's eyes just long enough to gesture a handsign.

<No.>

The rough treatment stopped moments later as Gregis chastised his people. "Let the Untempereds unload their precious cargo in peace. The lot of you can start in on the roast our dear Squires have labored over!"

More cheers and the Paladins fell upon the spits of meat brought out by dozens of sweating Squires. Felix caught the eyes of his team.

<Set it out. Quickly.>

Together, Felix and his team unloaded the best and most alcoholic of Palin's stock. It was all Journeyman Tier booze, potent enough to act as actual alcohol for the Tempered warriors, and in quantities enough to last them for days. The Dwarven laborers tapped the kegs, and soon full mugs were being passed around in the dry, thirsty air. Time fled as the Paladins feasted and drank enough to kill a thousand people back on Earth, their intense metabolisms and high Endurance and Vitality proving their mettle. Every once in a while though, a Squire would be too slow to get them some food or drink, and a cuff would send the poor dude into the dirt.

"Get a move on! Gregis don't wait for you, lilly boy!" Ioldo shouted at one such downed Squire. The apprentice scrambled to their feet, scalp still bleeding, and brought a tray of meat to the captain. Noxum simply took it without acknowledging the Squire, except to wave them away.

"Ripe pieces of shite. They deserve everything they'll get," Palin said, stepping up next to Felix. The orange haze of sunset had quickly transformed into the purpled shadows of early night. They had remained, hovering at the edges of the fort in case a barrel was tapped out and needed replacing. They had already gone through six man-sized kegs.

"You trust your concoctions?" she asked in a low mutter.

"You trust your brew?" he shot back. "They don't seem much the worse for wear."

"That's quality drink," she all but hissed. Her eyes darted among the walls and parade grounds, and fear rolled off her like a stink. "It'll impair them sooner or later, and keep your poisons hidden. Unless their Endurance is truly monstrous."

"Then it's just a matter of time," he said. "I had to guess on the dosage size for this many people, factoring in their Endurance and Vitality and how their Temper might affect it all."

"That mean it's not workin'?"

"That means it was complicated, lady," he said, forcing his voice to remain calm and low. He had no idea how good the enemy's Perception was, or what sort of sight or hearing Skills any of them might have. That lack made him more nervous than he cared to admit. He pushed steel into his voice, if only to hide his worry. "Trust. Just remember what you must do."

She looked at him, and the sense of fear redoubled. "A-aye. I will not forget."

Palin all but fled from him.

What was that about? he wondered. Pit trilled an uncaring shrug and huffed a bored breath. *Yes yes. I'm sorry you're bored. Soon we'll be hip-deep in undead, I'm sure, so enjoy boredom while it lasts.*

<Careful,> Vess sent to him from across the grounds. <You glow.>

<What?> he signed back, Perception peeled for observers.

<Your eyes. They glow.>

Shit. He blinked, trying to pull Mana from his eyes. He still wasn't sure how it happened or why, but now he knew why Palin got so spooked. *Hopefully no one else saw that.*

"Hey! Hey you! Why'd your eyes do that, eh?"

A Paladin, wobbling on his feet, jabbed a red-clad finger at his chest. Felix shifted just out of the way. "I'm sorry sir. I don't know what you're talking about."

"Don't—don't tell me...you callin' me a liar?" he slurred. The man suddenly went from tottering to wrathful, his finger jabbing with all the pent up Strength of a drunk and a Journeyman Tier warrior. It hit Felix square in the sternum.

"AIIIIIIIEEE!"

The Paladin howled in pain, his finger bent back on itself, crumpled inside the tin can of his gauntlet. Felix stood, utterly fine and equally annoyed. The nearest Paladins rose unsteadily to their feet, dropping bits of meat and beaten tin cutlery onto the flagstones. Without exception, they were all looking directly at Felix.

CHAPTER FORTY-FOUR

"What's goin' on here?" Captain Gregis slurred. He didn't bother standing like those near Felix. "Ioldo! Stop the screamin'!"

"He—this little townie attacked me!" Ioldo cried, clutching his broken finger.

"Oh really?" The captain stood...or tried to—he found his footing less than stable as he pushed up from his bench. He swiped his hand as if looking at his System interface. "Wha...what's—Inebriated. Poisoned!"

Goddammit.

Gregis roared from his half-leaning position over the bench. "They spiked the barrels!"

A wave of rage roared through the Paladins, shoving the lot of them to their feet, no matter how drowsy or drunk. Spectral flames flickered over the captain, a corona of light that burst in all directions, sweeping across his people and leaving behind pieces of its fire. Clarity surged back into their dulled eyes.

Plan B, then!

Felix let loose a burst of strained laughter, drawing every single glare in the crowd. "Yes! *I* spiked your booze, you giant...stupid...idiots! You think you could oppose the Prince of Kaldis?"

"Kaldis? That fop?" Gregis bellowed. "I'll wring your neck and send it back to the Prince on a platter! Kill that man!"

The Paladins charged.

Relentless Resolution!

Felix dove and twisted, evading three crossbow bolts by a hair's breadth. He rolled to his feet, already running as Paladins converged on his space. More bolts and javelins sliced through the air seconds later, clattering against the flagstones. Fire bloomed behind him as Felix ran, just ahead of their attacks. Back to the gate toward town.

"He's tryin' to escape!" someone shouted. "The Light Advances!"

"The Light Advances!"

A chorus of voices all cried the same words—a Skill, Felix quickly realized—and the light of a hundred burning blades charged and swung down. Felix leaped forward, his Strength and Agility easily keeping him out of range as the light and fire Mana slagged a molten hole in the parade grounds.

"How's he so fast!"

"Close the gate!"

Squires scurried among the battlements, and one kicked out a release lever on the winch. The portcullis crashed down, cutting off any escape, and the Paladins' roars turned to jeers. Yet Felix didn't stop, but accelerated.

And blew the thing apart.

Corrosive Strike!

Corrosive Strike is level 60!

Acid Mana and pure Strength hit the portcullis, warping the metal and tearing it free of the wood and stone enclosure. It fell with an almighty clatter, and Felix sped over its toppling remains, his footsteps sure and easy so long as his Relentless Resolution held.

C'mon, jerks! Follow me...yes! Felix cheered internally as the Paladins poured out of the ruined gate, heedless of the destruction Felix had wreaked, focused only on ending him. Pit squawked angrily, wanting to be let loose on the warriors, but Felix refused. *They don't need to know about you, bud. I got this!*

Felix slowed, letting the Paladins overtake him a little. Flaming swords and bolts of light flashed by him, brilliant with heat, but he dodged aside even as Gregis started laughing contemptuously.

"See? He cannot run forever! Stand and fight, Kaldis spy! We'll show you how the Hierocracy deals with saboteurs!" The big warrior leaped a final time, his massive armor lifting off the ground to eat up a good forty feet of distance and landing in Felix's way. "You'll never escape!"

"I was just trying to get away from everyone else," Felix said.

"What?"

Cardinal Flame!

Mantle of the Infinite Revolution!

Fire and cold spun off from Felix's body, the red-gold motes striking each and every one of his pursuers. It seized them with a blaring flash of light while a dire chill poured outward from his channels, coating the path around them in jagged ice.

You Have Enthralled A Paladin Of The Pathless (x45) For 10 Seconds!

Mantle of the Infinite Revolution is level 50!
Journeyman Tier!
You Gain:
+10 MIG
+10 INT
+10 END

Rime Shaping!
Spurred on by his Shaping, the ice surged from the roadway, climbing up the Paladins' legs in a flash.

Rime Shaping is level 23!
Rime Shaping is level 24!

"You—!" Gregis tried to shout through his immobile mouth, but ice soon coated that as well, leaving only his eyes and nose free. Felix grinned and took off, back toward the fort.

―――――

"Time to go to work!" Evie cackled. Her chain snapped like thunder, sweeping two Paladins off their legs. "Take em out!"

Her team moved at the same time Felix drew the zealots' attention, securing Palin and her workers while a few stragglers tried to attack. Evie disposed of them with relish, her chain making joyful loops of violence while the others threw bolts of fire and spears of air and force around.

Reap the Maelstrom is level 73!
Chain Mastery is level 74!

"Thought they were drunk and drugged!" Atar shouted, Imbued Sparkbolts whirling around him. He stood near one of the shattered wagons, his eyes scanning the parade grounds.

"They are! Were!" that tavernkeep shouted back. "Blessed Siva, that was enough to down an army!"

"Not *this* army, clearly!"

"Hey! I'm not complainin'!" Evie shouted, leaping over the mage to hurl a dagger at a Paladin. The blade tripled in weight the moment it left Evie's hand, slamming hard into their eye. They fell without making a sound. "Now get movin', lady! You and your people, into the wagon!"

Most of the wagons were abandoned at that point, but the first two were laden with food and drink, just as they had planned. Legionnaires and Giants had all emerged from the wagons, bursting them apart in some cases and driving even more of the Squires and lingering Paladins back in woozy alarm. Lightning crackled across the parade grounds as members of Arclight brought their magic to bear, while swords and maces and hammers swung out, engaging the enemy in an all-out brawl.

"Stop! Stop, damn you!" Darius hollered, pulling several of the legionnaires back forcefully. "Follow the plan!"

Evie wove among them all, getting everyone moving while distracting the remaining zealots. And she was very distracting. Her chain flitted among the ranks, slashing open leather armor and bashing metal as she increased and reduced its weight by turns. Silver spears flew among the crowd as well, though Vess was more directly contending with another squad that had emerged from within the wall. The heiress was almost overwhelmed, if not for Harn's axes cutting through two of the Paladins in quick succession.

Scorpion's Tail!

Evie's chain snaked out, wrapping around another Paladin's leg, and she hauled back with all her Strength. In the midst of running, the chain twisted him about despite his own clearly sizeable stat. Another thrown dagger ended him as well, the ghostly flame above his head vanishing.

Scorpion's Tail is level 65!
Thrown Weapon Mastery is level 52!

"What *is* that?" she asked.

"That leader of theirs used a Skill to purify their Status Conditions," Zara hissed. She swept her hand to the side, and a wave of blue-green Mana bowled over twenty armored figures, slamming them hard into the fortifications. "We do not have time to dawdle. That means you, too, Miss Aren."

"Yeah, yeah."

Evie followed at speed.

———

Felix tore back through the sundered portcullis, each step shattering the road beneath him as he hurled his Body forward. Still, Squires atop the battlements took potshots at him, crossbows twanging into the night and forcing him to swerve a couple times. He had no idea if those bolts could pierce his skin, but Felix wasn't willing to find out.

Adamant Discord!

Lines of lightning ignited in the air, snapping to life between him and exactly thirteen Squires atop the fortifications. With a grunt of effort, he hauled on every single link, turning it to steel in his hands. Thirteen Squires were simultaneously yanked from the battlements, their cries of fear and surprise lasting only a moment before they hit the hard flagstones.

You Have Killed A Squire Of The Pathless (x4)!
XP Earned!

Felix grimaced at the messages, slowing his pace just a touch. Nine had been knocked out, but those four had died. *Fuck. Why couldn't you all just go to sleep?*

A crash and clatter behind him made Felix whirl, only to find Gregis and three other Paladins staggering to a halt through the gate. The captain snarled, first in anger then in outrage as he spied the retreating forms of Felix's company.

"That Palin woman! She was involved with your treachery! I'll skin her and leave her bones to the desert!" His Spirit buzzed with violent discord, unveiling itself and pushing down on Felix with all of his might.

It tickled, a little.

Relentless Resolution!
Adamant Discord!
Shadow Whip!

Dual Casting is level 51!
...
Dual Casting is level 56!

Felix burst forward, his movement Skill mixed with the burst of lightning from behind. He charged straight at the captain. The man lifted his burning greatsword, ready for the impact which would never come. As Felix neared, he juked around the man, flicking tendrils of shadow Mana from his palms and hitting the three other Paladins. He grasped their breastplates and kept running, pulling them all off their feet with exclamations of outrage.

"Get off me!"

"Spy bastard!"

"You got it," Felix grunted, stopping and twisting. The tendrils snapped taut, spinning about him in a sharp arc and releasing the spell all at once, sending the three Paladins flying off the road and into the forest below. "Bye!"

The sound of ice breaking apart made Felix clench his jaw. *Running out of time.* He looked back to find the captain again, and a growl escaped his lips. Gregis, for all his faults, wasn't stupid enough to wait for Felix to come back. Instead, the man was running after the wagons, calling out to whatever forces were left within the fort.

Dammit!

Felix turned and ran after him, flaring Adamant Discord to pull the idiot off his feet and back into the parade grounds. It worked, and Gregis screamed as he flipped, ass over teakettle, to land in a pile at the center of the space.

Behind him, the rumble of newly-freed Paladins sounded along the road, all of them racing back. Huffing a frustrated breath, Felix called to his core space. Affinity sang, Intent shaped, and Stone followed, rocketing up from the flagstones and forming into a solid wall of sandstone he shaped up and over the Bogfeld-side gate.

"There. That'll do it, I think," Felix said, a bit out of breath. He'd spent a lot of Mana and Stamina in the last few minutes. "Now, for you—"

The captain rammed into him, sword-first.

"Move! Faster!" Lord Reed shouted from just outside the gates, and everyone raced to follow. Loquis' group hustled to keep up, none of them with the sort of Bodies designed for physical exertion, all of them heavily panting and sweating. It was full night now, but it felt hotter than ever, and the Half-Orc had to mop sweat from his brow with the edge of his battlerobes.

That was when he saw the leather-clad Squires creeping from a side hatch. Human, they looked no older than himself and just as frightened. Their eyes met.

"SQUIRES!" Loquis shouted, followed by the crackle of his most powerful Skill. "Fulminate!"

Lightning sparked outward, blue-white and fierce, striking one of the Squires dead.

Fulminate is level 31!

You Have Killed A Squire Of The Pathless!
XP Earned!

Loquis stared at the charred body for a second too long. His team shot off weaker Flashbolts, but they largely missed the other Squire, who had just enough time to kick free the wedge that held the portcullis winch secure.

Right onto an entire wagon full of people.

"No!"

Loquis shouted, his hands outstretched as if he could stop it when, miraculously, it did stop. A pair of huge blue hands held onto its frame, a Frost Giant stopping only a handspan from piercing several Henaari and legionnaires. Amazed looks passed among them all, a brief pause as their hearts hammered in their chests...followed by an explosion that rocked the parade grounds behind them. Everyone moved at once. A second giant joined the first, and together they lifted the big portcullis fully, holding it long enough for the last of their people to race through.

"Thank you," Loquis whispered as he passed the first giant.

The bearded warrior looked surprised before frowning. "Grmm," he said.

"Move people! Move!" Lord Reed shouted again, and Loquis picked up the pace.

Gods, but it's hot.

———

The captain's sword skittered off of Felix's now-scaled skin, and he looked up in horror as the wave of transformation lifted Felix until he was head and shoulders taller than the man.

"What in the light are you?" Gregis asked.

"Annoyed."

He swiped his talons across the captain's greatsword, shearing its steel in half. For his part, Gregis immediately dropped it and punched forward with a spike of incandescent light.

"Spear of Radiance!"

Chthonic Tribute!

The Skill vanished as it burst free, yanked into Felix's channels. Gregis' jaw worked soundlessly for a moment before he turned tail and ran.

"Hey!" Felix shouted after him.

Gregis moved with a series of bounding leaps, his low Agility proving to be less of an encumbrance than Felix would have thought. His Strength alone propelled the tin can forward like a ballistic frog, and in a few short jumps, he was going to reach Felix's team.

Adamant Discord!

At the apex of his jump, Felix crashed into the man, and they smashed up and onto the balcony above the gates. Felix rolled free of the captain, the both of them shattering through a set of double doors and barreling through the cozy furnishings of some sort of office. He flared Relentless Resolution and flowed to his feet as nimbly as he could, only to find the Paladin fetched up against the far wall.

He was on fire.

"You...you're no spy," he rasped. Blood flowed down across his face and the left side of his breastplate was crumpled in. A sword made of shimmering flame slowly coalesced in his hands. "You're an assassin. Kaldis sent you to...what? Disrupt the Knights? Surely he knew the Hiero-cracy had occupied this Pass. He knows the retribution such an attack would bring on his little Princedom. So why? Tell me!"

Felix said nothing, only lowering himself and bracing for whatever the Paladin might do next.

Gregis spat a mouthful of blood onto the carpeted floor. "Fine. Then I'll simply end you, creature...but not before you beg me for the Pathless' light!"

The sword in his hands bloomed, igniting the air as waves of Mana flashed outward in concentric rings of destruction. Fire and light obliterated everything in the room, ripping apart tables and chairs and scorching the carpets to nothing. Even Felix's Garment couldn't withstand the heat and radiance, burning away from his body as fast as it reconstituted itself.

Relentless Revolution!

Flaring his movement Skill, Felix rushed forward, ducking under the man's guard and grasping his armor at the elbow. The captain struggled, and was surprisingly strong in addition to being incredibly durable. Felix couldn't afford to be delicate. He thrust his arm into the man's armored elbow, snapping it the wrong way and ripping a howl of pain from the captain. Gregis' blade fell from his hand, but he was not unarmed. In his pain, he lunged forward, snapping his head into Felix's own.

Felix met him, head to head, a sharp report filled the burning room. The captain crumbled senselessly to the ground.

You Have Defeated Captain Gregis Noxum, Paladin of the Pathless!
XP Earned!

Finally.

Adamant Discord had him up and out of the fort, slinging his Body over the battlements in a single movement. Arrows followed him from a clutch of Squires who were hiding atop them. Several shattered against his scales, but a wash of fire magic burned the rest of their shafts to ash. Atar, on the rear of the wagons, stood with his hands upraised and a crown of flames atop his head.

Felix grinned.

He caught up with the wagons easily, landing about halfway in a dazzling crackle of electricity. The company was afoot and legging it through the Pass ahead. *Soon we'll be well out of range of these Paladins,* he mused.

The Paladins weren't giving up, though. Already, Felix could see that they had broken through his sandstone wall and were gathering atop mounts, ready to chase after their group into the desert.

So Felix did what he had to do.

Stone Shaping!
Stone Shaping!
Stone Shaping!

He yanked rock from the mountains beside them, his Mana reaching and spreading out in a net gossamer-thin and steel-cored. A wall, twice as high and thick as the battlements themselves, rose just ahead of him. This one, however, had no stairs or doors, no way to bypass it without breaking it apart. And it was made of the Tier III Stone of the mountain itself. Though it cost him almost his entire store of Mana, Felix figured it was worth it.

And stay out, he thought, a headache already clawing at him.

Stone Shaping is level 75!
Adept Tier!
You Gain:
+15 INT
+15 DEX
+15 END

They rode off into the night, with wrathful, frustrated screams the only thing following behind.

CHAPTER FORTY-FIVE

Gregis woke to smoke and flame.

Fire roared all around him, igniting the carpets and wooden furnishings in the office he'd once claimed. Tapestries were torches, and smoke crowded all but the few inches where he lay. Pain like nothing he'd experienced since Apprentice Tier wracked his Body, his *arm*, and he gasped in desperate agony. Then he coughed, his throat ravaged by the heat.

That...that burning whoreson...where...where is he?

There was no sign of the assassin from Kaldis, though the evidence of their struggle was written in the smashed doors, shattered glass, and torn stone. That *creature* had been stronger than anything Gregis had ever faced, stronger even than the Commanders, he feared.

Was it...was it of the Sworn? That thought chilled him, despite the flames licking his boots. If that thing was contracted to anyone with the coin, then nowhere was safe. *They need to know...the Commanders...the Justiciar must know.*

With all his remaining Strength, with his blood and Health leaking from him like a punctured wineskin, Gregis crawled to the door. Not to the shattered balcony, but a side passage yet free of flames. The captain tried, multiple times, to redirect the flames and light away. To seal them behind his conjured Blade of Sunrise...yet his Mana was spent, and his Stamina barely enough to propel him onward. His core twinged at each effort, its brilliance dimmed by that creature's assault.

Up there. I need to send a message. He gasped with the effort of simple movement, as if his legs had rebelled against him. *The Ffen...they can be sent....*

He dragged himself into the side passage, up stairs of crude stone, his Endurance flagging. He made it onto the first landing where he took a long, slow blink. When he opened his eyes again, the flames had crawled higher. Now they were behind him, on the stairs. He groaned and hauled himself upward. Upward. Finally, with a desperate cry, he fell atop the final landing. The top of the fort's only tower.

And found the final door broken. Slashed apart.

He shambled forward, holding onto the very last of his Health as if gripping a sheer ledge over darkened waters. His eyes dimmed before acclimating to the shadowed room beyond, only to find his hope...to find it dead. Torn apart.

"The Ffen..." He couldn't believe it. Their messengers, lizards no bigger than a cat, dead to the last. Green and silver scales sliced to ribbons, their Tier III Bodies no match for the monstrous assassin. One was still burning with a fitful silver flame.

"No..."

Only the fire answered—a roar from below.

———

"What was that?" the tavernkeep shouted once again from atop the rearmost wagon. She jabbed her finger back at the Pass and fort they had just departed. "You set fire to the fort! And—and that...that wall! How are we to return to Bogfeld now?"

"Ain't gonna," Harn grunted. "Sorry to say, you're mixed up in this too, now. You and your workers."

Harn's nod took in the Dwarven women still piled atop the rolling wagons, all three now pulled by a double team of avum across the sandy plains just outside the Caleph Pass. They were moving at a steady clip now that the slowest were stowed in the wagons, though they'd have to rotate a few of the weaker mages in a few glasses. As it was, the legionnaires, Henaari, and giants were all arrayed behind them, each jogging as best they could manage. He grunted, this time to himself. *Ain't gonna get stronger if they ain't workin' for it.*

Palin's face heated up, her face smudged with dirt and her hair frizzed. "And who's fault is that? Don't think I didn't hear your little leader's words! Blaming all this on Kaldis? That gets back to Prince Tevin, and I'll lose more than just my tavern! Kaldis will come for the entire town!"

Harn shrugged, keeping up with the wagon easily. Felix's secondary plan had been flawed, but not because of that.

"What does your leader plan to—AAHH!"

A shape fell from the sky, landing with a relatively quiet explosion of sand beside them. Harn's axes were in hand and shimmering with silver flames by the time the sand clouds resolved into the supersized form of Pit. The Chimera lurched into a run, wings half extended for balance atop the uneven sands but easily keeping pace. Felix was astride his back, waving.

Palin had cut her scream off once she realized who it was...or perhaps *where* she was. The woman looked around with wide eyes, suddenly terrified of the velvet darkness in all directions.

"Jeez, sorry didn't mean to scare you," Felix said, riding easily in the saddle. Harn didn't know if the kid realized how effortless he made it look, but that was high stats for you. Felix had stats like Harn had never seen—though it wasn't like he was privy to Master or Grandmaster-Tier Status sheets, or even been in the Interior for longer than a few weeks. For all he knew, having over two thousand Strength was normal for the true elite on the Continent. Harn shuddered. He hoped not.

"Harn, Pit and I didn't see any pursuit at all," Felix continued. He shook his head. "I doubt they could, given how I left things."

"Any flyers?" Harn asked, scanning the skies himself. His Perception was decent, but he couldn't make out much against the impenetrable dark clouds. The desert air was crystal clear, but so close to the Stormeaters and the skies were filled with thickening cloud cover. Unborn storms, drawn by whatever magic was in the mountains...or perhaps repelled by the desert. He'd heard it both ways from Guilders who came this way.

There were no moons, none visible at least. The night felt all the grimmer for it.

"Flyers? No, no monsters that I could see."

"Hrm," Harn grunted, replacing his axes at his side. "Good."

Felix shook his head. "The air is weird up there. Mana is coiling around the edges of those clouds, but it's behaving...strangely."

"It is a feature of the Expanse," Zara said, appearing beside them riding an avum of her own. It was an ugly beast, brown and ungainly, but she rode it as if with great familiarity. "The Scorched Expanse is not a pleasant place for water mages."

She didn't look the least bit concerned about that. For all Harn knew, she had a water core. Or something like it, anyway. *No tellin' with Master Tiers. She's likely got more tricks up those sleeves than Evie's got knives.*

"Storms are chased away. Huh. Makes sense why it would be a desert, then," Felix said. Pit cooed, the sound deep and resonant. The boy patted his beast and smiled. "Yeah. Probably keeps those undead fresh. Sundried."

His smile faded when he caught their eyes, especially Palin's. The tavernkeep had been pale, but now she was a bit green around the edges. Her eyes tracked from the horizon back to the smudge of mountains behind them.

"Palin. That was insensitive. You're probably terrified," Felix said.

"I am," she hissed, looking like she wanted to scream at the kid. "Why can I not go back to town? Other than the fact that you raised an *impossible* wall between us?"

Felix winced. "Well, the Paladins know you and all your people. Did you really think you could get involved and just walk away?"

"I—" Palin's face fell. She looked to Harn. "I had thought you—that you would protect us."

Harn's gut twisted. "Impossible. Not that we couldn't. But unless we killed every single Paladin in that place, there were bound to be consequences. It's why I told you not to come."

"Not come? They took all my stock! All my hard work, they wanted to *steal*, and you think I'd let you walk in there without me?" The tavernkeep and brewmaster scoffed. "It...if they want to come after me, then *fine*. Let them come. Everyone who works for me is here, so what more can they do to us?"

"Your tavern will not likely stand in the morning, for one," Zara offered.

"No! They *wouldn't!*" Palin gasped.

"They'd kill you in a heartbeat for suspecting you of sabotaging them," Zara said quietly. Intensely. "You think they would stop at burning one building? You might not be able to return to Bogfeld...not for a long time."

Palin sat back down, a thick hand reaching out to pat her consolingly on the shoulder. She turned to her people, gripping hands and sharing looks of commiseration. Harn was surprised that none of them looked particularly pissed off, at least not at them. He doubted he'd have taken that news quite as well.

Felix, for his part, looked upset about the whole thing. *And he should. He didn't listen.* Harn kept his mouth shut, though. Now wasn't the time.

"Palin, I am sorry for the way things turned out. But you will be safe with us. I promise you that. As far as Bogfeld goes," Felix paused, thinking. "We'll have to see how it all shakes out in the end. Maybe there's something we can salvage from tonight."

The tavernkeep only offered a mute nod before turning away, back toward her people.

She stopped yellin', at least.

"Felix? I need to speak with you at the forewagon. Atar is guiding us, but there is more to be done," Zara said. She didn't bother to wait for an answer, either, only spurring her ugly avum faster. "Haah, Grouse!"

Felix shared an annoyed shrug with Harn before taking off after her.

The night wore on, and soon the light sobs from within the rearmost wagon faded to nothing. The ground began to rise and fall, true dunes appearing as if by magic. Crimson soil became reddish-orange sand that scattered beneath their wagon wheels and booted feet. The company behind them began breathing heavily almost instantly.

Harn grunted. *Things are gonna get harder from here.*

———

Atar knew his way around the desert, apparently. He was guiding them with a combination of the stars and readings from his Mana Gauge Skill. It allowed him to read the relative levels of Mana in an area, sampling some of the kinds that were out and about. Basically, a crappier version of Felix's Manasight, but effective in its own way.

What Zara had needed Felix's help for, then, was using his Manasight to better chart the flow of power through the sands. Atar was following the strongest veins of Mana in the earth, which would fade and move from time to time. According to him, there was a puzzle to their movements, a secret passed down to him. Anything else, Felix was not allowed to know.

"This path is an ancient protection, meant to keep my home hidden from all but those entrusted with the secret," Atar explained.

"So how do people from Bogfeld trade with you? Or any other place?" Felix asked.

"Guides are offered. Men and women steeped in the ancient rituals that can lead them to the City. This way, we are safe from anyone, monster or mortal."

"Mysterious," Felix said, intrigued.

"And lucrative," Zara said, wryly.

"That too, that too." Atar smiled. "Give me some time, a day or two at most, and we'll soon reach Ahkestria, the City of Embers."

That had been an hour prior. Atar said he had a firm grip on their course, and Zara had wandered off to speak with Vess and Evie for some reason. He could have joined Alister, but he was back with the company, and Felix realized he wanted—needed—time away from everyone.

So Felix let Pit take off, burning off the energy that had been pent up during the battle. Pit's tread was light as wind Mana swirled beneath his wings, even while running atop the dunes. At the apex of each hill, they'd leap into the air, wings outstretched to let them glide atop the cold air currents. Each leap would carry them higher and higher, and in the distance, all Felix could see was more of the same—an endless procession of crimson sands that looked more like purple in the gloom. Behind them, his people moved quickly at the iron command of Darius and Harn, the lot of them all but running.

The miles vanished beneath them as the hours grew long. After the third, however, they had dropped to a slower pace while Darius rotated out people who were resting amid the wagons. These resting legionnaires and Henaari were fresh and took up the old pace within minutes. The Frost Giants never wavered, however, following their Battlelord and marching tirelessly. After all, a rapid jog for Humans and Dwarves and Orcs was a fast walk for the Risi's enormous stride.

The clouds had begun to thin above them, and now the occasional star peeked from behind their gauzy curtains. To Felix's Manasight, it was more than enough to see everything, and the air was so clear that his Perception could make out the smallest of details from miles away. Scouting while atop Pit was difficult, however, so thankfully they had sent out proper scouts ahead of them.

What will they find? he wondered.

"Felix," a gruff voice called from behind. "Run with me a bit."

"Oh, sure." It was Harn. Reining Pit to a stop with a thought, Felix hopped off his Companion. He could feel the tenku's urge to move further into the sands—his boy was hungry. "Go ahead, bud. Just stick close by. I have no idea what's out there."

Pit chirruped happily and took off into the night, sand scattered back from his huge, pumping wings.

Then Harn and Felix ran. No words, just movement. Harn's armor slid about itself, somehow soundless despite being made of thick plates that would have clattered on anyone else, while the man moved like a machine. Arms and legs pumping up and down, each step strong and steady, firmly planted beneath him. He was leagues above the small army behind them, who even now were struggling in the shifting sands. Felix had always admired the man's physical prowess, and though his stats were higher now, he was pretty sure Harn had forgotten more about fighting than Felix would ever know.

After a handful of minutes of silence, Felix nodded his head back at his people. "How much of this can they take?"

"More than they think and less than we need," Harn grunted.

"The martial orders seem decently strong," Felix judged, sweeping his Eye over them again. "Most aren't very far into Apprentice Tier, but I've seen worse."

"None of 'em have Endurance higher than 200, though most have a stupid amount of Strength," Harn said with an annoyed growl. "Their Stamina is low, and fewer still have decent movement Skills. Perhaps half have Runnin' up beyond Apprentice, while the rest are simply movin' their bodies however they see fit."

"You think they'll have Running by the end of this trip?" Felix asked.

"That or somethin' like it. Just a matter of pushin' 'em hard enough."

"Stress and need," Felix echoed, recalling his earliest lessons in Skill acquisition. Those rules applied to him as well, though it was easier for him, being Unbound and all.

"Stress and need."

They ran on, Felix sounding Relentless Resolution if only to try and level the Skill a bit more. He felt as if he could keep up their current pace for days without any Skills at all, but the use of his movement Skill put a little extra strain on him. It was a pleasant burn, like warming muscles and deep, steady breathing. It was almost zen, after a while. No thinking. Just advancing.

"Felix."

He tilted his head toward Harn some time later. How long had it been? An hour? Two? In his periphery, he noticed there was a different set of warriors trailing behind them now.

"We need to talk about the fort. About the Paladins," Harn said.

Felix frowned. "What about them?"

"You left them alive."

Felix slowed his pace, and Harn slowed down with him. The man was puffing a bit harder than usual. "I couldn't do what you suggested, Harn. I couldn't kill them just...just like that. Monsters, sure. No problem. And I've killed people, too, but it's always self-defense. Walking into that fort and slaughtering everyone feels like murder, man." Felix shook his head. "I can't."

"Mercy ain't somethin' you can afford, Felix. Especially not now, with the mantle of Authority on your shoulders. The bastards'll fight you, tooth and nail, and not a one will have a shred of mercy for you."

"Does that mean we shouldn't try? Maybe not here, but somewhere else?" Felix asked.

"If a beast were killin' people, is it a mercy to stay your hand? What if it would kill a hundred people if you let it live? One death balanced by a hundred innocents. I know which one I'd pick," Harn said.

"But they're people. Even if almost every one I've met was a rude, mean-spirited bigot, that can't mean every single person in the Hierocracy's orders are bad. Can it?"

"The Orders choose their people young. Four, maybe five years old and off ya go, whisked away to their citadels and fortresses. To be trained." Harn worked at his tongue as if he was trying to gather up what little spit was left. The air was utterly dry despite its frigid chill. "Trained to think like them, to act accordin' to their codes, to trust in the Order over all else. Maybe someone good can come outta all that, but I doubt it."

"Jesus. That's messed up," Felix said. "So they're all child soldiers?"

"A good way to put it. Of a sort. Youngest don't usually get outta their academies until they hit their majority, though. But all of 'em would be willin' to slit your throat if you went against their tenets or the instructions of their Order. They'd walk through fire to get it done, too," Harn growled.

Felix had seen the Inquisitors act pretty insane before, like that Creel guy in the sewers. "Why? Why would someone do that?"

Harn shrugged. "You forget. Monsters ain't just beasts. Many walk on two legs, preachin' about purity and the light." Harn finally spat to the side, his spittle thick and dark. "I killed their messenger lizards, but that'll only slow 'em down. There'll be consequences for leavin' them Paladins alive, I guarantee you."

Felix didn't have anything to say to that. He had known it, deep in his gut.

"Think on it, kid. I need some water."

Harn left him, jogging back toward the middle wagon. Felix stood there, frowning as the company swiftly overtook his position. When he started running again, it was from the back, where his gaze could linger on the smudge of mountains behind them.

CHAPTER FORTY-SIX

Felix kept an eye on the landscape behind them for the next six hours, through the darkest parts of the night. It was a fairly boring view, all told. Sand and dunes and dotted with the occasional rocky crags. The skies even remained dark and cloudy, the strange Mana currents of their formation pushing ever outward toward the Stormeaters.

The legionnaires and Dawnguard had been changed out multiple times, but all of the Frost Giants still plodded along steadily, never much altering their gait as they carried the barrels and crates strapped to their broad backs. For his part, Felix made sure to vary up his speed and stride, leaping atop neighboring dunes and sliding down the sides, moving twice the distance for every step made by one of the others. It wasn't *just* because he was bored, feeling guilty, and bored of feeling guilty, but those helped. He also wanted to push himself as best he could, and in the Stamina-eating sands of the Expanse, he found it was easier than ever to waste that resource.

For the first time in several months, he was *panting*. If he played his cards right, he figured he might even feel sore the coming day.

However, Felix never forgot his purpose during all that exertion. No birds or lizards of any sort had filled the skies, at least not in miles of their location, and the few monsters they encountered were herd beasts that bolted as soon as their column came close. Pit was up ahead, serving as a sort of vanguard with Vess and Evie, the latter having fallen asleep on the tenku's broad back at some point. He, too, had noticed very little in the way of life in the Expanse.

That's weird, right? The Prioress had said not to travel in the daylight, though...was that just because of the undead? Or because of the lack of monsters? But isn't night time the prime time for animal activity in deserts? I thought I read that some-

where. Felix jumped, kicking off a platform of condensed Mana and into the air over the caravan.

Cloudstep is level 43!

It was not a Skill he used much, but why have the spell if he wasn't going to utilize it? He came down on the far side of the caravan, arresting his fall with nothing but a triple stack of Cloudsteps. The first two layers shattered and cracked respectively beneath his weight, but the last held—barely. Felix hopped neatly off of its swirling, blue-white surface and onto the sands.

No matter how far into the earth he pushed his Perception or listened with his Affinity, he felt *nothing.* No slumbering animals or prowling creatures. It made him nervous.

A member of the Dawnguard loped up the side of his dune, approaching Felix at a steady if beleaguered pace. Everyone was tired. "My Lord! We've found a camp."

A thrill of fear raced up Felix's spine, but he squashed it. "Paladins?"

"Perhaps once. There is little of anything left, and few threats to be seen."

"Threats?"

"Monsters, minor Tier I and II beasts holed up near the waters. None left their dens at our approach, and our Blessings tell us that they will not attack unless threatened," the scout said.

"A handy Blessing to have," Felix murmured.

"The Raven protects and guides us."

"Sure. Are we headed toward it?" Felix asked.

"Yes, my Lord. Mage V'as is guiding the first wagons into the oasis now."

Oasis, huh. "Alright," he said. "Thanks."

"It is my honor, Lord Autarch," the Henaari said, bowing.

Cloudstep!

A series of self-contained hexagons appeared in mid-air, and Felix raced up them, slapping more down with every stride. The platforms were stronger now that he'd leveled them properly, and wasn't falling at speed. They still flexed beneath his tread, but that was part of the training, he supposed, as each footfall cost him a bunch of Mana to maintain its integrity. By the time he reached the front of the caravan, they were already winding into a series of those rocky ridges.

Cloudstep is level 44!

Felix landed just outside a narrow defile where the wagons could only barely fit. Their people were cautiously guiding the avum into the opening, but still the sound of wooden wheels scraping against the rock was unpleasant and entirely too loud. He followed along between the wagons, senses spread for any threats the scouts might have missed.

Within the defile, there was little but stone and sand, but once the passage opened up and Felix got a glimpse of the oasis, he almost gasped. Life Mana swarmed the area, crowding the air with water and earth and shadow and heat all mingling in a wild, lively chaos. It smelled of growing things, and for the first time since entering the Expanse, Felix spotted shoots of green grasses, ferns, and...and he heard insects. It was practically a forest, and all of it was bounded by cliffs on all sides. The oasis was perhaps a thousand feet in diameter, if he were to guess. Plenty of room for their people, even if most of that space was taken up by water. After the dryness of the Expanse, the air felt almost liquid with humidity, feeding off of the lake.

Felix found his friends quickly. Small fires had been kindled, the first in their long, cold march. They cast a surprisingly bright glow out into the fronds and palms.

"...and you have been here before?" Vess was asking. Pit had apparently landed earlier, though Evie was still snoring against his saddlebags. Vess had her spear out and was slowly prodding the shallows of the lake. "You are sure of the water?"

"It is clean," Zara said. She had waded ten steps out into the wate,r and the glow of her magic was around her hands and legs. Felix blinked. The Naiad was standing *on top* of the water. "Other than an abundance of Mana, the waters are as pure as any other."

"Like I said," Atar griped. "The oases are all repositories of water and life Mana. They are spots of fertility in a barren landscape."

"Does that mean monsters?" Felix asked, stepping forward. He could see Alister and Harn, too, now that he'd left the bulk of the wagons behind. "Dawnguard said there were some minor threats around the perimeter but didn't spot anything else." He pointed out into the lake, where the water was almost black. "What about in there?"

"Perhaps," Zara said. "The waters are willful here. They do not give up their secrets easily, nor would I force them to do so. But monsters are always a threat where there is a source of water and food. This place represents both."

"The oases are the place where the chance of attack is both high and low. Monsters will gather here, but the undead will not, for whatever reason," Atar explained. "So, I'd suggest we set out guards."

"A good idea. I'll take the first watch," Felix said.

"Surely you're tired, Felix?" Vess asked, wiping her spear with a cloth. "You have been running harder than all of us."

He waved off her concern. "I'm fine. Everyone should get some rest, though."

"You're not takin' first watch alone, ki—Autarch," Harn said in his gravelly voice. He stomped up from beside the nearest wagons, and Felix was suddenly aware of the company spreading out all around them, looking fearfully into the patch of jungle and the dark waters. "If'n you beg my rudeness, your Lordship."

"Harn—" Felix began, but the warrior lifted a hand, palm out to cut him off.

"I'll be havin' some teams do watches as well. These louts can use the Perception training, eh?" He said the last loud enough to carry to everyone. Felix heard some grumbling and tired groaning, but no one objected. Harn nodded to himself. "That's that. Reed! Help me make the selections."

Darius split from the bulk of folk, head and shoulders taller than most. "Aye. Form up!"

Felix watched, bemused, as legionnaires, Dawnguard, and giants alike shuffled about as if electrified. He read bottoming-out Stamina on almost all of them, even the Risi, but they fell in line with one another without complaint. Felix did notice, however, that they always seemed to group themselves by affiliation. Dawnguards separate from the Frost Giants, often with the four societies of the Legion clustered together between them. Yet even they were segregated among society lines.

As Darius and Harn picked out those with decent stores of Stamina left, Felix watched the lot of them. They were all so different—of course they were. But that difference was causing issues. They leaned on their smaller groups, but none of them leaned on the whole company. They followed orders, but Felix could sense the threads of tension between each and every one of them. Contempt, derision, disgust, envy, even plain rivalry spiked across their Spirits. Felix wondered at recognizing them at all, but each flavor of emotion felt drawn from his own memory, intimately familiar even if his own experience with some of them were relatively minor.

How do I fix that? Felix watched the first watch step away, breaking into smaller groups and marching out to the edges of their camp. The others were dismissed to eat and rest. *Even the watch groups are cliques.*

"Harn, I think we should send teams out to explore the oasis," Felix said. "Maybe mix up the squads a bit?"

"Hm? Ain't a bad idea, but I'd save that for daylight. Even if day is more dangerous, I'd rather not have 'em face death in the dark." He paused. "Potential death, anyway."

"Alright. That makes sense," Felix said.

"C'mon, kid. Let's get some grub and some shut-eye."

Felix let Harn guide him back to the fires, where the less than enticing smell of salted travel rations waited.

———

As dawn rose in the Expanse, Felix walked the jungle.

After eating enough food to put the Risi to shame, Felix had refused the offer of a bedroll and had joined the first watch. Partially that was because he wasn't really tired—a little muscle fatigue notwithstanding—and partially it was because he didn't really trust that the oasis was safe. It was too dark and too strange for him to feel comfortable at all.

As a tertiary bonus, he figured it would also let him get to know his people a bit more. Figure out what made them tick, what separated them and drove them into their conflicting groups. He had even approached several of the watch pairs, intent on engaging them in conversation, but not a single one would say more than three words to him. Fear, awe, nervous stress, all of them contributed to their silence, and nothing Felix said was able to break that ice. Not even with the Frost Giants.

So, having exhausted that avenue, Felix had begun exploring the jungle himself. It was mostly woody plants and heavy, oversized fronds with a healthy dose of stringy, hanging moss. Vines curled off branches, looping from one tree to another, something Felix mistook for giant snakes more times than he could count. No matter that his Perception saw them as plant fiber and his Voracious Eye cataloged just about everything he glanced at, the lizard-brain reaction to a snake on your face was probably the same from Beginner all the way to Paragon Tier.

Not to say that there weren't snakes. There were, but they hid higher in the branches of the trees, not interested in Felix or his face. There were also beetles, birds, and a plethora of rodent like creatures called Lesser Ratlings. They were all Tier II creatures, except the bugs, which were Tier I prey for just about everything despite their basketball size. The birds weren't nearly as large, but he caught surprisingly strong flashes of wind Mana surge in their tiny, flitting bodies. Twice he saw a Jeweled Thresher absolutely devastate one of the beetles with nothing more than its flapping wings.

Brutal.

Other wildlife was not so violent, but as the sun rose, the activity in the oasis burst to a humming crescendo. Throaty calls and trilling shrieks joined the endless rustle and splash of things moving all around him. It was pretty cool, actually.

Eventually, Felix made his way to the edge of the basin, where the cliffs rose higher than the trees and seemed to reflect the oasis' life-giving moisture back on itself. Felix eyed the sky, able to see it without a canopy for the first time in a bit, and saw that the clouds that had plagued their journey had all but vanished. In its place was a white sky, barely touched with blue, and the warm, buttery yellow of a rising sun. The shadows of the oasis were long and deep, but growing lighter by the minute. Felix took the moment to enjoy the heat as it pushed back the chill of night.

Felix sighed, loosening his sword and leaning back against the foot of the cliff. The edges of the oasis were raised just slightly, forming something like a bowl, and he could see a little ways into the center from this position. "Karys?"

"Yes, my Lord?" the green-gold light buzzed up from his blade.

"Relax. It's just us right now."

"As you wish. How might I be of service, Felix?" Karys said, his voice thick with...it wasn't sarcasm. Sort of the opposite, really, but somehow just as tongue in cheek? Felix shook his head.

"It's been a bit since my last check in. How is the Stronghold?" he asked.

"It is fine. The Risi and Henaari got into a minor tiff over a hunting accident, but other than a little bruised pride, no one had been hurt. The Legion has been...an irritant, but nothing I cannot handle."

Felix frowned. "An irritant how?"

"They have been consistently poking their noses where it is neither wanted nor needed, claiming a need to patrol 'the Fiend's holdings.' Thankfully, the wards on the Temple and Crafting Halls keep their curiosity out. It was wise of you to restrict access to those areas, my— Felix," Karys said.

"That was more Vess' idea than mine," Felix protested.

"A wise ruler both listens to and puts into action the advice of trusted experts," Karys said, almost sounding like he was quoting a passage. "Vessilia Dayne is a valuable ally, but always remember that it is you who is Autarch. The credit—and the blame—will always be on you."

Felix shifted uncomfortably. "What else is the Legion doing? You said they were patrolling?"

"Yes. The Farwalker has them patrolling the Stronghold same as the rest, going on hunts, getting stronger and increasing our stores little-by-little."

"They're not over-hunting in any one area, are they?" Felix asked. The Henaari had been adamant about that practice, as it depleted natural resources too fast for the Continent to reproduce them. Coming from Earth and the general shitshow of its own misused resources, Felix had latched onto the concept pretty quickly. "We need those plants and beasts to keep up with our production."

"Do not worry. The Dawnwalkers have sent at least a few of their members with every patrol, whether they are Legion or giant." Karys grunted, a metallic sort of sound from his Body transmitted through a sword. "No one is happy about that, but the Farwalker could not be swayed, even by his own Synod. I, however, believe it necessary. At this point, the Dawnwalkers know the area far better than anyone else."

"Make sure they keep it up. I'm running into similar issues here." Felix chewed on his lip, Voracious Eye scanning through the jungle. "Fractured factions. If we're all living together, then we're all gonna work together...*nicely*. They don't have to like each other, but make it clear I expect them to respect one another."

"It will be done."

"How's the healing stock coming?" Felix asked. "We had a good amount before, but I think we've found some buyers for the future. They've access to some interesting herbs out in the Ghreldan Hills. Called the Menders of the Blessed Fen."

"Healers? That is good news. Perhaps they may be swayed to join your Territory, like the Nagafolk."

Felix wasn't sure about that, but they were good allies, anyway. From what he'd learned of the Continent, healers and surgeons weren't all that common. Karys confirmed that he'd heard the same from his various inquiries. The Paragon turned Archonic Construct was at best out of touch with the state of the world, and he had apparently been interrogating people like A'zek and Wyvora for everyday information.

"How is the Mirk Enclosure doing? Still going strong?" Felix was most nervous about that one, even though they had figured out a temporary solution. The array that protected his Territory required him to feed it a ridiculous amount of Mana every twelve hours, an amount that no one in his Stronghold could produce so reliably. At some point in the future, he was told his Stronghold would generate vast amounts of ambient Mana, but that wasn't the case currently.

"I've had no issues donating the Spirit Fruit to the array," Karys said. That had been the temporary fix, though it was an expensive one. The rarefied Spirit Fruit would be rendered down to base Mana—which happened to be a *lot*—and fed into the Control Node once per day. "It has even afforded us a little surplus of energy, just in case the other arrays need to be used."

"That's...good, at least." Felix tried to suppress a grimace. The loss of one Spirit Fruit a day was a blow, as each one was several Essence Draughts he now couldn't use on his friends and allies. The Atlantes Anima may have been absolutely massive, but it wasn't infinite. It felt painful to waste it.

"Hopefully, we can resolve this soon. We're already in the desert, and Atar has us a few days out from Ahkestria." A bubble of excitement rose in his chest, and Felix realized he was happy to be traveling to new places, even if it was dangerous and expensive.

"Ahkestria was one of the ancient cities, though it must have changed vastly since I last laid eyes upon it," Karys said.

"You didn't mention that before," Felix said.

"It did not feel pertinent to your preparations. At the time, it was a city nestled upon an island in the center of an inland sea. Clearly, much has changed."

"Yeah, you could say that." A whole sea? It had been thousands of years since Karys' had fallen in stasis, but how did an entire sea dry up? Felix had an idea, and he didn't like it. "Did...have you heard of a Primordial in that inland sea?"

"A Primordial? Not that I—has something happened?"

"Yeah. I found—"

There was a scream, high and terrified.

"What was that?" Karys asked.

A dozen more voices joined the first, panic filling their throats. Felix scanned the jungle, pushing his Perception and Affinity to the limits. Ten thousand threads sprang into existence around him, some brighter than others, and some—*There!*

The earth jolted, and Felix fell to a knee, it was so violent. Rocks tumbled down from the cliffs above, but he shattered them as they landed near him. The jungle swayed, and what little he could see of the water was sloshing up into turbulent waves.

His people were being attacked on the far side of camp.

Adamant Discord!

Felix shot into the sky.

CHAPTER FORTY-SEVEN

"Walk lightly and with the darkness' Blessing," Osyk said, pointing at the cluttered undergrowth and placing his foot in demonstration. "Toe-heel, like so. If your tread is a whisper, then the story behind you will not overwhelm what comes."

Loquis attempted to copy what Osyk was demonstrating, but found his feet entirely too ungainly. His Half-Orc heritage left him with bonuses to Strength and Endurance, but nothing for his Agility or Dexterity. Training those had been a low priority, even after he'd gained admittance to the Arclight society—and by that point, he was all in on Willpower and Intelligence. At the very least, he wasn't the only one struggling. Their entire group was fumbling through the underbrush, robes and armor and weapons catching on every rock and root. A Bone fighter stumbled and got his head caught up in a vine, requiring one of the Blades to cut him free.

Pava leaned into his shoulder, her own sword out and low as she cut her way forward. "Did you understand any of that?"

Loquis shushed his friend. "He's teaching us about Stealth."

"...embrace the darkness, for it will hide you as it hides the rest. The light has its time, and all things must come to it eventually, but there is balance. Seek the balance, tip it in your favor, else your prey will hear your story before you can write its ending." Osyk stopped talking and smiled at them all. "Understand?"

"No?" said another Blade, like Pava. He was a strapping young Dwarf, beardless and all, and had a very slender thrusting saber at his hip. "Can you talk in normal words? The common tongue?"

A few of the other legionnaires laughed, though Pava frowned at the Dwarf. "Don't be an ass, Asaad."

"Me? I'm not the one explaining how to Stealth by talking about storytime!" Asaad shouted. The Dwarven Blade was always causing trouble, but usually that meant picking fights with the Fists or threatening a few of the Arclights. Loquis furrowed his brows. He was insulting their allies now, a people who were a part of the Autarch's Stronghold long before they had arrived.

"If you listen for once, then maybe you'd actually learn something," he grated out, and Asaad turned to him in surprise. Loquis was surprised at himself, in fact, but he kept going. "The Autarch has decreed that we all work *together*. Onslaught and the Lord Hand explained this."

"Well, well. The mage finally speaks up. You think I don't listen? You think I don't know we were told to pair up with some worthless mages and weaponless layabouts?" Asaad prowled toward Loquis and raised a blunt finger at the Half-Orc. "If you were a man, I'd fight you right here and now."

Asaad sneered, his fleshy, beardless face splotchy with the mounting heat. "But you're not. You're just a *mage*."

"*Enough*," a voice rumbled, and it was like rocks falling. An enormous blue hand reached across the forest and pointed at the Dwarf and Loquis both. "This talking is worthless. Unless you mean to draw blood, we move on. Now."

Loquis swallowed, trying not to show any fear of the looming Frost Giant. He doubted he was very successful. The creature—Geir, he was called—stood eleven strides tall, one of the shorter specimens, but still powerfully built and possessing formidable ice magic. There was no world in which the Half-Orc wished to oppose any of the Frost Giants.

"Bad enough they mingled us with trash like you," Asaad muttered at Loquis. "Now we have monsters giving orders."

"Shut it, *Ass*-aad," Pava said pleasantly.

The churlish Dwarf opened his mouth to say something nasty, but Osyk motioned them all to silence.

"Wary. Enemies ahead," the Henaari said softly.

Loquis crept after the Dawnguard scout, moving as quietly as his weak Body could manage. Pava and the others followed, even the giant, until they had emerged into a clearing by the edge of the lake. They had been told to hunt the jungles of the oasis, and while there were beasts aplenty, Onslaught had actually told them to find the true threats.

Designated as the squad leader, Osyk had quickly led them into the dense jungle and along a barely-there game trail for the last hour while the jungle woke up all around them. Now, the clearing buzzed with the sound of those odd beetles and the chittering noise of some sort of rodent.

"What is it?" Pava asked. "I don't see anything."

Loquis felt something crawling across his skin and shivered. There was nothing there, but a phantom pressure tickled his exposed hands and arms. In response, lightning crackled across his knuckles, and the mage looked sharply to the left.

"There!"

A shape exploded from the sand, a creature as big as an avum with eight legs and a dark carapace. Claws snapped at them, catching the hooked spear Osyk slashed at it and hauling the Henaari straight into the air.

"Aaah!"

"Cask Scorpions!" Asaad screamed. He yanked his sword from its sheath and thrust forward. A vibrant blue slash appeared across the scorpion's claw, scratching its chitin but not breaking it. Two more followed, the Blade engaging his Skills, sword moving in a devastating blur.

He didn't notice when the tail lifted and thrust, fast as his own strike.

"Fury's Ward!" Loquis shouted, pouring Mana from his feet even as he tackled the Dwarf to the ground. A sharp pressure hit him, slamming against the Half-Orc's body from all directions as the ward dispersed the Scorpion's attack. They rolled, both legionnaires a tangle of arms, legs, and sand.

Fury's Ward is level 28!

"Gerroff me!" Asaad threw Loquis from his chest. The Dwarf's Strength was impressive, and Loquis' body thin, so he landed with a pained cry a good five strides away. "Don't you dare interfere in my fight!"

"You were gonna die, you imbecile!" Loquis shouted over the sounds of battle and slithering sands. He looked up. The Scorpion came at them again. "Fury Ward!"

Another shield of crackling energy formed around the Dwarf just before the Scorpion's tail struck a second time. Loquis gasped, the pressure transferred to him. *Too much!*

A third strike, and the Ward shattered. Claws slammed into Asaad's blade, knocking it askew as one of its sharp legs slashed at the Dwarf's. Blood blossomed along his thigh, and he stumbled back. The tail came back, bobbing and weaving. It struck.

And skittered off an icy shield on the arm of Geir. The Frost Giant roared as he ducked under and thrust an ice-forged spear under the creature's carapace. The Cask Scorpion screeched, pivoting wildly, but it could not stop the giant's Strength. Another bellow and the overgrown pest was flipped onto its back...and Geir jumped atop it, shield and spear going to work.

You Have Killed A Cask Scorpion!
XP Earned!

"Fiend's fury," Asaad gasped. "I had it!"

Geir rumbled. "You did not. Stand. There are more."

Loquis had been so consumed by the fight, he hadn't noticed anything else, but now he shouted in surprise. All around them, the sands at the shoreline had burst asunder, and a dozen Cask Scorpions had rushed their people. Battle raged as groups of their squad—two or three at a time —all tried to fight off one or two of the creatures, but blood was on the ground. And it wasn't monster blood.

"Form up! Form up!" Osyk screamed, desperately slashing at an advancing Scorpion. "On me! For the Raven!"

No one listened. The Blades and Bones were busy engaging their own foes, strides away from one another but without a single attempt toward cooperation. Nevin, the only other Arclight, was all alone. Before Loquis could move or cast, a barbed tail burst through Nevin's chest, killing him instantly.

The Scorpions charged through them, driving them into even more fractious pieces, and Loquis despaired.

"We fight!" Geir rumbled, grappling with the nearest Scorpion. "*Tu Krakora!* Thunderweaver! Muster your strength and hurl it at this foe!"

Pava dove in, a slashing cyclone. Her longsword smashed aside the Scorpion's flailing claws and jabbing legs. Asaad even thrust, knocking its weaving tail askew. Loquis gasped and brought his hands together with a clap of thunder.

Fulmination!

A double-finger-thick blast of blue-white lightning snapped out of Loquis' palms. His friend and allies leaped aside at the last moment, just as the bolt hit the Scorpion dead in its drooling mandibles. It screeched in unholy pain and horror, and a piece of Loquis felt a furious glee.

Fulmination!
Fulmination!
Fulmination!

Bolt after bolt seared the beast, until its dark carapace was charred and sparking. Until his use of Mana made him feel suddenly lightheaded and sick to his stomach. He worried, for an instant, that the creature would attack in his moment of weakness, but it was unfounded. There were cracks and wet, squelching sounds before the trilling sound of a System notification.

You Have Killed A Cask Scorpion!
XP Earned!

Congratulations!
You Have Earned A Title!
The Wrath Of The Heavens (Rare)!
Lightning comes to you easier with each passing day, forging your being into one of galvanizing force.
+5 WIL, INT, PER

Power surged into Loquis, flaring across his channels and core space like a black storm. His Mana was low—too low—but every other part of him jittered and spasmed. Combined, it was all he could do to take a ragged breath and look around him. His squad was falling back, the tide of Scorpions still too much. Geir and Asaad and Pava were all breathing heavily nearby.

"We—we move on to the next one," Loquis said, a bit tremulously. He fumbled with a Mana Potion and took a swig. "Take on the two fighting the Blades."

"Do you have enough juice left?" Pava asked. Her own arm was trembling, the defined muscles twitching despite her white-knuckled grip on her sword.

"I'll...I'll be fine," Loquis said. Geir rumbled, but whether it was in disbelief or agreement, the Half-Orc couldn't tell. "We need to rally. We—"

The earth bucked, rising beneath their feet and dropping so hard all of them were thrown. Loquis cried out, his back smashing into a rock as the groaning, shaking sands exploded into a frenzy of motion. The waters surged, and waves of dark, cool liquid hit them and hurled their prone bodies back into the treeline. Loquis gasped for breath amid the foam and spray, barely regaining his feet as something *immense* rose from the waters.

It was a Scorpion, three times as big as Geir. So big that it could not possibly be the same creature. He flared his Analyze, only able to catch its name.

Name: Manadrenched Scorpion

Its claws came down, and the shoreline was obliterated. Legionnaires, Henaari, Giant, none of them were immune to the sheer force of its impact. Had Loquis not already been fetched up against a tree, he would have been tossed like a child's doll into the jungle, where even now more Cask Scorpions were skittering and attacking with abandon.

The Manadrenched Scorpion scuttled forward several steps, raising its claws again. This time, it aimed at the trees. At them. Loquis tried to cry out, but his breath wouldn't come. Lightning skittered from his channels, unformed and unfocused.

The claws came down.

And were seized by a burning, red-gold flame.

"Fiend," Loquis whispered, heart in his throat. "Oh thank the gods."

The flames spread, splashing down over the beach and sweeping into the trees. All around him, the mage saw hulking forms stopped in their tracks as fire ignited their chitin, while the Manadrenched monstrosity shook above.

"Fucking bugs!" the Autarch shouted, and the force of it was enough to shake the trees around them. "You want to crush something? I'll show you how!"

An impact sounded so loud that Loquis felt his Health drop, and the two-dozen-stride scorpion lurched to the right. Lightning crackled around its too-large body, and the thing *screamed*.

Loquis stumbled into the jungle, quickly finding Pava and Asaad behind a grove of tangled trees. Together, they ran to the nearest Scorpion, where Geir was already attacking its paralyzed form. It was half-eaten by the Fiend's hungry flames, but died to a saber thrust between its mandibles and through its brain.

You Have Killed A Cask Scorpion!
XP Earned!

"To the next!" Loquis shouted, already running. The huge beast behind them screamed again and again, but the Fiend did not stop.

And neither did they.

———

Cardinal Flame is level 81!
Adamant Discord is level 80!
Rain of Cataclysm is level 51!
Corrosive Strike is level 64!
Wild Threnody is level 68!
Armored Skin is level 76!
Cloudstep is level 48!

"Goddamn, that was a workout."

Felix stood atop the now-still form of the Manadrenched Scorpion, nursing his shoulder as he kept Sovereign of Flesh on a low burn. He could feel the injury knitting itself back together and eating up his Essence stores as a result. He'd used his battleform during the fight, as with the Dustborn Wraiths, hoping to get it to Tier up but it hadn't been enough. "That last level before Tiering is always such a pain."

Chthonic Tribute!

The mass of monster beneath him sublimated into a dense, black cloud streaked with blue-green light and a deep, pulsing purple. He dropped through it, splashing right into the shallow water.

Oh right.

His Garment shifted into swim trunks, letting his naked calves soak in the wonderfully chilly waters. Felix scanned the beach as he walked and ate Essence. A few more of those giant scorpions were around, but they had been surrounded by his people, all of whom were hurling Skills at it from a distance. Two more monsters died as he observed. The squad had done a decent job with these monsters, though he didn't miss several bodies washed up against the trees. That stabbed at him more than a little, guilt and sorrow warring against the anger in him. Of them all, the guilt was almost as useless as the anger.

I was the one who sent them out like this, who brought them along, he chastised himself. *The monsters killed them, but I'm the cause. I have to be better.*

And, he admitted to himself. *They need to get stronger. Or else, they'll never survive this desert.*

A giant spotted him as he came ashore, and it dropped to a knee before him. "*Tu Ostakkur.* My Lord."

Felix waved him back to his feet. "Where is your squad leader...Geir?"

Geir stood, all eleven feet of him, and looked proud that Felix knew his name. It didn't seem to occur to the giant that Felix might have just Analyzed him. "Osyk is there, leading the squad against the last insect. It is nearly dead, so he sent me here to see how we could aid you."

Obviously, Felix could feel the squad fighting not twenty yards into the dense jungle, though he couldn't see them by any standard definition of the word.

"Gather the dead. Teammate and monster alike. Do any of you have the Butchering Skill?" he asked.

"No, my Lord. But we all have the dressing-knife your Forgemaster made for us," Geir said, displaying a blade more like a machete on his hip. One of the simpler enchantments Rafny had taught Harn, the dressing-knives were inlaid with an array to stop monster corpses from decaying for a period of time.

"Good. Use it." Felix's ears perked up. In the distance, he could feel more things waking. He could almost hear the volley of spells and Skills against them, and it wasn't more Scorpions. It was too far for that. "Return to the camp and report back to Harn or Reed. There's more out there."

Adamant Discord!

Felix burst up through the trees, his Body and Mind sore but pressing on anyway. He flared the Skill again, shifting directions so he was yanked along the top, inches from the canopy. The sound of battle grew louder.

He dove into the trees once more.

CHAPTER FORTY-EIGHT

Felix found two squads battling an altogether different sort of enemy. Greater Ratlings, each one as big as a tiger and just as fierce; they were accompanied by a swarm of their Lesser brethren. Blades and Bones engaged them directly while Henaari used their polearms to stab over their shoulders. A small number of Fists were weaving through the mess of smaller foes, dispatching them as quickly as possible with their weighted gauntlets, while the Arclights dropped sparking bolts from the sky along the Greater Ratlings' backs. Vess, wonder that she was, stood atop two of her own floating Spears and was shouting out orders and directions to them all.

He flared Adamant Discord and stopped himself, pulling in multiple directions so that he floated about a hundred feet off the ground. It was difficult, holding his Body up like that, but it felt like exercise to the Skill. If he had the time, Felix figured he should start carrying boulders into the sky to train up his tolerance for Aspect strain.

In any case, he was relieved that this group seemed well-off. Ish. He saw quite a few fighters not listening to Vess' orders, causing problems across their battle lines that led to no less than six Blades becoming overwhelmed. Greater Ratlings pounced, slashing with foreclaws like knives and razor-sharp buck teeth. Felix almost threw himself into the fray, but Vess was faster—her Spears flashed forward, each one taking a Greater Ratling through the chest or open mouth. Their bodies were carried backward by the force, just enough so that when she detonated them, the storm of air and metal Mana obliterated them without harming a single legionnaire.

Shit. She's good. Felix grinned watching his friend fight. The heiress was impressive, as always, in her white-enameled half-plate, sleek pauldrons etched with draconic shapes to match her partisan. Her face was bright, despite the frenetic pace of battle, content and excited at the same time. *Dang, she's beautiful, too. GAH.* He shook his head. *Don't be weird.*

It didn't matter that he looked the same age, thanks to the magic of Tempering. It felt...It didn't matter. He didn't have time for relationships, anyway. Felix had a whole damn Territory to figure out, after all. He needed allies...*friends*, more than anything else.

Things were fine with the Ratling battle. In a flash of blue-white lightning, he moved on.

Felix maneuvered over the oasis like a crackling ghost, peering at battle after battle around his campsite. Monsters abounded, appearing as if from nowhere the moment the sun had risen above the horizon. The squads were fighting on every single front, and it was not all going as well as Vess' team or even the one against the Scorpions.

More and more of the squads were failing, taking grievous injuries, or simply running out of Mana or Stamina and dropping where they stood. The idiots barely even used the potions he had made for them to account for their usage, and it was only the interference of the Dawnguard that kept those people from being slaughtered. Yet the Dawnguard, though they had greater discipline, were not trained to fight with the Legion, and the Frost Giants...the Henaari and Risi avoided one another wherever possible, it seemed.

It was a mess.

None of them were working together, whether that meant chaining Skills or even thinking tactically. Felix shouldn't have agreed to let the Legion come, not if they were going to kill themselves in their first real combat. Atop the Nagafolk or against the Paladins earlier, they had barely contributed, and that was fine. Felix hadn't expected them to, nor that they would have made a difference against those enemies.

But the vast majority of these enemies were Tier II with only smattering of Tier III beasts, and the Legion were all in the middle reaches of Apprentice Tier. Each squad should have been more than able to hold their own. Instead, he saw time and again that his friends were pitching in to keep everyone from falling apart. Atar, Alister, Evie, Vess, even Harn and Darius were out among them slinging Skills and spells to keep the hordes from overwhelming the squads completely.

Felix did what he could, slowing down the rush of Lesser Ratlings or trapping the legs of a good number of Vine Wolves with Cardinal Flame and Rime Shaping respectively. It meant the monsters couldn't swarm the squads, trickling forward in groups of ten or twenty instead of fifty. He could have killed them all, probably just drenched the entire jungle with Rain of Cataclysm and burned them out...but not only would that have ruined the place, but it would have meant valuable leveling and training would be lost.

You cannot coddle them forever, Felix, Zara had said to him many months ago. He was realizing she was right.

Still, stone and vines and ice would nudge potions to injured mouths or trip up charging Greater Ratlings. Red-gold flames would wrap around a beast just long enough for a squad to surround it and cleave its head from its shoulders. Never too much and hopefully subtle enough, but Felix couldn't just stand by. He wouldn't.

Rime Shaping is level 25!
...
Rime Shaping is level 27!
Apprentice Tier!
You Gain:
+5 INT
+5 WIL
+5 DEX

Green Shaping is level 26!
Apprentice Tier!
You Gain:
+5 INT
+5 WIL
+5 PER

Obstinacy had the secondary benefit of pressing his lower-ranked Skills to their limits, at least.

Pit joined him at some point in his tour of frustration, flapping up from a patch of jungle that had been devastated by ice spears and slashed trees. He chirruped, a high, happy greeting that belied the blood on his beak and claws.

"Having fun?" Felix asked, trying to keep his tone light.

Yes!

Felix snorted, landing among a number of giants and Henaari nearest the camp who were anxiously looking at the sky. Pit landed with a dull thud shortly after. A wave of relief swept through the assembled fighters as they spotted him, but he noticed that there were none injured or dead there. He also only spotted four legionnaires, so that might have explained it. Regardless, he ignored them all and looked for the one with a green scarf around their neck. Harn was using them to denote rank, apparently. The one wearing the squad leader neckerchief was...he grimaced.

"What's the situation, Ifre?"

"Birds, my Lord," Ifre said. The captain of the Dawnguard had come along on the expedition at the behest of the Farwalker, but she had avoided him so far. He didn't mind her being there, nor her junior Isyk; she had chosen to defy her orders to kill him, after all. That had to count for something. Ifre likely didn't feel the same comfort—she wouldn't meet his gaze. "Very large birds."

"Birds?" he asked.

"Darkmantle Vultures," Battlelord Ari said from the side. He and six other Giants stood with ice-forged weapons gripped in their meaty hands. Ari grimaced up at the cloudless sky, which was almost blindingly bright and made his beard look dingy by comparison. "Two score flock."

"We've seen these before, and they are not kin to the Raven, nor appreciated," Ifre continued. She licked her lips. "But I am told they taste very good."

Ari rumbled in agreement, and Pit quirked his head up at the sky. Eagerness and hunger bled across their bond, and Felix smiled fondly at his Companion. It wouldn't hurt to get some fresher meat for their meals.

"They're back," someone said.

The birds came, faster than Felix expected. While they didn't match his Agility, and his Perception easily spotted their movements, the monsters were still remarkably speedy. Half as large as an avum, they had cruel, hooked beaks and iron-gray talons, both of which they attempted to slash and rake at the assembled team. Despite his promises to himself, Felix blatantly stopped two of them from smashing into a Dawnguard, and a third he punched out of the sky, killing it instantly. But then the Vultures were on them, and chaos reigned.

Felix stepped back from any further action, letting Pit join in the fray but otherwise leaving it to his burgeoning army. The sound of level-ups and Skill progression trilled across his Affinity, literal music to his ears as his people got better at a visible rate. Stress, challenge, and opportunity, the three critical things necessary to advance in power on the Continent. *How much more would they gain if I wasn't here, though?* He clucked his tongue, idly dodging a Vulture's slashing strike. *Ugh, this leading thing is hard.*

He retreated slowly, a casual stroll through the frenzied battlefield of ice, blades, and fluttering feathers. When a stronger than usual Vulture descended, this one colored an odd blue, he still held his hand.

But Pit didn't.

The Chimera leaped into the air, immediately challenging the Mana-drenched Vulture to aerial combat. Wings and claws flashed and snapped, while beaked mouths screeched and stabbed with abandon. Wingblades and Frost Spear splashed against reinforced feathers and a neck that seemed made of steel, while metallic needles rained down from the Vulture's wings. Pit dove, placing his armored body in front of the attack rather than risk his allies below. The Master Tier barding, now extending down the outside of his wings, deflected the projectiles like rain on a tin roof.

Kick his ass, Pit! Felix sent.

Pit obliged.

The Vulture grappled with Pit again, raking against the chimera's underbelly with its savage claws. Felix watched Pit's Health drop as bloody furrows were carved into his chest, but he didn't push the Vulture away at all. Instead, the tenku's immense wings wrapped around them both and a keening surge of air Mana billowed in Felix's vision. The

Vulture squawked in terror and struggled to escape, but Pit was too strong. There was a pulse—a wet, gooey *pop*—and the Vulture was no more.

Your Companion Has Killed A Manadrenched Vulture!
XP Earned!

Pit's Wingblade is level 73!

Pit screeched his victory into the morning air.

———

And so the day went. Felix and Pit raced from spot to spot, six in total, each time watching and involving themselves only if a creature too strong to face reared its head. Pit threw himself into the fray again and again, often facing a surge of territorial monsters all alone. He was still pushing toward his first evolution, whatever that was going to be, and needed to push himself to his limits. Felix was fine with that. Pit wasn't a weak puppy anymore.

Again and again, Felix heard the chorus of countless level gains and Skill progression from among the company. It was encouraging, even as his own Skills languished at the upper end of Adept Tier. But fighting off a jungle's worth of Tier III creatures would barely put a dent in the progress he needed to advance. Felix required stronger foes to challenge himself as well, just as Pit did.

It wasn't to be, unfortunately. The strongest creature to appear had been the Manadrenched Scorpion, with the Vulture as a distant second. That was good for the squads, especially as they all hit the wall far sooner than Felix expected. Stamina and Mana and Health dropped *fast*, their potions and tinctures mere patches on the greater problem. Squads were rotated out, allowed to rest at the campsite for a few hours before going back out into the dense jungle. They wanted to train Endurance and Stamina use, not drain them completely. There were miles of marching ahead of them, after all.

By early afternoon, the waves of creatures slowed. The Ratlings in particular showed a greater amount of intelligence than Felix was expecting and split into smaller groups. They attacked from ambush whenever possible, and two Greater Ratlings almost managed to down one of the Frost Giants for good.

The oasis was dangerous during the daylight hours, that much was clear.

Then the long shadows of night began to creep across the jungle. Long before the sky changed to sunset colors, the ridges all around pushed the hidden oasis into twilight, and the monsters fled. One minute, the Ratlings and Scorpions and Darkmantle Vultures were attacking, and the next they had scurried or flown off. Just as the Prioress had suggested, nightfall meant that the creatures of the desert simply...went away.

It raised a good number of questions, as the same was likely true in the desert itself given that they had seen no monsters or life of any kind out in the sands. While beating back the monster waves, a few squads had found dens beneath groves and against the sandy bluffs, so when the creatures fled, the Dawnguard had followed. Their homes were marked off on a map, and a plan was formed. But first, rest.

They were afforded a few hours before true dark settled over the Expanse. Only then, Atar confirmed, was it safe to travel the rest of the way to Ahkestria. Meals were made and bedrolls unfurled, wounds treated and the dead...the dead were burned and mourned. That part was the hardest for Felix, though it wasn't any easier on the others. Pyres were built along the edge of the lake, and the eight fallen warriors were laid on top while the entire company looked on. Felix felt like he should say something, but he didn't know them, only their names, memorized in passing before they had even left.

Tetra. Ciami. Nevin. Lesaan. Jiof. Werdan. Mi-ald. Tabanth. And Jadon in the Shadowgate.

Only the sound of lapping water and crackling flames broke the night. It was somber and blessedly quick. Atar lit the pyres, and his Primordial-touched flames reduced all eight stacks to brilliant pillars of light and smoke...smoke that Darius and Vess worked to disperse before it had a chance to leave the bowl of the oasis.

Eight dead. Nine since we left the Stronghold. That number weighed against Felix's Mind as he wandered from the funeral and drifted toward where Pit sat curled around the central campfire. The cold was rising as the shadows deepened, and though weather hadn't bothered him in a long while, Felix was grateful for the light and warmth. *Nine dead and nothing I can do about it. More are gonna die. This was just a skirmish with monsters in the woods. What happens if we fight the Paladins for real?*

Fight? Pit asked, face stuffed with a bowl-full of roasted meat.

No. Not right now. Felix patted his friend and settled back, feet to the fire. He dismissed his boots and greaves, letting them shrink into a thick band around his ankles, just to enjoy the flames a bit more. *I'm just thinking. We've a desert to cross, Paladins to avoid, and a Minotaur to find in the middle of it all.*

A lot, Pit sent, face shoved back in his bowl. *Dangerous.*

Felix chuckled. "It is. Probably for the best that we're headed to Ahkestria first."

"Only if the Paladins haven't torn it down yet," Evie said, carrying a pair of bowls in her hands. "Here. Eat."

Felix took the rough wooden bowl from her hands. It was piled high with roasted meat and some sort of fragrant stew. A hunk of dark, coarse bread was laid across the top—spoon and carbs in one. "Thanks. Didn't realize someone made stew."

"Really? The smell's all over the camp." Evie eyed him. "Those deaths really shook you up, huh? I heard Zara and Vess arguin' about you not saying anythin' at the pyres. Ol' Sharptooth was mad. Vess told her to leave you alone."

Felix frowned. "What exactly did she expect me to say? 'Sorry I dragged you into the desert to die' doesn't have the right ring to it."

Evie grunted. She'd been hanging around Harn too much. "They chose this journey. We all did. Just because they died doesn't mean it was a bad choice. Good or bad don't figure, least far as the Sorcerer says, and I'm thinkin' I agree with her."

"I could've prevented them from coming."

"You could've, yeah. But you made a choice too, right?" Evie shrugged. "What're you gonna do about it?"

Felix's frown only deepened. Evie's words caught at him in a way he hadn't expected. His Mind whirled, so lost in thought that he didn't notice when Evie drifted off into the night, or when his food grew cold and congealed. Pit fell asleep at his side, but Felix stared into the fire until it burned down to nothing.

Thinking.

Planning.

CHAPTER FORTY-NINE

They rode out into the sands as true night fell on the Expanse. Atar led them as before, his Mana Gauge finding the secretive trail to the City of Embers after only a few minutes. The rest of the caravan trundled on in his wake, though Felix imagined the quiet was more contemplative than a day ago.

It was odd. He felt as if everyone's guard was both lowered and heightened. No monsters prowled the sands, no undead in the dunes, but the fighting of the day—and the deaths—were too recent to be put off completely.

Felix saw the company still moving in discrete squads, the Legion, Dawnguard, and Risi all intermingling. He was happy that they were sticking with it, but it was clear that it was the result of orders. All of them needed work. He had puzzled at the problem for hours in camp and again as he rode Pit at the head of the column. What did he and his...his people, need?

Growth. To be challenged. But they can't be challenged until they can work together, and they can't work together until they trust each other. The real question had been how to achieve that trust.

The answer, he had accidentally realized, was Affinity.

The fighting at the oasis had forged a few bonds between the groups, that much had been clear as squads had wandered the oasis camp, ate their meals, and struggled to get a few hours of sleep. A couple legionnaires, a Blade and Bone, commiserated over the fire. A giant spoke with a Half-Orc Arclight about lightning versus ice magic. Little snippets, scattered across the campsite, of something more than the casual disregard or vague dislike that sat between all the rest.

When Felix had noticed this, he immediately felt their Spirits in an attempt to understand their feelings. But he pushed too far, and instead he saw a set of flickering threads. Cords of connection spreading in all directions, to all people and things. The Harmonic stat of Affinity was a delicate instrument he'd found, and flaring it too hard led to strange interactions with his Perception and other abilities.

It also included links to physical objects like the ground and the air, or that tree someone just touched, and those blades of grass where blood had been spilled. Those were like background noise to the rest, a song sung in another room. It had been a *lot*, almost too much for his Journeyman Mind. He had started to ease off his Affinity, until he noticed that the connections between those friendly conversationalists were brighter and louder than most.

That was eye-opening. He had immediately begun to study the connections among those he knew the best: his teammates. The strongest links—excluding his bond with Pit, which was another thing entirely—existed between Atar and Alister, Evie and Vess, Harn and Evie, Zara and himself, and...Darius and Zara. The last was surprising.

Despite his study, Felix couldn't intuit exactly what the links signified, other than a certain closeness. Atar and Alister were obvious, as was Evie and Harn. Both were intimate relationships, though they differed in the details: one was romantic, and the other was more like a father and daughter. Or perhaps a fond uncle and his favorite, very stubborn niece. Evie and Vess also felt similar in tone to that one, though a touch less potent. Friends. The one between Darius and Zara was weird. It had a flickering quality to it that Felix couldn't parse, as if it was fading in and out, waxing and waning in strength.

Affinity is weird.

The link between Zara and himself was obvious. The strength of it, however, was perhaps the most surprising of all. It was an orchestra to the simple string quartet of the others, involving so much more depth than he had expected. If Affinity was a representation of the desires, sympathies, and fears of a person—and Felix was beginning to understand that it was, to a large extent—then whatever Zara felt toward him was immense. But Affinity was also ineffable, to a certain degree. The connections existed on a metaphysical level that Felix still didn't understand, one that was deeper than just emotions and the amount of times someone interacted.

His connections with the others were...well. Felix didn't try to examine them too much.

Still, understanding the shape of his army's connections made some things far, far easier. He knew, for instance, where ties were strongest and where they were weakest, and the general feeling associated with them. It wasn't so clear-cut as "hate" or "love" or even "loyalty," just a sliding scale of positive and negative sensations. Best he could manage was spying on their Spirits as the squads interacted and mentally flagging those who worked well together. If only he could find a way to engender and reinforce the benevolent connections, few as they were.

Felix made a mental note to speak with Harn about it later.

His musings kept him busy, at the very least. There was little else to ponder on the long, boring journey. Felix wanted to be happy about the quiet, but the lack of action nagged at him. Fighting that morning had reminded him how much *fun* it could be, as twisted as that seemed. The first few hits he'd taken from the Manadrenched Scorpion had been thrilling—Felix hadn't been sure how strong the thing was—sadly, the rest of the fight was far less exciting. Other than a potent durability, the huge arachnid had been just another punching bag. Ironically, though he wanted to avoid conflict to keep his people safe, there was a large part of him that wanted to dive headlong into whatever dangers the desert had on offer.

Foolhardy, he chided himself. *When is Zara going to stop being right all the time?*

The sands slithered and shifted around them, the winds blowing cold and frequently. Cloaks and shawls had been fished out of packs and satchels and drawn tight against the chill, while the giants finally looked comfortable. Many beards were split with moonlit grins. For his part, Felix had shifted his Garment into a short jacket with a high neck and full-length trousers, eschewing any sort of cape or cloak. As dramatic as a cloak might look, the constant snapping and rippling in the breezes was irritating, and it wasn't like he needed the protection from the cold, even as it deepened.

Above them the sky was a dense field of stars, so clear it looked as if he could reach out and grab one. The Twins had risen above the horizon an hour past, along with brassy Yyero, and their waning illumination was more than enough to light their way. The desert swept beneath their feet, their speed incredible despite most not having a mount of any sort. Hours drifted this way, in silence and gelid solitude, until sometime after midnight they spotted a shape in the distance.

"What is that?" Vess asked him. Her eyes spun with a dozen colors as she engaged her Elemental Eye. "It looks like a...skeleton?"

Felix focused, and the miles-distant shape leaped into immediate clarity. He saw a town-sized collection of blackened bones emerging from a collection of those rocky bluffs. That was amazing enough, but he also saw people moving among the bones. "I think it's a settlement," he guessed. "I see small people, Gnome-sized, covered in...bandages?"

"Yttins," Atar said as the wagon crested the dune. "Strange folks, but good enough neighbors. It's encouraging that they're still here and unharmed. Means the Paladins didn't come through."

Alister peered into the distance. "Why would the Paladins care about them?"

"Yttins aren't the prettiest," Atar said. "That and their diet are usually reason enough for some to kill them on sight."

"Diet?" Vess asked.

"They like to eat their prey while it's still alive." Atar flicked the reins on the wagon, and the avum lurched forward.

Felix traded a glance with Vess, eyebrows raised. "This should be fun," he said.

"A delight," she muttered.

It took them a half hour to reach the settlement, and the entire time, Felix studied the blackened bones that jutted from the ground. He had estimated their size based on the Gnome-like dimensions of the Yttins, but it was still jaw-dropping as they drew closer. The bones that stuck up were a rib cage and a gnarled line of vertebrae, the ribs reaching somewhere around four stories tall, and the spine tracing back up and over the bluff before sinking into the sands. Cloth and leather had been stretched atop the rib cage, forming a sort of roof, and a darkness pooled inside that Felix's eyes couldn't pierce. At first he thought it was the distance, but even a half-mile out, he spotted nothing within that cavernous space, not even the swirl of Mana.

The Yttins noticed them well before they arrived, and while they weren't running outright, they did scurry with significant urgency. All while casting glowing glances at Felix's slow approach.

Zara appeared at his shoulder as they drew rein on the settlement. Her avum, Grouse, tossed his blunt head in agitation. "Be careful what you reveal," she said to all of them. "The Harmony...twists here."

What does that mean? Felix wanted to ask, but was afforded no time. A contingent of tiny, bandage-wrapped figures in loose flowing robes approached them on foot. They had sun-dried yellow skin and bright, glowing copper eyes, all wrapped in blue cloth so that nothing showed but their mouths and eyes. Even the twitching stumps on their backs were coiled about with cloth, though Felix couldn't decide if they were vestigial limbs or like...wing stumps.

Voracious Eye!

Pressure pushed against Felix's Mind and Spirit, harder than anything he'd felt in a long while. He twitched and dropped the Skill instead of pushing past the aggressive resistance. He had a feeling that they would notice if he forced the issue, and frankly, Felix wasn't entirely certain he wouldn't be injured by the attempt. His head *hurt*.

The lead Yttin started talking in a series of chittering clacks and wet snaps, as if they were rolling a set of dice in their too-wide mouths. Felix tried and failed to parse any meaning from it. He had no clue what they were saying and was about to confess that fact, when Atar spoke up in the same clattering language.

"They wish to know why we have come to their warren," Atar translated after a moment. He grinned at Felix's shock. "I *do* have talents outside of spellcasting."

"It's just, this is the first we've seen it," Evie said.

Alister nudged her in the upper arm, making her grunt through her grin.

"Tell them we have come for information," Zara said, overriding their banter. "We wish to know if they have news of goings on in the Expanse."

Atar chittered at the Yttins, who listened with a tilted head. Felix didn't see any ears, so he was curious how they made out sounds at all, but they obviously did. The lead Yttin smiled and pointed at their caravan before replying. Atar frowned.

"'Information for information,' he says. He wants to know why we brought an army to the Expanse, and a strange one at that." Atar looked at Felix and Zara, clearly unsure how to answer.

"We are simple travelers. Nothing more," Zara said with a laugh. "We have precious little information for you. But we have food and water to barter in its stead."

The Yttin clicked rapidly and waved a hand, clearly uninterested in either. When Vess stepped forward to suggest coin, they laughed outright.

"They've no need for coin. They—" Atar halted as the leader kept speaking. "They follow the Beast and its Signs. They thrive."

The Beast? Felix furrowed his brows, scanning the settlement once again. There were no houses in the rocks, none that he could see at least. *Is the Beast the skeleton? Do they live in the skeleton?*

That thought was interrupted by the approach of more Yttins, all of whom began to walk closer to the wagons and around Felix and Pit. Several of them poked at Pit's wings, causing the tenku to twitch back. They chittered to one another, their small, two-clawed hands clapping and grasping at fur, feather, and forged barding. Pit squawked indignantly, but the small pests kept on, patting and petting no matter how Pit stomped and flapped his wings.

"Back away," Felix growled, feeding on his Companion's agitation. A thrum shook through him, a rapid tattoo just above his navel that sang along his channels. He could feel his eyes glow, a blue to match their own copper orbs. "Now. Or else I'll let my friend here eat your bones while you watch."

Wild Threnody is level 69!

The Yttins froze, staring at Felix wide-eyed as their Spirits quivered strangely. Fear and...something else.

Pit chuffed a breath and brought his armored wing down, startling the little creatures and sending them scurrying backward with a series of rasping clicks. Felix glared, not caring that the negotiations for information had died away, and everyone was staring. The Yttins pressed together, congregating around their chief or leader, though it was hard to tell who was who—their bandages and his lack of Voracious Eye really hampered that effort. They chittered away, a wet clicking and clacking like a bony haunch clattering into a wooden board. Suddenly, one of their number rushed off, back into that cavernous rib cage.

That's...probably not good.

A Yttin extricated themself from the pile of prattling creatures and spoke forcefully to Atar again. They pointed directly at Felix.

"What is he saying?" Evie asked.

"They are asking 'who?'" Atar said. "'Who is he that rides a Chimera like an avum? Why can we not see him?'"

See...They tried to Analyze me.? Felix was glad for his Veiling Amulet, still going strong after all this time. "Just a man," Felix said, attempting to project a sense of nonchalance. He was distracting from the information gathering efforts, he knew. Now one of them had run into the skeleton for some reason. "Looking for information."

"'No man may touch the feathers of a tenku,'" the leader said, with a surprising amount of heat. Atar raised an eyebrow as he translated. "'And to hide one's truth is to break the weaving.'"

"He's my friend," Felix said, patting Pit on the neck. Pit chirruped in agreement, and from the way the chieftain jerked back in surprise, Felix knew they didn't need to translate that.

The chieftain clicked out a long string of sounds, gesturing first at Felix then at the skeleton, before pointing at their caravan as a whole. Atar blinked and licked his lips, but before he could translate, another Yttin ran from the skeleton cliffs and gestured sharply to the chieftain. The leader made a barking-click, once, then a string of harsh consonants to Atar.

Vess looked between the bandaged folk, her body as tense as Evie and Harn beside her. "That does not sound promising, Atar."

"They said, 'The weaving brings surprises anew, and if he is a Human, I will eat our home. If you wish information, then the Beast wishes to speak with this one. Alone.'" Atar's gaze flicked between the dark ribs and Felix. "The Beast is down there."

Felix eyed the dark recesses of the blackened bones and night-drenched cliffs. Something shuddered within those bones, like the sands were breathing.

"Great."

CHAPTER FIFTY

The others tried to protest putting himself in danger, but Felix ended the arguments by simply walking toward their creepy bone house. They needed information, and aside from the doom and gloom of the skeletal remains, Felix knew he could handle himself against most things. So what if the place looked like death's vacation home? He'd eaten Primordials and gods. Well, one god. Part of one.

"Felix!" Zara said, her tone sharp enough to cut stone. His team was gathered at the first wagon, with the company spread out further beyond it, and everyone was watching him walk across the night-purpled sand. "Have a care. The Song does not sit well within."

"...Right." He nodded, acknowledging her warning. She offered nothing else, so what could he do? *Be right back, Pit.*

Worry filtered back to him, hidden by a bright confidence. *Be safe.*

You know me.

Felix turned away from them all and tried to stride confidently up to the blackened corpse. It loomed over him, easily four stories tall, but the gaps in the ribs were narrow where they were not filled in with rock or covered in flapping leather sheets. The only entry was a gaping hole, where one massive, redwood-thick rib had been smashed apart. Without breaking his stride, Felix ducked into the dark.

And dark it was. The way ahead was utterly impenetrable even to his Perception, and the breeze that traversed the interior was hot and moist, like breath. If that wasn't unnerving enough, the floors were sliding sand, and the walls were a mix of stone and bone, barely wide enough for his shoulders. Felix followed it by touch, mostly, following a solitary path that wound around inside the structure like a maze, flaring his Manasight as best he could. He was able to pick up the barest hint of earth Mana from the sands and stone, but they were thin and dull. The bone all around him buzzed at his Affinity, a resonance that seemed to drag the Mana down and away. It was like walking through a dark room with a dying flashlight.

The path soon splintered in many directions. His Manasight and perfect memory served him well, allowing him to at the very least know his way back out. But finding his way forward and remembering the way back were two very separate things. Felix simply guessed at each junction, following the warm breeze whenever he could feel it. More than once, he had to turn back as he hit dead ends and small alcoves filled with bones and tattered cloth. After the fourth such misstep, Felix growled in annoyance and yanked his khopesh free of its sheath.

"Karys? Do you know anything about all this?" he asked. The sword buzzed, its timbre almost an exact opposite for the numbing sound from the bone walls.

"Oh," Karys' voice said, sounding far away. "That is remarkable. Where are you, my Lord?"

"Alone in a house made from a giant skeleton," Felix said. He gave his Chancellor a quick run down of the Yttins and their odd home. "What's remarkable?"

"The sensation of resistance. My Perception cannot gain purchase around anything but the sand at your feet and your own body." Karys still sounded like he was down the hall and behind a closed door, so muffled was his voice. "Only a truly powerful creature could exude such a forbiddance, even were it still alive. It is likely encompassing the entire settlement, and why you cannot Analyze them."

"Ok, one question down," Felix said. He grimaced as his foot went through something that cracked and then was upsettingly soft. A bug of some variety. "A thousand more to go. What do you know of the Yttin?"

"Yttin," Karys said. He went silent for so long, Felix was worried he'd lost him. "I—I am unsure if this is a correct memory, but I believe they were among the elite in Ahkestria. Warrior-monks of some variety."

"Bit spindly for warriors," Felix said, ducking beneath a thickened clump of cobweb. It stretched across the path, almost invisible in the gloom.

"Perhaps they used Agility-based Skills...My experiences with the Sunbright Jewel and its citizens was limited, that much I do recall."

"Hm. It was called the Sunbright Jewel before the sea dried up?" Felix asked.

"Yes. It was renowned for its crafters, even among the Golden Empire, and that is saying something," Karys said. "Lost, as all the rest was, during the War."

"You've mentioned this War a few times. War with who?" Felix asked. He stepped up and over a collection of bones that formed an odd, pyramidal staircase. Up and then down, back to the sand.

"The War against the...against the Enemy..." Karys struggled, and the green-gold Mana, already muted, flickered uncertainly. "I cannot recall their names. They were opposed to the Empire, sought to bring us low, to eradicate the works of our people and allies. Descendants of the Deathless."

"The who?" Felix stopped in his tracks, staring at his blade. "What are the Deathless? Karys?"

But Karys had gone silent.

Felix panicked for a few minutes, which was how long it took his Cardinal Flame to quest into the sword and check on its integrity. Its deepest recesses were opaque to him still, but the glow of life Mana was still there, just heavily muted by the bones all around him. Frustrated, Felix slammed the blade home in its sheath and prowled forward. The sooner he was out of the bone maze, the better.

Rooms and alcoves dotted the halls, small spaces meant for a small people. Many were festooned with cloth of various garish colors, as well as creations of paler bone. Furniture, made of their food, clearly. Tables and rudimentary chairs, all bound up by thin white cords that looked a lot finer than the hempen rope he'd seen in Haarwatch. They were interesting to see, but he kept moving, following the hot wind deeper and deeper down into the earth.

Finally, after a half hour's descent, he felt a strong breeze roll across him. His Perception followed the currents though he couldn't see around the maze-like corridors, the darkness having gotten only deeper as he went. He didn't look forward to fighting in it, if he had to, but that's what his Blind Fighting Skill was for, he supposed.

I should train that more, he mused as he ducked under another thick, wavering cobweb. The tunnels weren't made for tall people, at least not explicitly. There was a lot of ducking. *I can't expect to always have the upper hand on sightedness. If the Raven and now this place teaches me anything, it's that even my Perception can be stymied.*

He took a couple more wrong turns following the strengthening wind, but eventually he found a large antechamber somewhere deep below the bluffs. Blackened bones traced the walls and ceiling, reinforcing it like support beams, and the floor was just as sandy as the passageways.

What *was* different, were the hundreds—no—*thousands* of threads criss-crossing the ceiling and walls. Some were just layers and layers atop one another, until pieces of the bone and stone were obscured by a gauzy white. Others were delicate and complicated looking webs spun between prominent vertical bones, as if they were on display.

Shadows edged the corners of everything in a way that Felix didn't notice at first, but movement caught his eye. Then a sound, like falling tiles or hollow heels on wooden floors.

"Who's there?" he asked.

The clicking sped up, until it resolved into a new noise. A voice speaking the common tongue. "New. You are."

Felix turned toward the voice, but whatever it was had already moved. He could feel the wind of its passage, like a car passing too close on the highway. "That doesn't answer my question, creepy voice in the dark. Are you the...Beast?"

"Hmm," it said, clicking more furiously. "Small. Small and yet."

The ground thumped, and sand skidded across itself. Felix spun toward the sound and couldn't help it: he took a step backward.

"And yet so potent."

It may have once been a spider, but that was several mutations ago. Rippling flesh covered its many limbs and bulbous body, all of which was roughly the same size as an elephant. Rows of jagged spines traced along its back and legs, and each movement made them twitch and flutter as it shifted across the sands. Felix swallowed involuntarily. Its head wore a grotesque mask of carved bone, all teeth and eyes and grimacing muscles, but below it was a mouth of clacking mandibles and sideways incisors. Between those was a nightmarish, humanoid face, eyes glowing copper.

"What the hell are you?" Felix let his Cardinal Flame sing, and his body shimmered with pent up red-gold light.

The creature skittered back, half up the wall behind it. Its legs—oh god—its legs all ended in thick, Human hands, and each one grabbed onto the webbing between bone pillars. Felix stared at it, unwilling to even blink. It was using some sort of movement technique, because every couple of seconds, its sound and smell would deaden or twist. He was afraid if he even blinked, the thing would get behind him again.

"What are you?" he asked again, and tried to use Voracious Eye.

Tried being the operative word.

Pain lanced across his Mind as the Skill tried and failed to move the weight all around them. Felix screamed, his vision going white as the buzzing dissonance all around him intensified. The thrum of his cores sped up, a sound pressing back against it as his Bastion flared, and suddenly Felix found himself kneeling in the sands while blood dribbled from his face.

"Haah," he panted, wiping at himself. The blood was coming from his eyes.

Fear spiked through Felix and he surged to his feet, looking wildly about the room. His Cardinal Flame had been squelched by the...reverberation of the bones, and it took him a moment to find the creature. It had retreated back up to the ceiling, where it crouched in the unnatural darkness, peering at him with gemstone eyes and glowing copper orbs. It tilted its head, curious.

"You sing..." it said. Its voice was like whispered thunder, flexing the air in a way that Felix couldn't understand. "You sing, and the bone sings, and...you bleed."

Felix wiped at the blood on his face, not taking his eyes off the monster. "I'll ask again. What are you? Are you the Beast?"

A high giggle came from the elephantine creature. It made Felix's skin crawl. "No no. I am—I *was*—the shaman of my people. I read the Weavings and the weather and the stars in the Great Nothing."

"You're Yttin?"

Ten glowing eyes bobbed in the dark. "I was cursed by the gods for peering too far. Too far! I saw too much!" It tittered again. "The Weavings of Fate are not for mere mortals. No, no. Not for us. Never for us."

"You were cursed?" he asked. Felix licked his lips, keeping the exit to his back. He had zero idea on the thing's strength, but it was fast, and it could hide from him. If this thing was crazy and wanted to kill him, he'd have to run. Getting outside of the skeleton might give him a chance to kill it.

"The flesh turned, the blood soured, for the gods allow no intruders in their Domain," it said, its voice distorted as if by static. But the static was composed of sub-audible clicking, as if its vocal cords still remembered being Yttin. "We are not meant to know the endings that they Weave."

Felix watched the thing carefully, his senses buzzing against the dissonance all around him. How much was from the bones, and how much was from the creature? It looked—and felt—like Primordial spawn, just a lot more potent than the Dustborn Wraiths he had fought. His Affinity swam in the static around him, and he could feel a resonance between it and the song that coiled within his core space. The dark abyss roused, trembling as it scented the spider-monster, and Felix had to shove its sudden Need from his Mind.

Quiet, you.

"Who are you, Human, to have tamed a Chimera?" it clicked at him. Five-digit hands padded across the ceiling as it came closer, not dropping from above but stretching its head and abdomen down closer. The face hidden in its jaws pivoted and turned, until it was looking at Felix right-side-up. "Who are you to have such a song in your blood?"

"He is a friend. A Companion," Felix said.

"Chimeric Companion...an ephemeral tie to Harmony." The shaman giggled, and warning flares went off in Felix's mind. "They do not *like it*."

The bones around them groaned at its words, and that buzzing discord increased tenfold. The bond with Pit constricted, a foreign pressure squeezing down on it with insidious strength. His eyes opened wide, and Felix saw the darkness of the room crackle with blue-white light. "Do not touch my dog."

Felix felt his Will press against something alien and vast, a Will and Intent that moved like a mountain, slow but inexorable. Immediately, his Aspects burned, like he was leveraging that mountain with his bare hands. Felix locked his knees and strained against its weight...while the shaman's mouth-face crawled closer.

"You resist? The gods...they do not want resistance. They ask me, they ask-ask that you stop, that you cease." The shaman's copper eyes blinked, flashing brilliant streams of light that seemed to worm into Felix's Mind. His Bastion quaked, off-kilter by the weight he held aloft. Its voice continued on, whisper-thin, but surprised. "But you don't. You ask-ask, too. Of those who pass. My people, the People, once-warriors and once-proud, they speak to me of your caravan. What do you want, Human-who-is-not?"

Felix gritted his teeth against the pain, the mountain growing neither lighter nor heavier, but everything within him pushing back against it. "We...want to...avoid the Paladins...of the Pathless."

The shaman sniffed at Felix, lifting two of its disgustingly Human hands and pulling webbing from itself. It blinked, twice more.

"More. There is *more*. You tell us so little, yet you *vibrate* with potency. What are you?" The shaman pressed into him, poking, prodding with its vile hands. "The blue of your eyes. The glow of a Body attuned to fire?"

Poke.

"No."

Prod.

"Attuned to lightning?" It grabbed him with two hands, four, and squeezed his shoulders and neck. "No, no, no. *Tell us. What are you?*"

"Enough!" Felix screamed and flared Adamant Discord. Lightning lit up around him as connections sprang into his vision. They were thin and dim, but not the ones attached to the shaman. There was a link between them that was as thick as a keg and too bright to look at directly. Lightning surged along its length as he *pushed*, and the shaman's hairy limbs were wrenched back inch by quivering inch.

The shaman hissed, and two other legs speared at his face. Felix ducked his head, letting them hit the crown of his skull. It sent him skidding backward across the floor, and the mountain leaning against him vanished entirely. The creature skittered backward, two of its eight limbs blackened by Felix's power, and it hissed at him again.

"Cursed! We are both of us cursed!" it howled, before it lunged for him.

Stone Shaping!

Stone Shaping is level 76!
Stone Shaping is level 77!

Spikes of stone ripped from the earth, stabbing into the beast over and over, while more blocked its path. Felix saw fully half of his Mana vanish in an instant, as the pattern of the Skill had all but refused to cooperate. *It's this damn skeleton cave! It's fighting everything I do!*

The shaman tore through the rough-made sandstone, screaming in pain and rage and—

And he punched it in the face.

Corrosive Strike is level 65!
Wild Threnody is level 70!

The creature's head snapped up, its disgusting legs flailing and grasping at Felix as it tumbled backward.

Shadow Whip!

Felix grappled the spider horror, dark tendrils wrapping around its fleshy neck and yanking it forward. But he stumbled. That mountainous Will crashed into him at the same time Felix's second fist hit the shaman, and both of them were hurled back into the sands.

FELIX!

Pit's voice was thin, but terrified. All Felix could do was push against the weight bearing down on him, a weight that was so very familiar and utterly unknown. *Primordial.* It hissed and burned across his arms and chest, against his throat and face, but it did no more than scald. It was hot and dry, an oven wind filled with countless motes of sand, a million teeth tearing at him, crushing him.

Get...OFF!

Adamant Discord flared and flashed, sending pieces of the Will blasting off of him, but it simply reformed. It slammed down at him once more, and the chamber of bones vanished. Images flashed instead, of wind and sky and heat and the merciless sun, all of it cutting at his Will like knives. Felix pushed back against it, but it was like fighting a landslide.

And yet... he felt a hard nodule within its mountain, something firmer than the indestructible sands. Felix reached for it, shaping his Intent into a razor's edge and cutting upward through its Will for the briefest of moments. For a desperate instant, he could find no trace of what he sought, but his blade of Intent struck true. A bead of bizarre potency crackled across his senses, worse than all the weight of its Will.

"You're not the first abomination that demanded things from me! I'll tell you what I told the Unending Maw!"

Felix screamed.

He seized it.

"Fuck off."

Chthonic Tribute!

Unite the Lost!

Light and shadow slammed into Felix in a hurricane of force while streamers of red-gold flame and blue-white lightning surged back out. He lifted from the earth, buoyed bodily by the immense streams of Essence that dove into his channels, searing him and his core. Bone shattered, and the screams intensified, two voices raised in agony...until he fell to the sands with a final, heavy thud.

CHAPTER FIFTY-ONE

Felix woke still atop the hot sand of that antechamber, and he scrambled madly to his feet though everything in him wanted only to lay down and sleep. Notifications blinked at him, but he forced them away. Instead, he swept the chamber, looking for the monstrosity that had attacked him.

He found instead a frail-looking Yttin huddled in the center of the chamber. Their back was a mess of oversized spider-like legs connected to its spine, each hanging limp in the sand. Their face was uncovered, showing a mouth as wide as their jawline filled with small, sharp teeth and a sharp, hooked nose. Their skin was yellowed like withered parchment, and they were totally and completely nude. They looked at Felix with dull, awe-filled eyes the color of brass.

"I...my Body," they said, in a voice far...flatter than it had just moments before. They trembled. "My curse...it is gone. It is healed."

Felix let loose a relieved breath, sagging with the exhalation. It had worked. He hadn't been sure it would. "The Primordial curse is gone now," Felix said wearily. He felt the last of it drift down into the hungry abyss within him. "You're free. The Beast is gone."

"The Beast..." they muttered. "The Beast..."

Felix tore a piece of web-clotted cloth off the wall and handed it to the shuddering Yttin. They took it gratefully and wrapped it around their waist, but shook their head as they picked up a gruesome bone mask. It had survived Felix's power. "The Beast remains," they said.

Felix looked around, his senses finding no trace of the Primordial's Essence. "What do you mean? You're better now."

"I was never the Beast," they said.

"I—then what is the Beast?" He pointed at the mask. "The mask?"

"A symbol. A...warning and a promise." The shaman gathered themself and shuffled across the chamber to where the complex webbing stretched across the walls. "All the message I could preserve from what I had seen in the Weavings."

The shaman ran their hands across the webbing, each string producing a clear, resonant note. The patterns of it were confusing and interconnected in a way that looked like nonsense shapes and connections. "The message fades now. My connection to the Weaving is lost with my abominable form. I am lessened by its leaving...and blessed. My Mind could not take the warp and weft of the gods' Intent."

"What did you see?" Felix asked. He had no interest in getting further involved with the gods, but intel was intel. "Can you remember any of it?"

"Only that the true Beast will come," they whispered, and in the acoustics of the chamber it was like they yelled it. "And the sands will flow as blood."

Cheery.

"What's it mean?" he asked.

The shaman's eyes burned a brilliant copper and their uncovered face twisted into a too-wide smile. "That the ending comes, and we will see the end of this desert, one way or another."

They just get creepier the longer they talk, huh? Out loud, Felix tried a different tack. "I came down here for information. They told me the Beast wished to see me...I assume they think that's you?" The shaman nodded.

"A confusion I was not able to correct them on, not in my previous...state."

"Okay. And you planned to eat me?" The Yttin nodded, seeming unashamed. Felix decided not to take it personally—they had been influenced by a Primordial's flesh curse, after all.

"Information was on the table, of course. I...the desert requires a savage instinct to survive it. Yet you have shown compassion and, impossibly, Skill enough to end my long imprisonment." The shaman dropped to their knees and prostrated themself on the crimson sands. "I will be forever in your debt. I do not know how to repay it, in this life or another."

Felix grunted. "You can start by telling me what you know about the Paladins."

They sat up, and the glow in their eyes was contemplative. "Only that the warriors were seen two days eastward, chasing down one they called a heretic. My people heard them claim it was holing up in Ahkestria."

That's in line with what we figured. I doubt Michael shacked up with Yttins or others like them. Felix scratched his chin, wondering what else he could ask, when the shaman spoke again.

"We have seen this heretic."

"You have?" Felix leaned forward, eager. "Where? Do you know where he is?"

"South to Ahkestria, as the warriors assumed. He was chased by the

Cursewinds." They shuddered. "Far too close to the City than ever before."

The Cursewinds sounded like the cyclones of sand and undead monstrosities he'd seen in his visions. "The Cursewind carries the undead, right? Why doesn't it go near the City?" Felix asked.

"It simply does not. It is how it has always been, since the waters vanished."

So Ages ago. Probably some sort of warding around the city. I know I would have attempted to do something like that if I had airborne zombies flying around. Felix bit the inside of his cheek as he thought. *So onward to Ahkestria. Hopefully to find the Unbound there and—*

"Will you protect the City?"

Felix frowned at the interruption. "Sorry?"

"You do not like the Paladins. That is clear, even to my muddled Mind. Yet you chase after them. Why?" They tilted their head, a movement so like its former, monstrous self that Felix recoiled. The shaman didn't seem to notice. "Have you professed yourself to the flame? Is that why the gods could not burn you when we fought?"

"What?" He set aside the fact the shaman thought the Primordial was a god and focused on the weirder part of his sentence. "What flame?"

"The light and flame of truth, That Which Burns and fuels the passion of the City for an entire Age."

"Fuels Ahkestria?" Felix felt his stomach sink, just a little. "What exactly are you talking about?"

"An Urge of great strength. A goddess, minor though she be, one of unquestioned power."

"An Urge," Felix muttered. Exactly what he feared coming out of the shaman's mouth. "What's her name?"

"The Highest Flame."

Felix felt a tugging tingle in his memories as connections jolted and sparked behind his eyes. Highest Flame. He knew of only one person to have spoken that name before. *Why didn't you tell us, Atar? Or do the others already know?* He had to imagine the Paladins hated Ahkestria for the presence of an Urge alone; he'd been told before that the Pathless did not like Urges. The presence of an Unbound hiding among them was reason enough to wage war on the city, apparently.

Complications for later. "And what of your...gods? The one that cursed you? Do you know where it is located?" If Felix could find the Primordial, at the very least he could take steps to give it a wide berth.

The shaman gestured, arms spread wide. "It is here. All around us."

Felix looked at the bones in alarm, but the shaman only shook their head. "No. The greatest of gods, He who laid my people low Ages ago...it is the desert itself."

"I'm tellin' you, the ground shook," Evie said. She knelt against the sandy slope and stared upward at the black skeleton as the moons set beyond it. "Felix probably got in a fight."

"Perhaps," Vess said. Evie noticed how her gaze lingered over the monstrous ribcage, no matter how she tried to hide it by checking on their troops. "Unless we wish to break hospitality with the Yttins, there is little we can do until he returns."

"And if he doesn't?" Evie nodded at the wagons, now circled up near the Yttin cookfires. "Pit's awful nervous-lookin', and his Spirit is a mess."

"You can feel that?" Vess asked.

"Tch, don't be so surprised. I've got this Affinity thing down pat," Evie said, and it was even sorta true. Her Affinity had grown a lot in the past week, rising by ten whole points. She stood up and dusted sand from her knees. Evie had to be careful, or else her armor would fill with the stuff, and it was damn hard to clean out. "Pit feels like two pit vipers in a bag, wrestlin' over each other and bitin' all the while."

"That is...apt," Vess said with a nod. She closed her eyes, focusing on the Chimera. "He's concerned, worried, afraid...and there's pain, too." She opened her eyes again, and Evie saw a flash of white-green Mana in her pupils. "Ever since Felix left."

"Yeah, and he's been pacin', too, worse since the ground shook. Hence: fight."

The company had circled the wagons and brought all of their soldiers between them for a little rest and meal. That Palin lady was busy—she and her employees were busy cooking up food and handing out drinks to everyone. It wasn't anything much better than trail rations, though they had a little more of that Vulture meat. Evie thought it was a bit gamey, but it filled the belly well enough. As it was, however, she wasn't particularly hungry. That came with advancement, she was happy to find. Evie could go longer without any sustenance at all...but when the bill came due, she'd clear out a tavern's stock in a night, or it felt like that at least.

Harn was in the thick of it, talking to the legionnaires and Henaari, most mostly chatting in low tones with the Hand. *Strange allies.* She supposed they had training stuff to talk about; Felix's little followers were *rough. Damn near got me killed twice yesterday. Damn Apprentice Tiers.*

That wasn't entirely fair, but Evie wasn't feeling all that charitable. The company of followers were all dead weight. All except the Henaari and...and the others weren't to be trusted. Everyone was shoved together by Harn and Darius, intermingling despite the tense silence that threaded through the group. Waiting while their illustrious leader did some negotiation. That part, at least, sat just fine with Evie. If the man wanted a crown, then he'd better get used to the responsibilities involved.

I can do without all those chains, she thought with a chuckle. She patted her bladed weapon around her waist. *This one's all I need.*

"Reed and Harn are getting along well," Evie pointed out.

Vess' mouth flattened. "Yes," she said. Sounded right sour about it, too. "I worry at what his angle might be."

"Your minder? I thought he gave up that whole...thing of his?"

"So he claims. My father would never let him live down such a breach of duty, however. Darius knows that." She idly made small circles in the sand with the butt of her spear. "Yet he has been nothing but conciliatory ever since the duel."

"Concilia-what? Listen, if he doesn't want to make waves anymore, I'm fine with that. Is he still helping you with your Dragoon-ness?" Evie asked.

Vess grumbled, though it was less earnest than a moment ago. "Yes. He has even handed over the tomes my father entrusted to him."

"Skill books?" Evie gasped. "Those are rare!"

Skill books were exactly what they sounded like. Tomes designed to impart the knowledge of a Skill, greatly increasing the chances of learning it. When Evie had first heard of them, she'd thought they'd function in an instant. Read it and *bam!* Instant Skill gain. Mags had taught her different—she'd run into a couple, such as the one that let her learn her shielding spell.

Vess nodded. "Exceedingly. They detail the Path I follow, but they are not useful until I have reached Adept. The techniques are too advanced."

"Pity. How close are you to Tiering up?"

"Close, but so far. My Body and Spirit are reaching a high point—each Skill about five levels off Tier—but my Mind lags behind by seven entire levels. Only my Spear of Tribulations is within a single level of Tempering, and it has proven difficult to budge." Vess ground the butt of her spear through the doodles in the sand. "It is frustrating."

"Hm," Evie grunted. When the silence stretched on too long, she realized Vess was glaring at her. "What?"

"How close are you?"

"Oh I dunno. Close enough," Evie hedged.

"Evie."

She winced and let a grin through. "Body is one level away from Tiering up...in every Skill I need."

"Siva's grace!" Vess spat what amounted to a curse for the proper noblewoman. But her mouth split in an easy smile regardless. "What of your Mind and Spirit?"

"That's less good. Still a couple levels shy." Evie shrugged. "Could be worse."

Vess laughed. "Could be, indeed."

A companionable silence drifted over them after that, each of them in their own thoughts. Well, Evie was. Vess was likely detailing some sort of training regimen for herself. She was almost as bad as Felix.

Can't we just take a night off? I could use some good shut-eye. Evie leaned back, but despite her intentions, her gaze alighted on the knot of Felix's troops. On blue skin and thick, white beards. *Damn giants.*

Evie caught Vess watching her, and she scowled at the soft set of the heiress' mouth and furrow on her brow. Evie knew what her friend was going to say before she opened her mouth, but it still burned to hear. "How are you? With the..." Vess gestured with her chin toward the clutch of Frost Giants in the distance.

"I'm fine," Evie said. She forced a shrug, keeping the movement smooth and not jagged at all. "It's fine. Nothin' I can do about it, so..."

"I must admit, I was wary of their presence in our Stronghold as well as on this mission," Vess said. "Yet they have been surprisingly tame, even helpful."

Evie grunted. She wasn't about to go complimenting the brutes just because they hadn't stabbed anyone in the back yet. "*Maybe* they were useful in the oasis, but that don't account for their past. For what they did."

"Evie..."

The silence was broken by an explosion of sand from the skeleton.

"What in Yyero's sour ass is that?" Evie shouted. Her chain had already jumped into her hands.

Atop the slope, the sand settled and Felix appeared from its midst, his eyes glowing like little lightning bolts. The Legionnaires leaped to their feet, scrambling for weapons, while Zara calmly walked up toward the guy. Evie saw that his Garment was torn across the chest and arms, but it was repairing itself as she watched. And he was talking to himself. No. Talking to his sword.

What a weird guy. Evie scanned the half-buried skeleton, flaring Night-eye. Had something attacked him? That Beast thing?

That was probably why she was the first to see a figure appear on the rocks above the bones, where part of a skull and horn stuck out. It was ragged and without those blue bandages, but it was clearly another Yttin. It lifted something—a mask—above its head. It looked like a monstrous head.

In perfect, if accented common, it screamed. "The Beast will come! The Devouring begins!"

It hurled the mask and it shattered against the stones below. The Yttin all around them gasped and paused for only a beat before *all of them* rushed Felix's position. Evie whirled toward them, but her Affinity picked out strains of joy and glee among the shock in their Spirits.

"I...think your boyfriend just recruited another batch of misfits," Evie chuckled, stowing her chain. "How's he keep doing that?"

"I have not the foggiest," Vess admitted, only belatedly saying. "He is not my boyfriend."

"Sure."

CHAPTER FIFTY-TWO

The "Devouring" wasn't as bad as it sounded.

The shaman led their people in an impromptu feast—celebrating their new, curse-free existence. The Yttins cavorted and clicked joyously as they shared their roasting meat and savory flavored dishes with Felix's people. Felix's Eye worked overtime, quickly confirming that none of the meat on offer had ever been a Human or something. It was mostly a creature called a *fouval*, a sort of long-eared beast that grew the size of a large dog and bred like the rabbits they resembled. The only real difference were the short horns on their foreheads, like tiny, fluffy unicorns.

They tasted delicious.

His people conversed among themselves, spread among the cook fires and laughing. It was nice to see, especially after earlier that day, but Felix could still see a thread of tension among them all. That tension eased considerably when Harn announced that they were staying the last few hours of the night. They had time to eat and rest up before dawn, when they expected to see more conflict.

Harn and Darius had come to Felix with the suggestion that they stay, and he'd agreed easily. According to Atar, it was unlikely that they would reach Ahkestria before dawn, and even less likely that they'd find a better place to stay the dangerous daylight hours. The skeleton was potent, however, and according to the shaman, it kept most monsters away from the area by sheer presence. Zara had claimed it was accumulated significance, baked into the creature's bones, and Felix couldn't argue. Even in death, the beast exuded a solidity that made it unsettling to dwell within, even with *his* Willpower.

"Will that pose a problem to the troops, then?" Felix had asked.

"No. It's an unconscious effect; anyone with enough Will and Intelligence can get through it." Zara had waved off his concerns while eating a haunch of *fouval*.

"Dunno if they qualify," Evie had said, nodding at the legionnaires.

"They'll be fine. Consider it Willpower training."

That had been an hour ago, and things were starting to settle down. Felix assessed the night sky, Pit at his side. The thing was clear as crystal and chock full of stars in great, cloudy swaths. Galaxies, he figured, so similar to how the Milky Way had appeared back on Earth. The moons were close to setting, and Felix judged there was approximately three more hours before the sun began to rise.

Time enough to handle a few things, he thought, scratching the tenku behind his ears. The great lunk had all but tackled Felix when he'd emerged from the skeleton, and their bond had reaffirmed itself. Like a kink in a hose, pent up feelings of anxiety, fear, and a familiar bloodlust had slammed into Felix, but he weathered it just as he tanked the full-body slam. He'd been worried, too. About Karys as well, though his sword was also responsive again. The fact that either one had been disrupted, let alone both, put him on edge. *How do I stop that from happening again?*

Felix had some ideas, but he sought out Atar, first. The man was studying the skeleton. A dagger in his hand scraped ineffectually at the material, not so much as scratching its surface.

"Don't think that'll work," Felix said.

"Oh!" The fire mage jumped, startled enough that he fumbled his blade into the sands. "Burning ash! You move entirely too quietly, Felix."

Felix shrugged. "What are you doing?"

Atar straightened his robes, plucking at his shoulders to adjust their drapery. "A material like this would prove excellent for enchanting. I don't doubt the strength of its composition could hold a great array of enchantments." He looked at Felix, eager. "You don't suppose they'd give us some?"

"I mean, I could ask," Felix said. "Might be that they have some broken pieces they aren't too attached to."

"Excellent," Atar said with a grin.

"But I have a question in return. Or a request, I suppose." Felix folded his arms in front of him. "Tell me about the Highest Flame."

"Ah," Atar said, his bright smile withering. "Did Vess or Zara mention it?"

"The shaman, actually. Is this not a secret?" Felix asked. It had *felt* like a secret, somehow. "It's common knowledge?"

"I wouldn't say common, no. But it isn't a tightly guarded secret, either," Atar said, licking his lips. "It is simply not...announced at every street corner. Not everyone has a good view of Urges."

Not hard to figure why, he mused, thinking back on the Urges he'd fought. "I know they're not all like the monsters I fought in the Waterfall Temple. I also don't know enough about Urges to have a good or bad view of them...only that they're strong. That alone makes me nervous."

Atar sighed. "You're not alone in that feeling. But, trust me that there is nothing to fear from it. The Council of Masters may be beholden to certain rituals, but the Highest does not hold us even half as tightly as the Raven holds the Henaari."

Felix breathed a little easier. "Well that's good. What sort of rituals?"

"I really cannot say."

"More secrets?" Felix asked.

"Only by necessity. Even I, favored pupil of the greatest Master on the Council, was kept from its inner workings." Atar sheathed his dagger, as if surprised he still held it in his hands. "The Temples of Elemental Flame work with the Council in many ways, and I understand the protections around the city are due to their cooperation. That is truly the extent of my knowledge."

"That's right, you mentioned your Master before." *A few hundred times, in fact.* "I didn't know he ruled the city. Is this why you insisted on us coming to Ahkestria?"

"I only wished to protect my home from the danger you foresaw. That my former master is on the ruling Council has little bearing on my desires," Atar said. "In fact, I expect it will help us convince the Council of the threat the Paladins represent."

"Still, that's the kind of thing I need to know ahead of time, dude," Felix said, a little annoyed. It felt pretentious, but if he was expected to be leading them, then he needed to know all the details.

"I, damn, you're right." Atar ran a hand through his curls and scratched the back of his head. "I thought—well, I assumed that Zara would have told you. She knows who my former Master is."

Felix clenched his jaw. "Really."

"She asked me about it before we left. I thought it only natural she pass that onto you," Atar said with a frown. "Annoying that she didn't."

You're telling me. "Thanks Atar. I appreciate the information."

"Ah, sure."

———

"Hrm, a decent size," Harn said. He held a shard of bone, two strides long and half that wide. It glimmered, blue-black in the fading moonlight. "Add it to the pile."

"Grrm."

The giant, Geir, grunted as he took the piece from Harn. It looked comically smaller in his hands, and the Risi easily placed it in the growing stack on the wagon.

Harn considered the bone shards before him. After Felix had said something to the shaman, a tide of Yttins had come out bearing these broken slabs. Apparently, they were gonna take them, which hadn't been welcome news. They were having trouble enough with the sands, and adding more weight to the wagons was a good way to kill the avum teams. Yet, once he'd gotten a chance to inspect the material, Harn had eagerly changed his mind.

Damn good structure. Mana lattice is more solid than Tier III metal, I think. He rubbed his chin in thought as he sifted through the pile. Not all the pieces brought out were useful. *I think this could make a good weapon, a pike maybe. Legion could use pikes.* A line of pikemen was a great defense against larger monsters, especially when they charged. The problem was usually an issue of materials. Wood was typically too weak, even higher-Tier materials, and the better metals were too expensive to waste. *But this bone...Hmm.*

More shards were dropped in the sorting pile, clinking together like metal, and Harn looked up from his thoughts. "Evie. Did you have to drop it right in front of me?"

"You didn't look happy with that selection. So here's a new set," she said. "Those walkin' bandages have piles of the stuff. Couldn't wait to shove it in my arms."

Harn pursed his lips. The pieces she'd brought over *were* better than the scraps he'd picked over, many of them eight or ten strides long. His Mind whirled, already sketching out ideas for weapons and armor, and he couldn't help the excitement that rose in his breast. It was very different from his battle fury, but very welcome.

"What's goin' on?"

"Hm?" he asked.

Evie crossed her arms and looked him up and down. "You're different. If I didn't know you better, I'd say happy. You roll in the sands with that tavernkeep?"

Harn frowned. "Watch your mouth, kid." He grabbed a piece of bone and handed it off to Geir.

Evie raised her hands in surrender. "Just a question. Don't think I didn't notice those looks you two have been tradin'."

"Nothin' I can do about that," Harn said. "Ain't got time for distractions, now."

"Distractions ain't all bad," Evie said. "Sometimes unwindin' is what the healer ordered."

Harn handed off another bone shard. "And when was the last time you relaxed, kid? Who are you datin', except that chain of yours?"

"Fair point. I'll shut up," Evie said, her mood not dented in the slightest.

The two of them sorted bone shards a while longer without speaking at all. Sort, shift, toss to Geir. Harn let the work engross him, excitement growing with the potential of each new piece. That didn't mean he missed how Evie shied from Geir's closeness, or how she stared daggers at the giant's back whenever she thought Harn wasn't paying attention. It put a damper on his enthusiasm.

Harn cared a great deal for Evie. She was the kid sister he never had, and he'd taken up training her after Magda's death. Cal too, though the now-Lady had bigger issues to worry about. That meant the tough stuff was on Harn's shoulders...but there was only so much he could do for this.

Kid's gotta work her own way through it, he reminded himself. *Can't do it for her.*

Still, he could give her reasons to trust. The giants hadn't proved too bad, and their discipline was strong. True, that was mostly due to their fear of Felix, but that hardly mattered. They'd given their Oaths. He was more worried the legion would set fire to their camp before any of the Risi would betray their new Lord.

"Evie, take Geir to get their largest pieces, the ones they might have trouble moving," Harn suggested. To her credit, she'd only glared a moment at the Frost Giant before stalking off. Geir rumbled in confusion but followed her without complaint.

One step at a time.

———

Ultimately, Felix decided to leave Zara to her own devices for a little while longer. He had notifications to resolve. So, he'd found himself a small chamber inside the skeletal Warren where he could have some privacy, and he eagerly brought them up.

Chthonic Tribute is level 84!

Unite the Lost is level 50!
Journeyman Tier!
You Gain:
Reduction of Significance Consumed In Skill Activation
+50 RES
+50 FEL

You Have Gained 1 Level!
You Are Now Level 57!
+20 to STR! +22 to PER! +22 to VIT! +26 to END! +24 to INT!
+28 to WIL! +26 to AGL! +29 to DEX!
+20 All Harmonic Stats!
You Have 15 Unused Stat Points!

System energy flooded Felix's core, rebounding back out into his Skills in a blaze of red-gold and blue-white light. It was painful, as always, but manageable. The boosts to his stats were insane, but then again, it was his first level in nearly two months—gaining levels was far slower at his stage, according to everyone he'd spoken to, and adding the XP penalty from his Race only slowed him further. Even with his new Path, was it enough to go toe-to-toe with a Primordial? He'd fought the Maw, and then the Ravager King, but both had been weakened or limited.

"...it is the desert itself."

The shaman's words echoed back at Felix, just as unnerving as it had been the first time. Who could fight an entire desert? How would he even begin? He growled in frustration.

"Okay. Training, then." Felix said. Pit chirruped in excitement from within his Spirit. His Companion had refused to be separated again, so once Felix indicated he was entering the Warren, he'd hitched a ride. He found their bond unaffected this time around. The why of it was a mystery, as he still felt that distinct pressure from the blackened bones all around him. In fact, that was part of why he was sitting inside of the Warren again, as he'd planned to practice his Voracious Eye and push it to Tier.

Voracious Eye!

Voracious Eye Failed.

The skeleton refused to be analyzed. It didn't push back so much as simply refused to be moved at all. Felix licked his lips. He considered this a sort of resistance training for his Skill, but he vividly recalled the pain he'd felt further below when he'd pushed too hard. Now though he felt sturdier than ever. A new level and stats, an infusion of Essence and significance, all of which should anchor him against the pain.

So he pressed forward again.

Voracious Eye!

Voracious Eye Failed.

Jagged pain stabbed at his eyes and snaked among his core, but it was only pain. He'd dealt with worse.

Voracious Eye!

Absorbing the flesh curse from the mutated shaman had awarded him a sizable increase in significance. It had even given him more than he'd spent on Unite the Lost, the very action that turned the shaman back to his natural form.

Voracious Eye Failed.

Felix's nostrils flared. All in all, there was an odd balance to his Unite the Lost. He could use it frivolously, he knew, but it was like the actions he had taken so far were...approved, somehow. The System rewarded him for turning back the flesh curse, for curing the Archon's twisted creations, for saving that chorister back in the Nest months ago. That indicated it *wanted* him to continue to do so, at least if it had any sort of intelligence behind it. Felix still wasn't sure of that. It had spoken to him, but was that a mind? Or just clever, magical programming?

At a certain point, was there even a distinction between the two?

Guess that depends on whether the System is making plans or not. He frowned, idly crushing a sandstone rock in his hands. *I don't want to be under the gods' thumbs, but do I avoid doing the System's bidding? Would I want to?*

So far Quests given to him had only been for the better, except those that were clearly tampered with by the Maw or the gods. He couldn't go around questioning every single decision he made forever, though. Felix decided to let it ride, at least for now. He had goals of his own, and if the System helped him in that? Excellent.

Voracious Eye!

Voracious Eye Failed.

Voracious Eye!

Voracious Eye Failed.

Voracious Eye!

Voracious Eye Failed.

It was like beating his head against a wall, but each time, he felt the skeleton's resistance bend just a little more. Maybe that was all in Felix's imagination, but it fed his resolve. He wasn't leaving that room until he'd Tempered his Mind. Felix tried a different tack.

He dove into his core space.

It had once resembled a solar system—if a poorly scaled version. But now it was...well, strange was one way to put it. His Skills still revolved around the center in large, elliptical orbits. The highest-leveled Skills were nearest the center and shining bright, while those that lagged behind were further out and dimmer. Their rotations and revolutions provided the constant, steady song that threaded through him, loud as ever—a strange intermingling of tones and chords, all working to project a delicate Harmony.

Atop that, however, was a rival Dissonance. At the center, where typically there was a single core, Felix had two. They were formed as rings of liquid flame, the bottom a blue-white hue and the top a red-gold, stacked atop one another like a pair of wedding rings, and rotating in opposing directions. His [Thunderflame Core] and his [Cardinal Beast Core].

Where their surfaces ground against one another, lightning and flame burst and danced, generating that atonal Dissonance. It competed with the Harmony, but not nearly as much as it once had—Felix had reached a point where the two sounds had melded together into a single, rousing sound. For the most part. Peaks of wild Harmony and valleys of burring

Dissonance still crept through, each one a tremor that spiked through his core space.

Below the rings and spinning Skills were pillars, two of them now, that were the beginnings of his Weaving Stage. What they did Felix was a bit unclear on, but Karys assured him it was the next step in advancing his power. He ignored those for now. Felix knew he couldn't form another pillar until he'd reached Adept anyway, or else he'd risk weakening his foundation.

And all of that would have been fine, if a bit weird. Except, where Felix should have been able to see through the two cores atop another another—right through the center and down to the pillars—instead, he could see only a thick, pervading darkness. A hungry abyss, responsible for eating up the nastier portions of the creatures he devoured. It was sleepy and lethargic right now, as the shaman's curse had been quite the meal, and Felix was just glad he didn't have to contend with the thing.

And that brings us to the Tree.

Divine Tree, actually, though Felix didn't know if that was its name. It stuck up through the center of his cores, ignoring the dark abyss as if it weren't there, connecting his pillars to the upper reaches of his core space. There it branched out, just as a tree might, its bare branches clothed not in leaves but in thick, shimmering Essence and motes of resplendent light. A nebula, trapped above his solar system, glimmering in the endless dark.

God, I can't believe this is all inside of me, he thought, not for the first time. It wasn't *really* inside his body, that much Felix had ascertained, but was instead some sort of metaphysical other space that people could access. It related in some fashion to his Aspects, but Zara had not been able to explain it to his satisfaction. It *felt* like it was inside him, especially when his Voracious Eye spasmed against the restrictions of the skeletal Warren, like a sharp stomach cramp mixed with an ocular migraine.

Focus.

His Voracious Eye swirled down among the Skills nearest his cores, bright and shining with two Tempers behind it. The pattern of it was convoluted and confusing, much as any of them were, and it thrummed each time he activated the Skill.

Voracious Eye!

Voracious Eye Failed.

Felix frowned and narrowed his Intent. His Affinity sounded the pattern of his Voracious Eye, and his Intent shaped its power while his Willpower carried the Mana through his channels. It was like doing brain surgery with someone else's arms from across town, unwieldy and awkward. Yet Mana surged regardless, flaring up into his eyes and out into the world.

Voracious Eye!

The skeleton fought back, no longer passive, and that migraine turned to a stabbing, tortuous agony. Felix didn't relent. He was stronger now. *I can do this!*

Voracious Eye!

Affinity, Intent, and Willpower all converged atop his Skill, forcing it to new heights. His Eye tore into the skeleton's resistance, shredding it piece-by-piece until it vanished, all at once.

Name: Leviathan Bone
Type: Material
Lore: This is part of a once-mighty creature's Body, an apex predator that ruled the depths of an ancient sea. Leviathans are rarely seen, not because they are few in number, but because there are rarely any survivors. Leviathan Bone is a highly advanced material that is stronger than orichalcum and more dense than adamant. Due to the nature of its demise, this Leviathan Bone contains a portion of the significance it had in life, increasing its durability and value.

Voracious Eye is level 75!
...
Voracious Eye is level 79!
Adept Tier!
You Gain:
+100 PER
+50 AFI
+...

Legendary Essence Detected During Formation!
[Essence of Earthen Panoply]

Felix immediately felt the Essence that sang the most to his Skill, and plucked it straight from the branches of his Divine Tree. The mote of light careened downward until it splashed with a burst of resplendent light against his [Cardinal Beast Core], and the choices cascaded across his vision.

Broken Path and Fatebreaker Titles Found!
Adept Tier Bonus Added!
Calculating Effects...
Choose A Feature:
Armor - Fortified Monolith
Arms - Brandished Obelisk
Skyclad - Forsaken Foundation

Felix was beyond questioning why this Essence called to his Skill the most, but he was surprised to realize that it had originated from the

Atlantes Anima. His Spirit Tree had given him a few Essence Motes, likely during its tumultuous birth. Above all else, that meant he had less to worry about with regards to its consequences. Compared to the Urges and Archon, his Spirit Tree was basically benevolent.

He decided to trust his instincts. Voracious Eye, though it was twisted by the Maw all those months ago in the Void, was about gathering information. Knowledge was power, and Felix needed his Skill to retain its edge so that resistance like this Leviathan couldn't impede him in the future. It was a tool of his Mind, and with it he would seize that which threatens him and his people, and shatter it. Armor sang to him, while Skyclad did not, but neither so much as Arms. The Brandished Obelisk was a tent pole, a stele reaching toward the heavens...but it was also a spear.

He chose.

Congratulations!
You Have Absorbed The Essence Of [Arms]!

The power sank into him, bursting across his cores in a wash of red-gold radiance. His [Thunderflame Core] responded, crackling back, but it was the [Cardinal Beast Core] that raged the most. Pain swept out and into his core space, striking the pattern of Voracious Eye with a ribbon of iridescent power.

3 of 3 Mind Essences Formed!
Tempering Has Begun!

Everything went white.

CHAPTER FIFTY-THREE

"Is that...what is that?" Loquis asked, staring into the east. The Half-Orc stood with Pava and Asaad atop the ridge, one of several squads that had been set as lookouts. Henaari scouts were prowling the sands somewhere nearby, but the top of the bluffs had the best sight lines. Loquis shaded his eyes against the rising sun, just barely peeking over the horizon.

"What's what?" Asaad demanded. The Dwarf squinted eastward for all of a moment before sneezing violently. "Damnable sun! I don't see anythin'!"

"Clouds. I see clouds," Pava said. Loquis could almost see the wisps of Mana flutter around her eyes, enhancing her normal Perception. "A lot of clouds."

Elemental Eye is level 27!

The clouds were lit by the golden light of the rising sun, but his Elemental Eye saw it as a dark storm front. Black threads roiled among the dunes, and an unnameable dread seized Loquis' soul.

"Those aren't just clouds," he whispered. "We must tell the Autarch."

"Oh aye? You gonna be the one to do that?" Asaad said.

"He's been sequestered for hours now," Pava added. "Geir spotted his Companion down the second passage."

"Hrm. Yes," Geir said. "None were allowed near."

The storm was coming closer. It appeared slow, but that was an illusion of the distance. Loquis had no clue how quickly it could be upon them.

"I'll go. He needs to know. Everyone needs to know."

———

Congratulations!
You Have Tempered Your Mind!

You Have Formed: the Fiendforged Mind
+50 PER
+50 INT
+100 WIL
+100 INE
+40 ALA

Felix woke to the final notes of a dwindling concerto in his head, pillowed upon the soft, warm cushion of Pit's belly. That sound resonated as his eyes cracked open, fading to tremors of exquisite, jeweled tones that vibrated his fingers and toes.

Huh. Fiendforged Mind? Felix licked his lips, but it was like rubbing two dry stones together. There was no moisture within his mouth at all. He sat up, Body protesting and Mind quaking just a touch. It was the world's worst hangover. "Water," he croaked.

Pit chirruped and nudged a sloshing skin toward Felix's hand. He grabbed it and slung back the entire thing in four big gulps, only surfacing when the skin had hollowed out. He didn't even care that the contents had been warmed by contact with Pit's haunches. He worked his tongue against the roof of his mouth until crude functionality returned to his throat. "Gah, that feels awful. Remind me never to get dehydrated in a desert again."

Pit tilted his head, then nudged another full water skin toward Felix. He laughed, taking it gladly. "Thanks, buddy." He sipped at this one slowly, grimacing at the warm taste. "How long have I been out?"

Six glasses, Pit sent. *Sunrise is here.*

Six hours was about the same amount he'd slept off his Spirit Temper, so that tracked, but Felix didn't like that he'd lost so much time. There was too much to do before they headed off to the City of Embers, not the least of which was fit in a bit more training—for himself and the others.

Focus. Status check first.

Name: Felix Nevarre
Level: 57
Race: Primordial of the Unseen Tide (Greater)*
Omen: Magician
Path: Cardinal Fiend
Born Trait: Keen Mind

———

Health: 7692/7692
Stamina: 7212/7212

Mana: 6366/6366

STR: 1544
PER: 1857
VIT: 1508
END: 1304
INT: 1960
WIL: 2372
AGL: 1240
DEX: 1395

BODY - Calamitous Dawn (Journeyman)
Resistances: The Song of Absolution (L), Level 86

Combat Skills: Dodge (C), Level 63; Heavy Armor Mastery (C), Level 1; Blind Fighting (R), Level 45; Corrosive Strike (R), Level 65; Wild Threnody (E), Level 70

Physical Enhancements: Armored Skin (R), Level 76; Relentless Resolution (L), Level 71

MIND - Fiendforged (Adept)
Mental Enhancements: Deception (C), Level 30; Meditation (U), Level 69; Negotiation (U), Level 26; Bastion of Will (E), Level 85; Deep Mind (E), Level 75; Manifestation of the Coronach (E), Level 67; Chthonic Tribute (L), Level 84

Information Skills: Alchemy (C), Level 49; Tracking (C), Level 30; Exploration (U), Level 63; Voracious Eye (E), Level 79; Aria of the Green Wilds (L), Level 85

SPIRIT - Eldercrowned (Adept)
Spiritual Enhancements: Dual Casting (U), Level 56; Manasight (U), Level 63; Manaship Pilot (R), Level 22; Etheric Concordance (L), Level 76; Sovereign of Flesh (T), Level 74; Unite the Lost (T), Level 50; Fiendforge (Un), Level 1

Spells: Abyssal Skein (R), Level 49; Cloudstep (R), Level 48; Green Shaping (R), level 26; Invocation (R), Level 59; Oathbinding (R), Level 35; Shadow Whip (R), Level 46; Stone Shaping (R), Level 77; Sunken Ward (R), Level 1; Rime Shaping (R), Level 27; Mantle of the Infinite Revolution (E), Level 50; Arrow of Perdition (L), Level 42; Cardinal Flame (L), Level 81; Rain of Cataclysm (L), Level 51; Theurgist of the Rise (L), Level 80; Adamant Discord (T), Level 80

Unused Stat Points: 15

Harmonic Stats
RES: 724
INE: 1160
AFI: 2180
REI: 812
EVA: 871
MIG: 624
ALA: 1395
FEL: 1875

He had no active Status Conditions, thankfully, and his Health, Stamina, and Mana were all topped off. However, Felix swallowed audibly at his stats.

Twenty three hundred Willpower and over a thousand Intent? Dang. What does that mean, in practical terms? he wondered. *My Willpower is tied to things I can do with my Mind and Spirit, so that's my magic and just sheer stubbornness. Intent is tied to making the Grand Harmony move as I want it to...but there's a limit to that, isn't there?*

More than once, Felix had encountered obstacles his Willpower and Intent couldn't get past, and he likely would again if he continued to face off against Primordials and gods. If nothing else, however, his risen Intent meant that it would be that much easier to activate his Skills in the Chanter fashion. Affinity to make his Skills sing, Willpower to seize and force it through his channels, and Intent to shape the pattern of his Skills as he desired.

That's worth it, at least. And fifteen more points to invest. He thought only a moment before dumping all fifteen into Agility. It was the lowest of his Primary Stats, and while he was certainly very fast, he doubted he would be able to keep up with the true threats. *That's what Endurance and Vitality are for, I suppose.* Felix knew he could take a hit.

That done, Felix felt at his Mind. Despite the quivers of weakness when he'd first roused, it felt no different than before his Tempering. At least, until he flared his Cardinal Flame. Since it had evolved from his Fire Within, his first visualization and internal Mana Skill, it retained its sensitivity to his Aspects and core space. More than retained, in fact, as he could clearly sense the heft and density of his newly acquired Mind. Like his Spirit, it felt as solid as the earth itself. The strain that had hounded him since fighting the cursed Shaman had vanished from all except his Body, and even then, it was a manageable ache.

Fiendforged Mind. What determines these names? Felix had a Skill called Fiendforge, so maybe it had to do with that. That Skill had catalyzed from his efforts to build his own Path, and could be used to help his allies in some fashion, so that was encouraging as far as labels were concerned. He wasn't sure how it could help his friends, exactly—there had been not a single opportunity to experiment with the Skill. He planned to change that soon, now that he had a mess load of Essence Draughts on hand. If he could get the legionnaires to Tier up then imbibe a Draught, he could see what his Fiendforge could do—perhaps that might lead them to developing a more powerful Temper? He wasn't sure, but the idea of it excited him. Ideas and possibilities formed and were discarded in a blink, half of them silly fantasies while the rest were potentially useful. So long as the Skill worked as Felix hoped.

Felix?

He brought up the Skill again, checking on its details.

Fiendforge (Unique), Level 1!
You've proven yourself capable of Forging Paths from the threads of Harmony and Dissonance both. This Skill lets you do the same for others, but the learning curve is great. Dare you tempt fate again? Risk of failure decreases per level, risk of permanent damage to core decreases per level, speed of Forging increases per level.

Forging Paths. So, does that mean others won't need an Omen Key? Or would they still require one for me to use this on them? Felix drummed his fingers on the sand, but made a face at the way it just sprayed sand over his legs. *Ugh. Where's a good hard surface when you need one. Where was I? Right. Omen Keys.*

Felix.

How would I go about getting them for my people? They're System rewarded. I can't just...make the System give me some. But does that mean there's no way around it? Damn. What if I—

FELIX!

Felix blinked, and tore his eyes up from the sand, only to find Pit's large, golden gaze inches from his own. "What?"

A flutter of worry crossed their bond. *You're wrong.*

"What?" Felix frowned, looking himself over. His Health was fine, and there was still no Status Condition. "What're you talking about?"

I called you many times. Frustration, now. Pit let out a growling chirp. *You did not respond.*

Oh. Felix blinked, thinking back...only to find that his memories of his surroundings was almost totally blank for the last...five minutes? Instead, he felt a manic sort of energy fizz across his Mind. "Oh. Holy shit. My Mind's going too fast to keep up with everything. Is it a stat discrepancy?"

He stood up, feeling the world lurch slightly, like it was lagging just a touch behind. Felix held a hand to his head as if to steady his inner ear. "Whoa. That's not great. Definitely a problem with something."

His Intelligence increased the speed at which he thought, while Perception increased his sensitivity and breadth of what he could perceive. Together they worked to keep him ahead of others in most situations, even slowing things down at times as Felix reacted faster than events could occur. But...the Thresholds he'd been through meant that his stats were working together in concert, making them more effective than on their own. His Agility and Dexterity might be lagging behind all of the rest of his Primary Stats, but why would that be a problem now and not before?

Felix, Pit sent. A warning.

Felix shook himself. "I did it again, huh? That'll be annoying." He pressed a hand to the bone walls, steadying himself. His legs felt weird under him, or maybe it was the ground itself. Like if he walked too fast he'd fly off the surface, somehow. "Shit. That's it, isn't it."

It wasn't his stats. It was his Body. Felix could feel the strain accumulate as he moved, slight as it was, just from his Journeyman Body keeping up with his Adept Mind and Spirit.

"Karys?"

His sword ignited. This close to the exterior of the Warren, the sword still had a solid connection to his chancellor. "Yes, my Lord?"

He quickly explained what was going on. Karys made a few clucking noises before sighing.

"You have grown too quickly. And conversely, not quickly enough," Karys said. "As you suspect, it is clear that your Body cannot fully keep up with your Mind and Spirit. I mentioned before that the gulf between Journeyman and Adept is quite remarkable. If Beginner to Apprentice is a thimble to a spoonful, and Apprentice to Journeyman is a spoonful to a teacup, then the leap to Adept is akin to a lake. Crossing that expanse is difficult, and must be done swiftly, or else you risk drowning in your own power."

"Easier said than done," Felix groaned. "My Body Skills are close, but not enough."

"Then you must focus on them. Press them as much as you can and glean what understanding you must, because if the imbalance continues, you will see greater issues to come."

"Cool." Felix leaned against the cold bone and sighed. "I'll get right on that."

A timid knock interrupted his thoughts only minutes later. "Sir?"

Felix pulled himself into a standing position, bracing against the slight blur in his perceptions. He could still sense things around himself, but acting on it was hard. If he could keep his actions limited, though, then it was almost normal. "Come in."

The thin cloth at the entry to his small chamber was twitched aside, and a Half-Orc legionnaire stepped in. He wore battered battlerobes and bore the forked lightning of the Arclight society. Loquis, as his Eye determined, pressed a fist to his chest and kneeled. "My Lord Autarch."

Oh, jeez. "Don't do that. Stand up." The kid stood up, blushing awkwardly. "What's going on, Loquis?"

"Ah, um, I was, I decided to come down here to see you because, ah," the Half-Orc swallowed twice, his blush darkening his green face even further.

"Calm down," Felix said. "I'm not gonna bite, dude. Why did you come to see me?"

"The desert, sir. It's the desert." Loquis straightened up to his full height. "It's dawn, sir. And a storm is coming."

Monsters? Felix tried not to enjoy the thrill that shot through him, but it was hard. "Show me."

———

Felix emerged from the Warren to find the sands about the massive skeleton whipped into a frenzy. Pit squawked indignantly and refused to follow, eyes lidded against the wind. The sky had darkened, but not because of a lack of sun. It was due to huge, vaporous threads of blackened-green and dusty brown Mana that filled the horizon, all woven into the shape of an advancing storm cloud.

"Alright, stay here for now. I'll be back in a bit."

Relentless Resolution!

Flaring his Skill in the hopes of steadying his Body, Felix leaped straight up the side of the Levianthan's corpse. His feet hit once or twice, each time propelling himself up higher and farther, until he landed atop the sandy bluff the creature had embedded itself within. From there, he could truly see.

A roaring storm of sand and lightning surged across the horizon. It was a force of nature, so primal and impressive that Felix forgot to breathe for a few seconds. When he remembered, he still couldn't quite shake his awe. It was like if a twister and a hurricane had a baby, then dried it out. It was sweeping across the dunes like a rainstorm...yet Felix saw no water Mana within its structure—only earth, air, and a huge dollop of necromantic power.

It was terrifying.

"That is not a natural storm."

Felix started. Zara was beside him, staring at the storm as well. His imbalanced Aspects and distraction had conspired; he hadn't sensed her approach at all. "That seems obvious. Can't recall the last storm I've seen that was even a little necromantic."

"Indeed. It is also..." she tilted her head, listening. "*Filled* with an inert Intent. Interesting. I assume these are the Cursewinds."

"Yeah, seems likely." Felix licked his lips. He was thirsty again. *Damn dry desert air.* "Will this place hold against it?"

"The shaman seems to believe so. They were unconcerned when the storm was revealed to us."

The sound of hard boots against harder stone clattered behind them, and this time Felix easily sensed Evie and Vess' arrival.

"What's goin' on? Holy—" Evie looked at Zara, cutting her words short. "What're you two just out here standin' around for? That thing gonna hit us?"

"No," Vess said. To Felix's eyes, air Mana coiled around her upraised hand, feeding down into her eyes where it swirled in brilliant flashes of multi-colored light. "The prevailing winds have it headed south. It should miss us by a close margin."

"That's a relief. The idea of bein' buried alive in sand isn't much appealin' to me, personally."

"It would likely scour the flesh from your bones first, if that's any consolation," Zara supplied helpfully.

Evie sucked at her teeth. "Can't say it is, no."

They watched as the sandstorm rolled ever closer, though it appeared Vess had been right. It was going to bypass them on its way south. Toward the Stormeater Peaks, he didn't doubt, where it'd hopefully dash itself apart. Unless it hit the Caleph Pass directly. Could that happen? What if—

Without warning, there was a flare of piercing Dissonance, and all four of them reeled backward. Felix heard someone scream, even felt blood drip down his nose, but couldn't pay them much attention. All of his Mind was fully engrossed in the undeniable certainty that the storm was *looking at him.*

"It's...sensing you," Zara said from behind.

"Impressive, Felix," Evie snarked breathlessly. She had fallen to her knees after that Dissonance had hit. "I can be a thorn, but I've never made the *wind* mad."

"It's not the wind," Zara said. Her voice was heavy and thick with apprehension. "Feel its Intent, child. You too, Felix."

He did.

The inert Intent Zara had sensed was rough and grey, like a beast that had been slumbering for years. Or a corpse buried for decades. But there was a rousing acidity to it, an electric charge that suffused its core. It smelled of violence, tasted of Dissonance and thin, dusty blood. He recognized it, having tasted its Essence twice now.

"Primordial," he growled. "Or Primordial-generated, at least."

"It knows you," Zara said.

"Because of the spider monster? Because I cleansed it?"

"Perhaps. The capabilities of Primordials are unknown. The greatest were calamities, but even the lesser ones were forces of nature." The Naiad swallowed and helped Vess back to her feet. "If this is a mere branching of its Will and Intent, then it is one of the former. It is stronger than the Ravager King by an order of magnitude."

A scream shredded the air and shook the rocks they stood upon, as the winds shifted and the *entire* storm followed suit. Right toward them.

CHAPTER FIFTY-FOUR

Stone Shaping is level 78!

Extended from the dun-colored bluffs that the Warren was built into, Felix had formed squat structures that ran alongside the skeleton. Mostly, they were walls, curved up and designed to block as much of the savage wind as they could. The rest were choke points around the more wide-open sections of the blackened Leviathan skeleton, where his people could fight if needed. He wasn't an architect or an expert on fortifications, but he did his best in the time they had.

"Back! Back! I want a line of defenders here and here!" Darius shouted, pointing at places in Felix's impromptu structures.

"No archers until we see how this hits!" Harn bellowed right behind the Hand. "Henaari! Focus on spear work and maintain distance!"

The shaman and Atar and even that Palin woman had been clear about what was coming. The storm, the Cursewinds, were harbingers of the desert's worst foes, and no one was taking it lightly.

The stormfront was far larger than Felix had anticipated. From an indeterminate distance, it had seemed simply massive, stretching across a portion of the horizon and blocking the flare of the rising sun. Yet as it roared toward them—quite literally too, according to their Affinities—the Cursewinds proved itself thousands of feet wide and as tall as any skyscraper Felix had seen. The sheer presence of it filled Felix's senses, a behemoth of wind and sand and death.

When the storm hit, it hit Felix's fortifications first.

Sand scoured them, like a roaring curtain of miniature hail. Shields were raised, and Skills were used, but the sands tore into them mercilessly.

Not even Felix's shaped defenses were immune as the stormwall passed, the thickest and most intense portion of the tempest. They were scratched and pitted by the relentless assault. Felix was only thankful no one had taken undue damage from it; his protections had worked.

"Arclight!" Darius bellowed over the howling winds. The stormwall passed them, but the winds from within the sandstorm were gale-force at the very least. "Send first volley!"

Mages all along their impromptu battlements raised their hands, ensconced behind shaped fortifications and the upright slats of Leviathan bone. Blue-white lightning kindled in their palms, Mana Gates spewing out flickers of condensed power as every mage in their company shot out a spell. It was the most minor of spells, intimidating in number if not potency. Still, the spells were caught by the Cursewind after traveling about ten feet, twisting them astray until they were snuffed out entirely.

"Keep all magic close! The winds will skew your aim!" Harn bellowed. "Be ready! They're here!"

From his own, higher vantage, Felix watched as the boiling hurricane spewed torrents of sand. Among the sand, riding atop the winds itself, desiccated warriors with rusted armor and broken weaponry appeared. They dropped to the earth, landing on walls and sandy dunes, dozens at first and more on the way. The moment they touched down, their eyes swiveled toward Felix and his people, and a blackened green limned them in hissing light.

"Undead! Brace!"

The creatures charged, flailing their ragged bodies toward them all. Felix squinted through the winds and activated his Eye.

Voracious Eye!

Name: Dustwight
Type: Undead
Level: 39
HP: 0/0
SP: 3412/3422
MP: 1189/1189
Lore: Undead are once living creatures bound by necromantic Mana to the Will of another. Some monsters use necromantic Mana in the natural course of their lives, though they are hunted avidly when found. In either case, such creatures do not have any Health, instead suffering all damage to their vast Stamina. When their Stamina is reduced to nothing, only then can they be killed for good.
Strength: More Data Required
Weakness: More Data Required

Damn, they're strong. And hard to put down, Felix grimaced. He called up

Stone Shaping once again and attempted to adjust his fortifications. They weren't bad, but now that the Dustwights were coming at them, he could see places where they could be improved. Yet, when his Mana traveled outward, it was eaten up by the storm winds, until only a whisper of his power reached its destination. *Shit!* It wasn't nearly enough to do what he wanted. *I'll have to get closer.*

The undead didn't let him. There were so many now. Their shambling movements were faster than Felix realized, because they had reached his people below.

"Fire!"

A wash of flame erupted from Felix's left, where Atar held his arm up and out. His Field of Flames drenched the sand with almost-liquid orange Mana, all of it blazing with fire, setting even the stone ablaze. The Dustwights made no screams or wails, only pushed through the fire as if it weren't there, even as it ate into their ragged leather and papery flesh.

"Bolts!"

Lightning bolts shot out once the undead crossed within a dozen feet. They were mashed together so tightly that even those that missed their target still hit a creature, though Felix could see the Cursewinds taking a bite out of their power. The bolts drilled through flesh and withered muscle, but again that did not stop many. Hooked spears came down, thrust through chests and skulls with equal ease, demolishing the Dustwights one-by-one while the tight corridors of shaped stone kept their advance manageable.

The real problem was the overflow, as the undead did not stop coming. More and more were disgorged from the storm every second, until the dunes before them were teeming with their number. Most were dressed the same, in rusted metal and leather armor, perhaps with wrappings of ragged cloth twisting in the wind. A few, however, were equipped with hulking plate armor and weapons as big as any Felix had seen. Warhammers, mauls, and great axes to name a few, these Dustwights lumbered with the steady, slow gait of those with great Strength and too little Agility.

Paladins, Felix realized. He could make out their emblem, rusted and sand-scoured though it was, centered upon their breastplates. *A lot of Paladins. How many have died since coming here?*

Of the mass that was before him, Felix spotted at least a third wearing the distinctive armor of a Paladin or a Squire. The Pathless zealots had faced the Cursewinds more than once, it seemed, and as much as that thrilled Felix, it also left him with the annoyance of fighting their undead corpses.

The Dustwights pressed forward, no longer running, but clambering up and over one another. It was a wild, chaotic mess, and Felix figured it would just tire them out or damage them in some way...until he saw them scaling his fortifications. When he saw the first armored Dustwight stumbling forward along one of his walls, his gut soured.

Rain of Cata—

Before the spell fully sang to life, a silver spear caught the former Paladin straight through the chest. It exploded, leaving nothing left of the undead save for some mangled boots. Felix grinned as Vess appeared, leaping across the fortifications to plant two more Spears into the press of withered flesh. Air and metal Mana exploded, their radius so much greater than it had been a few months prior, killing ten or fifteen in a single blow.

Evie followed, her chain dancing across the top of the crowd and tearing heads from necks with every revolution. She flipped and was flung; her Body's mass moved into her chain as she whipped it across the battlefield, only to land in a flurry of ice and spinning blades. The Dustwights proved themselves to be more than unthinking beasts, as they began avoiding the two of them in short order, scattering whenever they saw one of the women coming from above.

They were rarely fast enough.

Beyond that, Alister stepped among the dunes, his feet planted atop columns of summoned blue force. Each step would lift him up and outward, traversing the walls and crushing undead with each stomping foot. Force Mana surged from him, hitting the sands like a man-sized hammer and reducing Dustwights to desiccated paste. His rapier did not pause, either, as the force-attuned ward around him blocked the sandpaper wind but did not stop his blade from stabbing bolts of kinetic power atop choice targets.

Atar was there too, though he kept closer to the Leviathan skeleton than the rest. While the others were using shields or simply the strength of their Bodies to tank the abrasive nature of the storm, Atar simply *burned* it all away. He was a column of fire among the dark sky and orange dusted air, and all who drifted near him were subsumed by his flames.

Damn, dude. He could *feel* how much Mana that must be costing the guy, but Atar didn't seem to care. His Imbued Sparkbolts whirled around him, occasionally spearing outward to melt two or three Dustwights to stinking puddles. *He's gonna run out of Mana too fast.*

Pit chirped from his side, eagerness clear in his tone. "You too? Can you even fly in that?"

Yes.

"...Alright, fine. Just be careful." The words were barely out of his mouth when Pit leaped past him and into the air, thundering away on streamers of air Mana. *Keep an eye on Atar. I'm worried about his Mana use.*

Elated confirmation whispered back at him before Pit wheeled through the sky, wings disrupting the orange sands in the air. The Cursewinds howled, and Pit shrieked right back, summoning Frost Spears before dive bombing the undead in the further back. Tension curdled Felix's stomach until he realized his Companion's Health was dropping by the tiniest of amounts before his natural regeneration ticked it back up.

He'll be fine, he reassured himself. *He's certainly tougher than Atar and Evie.*

"They have things in hand," Zara said from behind him, almost mimicking his thoughts. She had her arms akimbo, and her ice-blue eyes flicked among the horde. "The Legion and your team. I see no reason for my presence. I shall retire to the lower chambers to study those weavings the Yttin made. If you have need of me, simply call."

She nodded at a brightly feathered kingfisher that had appeared in the room. It was her familiar or something, named Keru, and it hopped once atop the window sill. Felix pursed his lips but nodded. She left moments later.

Felix didn't like it, but Zara had a point. Either of them could have ended this fight quickly, but so long as his people weren't in imminent danger, this was a great chance for them to grow, even Pit and the rest of his team. Felix had been tempted to cull the Dustwights' numbers before, but with his team chipping in, there was no need. Already the undead had stopped crowding as much, fleeing his people even as they were whittled down to more manageable numbers.

Training. Hm.

Hours passed as Felix sat within his Stone Shaped chamber near the Leviathan's sternum, watching as the waves of undead thinned but never faltered. More came, as if the storm carried an endless supply. He wondered at that, in fact, as the Dustwights came raining down from the sky. Were the Cursewinds just a way to transport undead across the Expanse? Why? What was the point, other than mayhem and violence? He could feel the Primordial's eerie Intent all around him now, present but not overwhelming, but there was no meaning behind it. It simply felt...instinctual. Like it *needed* whatever this happened to be, whatever function the Cursewinds served. He'd put the question to Zara, dragging her back up to his outpost, but she'd professed that it was one of the many mysteries of the Continent.

"Greater Minds than my own have attempted to unravel the Scorched Expanse's deadly secrets, but none have succeeded. Few, in fact, ever returned from such inquiries," she had said before vanishing below once again.

Danger and more danger. Felix drummed his fingers on the bone next to him. *A withering Primordial and a vast desert of tireless guardians, hunting down anyone crossing the Expanse. It's a wonder anyone bothers to come into this desert at all, though Zara had claimed to be surprised at the knowledge of a Primordial here. Had it not been active before?* He thought on the Dustborn Wraiths, on what the Prioress had said. *They'd never seen the Wraiths before. So does that mean something woke this Primordial up?*

He groaned.

What are the odds that it was this other Unbound?

Felix didn't like how likely that felt, considering his own history. For now, it was speculation, though.

The battle still raged as midday approached. The undead were seemingly tireless, but his people were not. The legionnaires were swapped out in groups to let them stay fresh, but the groups were kept relatively small. Darius claimed it increased the stress and tension within the fighters, giving them a greater chance to advance their Skills or even learn new ones. Felix would have called bullshit on that, if Harn hadn't agreed. Felix knew stress increased the rewards from battle, but increasing it on purpose felt perverse.

He could not, however, deny its effectiveness. The dulcet tones of Skill-ups and level gains reached Felix even over the roar of the Cursewinds, while the collective Spirit of his people rose to shattering crescendos with every passing hour. They were exhausted and bleeding, but there was a joy baked into their collective strain and conflict with the undead.

Felix found his own joy along the way, focusing on his lesser used Skills and attempting to push them in new directions. He Eyed everyone he could see, watching the Dustwights as they fought and died. All of them had the same information, plus or minus a few levels and Stamina totals. What benefited, however, was the updates to their Strengths and Weaknesses.

Name: Dustwight
...
Strength: Movement and normal attacks do not use Stamina, and Stamina recovers rapidly when not in combat.
Weakness: Agility is low as is their Perception. Strength is tied to remaining Stamina.

Voracious Eye is level 80!

Mostly obvious things, but he passed the knowledge down to his commanders Harn and Darius to use as best they could. Every little bit helped. Even the Leviathan skeleton was useful, as the pressure they all felt was apparently far worse on the undead.

Any undead that came closer than twenty feet were at some point afflicted by a Status Condition called Forbiddance. It slowed their movements just a tad, manifesting as a haze around their limbs that ebbed and flowed into the visual spectrum. It grew in strength the closer they drew to the skeleton, but Felix hadn't had a chance to see if it'd stop them from entering. The Henaari, Risi, or Legion would kill them before that ever happened.

Things were going pretty well, all things considered. Everyone was tired and aching, and Felix was a little bored, but they were doing it. The Legion was cooperating, or at least following orders. It was looking up.

Which of course was when the battlefield exploded.

Ice and fire burst, ripping through ranks of the undead and shattering one of his weakened walls. Felix surged to his feet, eyes panning the scene, only to land on the ice-burned epicenter...where Evie and Atar writhed on the ground, *screaming* as Mana boiled in and out of both of them. A set of brassy horns, crashing cymbals, and rolling timpanis tore into his Mind and Spirit.

"Felix!" Vess yelled. She stood closer to him and jabbed at their friends with her spear. "They're Tempering!"

CHAPTER FIFTY-FIVE

Felix landed among the desolation seconds before Vess herself. The sand around Atar and Evie had half-frozen into undulating waves, while the other half was charred and slagged into streaks of glass. An incredible combination of temperatures emanated from them both, and in his Manasight, their orange and purple-white Mana splashed and coiled against one another. Where they met, steam gushed upward.

"What's happening to them? Tempering should not strain them so!" Vess cried, kneeling to grasp Evie's hand. She hissed in pain. "She's ice cold!"

Evie and Atar weren't convulsing anymore, not physically at least. Their Spirits were undergoing wild quakes however, and Felix knew they didn't have much time. "They're holding off their Tempers. Find their Essence Draughts! Feed her one, I've got Atar!"

The two of them fumbled with their friends' pouches, and soon found the stone vials Felix and Aenea had made. Quickly, Felix uncorked his and tipped it back into Atar's mouth. Vess did the same.

Immediately, their Spirits calmed. Felix pushed his Affinity and Perception across them, hunting for signs of further issue...but he couldn't be sure. Chaos was erupting all around them as the Dustwights regained their bearings from the explosion of Mana. In almost every direction, the undead swarmed toward them on shambling feet.

Felix raised his hand, and lightning answered.

Adamant Discord!

Dustwights were seized by his Will, and their connections shoved back. The stress on those links spread lightning in a radial arc around Felix and Vess, blasting the undead back off their feet. Pillars of blue Mana dropped among them, crushing more of the monsters into the earth as sand fountained around them. Alister, wide-eyed, slid through the gap he'd created and down into the shallow crater.

"Atar! Is he—?"

"He's fine, for now. But we have to move them," Felix growled. "Pit!"

His Companion dove out of the twisting winds, landing heavily. Vess turned to the others. More Dustwights rushed them, and a few even hurled their broken spears and swords at the group. A sharp word from Alister deflected the projectiles in a flash of kinetic blue.

"Go! I'll keep them distracted!" Vess hefted her partisan and summoned her Spears all around her.

The Cursewinds crackled, a deep rumbling tearing through them. Felix glanced up, sharply. The skies were black with twisted Mana while the intervening air was a haze of crimson sands, but he saw no lightning among the swirling storm. He could only feel a sharpening of the Intent within its core, but Felix couldn't guess what that could mean.

"Go!" Vess shouted before rushing toward the nearest cluster. More burst from their left and right as Alister lifted Atar onto Pit's back.

"Get on, Alister! Pit! Fly them into the Warren!" Felix didn't wait for them to answer but scooped Evie up into a fireman's carry. Her body was heavy, and that chain of hers dug into his shoulder, but the worst thing was how bitingly cold she was—it was like hefting a block of ice.

Rain of Cataclysm!

Felix sounded the spell, letting it form and flow from his channels in a tightly controlled burst. The Skill was an area of effect—quite a large area, in fact—but for this he restricted it, clamping on its pattern with his Will and Intent until it was no more than forty feet in diameter. Mana streamed into the air, coalescing in a snap above the undead. A deluge of flashing green rain dropped within that space, melting every single Dustwight caught within and freeing Vess' advance.

She grinned back at him, her dimples deep and her Spirit soaring.

Rain of Cataclysm is level 52!

...

Rain of Cataclysm is level 55!

"Take care of her!" she shouted, before leaping up and into the storm.

Pit! Go!

Pit launched into the sky just as more undead clawed their way out of the sand, and Felix did the same. Holding Evie closely, Felix hauled on the connections between himself and the air, arcing over the battlefield and back toward the Leviathan skeleton. He landed at a run, weaving through the legionnaires that started in shock.

"Make a hole! Coming through!"

Behind him, the undead attacked with renewed fervor, as if they were aware that Felix was out of reach. The sounds of conflict rose, but Felix couldn't care. He had his team to worry about.

———

Quickly, Felix and Pit brought their friends to a fair-sized chamber, one that had been used as a sort of dining area at one point. Felix kicked aside stones and charred remnants of a fire, clearing the ground so he could lay both of his friends down.

"Atar's burning up, Felix," Alister said, dabbing at his boyfriend's forehead with a cloth. "Are the draughts not working? What's taking so long?"

Evie was the same way, just cold, the both of them reacting in accordance to their core attunements. "I don't know. Adept Temper takes more out of you. Took me hours to process my Mind last night. It could just be that, but..."

"They are struggling."

Zara stepped into the chamber, shoving aside thin cloth draperies. "You can hear it, Felix. Open yourself to it. They aren't just Tempering themselves. Both of them are also hitting their next core stage, right now."

Felix's eyes widened. He flared his Affinity and Perception, straining his Fiendforged Mind in the process. Their Spirits were chaotic, and their breathing erratic, but that's all he could truly make out. "I don't hear it."

Zara looked outward, toward the battle happening a level above ground. "You have a choice, then. I can aid one of them, but not both. I will need you to handle the other. Are you up for that?"

"Yes." Felix didn't hesitate and could almost hear Alister's muscles relax. "They're my friends."

"Good. Then follow my lead," Zara said before summoning a wisp of her Mana from her right palm. It curled like a hypnotised snake in her palm and was dense enough to appear liquid. "I shall handle Evie, for our cores are similar. You shall take Atar, for the flames you both bear. Press your Mana into their channels and seek out their core space. Once there, exert your Will over it. Your Intent must be to stabilize things while they advance their cores. Watch me as I show you."

Cardinal Flame.

Felix's own crackling Mana manifested, a thin stream of liquid Mana surrounded by its more vaporous state. "I've done something like this before."

Zara pursed her lips, though her expression was more pleased than upset. "Good. Let's begin."

Felix caught Alister's eyes. "Hang close. We'll get them through this."

Alister swallowed and nodded, not releasing Atar's hand from his grip.

Felix sent his Cardinal Flame in through Atar's other palm Gate and delved into the convoluted network of looping pathways within him. Just as with Pit, Atar's channels were utterly foreign compared to Felix's. It seemed everyone developed their own pathways, though at least the fire mage's Mana Gates were in all the same spots he knew. Skull, palms, elbows, knees, and feet. Where normally there would be a constant flow in and out of someone's channels, Atar's were silent and still, save for a spasmodic twitch. Like a man gasping for breath.

Atar!

He was failing.

Forgoing finesse, Felix flared his Cardinal Flame, and crackling Mana flooded Atar's channels. His senses whirled down looping passages before emerging into the metaphysical space at his center. Fire greeted him within a vast chamber decorated in gold, black stone, and soaring natural monoliths of orange rock. Flames littered the entire space, though it did little for the illumination of the space, and a heavy, fragrant scent of charred wood pervaded it all.

How—? The last time he'd perceived a core space, it had been Pit's, and that had required him to flood the space with his own Mana to read the strange fluctuations within. Now it was like he was actually here, in much the same way Felix could materialize a sort of mental body in his own core space.

Fiendforge is level 2!

Felix's nostrils flared. *Right. That one. But that's for forging Paths, isn't it? How does it—Stop. It doesn't matter. Help Atar. Worry about Skill possibilities later.*

Step by step, Felix padded down the cold stone platform, idly noticing the radiating lines of gold-inlaid into the black floor slabs, beautiful sigils, and array lines that skittered under close examination. The open floor plan was interrupted by those large monoliths of crudely formed rock, each one a different thickness but all of a height. Atop them were basins, formed of more gold and filled with wood and sweet smelling oils, fuel for the fires that burned atop them.

His Skills are the flames; that's easy enough to reason out. He moved faster, toward the center, which was partially obscured by the bright pyres around it. *That is the core, then. How am I not surprised?*

A huge bonfire the size of a three-story building burned atop another orange rock monolith. This one was the thickest by far, and it was decorated with more of those golden inlay and black detailing. The flame was hard to look at, even with his stats somehow, colored orange and yellow with a significant tinge of bloody crimson. Oil and aged wood fell from somewhere far above, the details hidden in the shadows of the coffered ceiling, and each piece set the bonfire to raging.

Among the flames, Felix could even see the rainbow shimmers he'd recognize anywhere. The first Essence Draught had been consumed by his core...but it hadn't been used to Temper anything. *Why? Where the hell is Atar?*

Without warning, everything pulsed, and Atar's core swelled to twice its size. Constructs of fire Mana lashed outward, splashing into the monoliths closest, yanking pieces of their fire into itself...and yanking on Felix, too.

Bastion of Will is level 86!
Relentless Resolution is level 72!

Felix could not be moved, not by Atar's core. A simple refusal made the entire construct of Mana collapse on itself. As if in defiance, he took steps closer anyway, batting away the questing reach of the core flame.

"Atar!"

Hidden next to the great inferno, a figure stood as if frozen. His face was fire and char, as if the man were rendered into wood and set ablaze. He quaked at each new pulse from the core, blinding flames that burst against his wooden flesh and sent ash and sparks scattering off into the distance.

"What the hell happened to you?" he said, horrified. "Hold on!"

Cardinal Flame!

A surge of new Mana spread out and around Atar's strange, immobile body. It felt like a tree on its last legs, dried and crumbling save for the heartwood, where he could feel the faint but distinct pulse of life Mana. He reached for that life, hoping to connect, to use Unite the Lost perhaps. But instead, Fiendforge sang from within Felix's distant core space, a song he'd never heard before.

Fiendforge.

Felix immediately felt his being settle against everything around him, and he was possessed of the curious sensation of holding Atar and his core space in the palms of his hands. Of holding himself, too, which was trippy and hard to parse, but harder still were the vibrations that twisted and spun between his palms. Not his own, not his Skill's, but the vibrational signature of Atar's core space itself.

That's...What?

It felt broken, or on the cusp of breaking. Cracks ran its length, spiderwebbing outward from the core flame itself and growing with every passing second. He knew, in the way of dreams and System-enhanced knowledge, that Atar's core space was seconds from ripping itself apart entirely.

It gets harder with each advancement, Karys' voice echoed in his memories. Atar was breaking apart as he attempted to Temper and press himself toward his next core stage all at once. Did he know what he was doing? Was he in control? One look at the paralyzed effigy of the man suggested he wasn't at all.

Then allow me. Indistinct impulses from the Fiendforge spread through him, and through him into Atar. His hands pressed and pinched, surrounding and pervading the core space with swells of Felix's potency. The vibrations of Atar's monolithic altar sang as its cracks pressed shut, and Felix's Fiendforge met that song with a low tone of steady, uncompromising strength.

Harmony flowed, and everything—even Felix himself—shuddered.

Fire blossomed, shooting upward to splash against the coffered ceiling.

Melted stone and gold rained down on them both, but Felix paid it no mind at all. All of his Will and Intent and the last vestiges of his Fiend-forge grabbed at Atar's wooden form. He drew at the life within its heart-wood and hurled his own Mana at it, letting his perfect memory replicate the man's face and robes and annoyingly perfect curls.

Fiendforge is level 3!
Fiendforge is level 4!

Wood became flesh and hair and cloth, while life and flame turned to power enough to throw Atar's once-wooden form back into the nearest monolith. Flesh flushed with crimson, and Atar drew a pained, exultant gasp.

Felix sagged, suddenly tired, only managing the smallest of smiles for Atar's confused, startled stare.

"Wh-what happened?" he said, leveraging himself back to his feet. He held his ribs as if he'd truly hurt them.

"Adept Temper isn't an easy one," Felix said, breathing hard himself. It had taken more mental energy than he had expected, even with his newly Tempered Mind. "And you're also pushing toward the Ring Stage of your core, according to Zara. What Skill did you Tier up? We need to find it."

"This is my core space," Atar said, wonderingly. Then he looked at Felix in accusation. "What are you doing here? *How* are you in here?"

The core space shook around them, and the fountaining flame began to die down. Power was waning all over, they could both see it in the dimming of the light.

"No time! Skill! Aspects! I need to get you another Essence Draught. It looks like your core already consumed the first to stabilize itself."

Atar threw up his hands. "I leveled Focus, right over there. Imbued Sparkbolt and Fields of Flame are over on the opposite side."

"Ok, go to Focus; I'll be right back."

"Where are you—?"

Felix Willed himself away, resurfacing into his own Body with a painful snap. Blinking at the mounting migraine, Felix whirled on Alister. "I need three Essence Draughts!"

"Three?" the man asked, fumbling to get them uncorked. "Why?"

"Atar's core had already metabolized the first one, using it to boost its growth. It doesn't matter. Pour the next one down his throat, now," Felix ordered. "I'm going back in."

Pain branched through his Mind as Felix blinked back into Atar's core space, startling the fire mage.

"How in Avet's name are you doing that?" he demanded.

"Not really the time to explain, man," Felix said, eyeing the dark architecture around them. There were walls, but they were as drenched in shadows as the coffered ceilings and the flames all around them had dimmed a great deal more. "Our first step is to Temper you, then we'll worry about getting to Ring Stage. Alister is feeding you another Essence Draught. Can you seize it as it arrives?"

"Yes, of course I can," Atar said, offended. "I've done this before."

"Not like this. Adept Tier is harder," Felix frowned into the dark, and inspected the monoliths all around them. "C'mon. Where is it?"

So long as they got the Essence Draught into his core space, and Atar made proper use of it, Felix was sure they'd be fine. Aside from their sheer potency, the primary benefit of the Spirit Fruit Essence Draughts were their universal nature. Body, Mind, or Spirit, it didn't matter. The real question was what Essences would be available, but Felix didn't doubt that all would be strong. A Legendary Spirit Tree wouldn't be likely to disappoint.

That said, Atar was the first to actually use one.

Fingers crossed.

"It's here!" Atar shouted, pointing into the dark.

The first of the Essence Draughts poured into Atar's core space like a liquid orange fog or roiling stormcloud. The moment it hit the light, however, it ignited into a conflagration. The flames everywhere burst alight in sympathy while the swirling orange and white hued Draught raged through it all.

"Grab it!" Felix growled.

"I got it!"

Felix grinned in approval as the burning cloud was wrested from the air above them and brought down into Atar's core flame. The bonfire burst alive, raging back to its original height as it processed the Spirit Tree's potency. More. It kept growing, expanding upward and outward until it was once again almost touching the charred ceiling. Atar gasped, but his gaze never wavered as tendrils of flame quested outward. Toward the monolithic altar that held his Focus Skill.

"I can handle it," Atar hissed to himself. "I can!"

Light and flame encompassed them both.

CHAPTER FIFTY-SIX

Atar's Focus (Rare) Has Evolved Into Lens of the Magus (Epic)!
Level Is Retained!

Atar's Imbued Sparkbolt (Rare) Has Evolved Into Stars Of The Sovereign (Legendary)!
Level Is Retained!

Atar's Fields of Flames (Rare) Has Evolved Into Incendiary Vortex (Epic)!
Level Is Retained!

Bastion of Will is level 87!
Relentless Resolution is level 73!
Cardinal Flame is level 82!
Fiendforge is level 5!

"Just keep rotating it as you Temper the last Skill," Felix encouraged the mage. "Feed it power and squeeze it while it spins."

"I'm—guh!—trying!" Atar's face was ashen, his olive complexion literally crumbling between moments of concentration, before reforming into his Human visage. Felix tried not to focus on that though—it was too disturbing.

Instead, he observed Atar's core space as a whole. The mage had impressed him; his Willpower was strong enough that he had suffered through not one but three Skill evolutions *and* their Tempering. The man was shaking like a leaf, holding his hands out and guiding a channel of flames between Incendiary Vortex and his core. It advanced, ever so slowly, prodded by the taxed mental faculties of the mage. But it did move.

Crimson-tinged flames were everywhere now, though most of it was concentrated on the core flame and the now-evolved Stars of the Sovereign Skill. A parting gift from the Primordial curse back in Haarwatch. It had marked Atar more deeply than Felix had realized.

The rest of Atar's core space was in a bit of a shambles. Rubble filled the floor, shaken loose from the walls and ceiling, obscuring the hazy sigaldry lines etched beneath their feet. Shelving Felix swore hadn't been there when he'd arrived had toppled and splintered, hurling tightly bound scrolls onto altars and catching fire. The monolithic altars and golden basins flared in random bursts, and not just the one's Atar had been Tempering. All of them suffered as the mage fought to spin the bonfire of his core.

Felix hadn't needed to step in during the Tempering so far, but it had been close. The final dregs of the last Essence Draught were swirling just above the core flame, a liquid cloud that burned and burned but never consumed itself. Atar had guided two other Essence Draughts into his core flame, each time feeding the power to the Skills he desired to Temper and struggling through the process. Felix hadn't been privy to the Essences Atar had been offered, only that Atar trembled after each Tempering.

The guy was wiped, but he didn't stop. He couldn't, Felix knew, because to do so would be to ruin his progress completely.

C'mon, Atar. You got this!

The last wisp of Essence Draught was devoured by the core flame, igniting an explosive *pop* within its depths. Felix frowned, and Atar flinched as the reluctantly spinning bonfire finally gained momentum. A lot of momentum, in fact. Too much.

"Atar! It's pulling in too much power!" Felix warned.

"I can't—I can't stop it!" Atar screamed, his shoulders bursting into charcoal ash and flame before reforming. "I can barely hang on!"

The mage's core whirled until it was no longer flame, but a solid beam of light. The gold altar beneath it dimmed as it brightened, condensing and rising higher and higher from its original position. A high, keening whine ascended with it, loud and sharp enough that Felix's ears buzzed, and the muscles in his neck spasmed wildly. It was familiar.

That's like Dissonance...but not. Felix pressed his Affinity as hard as he could, his Perception, his Cardinal Flame—whatever he could to see what was happening. Manasight caught it. Swirls of nameless Mana and Essence expanding and grasping from the core's gyrating form. *It's Dissonance Lite. Same great taste, none of the calories.*

The Maw's influence, again. Luckily, Felix had the solution to *that*.

Chthonic Trib—!

Wait! Felix's instincts screamed at him, and he cut off the Skill before it could fully activate. The ravenous abyss within him chomped in frustration, but he shoved the sensation aside. *That isn't right. The Primordial's influence...it's not there.*

Felix could sense that *something* was present in Atar's core, and indeed all over his core space, but whatever it was had been fundamentally changed. Transformed. *By something Atar did?*

It's not Dissonance, not as I know it. It felt hot and heavy, like a suffocating convection bent on burning Felix from the inside out. It was too weak to harm him, but it was growing. Fast. *It needs more power, though. That's Atar's real problem.*

Even now, those grasping tendrils of Intent spread outward, utilized by his core even if Atar didn't have the stat unlocked. Everything used Intent, it was just a matter of being in control or not, and this was wildly outside the mage's ability to command. Those tendrils caught up the walls, the broken shelving and mysterious scrolls, burning them all and sucking the fuel back into its center. The beam of crimson-orange light burned brighter with every passing second...and Atar's core space was falling apart.

Fiendforge!

That same out-of-body experience happened, as Felix took the core space in his hands and *pressed*. He could feel links forming between himself and Atar as his Aspects molded the mage's. They resonated, Skill and core space, until the transcendent Harmony overwhelmed the keening screech of spinning fire.

Fiendforge is level 6!

Things shifted. The hybridized archive/temple/ritual chamber turned and clicked. The shadows grew richer, more textured, while the golden inlay became more lustrous. The sigaldry on the black stone was refined, the haze of its meaning clarified as Felix called out to Atar's visualized space. Flames sharpened, brightened, but also that crimson glow deepened along the edges of each and every fire. Felix couldn't touch that part at all for some reason, but his influence magnified its presence until it suffused the stone itself. Crimson gems appeared on the stone pillars around him, studding the darkening rock and golden basins at their zeniths.

Power and strength flowed from Felix, Essence and significance burned alongside his own Mana, fueling the changes. No. Not changes, but affirmations of what Atar had already intended. The pattern of it was clear to Felix, the way the mage had visualized his space and what he wanted it to be—all Felix had to do was reinforce it.

The Skills all around them surged, billowing into columns of red-orange flame as Atar's core let out a powerful, singular roar...before folding in on itself. It spun, faster and faster, the Harmonics in the air spurring it onward as much as Atar's furious Will. The man thrust himself forward, all but jumping into the flames, and the power coalesced. His core shrank by half, but now was a hollow ring of liquid fire, similar to Felix's, just colored orange with bloody crimson haunting its edges.

Fiendforge is level 7!
Fiendforge is level 8!
Cardinal Flame is level 83!

Atar fell to his knees, and this time, they held their Human shape.

"You did it," Felix said, looking around. He was tired, but it was all mental. Physically, he felt fine. "You got it from here?"

Atar only nodded, too busy rapturously studying the space around him. He ran fingers over the golden sigils in the black stone flooring.

Felix let his Cardinal Flame relax and opened his real eyes.

The sandy chamber was awash in the smell of char, and a glittering shield of blue force Mana hung around him and Atar's body. Alister jumped when he noticed Felix's open eyes, and the ward vanished.

"I had to shield you because of all the fire Mana he was putting out. I barely stopped it all. What happened? Is he okay?" The words tumbled out of Alister's mouth as he crouched next to Atar's prone form. "Did he...did he Temper?"

"He's fine. He did fine," Felix said with a grunt of exertion as he tried to stand...and took a solid chunk of glassed sand with him. It clung to his legs and trousers where the apparent fire Mana had melted it—he could see several places where Atar's robes were trapped in the glass. A careful exertion of Will and Mana shifted his Garment, and the glass fell free. Even that much hurt him, the strain of his Mind and Spirit mounting after his efforts with Atar. They weren't debilitating, but Felix suspected it'd be at least a few hours before he'd be at a hundred percent again. "He's inspecting his core space now, but he's done. Keep an eye on him. He didn't fully Temper an Aspect, but he's gonna be tired for a while."

Alister nodded mutely before taking Atar's hand in his own.

"Felix."

He turned to find Zara kneeling over Evie's body. His friend was bleeding from the nose and mouth and shuddering violently, like she was having a seizure.

"What happened!" He rushed to her side, barely noticing that the sand was frozen solid beneath his feet. "She's bleeding!"

"Her core space is locked tight, I couldn't pry it open," Zara said, frustrated. "Damn girl has it frozen solid and wrapped all around with chains...and there's something else."

Felix looked up from Evie's face. Her jaw was chattering, and her lips were turning blue. "What?"

Zara's pale eyes met his own. "Something is stopping me from getting closer to her core."

"Stopping you? You're Master Tier. What could Evie do to stop you?"

"I could force my way in, but it would ruin her." Zara shook her head.

"She would never advance beyond Weaving, and could not even Temper to Master Tier were I to do that. But you...whatever you did with Atar worked. You need to do it again. Can you?"

Felix clenched his jaw and placed a hand on Evie's own. "Doesn't matter if I can. It's Evie."

Cardinal Flame!

He dove into her channels.

———

The sandstorm howled just beyond the barricades, and monsters raged in its midst. Vess spun through attack after attack, leaping and landing amid the undead horde with greater and greater ferocity. Spears burst again and again, tearing through the creatures without mercy as fast as she could muster the Mana to summon them. Bolts of lightning and fire still zipped out from the skeleton, along with carefully placed arrows packed with deadly Blessings and Skills. The Legion were holding their own while Vess thinned the numbers in the storm, and even when more got through than she intended, the Henaari's hooked spears and the Frost Giant's massive ice axes tore the enemy apart.

It was working.

You better be okay, Evie! Vess thought as she skidded to a stop on an angular ridge of stone. Dustwights streamed below her, pressing against one another in a mad dash toward the skeleton and her people. *Adept Tier is harder than those that came before. Father always told me that, but I did not think it would affect them so much.*

The sight of her friends on the ground had affected her more than Vess was happy to admit. That they could be struck down, even if it were only to their own advancement...it filled the heiress with dread. She dealt with it in the only way she had ever been taught.

You Have Killed A Dustwight (x3)!
XP Earned!

Vess had jumped up an entire level during the battle, but she was more concerned with pressing her Skills to their limits. She had to reach Adept Tier herself, and soon, or else she would be unable to protect anyone from the threats facing them. At least as Adepts they had a fighting chance against Masters, small though it was, and Vess could not foresee a scenario where they did not face the Paladins down. It felt inevitable.

Dragon's Descent!

She jumped and landed among another dozen Dustwights, their bodies exploding with the impact of her spear. Experience surged within her, and she nodded in grim satisfaction as her Skill grew.

Dragon's Descent is level 67!
PER +1

Vess paused as the Dustwights scrambled away from her blast, catching a sound on the wild winds. It was as if the storm had changed timbres suddenly, gaining a basso thrum to it that shook her teeth. *There. It is...growing?*

A single leap carried the woman fifty feet into the air, arcing up and over the battle before kicking off a bluff and leaping again. For a brief, weightless moment she hovered, over a hundred feet above the battle and braved the scouring winds. She squinted, pressing her Perception for all it was worth.

Elemental Eye is level 55!

The blackened green and dusty brown Mana all around them was darkening to the north. Strengthening.

Another storm. It is another storm!

She began to fall, but not before the second Cursewind hit them. Its unnatural strength added to the first, and the wind turned from powerful to undeniable. Vess was hurled from the sky out into the desert where she impacted and exploded an entire dune with her impact.

"Ungh!" She groaned, clawing out of the soft ground. "No. That storm is bringing more than just wind." The air was impenetrable with orange dust and foul, swirling Mana, but she could see shapes falling from the new storm. Dustwights by the hundreds joined the army already laying siege to their temporary fortress. "I need to get back."

Her Health had dropped to half, but it was making a slow recovery, and Vess limped down the face of the dune. She'd traveled perhaps two hundred feet in her fall and couldn't even see the enormous skeleton through the storm. Still, she would make it back and help. Darius and Harn would have already seen the danger. They would be fine.

Then, between her and her friends, a series of sandy explosions blasted apart the dunes. Shielding her eyes against the gritty winds, Vess could not spot what had caused it at first, but then forms began to crawl from the impact craters. Tall and hunched, thin as corpses and bearing claws like curved daggers, they clambered from the sands. Ten of them. Fifteen. Thirty.

Analyze!

"No," she whispered. She had recognized them from Felix's description, but Analyze confirmed it. "Dustborn Wraiths."

Vess began to run.

CHAPTER FIFTY-SEVEN

Icy water exploded all around Felix as he landed, absolutely soaking him. He stifled a gasp at the chill, which somehow bypassed all his resistances.

"It is a chill of the Spirit, not the Body."

Felix wiped his face, finding Zara standing right beside him, unruffled and entirely dry. She was even standing atop the ankle-deep water as if it were solid ground. Felix frowned, and with a gentle flex of Will, he rose to the surface as well.

"Do you see?" Zara asked. "Her core space."

Felix saw the chains hanging from the storming skies. Massive steel links looping across the undefined core space like lines on a Manaship. The water extended in all directions as a flat plane, but those chains hung from above in discrete clusters of white-frosted metal and crackling ice. The sound of clinking links, breaking ice, and sloshing water filled the space almost as much as the biting cold that drove deep into his flesh.

"The clusters are her Skills?" Felix asked. They were shifting in place, pulled this way and that by the chains that extended in multiple directions. Each moment saw the clusters shrink and grow by turns.

"Good eye. Yes, those are her Skill visualizations. Why she chose this arrangement, I do not know." Zara made a frustrated sound in the back of her throat and bared her sharp teeth. "The chains drag against one another while the ice among them actively halts movement and growth. It is suboptimal for any who wishes to reach the higher echelons of advancement."

Felix could recognize that, even as he felt his back go up in defense of the girl. "She clearly didn't know what she was doing when she visualized all of this. Who does?"

"I am sympathetic, but the facts remain, Felix." Zara's teeth vanished into a scowl. "And then there is her core."

The clear center of the web of chains was shrouded in a blue-white haze, preventing them from seeing much aside from a thick column of ice, fog, and snow. Chains, thicker than all before, spun within that haze, weaving among itself as fast and as deadly as Evie's own weapon of choice. The water churned the closer they drew to the core, until its surface was riddled with half-frozen waves that fell and shattered like glass daggers with every passing moment. Flaring his Affinity, Perception, and his Cardinal Flame gave Felix little else...save for the faint impression of a large structure contained within the occlusion.

"I can't see it. I'm assuming more chains?" Felix said.

"Indeed. Ice, water, and metal swirl in their greatest concentration there, forming an edifice of some design. When I approached I was...re-buffed." Zara pursed her lips and started walking closer. Felix followed.

"Rebuffed how?" he asked.

The chains rattled around them both, slipping and clattering against one another as the Skills shifted. Resonant twanging noises echoed as thinner links were pulled on, moving the ice-metal clumps higher or lower, left or right as her core dictated. The water churned, crackling with sudden miniature icebergs. The icebergs grew, until the smallest was twice his size and the largest was far bigger than that. The water fed into them, along with swirls of purple-white Mana vapor that crystallized along the waves, until a flotilla of glaciers loomed around Evie's core. Felix stopped walking, taken aback, but Zara didn't—she merely gestured.

"Observe, and tell me what you see."

With a report like a hundred gunshots, the icebergs all cracked in unison...and exploded.

"Holy shit!" Felix flinched. He was unharmed by the icy shrapnel, but his hammering heartbeat was convinced otherwise. "Those...those are giants?"

Enormous forms had emerged from the detonated icebergs, all of them just as craggy and blue as their real-life counterparts. That they could be anything *but* Frost Giants was laughable...yet Felix realized they were literally *made* of ice and hazy Mana. As if the glaciers had given birth to them in truth.

With a singular, wild roar from every one of their throats, the Frost Giants charged the icy fog. Hammers and axes and clubs of all shapes and sizes manifested in their hands as their legs churned the slushy water into chaotic spume, and every single one hit the hazy barrier at the same time.

Only to be thrown back by the titanic whirling of a wall of chains.

No. Not chains.

Ice cracked, and water fountained as the false giants roared in stymied rage. A wide, muscular figure stepped from the fog, taller than Felix by more than a foot, and holding two complicated lengths of thick chain in its hands. It tugged, once, and the wall of chains retracted and collapsed into structures affixed to the figure's forearms. Wide and wedge-shaped.

Shields, Felix thought with a ragged gasp. *Magda.*

The figure was made of ice and metal, but for all of that her resemblance to Evie's sister was uncanny. From her build to her bearing, to the oversized kite shields on either arm—all of it was as if someone had created a perfect statue of the woman, carved from ice and chains.

Once the shield reformed on her, the dead woman charged, taking a false giant down with a swift decapitation.

"How?" Felix asked. "You mentioned a barrier, and I thought...Evie is protecting her core with her *sister?*"

"A simulacra. A Golem, if you will, though it appears to be formed of Evie's untrained Intent and moderate Will as much as her Mana." Zara gestured and a ball of water lifted from their feet, containing within it swirling motes of Mana and chunks of ice. "A representation of Evie's memories, set to protect herself from invaders."

Magda and the giants clashed again, and this time, she held off a dozen of them with ridiculous ease. Her shields were made of chains wound impossibly tight, and more than once they exploded outward to tangle limbs or punch through the false giants' defenses. Whatever she was, she fought almost exactly like the real Magda, blocking and redirecting forces with an implacable Endurance.

"The invaders are made up of Evie's core space too, though...right?" Felix asked.

Zara worked the water and ice Mana between her palms, pressing and twisting it in complicated ways. "So it seems, but look closer." The Mana solidified into a foot-long dagger of ice, but that didn't catch Felix's attention. Instead, it was the wavy, liquid vapor that had begun to boil from the Mana construct. "The Essence Draught was absorbed by these waters. It is what drives these giants forward, that and the piece of her Will that knows what must be done. Advancement cannot be denied, not this long. I fear there will be consequences for her."

"What can we do?" Felix asked. "Fight...do we fight Magda?"

"While that would work in the short-term, it is what I hoped to avoid. Evie's sister is as much a part of her core space as everything else around us, and to destroy her would have cascading consequences. No. We must find a way to access her core without harming Evie's foundations."

"How?" Felix asked. His Mind spun with thoughts of his Unite the Lost or his Fiendforge, but both of those were constructive forces, and Felix wasn't even sure the former would work in another person's core space.

"The same thing you achieved with Atar," Zara said. "I could feel the power you exerted, even from within this place. The fine details are indistinct, but I could feel Atar slipping away before you arrived. After, it was as if he'd been...reforged." She raised an eyebrow at Felix. "However you managed that, you must do so again. You must restore the core space to Evie's control."

Felix frowned at Zara's probing look. "Where is she?"

"Within the center, of course," Zara said.

Right through "Magda," he thought with a dull ache. *Of course.*

———

"Haah!"

"Haah!"

"Haah!"

Loquis stood beyond the third barricade, watching in mild envy as the Henaari Dawnguard struck down the shambling undead. Each thrust of their hooked spears punched through withered flesh and desiccated leather armor, while the hooks on them maneuvered the creatures into the path of their fellow's follow-up attacks. A succession of unrelenting strikes that could have been overcome with a measure of coordination, but was impossible to avoid thanks to the Dustwights' tendency to group tightly together and attack alone.

They're no smarter than beasts, Loquis thought, scratching the note down with a grease pencil in his pocket-journal. *In fact, the Cask Scorpions were a good deal more intelligent. Is it because whatever drives them is mindless? Or...are there simply too many to accurately control?*

Loquis knew such vast control over Mana was no easy feat. Whatever was motivating the Dustwights was an order of magnitude greater than anyone he'd ever met. *Perhaps the Fiend could do such a thing..not that he would, of course. Defiling himself with necromantic Mana? Only a fool would choose such a path.*

A shearing sound tore through the air, like rocks breaking against steel, and the Half-Orc saw several Frost Giants wade into battle. Their massive axes and mauls tore through the Dustwights without resistance, and in fact often splintered the occasional Fiend-made fortification. Henaari redoubled their efforts, driving more of the undead toward the giants' assault, and Loquis imagined he could hear the levels they were all gaining.

"I'm losin' levels to those Henaari! Damnable rest!" Asaad grumbled. "Who says we cannot fight for longer, eh? I've got enough piss and vinegar in me to kill a town of those dry bastards!"

"A right natural piss master," Pava said, patting the Dwarf on the shoulder. "Is that what I smell leaking all over your leg?"

"That's blood, and you know it, lass!"

"And it's one of the reasons we got cycled out," Pava said pointedly. "I've got enough Stamina and Health to keep fighting, too, and Geir hasn't been winded yet."

"Hmm," the Frost Giant rumbled from beside them. The eleven-foot giant was folded up beside them, doing his level best to relax before they were set to move back to the battle line. "Battlelord gave orders, as did Osyk. That is enough."

Asaad spat to the side. "I don't listen to your Battlelord, nor to that Henaari scout. I listen to the Autarch and the First of Blade. That's it!"

"Why'd you cower when Commander Harn gave you a sour look, then?" Pava asked, smiling. "You certainly listened to him."

"That—I didn't cower! That was my injury, pressin' down on my Mind. If it weren't for that, I'd be out there fightin' now!"

"Sure."

Loquis blocked out their arguing voices. They'd been a "squad" ever since the oasis, Osyk acting as their scout and sometime leader, but the chain of command was fuzzy. Asaad kept trying to assert himself, but while he was good at fighting, that seemed to be the extent of his prowess. Well. Fighting and complaining—Asaad had rarely stopped bleating since they'd left the jungle.

Pava and Geir were far more agreeable, though Pava had a tendency to act before thinking, and Geir was more taciturn than a rock. Osyk was the chattiest of the bunch, but he'd been told to remain with the Dawn-guard due to his skill with the spear. He'd smiled and patted them on the back, ordering them to rest while he carried the load a while. Asaad had pushed back, but that was when Commander Harn had moved down the lines, pushing squads back to rest.

A casual Analyze told Loquis that his team was mostly back in fighting shape, save for Asaad's Stamina and the Half-Orc's Mana. He was exhausted, having spent himself against the undead horde until he had run dangerously low on Mana. Loquis had nearly passed out under the strain, and while he had a potion at his hip, he'd long decided to save it for an emergency. He had time to rest now, so he took advantage. If only his Mana didn't regenerate so slowly, the splitting headaches and heaving nausea might have been tolerable. As it was, they had been resting for a solid hour, and his Mana was barely back up to a quarter of his maximum.

"—aiths—!"

Loquis sat up, pointed ears twitching. "Quiet. Did you hear that?"

Asaad, mouth half-open in a rant, scowled at him. "What're you on about?"

"Dust—ths!"

"*That!*" Loquis said, leaping to his feet. "Someone is shouting out there."

"Who?" Pava asked, peeking around the barricade. "One of the Autarch's team?"

"Who else dares to be out there?" Loquis asked, breathless. He still felt dizzy from his Mana loss, but this felt important. Urgent. He peered into the crimson-orange haze, beyond the bunching horde of undead and into the swirling black winds of the storm itself. The sand was whipping fast enough that it'd tear even his flesh were he to remain out there for long without a shield or armor. "If it were a legionnaire, they'd have died by now."

"Dustborn!" came the shout again, this time far more clearly. Loquis gasped and saw the Lady Dayne falling from the skies. Two skeletal creatures fell with her, clawing furiously at the noblewoman's armor and head. "Fall back!"

Without warning, the undead horde before them surged forward. Milky, unthinking eyes suddenly gained a clarity that terrified Loquis, and the Dawnguards' unerring thrusts were turned aside or dodged completely.

"What is happening?" Geir asked, standing to his full height. "The undead, they are fighting."

"Been doin' that this whole time, tiny," Asaad said. "But damn if they're not fighting *well*, all of a sudden!"

Something exploded in the distance, and Loquis realized he'd lost track of the Lady Dayne...but six more of those skeletal creatures came bounding out of the Cursewinds, their faces half-covered in heavy bone plating, and eyes of pure darkness stared balefully at them all.

"Fall back!"

The shout boomed out, loud enough that Loquis' ears hurt. Harn was running past them, shoving his way to the front while still bellowing. "Everyone back to the Warrens! Now!"

The creatures barreled into the other undead, tearing through their ranks with sheer momentum and unnatural strength. Hooked talons the length of daggers slashed forward, ripping their way through the horde and toward the spear-line. With measured care, the Dawnguard and Frost Giants began to retreat, keeping their weapons and shields lifted and engaged. Dustwights died by the dozen, but still they came, more ferocious than ever.

Analyze!

Analyze Failed.

Oh no, Loquis thought. His Analyze couldn't identify the oversized undead even a little bit, but they exuded a pressure that he *did* sense, even from such a distance. "They're strong. Too strong. No wonder we're retreating."

"Oh fuck that," Asaad said, hefting his slender saber. "Retreat? I ain't lettin' all that experience go to waste."

"You idiot!" Loquis shouted as Asaad slipped through them all. He ran from their barricade and toward the retreating line, clearly aiming to claim a few more kills before they fully retreated. "Siva save us from fools!" Loquis muttered.

"Do we follow?" Pava asked, her own blade held in a white-knuckle grip. "Pull him out?"

Geir made a chortling noise like a bear with a phlegmy throat. "It would be...amusing to see."

Loquis grabbed at his hair. "Burning ashes! Follow him!"

CHAPTER FIFTY-EIGHT

Felix took off just as the next wave of ice-born giants charged. Chains descended, combining into spike-studded shields that stabbed and bashed in equal measure. The giants took the attacks head on, too dim to swerve or dodge, merely swinging their conjured weapons in roaring defiance. False Magda stopped them cold, every time.

Among the chaos, Felix flared his Agility and his Relentless Resolution. Water sprayed in his wake, and the core space blurred into smearing shapes, yet his Perception and Intelligence worked together to easily keep up with his speed. Evie's strange protector moved as if she were in slow-motion, but the chain shields at her disposal flashed about at far greater velocities. Felix ducked and twisted through the maze of false Magda's assault, doing his level best to evade the protector entirely.

She was making that harder than he anticipated.

From beneath his feet, chains of ice erupted in geysers of frigid water. It was all Felix could do to redirect his momentum, skidding to a startled stop to dive out of the way as the chains appeared. They sprouted blades and spikes, each of the dozen metal strands flailing in separate directions, and way faster than Felix expected. Though he was only a mental construct, his body as false as Magda's, he was solidly visualized—that was how he could be there in the first place, how he could traverse his own core space. The drawback meant that, as two chains clipped his shoulders, they drew arcs of blood that splashed into the water as he rolled, dodging another three.

Dodge is level 64!

...

Dodge is level 67!

Relentless Resolution is level 74!

Wounds clotted and healed as he ran, his overwhelming Vitality proving superior to Evie's conjured guardian, but the offensive was persistent. Chains followed him, forcing him to weave in twisted circles and patterns, jumping over and sliding under their sinuous lengths. His Garment was slashed to ribbons, and his skin was soon criss-crossed by welts and burning lines of crimson. He was stronger and more durable than Evie, but something about her defenses was transcendent.

How is this thing so strong?

She shouldn't have been able to contest him physically, or even mentally, based on their stats. Felix outclassed her in every way. Yet, as he ran for the deepening haze of her core, Magda was there, shields already bashing toward his skull.

Enough! Sovereign of Flesh!

Felix's skin transformed to scales as he punched forward, expanding as the muscles of his right arm ballooned with power. His fist met false Magda's shield with a cataclysmic crash, scattering the water for twenty yards in every direction...

...and hurling the false woman back into the hazy mist.

Felix recoiled from the strike, immediately canceling his Skill, because the crash did not stop with the impact. No, the sound reverberated, spreading out around them like a gong, until the world around him shook. Water surged and splashed and ice-born giants fell over themselves—even the Skills hanging above them groaned in sympathy, raining chunks of ice and snow from their twisted bulks.

That's...not good. Felix grimaced but took off again, heading for the core. *I can't afford to hit any part of Evie's core space. Another punch like that...*

Felix was certain that he would shatter it all.

Magda was not done with him, however, and she came surging out of the mist once more. Her arms bore the same pointed shields the real Magda had held, her face the same stoic implacability, and Felix felt a spasm of unease as he sidestepped out of her way. Chains followed him, unfurling from her shields and her icy back like serpents, stabbing at his chest and arms and legs. Anything they could reach. More of his Garment was torn, but his skin was toughening up against the constant onslaught.

Armored Skin is level 77!

His Spirit shuddered, buffeted by each touch of her chains, and it became a scream of agony as one of her shields clipped his thigh. He tucked into a roll atop the churning waters, slipping free of her melee range once again and gasping in revelation. He could see it—feel it—after that brief moment of contact. There was a cadence to the creature's being, and it danced along his Spirit like a jet engine, tearing at his Affinity with a wild ferocity.

Grief. Pain. Felix licked his lips, resetting himself before the guardian. *She's Evie's rage, personified.*

The giants were still attacking, conjured by Evie's conflicting forces to assault her core, and false Magda spun to face them as well. More shields of ice and metal rose, more forged tendrils of sharpened steel to bash and slash through their number.

The giants. Why giants? Felix watched carefully as his shallow wounds healed themselves. *Evie hates the giants, and the giants...killed Magda. Shit. Who else would defend Evie's core, then?*

She had unconsciously recreated Magda's death...and Felix felt a bone-deep certainty that she would never let her sister lose. Not again.

I'm sorry for this, Evie, Felix thought. He knew what he had to do...he just didn't like it.

Cardinal Flame!

Felix's Mana rolled into the core space, crackling with lightning and burning flame as it raced toward the charging giants. Sigils of rage and strength branded themselves into the icy behemoths, and the Essence Draughts that made them up ignited into violent flame. The giants roared and pressed forward, the lot of them moving far faster than they had before. Magda said nothing, but she raced to meet them. Massive chain-forged shields rose from the waters, bashing into her frost foes with abandon.

Distracted, there was nothing to stop him from taking off into the wintry haze, speeding atop the freezing waves.

In order for Felix to fix this, Magda had to fail.

The haze continued for some distance, occluding his Perception but not his Affinity. He could hear the pulse and snap of Evie's core, always just ahead despite running what felt like a half mile atop frigid waters. At the very least, there was proof of his journey. Beneath his feet, the waves had iced over in odd, floating sheets, each growing larger and larger until the haze cleared and Felix found himself standing atop a huge, storming swell...that was utterly frozen through.

Whoa.

Smashing up through the eternal ice, a gargantuan chain loomed ahead of him. It stuck up at an angle, extending somewhere into the misty sky above and deep into the bitter black below. Each link that composed the thing was hundreds of feet tall and coated in dripping hoarfrost. Icicles connected entire links with striated sheets of once-melted Mana, while smaller chains filled the vast spaces left behind. Shapes were in those complex, tangling intersections, forms that resembled architecture in its most rudimentary form. Bitter cold pulsed from its shape, and apart from a faint, almost imperceptible vibration, there was only utter stillness.

There, atop another wave and beneath the frozen core, stood a figure.

Evie!

Felix leaped, shattering the ice at his feet and soaring the sixty feet or so to Evie's side. A flare of his Will slowed him down, letting Felix skid to a more gentle stop next to his friend. A friend that he realized was completely encased in ice, until she was no more than a suggestion of a shadow within it.

Just like Atar, he realized.

Fiendforge!

The sensation of gripping the world returned to him, though this time it burned him far more readily than Atar's had. A numbing chill spread along his phantom hands as he pressed against her core space, the sheer cognitive dissonance of being in two places almost overwhelming his Mind. His Will and Intent, however, were not just for show. Felix steadied himself, and focused.

There are cracks everywhere. The core is fused solid, and the Skills barely move. He could see the giants still assaulting Magda, a constant wave of power that resembled nothing more than energy attempting to flood Evie's core, just as it did in Felix's during a level-up. *How do I fix this without breaking it all apart?*

Felix pressed ever so gently as his Skill pulled Mana, Essence, and significance from his own core space. The power flowed into Evie's core, swirling around her space like an invisible maelstrom.

Maybe she knows, he reasoned, and funneled his power into the block of ice before him. Much as it had with Atar, Felix's memories of Evie paved the way for his Fiendforge. He pulled the ice away from her form, chiseling the negative space away from the person he knew lay within. It happened far faster this time, owing perhaps to the levels he'd gained in the Skill.

Fiendforge is level 9!

Then it was done, though he held lightly to the Skill just in case. Evie collapsed to the ground, her armor-encased limbs unable to bear her sudden weight, but she was moving. She coughed and lifted her hands in confusion before staring up at him.

"Felix?" she asked, her voice breaking mid-word. She rallied and looked around. "Didn't expect you in my core space."

"Didn't expect to be needed," he said. "I'm here to help."

"Help?" Evie stood on shaky legs and looked closer at her core. "...Shit."

"That's what I said," Felix said, though it came out more deadpan than he wanted. "Is it normally this...still in here?"

"No, Avet take me," Evie said, the fear in her voice clear. Her cheekbone became a faceted, crystalline shard of ice though it faded quickly back to flesh. "My core's empty."

"Empty?" Felix looked again, flaring all of his senses. "I can sense power here. Mana and Stamina in the ice. Isn't this normal?"

Evie was sweeping her eyes left and right, almost frantic. "No. No, it's not. She's gone."

It clicked. "Magda. She's part of your core?"

Evie looked at him, guilty and worried. "For a long time now. She...she keeps me safe, Felix."

Felix grunted. "So I've seen."

She raised an eyebrow as her form flickered with ice again. She cried out, staggering. Felix reached out to help her, but Evie put out her hands, warding him off. She stood on her own. "What—what're you talking about?"

"Your version of Magda is preventing the Essence Draught from reaching your core," he explained. "It's preventing everything from reaching it...and that's bad news, because your core is trying to advance."

Evie paled, skin flickering between flesh and ice. "Advance...? To the Ring Stage?"

"Yeah. Your core space isn't doing great right now, and your Body...can you stop her? Tell her to stand down or something?" Felix asked.

"Stand down? She's my...she's my protector. I don't control her," Evie said. There was a smallness to her voice Felix had never heard from her before, stripped bare of sarcasm and battle lust. "I can't."

"You have to. Can't you feel it? The pressure?" Felix certainly could, so long as he focused on it, like a constant tugging on his soul. Only his Bastion of Will and Relentless Resolution kept him affixed in place, largely unaffected by the vacuum of Evie's power. "It's collapsing on itself."

Evie blinked, eyes flicking between her core and the hazy barrier just beyond them. Tears glistened there, but Felix didn't mention it and neither did Evie.

"Fine," she whispered. "Let's fix this."

———

They traversed the barrier of fog and frozen waves, following the sounds of battle as it raged. Felix's Perception picked up the enormous shapes of Frost Giants—the smallest of which were now thirty feet tall—battering uselessly against the utter and absolute guard of a woman made of ice and chains.

"Magda," Evie whispered. Her face twisted between sour guilt and sorrow.

"You need to stop her," Felix said again. "This is your core space. You're in control here."

Evie snorted softly. Fear and other, more confused emotions tangled in her Spirit, so loud Felix couldn't help but hear them. Still, the woman ran forward, her feet splashing through the ankle-deep waves.

Brave, Pit sent across their bond.

Yeah bud. She is.

"Mags! Stop!" Evie shouted, skidding to a halt before the hulking form of her sister. A head made of ice and hard, steel angles tilted at Evie in confusion. "It's me. It's just me..."

Without a change in expression, false Magda swung her shield at her sister. Evie rolled aside, springing up from a tumbling handstand to her feet, just barely evading the conjured shields as they bashed into the water behind her.

Felix watched, unsure how to help. He couldn't attack—he saw what happened when he struck parts of Evie's core space. Even with holding his Fiendforge loosely about them all, Felix dreaded that exerting too much force would shatter her core completely. Meanwhile Evie dashed about, uncoiling her weapon and warding off blows, but she clearly could not bring herself to hit her sister. Real or not.

"You need to return to my core! It's falling apart without you in it!" the agile fighter shouted. Beyond them, the giants had not stopped their advance. Enormous, hulking brutes stomped toward them all. "Let...let them in!"

NEVER!

The words smashed into Evie like a hammer blow, and even Felix was pushed back by it. They seemed to emanate from false Magda's form, but also reverberated from all over the core space at the same time.

"What the hell! How can it speak?" he shouted.

"I don't know! She's never—!" Evie screamed back. Her face had broken along her left jawline, revealing sparking ice and steel beneath. "Get the...get the giants in, Felix! Help me!"

"On it!"

NO!

Chains wove through the water, arcing toward Felix's position, but he was already on the move. Evie deflected more of the attacks, drawing Magda's fire as Felix flared his Agility and Relentless Resolution. He sped across the surface of her core space, his passage barely kicking up any spume at all, focused entirely upon speed and evasion as the very waters turned against him.

Ice spiked, shooting upward to spear at his body with razor-sharp formations. Felix tanked them, letting the magic shatter against his Armored Skin. It hurt, and his Health dropped, but he could handle it and barreled through it all. Which was when he ran headlong into the descending club of a thirty-foot Frost Giant.

Adamant Discord!

The spell burst from Felix before he could stop himself, electric force blasting aside the tree-trunk sized weapon that came for him. So strong, in fact, that it sheared right through the giant's hand and forearm, resulting in the collapse of a small hill's worth of ice and Mana.

"Shit!"

Yet the core space didn't quake. If anything, the pressure on his Fiend-forge lessened.

Kill the giants! chirruped Pit.

Yeah, I figured that out! The giants, or the manifestation of power that was shown as giants due to Evie's...imbalanced state of mind, were what was causing the pressure. It was the Essence Draught and the System itself. *But what if all that power wasn't there anymore? What if...!*

Sovereign of Flesh!

Felix's body shifted and grew, swelling with muscle until he was the same hulking monstrosity that had fought the Archon to a standstill. He leaped, talons leading the way, tearing into the ice-born giant's massive chest...and out the other side. Felix landed with barely a splash, already moving onto the next enemy. Yet, before the dead Frost Giant could dissolve back into another iceberg, he grasped it with all of his Willpower.

Chthonic Tribute!

The inert power in the ice was pulled into his channels. There, Felix held onto it as he moved down the line, refusing the hungry pull of his abyss.

Adamant Discord!

Lightning force ripped through the next giant, and his claws took the leg off a third construct of power. The wavy, liquid power of the Essence Draughts flowed all around him, dragged in his wake as it all thundered into his core space.

———

Evie nearly stumbled when she realized Felix was *attacking* the giants. She didn't understand it, nor why he was eating them like he did out in the real world, but she hadn't the time to figure it out. Her sister was taking all of her attention.

Not *my sister!* she reminded herself for the tenth time. *Magda would never be. So. Damn. Stubborn!*

Each thought was punctuated by Evie's chain meeting a shield, each one varying in size and style. Kite, buckler, tower, each one wielded with contemptuous ease by the Golem that faced her. Every attack Evie made was countered expertly.

The chains that her supposed protector had been using were absent, at least. A quick glance showed them—all of them—were focused on Felix and the giants.

Gotta keep her busy until he can do...whatever he's doin'.

Reducing her weight with her Born Trait, Evie jumped up and over her false sister, shifting the heft into her chain and flicking it sideways over Magda's head. Evie flew up, then jerked suddenly to the left, just barely dodging an overhand swipe of the creature's shield. Evie landed nimbly, rolling in the water to disperse the impact, barely evading Magda's counterstrike.

YOU LEFT ME!

Evie stumbled back at the force of Magda's scream, too stunned by the words to cope with dodging. Twin shields bashed into her, hurling her body backward and straight into an approaching Giant Felix had missed. Straight through, in fact, shattering the creature's icy form before she burst from the other side and splashed into the waves.

Gasping in pain, Evie leveraged herself up, only to find Magda there, double shields already descending.

Scorpion's Tail!

Her chain stabbed into the ground beneath the water and suddenly contracted, collapsing into its travel form and dragging Evie out of the way. She skidded back, just as a geyser erupted where Magda struck.

"You are stronger."

Zara?! The Naiad's voice sounded close, but Evie had to whirl to find her. Through her dripping hair, she saw the Sorcerer hundreds of strides away. *Why is Zara here, too?* "What the hell are you on about?!"

"You can overcome this. Stand, Evie."

"You think I was gonna take it lying down?" she hissed, surging to her feet. A charge, chain lash and yank, pulled her to Magda. When the woman tried to strike with her shields, she altered her mass again and threw her chain, swinging her away from the blow.

"Stand and face her."

Evie was getting winded. Her endurance had never been terribly high, and already her stamina was burning low. Each exchange had her panting, avoiding all harm but affecting no change in her sister. She stood there, implacable and unfazed.

YOU LEFT ME, AND I DIED.

"You're not my sister," Evie whispered. *She looks just like her...*

I AM ALL THAT SHE WAS.

"No you're not! You're just some ice monster I made up! Mags would never talk to me like that!"

YOU LEFT ME TO DIE. Magda walked forward, each step ponderous and sending waves of water surging in all directions. **YOU LEFT ME, AND THE GIANTS KILLED ME. IT IS YOUR FAULT.**

"No!"

Evie tried to scream, but the words only came out as a choked gasp. Magda was before her now, looming like judgment itself.

I AM DEAD, AND IT IS YOUR FAULT.

Images of her sister ripped through Evie's Mind, memories of their youth in the slums, of when Magda joined the guilders, of the day Evie herself joined. Pain lanced across Evie's heart, her soul. She fell to her knees.

A frost-encrusted shield lifted into the air.

More memories came. Of their battles, of arguments, and of Evie leaving Magda in the Frost Giants' camp. Of her embracing Cal. Evie's Spirit wrenched, overcome, and she only stared blankly as a second shield joined the first.

They dropped, descending like an executioner's axe.

CHAPTER FIFTY-NINE

The frozen waves of Evie's core were like mountains, grown somehow in the few minutes he'd been gone, and Felix's every step scaled them. Leaping from the crest of one, he soared through the air on the Strength of his legs alone, while the only thing preventing him from shattering the glacier beneath him was a hastily summoned Cloudstep. The platform exploded beneath his tread, but it served its purpose.

Evie's core stretched into the sky before him, as huge and as choked with frost as before. Essence—stolen from the now-obliterated giants—filled him to bursting as he hurtled horizontally toward the massive chain. He reached for its winter-locked shape with Will and Skill.

Adamant Discord!

A dim connection turned to a solid steel bar in his grip, filling Felix with a bone-deep chill even as he directed the stolen potency within him into the link. It warmed immediately, turning intensely hot as he hauled on it. Lightning sparked, generated by the sheer friction of his motion, and he found himself practically teleported to its side, so fast was his movement. Felix barely had time to flex his Will in the reverse, landing with entirely too much force on the craggy chain.

The entire thing shook, and broken ice rained down from above.

Felix grimaced, but couldn't afford the time to care. Gentle meant failure, and failure...Evie wouldn't be able to hold on for long. He grabbed at the Essence in his core, held separate from his Divine Tree and other gnashing bits of his core space, and focused. With a great heave, he shoved the lot of it out of his Mana Gates and into the chain core at his feet. Power, white-bright and thick, blasted forth from his palms and feet and mouth.

Ice turned to water then vapor almost instantly. Essence Draught and

System energy thundered from Felix, so bright he couldn't even look at it all, so loud he had to squeeze shut his Affinity to keep out the Spirit-splitting pain. Everything around him bucked, once, twice, before even the metal started to sag and warp.

Ice exploded above and below as the entire skyscraper-sized chain began to *move*. A huge detonation shook the core space, quaking everything, and Felix could barely sense the frozen waves all collapsing on themselves as they melted. An ocean of power heaved beneath him as the chain morphed, twisting on itself as ice was drawn upward from the surface, and clouds were pulled down from the sky. Purple-white and silvery-blue, the Mana burned as bright as the System energy, hotter than a sun and twice as brilliant.

"Evie!" he shouted, putting everything into his voice. "Now!"

———

Evie's eyes snapped open as the world fell apart.

Water surged, and her nearby Skills screamed in protest, metal and ice shearing against one another in a high-pitched cacophony. Magda, committed to her attack, was hauled off her feet by a sudden inexorable suction. Her sister's icy double was wrenched backward toward Evie's core, flipping over itself until it planted its jagged shields in the water and floor beneath it.

Evie felt the tug, but it was somehow far less disastrous for her. Water streamed past her body, swirling toward the center, but left her relatively untouched. She stood, still shaking. Her eyes were filled with her sister's Golem, its inanimate eyes seeming terrified and utterly unconcerned at the same time.

"I—I didn't," she whispered. Evie took several steps, not even feeling the frigid water on her feet. Memories still swam in her head, visions that refused to leave her. She didn't *want* them to. "Mags, you—I didn't kill you."

YOU LEFT—

"I DIDN'T KILL YOU!"

Evie screamed as she tackled the creature that wore her sister's face, knocking its shields loose and sending the both of them crashing into the water. Currents swept them away, pulling first Magda and then Evie under, tumbling them at increasing speeds toward her core. The creature's thick limbs pushed at Evie's smaller frame, but she had little leverage so close, and the younger woman clung like a barnacle on a sinking ship. They bobbed back up to the surface, both of them gasping for breath.

"I'm not to blame!" Evie shouted. A dagger appeared in her free hand and was brought down again and again. Ice chipped and flew in all directions. The creature twisted, kicking its legs and flexing its beefy arms.

THE GIANTS FOUND ME! YOU WERE NOT THERE!

"I saved them! I saved the people we were sent to save!" Evie rolled as the creature bucked beneath her, until they both flailed in the deepening water. Waves hurled them up and down, barely missing the broken ice flotillas all around them. "You fought them—"

I FOUGHT THEM ALONE!

A shield at least ten feet tall sped through the water, narrowly missing Evie's skull as it sheared through three burgeoning ice floes behind her. The force of its passage, however, sent Evie splashing in the depths, sunk below before bobbing up like a cork.

"You...did," Evie choked out as she climbed atop an ice platform about ten strides across. The creature that was—and wasn't—her sister did the same, at the opposite end. The water around them was racing now, the currents too strong for her Strength to overcome. "You saved everyone...Felix, me, Cal...everyone."

Evie looked down at her hands, which were raw and shaking from the cold. The bladed chain tumbled uselessly from her fingers. Her voice was a low sob that hurt her chest and throat.

"No one is to blame. You...you chose."

Magda regarded her, and for a moment, the violence paused. A shield half-formed from ice and metal chains, stuttered to an unnatural stop. Evie's breath caught as something manifested within the construct, something she could *hear,* even over her own ragged breaths. It was gentle and sudden, yet viciously guarded. Tears leaked from Evie's eyes at that sound, which felt so much like her sister that she had once known.

"Magda...?"

Magda reached out a hand of faceted ice layered with links of steel upon her shoulder, one and then the other. Beneath that touch, Evie's own form flickered, her visualized flesh giving way to ice and water and metal chains. For an instant, as they embraced, they were the same. Evie shuddered, her throat scraped raw, and collapsed into her sister's arms.

The construct's arms tightened just a little more. Evie gasped, and looked up...but its arms loosened without warning.

Core Space Authority Recognized.
Direct As Needed.

The creature's face was empty, and its song was gone, turning once more to ice and steel. Evie blinked back tears and pulled herself away.

"Y-yeah. Let's go back to my core."

Confirmed.

Evie pushed down her pain. She couldn't afford it. Not then. The currents carried them into her core faster than ever before, floating atop their frozen platform. The currents grew stronger and stronger, until everywhere there was a frenetic inward movement. She feared, for a moment, that they were headed for a waterfall. Yet she wasn't ready for the true devastation at her center.

She gasped as it came into view.

Chains and ice pulled inward, buckling huge sheets of thick hoarfrost before they were rendered into a thousand tiny pieces. The water below it all was sucked in as well, hissing as it hit her core and producing a cloak of choking steam. Her impossible chain, once frozen in place, now moved, spinning slowly as three distinct Mana types flowed into and around it all. Water, ice, and metal. They called to her in a cacophony of drums and crashing cymbals, a symphony of building rhythm...but empty just the same.

AFI +15!

Evie blinked in surprise as the sound deepened and expanded. The drums divided into sharp reports and low, sonorous booms, while metal crashed and vibrated in equal measure. It was the sound of her core as it spun, but it was incomplete. That emptiness was all the more obvious for its increased volume, a gaping hole where the rhythm died.

She saw Felix, hovering in mid-air in the blazing light of her molten core. His arms were outstretched, and red-gold flames licked along their length as he enacted some sort of Skill.

"Evie!" he shouted, not seeming surprised by her arrival, only relieved. "You need to spin your core! The power must be spooled together! Condensed!"

"How?" she asked, shouting with everything she had. She could barely hear him over the hollow music in her ears. "I don't know how!"

"Your Willpower! Focus on what you need to happen! Visualize it!"

Visualize. Just like Harn said, she realized. The warrior had beat the concept into her over the course of months until she'd formed this space, but even then Evie still questioned how it all worked. The why of it. *Don't think. Just do.*

The core he was stabilizing with Fiendforge shifted, its lazy rotations picking up by the barest of margins.

You got this, Evie. C'mon.

Fiendforge is level 10!

His Skill was working hard, filling Felix's channels with its strange, complex song. The pattern of the Unique Skill was all that was holding Evie's volatile core space together as the System tried to advance her—and he spotted more power incoming.

From the distance, waves of shimmering water Mana flooded, rising so high that they threatened to crash into the floating chain-bundles of her Skills. By the time the waves reached them, they had partially frozen into ice and slush, hitting Evie's core with a stentorian hiss and release of carbon-charred steam. Each wave hurt him more, wasting a ton of his Essence and Mana in the process, not to mention the shreds of significance that fed into his Fiendforge. It was far less than what Unite the Lost utilized, but Felix wasn't sure it was working.

Evie's core remained in its strange transitional state, even as her Willpower caught enough momentum to maintain a steady rotation. The core space was drawing in Mana from all around, not even counting the occasional System wave, and like debris in a river, Felix could feel that it would eventually dam itself up.

What's missing?

"Evie!" he shouted, forcing his voice with all of his chest. It was crazy loud so close to her core. "Evie! It's not catching! We're missing something!"

He had no clue what, or else he would have pointed it out. Frankly, thinking was getting harder the longer he maintained his grip on her core space. His Mind and Spirit were straining while he felt his Body distantly spasming back in the real world. Fiendforge was not a Skill lightly used, he was realizing, but it was too late for that. It was all that kept Evie from breaking apart completely, and he'd hold it until he collapsed, if it meant a chance for her success.

"I don't want to rush you, but this hurts. Like, a lot!" Felix grunted.

In response, he heard a high, blood-curdling scream. It was laced with frustration and...and grief and loneliness. The core before him began to hum as if in sympathy, and to Felix's amazement, it spun. Faster. And faster.

"You're doing it! I don't know what, but you're doing it!" Felix shouted in joy. He risked a look back at his friend, only to see her on her knees. "Evie?"

Her face was stricken, and her hand was outstretched but limp against the ice floe she was on. Felix focused, only just barely making out the shape of her Golem, the false Magda, as it raced toward her core.

"She's the missing piece," Evie said, her voice strained.

The creature, made of ice and metal, hit the spinning core in a single, colossal leap. It turned to liquid before ever touching it, the compression and friction of its spin too much for its form, and even the liquid burst into steam that was pulled whole-cloth into the roiling morass beneath Felix.

Evie screamed wordlessly, and her core pulsed.

A melody joined the insistent rhythm, a song that wove deftly within the empty spaces between beats. The whole of Evie's core surged, bucking in Felix's grip as Evie's fledgling Intent finally became realized. Molten metal stretched and twisted, spinning in greater velocities with every passing second. Ice from below was pulled into the weave, spiraling around the molten core of it like a strand of DNA. The ice melted, turning to water and then to steam as it rose to the topmost portions of the complex ring, where it once more condensed into ice—all to repeat the pattern over and over again. Deep blue and purple-white Mana spun endlessly in looping whorls around the molten silver core. A chain of power, endlessly wrapped within itself.

Evie's ring core was complete.

Three chains shot outward, glowing links of blazing silver and deepest blue that stabbed out into her core space. Each chain sank into a Skill, and power thrummed along their lengths. Ice shattered as the Skills cracked and twisted, the chains within them whirling to a life Felix had never seen them display. The thick ice that had choked them broke off in great sheets while in their center orbs of wobbling water formed, each of them illuminated by swirling motes.

Light inundated the core space, the same process as Atar's, and all Felix could do was hunch and weather the onslaught of power. It washed over him, burning at his skin and hair and face, but leaving him largely unharmed. Below, Evie shouted as the power altered her in a fundamental way, and she blossomed with a sympathetic radiance.

Felix closed his eyes and held on.

Fiendforge is level 11!

———

Above it all, hovering in a darkness beyond the sky, Zara watched. Water and ice and metal had swirled triumphantly into a thin ring of power, a core worthy of a nascent Adept, and the whole of Evie's core space shone with the baptism of resonant energy it had just undergone.

Zara was shaken.

The cracks that had crazed the girl's foundations were gone, healed just as completely as if they had never happened. The immense, vice-like grip of Felix's strange Skill had held it through the worst of her crisis, and the System's rush of energy had done the rest. It was not an impossible feat, achievable by many who called themselves true experts in the advancement of core spaces.

And yet...Felix had also reforged the girl's core in a way she had never seen before. He'd balanced the spin and twist of her attuned elements, giving a priority to metal as was proper to Evie's selected build, while also creating a cyclical representation of her ice and water attunements. His grasp of the intrinsic nature of Harmony, of the music behind the world, was growing at an alarming rate.

Zara felt hope swell within her breast at the sight. Perhaps doom wasn't certain, were Felix to join their side in the coming battles.

Perhaps...

For now, she would wait and watch. And pray.

CHAPTER SIXTY

Evie's Acrobatics (Common) Has Evolved Into Fleet of Foot
(Rare)!
Level Is Retained!
...
Fiendforge Active!
Evie's Fleet of Foot (Rare) Has Evolved into Undine Grace
(Epic)!
Level Is Retained!

Evie's Scorpion's Tail (Uncommon) Has Evolved Into Silver
Stinger (Rare)!
Level Is Retained!
...
Fiendforge Active!
Evie's Silver Stinger (Rare) Has Evolved into Tooth And Claw
(Epic)!
Level Is Retained!

Evie's Chain Mastery (Uncommon) Has Evolved Into Chain of
Thought (Rare)!
Level Is Retained!
...
Fiendforge Active!
Evie's Chain of Thought (Rare) Has Evolved into Bonds of
Dominion (Legendary)!
Level Is Retained!

Felix couldn't focus on the details of his friend's new and repeatedly changing Skills—too busy with holding the whole of her core space together—but he smiled at the elation he felt in her. That mounting joy was a balm after everything else that had happened. And it made him feel a bit better about the fact that his Fiendforge was directly influencing her Skills. Felix only hoped it was a positive change and vowed to ask her about them later.

The last Skill, however, struck through his split attention.

New Skill!
Chains Of the Protector (Unique), Level 1!
The best defense is a good offense. Forge chains of ice and metal Mana into a floating shield that can protect as well as unravel to entangle and damage nearby foes. Size of shield and length of chains increases slightly with level, damage deflected increases with level, damage dealt increases with level and Endurance.

Is that...that was the thing the Magda construct was doing. Shields of chains...Whoa. Felix jerked his head back in surprise as a new, glowing collection of power was ejected from Evie's core. It flew in a high arc until it landed somewhere farther out, at the furthest point of her core space, where it glimmered and uncoiled. Felix had to squint to make it out, but the new Skill looked like all the rest: a ball of frosty chains wrapped around a glowing, watery center. Still, it was cool to see a new Skill form in someone else's core space.

The joy turned complex at the introduction of the new Skill. All the intense emotions Evie had been experiencing during this process were still raw and unprocessed, and Felix honestly felt like a voyeur. He hated eavesdropping on her Spirit, but using his Fiendforge and stats to help Evie made that a necessity. He still wasn't entirely sure how his Skill worked, but Felix had realized that the best results seemed to stem from following the Will and Intent of his target...and that was impossible to do if he shut down his senses.

3 of 3 Body Essences Formed!
Tempering Has Begun!

In the distance, Felix sensed a powerful influx of System energy coming toward Evie's core. More than that, he also felt an abrupt slackening in the pressure against his Fiendforge. As gentle as he could, he eased off his Skill, letting its pattern silence within his core space...and Evie's held firm.

Oh perfect! She can handle the rest, I think. He pulled back slowly, letting his awareness of her core fade bit by bit. His Mana and Will retracted, until he floated at the edges of her channels. *You got this, Evie.*

A hand settled on his metaphysical shoulder.

Fire blossomed along his entire body, and Felix was halfway through a wild backhand when his arm was caught. Zara stumbled, her shape turning briefly to flowing water before she stabilized. Shock, pure and unfiltered, flitted across her face before vanishing into her usual staid expression.

"Felix, let us talk a moment."

———

She led them up instead of out, and it was Felix's turn to be surprised.

"Where are we going?" he asked.

"Somewhere we can speak without interruption."

Smooth as silk, Zara led up beyond the clouds of Evie's core space and into a greater darkness. It reminded him of his own core, though Evie's was less...refined? There were bits of debris floating around, remnants of Mana or inert matter from her visualizations...he wasn't sure which. Reality got hazy in core spaces, after all. But after a short while, Felix realized they weren't *in* a core space at all. He stopped floating after Zara and looked around in alarm.

"What is this?" he asked.

"We are...adjacent to Evie's core. Not quite attached to her Aspects, but related," Zara said.

"This feels familiar," Felix said, repressing a shudder. The last time he'd been in a similar place, he had been dragged there by an insane goddess. He pressed himself downward, easily phasing back into Evie's core space. A little of the tension drained from his shoulders, but he still looked up at Zara with a frown. "Let's keep this short."

Zara pursed her lips, giving him a look that might have cowed Felix several months ago. When he didn't respond or even alter his expression, Zara floated down to speak to him at the same level.

"Very well. I would ask you how."

"How, what?" Felix asked.

"How did you accomplish *that?*" she said, gesturing below them. Evie's core spun about, a crazy complex ring of multiple Mana types. "I could hear the Grand Harmony interplaying among her being, but yours is...it is opaque to me in a way that I find disconcerting, Felix."

"A little Will and Intent, but mostly it was two of my Skills," he said with a shrug. "Cardinal Flame for the Mana control and shaping, and Fiendforge. It's a Unique Skill."

"Fiend...forge? You spoke of Cardinal Flame, but I do not recall mention of this other, let alone that it was Unique." Zara tapped her lips with a long, ochre finger. Her hair looked like flowing water in the darkness, lit up by the flashes of power below them. "What can it do?"

"It was after I...survived my Omen Path. It allows me to shape the Paths of others, and apparently also means I can influence people's core spaces. I did the same for Atar." He grinned. "Worked so well both times, I hope I can use it on all of my teammates."

"...Impossible. That is not a Skill that should exist, especially not under the System itself. It has...restrictions..." Zara took a breath, and had she been less self-possessed, Felix was sure she would have slapped her own forehead. "Unbound. Right. The impossible does not figure into the calculus of your life, does it?"

Felix just shrugged again.

"How did you know to do this? To form her core in such a way?"

"I didn't," Felix said, nodding to Evie's shining form below. "She did. I just...listened, I guess." He laughed. "It's a lot less impressive in that sense. I'm a...battery, I suppose. Feeding her enough power to achieve what she always would have."

"She would not have done this alone," Zara said.

Felix blinked. "What?"

Distantly, he heard a scream. Zara looked up, too.

"That is coming from the external chambers," she said, concern creasing her brow. "Who—"

More agonized howls tore across them both, accompanied by a sudden and intense *fear*. Below, Evie's Temper suddenly bucked.

"That's Alister!" Felix shouted. "Watch Evie!"

He hurled himself from Evie's core space.

"FELIX!"

———

Felix rose from the darkness and moved. He surged up, cracking ice and sand from his knees and tearing his Garment apart, but it barely registered.

Screams filled the air.

Five undead scrabbled across the chamber, crowding in from the twisty corridor. Their wide mouths and grasping claws scuttled across the sands, held at bay by a plane of raw force Mana. Alister was on the ground, curled over Atar's still-unconscious form. His arm was upraised, bleeding and shaking as the undead slashed and scratched. Cracks splintered the shield, and the mage cried out.

The shield shattered. Alister shouted.

Felix was already moving. He leaped through the bursting shield and took the foremost Dustwights to the ground. They wailed in his face, but his hands throttled their skinny necks, cutting off the sound with a dry creak. The other three immediately dog-piled on him, their teeth and claws slashing his Garment further, but ricocheting from the scales that burst along his back and arms.

They were not enough.

Emerging talons tore undead throats apart, raining dark sand from the ragged wounds. The others he seized with fire.

Cardinal Flame!

Red-gold flame burned them, limning their withered bodies in carmine light that did little to hurt them. It had a terrible effect on Health, but these things were entirely Stamina-fueled. His claws would have to do, then. Seconds later, he stood among the shredded and twitching remnants of their bodies and ate them all.

Chthonic Tribute!

"You good?" he asked his friend.

"Y-yeah," Alister said, looking at Felix's claws and shuddering. He was shaky—a clear sign of Mana drain—but despite the bleeding, his Health wasn't too bad. After a lesser Health Tonic, even that went away. Atar was unharmed, thankfully, and Zara still hovered over the Tempering form of Evie. "Those things came out of nowhere. I-I don't know what's happening up above, but it cannot be good."

"No, it's not," Felix growled. The Leviathan's bones blocked his Perception and Affinity from reaching too far beyond their location, but the sounds of shouting and screaming hadn't stopped. The echoes of battle fed into their chamber. "I'm going up. Stay here."

Alister was downing a Mana Potion, already on his feet. "No, I'm coming with you."

"Someone has to protect them," Felix said, jerking his chin at their prone friends. "Zara is watching over Evie as she Tempers her Body, and Atar is still coping with his changed core. Here." Felix handed over two more Mana Potions from his satchel. "I'll block the door, but keep those shields handy. Focus on destroying their heads. If nothing else, that'll disorient them. Hopefully, I'll be able to stop any more from coming down this way."

Alister clenched his jaw, frustration clear on his face and Spirit, but nodded sharply. "Very well. Kill them all, Felix."

Felix only grunted as he stalked into the corridor, using a casual Stone Shaping to block the doorway. It was only a hardened sandstone, but it'd give the undead pause, at least. He ran.

The crooked hallway was tight, but Felix moved as fast as he was able, kicking off corners to increase his speed. The bone held strong, though the stone shattered in a few places. He slowed only once when a dozen Yttins fled past him.

"What's going on?" he asked, but only got terrified clicking in response. They ran back the way Felix had come.

Crashing sounded ahead, far closer than before, and Felix's head whipped toward it. *Damnit.* He increased his pace, rapidly hurtling around another two corners. *I need to be* faster. He promised to himself that his next free points were going to focus on Agility and Dexterity. It was past time those stats caught up with the rest.

He turned a final corner and nearly ran straight into another collection of the undead.

"GRAAOU!" they hiss-moaned. The creatures stumbled before him, flinching with every step, but they barely hesitated to attack.

Felix ripped through them like paper.

How the hell did they get past the Leviathan's influence? The shaman had assured him they wouldn't come close, and it had proven true before. *What changed?*

Then he saw.

Dustborn Wraiths, three of them, down the hall. They tore into two Yttins while slashing at more Dustwights to force them forward. The undead were being driven like murderous cattle.

Chthonic Tribute!

Luminescent smoke poured into Felix as he ran, and flame burst along his limbs.

"Get off of them!"

———

Vess coughed up blood onto the dusty stone. It was a brilliant red, compared to the dead winds raging around her, glowing with blood and life Mana. So very different from the Dustborn Wraiths she had fought. She'd killed two of them, but that hadn't been enough. Vess had thought she could take the creatures, but the claw buried in her gut spoke otherwise.

"Y-you...mi-i-ine," the Dustborn Wraith whispered to her, and Vess was so shocked she barely felt her body being slammed into the cliff again. She couldn't seem to move properly. "Mi-i-ine!"

They talk!?

Her Mind whirled, too groggy for thought, but that burned at her consciousness. Her Health slipped away, not terribly fast, but inexorable. Her potions were shattered on the ground, stomped by clawed feet, the first clue that these undead were not like the rest.

A mouth of fangs opened above her, and dimly she felt its Spirit. It was...happy. Sadistically so.

You Have Been Cursed!
Status Condition: Dustborn

D-dammit, the curse. Vess could feel its tendrils reaching into her, spreading across her Body like a wildfire. It burned with a sun-baked heat, like sand in her veins.

The Wraith leaned forward, pushing its bone plate-covered face toward her own. It sniffed deeply. It...hesitated. Between them, Vess felt an echo shudder into being, like the tread of someone down a city block, heels clicking against the cobbles.

A...something...approached, distant and indistinct, vast and powerful and so very, very old. She shuddered, quaking so hard she bit right through her tongue and did not care a whit—all Vess could do was stare at the call of it. The echo strengthened, a cry that threatened to split her apart if it drew any closer. Blood dribbled from her mouth. It *called*—

"FULMINATION!"

Lightning took the Wraith in the chest, followed oh-so–closely by a massive, ice-forged axe. It tumbled off of Vess and into the sands, spewing dark sand from its torso.

"Lady Dayne! Are you—" a sharp gasp cut the voice off, and a woman around her own age leaned over her. "H-here, ma'am—er, milady. Your Grace!"

A Health Potion was fumbled to Vess' lips, and she gratefully drank it down, letting the alchemical magic flare through her channels. Her descending Health began to rally, leaping a full five hundred points from that one vial, but it did nothing to touch the curse that burned through her Body.

Not enough to stop a Dragoon, she thought with a fierce burst of anger. The girl, Pava, handed Vess her spear, and she nodded in thanks and leveraged herself to her feet. *Not enough by half.*

A Dwarven Blade, a Risi Warrior, a Henaari Dawnguard, and a Half-Orc Arclight surrounded the Dustborn Wraith. Lightning peppered the creature, though the Half-Orc was all but breathing in Mana Potions. He was running out, fast, but his companions had Stamina to spare. They swung and thrust in an irregular tempo, none of them giving any quarter to the slashing claws of the hunched Wraith. Sand leaked from its body in lieu of blood, something Vess had noticed from the other Wraiths...the same Wraiths that suddenly emerged from the raging dust storm around them.

Not dead. Blighted undead!

"Two more?" Pava said and gripped her own longsword. "I need to help them."

"Not alone," Vess said.

"Ma'am?"

Vess snarled, baring her bloody teeth. "A Dragoon fights together."

Wyrmling's Call!

Spear of Tribulations!

A spectral dragon's head formed around Vess', and its roar blasted the Cursewinds around them in a forty-stride bubble of quaking air.

You Have Taunted A Dustborn Wraith (x3)!

Silver spears manifested around her, seven floating in the storm. "Go!"

CHAPTER SIXTY-ONE

Relentless Resolution!

Felix was atop the Wraiths before they had dropped the first Yttin, yet their claws met Felix's talons in a shower of brilliant sparks. His greaves vanished, retracting to thickened metal anklets and revealing clawed and scaled feet that swung in a horizontal arc into another Wraith's gut. That, at least, did some damage. The monster flew back and hit the far wall with a solid, echoless crack.

"Kill..."

Felix stumbled, surprised by the Dustborn Wraith's sudden words. Which meant the third Wraith caught him in a tackle from his blind side. They both went down in a tangle of limbs, claws flashing and clashing against bone plate and midnight scales. The latter held, but the former cracked and splintered beneath Felix's Strength. The Wraith screamed, high and shrill, then went silent.

Dark sand spilled over bone and stone.

One Wraith down, another with a twisted leg, and the third coming at him. Felix scowled. "You spoke."

"Kill...him...need...him...."

Need. Felix's scowl deepened. *Just like the Whalemaw. Fucking Primordials! Cardinal Flame!*

His body *blazed* with Cardinal Flame. The Skill morphed around his form, no sigaldry or paralysis-inducing spell, just a fever-bright flame from the center of his [Cardinal Beast Core], wreathing his fist as he drove it up into the jaw of his enemy.

Its head burst like a grape in a microwave. The other died soon after, rent asunder by claw and fire.

You Have Killed A Dustborn Wraith (x3)!
XP Earned!

Behind us! Pit warned from within his Spirit. *More come!*

Felix's head whipped up as a tall figure barreled into the corridor further up. It was Darius, his armor busted and bloody, and following him were five more Wraiths, their speed only countered by the tight confines and their sheer size.

"Fiend! They've entered the Warren! Soldiers are down!" Darius screamed at him. One of his eyes was swollen shut, and his skin had blackened along his jaw. Veins of corruption pulsed there, traveling up his thick neck from a bloody gouge in his breastplate. The Hand had abandoned his massive greatsword at some point, and now wielded a shorter, thinner weapon made *entirely* of air Mana. It keened as it swung, shearing through Wraith flesh like water, yet only barely keeping them at bay. "Help us!"

More screams echoed from up above, but Felix couldn't focus on them. His core *burned*, and the red-gold flames atop his flesh was joined by the crackling charge of his second core. Thunderflame raged.

Felix flared his Agility and Dexterity, Perception and Intelligence and Strength, pressing every stat to the limit of his ability as he took off. Sand erupted behind him, the stone cracked, and Felix plunged down the corridor toward the Wraiths. He flashed by Darius, the man moving as if underwater, and knocked aside the claws of two Wraiths that would have ended the man's whole career in an instant.

Their arms bent and snapped, buckling under the sheet power of his blow and catching on fire from his burning form. Simultaneously, Felix swung a wide slash into the chest and neck of the next two monstrosities. Withered flesh and rusted armor parted; the whisper and scream of both sounded weirdly echoed to his ears, and dark sand sprayed into the air. Still he did not stop, not until he speared straight through the last Wraith, pinning it into the stone wall behind them.

Time caught up, accelerating with a howl as he stopped running. Metallic claws slashed at Felix's back and shoulders, and a mouth of dark iron teeth tried to sink into his neck.

He headbutted the damn thing.

Stone detonated behind it, driven by the force of his attack, and its bony carapace shattered into a mushy, granular mess. With a flex of his shoulders, Felix tore the undead freak in half.

You Have Killed A Dustborn Wraith (x3)!
XP Earned!

"What the—!" Darius exclaimed, before screaming again, this time in pain. Still aflame, the two Wraiths recovered rapidly from the broken arms and pounced. Darius went down.

Cardinal Flame!

A Dustborn Wraith (x2) Is Enthralled for 0.08 Seconds!

What?

Felix barely had time to process that notification when a force slammed against his own Will, shattering his hold over the Wraiths and extinguishing not just the red-gold flames on them...but on Felix's body, too. He stumbled back, his Mind ringing with sudden agony as a clawed hand shoved him hard into the earth.

FELIX!

Pit's power raged within him, but the tenku might as well have fought a tsunami with only his beak. They were both swept aside by that vast and alien Will. The world shimmered before Felix's eyes, the cramped, bone-constructed corridor wavering with a deep and desolate emptiness. Threads hung across his vision like the cobwebs of death, stretching off into infinity and ending here, above his friend. The Wraiths slashed and clawed, deflecting off Darius' wind blade even as it flickered and failed.

No!

Title: The Call of Defiance Activated!
+25% Willpower When Contested By A Foe Of Divine Formation Or Greater

The immeasurable Will shifted, not lightening or breaking, but becoming textured. Something with handholds. Felix seized it and heaved, all of him shaking like a leaf as he strained. His Mind and Spirit burned and crackled, his cores spinning a cacophony of noise, while his Body could barely stand. But barely was enough. He stood.

And the Will fled from him.

Felix staggered two steps, lurching forward with unimpeded momentum, and drove his clawed fists into the Wraiths' backs.

"Get off of him," he growled, and tore their spines out.

You Have Killed A Dustborn Wraith (x3)!
XP Earned!

"Fucking...Primordials..."

———

Harn jumped over the busted barricade, his Strength propelling him just high enough to clear it. He hit the sand and rolled, his armor cushioning the twenty-foot fall, and kept running. His axes led the way through the press of undead flesh, reaping experience with every slash.

"There! Sweep out!" he commanded. From behind him, a contingent of Henaari Dawnguard fanned out, their lithe bodies loping through the storm. Hooked spears were traded for shorter blades, far more effective in the press of undead flesh, and they tore a swath of destruction through the Dustwight numbers. Visibility was still garbage, but none of them were without observation Skills. "Focus on bringin' back survivors! I'll find Lady Dayne!"

The line had been holding well during the battle. Darius and himself were overseeing the regular changing of the front line as Stamina, Mana, and Health dipped to dangerous levels, and the Legion had actually been listening. There were a few jockeying for advantageous positioning, but on the whole, the legionnaires had proven a measure of their mettle. The undead were being eradicated, one-by-one.

Blighted Wraiths, Harn cursed. His axes sliced through another three lesser undead, the silver flame of his Raze spreading across their bodies like fire on oiled rags.

Raze is level 77!

The damnable Wraiths had punched through their defenses, too strong and too fast for them to stop. Harn and Darius had taken the brunt of their strikes, but their assault had proven effective. The defensive line buckled, and the undead flowed into the breach like a wave.

Another two withered monsters leaped out at him, and Harn kicked the first in the chest and broke open its torso. Its ribs cracked like kindling, and it went down, clearing the way for his axe to cleave the second from crotch to skull. A negligent backhand finished off the wounded Dustwight.

Heavy Armor Mastery is level 74!

Harn felt a rush of excitement stir his veins. After years—*years*—of training and fighting, he was close to advancing. Even his core was ready to enter the Weaving Stage, held at bay for months now until his Formation could catch up. Ruthlessly, he pressed the feeling down. He'd have reason to cheer later.

Now he had to find the girl.

"Vess!" he boomed into the Cursewinds. The sound was swallowed up. "Blighted night!"

A sparking flash lit up the red-orange haze, and Harn focused on it through the slit in his helm. Another, and another. He could feel the clash of metal-attuned Skills, just ahead. *That's her!*

He rushed forward, his Brawler's Physique flared as he ran up the incline of a fallen wall. He paused at the top, taking in the scene in two heartbeats. Dustwights swarmed, facing off against a squad of Legion, Dawnguard, and a Risi Warrior of all things. The squad was pushing them back, but in the thickest of the fray was a lithe woman in white-enameled armor and a spear that shimmered blue through the storm. Vess was fighting two Wraiths alone.

Descent of the Barbarian!

Harn leaped off the rock, twin axes descending onto the backs of the undead. His axes moved in a blur, his Agility and Strength fueling the frenetic power of his evolved Skill. It had once been his Axe Mastery Skill, but it had enjoyed a rebirth during their confrontation with DuFont. Now he was a blur of silver death, too fast for the Dustwights to avoid in close combat and his axes too heavy to resist. They burst apart in showers of dark sand, and suddenly the Risi Warrior was free of foes.

"Go! Help the others!" Harn grated at the Frost Giant. He nodded and ran toward a Half-Orc struggling with a crackling shortsword.

Harn hewed through the crowd, cutting through limbs and necks with every swing, and his axes never stopped. Not until he made it to Vess' position...only to find the girl standing over two downed Wraiths, both of them pinned to the stone with several of her silver Spears. She whirled toward him as he emerged from the battle, but relaxed when she recognized his armor.

"Harn," she growled. Her face was bloody, and her armor broken in several spots. "These *things* will not die."

She was right. He could see their wounds repairing, stitching themselves up by some unnatural power. His teeth grated against one another at the realization. "Damn. Damn!"

"What?" Vess stepped toward him, but nearly lost her balance. "Harn? What is it?"

"More of them got into the Warren," he said, barely restraining his anger. "Darius faced them. If they ain't dying...if they just regenerate..."

Vess' eyes widened. "A lot of people are going to die."

"Yeah."

Pain Resistance is level 74!

A spike of power shot through Harn's core, flaring across his channels and sending a wave of dizziness through him. He twisted, setting his feet so he didn't tip over and rode out the sensation.

"What else is wrong?" The girl put a hand on Harn's shoulder, helping him steady even as she quivered in obvious hurt.

"I'm gettin' real close to Temper. Energy's makin' me unsteady," he grunted, then ran his eyes over her. "You look like your about to fall down, yourself." Harn handed her a Health Potion, noticing hers were all depleted. "Here."

She took it and drank it without a word, only grimacing at the sensation of wounds closing.

"That don't look like all of it. Another?" he asked.

She shook her head, the grimace turning darker. "Status Condition," Vess rasped. "Curse."

"Damn." Harn looked at the Wraiths. "Regenerating and curse-bearing. Felix warned us of the curse, at least. He never mentioned 'em bein' so tough."

"Perhaps he never noticed," Vess said before summoning another Spear and jabbing it through the nearest Wraith's chest. The thing writhed, attempting to reach her with its gnashing, metallic teeth.

Harn only grunted. That sounded like Felix. Too strong for his own good.

Then things went silent. The screams and groans of the undead, the clash of magic and Skills, the damn storm itself. A hush descended...before every single creature turned and ran off.

"Is...is the storm *leaving?*" Harn asked.

On the ground, the two Wraiths burst into a frenzy of motion, clawing at the conjured Spears and their own bone-plated flesh. Dark sand poured from them, more with every second. Vess and Harn shared a confused look as the storm well and truly dispersed.

"They fled. Why?" Vess asked.

A thump shook the earth behind them and showered Harn with sand. Harn spun to see Felix crouching there, at the center of a small crater in the dune. His clothes were shredded, barely covering his bits, though perhaps that wasn't an issue. The kid's skin was entirely covered in unsettling black scales, and his eyes burned a brilliant sapphire blue. He said nothing to either of them, though his eyes lingered on Vess for an outraged second. Then he stalked forward and slammed his talons into the skulls of both Wraiths. They shrieked, piercing whistles that made Harn flinch, before bursting apart into luminous smoke.

Felix stood, smoke pouring into his Body, before he clawed at the air itself.

"You're mine, too," he said. The air shuddered, and so did everyone else, even Harn.

Every injured person he could see convulsed, wracked by an intense, burning pain. In his channels, Harn felt as *something* was torn loose and extracted from him, an arrowhead of vile corruption he hadn't noticed building within his Body. It seared his channels as it emerged, manifesting in a long moment of excruciating agony.

All of it—every ounce from the legionaries and Harn and Vess—settled into Felix, who by then practically glowed with malevolent energy. Then it was gone, too, pulled into his core as if it never were.

Vess stabbed her spear into the earth, supporting her suddenly weak limbs, and Harn was right there with her. That wave of enervation nearly unmanned him, though it passed quickly enough. He straightened with a pained grunt and saw Felix grab her by the shoulders. The girl flinched.

Felix pulled back, and his hand shed its monstrous coating, each scale and talon fading to vapor that blew away in the wind. He turned to Harn.

"Get everyone inside. I'm sealing off the Warren."

"Aye." He could do that. "What about inside? Darius...?"

"He's alive," was all the kid said.

Harn hadn't missed the momentary hurt in Felix's eyes at Vess' flinch. It was gone now, replaced by a steady authority. Harn had the distinct impression he wasn't looking at Felix, but at the Autarch.

Stupid thought. It's the same kid.

Felix nodded at them before vanishing in a burst of sand and rising lightning. Up into the sky and the fading storm.

CHAPTER SIXTY-TWO

Stone Shaping is level 79!
Rime Shaping is level 29!
Green Shaping is level 28!

The Cursewinds had well and truly fled by the time Felix finished his protective enclosure. The wild, chaotic Mana had dissipated and run out of energy, fading into the blazing midday sun. Here and there, Felix could make out withered pieces of the Dustwights, but otherwise there was no sign of the undead that had assaulted them for the past eight hours.

They'll be back.

He was certain of that and told his people to keep their Perception flared. The Primordial behind the undead was not done with them. Even in that brief taste of its Will and Intent, Felix knew it was being drawn to him, like iron to a magnet. He suspected it had to do with his Primordial nature, but that was unlikely to be the sole reason.

It didn't want to eat me like the Maw would have, but it definitely sought me out. That Wraith spoke of a Need...just like the Whalemaw. He grimaced. *And it ran when I shrugged off its touch. Why?* Felix pondered atop the stone enclosure, hair blowing in the hot breeze. *It felt old and rotten. Withered. A lot like the undead it ordered around, I guess. Is it an undead Primordial?*

Felix shuddered at the thought, thinking back on the necromantic spirit he'd fought in the Haestus Temple. That thing had been weakened by its long imprisonment and was still a force to be reckoned with...he had no interest in facing down a Primordial version, too.

He stood up, Body slick with sweat beneath his restored Garment, and surveyed his work. While Pit had retired below, Felix had spent his Mana, over and over again, building a massive stone shell over the Leviathan skeleton, encasing them all in protective layers. Like the walls of his Stronghold, Felix utilized all of his relevant shaping Skills as best he could. If nothing else, pushing himself did wonders for the Skill. However, without the framework of his Stronghold to guide him, combining the three shaping Skills was a task beyond his current abilities. He achieved something approaching his goal, but it wasn't nearly as strong as the wall back home. The Leviathan's shape was covered in a mountain of muddy gray stone veined with glimmering red. At least it didn't stick out in the crimson desert.

Rime Shaping was especially hard to manage here in the arid desert. He leaped from the rounded top of his enclosure and let gravity take him. *Mana becomes ice as I manifest the Skill, but the environment clearly affects what I can do. Conjuring ice and water in this place feels like being squeezed by a vise. Ugh.*

Felix landed, flexing his knees to absorb the impact and scattering sand in all directions. A lone opening existed in his conjured defenses, and as Felix passed through it, he erased even that, allowing the stone to close over it all. His people—and the Yttins—would be screwed if Felix wasn't around to open it back up, but he felt it was a necessary precaution. At least this way, everyone could get some rest without any more looming threats.

He descended the winding paths, deeper into the Warren.

The pressure from the Leviathan was meager at the higher levels of its skeleton, though that might have been because he was more acclimated to it. The few legionnaires he passed had strained looks on their faces, even as they attempted to sleep. Felix decided it was good for them.

A little strain will help them develop their Willpower.

Aside from the Arclights, few of his followers had a sizable Willpower stat. The Blades, Bones, and Fists all focused on Strength, Agility, and Endurance with a minor focus on Vitality. Warrior stats, as Harn had explained. They patterned themselves after Felix, but all viewed him as a warrior first and a mage second. While Felix wouldn't claim himself a wizard, he was a powerful magic user, and the stats related to it were a large part of his success. Without his Willpower, he would have failed too many times to count.

The Legion, Henaari, and Risi were clustered all within the first few chambers. All of them were laid out on the ground or leaning against the walls, exhausted enough to drop off despite the Leviathan's pressure. A good portion of their Health Potions had been consumed in the aftermath of the extended battle and its unexpected conclusion, but Felix wouldn't have it any other way. He'd made those to keep his people safe. If it weren't for the potions and his Chthonic Tribute to pull the Dustborn Curse from their Bodies....

As it was, there hadn't been a single death this time around.

That's fucking progress, he thought with a pleased nod. Maybe they hadn't fought as well together as they could, but they listened to Harn and

Darius' instructions, for the most part. They were growing stronger and more capable.

He walked farther along the Warren's crooked corridors, finding Palin and her team busy making food. Yttin hovered around her, helpful in their own strange way. Palin flinched from their bandaged hands, but her Dwarven assistants smoothly accepted them into the process. Some sort of stew was boiling over an open flame, and it smelled good. Pit was there, poking his oversized beak into pots and pans and being chased away by angry Dwarves. Felix smiled, continuing to walk as the sound of chopping knives faded to nothing.

Atar and Evie were still recovering, he'd been told. Atar was awake but not moving much, while Evie was still in a deep sleep. Zara had told him that both of them had depleted their internal stores and would require an extensive rest before returning to battle. That made sense. Tempering one of his Aspects had Felix down and out for six hours, after all. Luckily, they had plenty of time before the sun set, and they needed to move once more.

Hopefully, Darius is in fighting shape by then as well. The Hand had lost a lot of blood during his battle with the Wraiths, but most of the damage had been due to stacking instances of the Dustborn Curse. Once Felix had eaten those up, the man had begun to heal.

Harn had been similarly damaged, as had Vess, but both of them were already back in top condition. A little tired, but able to fight if the need arose. Felix had no plan to involve them in any fighting that might occur that night, however. Everyone had put in plenty of effort getting to that point, but with them so close to Ahkestria, Felix planned to handle the rest of the fighting alone. He could have devastated the Dustwights before they'd ever posed a threat, leaving everyone to fight the Wraiths en masse. Felix wasn't about to deny the benefits they had reaped, but he had no interest in delaying any longer.

We still haven't even run into the Paladins out here, and that concerns me. Felix had figured he'd be happy to not see their plate-covered forms, but not seeing them only made him worry about their intentions. *The shaman indicated they were east of here, but headed to Ahkestria, chasing the Unbound. Will we find them inside the city? Is that vision correct? Are they attacking the city even now?*

There was no way to know, and not knowing was driving Felix a little stir crazy. A part of him wanted to head out right then in a mad rush to beat the Paladins to the city. It was stupid, he knew; the Paladins were likely already there, and travel under the sun was a good way to attract another Cursewind. So he stewed in his stress, Primordial and Paladins relentlessly picking at his attention.

So, Felix decided to distract himself with training.

Farther along the path was another antechamber, similar to the one he'd faced down the cursed shaman within, but at a higher level. He hadn't nearly traversed so deep as to feel the Mind-numbing pressure from before. Now it was a vague, unpleasant tingle in the back of his head, easily ignored. As he approached the antechamber, he heard the sounds of combat. Felix was surprised to realize that Alister had preempted his own idea and was fighting against a small cadre of Dawnguard.

Huh. Hell, yeah. Go Alister.

The mage was wielding his force Mana in powerful bursts, driving back the hooked spears of the Dawnguard before diving forward with his rapid, Agility-based rapier Skills. The Henaari were fast and strong, but their stat advantage couldn't quite overcome the oppressive advent of Alister's pillars and shields. Their interchanges were snappy and bright, neither of them able to find purchase on the other in the long minutes Felix observed them. That alone was impressive, as Alister wielded his Mana Skills with increasing ability, and the Dawnguard refined their edge with every misdirected blow.

At the first break in their composure, Felix stepped into the room properly.

"My Lord," the nearest Dawnguard said to him. Ryel, Felix recalled. The other Henaari all pressed their fists to their heart and bowed.

"Hey there, Ryel," Felix said, waving at them all as casually as he could manage. His body was aching to fight, and the last thing he wanted to do was scare them all off. "Alister. I see you've been sparring."

The force mage nodded, his mouth a grim slash across his face. "Attempting to, yes."

"You seemed to be doing quite well," Felix said. "Not everyone can hold over five Dawnguard at once."

Ryel and his people puffed their chests in pride. "Mage Knacht is a formidable opponent. He asked that we test out his Skill, what was it?"

"Pillars of the Domineering Sentinel," Alister provided. "I have been using it as a barrier and attack in one...but I think it can be more. Grand Impetus, too, though that is less faceted."

Felix nodded. "Good. Using Skills in new ways is always a great idea. I've noticed it drives those Skill levels higher at a reliable pace, especially if you press yourself while in danger." He grinned, and his Garment shifted until his sleeves vanished, and his pants gathered up at the knees, just above his silver greaves. "Why not let me join in?"

"Ah," Alister looked at the Dawnguard, but they merely nodded excitedly. "Any team you join will have the advantage, Felix."

"Then I'll be on my own team. Everyone versus me. How about that?" Felix asked, swinging his arms to loosen up his shoulders.

Alister and Ryel traded looks, the latter far more enthusiastic than the former. The noble cleared his throat. "Well, if you're certain..."

"Great!" Felix clapped his hands. "Let's begin."

"Grand Impetus!" Alister shouted, and a foot-thick lance of blue force Mana blasted off his rapier.

Relentless Resolution!

Felix flowed around the attack, evading its howling edge by inches, and tore through the bindings around his arms and legs with sheer Strength. Several of the Henaari grunted in shocked pain as their Blessings were torn apart—they looked like tiny bird claws attached to ropes, all made of shadow and metal—but the others of their number manifested speed that matched him. Ryel charged, twin short blades weaving in deadly arcs, before sparking off Felix's scaled flesh.

"Blessing of Stolen Light!" another Dawnguard gasped.

Felix felt the Urge-based Skill sizzle over his Body, like a wave of burning feathers. A Status Condition tried to root into his eyes, and he grinned and let it.

You Are Blinded For 1 Minute!
Status Condition: Blinded (Severe)

The room vanished from his standard vision, and immediately Felix felt the bite of two spears into his gut. They didn't pierce his scales, but they didn't feel great. With Sovereign of Flesh activated and plenty of Essence to fuel it, he had told them to let loose with their most powerful Skills. Alister had hesitated at first, but the Dawnguard had followed orders with gusto. And now he was blind, pummeled on every side by force Mana and cold blades.

Blind Fighting is level 45!

He caught one of the hooked spears, snagging it blade-first and yanking it out of the Henaari's grip. The Dawnguard shouted in surprise, but Felix only flared his Perception. His eyes might have been blinded, but he could *feel* everyone around him, a combination of his Skill Blind Fighting and ridiculous stats.

Another sword thrust for his face, and he jerked out of the way, utilizing the momentum to bash his skull into the fist of a separate attack. Warmth splashed against him as bone and skin split, and Felix laughed.

———

Blind Fighting is level 59!
Journeyman Tier!
You Gain:
+5 DEX
+5 PER
+5 AGL

Armored Skin is level 78!
Dodge is level 70!

Somewhere around the third hour had them all run out of gas, and despite numerous attempts at resting, the majority of the Dawnguard could no longer muster the will to fight.

"I suppose we can call it there," Felix said. He was feeling good, mostly. In fact, it felt as if his edges were being honed—he would have happily fought for another few hours, despite the weariness that had started to dog him.

The others groaned in mixed sentiment, relief the most evident emotion of all. Alister was clearly spent. He was slumped against a Stone Shaped obelisk Felix had conjured to counter one of the mage's Pillars of force. Felix was impressed, though. He had set a loose rule in his head about not using his more advanced Skills in the fight, but Alister had pressed him enough to force the issue.

Now, however, everyone was exhausted. Quite apart from their fight, the pressure the Leviathan put off was straining their Aspects, making Skills harder to utilize. As far as Felix was concerned, that was just additional training. His Mind and Spirit felt mostly fine—thanks to their recent Tempering—but his Body certainly felt the abuse he'd just put it through. The efforts of the Dawnguard and Alister weren't something that should have given him pause, but the combination of their fervor and the Leviathan's dominating pressure strained him. He was sweating, which hadn't happened in a while.

As the Henaari slowly picked themselves up off the sand, Felix nodded to them. "Thanks for keeping up the Status Condition like I asked. Really helped me out."

"I am pleased to be of service, my Lord," Ryel said with a shaky bow.

Felix grinned and walked over to Alister. The man was holding his head in his hands, clearly suffering from extremely low Mana. Felix took a small vial from his pouch and flicked it at him. "Here."

The vial pinged off Alister's head, moving too fast for him to catch it. "Oww."

Felix fought down a laugh, scooping up the vial and handing it to the mage. "Sorry. Here. It's a Mana Tonic. Should take the edge off that headache."

Alister wordlessly peeled the wax seal and drank the meager vial.

Felix sat down, leaning against the same irregular obelisk as the mage. "You did good out there. Surprised me a couple times."

"You were literally blinded," Alister said. "You had Ryel reapply that Blessing so many times that you shouldn't have been able to fight any of us." He laughed, a tinge of bitterness in his tone. "But yes. I surprised you twice."

The Blessing of Stolen Light stripped his vision at first, but each subsequent application had the potential to muffle your other senses as well. Felix could have easily shrugged off the effect—activation was a matter of contested Wills and Vitality—but he let them stack up. Each lost layer of his senses had only heightened the strain of his Blind Fighting Skill, and Felix had given himself over to its use.

It had been more than enough.

"Well, I have a Skill for that. I have a Skill for most things, now that I think about it," Felix said, contemplative. He snapped his fingers. "I don't have a Skill for cooking, though. Is that a thing? That's gotta be a thing, right?"

Alister snorted. "It is. Cooking is a Common-ranked Skill, but surprisingly hard to advance beyond Apprentice Tier. My father..." He sighed. "My father once had a man with the Chef Skill. Uncommon ranked. Made the most marvelous dishes."

Silence fell over both of them. Alister was clearly working through something, and Felix was happy with waiting. The man had been a steady friend for months, but he'd never had a chance to just sit and talk with him. *There were always more...important things. God, that sounds shitty.*

"I miss them. My family," Alister said at last. "My parents and I never got along well, though they cared enough to fund my entrance to the Guild. Cared about the status, at least."

"Are they back in Haarwatch?" Felix asked.

"In a sense. They died after the Eyrie fell. My old estate was swarmed by those Revenants." Alister looked up at the bone-buttressed ceiling, and a weary ache rippled across his Spirit.

"Jesus, I'm sorry Alister. I didn't know."

"I don't talk about it," Alister said with a dismissive shrug. "My family and I had been lost to each other for years before that, the monsters only cemented it. Still. It aches to know that they died while I was still unconscious. If I'd been hale, perhaps I could have...perhaps."

Felix didn't know what to say. Sadly, he didn't have a Skill for painful emotional conversations. He could only remain silent and listen.

"Atar is my family now. All of you, really. It's why I've put so much of myself in bettering your Stronghold, in improving myself. But today...today I failed. Those monsters would have killed us if you hadn't driven them back."

"That's why you're pushing yourself so hard? Alister, those Wraiths are *strong*, and you held them back for what? Thirty seconds? A minute?" Felix shook his head. "Atar and Evie would have died if you hadn't been able to do that."

"It doesn't feel like enough, though. I'm good with sigaldry and my blade, but Atar is better at the former and Vess or Harn could trounce me on my best day. I've not worried about that much, I am happy instead that you are all my allies. My rapier and meager magic were enough." He grimaced. "But when I thought death was coming for us in that chamber...Felix, I realized I need to be more. Stronger. I need to protect him."

"I get it, believe me," Felix said after a lingering moment of silence.

The torches along the chamber were burning a bit low, and the shadows pooled deep in that place. "I spent a lot of time fighting monsters by myself, even before I met Pit. Getting stronger was my way to survive, to push through. Sometimes strength isn't enough by itself, though, not when you're alone. But you're not alone, are you?"

Alister blinked at him. "No, I don't suppose I am."

Felix handed the force mage a couple Mana Potions and a Stamina potion from his satchel. "Here. Drink up, then we go again."

"What?"

"Replenish yourself, then we spar again." Felix stood and stretched, feeling his spine and joints pop pleasantly. "I'm not gonna hold back this time."

Alister grinned and downed the potions one after the other. His Spirit fluttered, a song stretching between anxious, drawn-out notes and a fluting, frenetic piping. He stood. "I can do this."

"Prove it."

CHAPTER SIXTY-THREE

Two hours later, Felix saw the Henaari and mage off to a meal and bed, the lot of them too drained of Stamina and Mana to do much more than shovel in food and pass out. Palin was still up, serving her food and ensuring everyone had gotten something. That included Felix, apparently, as the stout woman shoved a bowl of stew roughly into his hands before prowling away.

Still mad at me for the Paladins, he thought as he sipped his stew. *Well, let her be mad. At least she's alive—oh whoa. This is really good.*

The stew was a savory mix of blue root vegetables and marbled meats, worked heavily with some sort of earthy spice. The broth was a pale orange which was weird, but as long as he closed his eyes, he couldn't deny its delicious flavor. Felix managed to wolf down four entire helpings before his stomach began to protest and Pit, of all people, dragged him away to bed.

Which is how Felix found himself lying atop a snoring Chimera, entirely wide awake in spite of his aching Body. Pit was dead to the world, stuffed even more than Felix and taxed by their use of the Fiendforge. It hadn't been too apparent in the moment, but all the strain and struggle Felix had undergone within Atar and then Evie's core space, Pit had experienced as well. In fact, it was thanks to their Etheric Concordance that Felix had the Intent and Affinity available to spare. And, though the tenku had been protected within Felix's Spirit, the burden of all those forces was impossible to deny.

Long story short, Pit deserved his rest. And so did Felix. He just couldn't get any.

"Fuck." Felix stood up in a frustrated huff, careful not to jostle his

Companion too much. Pit merely grunted and tucked his huge wings a little tighter into his sides. Felix spent a moment just staring down at him.

You're up. Go do something useful.

A voice in the back of his head urged Felix toward action. It wasn't a *real* voice—he'd had enough of the Maw to be an expert on that—but behavior that he couldn't quite shake. He'd spent nearly every moment of his life on the Continent in some sort of peril, bouncing from conflict to conflict, dire straights to crumbling precipices...it felt strange to sit still. He'd had the same issue back in his Stronghold, and he'd often find himself working on alchemy or tweaking their defenses. Here, in the middle of the wilderness, Felix didn't have those options, not in the same way at least. But there was something he had been putting off.

He walked out of the chamber, tossing aside the thin cloth doorway. Two Henaari Dawnguard, eight legionnaires, and two Risi were standing guard in the corridor outside, and all of them snapped to rigid attention as he walked out.

"Why...what are you doing?" he asked.

A four-foot-tall Goblin in boiled leather armor saluted him, fist to heart. "Sir. Commander Harn told us to keep you safe."

"Really?" Felix Eyed them all, noting their levels and feeling the shape of their advancement. All of them were pushing into upper Apprentice Tier, though the Henaari and giants were closest. The Goblin, named Rog, bore a blue eye outlined in red-gold flame on his breastplate. It sat opposite the insignia for the Bones society of his Legion. "You're the...captain?"

"Aye sir. Captain Rog, sir," the Goblin saluted again, harder. "Commander Harn told us to stick close to you, sir. We're the Fiend's Shadows."

Felix looked at everyone else. He felt a vague sense of annoyance from the Risi and amusement from the Henaari, but not much. The other legionnaires, another Bone, two Blades, two Fists, and two Arclights. *Two of every group...Fiend's Shadows. Who came up with that name?*

"Fine. Just keep up," he said, and started moving.

Felix's Agility was quite high, and while it meant his body moved easier and with greater speed, he would not be able to use it properly were it not for his enhanced Perception, Intelligence, and Dexterity. Moving fast, after all, meant his ability to react and adjust had to keep up, otherwise he'd end up face-first in a wall somewhere. Thankfully, the use of stats was a lot like a muscle in that you had to "flex" it to enjoy the maximum effect of all the points you'd invested.

That meant most folks could walk around and interact with others without issue, no real fear of crushing hands in greeting or leaping over a house when you meant to hop a puddle. Felix...Felix's stats had risen quite high, however. So, while Felix only meant for a brisk jog toward his destination, it wasn't until he stopped outside a switchback path deeper into the Warren that he realized his Shadows were several turns behind him.

Ugh. "Down here," he called out, before descending the path. They'd either catch up or not.

Down below, the pressure from the Leviathan was more pronounced, even for him. He slowed to a walk, unwilling to further strain his Body, but there wasn't far to go.

"Klzix," Felix said. He walked into a rib-vaulted chamber, the same one he'd desperately fought the transformed shaman in, and found the Yttin clicking excitedly to a group of their bandaged brethren.

"Felix," the shaman said in greeting. Then they bowed. "Or perhaps I should call you Autarch? How might I help you?"

Casually letting his senses drift over the Yttin assembled, Felix smiled. "Funny you should mention that. You've told me that you struggle out here. Supplies, relations with Ahkestria, fighting off the undead...what if I could make that easier?"

Klzix tilted their head, and their copper eyes gleamed. "Please explain."

"Have you ever heard of the nation of Nagast?"

————

Congratulations, Autarch!
You Have Recruited A Faction!
The Yttin (Beastsworn) Have Joined Your Fledgling Nation!
+25% To All Positive Relations With Yttin!

Negotiation is level 27!
...
Negotiation is level 33!

Oathbinding is level 36!

Felix walked away from the shaman about as happy as he could be; recruiting them into his loose federation of peoples was a goal the moment he realized their vulnerability and worth. They might have been creepy, but he'd noticed quick and precise movements were consistent among every single one. They were all high Apprentices, and quite a few had broken into Journeyman Tier. The shaman had settled into near-Adept after recovering from their mutation. They were strong.

More than that, they knew the desert better than anyone. That would help them now and into the future, when trade was more of a concern for their growing nation. Now was the more pressing concern, of course. Atar had been guiding them capably, but only moments after affirming their new relationship Klzix had dropped knowledge that had changed their plans entirely.

There were tunnels under the desert.

"And they're safe?" Felix asked.

The shaman shrugged their thin shoulders, each of their back-bound limbs wriggling. "Nothing is truly safe. The tunnels were built long, long ago, before the sea vanished and our people were slaughtered. Many have collapsed, but those that haven't are warded by ancient sigaldry to remain watertight and dry, even beneath the waves."

Now they all ran beneath the sand dunes, but that made little difference. "And they will lead us to Ahkestria?"

"Yes. The Latticeways were trade roads, and all roads here lead to the City. That does not mean they are easy to navigate, however. The tunnels are a dense web, tangled in many cases, and collapses have made that worse."

"Can you guide us, then?" Felix asked.

"No." The denial had been swift and emphatic. "We do not go near Ahkestria. Not any longer. It is unsafe for our kind."

Felix froze in mid-step and stared at the shaman. These Yttin barely came up to his waist, but the stone certainty that poured off of this one was unnerving. "Why is it unsafe?"

"We are a memory of what once was," Klzix said. They sighed, an exhale filled with rapid clicks. "A few of my kind live beneath the City, but it is not a life any should desire. The comforts of the City are denied us, for our cores swirl with the ancient waters, and That Which Burns does not appreciate the reminder."

Urges. I need to ask Atar about this Highest Flame. I have a feeling they will be a problem.

"But if you have one that can read the earth veins, then that will guide your way to Ahkestria."

Atar could do that, Felix thought. "Thank you, Klzix. I appreciate the information."

"And I appreciate the offer of trade and resources...my Lord." The shaman bowed again. "We will serve as we are able, until the Beast comes to render our world undone."

"...Right." That had been a sticking point with the Oath he'd had them take, and was likely the reason he'd earned a level in the Oathbinding Skill. He didn't usually for these oaths of service.

The Yttin would serve in honor and Skill in exchange for protection and resources, following him until their dying breath...or until the Beast arrived, which would sever all bonds and "forge them anew." Whatever that meant. Felix had a sneaking suspicion the Beast had something to do with the Primordial, though. "We are looking to leave the moment the sun sets. Where is the entrance to these tunnels?"

The shaman pointed down.

"Into the belly of the Leviathan, I suppose," Felix said and laughed.

Klzix did not. They merely nodded. "Yes."

———

Shortly before dusk, the company set out. Or, the Fiend's Claw, as nearly everyone was now referring to their group. Felix hadn't the foggiest who had come up with the name, or how it had spread so fast, but he had to fight the urge to roll his eyes every single time he heard it. Each group within the Claw was further identified as a Talon: the Dawnguard, the Risi, the Legion, his original team, and Felix himself. Pit was included with Felix, for obvious reasons.

If nothing else, I haven't heard nearly as much bickering from everyone, Felix mused. He'd take his victories where he could.

The Claw followed Felix and the Yttin shaman down into the deepest levels of the Warren, where the pressure from its ancient significance was a literal assault on their Aspects. The majority of the Talons had to be carted in their wagons, and those wagons had to be pulled by Harn or Vess or Felix himself as someone led the trembling Avum by hand.

The passages were barely wide enough for said wagons, too, and they had to disassemble them several times to get through the narrower corridors in the depths. Eventually, Klzix brought them to a large door approximately thirty feet wide and twice that in height. It bore carvings of beautiful aquatic creatures swimming across its surface, with a complex insignia emblazoned in the very center. It looked like three waves chasing themselves in a circle, centered atop a spiraling shell.

Klzix ran their fingers across the door's surface, setting hidden sigils alight. Felix's Manasight tracked them as they activated and sent pulses of power through the stone's surprisingly complex interior. Mechanisms moved within, turned by magic but very much mechanical in nature, until the doors cracked open with a soft boom.

Their torches fluttered wildly as the air was sucked into the yawning darkness beyond.

Exploration is level 64!

"What're the odds that we fight a shiny new abomination tonight?" Evie asked. "Two silver says we get attacked."

"Two silver on it not happening," Atar said, sounding a bit tired.

"Five silver on more undead," Alister offered. His voice had an edge, an echo of their sparring matches. "I hope so, at least."

The shaman shook his small, bandaged head. "No, beasts and monstrosities are kept from these tunnels by the wards."

"And the collapsed sections you spoke of?" Vess asked. "The wards would have failed there, yes?"

"That is true, but there are few fallen tunnels near us. To have wandered so far afield as to threaten your journey..." The shaman shrugged. "It is not impossible."

The lot of them pushed into the tunnel, which proved to resemble nothing so much as a modern highway. The floors were a pale stone, formed so seamlessly that Felix was certain they were Shaped, and the walls were made of an identical material interspersed every dozen feet with thick, dark metal arches. At Felix's approach, the arches glimmered, revealing a smattering of sigils inscribed along their lengths. Together, they released a soft glow that approximated a dim sort of sunlight.

"Wow," he said.

The remainder of the Claw was brought from above. The most significant feature of the Latticeways was an incidental one: the moment any of them passed through the threshold, the pressure from the Leviathan's bones vanished completely. Arrivals were announced with gasps and groans of relief, until the entire Claw was once more whole. Wagons reassembled and teams re-hitched, Felix bid farewell to the shaman.

"I appreciate the help," he said.

"It costs me nothing to aid you, my Lord, and I owe you a debt of gratitude that cannot be repaid lightly." Klzix touched their chest gingerly, where once-chitinous monster flesh had adorned them. "Until the Beast ends it all."

"Until then," Felix said with a nod.

Their journey continued, into the dark latticeway tunnels at full speed. Thankfully, the glow of inscriptions provided a constant illumination that followed their company as they progressed deeper along the path. Ahead, arches would ignite, while behind the last of the arches would persist with their radiance for perhaps two minutes before fading to shadow. Though many of them could see quite well in the dark, the constant light was like traveling in a bright bubble through murky waters, obscuring observational Skills with the glare of weak sunlight. Felix kept to the front to address any unforeseen issues, while Evie and Vess hung in the back along with a rotating squad of legionnaires.

Their injured were in the wagons, Darius amidst them. The wounds among them all were many, but every single one was on the mend. So many of their potions were used, though. Thankfully, Felix and his team had made a *lot* before leaving...but they'd run out sooner rather than later if the battles kept being so costly.

Atar led them as before, sensing the flow of earth Mana in the sands above them, and parsing which tunnels they had to follow. The tunnels themselves forked quite often, heading in many disparate directions while also reconnecting in complex intersections. They were well-named. Felix couldn't imagine the Continent ever needing so many roads, though, and Atar seemed impressed as well.

"I cannot believe all of this was down here, below our feet," he murmured in wonder as more arches lit up around them. "Such perfect pathways...news like this would bring joy to the Council. Trade has always been the goal in Ahkestria, but the costs for overland travel could beggar a modest merchant. Factoring shipments through Manaship was even more expensive. If they had this latticeway to make use of...trade could expand. Boom, even."

"Why do you think the Council does not already know?" Zara asked.

She was once more on her ugly Avum, Grouse. The bird squawked, keeping up with Pit's loping strides.

"What do you mean?" Felix asked.

"Yes, just what are you insinuating?" Atar demanded.

"Only that you look before you leap, Atar," Zara said mildly. She nodded at the exquisite, if worn, workmanship of the tunnels. "Do you think these have remained completely unknown for Ages? Or is it more likely the Council knows and chooses not to utilize them?"

"I—" Atar sat back on the lead wagon. "You may have a point," he grumbled.

"Why wouldn't they use them? Threat of monster attacks?" Felix asked. He flared his Perception again, as he'd been doing the past hour, but he sensed nothing ahead of them but rock and dust.

"Perhaps. Protection is an easy answer," Zara said. "And perhaps they do not want trade to be so easy with the outside world. The products of Ahkestria are renowned for their craftsmanship as much as their rarity. If the market were flooded with work, then..."

She let herself trail off, but Atar frowned and finished the thought. "Then prices would drop. An understandable tactic, I suppose. Hardly sinister."

"I never claimed to know their agenda, Atar," Zara said softly.

Price fixing, basically. Slimy, but no different from what people did back home, Felix thought, trying to remember his old economics lessons. The exact term evaded him. His Mind, however, whirled on ahead. Societies keeping knowledge a secret was par for the course on the Continent...but if they kept something as simple as trade routes classified, then what else were they hiding?

One way or another, Felix had a feeling he wouldn't like the answer.

CHAPTER SIXTY-FOUR

Aside from being out of sight, the Latticeways' greatest feature was their utterly flat design. No more rolling dunes to contend with or constantly shifting sands. The solid footing let the Claw move with blistering speed. So fast, in fact, that Atar had to bring them to a halt several times to consult the Mana flows in the earth.

The speed of their travel allowed Felix to contemplate the advantages of building real, quality roads. Vess had told him most nations had their own network of roads, but maintenance was rarely done except in the more prosperous areas, such as around the various capitols. The bigger empires and kingdoms in the far east were said to have brilliant road-works...but little could be trusted of those rumors. It was too far away.

That's part of the problem, he mused, idly tapping Pit's saddle. *Everything feels so...disjointed. The sheer size of the Continent, as it's been explained to me...it's bigger than any landmass back on Earth. I'm worried about the Hierocracy, but what else is out there? God, I need a map.*

He'd never had the chance to peruse the Archives back in Haarwatch, and there were no "world maps" available for sale at the few cartographers that existed in the city. Maps of Haarwatch? Yes. Map of the Verdant Pass? Yes. They were also poorly made and wildly different from one another; it had been clear that neither of the shops he'd visited had any levels in Scribing or Cartography. If those Skills even existed.

Atar says there's a great library in Ahkestria. Maybe I can find better maps there.

A pained grunt came from his side, where a blue-skinned giant was running alongside them. Others were there, but the two Risi Warriors had been running the entire time, and keeping up with Pit's Agility was tough for anyone. He was riding atop the tenku at the forefront of the group still, and Pit raced forward with unflappable energy. He was pretty sure the guy was loving it, running so freely. Even the giant's vaunted Stamina was bound to run out eventually, though, and from the way they were sweating, it was close to bottoming out.

At least two of the Fiend's Shadows kept wherever Felix roamed, running alongside Pit in shifts. They had claimed Harn had sent them, but Felix soon discovered that was only partially true. His honor guard had been mobilized by the members of his company after rumors went around that the Wraiths were specifically targeting Felix. Apparently, a few people heard them speak about needing "him" and assumed they had meant the Autarch. A complete stab in the dark on their part—Felix wasn't even sure who the Wraiths needed, only that it was a "him."

Regardless, formed of their own volition, members voted by all of his Claw, the twelve men and women took their job as honor guard very seriously.

"Hey, both of you. Go rest," he said.

The big blue warriors looked askance at one another, their sweat-soaked beards sticking to their breastplates. "My Lord, the others are rest-ing. We cannot—"

"It's fine," Felix cut in. He patted Pit's neck. "Pit will take care of me in the meantime. Cool?"

This time, the giants traded genuinely confused looks, and Felix had to bite back an annoyed sigh.

"Just...go. That's an order."

Perhaps the steel in his voice did the trick, or it was as simple as ordering them, but the Frost Giant Shadows dropped back without another word. Felix let himself groan in relief. He wasn't a fan of having people watching over his shoulder all the time. It was eerie.

"Pit, you good to keep running alone for a bit?" The mental equiva-lent of a shrug came back to Felix, and he patted his friend again on the neck. "Alright. Gonna go talk to Atar for a sec."

Riding at the front, Felix was parallel to Atar and Alister's wagon, where the mages sat testing Atar's Mana Gauge every few minutes. He urged Pit toward the team of Avum and very carefully climbed atop his saddle. The Master Tier barding creaked a bit as he jostled around, but it held just fine as he leaped gracefully up and through the air.

He landed in the wagon with a muffled thump, sending the whole thing tilting dangerously to the side.

"Ahh!" Atar screamed, almost wrenching on the reins before Felix grabbed his wrists. The wagon slammed back onto all four wheels a moment later.

"Ooh, sorry! Don't do that!" Felix laughed. He released Atar's hands once he knew the mage wasn't so spooked. "Didn't mean to tip the thing...or scare you."

"Didn't mean—! You jumped out of the burning air!" Atar sputtered.

Alister, however, looked around Atar and saw Pit's departing form. "Did you jump from Pit's back? At full speed?"

"Yeah," Felix grinned. "Pretty cool, right?"

His time on the Continent had been rife with death-defying stunts that he miraculously had lived through, but every once in a while, the extent of his physical abilities made him giddy. Jumping between what amounted to two cars driving down the highway sat firmly in that area of his mind.

Alister copied his grin and shook his head. Atar, however, snorted. All evidence of his earlier panic was gone. "At least warn us, next time."

"Sure. Sure. Hey Atar, I've been wondering something. What exactly are Blessings?" Felix asked. He'd meant to broach the subject earlier, but things had been chaos. "They looked basically the same as Skills in your core space. And the way the Henaari talk about them...well."

He let that last sentence hang there, hoping that Atar would sense his unasked question. Felix wasn't sure how rude it was to accuse one's friend of worshiping an Urge. Vess didn't seem to like it, at any rate.

"Blessings," Atar said. He took a deep breath, as if to launch into some lengthy explanation, then let it all out as a weary sigh. "You know."

"Hard to hide it from the guy who fixed up your core space," Felix said with a shrug. "Mind you, I'm not judging. I certainly don't give a crap about where your abilities come from."

"That is...a relief, I suppose," Atar said.

Alister looked between the two of them, confused. "Atar? What's he talking about?"

"I...no reason to pretend anymore, Alister."

Alister's face eased from confusion to acceptance. "I see."

Felix glanced at their faces. Clearly not many secrets existed between them, but this was not the reaction he'd expected. "Do people hate Urges so much?"

"Many do. It is seen as...false power among the upper Tiers," Atar explained. "Blessings *are* the same as Skills, but they originate with the Urge one has made an accord with...and if the accord is violated, those Blessings may be removed. Forcefully."

Felix grimaced, recalling the anguish he had felt from the former Matriarch. The Raven had pulled its power from her entirely. Or at least, it hadn't resisted when Felix did it.

"Yeah. Those among the conventional powers of the Continent do not condone an accord with an Urge, no matter how benign they may be. The Protector's Guild is one of the few places that are relatively egalitarian in their views. To them, only coin and the influence of status has any weight, and power brings both." Atar shrugged. "I've never been embarrassed about my abilities, or their origins, but caution sealed my lips."

"Believe me, I know the feeling," Felix said wryly. "But I need some understanding of your hometown. Of the people who rule it, and the Urge. The Highest Flame, right?"

"Yes, that is her name. She has an accord with many in Ahkestria, but not all. Still, she is very, very powerful. Were she not, the amount of accords she could maintain would be far less."

"What do you mean?" Felix asked.

Alister answered that one. "Urges are a finite conglomeration of power, and an accord borrows a piece of that power, enhancing your own. Mana and other things that aren't well understood compose their beings, which are largely Cognitive and Ethereal in nature. The strongest of them have a presence here on the Corporeal, but they are rare beings who have amassed some form of sustenance to fuel their being. I doubt even the Endless Raven can manifest itself outside of that little Domain the Henaari carry."

Felix nodded along with Alister's words. It made sense. Urges were born from the collective Intent of beings the world over, and so long as some of it existed, so too would the Urge. "Okay, so that would mean they're diminished by making these accords with people?"

"It does," Atar said, but waggled his hand back and forth. "But there is a return. When someone with their Blessing advances, a portion of that energy is siphoned back to the Urge. So, for those like the Endless Raven —or the Highest Flame, in my case—it behooves them to set up a supportive community and to treat them fairly." Atar grimaced. "That said, it is not...unknown for particularly nasty Urges to prey upon a community and use them up like matchsticks."

Like the Urges I ate. "Why would that be a good idea?" he asked.

"Depends on the Urge. Some revel in despair and bloodshed, and driving a Blessed toward such an end would strengthen it. From what you told me of the Urges you defeated at the Waterfall Temple? Sounds right up their alley."

Felix nodded, putting pieces together. "They were ravaging the populace and growing stronger by it." Felix curled his lip in disgust at the near-perfect memory that flashed through his Mind. Their waterlogged and bulbous forms were something he'd rather not recall in detail. "Glad I ended them."

"Might want to keep the 'Urge-ending' part of your accomplishments quiet once we're in the City," Atar said in a low voice. "The Highest Flame doesn't necessarily rule Ahkestria, but it is a great power and holds sway over half of the Council of Masters."

Felix leaned toward the two mages, eyes intent. "Tell me more about this Council."

———

They ended up talking for another hour or so on the subject of the ruling Council of Masters, as well as the secondary governing bodies in the City of Embers. Turned out there were merchant guilds (four of them, actually) that headed up a Trade Council, and the Priests of the Highest Flame had the Court of the Flame. The former dealt only in economic issues and the latter only in matters of worship, but both were tied intrinsically to the Council of Masters.

Unlike the Gold Ranks of the Guild, the Council was composed entirely of true Master Tiers. Or, as Atar called them, "old monsters." Atar's former Master was a part of the Council, and was confident they would treat with them fairly. Felix certainly hoped so.

The Latticeways extended for miles. Even with his senses, Felix had no clue how close they were coming to Ahkestria. Seven hours in and rapidly approaching sunrise, they still traversed the endless roads. It was not an uneventful journey, however. There were many places where the latticeway was broken or disrupted, and often those were cave-ins or the like, but sometimes it was crystals. Huge, faceted growths would overtake swaths of the road, slowing their progress for a few miles each time. They were all a deep, fathomless blue and shined bright enough to banish shadows completely, while small creatures flitted at the edge of Felix's senses. Bugs and mice, it had felt like.

"Crystallized Mana," Zara had pointed out, the first time they encountered them.

"Really?" Felix had asked. He had felt their potency as a buzzing hum against his skin that only intensified the closer they came. The sense of those tiny creatures also came into focus. There were a lot, but they were all low-leveled and seemed entirely passive. Just beasts living their lives. "Wait. What's the difference between solid matter and crystallized Mana? I thought everything was made of Mana?"

"It is, but what you call solid matter is joined by Essence and the ineffable movements of the Grand Harmony. That is what defines the Corporeal Realm." Zara had gathered up a measure of blue crystals in her hands, floating them on currents of her own liquid-like aquamarine power. "Pure Mana is a distinct vibration of that Harmony, similar to what we all generate within our cores. The more pure it is, the more steps toward solidity it can take."

"So the advancement of our cores from a vaporous shape to more liquid is the same thing? Mana...condensing?"

"Precisely. The Ring Stage is a stage of condensing power, though in practice, it functions a bit differently for everyone. Eventually, your core will harden to a true solid core, increasing its potency once again." The blue crystals chimed in her hands. "Much like this."

Felix had seen solidified Mana before, from the Archon most recently. Before that, the Farwalker had a construct of crystalline Mana in his hut. *Is that the same as these crystals? No, but his construct moved, like the Archon's manipulated Mana.* When he asked for clarification, Zara had only said the truth of it would unveil itself with time. To tell him outright would be to spoil the process itself, she had said.

She did, however, suggest they gather what they could of the crystals. They were condensed water Mana and could be used as a source of hydration, which was a relief to their already straining supplies. A few crystals dropped in their water barrels, and the things had slowly begun to refill. How they sensed the limits of the barrel, Felix had no clue, but the water stopped right before it would have spilled over.

They grabbed as many as they could, and Felix personally snagged a particularly large sample. About the size of a basketball, it barely fit in one of Pit's saddlebags, but he managed to strap it down. His friend was already piled high with Spirit Fruits, Essence Draughts, potions, and his massive Blade of the Fang. Felix supposed the saddle was reaching the limits of what it could store, even on a creature as large as Pit.

For his part, Pit never complained. He was strong and durable enough that the extra weight was barely an inconvenience. Even Felix atop his back didn't bother him anymore, and Felix was heavier than ever. Despite his reassurances that he was "fine" and that Felix should "stop worrying," the Autarch hopped off his Companion as the seventh hour rolled into the eighth. He was more than able to run the rest of the way.

"Converge if you want a rest, bud," Felix offered, pulling his Blade of the Fang free of its saddle-sheath. Pit chirruped warmly at him, but refused. "Alright. I'm gonna check our perimeter again."

As he had at least a dozen times now, Felix sprinted back among the column, senses extended in case any more undead had decided to chase after them. And as he had discovered every single time before, there was nothing. The Latticeways, like Klzix had said, were free of monsters.

"Just a little longer," Atar said, flicking the reins as Felix returned to the front. He jogged beside the mage's wagon, keeping pace without much issue. "Ahkestria is close. I can feel it."

———

Miles back, the last crystal colony in the tunnel glowed with a lush vibrancy. Small creatures, insects and mammals both, drank from the moisture beading along those crystals. The scent and wafting vapor of life hung around the area, richer here than anywhere outside an oasis.

Or it should have been.

One by one, the crystals dimmed. The glow of their power faded from brilliant to merely bright...until the farthest crystals went utterly dark. There, in the fading light, clawed hands and withered limbs prowled.

Jaws of bone and teeth of iron shattered one of the largest growths, sending a ripple of hot air flowing across the colony. More lights flickered and died, their moisture boiled away by an intensifying heat.

"Find...him..."

A Dustborn Wraith, twice as large as those behind it, lurched into the growing dark. The crystals all failed, water vanishing beneath the pressure the creature exuded, and shadows claimed the path. It hissed and began to run. Trailing behind it, the roadway shuddered beneath the tread of many, many more.

"Find...Fe-lix..."

CHAPTER SIXTY-FIVE

"How did you come to the Blades, Pava?" Vess asked.

The two of them ran in the back of the column, and along with the rest of her squad, were meant to keep an eye on their rear. Two other squads were nearby, spread out so that they could better canvas the Latticeway with their Perceptions. Pava was panting, but her Endurance was decent and her Running Skill was nearing level 40; she had plenty left in her, unlike her poor Dwarf and Half-Orc companions. They had been sent ahead to rest in the rear wagon half a glass prior. It was why Vess was there, in fact.

"Oh? I, hah, I saw a place I could earn myself three squares and some real, actual training?" Pava laughed, flyaways bobbing with her steady gait. "Never could get past the Guilder tests, and my mom..."

Vess' heart twisted. She felt the spike of anguish that vibrated Pava's Spirit. It was only a moment, but it was dreadfully familiar.

Pava smiled through it. "Well, she used to worry. But I proved my bladework to the First, and he let me join. After that, it's been training non stop against the monster waves in Haarwatch. Though those stopped right before all that fog rolled in."

"Do you know where the First of Blade received his training? Was he a Guilder?" Vess asked. If Pava did not wish to dwell on her past, then so be it. "I only ask because I've noticed some...flaws in your form."

"Flaws?" Pava asked, but her eyes lifted to gaze at Vess, and she missed the crack in the causeway. She stumbled.

Dragoon's Footwork!

Vess slip-stepped and caught the warrior with a single hand. In a simple, graceful twist, she deposited Pava back on her feet, and their gait suffered nothing more than a slight hitch. Pava stared. At the speeds which they were running, such a fall would certainly tear flesh or break bone.

"You—you caught me, and—" she stammered.

"We all make mistakes. It is up to us, however, to seek out ways to correct those mistakes." Vess kept her eyes ahead and her Perception trained behind them, sweeping for enemies. "Like increasing your Perception stat, perhaps."

Pava blushed, and Vess laughed.

Diplomacy is level 69!

"Perception or a solid observation Skill would do you a great service in remedying the flaws in your sword form. I am not focused upon the blade, but I have studied it for a long time," Vess said with a wry grin. "We could start even while we run here now, if you are willing."

Pava nodded enthusiastically. "Oh please! I would be honored. Let me go grab Asaad and the others!"

She took off, running to her squad before Vess could say otherwise. Ultimately, the heiress shrugged. *What's a few more students?*

———

Evie ran alone. Or tried to, at least.

Scattered along the right side of the Fiend's Claw—she still snorted at the name—Evie kept watch along the racing column's side. Quite frequently tunnels would open up in all sorts of directions, leading to Noctis knows where, and so the squads had started guarding each cardinal direction. Just in case. Evie had been among the first to choose the right hand side of the column, but was soon joined by almost the entire contingent of Frost Giants.

At least they're keeping their distance, she mused sourly. She could have left, could have moved to the left side and guarded there, but stubborn pride didn't allow her to shift her position. She'd chosen this spot, and the giants had moved in without any regard for her opinion. *Why should I leave first?*

They reminded her of many things, but most recent was the assault on her core space. Giants of ice and metal had attacked her core for a reason, at least according to Zara. Her core protected itself from the Essence Draught, and in her confusion imbued her rage and distrust in the System power, forging giants from it all. If she had been able to let go of that rage sooner, to let Magda rest....

It wasn't my fault. I almost wish it was. There was nothing I could have done, Mags. She took a breath. *But it wasn't these particular giants' fault, either.*

The Frost Giants that had killed her sister were all dead, along with their leader. The destruction of the Labyrinth had seen to that.

Sometime after waking, Zara had been there. She had informed Evie that Intent and Affinity and Will determined so much of what was incorporated into one's core spaces. "Chains are how you see yourself relating to the world around you, so chains are what proliferate. Ice and water and metal for the attunements you made, and though I normally advise against three, you have successfully incorporated them into your core."

Didn't do it alone, Evie thought. Could she have, had Felix not helped? She snorted. *Of course I could have. Onslaught and the Shieldwitch trained me personally. I'd be a pretty sorry student if I couldn't do something so simple as advance on my own.*

The lie was a cool balm against her pride, even if Felix hadn't made a big deal out of it. Allowing him into her core space was...well it was intimate and revealing. She had felt excruciatingly vulnerable in the aftermath of her Tempering, but Felix hadn't gloated or even much mentioned what had happened in her core. Evie knew the guy wasn't the sort, but it would have almost been more comfortable had he sneered at least once. Instead, he was just...supportive, same as Vess.

Friends are weird, Evie marveled as they approached another intersection. Growing up, she hadn't had many, not with the way Magda and she had continually bounced around the slums of different cities. Once they'd settled down a bit, their training took up so much time, and fear of Magda's growing prowess had driven away those who tried to draw close. Magda had always been protective of her little sister, and Evie had relied on her for such a long time.

Still do. Magda, or the memory of her at least, was still in her core. She could feel it, though it was faded. The formation of her new Body had drowned out so much of what she had come to understand with her fledgling Affinity and Apprentice Tier Body. The sensation of her new, Adept-Tier Body was almost overwhelming. The System called it the Galvanized Dominion Body. Running was simple and easy, her Stamina barely dipping even after hours of uninterrupted exertion. The efficiency was amazing, her Agility, Dexterity, Vitality, Endurance, and Strength all enjoying big bonuses upon its formation.

She clung to that fading echo of her sister, though. Maybe it wasn't healthy or wise, maybe it would cause her problems in the future when she Tempered again. *Maybe, maybe, maybe. All I got is questions thrown in my face. I don't care that she's not real. Ain't no one gonna tell me when to let go. Wait.*

Something tickled against her senses. Wind from far off coiled at the nape of her neck. It wasn't anything more than a puff against her skin, but Evie bent her Perception toward it.

Down the rightmost side passage, light flashed on metal.

Nighteye!

The world shimmered green, and the darkness fled before her eyes...revealing claws and withered limbs. They screamed, howling as they barrelled forward. Evie hissed. "Undead! To our right!"

At the same time, from all around the Claw, the howls of the undead rang out.

"Undead to the left!"

"—to the rear!"

Discharged Skills lit up the dark, and the howling monsters were met by exploding bolts of lightning and shrieking arrows. To their right, the first of the Dustwights tore into range, and Evie unleashed her chain.

Tooth And Claw!

Her whirling, expandable chain sprouted jagged protrusions all along its length. It normally bore spikes and blades, but these were far larger and barbed, each one a miniaturized picture of violence. Evie twisted, flicking her wrist, and the chain lashed into the front four undead, lodging into legs and hips and chests. She flexed her Will and feeble Intent, though, and the jagged barbs began to spin.

The chain chewed through the undead in seconds before snapping free and returning to her hands.

You Have Killed A Dustwight (x4)!
XP Earned!

Four was a meager number, however, and a tide of Dustwights flooded out of the side tunnels. Their eyes burned with a blackened green intensity, and their withered mouths howled. Tooth and Claw tore through them while her Undine Grace let her flow among the rampaging horde, letting loose with her new and improved Body. Bonds of Dominion, once her Chain Mastery Skill, shined within her core space. The twisting ball of ice and metal links glowed with a furious power as Evie bashed and cut and shattered her way through them all.

Breaking Wheel!

Reap the Maelstrom!

Bindings of the White Waste!

Skills surged from her channels with the ease of long practice and steely resolve. Evie flowed and slid among them, breaking their front line even as they kept pouring over themselves in an unending wave. She quickly lost sight of the caravan, of her friends. She had no clue if the undead were overwhelming them and couldn't spare a single instant to contemplate it; there was only the fight.

There's too many!

More Dustwights, bigger ones now with less withered muscles. Blow after blow made it through her defenses, if only due to the sheer amount of flesh that slammed against her. She was greased lightning in her movements, but they were *everywhere*. A claw dragged her down, tripping her legs despite her careful movements. She hit the ground, rolling up to her feet again.

Bindings of the White Waste!

Icy chains seized six undead around her, halting their movements, but four others ripped through their brethren and struck at her. Her pauldron broke, and Evie screamed as fire lanced across her arm and shoulder. She fell.

"Hoar Hammer!"

A maul of cloudy ice slammed into the undead, crushing them beneath its heavy weight. Ice ripped across another two, freezing them into jagged shards that a second maul shattered. Frozen sand rained all around her, and Evie spun to face the advancing tide of blue-skinned giants. A hand the size of her torso offered itself to her.

"Lady Aren. We are here," Battlelord Ari said. "We will hold this flank."

Before she could overthink it, Evie grasped the giant's hand and let him haul her to her feet. She grunted and took a swig of a Health Potion. "Let's kill 'em all."

Ari nodded. "We shall follow your lead, Chainmaiden."

Evie blinked, but refused to think. She couldn't. There was only the fight.

She screamed as they charged, ice axes and chain meeting undead brawn.

"ATAR OWES ME MONEY!"

———

"Ahkestria is just ahead! Half a league at most!" Atar shouted over the din of battle.

"Keep going!" Felix ordered, wheeling Pit around. "Get everyone out! I'll handle this!"

Pit let out a savage shriek and leaped into the air above the Claw, manipulating air Mana until it sent them rocketing back along the caravan. From the top of the vaulted tunnel—nearly sixty feet high—he could see that his people were running ahead with everything they had, but a number of squads had resorted to running defensive measures. Hordes of Dustwights poured in from the rear and both flanks, but they were being held back...for now.

They ambushed us at the intersection, Felix thought as his Mind whirled through plans and points of attack. *That's...that's way too smart for my liking.*

The right tunnel was being handled by Evie and—surprisingly—some giants. Their tactics were freezing swaths of the ground and shattering the undead before they could advance. In the rear, several squads had gathered under the leadership of Vess and were putting up a powerful effort. Arrows and spells ran amok in that direction.

And to the left, Harn and another three squads were cutting through the horde as they ran. Felix's Voracious Eye burned, and his Mind soaked in everyone's information as fast as he could. The squads were moving, attempting to keep up with the caravan, but already he could see some of them burning through more Stamina than they could afford.

"Pull back! Retreat!" he bellowed, his Journeyman lungs rising above all the noise. "NOW!"

A Skill pattern sung within him, and Felix let it build, marshaling

Mana and Intent within the frothing power that escaped his channels. Clouds manifested before him as he and Pit maintained their altitude, and Felix poured more and more Mana into the spell. As his people disengaged from the horde below, Felix fashioned a present for the undead. He held it, letting them follow his people into the intersection in their multitudinous throng, until everything below him was monster.

Rain of Cataclysm!

The clouds flashed with virulent green Mana before disgorging a torrential downpour. Acid rain tore through the undead, sizzling through skin and muscle and bone and dropping hundreds in seconds. Felix let the kill notifications wash over him, too focused on harnessing his Skill to pay attention to the System. They died below, yet their numbers did not dwindle. Fresh monstrosities raced from the dark, more and more, until his rain could barely keep up.

How many are there?!

Felix focused, sounding his Skill's pattern through the twin focus of Intent and Affinity. Chanting, as he understood it. Rain of Cataclysm was a Skill meant for armies, for monsters that sought to end everything. Memory of his Paths flashed before his eyes, of the great horde that had come for him in that vision of what might have been. The Skill had been so much more powerful in that place, but Felix could remember the texture of it. There had been a *weight* to it.

Trusting that feeling, he siphoned off the significance that dwelled within him, peeling pieces of it from his core space with Cardinal Flame. It was hard to do, but he'd managed it before. Red-gold sigils flared and burst, guiding the weight through him and into the pattern of his Skill.

It convulsed. It *burned.*

The clouds rippled as the power within his channels shifted. Leaden liquid flowed from him in a gush, saturating the clouds of Mana until a wave of dark, almost-black acid poured from the skies. For a few, terrible seconds, each drop hit the earth like a gunshot, drilling into stone as if it were tissue paper.

The Dustwights didn't stand a chance. Even a single raindrop burned through them, skull to spine, and they collapsed as if puppets with their strings cut.

Rain of Cataclysm is level 56!

...

Rain of Cataclysm is level 65!

The horde fell apart. By the time his Skill exhausted the small store of significance he'd sacrificed, the intersection below him and Pit was a pitted abattoir. Acid pooled in shallow craters, and bodies were rendered into flesh and dark, dusty sand. Not a single Dustwight remained.

But there was movement.

Felix narrowed his eyes, and Pit let out an involuntary snarl.

Dozens of creatures stood up, many of them rapidly healing from their acid bath, and all of them too tall and covered in bone plates.

Wraiths.

More stepped out of the side passages, iron teeth gnashing and heads swiveling up. Looking straight at Felix.

CHAPTER SIXTY-SIX

"Hiyah!"

The Avum squawked in fear and distress, but Atar snapped the reins regardless. He had no choice. "Can you see them?" he called out.

Atop the covered wagon, Alister perched precariously with his rapier drawn and extended for balance. He peered into the darkened distance, where Felix and Pit had gone to take on the undead.

"The squads caught back up! Evie and Vess and Harn are at the edges of my Perception, but I cannot make out anything else." The wagon lurched, and Atar's heart did the same. But Alister maintained his footing, only cursing slightly. "I don't know if the monsters are still after us or not!"

"Felix went after them. They're good as dead!" Atar shouted back. "Get down here! We're coming to another intersection!"

Mana Gauge!

Atar swirled his forearm in the air and held it up. Bands of various Mana types swirled atop his arm, though dusty brown earth Mana was the greatest presence. "Left fork! We're close!"

The way to Ahkestria was hidden, the path winding by shifting terrain and complex wards, but Atar knew the path even in these deep tunnels. The readings were impossible to deny, not so close to their destination. Atar's grip on the reins tightened, and his ears strained for any sounds behind them. All he could hear was the creak of traces, wagon wheels, and the countless tread of the Claw's advance. "Felix killed them all. Thank the—AHH!"

Withered Dustwights leaped from the shadows ahead, too close for Atar to swerve around them. The Avum squawked in terror and mowed them down.

Stars of the Sovereign!

Three blazing white stars launched from his outstretched hand, each one trailing a blaze of heat and light. They impacted more undead, ripping through them as if they were made of parchment. Then they exploded, lighting up the looming darkness ahead. Atar's eyes bulged.

You Have Killed A Dustwight (x24)!
XP Earned!

You Have Gained 1 Level!
You Are Now Level 52!
You Have 3 Unused Stat Points!

More came, trampled under the claws of his charging Avum. The frightful heat of System energy built up just above his navel and through his channels. *There's hundreds of them!*

Atar hurled a fourth star to his right, narrowly missing the just-landed form of his boyfriend. Alister fell backward onto the bench and nearly dropped his rapier onto the road. "Blighted Night, Atar! It's me!"

"GAH! Sorry!" The fire mage hauled on the reins, coaxing what speed he could from the frightened birds. "More Dustwights ahead!"

"I see them," Alister said, and despite the chaos, Atar noted his curious tone. He almost sounded *eager*. "I'll reinforce our caravan. Focus on bringing us to the end!"

Alister thrust his two hands, palms out, toward their speeding team. Waves of blue Mana surged from him, barely visible to Atar's senses, and they swiftly congealed into a wide-angled barrier that slammed down ahead of the Avum. It was large enough that it covered most of their caravan before tapering off toward the edges of the roadway.

"I read about these, once," Alister panted, clearly depleted. "Commoners use them for tilling the earth!"

With a deft twist, Alister anchored it all to their wagon, just as they reached the first wave of charging undead. It slammed down, sending sparks flying from the stone and *demolished* the Dustwights.

You Have Killed A Dustwight (x31)!
XP Earned!

Atar's share was far smaller this time, the experience splitting between the Avum, himself, and Alister. The man grinned through the Mana Potion he was swallowing. "It's working!"

Undead threw themselves at their charging column, but none could withstand Alister's shield coupled with the sheer momentum of their charge. Until the damn things started *climbing*.

"Burning ash!" Atar shouted. "*Stars of the Sovereign!*"

White-hot projectiles spouted from his extended palm, burning through those undead clever enough to leap atop the barrier. Most died, heads and shoulders set aflame like kindling. Others were cut through, the Stars acting as burning blades that cut neat holes into their torsos, before flying off to impact the ceiling and explode. Those kept moving and jumped off the top of the barrier.

"Some help would be nice!" Atar screamed to anyone who might be listening. More Stars caught the leaping undead, this time burning through their skulls. They fell to the earth, trampled under claw and wheels until they died. Yet no one from behind answered him. *Are we too far in the lead?*

More climbed, readying to jump at them.

Crown of Ignis!

Atar stood as a red flame crown formed atop his golden curls, filling him with a fearsome might and a giddy, riotous sense of mastery. The Stars around him multiplied, two dozen forming a majestic, rotating constellation around his body. Atar laughed, and that authority within him shrieked in glorious revelry. *This* was how a mage of his caliber should be acting! Atop a charging steed, the fires of creation whirling around him, while his enemies fled before him like chattel. He burned to set them all ablaze.

Stars ignited and sped from him, hitting the vile undead that dared oppose him. They died, the Stars exploding into unsurpassed conflagrations that rendered them as nothing more than charred flesh and slagged glass. None of them could stop his advancement before, and now his magic was all the more potent. It surged in his channels, raw and untamed, the sun had come to burn away all that opposed it. Kill notifications streamed across his vision, and his Crown flared in triumph.

Stars of the Sovereign is level 76!
Stars of the Sovereign is level 77!
Crown of Ignis is level 71!

"Atar! Calm down!"

A hand tugged at the collar of his battlerobes, but Atar slapped it away. "I am in control! Do not interfere with my power!"

A line of red-gold flame, so similar and yet unlike his own might, tangled within his core, leading...backward. *What is THIS? Someone has laid a tether on my Spirit? On my core itself? What treachery—!*

White light flashed across Atar's eyes, a burst of light that sent a shock of cold sensation down his spine. The man in blue had *slapped* him! Fire gathered in his channels as he spun on the bastard mage. "How *dare* you!?"

"Get a grip!" Alister screamed, shaking him by his robes. "The Crown has you! Master it!"

The words, far more than the slap, shook him. Resonated. His Mind shuddered, and without warning, the Crown bucked. Atar gasped and fell onto his ass as all of his Stars blipped out of existence.

"Blighted Night," Atar said, grabbing at his skull. The Crown flickered and vanished from above his head. "How did that get so strong? I thought I had it under control..."

"Doesn't matter right now! I need your help!" Alister grunted as more undead bashed into his force barrier. "This plow is taking everything I have to maintain. Can you muster up the energy to barrage them again?"

"I—yes," Atar said. He realized Alister had the reins as he fumbled for a Mana Potion. Atar had dropped them in his...fit. "Yes. I can do this."

He stood again, but the Crown did not return.

I don't need it, he told himself. *Even if it multiplies the damage my Stars can do...I can't afford to wear it. Not yet.*

Lens of the Magus!

His evolved Skill—once called Focus—allowed him to reduce the Mana cost of his spells, but made them weaker in exchange. But the undead before him weren't powerhouses...they were simply hundreds of them. *Stars of the Sovereign is strong enough. Too strong. I can do this!*

Stars of the Sovereign!

Mana pulses flowed from his blazing core with a fluidity he hadn't experienced before. His Lens hummed within him, a strange sound Atar had never heard so clearly, and the torrent of Mana was split into dozens of gushing streams. Each burst out of him, manifesting into a white-hot Star that hovered about his head. He barely felt their strain.

Stars of the Sovereign is level 78!
Lens of the Magus is level 76!

Atar thrust his palms forward, and the Stars shot forth. Every single one streaked into a Dustwight as it climbed atop the barrier. They didn't explode so gloriously, but there were so many that the creatures were torn apart as easy as parchment.

Arrows joined the effort shortly after, several Henaari Dawnguard racing ahead of the others as they fired shot after shot. Some arrows burst into tendrils of sticky darkness, binding clumps of creatures together, while others somehow multiplied and rained down on the horde like stone-tipped death.

"Yes! Hiyah!" Alister cheered, urging their mounts ahead. "Another fork! Which way!"

Atar hastily checked his Mana Gauge, and pointed to the right. "That way!"

"On it! Brace!"

They turned at speed, the wagon tilting dangerously while the force plow scraped a massive furrow into the road. Sparks flew in all directions while the undead were hurled bodily. The only problem was that this opened their flank to an entire tunnel...and the Dustwights were still coming from that direction as well.

"Dawnguard! Fire!"

Zara's voice shook Atar from the horror that seized him just in time to witness a rain of arrows fall on the approaching mob. Undead fell, darkness and sparking wood bursting among their numbers. He mustered up more Stars, sending them flying into the breach to explode those in the lead, their burning corpses sudden impediments to the rest. Yet he need not have bothered, because a wave of aquamarine power slammed into them shortly after and crushed them into the earth.

All of them.

Zara rode abreast of Atar, her face tight. She nodded. "Almost there, are we not?"

Atar fumbled for words, his Mind still tumbling with the sight of her power. "Just...just about. The next intersection should have a gate or entrance of some kind."

"Very good. We've managed to hold together for the most part. We must make the gate then hold them off until we can open it." Zara glanced backward, and her ugly, scarred Avum snorted.

"Where's Felix?" Atar asked. Stars manifested around him and he threw them over the barrier with little thought. "He went back to—"

"I do not know," she said. Her sharp teeth drew a bead of blood from her bottom lip. "But I trust...I trust he will be along shortly."

Howls shook the air.

Atar gasped, attention pulled forward once again. "It's there!"

He could see it now. A massive ornate gate of dusky metal shaped into a stylized wave. A ramp led up to it, as wide as the tunnel itself. It started to light up as they approached, still three hundred paces distant, but already it gleamed.

And between them was a fresh army of undead.

More than that, tall creatures covered in plates of jagged bone prowled out of the darkness. Their bodies were gaunt and withered, but somehow they glowed with a dark blue luminescence...and crystals surmounted their jagged shoulders. Easily a hundred of the monstrosities were there, flanked by an equal number of common Dustwights.

Atar hurled his Stars at them, and the Wraiths didn't even flinch. They burst against them, explosions of heat and force that made them take a single step back. Their Claw did not stop, and as they drew closer, Atar could see the creatures' wounds were already closing.

"Blood and ashes," Atar whispered. They were closing, fast.

"What in Avet's name?" Alister said. "Those are Wraiths but—"

"Go!" Zara shouted. Atar's eyes snapped to her, and she looked grim. "I will keep them at bay."

Before either of them could argue, Zara and her mount leaped forward, borne atop a massive wave of blue-green power. Her dull brown mount arced over the barrier and landed on the other side, running at full speed. The wave started again, gathering beneath them as she set upon the horde, crashing into them all. Teeth and claws flashed, only to be met by tendrils of Mana that shattered arms and jaws with equal ease.

"GO!"

"Alister!" Atar shouted.

With a scream of effort, Alister altered his barrier. It shimmered and bucked, twisting on itself as it became a simple plane of force, wedging their Claw through the chaos of undead monstrosities. Zara's magic must have helped, because the Dustwights and Wraiths couldn't even close with their column...but that was all Atar could pay attention to; he had come to the gate.

His team stormed up the ramp, the doors now shimmering with sigaldry, and Atar hauled on the reins. The Avum slowed, but not fast enough. They twisted sideways, and their entire wagon smashed into the huge, metal gate. Wheels buckled and shattered.

"Shit!" Atar screamed, shock eliminating the pain he was doubtless to feel later. *If you survive, you idiot!* "Gather close! Everyone! Up the ramp!"

Thunder behind him, Atar glanced anxiously back to see a flickering shield now at their rear. It was blue, but tinged heavily with green now. Alister grimaced, sweat coursing down his face as he quaffed another Mana Potion. "She's helping me hold it, even as she fights...hurry! Open the gate, Atar!"

Wagons and people pressed forward, all of them managing to stop with far more grace than he had, but Atar couldn't focus on any of them. He leaped off the tilted wagon seat and pressed closer to the metal gate.

An array here, and here. It...this means sealed. This is...water and force? Fire and...is that thirst? Atar licked his lips. "I-I can't understand this. It...it requires a key."

"Then break it down," Harn growled. His axe swung into the metal gate, but the kinetic force and even the silver flame atop it was simply absorbed. Dispersed into the metal. Harn stared at his axe, confused. "What?"

"It's absorbing anything used against it," Atar said. A nervous titter rose in his chest, but he pushed it back down. "We can't force it open."

"Think, kid! You know this stuff," Harn urged, turning to grab him by the shoulder. "You're the damned Glyphmaster of Nagast! If you can't figure it out, no one can."

Through his panic, Atar felt a surge of shock and alarm. "You're complimenting me. You never compliment me."

Harn shrugged, then pushed through the gathering crowd. "I ain't lyin', either. But you either open that now, or we might die here."

Atar's guts chilled, and lightning fear raced up his spine. Harn cried out for the squads as he walked back to the barrier, and warriors assembled. Atar looked at Alister, who was mumbling to himself and weaving his shaking hands together, putting everything he had into the shield as undead began to assault it.

We're not dying here, he swore.

"You and you! Can you read sigils?" A man and woman in robes, Hobgoblins both, nodded. "Go, look for anything that resembles a standard opening sequence. You know it? Good. Go!"

Atar poured himself into studying the gate.

CHAPTER SIXTY-SEVEN

Chthonic Tribute!

A storm of Essence and Mana thundered into him as he ran, massive Blade of the Fang slick with molten sands and granular ichor. The blade of the weapon glowed brilliantly with an acid-green virulence, which proved immensely useful in mowing down dozens of the Wraiths at a time. He had killed almost a hundred by that point, butchering at least one with every swing and ensuring their death with liberal uses of his Tribute.

Yet more kept coming.

His Skill levels were stacking up, streaming past his face in bursts. His lesser used Skills got a chance to shine, certainly, all channeled along the length of his Blade.

Wild Threnody is level 74!
Corrosive Strike is level 70!
Arrow of Perdition is level 46!
Green Shaping is level 34!
Rime Shaping is level 37!

Each Skill transformed his weapon as he summoned it through his Wild Threnody, which allowed Mana to imbue his strikes. Rime Shaping expanded the already-huge Blade to twice its width, forming a massive cutting edge of ice that sundered a number of Wraiths. Green Shaping was harder to utilize, only making the Blade glow green-gold. Once it made contact with the enemy, however, woody growths sprouted from their wounds. This not only slowed them, but sometimes ended up binding a few in a tangled nest of vines. Arrow of Perdition, of all of them, had been relatively useless. While the golden-azure energy shined and burned the Wraiths, it didn't affect them like it would a normal opponent.

"They do not contain a core, Felix! That Skill is useless against them!" Karys had buzzed at him.

He soon dropped it in favor of his old standby. Corrosive Strike had fallen by the wayside when he earned himself Wrack and Ruin, now Rain of Cataclysm. Now, however, his Rain had proven too unfocused. Adding the sizzle of acid to his six-foot-long sword meant it cut through them in a much more direct way.

And down there, on the ground, he could rip their Essence out with ease.

"Fee...lix!"

"Find..!"

"Bring!"

They're not stopping, he thought while ducking below another iron-clawed swipe. His own transformed hand tore upward, frost glittering off the tips of his talons and sending a spike of ice up through the Wraith's braincase. *They're streaming out of the tunnels like a river of bone plates and iron teeth. Where are they all coming from? How many of these things does the Primordial have?*

He'd absorbed over a hundred of them already, until his core space swam with diluted pieces of Primordial. Felix had hoped that by consuming so many he would be able to salvage a Memory or even a Skill or two. It was all scraps, however, too shredded and malformed for it to carry anything more than the physical potency of their Bodies. Whatever constituted their Minds and Spirits, or of the Primordial itself, was too mulched to result in anything more than a swelling sense of satiation.

Adamant Discord!

A blast of omni-directional force swept from Felix. He drew on the connections he had to each and every one of the Wraiths, one of shared curse and blood, stronger than most links he made use of; it blasted a full thirty of them in half. Before they could heal, he sent his voice ringing into the air.

"Pit! Lay it down!"

His Companion shrieked, and the area around Felix was suddenly bombarded by thick, eight-foot-tall icicles. The undead annoyances shrieked and skittered backward, only a few slow enough to become impaled. Either way, it allowed Felix to disengage from them with relative ease.

Let's get back to the caravan! he sent to his friend. *This fight is pointless, and I'm worried about what they may have run into!*

Pit sent back a soaring affirmation before he sped off along the ceiling. Felix flared his Agility and Strength and kicked off. The stone roadway shattered and burst, flinging razor-edged debris behind him and into the undead horde.

In seconds, he had left them in the dust.

"Karys! You still there?" he shouted as he ran.

"I am."

"You said the undead didn't have a core. Explain, please."

Karys hummed to himself, the sound transmitting as the droning of a soccer ball sized bumble bee. "They do not need one. They are controlled creatures. Puppets, unable to move without the Will of another. Necro-mantic Mana invigorates their flesh and bones, strengthens them, but it does not return life to them. No Skill, no matter the rarity, can resurrect the dead."

"Puppets," Felix said, stretching out the word in thought. "And their connection to the Primordial is—"

"Very strong. A normal necromancer would have a limit on the range of their control. This Primordial...I cannot get a sense of its limits. Perhaps it does not have them, at least not in the same fashion as you or I."

"A Primordial without limits, how new and exciting," Felix joked. His steps broke the road beneath him, but Felix fought back the wince with each footfall. No one used the Latticeways, regardless.

"Find out if it is a Lesser or Greater Primordial, Felix. I...I cannot recall what that should tell us, but there is something there," Karys said. "Be careful."

The Wraiths appeared to be gaining on him again, and Felix flared his Agility once more. Within his core space, he fed the glut of Primordial Essence into the dark abyss. The pressure of it all vanished. "I'm...unf...I'm always careful."

———

Kuyyt Ma'ar, neophyte of the Temple of the All-Burning Flame, did his best to scrub the Cathedral's floors. His thin arms quivered beneath the strain of his fourth hour toiling atop the white marble tiles and gemstone inclusions. His skin was cracked with repeated exposure to the harsh soaps and scalding waters, split but not bleeding. Never that. If he bled, it would get in the cleansing solution and that...that would be bad.

Kuyyt shuddered. He couldn't help it. *Holy Flame, please forgive me. I shall not spill my blood upon the Walk.*

The Walk of Scintillating Facets had existed since time immemorial. Since the founding of the City, according to the Matrons. It was main-tained by the neophytes of the Temple and contained the Altars of Ancients. He didn't know what the Altars did, or who the Ancients were, as that was not information given to neophytes of the Temple. His role was to cleanse.

So when one of the Altars began glimmering with swirling, sparking vapor, Kuyyt was frozen with sudden fear. Wordlessly, he dropped to his knees and prostrated himself before the Altar, as the vapors of power washed over him. The billowing light tingled against his skin, drawing a pleasantly surprised gasp from his chest. A note, proud and pure, shook through the air like the tolling of a tiny yet profoundly resonant bell. It...rippled his soul.

And then the voices came.

"What in Yyero's blighted backside is this?"

"It's a message array, you uneducated lout! Get away! Hear me! This is Atar V'as, once an apprentice of Sig'nyh Kel'lyv, Grandmaster of the Desert's Fire and sitting Council member! We are under siege! We require you to open this gate immediately! Hello? Hello!"

The neophyte stood on slow, shaky legs. His skin still tingled with the light that caressed him, and his mind was awash with mad voices. This was the work of gods, he was certain. Of She Who Burns. Yet...it spoke of one of the Masters. Trembling, he stepped toward the Altar, screened away like all the others by an intricately carved wall of stone.

Atop an ornate marble plinth shaped as a rising wave of...sand? The shape confused Kuyyt, but he quickly disregarded it, for atop the plinth was a green crystal. The crystal was the size and general shape of his head and polished until it was utterly smooth. From within it, the vaporous light emanated, flaring now with purple lights, interspersed with intense golden shimmers. The lights intensified as Kuyyt drew close, causing him to squeak in terror. But when he opened his eyes, the lights had congealed into an illusory image of a bloody and tousled young man. Their eyes met, and the bloody man smiled.

"Ah! The priesthood! Please send someone down to open this door! Notify the Council! By She Who Burns, I swear we are without guile in this!"

The man's image briefly glowed with a brilliant yellow flame. A testament to his word.

Kuyyt gasped and stumbled away, body clipping the carved wall and skidding across the slick marble tiles. He did not care. *The Matrons must know!*

"Hello? Where did you go?" Atar shouted into the door. The Mana construct that had formed from the door's frame fizzled and popped, vanishing entirely. "Damn it!"

"You scared him off."

"Shut up, Evie," Atar said off-handedly. He'd spent entirely too long frantically searching the door for some way to operate it. The sigaldry was all but impenetrable, however, so dense with restrictive layers that he would need to break them all to get at the opening mechanisms. And if he could do that, he wouldn't need to open the damn thing. "The door won't open. Not from out here. We need someone in the City to open it."

Evie paused after drinking another Stamina Potion. "I thought you said no one knew about these roads?"

"The common folk do not," Atar corrected. He ran his hands through his hair, for once not caring that it made him look a madman. "I am hoping that those on the Council do, however. And that the neophyte we just spoke to isn't as idiotic as he appeared."

The battle was not going well. Zara had fallen back behind their shields before taking them over entirely. Alister had passed out, too strained by the effort of holding that working together. Darius, at least, had woken from his healing slumber and pitched in—his spinning air attacks scythed through the undead without mercy. Vess was out there, as was Harn. The rest of the Claw contributed, too, all of the squads pouring their Skills and Stamina and Mana into the horde, hoping to see the end of the night. Hoping that Atar would save them.

And he'd failed.

Panic clutched at his chest, but Atar shoved it down. He had long since resolved to break down later, when there was time. His elevated Willpower was a boon—if a temporary one—in suppressing his emotions and unhelpful worries. Long ago, his master had told him of such benefits, but Atar had not appreciated their true applications. Now he understood, though he almost wished he did not—it would mean they weren't in terrifying mortal danger.

The shield that Zara had created was buckling. Everyone knew it, most of all Zara. She had...expended herself, somehow, fighting the Wraiths. His heart raced at the thought, and his core churned as a cold sweat manifested across the nape of his neck. For all the vaunted power of the Chant, the unflinching endurance of the Primordial Spawn had exhausted it. His Willpower felt as if it creaked with the force of his emotions.

"She's got the curse," Evie said with a sour grimace. "*Where* is Felix?"

"I don't know!" he snapped. His control slipped and a bundle of lit coals tumbled into his gut. "I don't know! And I don't know how we'll survive, Evie! I don't!" He spun back to the impenetrable door and slammed it with his fists. "Blood and burning ashes! OPEN UP!"

All at once, the sigaldry flashed with green, gold, and deepest blue light. The massive door shuddered, and a section perhaps twenty feet tall and twice that wide...opened at the base.

"Are you kidding me?" Atar whispered. His Mind felt suspended in mud. "I just...had to ask it?"

The opening door blazed with a brilliant, fiery light, and no less than thirty figures in orange robes trimmed in gold. Armor was placed atop the robes, each piece seemingly also made from gold, and they bore staves and blades that raged like tiny infernos. A young woman was in the lead, a Faun with tiny horns atop her head and white tattoos across her brow and cheeks. She stepped forward.

"Who dares step upon the Ancients' Causeway?" she intoned.

Atar and Evie shielded their eyes against the sudden blaze of light, and the mage spoke up. "We did. A special delegation from the north! Help! We are under attack!"

"Who is 'we?'" the Faun asked. "The Causeway is not for the—AAH!" Her eyes widened in alarm, and the weapons of all her associates rose in answer. Atar heard a tremulous note alternating between basso and tinny from them all. "You have brought an army to our gates!"

"No we didn't, you fire-blinded matchsticks!" Evie shouted right back. "We're runnin' from one!"

Only then did the fires among them die enough that the massive barrier was clear...and what lay beyond it.

"Burning ashes," one of them said, and the tremulous note was back. Atar recognized it this time as fear.

"What have you done?" the Faun demanded. "You've led the Cursewinds to our gates? How?"

"Shut up and let us in!" Evie demanded.

"Answer the Disciple!" another said, leveling their burning staff at the chain warrior. Evie didn't even flinch. "You—"

"I am the former apprentice of Sig'nyh Kel'lyv, Grandmaster of the Desert's Fire! I am Atar V'as, citizen of this City, and I demand entry!"

The Temple Guards—for they could be nothing else—went still. The Faun peered at him with wider eyes than usual, as if peeling back the blood and sweat that coated his face. "Atar?"

Atar blinked as well, realizing he knew the woman. "Fiammetta? Thank the Flame, you must let us in!"

"I—" She hesitated then nodded firmly. "Bear witness: I stake my Oath upon this man. We will bring them within."

The others all nodded in unison. "Witnessed and accepted."

The Faun's serious mien broke into a wide, if frightened grin. "Let's save your people, V'as."

Atar felt his chest unclench, and an answering grin spread across his face. Which was when, of course, the shield behind them imploded. The undead surged, slamming into their frontline fighters.

"Get everyone out!" Evie said before leaping up and hurling her chain into the air. Some trick of her Born Trait sent her flying after the weighty thing, straight for the thickest of the battle.

"Go go! Now!" Atar screamed to his people. "Everyone! Into the gate!"

Those nearest him were already running, having watched the interaction go on, but now others turned from the horrifying carnage. Eyes brightened as they ran through the gate, the Temple Guards letting everyone pass with stoic gazes. Atar hefted Alister onto his shoulder, but soon realized a second pair of hands was helping him. Fiametta nodded, and the two of them carried the force mage into the gate before setting him down to the side.

"Ensure no one harms him!" Atar demanded of one of the Temple

Guards, who only raised an eyebrow at him before nodding. Atar tore back into the tunnel, the Faun on his heels.

"What are you doing, Atar? You're a mage, not a warrior!" she shouted after him. "Get into the gate!"

"They need more time!" Atar said, conjuring three Stars between his hands. "Get everyone out, please!"

He took off into the crowd.

———

He's gone mad, Fiammetta thought. *That fire has burned his last sense clean out.*

The Causeway was in turmoil. The men and women raced past her and into the gate—which was thankfully big enough for all of them and more besides—their appearance startling her more than anything else. Half-elves, Hobgoblins, Dwarves, Orcs, Gnomes, burning *Henaari* and *Frost Giants*, of all things. All together.

How? What is this assemblage? Why?

The Faun's Mind raced, positing theories while she ensured that the wagons that rolled up were brought safely within the gateway. She could come to no satisfying conclusions, however, before the flow of people dwindled, and all that she could see was a sea of ruinous undead.

Vile cursed ones, she thought. *How could they come so close? Are the Causeways no longer warded? And...and how...*

Words failed her as no more than six people held back the raging flood of monstrosities. A woman with sea-green hair wove strange, watery constructs that tore apart the enemy while beside her a bandaged man wielded a blade made entirely of white-green light.

Some distance from them was a woman who danced among the undead, silver spears floating and thrusting in a wild, incomprehensible rhythm. That chain wielder was nearby, a graceful force of violence, a whirling dervish that sent the undead falling backward, most severed in half by her spinning chain. A man in full armor wielded axes that sent slashes of silver fire careening through the enemy, a tireless engine of destruction.

And Atar...he *burned.*

White-hot shapes surrounded him, four-pointed conjurations of heat and flame, and they spun in a complicated dance. Any undead who so much as approached was cut apart or set aflame. Often both.

And still—*still*—the undead pushed them back. Sheer numbers could not be overwhelmed, and if her Analyze was not failing her, Fiammetta noted many dozens among the hundreds that were evolved versions of the common Dustwight. She licked her lips, judging the battle, but no calculation she made ensured that she could save these five *and* prevent the undead from entering the gate.

Atar...you brave, stupid man. You still haven't seen how much higher I've risen than you. Dying now...

She had no choice. Fiammetta turned and ran back to the gate. "Morren! Close the—!"

An explosion swallowed the sounds she made, so vast was its roar. Fiammetta skidded across the stone ramp, her armored robes striking sparks from the ground that were likewise overwhelmed by a blue-white radiance. A heat rose in her breast, one that shimmered into two System notifications.

Status Condition: Stunned!
Slowed Cognition For Duration!

Status Condition: Rallying Cry!
Double Regeneration For All Allies In Range for 45 Seconds,
Reduce Chance Of Frightened Status By 50%

What—what is this?

Her head spun. She couldn't figure out how to stand, until two sets of arms scooped her up. A man in full armor, the one with the axes, held her up. The woman with the spears was there, too.

"Ho there, kid. Best not to linger," he grunted.

"Wha'?"

The spearwoman looked back, and her face flickered with that blue-white illumination. "He arrived just in time again. I have a feeling he has grown a taste for the dramatic."

"Not gonna argue with a good Rallying Cry," the armored man said. They were still dragging Fiammetta toward the gate. She valiantly marshaled her Willpower and planted her feet. "Hm? Kid, I don't recommend stayin' here. Felix is good, but he can't hold all of 'em."

Fiammetta shook her head against the clinging tendrils of her Stunned condition and turned.

She gasped.

A figure stood behind them on the Causeway, a massive sword in his grip and lightning—*lightning!*—playing about his body in brilliant arcs. The undead were burning and dying in droves, their withered bodies bursting apart whenever that strange energy touched them, and not even the evolved versions could draw close enough to harm him.

One man held back a horde of nearly a thousand undead.

Who are *these people?*

CHAPTER SIXTY-EIGHT

"Close the gate!"

Felix hollered with all of his Journeyman lungs as the Dustwights threw themselves at him. He paid them little mind. They couldn't penetrate his Armored Skin, let alone his transformed hide, and his Blade of the Fang reaped them like wheat. The Wraiths were more of a concern, but that was why he was still running his Adamant Discord. He had to pulse the Skill to take care of the more powerful undead, but the rest were tossed about like leaves in a storm. The glut of galvanized links filled the tunnel with crackling light, each tie to the undead snapping in such quick succession it felt like he was inside one of those plasma balls you could buy at a mall.

Just way, way more violent.

Flesh burst and sand scattered with each pulse of his Skill, the Mana ebbing and flowing within his core as his regeneration replenished what it depleted. He could hold them back for a while, even with the extra effort the Wraiths cost him.

A plaintive warble came from within his Spirit, but Felix quashed the argument before it could begin. "I know you want to fight, but now's not the time!"

I am growing! the tenku sent.

"I know you are, but...there! See?" Felix's gaze flicked back toward the distant gate. The smallish section at the bottom had started to slowly close. "They're all in and closing up! Either you fly ahead without me, or stick around, and we'll get in together. Your choice!"

Fine, Pit chirped. It was weird, hearing the sheer *sulk* in the sound.

Felix grinned, too relieved to feel bad. He dropped his Adamant

Discord and kicked off the stone. Cloudsteps formed beneath his feet, pushing him back ten and then twenty feet as he accelerated. *Time to go!*

A bellow like a dying, thirty-foot walrus shook the air. Stone dust drifted from above, and even Felix winced at the utter volume of the cry. He looked back toward the horde and spotted another undead.

"What the actual fuck," he hissed to himself.

A huge, hulking creature on par with the largest of Frost Giants ripped through the horde of undead. Its body was covered in bone plating and cruel, hooked barbs along its shoulders, back, and the outside of its limbs. Many of them even glowed a deep blue and looked...almost crystalline. A face that was nothing more than a dark, iron skull roared at him.

It looked like a gladiator from hell.

Voracious Eye!

Name: Dustborn Behemoth
Type: Primordial Spawn (Lesser)
Level: 73
—

He'd barely had time to read the notification when the Behemoth tore through the crowd of undead. Sand and limbs flew in all directions, its barbed spikes catching and ripping through its alleged allies. The thing was *fast*, too—Felix barely had time to bring his Fang to bear, but he managed. The Blade shimmered bright green, and Felix brought the sword up in a diagonal slash across its chest and knocked the thing back a single step.

It didn't even flinch.

Still roaring, the Behemoth caught Felix in a devastating backhanded slam. Committed to his own attack, Felix had no choice but to take it head-on, and he gasped as he was crushed into the roadway. The ground cratered around them both, and his gasp became a shout of pained surprise. Blood splattered from his nose and mouth.

Faster than Felix could track, the Behemoth swung down again. And again. Each time smashed him farther into the crater.

Status Condition: Broken Rib (x3)
Status Condition: Internal Bleeding
Status Condition: Punctured Lung

The Behemoth opened its massive, iron jaws and roared in triumph. It slammed both fists down a final time, exploding the ground for twenty feet in all directions. Stone dust obscured the crater, and the cacophony of the other undead quieted to a low rumble.

"Ooh ow, my bones, ahh," Felix rasped, as he rose from the gel-like stone just outside the attack's range. The rock firmed beneath his feet, and he wobbled, holding his ribs gingerly. "I'm giving you shit, but that hurt a *lot*. So, uh, credit where credit's due."

"FEEEELIX!"

"Oh, I don't like that you can all talk," he muttered. The Behemoth's muscles bulged, snapping through several of its bone plates, and it leaped forward. "Nope! Not today!"

Adamant Discord!

A cord of connection, larger and thicker than all the rest, snapped into place between them. Felix shoved, hard, and the kinetic force and lightning demolished the Wraiths beside it. Yet the Behemoth was only forced back by a single, staggered step.

"See ya!" Instead, Felix was sent hurtling back with all the force he had mustered.

Felix grinned as the world was whipped into blurring shapes. Perhaps he could have fought the thing, but he wasn't willing to try. Not at the moment. With a grunt, he shoved his hand down onto the ground below, jamming his talons into the stone ramp as he flew. Four narrow furrows ripped into the stone, slowing him down until he jerked to a sudden stop just outside the gate.

Can't believe that worked, he thought as he stared at his hand. His talons were a bright, cherry red and sizzled in the air. He looked at the Behemoth, who was only now recovering from the staggering shot of his Adamant Discord. Felix raised his still-sizzling talon and flipped the damn thing off.

Pit squawked in alarm, and Felix hopped backward, ducking under just as the gates closed.

Through the split second the huge gate door was swinging closed, the Behemoth rushed forward. Its massive bone claws hit the metal gate hard enough that Felix flinched backward, and the damn thing *dented*. Someone screamed. Cracks spread across the inside of the gate, though it was closed, spreading wider and wider as the furious impacts hit one after the other.

"Out of the way!" someone shouted, and a man in golden armor and an orange tabard shoved his way toward the side of their strange chamber. Felix felt the whisper song of a Mana Skill, and the sounds cut off completely. A complex network of arrays ignited within the chamber, cutting off all sound and arresting the cracks before they spread. The man nodded at the gate. "There. Bastard is cut off."

Felix wiped a smear of blood from his nose. "Well. That was..." He paused and quaffed one of his heavier duty Health Potions before checking his Status. His ribs had mostly healed, and the internal bleeding and punctured lung had gone away thanks to his accelerated Health regeneration when he held Sovereign of Flesh. It had eaten through a *lot* of his Essence, but Felix wasn't about to complain. With a sigh, he let his transformed skin fade back to normal. The cracked ribs would heal up eventually, but he sensed new people among them. Terrifying midnight scales and fangs weren't the best icebreakers.

The entirety of their company was contained in the long chamber, though it was a tight fit especially with the space the Frost Giants took up. Felix didn't sense another door or even passages beyond the walls of the space, but the wards could have been throwing off his Perception. It wasn't worth worrying about just then, so he sought out his friends instead. "How is everyone?"

Atar, Vess, Harn, and Zara were the closest, and all four were in bad shape. Wounds covered their exposed skin, and in the case of Harn, his armor was dented all to hell. Zara especially looked bad, and Felix's nostrils flared in recognition.

"Shit, Zara——" he started, but she cut him off.

"I'm fine for now, as are our people. The efforts of the Claw have proven more solid than I hoped. Few were injured, and only a single death," she said. Felix felt the last word like a blow to his gut. He had feared it, but hearing the results of their fight was a burden he'd hoped to avoid. "I believe we have other, more immediate concerns."

The Naiad's eyes flicked sideways, and Felix saw a young...deer-woman step out of the crowd. Around her were six Humans in similar armored robes in orange and gold. Both shades were almost precise replicas of how the Mana for fire and light looked to his Manasight. The deer-woman cleared her throat.

"Right. This is Fiammetta, a Disciple of the Temple of the All-Burning Flame," Atar said wearily. "Fiammetta, this is——"

"A representative of the Territory of Nagast," Zara interrupted, a hitch in her voice. The way she was holding a hand to her side concerned Felix, but he didn't miss what she was doing. He nodded at the deer-woman.

"A pleasure to meet you," he said and activated his Voracious Eye. The woman was a Faun, a sort of deer-person in the same way Zara was a water-person.

Lore: Fauns are believed to be descended from nature elementals in the First Age, and often have characteristics in common with the bestial creatures of the wilds. A nomadic people, little is known of their deeper histories, even to themselves. Much as Goblins and Hobgoblins are close cousins, many believe Fauns are closely related to Alseids, Nixies, and Naiads.

All in all, cool information that told him relatively little. She was level 61, had less than half of his own Health total, and hadn't yet fully reached Journeyman Tier. Why she was in charge was a mystery, as he could sense the others with her were all well into that same level of advancement. *Perhaps,* he thought, *there are other considerations for leadership in the Temple.*

"Nagast," the woman said, slowly. "I have heard of this Territory. It caused quite the commotion recently, did it not?"

"So I hear," Felix said, shaking his head. His Mind spun, and his Deception flared within his core. "I'm Silas Veil, diplomatic representative sent on behalf of the Autarch of Nagast. The commotion you mentioned is exactly the reason we've been sent on this mission."

"And what mission is that?" she asked, her bright eyes peering into Felix's own. "And how did you access the Latticeways? All proper entrances are sealed."

Felix smiled, but evaded the question. "Trade is of interest to us. Perhaps more...but I believe all else would be better discussed with your Council."

The Faun's expression tightened, and her Spirit trilled. Wariness and excitement flared beneath her agreeable facade. "Of course. Devoted Tem?"

"Aye, Disciple," said one of the golden armored warriors, before he walked over to join the man that had enacted the wards. Felix's Perception flared, and he spotted thirty-two of them interspersed among his Claw. Shifting very slightly on the balls of his feet, Felix prepared himself for whatever these warriors were going to attempt. The two warriors by the gate held their gauntleted hands over a rotating Mana construct that had extended from the wall. "By your leave, Disciple."

"Let us rise," she said. Her voice and Spirit were matched in relief and joy as she grinned at Felix. "I believe you will enjoy this, Representative Veil."

The ground lurched beneath his feet. A series of startled oaths tore from his Legion, even more so when the odd sensation of movement began to press at them all. Felix felt a touch of nostalgic wonder as he realized he was in a giant, industrial elevator.

"Mind the sides," a few of the warriors said, shepherding folks away from the now-moving walls.

"A lift?" Vess asked. She peered at the walls and the complex, flashing threads of sigladry that fluttered past them with gathering speed. "The power required to move so many at such speeds is considerable. How do you afford it?"

"These lifts are not available to the wider populace," Fiammetta said. "The cost of their operation is handled entirely by the Temple."

"Because the populace doesn't know about the Latticeways," Atar said, grimly. "Why not?"

"It is not my place to question the orders of the Matrons, nor the Council of Masters."

Felix kept his face mild, but his Spirit rumbled. He didn't like the feeling the temple and Council were giving off already. *If they're as corrupt as the Guild and Inquisition....*

Either way, Felix was not going to be caught unaware ever again.

The elevator sped up, powered by a prismatic swirl of Mana types, but primarily deep blue water and lighter blue force Mana. Felix thought that strange, especially in a desert, but the thought stalled out as they emerged into the light of day.

"Siva's Grace," Vess gasped.

"It's beautiful," Evie said.

Harn grunted. "Eh."

The walls of carved metal and stone had vanished, replaced instead by a sheath of transparent crystal. Through the crystal, Felix could see the Expanse spread out in almost every direction, save for directly behind them. That was dominated by a craggy tract of a mountain, barely lit in the pre-dawn dark. They rose along an elevator shaft fastened to the outside edges of a huge edifice, so big Felix couldn't get a good sense of its true dimensions. Instead, his vision was arrested by the dark night. Stars wheeled in the black sky, brighter than they had appeared from the desert's sands—thick swaths of distant fire that paled in comparison to the moons already dominating the heavens.

Yet all of that was distant and frankly hard to see through the crackling sandstorm that surrounded them.

"The Cursewinds?" he asked in alarm, but as they rose through the storm, he realized it bore none of the torpid aggression he'd sensed before.

"No, these are the unique defenses of our City of Embers," Fiammetta said proudly. "The single greatest Blessing ever bestowed upon our people. It protects us from the dire Cursewinds and repels those who have...less than honorable intentions with Ahkestria."

The sandstorm was thick with earth Mana, but even more so, it was filled with searing flashes of fire. It felt hot and protective to Felix's senses, and the Mana would have been blinding to him only a few months prior. Now his Manasight picked out the strange flows of power swirling around them, enough that he could tell how utterly complex it all was. The storm was a tightly woven net that rarely repeated any sort of pattern, except for occasional knots of earth and fire and purple augmentation Mana. Even those were sporadic and appeared randomly in the swirl of dire winds and corrosive sand granules.

"I have never stood so close to it," Atar said from beside Felix. He coughed. "It's beautiful."

"The Highest Flame Blessed us all with its creation, and the Matrons maintain it daily with their mighty power," Fiammetta said. The Faun looked at Atar and pursed her lips. "You are quite fortunate that a neophyte was cleaning near the Altars of Ancients when you activated the messaging array. Luckier still that the Matrons deigned to send us to greet whoever had lost themselves on the Causeway. Perhaps the Highest Flame has Blessed you more than you ever acknowledged."

Atar smirked. "Perhaps."

Felix frowned but ignored their banter. There was history there, and he didn't care to piece it together, not now. If Atar wanted to share, he would do so later. Instead, Felix's attention was taken by the glimpses of the Scorched Expanse he could make out beyond the storm. The dunes rippled, carved by winds and painted by soft moonlight and blue shadows. They were frozen waves, like Evie's core space. A huge sea, like how Klzix had described it being in the past.

Did the Primordial cause the sea to dry up? If so, why? And why hasn't it shown its face yet? That last part was frustrating Felix more and more. Not that he wanted to go head-to-head with another Primordial, but the fact that he had no idea what the creature wanted or planned to do. Add in the fact that it was hunting him specifically, and it was all Felix could do to keep his skin from crawling right off. The direct clashes he could weather but his people getting caught in the crossfire was unacceptable. *And now we have the Behemoth. That thing was strong, too. If this Primordial sends more of them, we're screwed.*

He drummed his fingers against his thigh as the elevator rose higher and higher, and the storm outside intensified. The light of the moons could no longer penetrate the covering, but Felix noted a steady glow from their rear. He turned toward the cliff face they climbed and was surprised to see the rock give way to gargantuan crystalline shafts of solid Mana. A ripple of awe went through the Claw, while the Temple Guards all smiled.

"Now *that's* impressive," Harn said.

Felix could tell now that what he beheld was a mesa, a huge table of stone in the middle of the desert. Except the top third of it was composed entirely of solidified Mana, all of it colored the deepest blue and a vibrant green-gold. Water and life Mana surged through his Manasight, smelling of old stories and petrichor and tasting of a long nap on a summer's evening. People around Felix, especially those with higher Mana pools, found themselves wobbling on their feet from the sheer immensity of pure Mana before them.

Then they rose higher, and crystalline pillars were clearly delineated from the bulk of the mesa. Each pillar supported a stone platform, which in turn supported another and another, clusters buried in stone utterly beyond Felix's ability to affect with shaping. He couldn't even tell what Tier it was, only that his efforts would likely shatter the teeth of his Skill. And atop it all, came the City.

Ahkestria, City of Embers.

The lowest layers were obscured by thick, granite walls, but the elevator rose rapidly past them. Atop those, four other layers were more open to the skies and sun through a series of clever passages and skylights. Buildings hewn from the rock itself filled the layers, extending in deep, complex neighborhoods filled with the dim lights and thin cookfires of people only just waking up. Up and down the streets, solidified crystals of orange and gold seemed to grow naturally all around the city.

"Fire and light Mana, solidified by the tireless efforts of our powerful ancestors," Atar said with pride. His face glowed with a measure of happiness at seeing his home—it was nice to see, even if it sent a pang of jealousy through Felix's chest. His own home had never felt quite so far.

"Those crystals are more precious than anything in the wider Continent, you know. Even here, they would have been hoarded if they could be moved without destroying them entirely." Atar laughed, and the happiness shifted into a faint bitterness. "So the Council decreed that they were to be used to spread light and warmth throughout the city. A boon, they call it, ignoring the fact that the light does not reach all layers of Ahkestria."

"What?" Felix asked, but the fire mage just clenched his jaw.

"It is what gives the city its name," Fiammetta said. The pride in her home was also clear, but it burned like a sun next to Atar's moon. "The City of Embers, glimmering through the night. Beacon of the Scorched Expanse."

"I'm thinkin' all the fires help, too," Evie pointed out.

They had reached the very top layer, the one exposed to the sky above, and huge golden braziers were placed around towering edifices of crystal and stone. Soaring structures surrounded this area, many of which were contained by high walls and clear defensive structures.

Felix found that odd. Those braziers burned with bonfires that lit everything. Felix could almost imagine the heat they threw off. In the far distance, perhaps miles away, the swell of what must have been a palace dominated the skyline. Its very tip was alight with flame as well, and this one fluttered against his senses with more than just heat.

Exploration is level 65!

The elevator slowed and came to a soft, hissing stop.

"Welcome, envoys of the Territory of Nagast, to Ahkestria." Disciple Fiammetta spread her arms and stepped toward another metal gate as it opened into the city. "May your Flame burn in the Night."

She gave Felix a slight bow. "If you would deign to follow me, I shall arrange quarters for you and your people."

Felix pasted on a smile and nodded back. "Lead the way."

CHAPTER SIXTY-NINE

The Claw left the large industrial elevator and found themselves within a squat building at the very edge of the Risen Ward, as Atar informed him the topmost layer of Ahkestria was called. The building itself was simply a series of empty storerooms and service hallways that led out onto a shallow portico. Columns of orange stone rose all around them, their centers striated with more of those ember-hued crystals. They gave off a cheery glow that lit their way down the steps and onto a wide thoroughfare.

Fiammetta led the way, and Felix did not miss how her Temple Guards spread out among his people. They acted as shepherds, corralling his Claw without seeming to, and though he didn't sense any malice in them, Felix could hear a dense wariness that strummed through every single one of their Spirits.

What are they afraid we'll do, exactly? The Continent wasn't exactly a trusting place, so perhaps that was the full extent of their wariness. Who could be comfortable with having a foreign militant force in their home? *I suppose we don't look all that peaceful.*

The Fiend's Claw was bedraggled and bleeding, but their faces were fierce, and their weapons were all to hand. Felix silently cheered the grit that drove them, even though he knew many were only steps from exhaustion. No. They did not look peaceful or compliant, and that was fine with Felix.

The streets were empty of people, the few hours remaining before dawn proving the darkest and quietest. The opulence of the Risen Ward also lent itself to that impression—there were no bakers or laborers up at ungodly hours to begin their days. The topmost level of the city was filled with the rich and their servants, though perhaps Felix would begin to sense the latter rushing about in the coming hours. For now, it was deathly still and filled with the thump and clatter of their boots and wagons.

"These crystals..." Felix ran a hand over the nearest example of blooming Mana crystals. They hummed with a potent fire, banked behind its strange matrices. "They're beautiful."

The wide streets, paved evenly with huge slabs of white stone, were lined with the crystalline growths. Some were simply waist-high clusters, while others towered twice the size of the two story buildings around them. Every one appeared as flowers or fountains of crystal growth, none the same yet all grown in line with some sort of aesthetic.

"I am impressed," Zara admitted. She walked by Felix's side, just behind the Faun. "The power needed to shape such purified Mana would have been extremely taxing." *Even for me*, her words suggested. "To compress enough to manifest even a handful of Mana is a feat worthy of legends. Most will never reach such heights."

"The founders of our City were the strongest of their Age," Fiammetta said. The conviction in her voice was a literal heat in the air—from her channels, Felix spotted wisps of heat Mana escaping to swirl around her form. "The knowledge of their making is lost to all but the Matrons and perhaps the Council, but few could replicate the founders' feats. Instead we thank their departed Spirits for the boons that light our lives, and we give glory to their memory."

Felix remained silent as they kept walking. Most streets appeared very similar, with wide avenues for traffic and smaller sidewalks for pedestrians. Forty to fifty-foot walls were everywhere, blocking the sightlines of the Ward as each estate they passed did their best impression of some warlord's citadel. Opulence shown in the stone and metal used on the walls, all of it Tier III or higher, with filigree and gemstones inlaid along the tops and surmounting the small watchtowers.

"Who lives in these estates?" Felix asked.

"Those are the mansions of the Patricians of Ahkestria," Fiammetta said. "A vital force to our City's wellbeing and economy."

The woman obviously had great pride in her city, but the longer Felix listened to her, the more she sounded like a tour-guide. Atar laughed. The sound was loud in the still night, and the red-headed Faun snapped her gaze to him.

"You mean merchant lords," Atar said, ignoring the narrowed eyes of their guide. "They're the backbone of power in the City. The unofficial third council, if you will, behind the Masters and the Matrons."

Felix kept his expression bland, but wanted very badly to roll his eyes. "Merchants, Masters, and Matrons? Was that intentional?"

Atar shrugged, a grin tugging at his lips. "I didn't name them."

"Representative Veil, while the Patricians..." She emphasized the word so hard Felix could hear the capital letter. "Hold a great deal of power in our city, they are by no means a guiding force. That is the role of the Matrons of the Highest Flame."

"Then shouldn't I speak to them instead of the Council?" he asked.

Fiammetta flushed, the freckles across her deer-like nose vanishing for a moment as she stammered. "O-of course not. The Matrons do not speak to those who—that is, ahem." She straightened her robes and faced forward once again. "The Council deals in matters political. If you've spiritual concerns, then by all means please come to the temple and seek out my fellow Disciples."

In a low, almost sub-audible tone, Atar muttered. He was clearly addressing Felix, trusting that Felix's Perception would pick it up easily, which it did. "The Matrons influence things more than they like to admit. The Council is not under their thumb, but that isn't how they see things. It's simply considered rude to point it out, among those in the know."

More politics. Felix kept his sighs to himself and listened with half an ear as Fiammetta kept rattling off the highlights of living in Ahkestria. *I imagine if I'd introduced myself as the Autarch, our party would be steeped in even more politics. Masquerading as a representative should be enough.*

It was decided among their team that arriving as the Autarch could prove...complicated. Outside of his powerbase, even with the support of his small army, he would present a ripe opportunity for an attack. The Continent-wide notification had painted a target on his back, after all. His Authority did not work outside his Territory. No strange rituals and spells were at his fingertips, nor deep wells of power from the System itself. Here, he was just a mortal man.

Or so they thought. And according to Vess, Deception was Diplomacy with the edges rubbed off. Power was perception, even in a world where people could shatter stone and bend metal with their bare hands.

Felix still wore his Veiling Amulet, which kept him from being Analyzed by anyone below Master Tier. That meant they'd have to give up the charade eventually—Felix very much doubted the Council of *Masters* would be fooled by it for long. But even Zara approved of keeping as low a profile as they could; they weren't really here to broker some trade deal with the Council, after all.

In the distance, Fiammetta pointed out the rising tower of the Temple of the All-Burning Flame, and the relatively squat shape of its neighbor, the Council Rotunda. Both of them were blocks away, at the far reaches of the Risen Ward, and not their current destination. That lay just beyond a large round common area, one that was dominated by a huge water fountain.

The fountain centerpiece was a statue formed *entirely* of Mana crystal, ranging in colors from orange and blue to green-gold and white-green. Fire, water, life, and air all intermingled, grown into the shape of a tremendous warrior bearing two spears that glinted with the deepest colors of water. Their features were muddled, either by the medium or by time itself, but Felix wasn't really paying much attention. His eyes were instead on the gates of a small estate that had been thrown open.

"Welcome, Representative Veil, to your accommodations for your stay. You and your staff have the run of the compound, though for safety's sake, my Temple Knights will provide security."

Fiammetta's words drew Felix up short, and his attention flowed to the men and women who stood along the courtyard as the Claw entered. All of them were wearing heavy golden armor and bore swords, shields, and halberds.

"When will we meet your Council?" Vess asked.

Fiammetta's eyes snapped to the spearwoman, easily her opposite—tall, dark, and possessed of a casual strength that the Faun hadn't missed. The girl had peered at all of them on the overly long journey to this walled estate, likely gathering as much information as she could.

The redheaded Faun only smiled. "The Council will convene in the afternoon, once the worst of the day's heat has passed, as is their way. I shall send a messenger to you all when your meeting will occur, but I imagine they will wish to greet you with as much haste as they can manage." She gestured, and the thirty-odd guards began filing out of the heavy front gates. "The gates will close and seal behind me with a net of wards designed for your protection. Please do not be alarmed. They are merely a precaution against the Cursewinds."

"The Cursewinds do not reach the Risen Ward," Atar said. His expression was mild, but his Spirit thrummed with anxiety. "I am not aware of—"

"Much has changed in your time away, V'as," she said, her excitable voice subdued. She blinked, blanched, and drew herself up to her full height. "I will leave you to rest. Good evening, Representative Veil."

"Good evening," Felix murmured. He watched Fiammetta and her team exit and the gates close with a slow, inexorable boom. Arrays flared along their lengths, six or...no eight layers of them. His gaze returned to the Knights, who were still posted on the walls but had their backs to the inner portions of the estate.

"Feels like a trap," Evie said. Her fingers squeezed at her chain. "Don't like the look of those Knights or those wards."

"She wasn't lying about sealing us in," Atar said. His voice was weary, as if his earlier anxiety had worn him out. Or perhaps all the fighting they had just pushed through. "I *believe* I could unlock them, but I'd have to figure out the ward key."

Felix waved a hand at the gates. "I don't care about them. Not now. Zara, Harn." He looked to his mentors. "Gather all the injured within the main hall, here. Atar, do you have enough juice to muffle the sound?"

"Yeah, think so," the mage said. "I'll help get everyone in—"

"No, we have this," Vess said, putting her hands on Atar's shoulders. "Go inside. I will bring him in."

Atar sagged, slightly. "Thank you."

Felix frowned at the Knights, who were very obviously and pointedly *not* listening to them. He was positive they heard everything. "Move, people. We all deserve some rest."

———

It took Felix about an hour to devour the Primordial curse from all the afflicted, see to the healing of those with more serious wounds, and ensure that everyone had a bed to sleep in. Well. He accomplished the first part relatively quickly, and the rest was just trusting his friends to do what was best. Zara and Vess—tired as they were—both oversaw the healing of the Claw, while Harn and, surprisingly, Palin had proven to be a pair of deft hands at distributing supplies and quarters.

So it was all too soon that Felix found himself settled within the master chamber of the estate. He and Pit were cuddled together on a massive bed that, while extremely soft and inviting, was nevertheless not equipped to withstand their combined weight. It creaked alarmingly with every shift or restless kick Pit made, which had Felix feeling more tense than ever. It felt like a violent sneeze would send the whole thing crashing down. So he laid there, wide awake and staring at shadows playing across the coffered ceiling.

He felt tired, sore, and a little guilty.

Felix had waited to use his Chthonic Tribute until they were well out of the range of unfamiliar eyes...but he had not liked doing so. His people were in pain, and it chafed that he had to be so secretive. Zara had approved of the move, obviously, as she maintained that one could never know what knowledge the enemy had at their disposal. Last thing he wanted was to be associated with a Primordial, and Chthonic Tribute had the Maw's stink all over it, even now.

Do the people here even know a Primordial is attacking people? That it's controlling the Cursewinds and the undead hordes? His Mind rolled through his memories, to what the Prioress had said to him. *She didn't know they were Primordial Spawn, either. So either they can't Analyze that part of them, or the creatures are new arrivals...but I'd bet on the former. The Revenants had also hidden their Type, back in Haarwatch.*

The real question was whether he wanted to announce the details of their foe to the Council later. Doing so would require proof, he imagined, if the Council was ignorant of the threat. If they were not, and were simply keeping it under wraps...Felix wasn't sure what the point would be in revealing his knowledge.

He sighed, and the bed groaned. Felix had a feeling remaining anonymous in Ahkestria was going to be troublesome, but he only had to maintain it for a few days. Once the sun rose, they would be able to start quietly canvassing the city and searching for evidence of the Minotaur. Felix doubted the guy would be hard to find; a seven-foot-tall bull man would likely stick out like a sore thumb.

Nothing to do about it now. Just rest, you idiot.

Felix took a soft, steady breath—careful not to rock the bed—and flared his Meditation Skill. It soothed him as he laid there, trying to sleep. The familiar pattern of the Skill was a calming song within him, coupled with one of his first memories on the Continent: of the Kingsap Tree where he had sheltered during his first, terrifying night. The recollection was warm and comforting, even if Felix had moved so very far away from the man he had been in those early days.

Yet his core space was distracting. Spinning large and fast near his dual cores, two Skills in particular were giving off a faint keening sound, like a tea kettle about to boil. Relentless Resolution and Sovereign of Flesh, both of them a single level off of Tempering into Adept Tier—the final barrier to forming his Adept Body and fully advancing to the next stage of power.

Felix scowled at them, spinning like slow gas giants in the multicolored light of his cores. He had used both Skills *extensively* since leaving his Stronghold, yet they refused to shift over that final gap. Felix had a sinking feeling that neither required brute force or stress, but something else. A fundamental understanding, perhaps.

Sleep refused to come, so he gave himself over to such musings. He started with the easier of the two.

Relentless Resolution was about primal movement. Beyond thought or reason, it was his Body's reaction to the world around him. In its previous form, it had drawn on his Willpower, but now it drew deeply on his Perception and Affinity. There were even hints of Evasion, Might, and Felicity in there, swirling among the convoluted patterns of the Legendary Skill.

The higher the rarity, the more complex his Skill patterns appeared— Felix could feel them like unfinished songs, and the further their rarities rose, the more complete they sounded. But it also meant there was more nuance than Felix could parse with a simple investigation, even from within his core space. At the very least, he knew all of those stats and information from the outside world was gathered and fed directly into the Skill, which translated it all into direct physical motion.

He had thought that absorbing more information, reacting, and fighting would advance the Skill. It had, to an extent. As he'd learned to press his stat advantage to its limit, he'd moved forward in a number of Skills, but the final level before Tiering up was always a struggle. It was like the System wanted to make sure he knew this was *important.*

The most curious feature of Relentless Resolution was one it shared with several others. Deep Mind, Meditation, and even Oathbinding were all connected by a delicate tracery of linkages to the hub that was his Bastion of Will. On a whim, he descended into that Skill, the only one in his core space that held a tiny little world within it. The patterns parted to reveal a curving landscape of green forests, fields, and distant craggy mountains near a familiar sea. Centered within it all was a squat fortress of dark stone. His Bastion.

He landed there, atop the sole tower, and assessed the area.

A silver needle extended beside him, reaching up and stabbing into the sky. Ephemeral, multi-hued strands of light passed through that needle, coming from all directions like a spiderweb. It was his Oath-binding rendered into a semi-real form; a manifestation of the connections that Felix had established and continued to grow. A quick glance told him this one belonged to the Frost Giants, and this one belonged to the Nagafolk, both of them thick and potent. The connections sang in a muted, sub-audible sort of way, humming at the edges of his senses. Felix ignored them for now.

The tower beneath his feet was the binding point for the Skills that had glommed onto his Bastion. With a minor flex of Will, he rose into the air and descended down to the inner bailey, rotating all the while around the full circumference of his tower. The structure was not round, but faceted with five flat planes. Three of the sides were marked with the pattern of another Skill: Relentless Resolution, Deep Mind, and Meditation. Oathbinding was the exception, having manifested up above for some reason.

Why, though?

Felix alighted on the thick grass of his inner bailey and stared at the tower. The patterns glimmered with light, and if he focused too long he could hear their unique vibrations. They were both here and outside in his core space, at the same time.

"Karys, you awake?" he asked the sword at his hip.

Surprisingly, the blade flared with more green-gold light than Felix had ever seen it handle. With a near-blinding flash, a shape was manifested next to him.

"This is...quite unexpected," said the shape. It had resolved into the form of an elderly but vital-looking man with dark skin and tightly curled hair dusted with gray. A smile stretched his mouth. "Delightfully unexpected."

"Karys?" Felix asked. He'd seen the former Nym once in a stolen Memory, but he'd looked a good deal more frail then. "Are you being projected here through the sword?"

"It would seem so, Felix. Your Bastion...it is quite remarkable." Karys stretched his arms and patted his torso and legs, all of which was covered by a sort of black and gold uniform. A military one, judging by the sharp cut of it, though of an unfamiliar style. "This...this is wonderful."

Felix grinned. "Well, it was unexpected, but I'm glad you like it."

"I truly do. To experience my original Body again...it is a pleasure I had thought lost to me," Karys said, turning his closed eyes up toward the bright sun above them. The man's Spirit trembled, though Felix felt it through the sword at his waist. "Yes. I had missed this."

He sighed after a long moment and turned back to Felix. "But you did not call on me so I could take a vacation. How might I help?"

Felix scratched the back of his neck. "Well, now I feel bad. If you want to just wander around or something, you're more than welcome to. Anytime you want, really, if you're able to come here without me."

"That would be wonderful, Felix. Thank you." Karys' smile was infectious, and the sword buzzed with barely suppressed joy. "But I do wish to help."

Felix smiled and slapped the man on the back. He felt like a solid wall of muscle. "Excellent."

CHAPTER SEVENTY

"Almost...there!"

The entire hundred-foot-long stone wall ahead of Felix exploded. Rock and dust and Mana expanded outward in an eruption he had handled three times before. Once again, he flexed his Will and seized it all. The explosion stopped, the stone and even misplaced air frozen under the force of his regard. Felix marshaled his Intent and burned Essence to fuel it—but the wall all but leaped at the chance to change. He wasn't creating so much as containing a vast force that simply wanted to *grow* and *expand*. Felix wrestled with that force, folding it into the design he held in his perfect memories—and once given an avenue of approach, the wall transformed.

When the smoke and dust cleared, the wall was there once again. But instead of the huge stone blocks, the wall was now a single, monolithic structure that towered at least twice as high as it had before. Not only that, but it resembled the walls of his Stronghold in composition and coloration: a glassy, dark blue-black stone veined with a luminescent red-gold. The veins were more stark here than back in Nagast, but it otherwise looked the same, even the towers at each of the four corners.

Stone Shaping is level 80!
Rime Shaping is level 40!
Green Shaping is level 39!
Cardinal Flame is level 84!

"Damn, that was hard," Felix said. "I think I used up more than half of my remaining Essence store...and I got *a lot* from those undead."

Karys stepped up to the wall and peered at it. He ran his thin fingers across its glossy surface. "It appears identical to the other three walls you've raised. The material is interesting...it resembles the construction in your Stronghold, but its texture is different. This is so polished as to have almost no friction at all." Karys nodded, seemingly impressed. "A force laying siege to this place would find themselves hard-pressed to scale these fortifications."

Which meant his Mind was that much more protected, according to the logic of the Skill. Felix let out a relieved breath. He didn't entirely understand the underlying mechanics, but his Bastion had stagnated in its original form for too long, and part of the reason was that he'd not put the conscious effort—read, *Will*—into its transformation. Karys had pointed out how the pattern of the Skill had become quite convoluted, but that complexity had not been reflected in the little world inside of his Bastion. Changing the fortress was the first step to rectifying that.

Bastion of Will didn't level at all, though my Skills related to shaping the walls all did, Felix noted. When he'd mentioned that to Karys, the Paragon had explained that he was simply altering the contents of his Bastion to match its current advancement. More levels would likely not result from the changes he wrought, but his capability would increase. The shaping Skills, however, were due to the process of creation...and fed by his Essence.

The Essence provided the fuel necessary to level his Skills, cementing his progress within reality even as he ostensibly built an imaginary wall. Except...Felix placed his hand against the slick stone. It felt almost oily, though it left no residue. *It feels real. More than the old Bastion did. Was that a result of Essence?*

"Do you feel it?" Karys asked.

"Yeah. I think so." Felix rested his hands on his hips and twisted to catch all of his Bastion in his gaze. "Feels...sturdier, somehow. More real. Did Essence do that?"

"Perhaps. Essence is an unfamiliar avenue of growth for me. But it is clear that it has changed your Bastion and you in very palpable ways." Karys pulled his hand back from the wall. "I feel a vibration in the stone now, where before it was all but inert."

"Why?" Felix asked.

"You have spent a long time undergoing challenges to your Will, Mind, and autonomy. It is no wonder this place is leaping at the chance to change itself, to evolve and become something more." Karys nodded to the grass beneath their feet, which had grown into complex patterns of lush, vibrant life. Stone, moss, and small, jewel-colored flowers abounded all around them, filling the inner bailey with a riot of color.

Pathways were carved into that life, ones that resembled sigaldry, but not the somewhat limited form of modern written magic. Instead, they held a breadth and sweeping potency that echoed with his Theurgist of the Rise Skill. Karys' memory of it was patchy, but he claimed it was a precursor language, one that few Nym at the height of their power had known. "Do you know what this means?"

Felix shook his head. "Not a clue. It feels like protections, maybe a warding of some sort, but even my Theurgist of the Rise isn't clocking its meaning."

"A warding seems likely, simply from its arrangement. Assuming the language functions the same as normal sigaldry, that is."

Reminds me a bit of the Sigils of the Primordial Dawn I'd learned a long time ago...and even has echoes of the Archon's Profane Sigaldry. He could see pieces of both in the looping array, and more besides. "The new walls I understand. They're copies of what I've already made. But how can I do this?" Felix asked, pointing at the sigaldry.

"This is a manifestation of the Skill itself, if I were to guess," Karys said. "A common occurrence, once you reach the beginning stages of true power. Skills of all rarities have hidden depths that deep understanding may reveal, but those ranked Epic or greater will have a heavier history."

"Hm," Felix grunted. He walked down the most direct path and focused on the tower at his Bastion's center. "And how'd this change?"

Where before the tower had been a pentagonal construction that barely rose above the tops of his walls, now it was easily twice the height and thickness...and had six instead of five sides.

Karys hummed in appreciation. "Curious. The array grows..."

"Array?" Felix asked. "The sigils?"

"Hm? Oh, no. I mean the Skill Array you created," the man's words trailed off as he watched Felix's confused face. "You...did you do this on purpose? Placing these other Skills within your Bastion of Will?"

"Not exactly. It was more of a 'react without thinking' than a conscious decision. I was fighting off one of many attacks by the Maw at the time, and there was a resonance between some of my Skills." Felix nodded at the tower. "Before I knew it, they were up there. Etched in light. That's why I came into my Bastion in the first place, really, because I'm interested in advancing my Relentless Resolution. It's all tied up in here, too."

Karys shook his head, but he had a smile on his Human-like face. "I do not know whether to chastise you or congratulate you, Felix. You have unintentionally created a Skill Array, which is a useful if dangerous tool."

"Alright, cool. Excellent," Felix said. "What's a Skill Array?"

"I had assumed you knew, otherwise I would have explained far earlier. A Skill Array is...difficult to form without mishap, but that is due to System restrictions that do not bind you. They are part System feature and part Chanter magic, actually, but even in my day, they were not common despite their benefits."

Karys took a breath and couldn't suppress a smile. "That is nice. Breathing. Anyway, a Skill Array is accomplished by establishing a single Skill as the Primary or hub. This Skill is typically higher in rarity and level than the others, which comes into play later. Other Skills could then be linked to this hub—the number being determined by the Primary's level, rarity, and Tier—and these were called Secondary Skills."

"Okay," Felix said. "That makes sense so far. What's the benefit of this arrangement? I honestly haven't noticed one so far."

"Ah. Well, the Primary Skill would, ideally, provide a measure of meaning and weight to the Secondaries to which it was connected. This would generate benefits for those Skills, ranging from increased leveling speed, greater efficiency or potency, even range. Each of them would in turn offer a measure of their own potency to the Array, but typically far less than the Primary. The actual benefits vary depending on the Primary Skill's purpose, while the rarity, level, and Tier affect the *amount* it affects the Secondary Skills."

Felix tapped his lips, thinking. "Okay, so my Bastion is concerned with fortifying my Mind with my Willpower. It was an evolution of Mental Resistance. All of my other Skills tied to it have a through line of being Mind Skills or concerning my Willpower. I haven't noticed any benefit, though."

Karys laughed. "Do you think it is common for people to survive encounters with a Primordial and a goddess? Even if both were restricted or restrained, your Mind should have popped like a grape. It is likely your Titles and this Skill Array saved your life many times over."

"Huh." Felix couldn't deny that he'd gotten out of more scrapes than was likely, especially considering the power level of his foes. He'd almost chalked it all up to being Unbound, really. "Huh," he said again.

Felix marshaled himself, flexing his Willpower to stay on task. As he did so, he thought he could hear a faint hum from the walls around him. "Okay. Alright. Well, I can't argue that. But I doubt a Skill Array is all flowers and rainbows, Karys. Not on the Continent. What's the catch?"

Karys amused expression grew stilted. "The catch is if your Skills undergo any damage or significant changes, then the Array will unbalance and dissolve. The...consequences of such a dissolution could break your Skills, sunder them completely, or worse."

This time, Felix laughed. That felt more like the System. "So good benefits with potentially life-ending downsides. That's quite a risk to take. Why would anyone do this at all?"

Karys didn't answer at first. Instead, the Nym contemplated the sky, the walls, even the sigil-laden landscape. "I find myself with remarkable clarity within your Bastion, Felix."

"That's...that's good. Great, even. I know your memory has been troubling you," Felix said, a bit confused. He was tempted to ask where Karys was going with things, but held his tongue.

"Yes it is—it is terrifying to see yourself slip away, to lose pieces of who you are." Karys shuddered. In his Nymean form, he appeared so...fragile. "But I've a focus within your Bastion that feels good. My memory remains foggy and distorted, but what I do recall has become sharpened. And I must tell you that the secrets of advancement are kept secret for a reason, Felix."

"What?" he asked. "Is this about the Skill Arrays? Why—?"

"They are kept secret because the act of knowing hinders all attempts. Expectations cloud our Minds, frivolous details derail our Spirits, and our Bodies are weighed down by the impossible standard that lies in wait. Just as your core space was developed alone, subconsciously, the way forward is meant to be similarly uninhibited by those that came before you."

"That...is a convenient excuse to hoard knowledge and power, Karys." Felix shoved away the anger that tried to bubble up at the thought. "I've seen way too many people struggling to survive to accept that reasoning."

Karys held up a hand, forestalling Felix's tone. "Assumptions shape our approach, Felix. I, too, believe in arming the people with the knowledge they need, but at a certain point, the Paths toward true power are far, far more treacherous than I can accurately describe. Some is clear, while other bits are hazy or missing, but I know that much." Karys licked his lips, clearly considering something. He nodded to himself. "But...I know you are strong, Felix. Even if I was unaware of your history, this Bastion alone speaks to your unshakeable Willpower. So, I shall tell you this: look to your core space. And since you have the ability, look to the core spaces of your friends and allies. Think on their similarities...and their differences."

Karys swallowed, and his dark skin appeared suddenly ashen. Bits of him flickered out, replaced by pitted pieces of bronze metal, before settling again as flesh. "I...any more than that, and I fear the consequences. For both of us."

Felix let silence linger between them for a while. He knew Karys was neither malicious nor particularly secretive. If the man said he couldn't tell him, then Felix had to accept it. "Alright. I don't entirely get it, man, but I appreciate what you've been able to tell me so far."

Karys nodded, but his form settled back to that of an old man.

"Would it hurt to add more Skills to the Bastion's array?" Felix asked, partially to move the conversation on and because of a notion that began to percolate in the back of his Mind.

"Other than the dangers I've already outlined? Likely not. I would choose wisely, however. Typically, someone would group a Skill Array based on commonalities in the Skills themselves, but it is never a sure thing."

"Nah, don't worry about that," Felix said, letting himself grin. "I cheat."

CHAPTER SEVENTY-ONE

Felix blinked blearily into a beam of golden sunlight. He groaned.

"Not nearly enough sleep," he muttered. "Pit?"

Beside him, the large bed was empty. It was also fully on the floor, the mattress perched precariously on the shattered remnants of the over-stressed bedframe. Across their bond, Felix sensed his Companion some-where close by, eating. Felix grunted and swung his legs over to the side. He scrubbed at his face, briefly blocking the lancing streams of light from the tall windows all around the master suite. Judging by the angle of those beams, it was mid-morning.

I was more tired than I thought. Not too much time left before we meet the Council. He stood, feeling his muscles stretch pleasantly. Rest had been good for him. That deep ache in his Body had faded to a dull buzz, no longer strained so much as just a touch weary. *That Behemoth was strong. On top of everything else, my Body wasn't ready to contest it directly. Maybe with my Skills, but...*

...how many of those could the Primordial summon?

His master suite was a wide room filled with windows and two doors. There weren't any sharp angles in the place, with walls and ceiling all meeting together in curving, organic shapes. The main door itself was rounded, large, and made of ornately carved stone flecked with shiny crystals. Felix's Eye found those flecks and confirmed what he suspected: they were tiny, minute pieces of Mana crystals. They barely held a smidgen of potency, but it was a display of opulence and power that wasn't wasted on Felix.

The secondary door was more modest, but still carved into curved, organic shapes. It, he discovered, led into a bathroom. A real, honest-to-goodness bathroom. A shallow wash basin sat in a corner, along with a sort of proto-toilet. All of that would have been wonderful enough, but there was also a huge bathtub that dominated the space. Linking it all together were a series of pipes and valves that made a little part in Felix almost scream in excitement.

They have running water? He flipped open the valves and watched in amazement as various-temperature waters poured into the deep tub. *They have* plumbing?

Felix had no clue how plumbing worked back on Earth, but here there seemed to be sigaldry etched into the pipes where they met the valves and again at the ground. They were modified *force* sigils, along with a slew of secondary modifiers that he technically understood, but didn't care to investigate. Simply put, they pulled water up from somewhere below when the valve was turned. Easy enough to understand. A thumbnail-sized faceted crystal—deep blue water type—was set into each valve and clearly powered the whole assembly.

He let the tub fill up until it was visibly steaming, then stripped off his Garment, vambraces, and greaves before stepping in. It felt glorious. Felix had been making do with rivers and lakes recently, and even if he could ignore the cold, it was still a far cry from a real bath. He groaned in relief as he settled into the scalding, almost boiling water. He could feel it soothing his muscles already.

A benefit of his high resistances, Felix could ignore a high degree of heat and cold, but it never reduced his ability to feel it. Just as with pain, he could stop it from affecting him, but the knowledge that he was in pain was still very much there. In battle, that was something he had learned to ignore, but here he let his awareness sink into the tub with him. Heat became his world for a little bit, as Felix soaked and merely existed.

He'd overslept and was short on time, but this was something he was determined to enjoy. The hot water, the old ritual of bathing, all of it conspired to make Felix feel more normal than he had in a while. His Body was too heavy to float, so Felix simply let himself drift below, until he settled at the bottom of the wide tub.

It was wonderfully quiet.

By the time he resurfaced, the sun in the windows had shifted its angle again, now pushing into midday. He regarded the light playing off the walls and ceiling. The ceiling was tiled with wide panels of tin, each stamped with a swirling design. The decor of the room was the same, flames and fluid lines. Even the windows weren't straight, forming teardrop shapes of various sizes. It was something he had seen during their walk through the Risen Ward, but Felix hadn't really paid attention to: the predominant style in Ahkestria was this flowing, organic construction. As if every building was very slightly distorted through a haze of heat.

Magical construction. Like the Henaari, maybe. The use of Mana crystals set Ahkestria apart, however. *If they're so expensive and rare; where did they get them all?*

His thoughts drifted in lazy, relaxing circles. *Karys is probably done in my*

Bastion by now. A quick pulse of his awareness, and Felix confirmed it. His Bastion was empty. After he had stopped consciously keeping the connection between them going, it had been on Karys' shoulders. Keeping up the connection was hard work on his Chancellor's part, costing an exorbitant amount of Mana, and was only worsened by the distance. *Probably couldn't maintain the connection for too long alone. Ah, we'll figure a way around that. If nothing else, it's nice to have someone in my Bastion who doesn't want to kill me.*

A faint indignation drifted across his bond, and Felix snorted, then coughed the water out of his nose and mouth. *Gah. You know I don't mean you.*

Satisfied amusement answered him back.

Ha. Ha. He leaned into the water again, still thinking on his Bastion, this time with a faint excitement. Together, Karys and Felix had completed his Skill Array, connecting a full *seven* Skills to it. Previously, it had contained Relentless Resolution, Deep Mind, and Meditation on each wall of the tower, with Oathbinding up on top.

Utilizing his Affinity, Intent, Willpower, and his Fiendforge, Felix had sought out the remaining three that would fit the Array best. Just as he did when combining Skills, he listened to their patterns and searched out compatible vibrations. Sometimes they shared a sort of melody, while others it was simply the beat at their core, but always they complimented the Array and his Bastion in some way.

Connecting them, in the end, had required less effort than combining Skills; Felix had simply engaged his Fiendforge, and they smoothly integrated into the Array. Conversely, finding and identifying the Skill had taken Felix longer than he had expected and tired him the hell out. Yet by the end of it, he had added Voracious Eye, Aria of the Green Wilds, and Chthonic Tribute into the Array.

Fiendforge is level 12!
Fiendforge is level 13!
Voracious Eye is level 81!
Aria of the Green Wilds is level 86!
Chthonic Tribute is level 85!

Now the tower blazed with etched light and tumbling sounds.

It had made a world of difference. His Bastion was now...he smirked, thinking of it. Of the changes. Still, Relentless Resolution remained firmly at level 74. He hoped that it would level faster now that the Array was full up, but Felix would have to wait and see.

No observable benefits yet, Felix thought with a sigh. He sank just a bit more into the hot water. *The sound of the Array is...evocative, though.*

The completed Skill Array filled Felix with a strident song, just at the edge of normal hearing. Threaded through the chaotic interplay of his dual cores, of Harmony and Dissonance, the Array's voice was influenced by the Skills within it. Felix heard the song like golden sunlight through verdant boughs, heating the surface of a blue-black stone wall and sending trilling gusts of wild wind through the leaves. And buried within it all, hidden in the folds of emerald jungles—the distant bellow of a beast.

It felt...good. Ominous and powerful.

With the promise of higher leveling speeds for associated Skills and a variety of benefits, Felix couldn't help but wonder if his people could benefit from something like it. He'd asked Karys about it, but his Chancellor was cautious.

"It could prove beneficial, that is certain," he had said. "But your allies are not as durable as you are, Felix. If they encounter problems, then their Arrays would degrade and severely harm them."

It was a viable way forward, though. Karys had admitted that much. Felix had to give it some more thought and ask Harn and Zara about it. Maybe even Darius. *That guy's been doing high-level training for a long time. He has to know more secrets about advancing, right?*

Given the right knowledge, Felix was excited to see what his Fiend-forge could provide to them all.

Finally, he climbed out of the tub and let water stream off his lean frame. The tiled floors were tilted and set with a drain, which was wise, considering Felix didn't see a towel anywhere nearby. *Did they not use them?* He sighed.

Mantle of the Infinite Revolution!

Mantle of the Infinite Revolution is level 51!

Mana flowed from his channels and around his form, spinning tightly and burning bright. Heat seared his skin and hair, roasting his Body and drying him in a single second. Felix released the Skill, but not before he caught sight of another unique feature in the room.

A full-length mirror dominated one of the walls, and for the first time in a long while, Felix got a full view of himself. He had grown older in many ways, which was almost a relief. His face was youthful, but hard. The baby fat he remembered carrying at this age on Earth wasn't present. Everything about him was angular, too, from his cheekbones and jawline to the shape of his shoulders and hips.

You need a fucking haircut, though.

He thought of putting it up in a hair tie or something, but immediately shot the idea down. Felix found the idea of a ponytail...kind of embarrassing. No, he would rather have it hang loose around his ears and neck, at least until he could get it trimmed.

Sovereign of Flesh.

His eyes pulsed, igniting like sapphire flares. Dark scales crept over every inch of his body, and from his forearms, elbows, and knees spikes of ivory bone erupted outward. It hurt, same as always, but Felix buried the pain beneath his resistances. A mask of tooth and scale formed around his lower face, a nightmare visage that he rarely used—it even moved and opened with his own jaw, revealing a mouthful of true fangs. With an experimental effort of Will, he managed to reverse the change on his own teeth, then banished the half-mask. While one was pretty cool, reshaping his teeth had always unnerved him.

"I still look like a monster, though," he whispered. "No wonder she flinched."

The thought of Vess was like touching a hot stovetop in his brain. He shied away from the memory, and focused on his Skill. *If I can keep my teeth from turning, and if I can flare this to double in size, then what else can it do?*

Sovereign of Flesh was even more hellishly complex than Relentless Resolution, being an entire rarity higher. The Skill was of Transcendent rarity, which meant the vibrational pattern was larger than many others in his core space, and the intricacy of its composition was something that completely befuddled him. He had only briefly perused the Skill the night before, and hadn't the mental energy to delve further.

A Primordial Skill. Transformation and...control. When he used the Skill, he was stronger and more vital and durable, his Body turned into a weapon. Claws, spines and spikes, even growing wings when Pit was Converged within his Spirit. It was a shaping Skill, of that he was certain, but the medium wasn't some Mana type but very specifically his own flesh. Essence fueled it. Was that because the Maw operated on a diet of Essence?

With an annoyed grunt, Felix let his scales dissolve into dark smoke. *Figure it out later. You have things to do now.*

———

Felix quickly left his rooms, transforming his Garment into a long coat split at the tail with a loose white shirt underneath. The heat of the desert made his choice on the shirt, but he wasn't about to abandon his jackets. Being all but immune to the dry, baking heat had its advantages. Pants, too, though he kept the green material loose and thin like cotton and tucked in at the knees into his silver metal greaves. He strode through the hallways of the estate, following the sound of clattering wood and steel to the courtyard.

Ah. Excellent.

The sun was bright and shining from a blindingly blue sky, and his people were sparring. Squads were paired off against one another, attacking with controlled bursts as Harn and a still-bandaged Darius walked among them, shouting instructions and insults.

Felix stepped into the sun, enjoying the warmth of it. He tried to push down the sensation that he was exposed to enemy eyes. After fighting monsters for a week, it was a hard habit to shake...and he wasn't entirely sure he should. Felix's Perception quested outward, rolling along the battlements where Humans in gold and orange armor stood guard. His

Affinity snaked after his Perception, pulling in the ambient noises of their Spirits.

They were all curious and a little contemptuous of the Claw's abilities, but that was strangely directed. It took him a moment to realize they were sneering specifically at the Giants, Henaari, Gnomes, and Goblins; essentially anyone who wasn't Human earned a little burst of derision from the Knights.

Great. More fantasy racism bullshit.

Felix shook them off and refocused, watching the squads for a time. As a whole, they had improved dramatically since the oasis. A woman with a sword was teaching a man with a mace how to use the bladed weapon. Another group was demonstrating a spell, and a woman with heavy gauntlets was listening intently. These examples were few and far between, but the lines were blurring. Clashes of personality and bickering still happened, and divisions clearly existed between the Legion societies, but seeing them fight together began to assuage his worries. *Maybe they'll actually be worth something in combat soon.*

"Felix!" Vess called. She was wearing her armor, as usual, and was soaked in sweat. "Did you sleep well?"

"Better than I have in a while," Felix admitted. He scratched his neck and frowned at his long hair again. "Even had a bath."

"Oh, that sounds wonderful right now," Vess groaned. She leaned against one of the pillars on the portico behind them, planting her spear and wiping her forehead. "I have been helping the Blades with their sword forms, which soon ended with me helping the Bone and Fist Legionnaires as well. Even a few of the Arclight mages joined in." She laughed. "Not for long, though. This heat is brutal. It feels a good deal greater than the desert floor."

Felix smiled. "That's great. I didn't know you knew the sword."

"I was raised by a warrior, for all that he carries the title of duke." Vess shrugged a single shoulder. "I would have had to been blind not to pick up a little. And a little is far more than any of your followers know, sorry to say."

"They're rough," Felix agreed. "Getting better, though."

"Oh, I agree. Our training led to this," she gestured to the intermingling squads. "They're learning from each other. Only a little and only some of them, but it's a start."

Felix watched the squads sparring, clashing over and over in the rising temperatures. "I don't know where they got the idea of separate weapon-based societies from, honestly. They want to follow in my footsteps, but I don't lean on any one style over the others. I'm kind of a mess, technique-wise."

"I am aware," Vess said with a small smile. "They, however, know you're strong. That encourages them, even if they haven't the talent or..." she shrugged. "They aren't you, and they know it. Better to specialize than attempt your mad rush at general mastery."

"Jack of all trades is a master of none," Felix said. The full phrase came to him, unbidden from some decades-old vault of memory. "But oftentimes better than a master of one."

Vess tilted her head, and her loosened hair fell in a curtain over her high cheekbones. "The System does not encourage that outlook."

Felix shrugged. "I don't think the System wants anything, really, only giving everyone the power to Choose for themselves. If they want to specialize, then so be it. But like you did, we can show them other paths, other viewpoints to better themselves."

Vess regarded him for a few silent moments, a small smile never leaving her face. "You are getting better at that."

"What?"

"Leading." She stood up straight again and reached out to squeeze his shoulder. "I'll go help our Legion some more. What is your plan?"

"Well, Fiammetta said the Council won't convene until later this afternoon, so I had planned to take a look around the city." Felix sighed. "But I suppose I slept in too much."

"Zara beat you to it, anyway," Vess said.

"What?"

"She took off shortly after we settled in, said she was going to search for an old friend," Vess said, giving Felix a look. It was a look that tried very hard to be casual. *She means Isla. The other Chanter.*

"Hope she finds her friend, then. At least one of us gets to see the city. That...puts me at ease," Felix said. Vess nodded, agreeing with his unspoken words.

"She said to head to the Council even if she has not yet returned," Vess said.

"Hm. Then there's not much else to do but train. Or..." He shifted his attention. "How close are you to Tempering?"

Vess blinked at the shift in topic. "Close, a few levels off in most of my Skills. Frustratingly so, I will admit."

"Glad it's not just me," Felix said with a grin. "After helping Evie Temper her Body, I've got...questions, I suppose, about other people's core spaces. Do you mind if I see yours?"

"Um," Vess blushed and sat back down. "I suppose not. Evie mentioned that you helped her—but she was Tempering. Why do you need to see my core space?"

"A comparison. Karys brought something to my attention that—well, if I can make sense of it all, then I might be able to help everyone grow."

Vess pursed her lips and looked to the courtyard. Harn and Darius—the latter looking much better now—were drilling the Claw in basic maneuvers again. She nodded, decisively.

"Alright."

CHAPTER SEVENTY-TWO

Felix walked up a mountain, and the winds tried to tear him off.

This is... He was astounded at the detail all around him. After using his Cardinal Flame and Fiendforge to peer into Vess' core space, he hadn't quite known what to expect. Something to do with the spear, he imagined. But this...

Everything looks and feels real. *How did she do this?*

Felix was climbing up a winding staircase carved into the mountain, one that was as ancient as the peak itself. Its sharp edges were worn smooth by the ceaseless wind, but in its recesses clung small bits of moss and plant matter, surviving in the lee of their age-old shape. At the base, where he had entered her core space, clouds covered much of his vision. But each step increased the power of the wind and those clouds were pushed away. He took the steps slowly, but soon he rose to the very top, where the peak flattened itself out into a wide plateau, as if a god had sheared the top off with a sword.

He blinked at the swirling gusts of winds, stepping through them to emerge onto the top layer. Dominating the area was a massive temple that looked like a fusion of many eastern styles back on Earth, yet was heavily mixed with details that were wholly of the Continent. Thick, unadorned pillars were holding up a curved, pyramidal roof, and red tiles overlapped across its top. A wide porch surrounded the temple, adding about twenty feet of polished wood and stone before someone could even walk through the temple's main doors. Said doors were metal and gleamed in the omnipresent light.

Her core is in there, he thought. He was certain of it.

"What, ah, what do you think?" Vess asked.

Felix turned from the sight of her temple and gazed outward. Other peaks stretched into the distance, each of them only lifting a few hundred feet above the cloud layer. They stood on the tallest, of course, but those that clustered closest to the temple were taller than those farther out, with some only barely peeking above the clouds.

"This is amazing, Vess," Felix answered. "How the hell did you do this?"

"Do what?"

Felix turned to look at her, his eyebrows raised. "Do what? The detail! The amount is staggering, and—" Vess stood before him, garbed in her usual white-enameled armor and spear, but she was *glowing*. "Whoa. Why are you glowing?"

Vess looked at her arms, confusion clearly etched across her features. "I am not? But the detail is a mental exercise given to me by my tutors. They explained that specificity was helpful in visualizing one's core space, though the reasons behind that have never been clear." She shook her head, and to Felix's eyes, a puff of shimmering annoyance followed after her movements. "I have practiced every day for multiple hours to get to this level of detail. In the core space and my own appearance."

That's *what I'm seeing. She's so viscerally* here *that it's...resonating with her core space.* "Huh. Well, I don't know the reason, but I could stand to try those exercises you're talking about. I'm sure your tutors weren't pulling your chain."

Vess smiled, cheek dimpling. "No, I imagine not. It is just disheartening to strive toward a goal without knowing the purpose of so much of the training. At least spear work is straightforward." She whirled her partisan, performing a simple thrust. Yet, the moment she did, the wind *howled* in its wake. "Simple and easy to understand."

"Uh, yeah." Felix's eyes tracked that wind. It impacted the clouds many mountains away, splashing into them. "Are all these peaks your Skills?"

"They are," Vess said with a nod. "Is this...how do I compare? To the others?"

Felix laughed before he saw how serious the Heiress of Pax'Vrell looked. "You're a thousand times more stable than Evie, and your space is far more detailed than Atar's. Better than me on both counts, I think," he finished with a laugh.

"Really?" Vess' face lit up, and she tucked her hair behind her ears. That glow increased across her chest and arms, pulsing like a heartbeat. "I must admit, that is a relief. I have not had my core space checked since I left home. Not even Darius can perform a Sounding."

"Well, glad I could help. Interesting that there's a Skill to do this. I'm just cobbling techniques together to be here," Felix admitted.

Vess flashed another smile. "Do you want to see more?"

"More?" Felix asked. "Inside the temple?"

Instead of answering, the spearmaiden stepped past him and walked up the large, beautifully ornamented steps of her strange core space. Felix followed behind. They passed the wide, smooth columns and across the wooden expanse of the portico. The door, a metal portal built in a dark, cherry-wood frame, was surmounted by complex knotwork designs. On the door itself was an etching of a dragon, picked out in gold upon the weather-tarnished silver. It was maned and antlered, and in its long, serpentine body was held a spear and an orb of swirling winds.

"That's a Dusk Dragon," Felix said in surprise. "I recognize it from my Omen Path."

"Truly? You saw a Dusk Dragon?" Vess ran her hand across the polished gold features of the creature. Rather than a lizard, it had a decidedly canine set to its face. "They were our protectors in the last Age. The Dragoons were formed because of them, because of the knowledge they imparted upon our Order. They all perished in the turning of this new Age, a long, long time ago."

"Well...I didn't see one living, no. Sorry. It was a statue in my Path," Felix said.

"That is odd. My Order claims only our Path touches upon their memory. Why would your Path take you before them?" she asked.

Because of you, I'm pretty sure. That's what he wanted to say, though it felt awkward to admit. Felix felt close to Vess, but they hadn't ever said anything aloud. *And she's too young,* he told himself, for probably the hundredth time. *I mean, not* that *much younger than you. But shut up. Focus on the details. You're here for a reason.*

"I'm Unbound. Who knows why anything happens." Mentally slapping himself, Felix ran his hands over the door as well. "It is beautifully carved."

Vess regarded him with her dark brown eyes. Felix could feel her regard but refused to look at anything but the fine detail on the door. The gold was polished and shiny, with small scratches on the metal, but here and there, he spotted a faint haziness. More a suggestion of shape and color than reality.

"It is a faithful replica of the Temple of Winds, in my home," she said. Vess' hand pressed right near his face and shoved open the door. "As faithful as I could make it to be, that is."

A chill wind sprang from inside the Temple of Winds, cutting right through Felix's resistances. He blinked and beheld a single large interior of polished wood and stone flooring, delicate tapestries, and thin columns around a central space. There, in the center, was a massive dragon.

And it was glaring at him.

Felix hissed, fire and lightning blooming along his visualized limbs. He set himself, but stumbled when he heard a high laugh from his side.

"I am sorry to laugh," Vess said between breaths. She stuttered with brilliant light, rolling from her dark hair and armored shoulders. "But it is only a statue, Felix."

She was right. Felix stood, feeling more than a little embarrassed. "Your core?"

Vess only nodded, eyes still bright.

Felix stepped closer, actually paying attention this time. The dragon *was* a statue, but it was also more than that. It was made of blue and silver stone, veined with milky white that pulsed in time with the white-green light that floated within. Pieces of its body were segmented, too, filled with that swirling white-green light, so cleverly designed that even the hair of its mane waved in that wind.

It was clearly another Dusk Dragon, with its elongated, dog-like face, antlers and serpentine body that resembled Asian myths back home. There was an...intensity and resonance with the sculpture that gave it a sense of life, though. As if it could spring from the light at any moment.

"It's beautiful," he said.

"Thank you. It is a memory, passed to me from my mother," Vess said. Felix glanced at her and found her gazing fondly at the dragon. "We do not even know if it is a true recollection, or if it has been warped by time and the hands that held it. I built my core space around this idea. The same one my mother had."

"And your mom is—"

"Passed. Many years ago now."

"I'm sorry, Vess. That's...I'm sorry," Felix said, lamely.

"No need. I miss her terribly, but that was not your fault." Vess sighed, but a pulse of happiness shivered through her frame. "Finding out she had worked with Zara in the past, that she had used the Chant, that was nice. Learning a new thing about her, something so few knew, it was like having her here again. Just a little." Her smile returned, dimple and all.

Felix shook his head, his own smile impossible to repress. "I get that. I...well I miss my own mom a lot. Her and Gabby, my sister, they're back home. On Earth." Felix's smile faltered a bit. "It's hard to think of them dealing with my disappearance. I can't even send them a letter or something, let them know I'm alright. So it's like I lost them both."

Vess reached over and squeezed his shoulder again. "It gets easier. That is a cold comfort, but I found it helpful to get through my longest days."

"Yeah." Felix looked back at her core, vaguely ashamed at the tears in the corner of his eyes. He forced a smile. "Well. Better to survive, or else I'll not even have cold comforts to look forward to. You've given me a lot to think about."

"I am pleased to hear it." Vess hesitated a moment before, all in a breath, she spoke. "Do you want me to show you my visualization exercises?"

Felix's grin this time came easily. "Absolutely."

———

Some hours later—well after Felix shook off the mental fatigue of Vess' exercises—Felix gathered the inner team within his master suite.

"Why is this so much better than my room?" Evie said, immediately claiming a couch and a bowl of dates. "What're you, some kinda king?"

"When is this damn Disciple coming to have us visit the Council?" Alister snapped. "I don't like how those Knights have been looking at us."

"She will be back soon, no doubt," Atar said to them all. "That little...firebrand was always very punctual."

"How do you know this lady?" Evie asked from her position on the settee. She lazily chewed another candied date. "Old flame?"

Alister laughed. So did Felix. "Is she trustworthy?" he asked.

"Enough. We had a rivalry going back when we were vying for apprenticeships." Atar leaned back against the overstuffed leather chair. "She was pushy then. A little rude and self-centered, but that's been polished out of her, apparently."

"What about the temple?" Felix asked. "We haven't had the best of luck with religious types. Or Urges."

Atar nodded seriously. "I know. The Highest Flame is..."

"What about this Council?" Harn grunted from the corner. He was still in full armor but had his helmet dangling from his hand. "A whole set of Masters puts my teeth on edge. And what's this about your old boss? A Grandmaster?"

"Zara knew of this and had no issues!" Atar protested. "She and I spoke of this before we left your Stronghold, Felix. I told you this."

"You did. Don't worry, man. You're not on trial here. But I also haven't had a chance to talk to Zara about it. Or why she was so comfortable with this interaction." Felix ran a hand through his sweat-slicked hair. He could ignore the heat and its pains, but apparently his Body still had to sweat. "Since she's not here, we can't know. But there's no reason for this meeting to turn violent. We're just paying a visit to their city for trade, that's the story."

"And to warn them," Atar insisted. "About the Paladins' attack."

"Love, I don't think they'll believe us," Alister said. "We have no proof."

"We saw them in Felix's vision. They are gathering their forces in the desert," Atar said.

"We didn't really see 'em, though," Evie said. She had somehow twisted so her head was hanging off the edge of the settee while her boots drummed against the tiled walls. "Not since the pass."

"But—"

Felix held out a hand, and everyone quieted. "Listen. We know they're a threat. The Paladins are here to look for the Unbound, and he's here. I don't doubt they'll lay siege to this city to find him. But we can't mention the Unbound to the Council or anyone else. You saw how freaked out Darius was when he was told, and he's on our side."

"In my defense, the concept is terrifying," the Hand said from the far end of the room. "The Ruin and Unbound and all of you just...running in its direction. Madness."

"Sometimes the proper direction lies along the most dangerous Path," Vess said.

"Did you just quote your father at me?" he asked, a small smile on his face.

"The point stands. The Unbound are too tempting a target to try and control. I'm not worried about me, but this Minotaur. He's strong but is clearly just coming into his own. We can warn them of the Paladins, but leave it to me. I need to find a way to approach it that isn't too insane or a death sentence." Felix shook his head. "What a pair of options."

"Regardless, our primary goal should be to establish good relations and give us a reason to stay in the city," Vess said. "Once we find the Minotaur, we spirit him away and leave."

"Exactly what I was thinking, Vess. Perfect. Any objections?" Felix looked around at the core team, waiting for someone to point out an issue or complain, but all he saw were steely eyes and iron resolve. "Alright. Let's do this."

Felix looked at the door.

"Just as soon as Zara's back."

CHAPTER SEVENTY-THREE

Zara stepped carefully, keeping her boots from the fetid water. The underbelly of Ahkestria was as ruinous as she had heard. Potholes studded the pathways, sewage filled broken gutters, and the dwellings turned from well-appointed, if modest homes to ramshackle huts. The people were dressed in serviceable clothes, sturdy tunics and breeches hemmed at mid-calf, but they were caked with soot, dust, and dirt. All of it was evidence of their primary occupation: mining Mana crystals.

Men and women, mostly non-Human—and a surprising amount of Yttin—walked with heavy gaits and morose expressions. Little light made its way down into these bottom layers, so torches were set up at regular intervals. Soot and greasy smoke congealed in corners and ceilings, while ragged cloth coverings were used in place of wooden shutters on the dwellings. Not even Haarwatch's Dust Quarter had been so destitute or ill-kept, and for good reason. A great majority of Haarwatch's industry was powered by the laborers in the Dust Quarter, and not even the Guild was stupid enough to discount that.

Here, stupidity abounds, she thought. These people were the engine that drove Ahkestria's industry, providing the raw materials for all their vaunted crafting. Without the crystalline dust and larger chunks, the city's economic heart would fall to ruin. She spotted a line of folk carefully apportioning water from a dusty well that had clearly seen better times.

Running water for the nobility, and this for the people? A part of her raged at the conditions, at the memory of other places, other times. It was hard to live as long as she had, to have seen so much suffering in so many nations. Surviving all of that left its mark on you, she found, which had required Zara to develop a control over her emotions like few others. As much as she would give to vent her spleen, now was not the time. She pulled her hood tighter over her face and kept walking.

The number of tails she had to shake just to escape their warded estate was impressive—less so their Skills, but Zara was a Master for a reason. She had left all of them chasing shadows across the Risen Ward. Now, she had descended quite far in her search, and poor conditions aside, the amount of armed and armored soldiers in the slums was telling.

There was little chance of them rising up against the upper layers, but it was clear that *someone* was worried they might make the attempt. There was a palpable tension between the soldiers and common folk, and the latter gave the former a wide berth wherever they were found. The soldiers were like stones in a river, even when moving; the crowd flowed around them without even coming close.

It is good Felix was not able to come with me. His compassion is laudable, but the boy has little control over his desires. A Yttin stumbled nearby and splashed into one of the deeper and more foul puddles. The soldiers only laughed. Zara flared her nostrils but kept walking. *He needs to learn when it is appropriate to exert your Will. And when to bide your time.*

Zara sighed and turned a corner, heading down a sloping ramp along-side a clutch of cowering Yttins. They chittered at each other through their bandages, but kept their eyes away from hers. Fear quivered their Spirits like a parasite, an infectious cough with its hand around their throats. The path extended a ways through the open-air layers, the Lower Wards as they were called, too numerous to be named anything unique. She was growing more and more frustrated as she traveled, however. There had been no sign of Isla on any of the layers before this one. Zara's only hope was to keep descending.

Felix and crew will likely meet the council soon, she mused as she crossed over a crumbling bridge. The drop was considerable, and there were no guardrails, so the Yttin and Goblins with her crossed with mincing steps. *Vess can handle the politics, so long as Evie doesn't interfere.*

Zara hummed to herself, keeping it quiet. Evie had been much more contemplative since she had advanced her core. She was unlikely to cause trouble in the short-term. *No. it's Felix I'm worried about. He needs to handle his approach to the Council delicately.*

She had wanted to be there, but finding the Unbound Minotaur quietly took priority. The threat of the Paladins still loomed large, though Zara was put a bit at ease upon seeing the effectiveness of the city's defenses. It was a foolhardy few that would brave the cutting winds of Ahkestria's private sandstorm. The true, immediate danger was making their case to the Council of Masters, buying themselves time to get what they needed. She had spoken with Vess and Harn; they knew to focus on goodwill and discussions of trade.

A swell of a mournful dirge caught her ears as she walked past a dilapidated tenement. Zara slowed to a stop, boots grinding on the dirt and stone chips. She peered into the darkness of its side alley, only to hear the sound once more. With carefully measured steps, Zara stepped into the shadows...and found a Mark upon the wall. A very familiar one.

Isla. Finally. The dirge faded as soon as the Mark was found, and another slow song pulled her deeper into the warren of passageways.

A trail of breadcrumbs attuned to our Order. Why? She couldn't have been expecting company so soon. Zara stepped off a ledge and dropped fifty feet onto a narrow outcropping. The second Mark was there, etched into the pitted stone. It flared in her ears, then faded from existence. The next came into being, and it was far below, through chasms torn in Ahkestria's base.

She must be buried deep in these slums. To escape the attention of the Urge? Or some other reason?

Zara was eager to find out.

———

"Envision your core space, but do not delve into it. Not yet. The first technique requires you to split your focus between the real and the visualized," Vess explained. Her voice was soft and melodic, yet it threatened to topple him. "Claim that focus."

Felix teetered, his Mind balancing precariously on the edge as she requested. It was unreasonably difficult in Felix's opinion. He had expected to grasp this training technique immediately...though he was glad that he'd never declared anything of the sort. This strange balance was only the first step to honing his core space, and he'd only just managed it.

"I do not have the Sounding Skill, Felix, so I cannot tell if you are primed properly," Vess said. She was very close. He could feel the heat of her body, just as he could feel the chaotic hum of music within his darkened core space. "Tell me: are you balanced?"

"Y-yeah," he said. He could smell a faint floral soap from her, undercut by the gurgling growl of the abyss within his cores. "I got it."

"Perfect. That is far faster than I managed it," she said with a breath of pleased surprise. "Concentrating was very difficult when I was six years old."

Felix huffed a surprised, rueful grunt. His pride collapsed, but he let it bleed out. He didn't need it anyway. "Why...do I...have to do this?"

"Hold it for at least a quarter glass. Sharpen your focus. That is the first goal. After that, I can tell you more."

Felix managed to last all of five minutes before the front door crashed open, shattering his concentration and admitting a blast of furnace winds. "God damn it, why'd we do this in the foyer—" he paused as his senses registered the form of Fiammetta and her thirty-some Knights arrayed behind her. "Ah. Is it time?"

"I apologize for the intrusion, Representative Veil, but yes. It is." The Faun looked between him and Vess. "Did I interrupt something?"

Felix glanced at Vess, only to blink in surprise. They were...very close. Felix was wearing his Garment, which he'd changed into a loose cotton shirt and pants, both a slate gray. Vess was likewise wearing a breezy sort of blouse with an open collar and some sort of layered skirt. He spotted sweat beading on her neck before turning his gaze. *Has she been wearing that this whole time?*

"Simply training," Vess said to the Faun. "Normally, one would knock before entering another's residence. Is standard civility not taught in your temple?"

Fiammetta's sly smile tightened into an almost grimace. "I apologize again. I did not expect to...inconvenience you both."

"No inconvenience." Vess adjusted her blouse ever so slightly. "Armor gets quite uncomfortable after a while," Vess said, and her smile was sharp as a wolf's.

"I can imagine," the deer lady said. She looked slowly between Felix and Vess. "I advise you to look more...presentable before the Council."

Felix frowned and made to stand up, but Vess' hand on his forearm pulled him short. He looked down, then back up at her, only to find her eyes still fixed on Fiammetta. "We will be ready in a short moment. Please, avail yourself of the refreshments in the parlor."

With a sharp nod, Fiammetta led her Knights into one of the side rooms, where indeed there were refreshments laid out by the servants. Servants that Felix had yet to spot even once.

"What was *that* about?" he asked.

Vess simply stood. "I will find Evie and don my armor. Please let everyone else know it is time."

"Uh, yeah. Sure," Felix said. He felt like he was missing something in that interchange, but shifted gears. "I'll get everyone ready."

———

In a few short minutes, the lot of them were striding out of the manor's gates. Felix (with Pit nestled in his Spirit), Evie, Vess, Atar, and Alister walked within a cordon of Knights down the wide boulevard as the sun began to set.

"I don't like leavin' Harn behind," Evie complained again.

"He'll be fine," Alister assured her. "Besides, someone needs to watch over the Legion."

"Darius is there, too, and he is well on the mend," Vess said. "I would not worry about those we left behind, Evie."

"Oh, it ain't *them* I'm worried about," she muttered.

Fiammetta led their little entourage, and they kept a brisk pace across the Risen Ward. People were out and about this time, as the sun's fading light created a much more hospitable atmosphere. Men and women, all Human, walked past them wearing robes and dresses and talking in light, cheerful voices. Laughter danced from one of many eating establishments, where glowing lights and the clink of glasses and dinnerware drifted on the breeze. To the east, stars glimmered in the approaching dark, and the west was a blaze of blood-red light that soaked the district in tinted shadows.

It was, in short, beautiful.

More of those crystalline formations dotted the streets, their orange glows growing more pronounced as the day fled. It was weird for Felix, as whenever they passed too close, he heard a sharp ringing in his metaphysical ears. The potency of the Mana crystals was intense, far more so than the weakened crystals on display in the Farwalker's hut—or even the ones the Archon had used against him. Felix gathered that their compression and hardness was an indicator of just how much Mana was packed into them. *And Atar said that people couldn't even scratch the things, which is why they're still standing instead of being long-since picked apart.*

The buildings continued on as he had first seen them; beautifully shaped and structured, glittering with inclusions of Mana crystals and carvings to accentuate their wavy, organic shapes. More than a few manors and public buildings were rounded and oddly malformed, firming Felix's notion that it was an artistic choice. Heat and flame was given a lot of weight in Ahkestria, that was clear. Perhaps back on Earth such architecture couldn't exist, but there was no doubt some Skill at work to make the buildings functional despite their eccentric shapes.

"Ah, Atar, it is nice to have you back in the city," Fiammetta said after a while.

Felix could feel the fire mage's surprise ripple across his Spirit. "Nice? When last we met, you cursed—what was it? 'Every demon get from my loins?'"

The Faun blushed and waved her hands. "That was—well, I was not very gracious, was I? But then, neither were you. Refusing to speak on why you were leaving! Did you know your master refused to take on any further apprentices? Not one, since you've been gone."

"Really?" Atar looked a touch nervous. "Well, opportunity knocked, offering me knowledge I desired. I greatly appreciate the Grandmaster's guidance, but he has always viewed sigaldry as a crutch of the weak and mentally infirm. Magic, to him, is power to be conquered...not a mystery to be investigated."

Alister's hand found Atar's and squeezed.

"Sigaldry. I see. I joined the Temple shortly after you left, having few options. But the Matrons have been kind and my training extensive." The Faun puffed out her chest in her robes and golden breastplate. "I am the youngest Disciple in the last half-century."

"Congratulations," Atar said. It even sounded like he meant it.

Felix patted the fire mage on the back. "Atar is modest. He is quite accomplished on his own as well, in research and the battlefield."

"Truly?" Fiammetta asked. "I saw you all fight against those undead. The Temple often sends its Knights and Disciples into the lowlands for training, but we've never faced so many before." She shuddered. "A nightmare in the flesh."

"I imagine your heat magic would do well against them," Atar said.

"Perhaps." She tilted her head, as if considering the mage for the first time. "You are much nicer now, you know."

"And you aren't half as annoying anymore," he shot back. Then in a kinder tone, said, "And authority looks good on you."

Fiammetta didn't say anything to that, but her freckled nose blushed. On a hunch, he flared his Affinity. Aside from the incessant, piercing hum of the various Mana crystals, he could sense threads tightening between Atar and their guide. He had remained suspicious of the woman's intentions and allegiances, if only because he had to be, but the link between her and his friend was encouraging. *I can't argue against an another ally,* he thought. *We need all we can get.*

Zara still hadn't returned, but Felix tried not to let that bother him. He was more than capable of operating without a babysitter. Yet they were walking into the den of several Master-Tier individuals. Felix couldn't deny the comfort of having a Master-Tier on their side. He didn't expect this meeting to go bad, but he'd been wrong before.

When they reached the Council building, it defied the standard set by all the others. It was a domed rotunda, relatively squat and fitted with many thin pillars around its exterior. The copper dome gleamed in the setting sun, while the grounds around it and the stone-lined pathway leading to its doors was drenched in wall-cast shadows, deep and purple. Sconces of crystals were set into the sides of the path and again by the huge, double doors, though there the crystals were half again as large and *thrumming* with power.

Felix suppressed a wince as they drew closer. It was like standing too close to a speaker at a concert. Fiammetta began talking, but part of him only heard the ceaseless waves of sound.

"We shall enter the Council chambers together, Representative Veil," she said. Felix closed off his Affinity and focused on her words. "My men will wait out here. If you would follow me?"

"Lead on," he said.

The door opened slowly and ominously, admitting them all into a half-moon shaped antechamber that contained two curving staircases on either side and a somewhat smaller door going farther inward.

"What's up there?" Evie asked.

"Balcony seating," Atar said. "Council gatherings can draw a crowd sometimes."

Felix frowned at the movement he sensed up those stairs, but Fiammetta marched them onward through the next set of doors and into a vast, vaulted chamber. It reminded him of a small stadium, with tiered seating all around them leading down to a lowered area at the center. There the ground was open for a sizable portion of polished stone, while beyond that were a series of five raised benches made of dark, pitted stone. Chairs made of glowing Mana crystal were mounted behind them and contained three men and two women, all Human, who were conversing animatedly among one another.

They walked down the carpeted steps slowly. Felix spotted a dome of sigaldry covered the councilors' benches and central area. It appeared complex, but after a moment, Felix had its measure: it was a muffling array, which explained why he couldn't hear anything from the seated Masters. He nodded at it.

"Why does it feel like we're on trial?" Felix asked. "Will the Masters not meet us face-to-face?"

Fiammetta frowned, but not at him. "The Council has spent much of today considering proposals from the patricians and merchants, I have been told. This is the soonest we could fit you in to see them."

"I had wondered why we'd been kept waiting," Atar said. "Not meeting in an audience is...not ideal, but this should serve our purposes."

They breached the line of sigaldry, and active Mana crawled across Felix's body like stepping through a thin sheet of water. Something about it snagged at Felix for a second—a brief heat—but it faded quickly as he shrugged it off. Humming filled the inscribed bubble, which Felix attributed to the opulent crystal chairs, but otherwise, their approach was as silent as the grave. Fiammetta led them onto the wide, open area and motioned them to half.

"Who comes before us?" a woman with silver hair and unlined face demanded. It had the sound of ritual to it.

The Faun took a single step and raised her chin. "Disciple Fiametta of the Temple of All-Burning Flame."

"Why do you seek the Council of Masters?" asked another, a portly man with a spade-like beard and a bored expression.

"I bring before you those who seek wisdom and guidance," Fiammetta intoned. "Representative Silas Veil, of the newly established Territory of Nagast."

Two of the Masters exchanged a short glance, but otherwise they all simply stared. Felix tried to feel at their Spirits, but each one was a brick wall to his senses. Not to mention that the entire building was awash in vibrations. The Mana crystals, the sigils, even the wards woven into the benches and floor that Felix could only barely perceive. Protective measures, no doubt. All of it was a *lot* to parse, even for Felix's impressive senses.

"Good evening, Councillors. Masters," Felix said, reciting the greeting Vess had made him memorize. "We are here as a representative arm of Nagast to the north. I had assumed we would be meeting in a more informal setting, but we are nevertheless here to establish relations between our Territories."

One of the Masters, another man with reddish-brown skin perked up. "Do you speak of trade, Mr. Veil?"

"Trade is one of our goals, yes. In fact—" Felix tried to go on, but Atar of all people pushed forward.

"Paladins seek to destroy Ahkestria!" he said. Atar's eyes widened, and he looked at the others in shocked dread.

Atar? What the hell dude?

Silence followed Atar's outburst. A man at the center watched them over steepled fingers, and the force of his regard was a physical weight. He had an entirely bald head, skin the color of basalt, and sharp-lined tattoos covering the little flesh exposed by his off-white robes. The Grandmaster, Felix knew. He could *feel* it as the mage leaned forward on his crystalline throne.

"Explain."

CHAPTER SEVENTY-FOUR

Layer after layer, doggedly pursuing the meandering Marks of her associate, Zara had delved truly deep. While above the ramshackle huts and destitute streets had been atrocious, here in the true slums, it was one step away from starvation and death. Lean shanties were constructed in hollow nooks along the rugged passageways, and huge chasms tore through areas, all without wall or rail to prevent an untimely fall. Glowing copper eyes stared out from the darker crevices, children mostly, hiding while their parents traveled the jagged roads farther inward.

The sound of pick on stone rose from the chasms, individual strikes overlapping until it was simply a ringing chorus from the earth's wound. Here and there, the stone was open enough to expose crystalline pillars that filled their area with soft, elemental light.

The bones of Ahkestria, she thought. *And they are sent down to pick at what remains.*

Zara had reached the mines. The number of guards had increased from above, sent to corral and police the miners, most likely. But where she had expected to see them indolently drinking or smoking their long pipes while the miners toiled, instead Zara saw Humans in dark mail with a single golden pauldron, fashioned to resemble flames.

Disciples of the temple? What are they doing here? Zara stood, cloaked in shadow and her own power, careful to keep out of their sight. *They're rounding up the Yttins?*

The Disciples had commandeered the soldiers-turned-guards, using them slowly gathered up the miners from their huts. More filtered up from the chasms, marching behind a long line of nervous Yttins, Dwarves, Orcs, and Goblins. Zara read fear and confusion in their unguarded

Spirits—in fact, it was so vibrant, it was all she could hear for a moment. It came from everywhere, throughout her Affinity's range.

What is going on?

It reminded her of another time, in a city by the Ending Sea, where the Pathless once reigned. Of cold nights hiding in woodsheds while patrols hunted for her family, all of them deemed heretics and anathema to the faith. Zara hissed, her breath sharp between her pointed teeth, and forced herself to relax. Shoulders came down, breathing slowed, and she unclenched her fists to find small crescent wounds pressed into her palm.

Find Isla. Then discover what is going on, she told herself. *Go.*

There was another Mark across the street, between two boulders. She stepped across the path, walking behind one of the Disciples as they passed. She was tempted to reach out...but Zara had control of her emotions once more. She let the Disciples pass without interfering. At the other side, she slipped between the boulders and engaged the Mark.

The softest song yet filled her ears, pointing her senses in the final direction. The space beyond the boulder was a switchback path that led Zara farther down the nearest chasm. She followed it, stepping carefully. The path was well-trodden, which spoke to Isla interacting often with the locals, but there were a few cracks and scars in the stones that told a tale of violence. She sped up her pace.

After the fourth switchback, Zara rounded a corner and found a wide ledge dominated by two large stone buildings. They were crude structures and very old, little more than caves with a bit of edifice carved out of them. That wasn't what made her draw up short, however, nor what made her pulse her illusory magics a touch harder.

The door to the dwelling had been kicked in, and pieces of paper and pottery were strewn about the ledge. Faintly, she could hear the low sound of talking.

Someone is inside. Several someones, all around the Journeyman Tier. Zara narrowed her eyes and slowly edged forward.

"Explain."

The moment the Grandmaster spoke, a compulsion reached up and tried to seize Felix. With an annoyed grunt, he swatted it away, his Willpower too much for the working. However, his Manasight followed the tendrils of magic that spread upward from the polished flooring beneath them all.

An array, carved beneath their feet, and he had missed it in the plethora of interference. The humming of crystals, the shimmer of the muffle ward, the various protections that simmered just beneath the council members' benches. All of it was ringing in Felix's ears.

The array felt very familiar but also utterly foreign, and it took him a second to realize why. The pitch and pattern of its faint song sounded like his Deception Skill...but inverted.

It's a circle of fucking truth, he thought.

Rage kindled in Felix's chest as the wispy tendrils reached out and sank into the Spirits of his friends—rage and fear. No matter how personally powerful Felix had gotten, he doubted he could go toe-to-toe with a Grandmaster. He couldn't risk threatening the guy, not overtly.

But the array would not stand.

Cardinal Flame!

Chthonic Tribute!

Felix fixed his attention solely on the truth-compulsion array and sank his metaphorical fangs into it. It resisted him, but his Intent and Willpower were sharpened by adversity and monsters greater than some scrawled lines in stone.

"The Pal—" Atar started, but Felix put a restraining hand on the man's shoulder. The array pulsed, once, then its power vanished into Felix's channels. Atar sagged like his strings had been cut; he looked at Felix with fear and sudden relief. Felix nodded and stepped forward.

"I will answer your questions," he said.

Looks rippled across the others, but the Grandmaster merely narrowed his eyes. "Very well. My former apprentice spoke of Paladins seeking to destroy my city. Explain this."

His city, huh? Felix nodded. "In our journeys here, we have encountered a number of the Paladins of the Pathless. Most notably were the forces that hold the Caleph Pass. Several battalions, we were told, were on their way to your city."

The Grandmaster drummed his fingers across the top of his desk. Felix could feel *nothing* from the grey-skinned man, but the others around him were giving him something. It was hard to parse in all of the magical interference, though. "And you have seen these forces around Ahkestria?" he asked.

"Our approach to your city was underground, so we did not see the area closest to it," Felix explained.

"Yes, the Disciple mentioned that you used the Ancients' Causeways. How did you gain access to them?" One of the other Masters—Llathyn—spoke up. Felix's Eye could see their name, but the rest of their information was blank, much as the rest. His newly Tempered Voracious Eye could *maybe* rip through their resistance, but now wasn't the time to provoke anyone. "The Causeways were sealed, and for good reason."

"We found our way through a breach. It was an alternative to the constant storms and attacks by undead," Felix lied.

Deception is level 31!

"Damnable storms. And those breaches should have been repaired years ago, Sig," the Master said, his ruddy face flushing further.

"The undead are an eternal problem of the Expanse. It is the price we pay for the failures of our past," the Grandmaster said, and the round-faced Llathyn pressed his lips closed.

What failures? Felix thought.

"Regardless, the Causeways are not to be traversed. For that alone, this Council should censor you, but the addition of lying about an invasion of Paladins that you cannot even confirm to have seen..."

"Lying?" Atar said. He stepped up, despite Evie's grip on his robes. "Grandmaster Kel'lyv, I would not lie to you!"

The gray-skinned mage furrowed his brows, and Felix swore that the entire room warmed by several degrees. "Do you think me a fool, Atar V'as? The Hierocracy has never invaded our lands. We have not enough to tempt them, nor is the Expanse hospitable to their armies. To bring even one battalion into the sands is an endeavor that they cannot afford, least of all now, with an insurgent Territory in their midst." The last was said with a sneer. "What proof do you offer me of these Paladins and their hostile intent?"

"I am a Seer."

Deception is level 32!

The words tumbled from his mouth before he could consider them overmuch, but it was a fair gamble. According to Zara, few people knew how Seers operated, except that they "read the near future" and could scry distant places. Felix looked into the shocked faces of the Council, their expressions varying from smug disbelief to worry. The last struck him, but he couldn't afford to stop once he started talking. "I have had a vision of the Paladins of the Pathless attacking the city of Ahkestria. In it, they are attempting to breach the storm around your city. There were many hundreds of them, all come here, for you."

Deception is level 33!

"You lie," said a female Master. Her hair was a bright, fiery red streaked liberally with white. "None have breached our storm since its raising. None can."

"They *will*," Felix insisted. He hadn't seen this during the ritual, but he knew it to be true. The Unbound was too tempting a target. "I don't know how, but they will."

"A Seer is a rare thing," Grandmaster Kel'lyv said slowly. "A combination of Skills and Titles that can only come about through years of concerted effort. How did you come to work for your master, this Autarch?"

"We've been together all my life," Felix replied honestly.

"Disciple. Is this true?" the red-haired Master asked. Fiammetta stepped forward nervously, casting a strange look at Felix.

"I-I cannot say if he is a Seer. But I know him to be a powerful mage," she said, licking her lips nervously. "I personally witnessed him hold back a horde of undead in the Causeways for a span of time. There were at least a thousand of them, if not more. Representative Veil did this alone."

That gave the Council pause, and even the Grandmaster graced Felix with a look of curiosity and interest. Then, without warning, a secondary array activated around their benches, and a curtain of silence and distorted air descended upon the Masters.

"What's happening?" Evie asked.

"They are conferring," Fiammetta said, her voice a little shaky. "They-they will continue their discussion momentarily."

"Discussion," Evie snorted. "This is a tribunal. I've been in one before, I know what it looks like."

<Quiet, Evie! Handsign only. I do not wish to gather the Grandmaster's ire, and neither should you,> Atar signed.

Evie pressed her mouth closed, but wasn't happy about it. <Fine.>

<Why are they questioning us? Evie is right, this feels like a trial, and that we're already guilty of something,> Felix signed, using his body to block the view of their communication.

<I am unsure, but more importantly, when did you decide to tell them you're a *Seer*?> Vess asked, eyebrow raised.

<Best I could come up with on short notice,> Felix signed, surreptitiously. <There was a truth compulsion array at our feet.>

<Oh thank the flame, I thought I was going mad,> Atar gestured.

<I almost thumped you one,> Evie said, and she sounded disappointed. <Sure you haven't turned traitor?>

<I had to get rid of the array, but I doubt that's it. This place is full of them. Watch out for more tricks.> Felix warned. Seconds later, the Masters' privacy screen dropped, and Felix blinked in surprise. While the area had been obscured, a number of other figures had entered, all of them women and wearing robes of orange, white, and gold.

"Matrons," Fiammetta uttered in surprise. She executed a low bow, almost prostrating herself.

"Stand, Disiciple. We are here as a formality," said a woman with silver-white hair and an unlined, almost ageless face. "This threat to the city is too great to not take seriously."

"Then you believe us?" Felix asked. "We would not press the issue if it were not a real concern. The people of your city—"

"Shall be protected, Representative Veil. Do not doubt that," the Grandmaster snapped. The heat that had faded returned again as the man gave off waves of Mana vapor into the air around him. "Our people have faced a great many crises in my time here. From famine to civil unrest to dangerous, wild beasts. All of them were surmounted.

"Now the Continent is undergoing a new period of unrest. There is conflict in the Ghreldan Hills, as always, but also the provinces to the East and to the South. Rumors of larger and more vicious monster hordes appearing within civilized lands. And to the distant Northwest, there is tell of a Beast turned Man that ate half of a frontier town. Of your master, this Autarch of Nagast."

A ripple of disquiet spread from Felix's chest. He couldn't place it, because it wasn't from the emotions of the Masters or the Matrons. They had returned to being solid walls of control.

"This Felix Nevarre is a puzzle, Representative Veil, and your presence and potency offers us no clues to its solution. Why have you come to us? To warn us out of the goodness of your heart? Or do you carry dire intentions of your own?" Kel'lyv bared his teeth, bright white against his gray skin.

"Dire—? We came to warn you, yes, but also to establish relations. We had hoped to seek trade agreements—" Felix's voice was cut off by a sharp, bitter laugh from the Grandmaster.

"I am not a fool, Veil. Perhaps your Nagast has treasures to trade, and perhaps not, but to come so far from your borders for that? There is more to you than can be accounted for." Kel'lyv gripped the arms of his crystal throne. "Why would a man of honest intentions hide themselves? How are you blocking our Analyze, Veil? If you intend no dishonesty, then unveil yourself to us."

The sound ground against Felix's senses, a disturbance that rode sideways across the discordant hum of so many powerful Skills, arrays, and crystalline Mana. He tried to respond to the Grandmaster's intimations, but the noise was like a burr catching at his thoughts, pulling at him. Insistent.

"It matters not what secrets this Autarch chooses to hide, or what his Representative deigns to tell us. We know what must be done," said the silver-haired Matron. "The city is in danger. The Highest Flame dwindles, and we've one chance at atonement. You know this, Sig'nyh. Let us do what you have called us here to do."

"What?" Felix asked. His friends shifted, moving up behind him. "What is she talking about?"

"The Highest Flame is dwindling?" Atar asked. "That's insane!"

An array burst to life beneath their feet, and this one was many times more complex than the simple truth-compulsion. Felix and his friends were grabbed by tendrils of dire force, all of them yanked to their knees.

"The Highest Flame is dying, Representative Veil," the Grandmaster said. He stood from his throne and gestured. Doors at the far end of the chamber boomed open, and the sound of booted feet filled the air. "The Paladins of the Pathless, however, have offered a brilliant solution."

Blood-red armor stomped into view, and a man at the lead with bright yellow eyes, a scar across his chin, and a sunburst at his breast.

"High Justiciar Haim, just in time. I believe I have several more volunteers for the ritual. I believe a Seer would prove quite significant."

CHAPTER SEVENTY-FIVE

"Sacrifice?" Felix grunted.

"Mhm, oh, you're all still conscious. Curious." Grandmaster Kel'lyv leaned over the edge of his bench, peering down at them upon the smooth stone flooring. "I see. Llathyn, your truth array has fallen apart."

"What? That's impossible!" The ruddy-faced Master leaned over his own bench, but the moment his eyes caught sight of Felix and the others, his eyes rounded, and his mouth gaped like a fish. "That sigaldry has lasted for a century!"

"And was maintained last decade," said the red-haired Master. "Pathetic, Llathyn. Forget about consciousness, look at him! He is still on his knees!"

The power of the array was *intense*. Whatever complexities powered it, the sigaldry was clearly leveraging itself against all of his Aspects at once. Felix could feel his friends beside him, aware but flat on their faces and unable to move.

"Sup—suppression array," Vess gasped.

It dug needles into Felix's Body, but it was his Mind and Spirit that it gouged. An immense weight and heat had settled on both, like he had been buried under a burning building. Pit screamed, the illusory flames singeing his tail and feathers with unremitting pain. Felix shook, his Body barely able to cope despite his Song of Absolution. It was as if the Skill didn't even exist. In fact, it was as if none of his Skills existed, for all the good they did him.

Chthonic Tribute!

The Skill hummed before shuddering to a sudden stop.

"Yes. An array we have found quite useful in recent days," said the Paladin. It was the man identified as High Justiciar Haim, and his bright yellow eyes creased in clear pleasure as he watched Felix struggle. "The greater one's Aspects, the better it suppresses, though that is hardly needed on the pitiful ragamuffins we removed from the city's lower layers."

"Trash," Llathyn sneered. "Hardly worth the expense such an array cost to construct. That takes nearly forty pounds of Mana crystal dust, you know!"

"The cost is irrelevant," the Grandmaster said. His gaze never left Felix's, and for a moment, the Autarch thought he saw a flicker of disappointment in his expression. "No cost is too great to keep our patron from Her demise."

Gears turned in Felix's Mind, far slower than normal thanks to the array. "You...you're sacrificing...your own people, too? These...idiots...want you...all dead..." He tried jabbing a finger at the Paladins, but his arms wouldn't work right.

"Tch," the Grandmaster shook his head, as if disappointed. "Whatever your personal power, it is clear you are new to politicking. This alliance is one of mutual benefit. We provide our peerless crafts and Mana crystals for their new war efforts, and they aid us in return. Truly, if you had wished to strike a better deal, then you should work on the one thing effective statesmen have honed: timing."

The Grandmaster stepped down off his throne of crystal, followed closely by the other Masters, and descended to join the Matrons and Paladins at the base of the array. "The High Justiciar arrived here days prior. They even warned of your coming, Veil. Of the insidious influence you walk under, one whose true nature was proven when your people assaulted and killed the Paladins left at the Caleph Pass. What sort of man would order such bloodshed?"

The Grandmaster fell silent, but the red-haired Master picked up the thread of his speech without faltering. "Where does your allegiance truly lie, Representative Veil, Seer of Nagast? Your Autarch is said to pay deference to the Endless Raven, Lost Gods, and worse. A hideous abomination in the false shape of a man, who has countless dead at his claws...You think we will trade pleasantries with such as you? Who travel in the company of Henaari and Giants?"

Pain! Fight! His Spirit surged despite the suppression, and Pit tried to claw his way free. Felix winced, falling to his hands and knees. *Fight!*

Hold on, Pit! Stop! Felix sent, but it wasn't his words that stopped the tenku. The suppression array flared higher than ever, drawing wheezing groans from his friends and sending Pit rebounding off the edge of Felix's Spirit.

"Hah, look at him, still struggling," one of the Masters said. Felix couldn't tell who through the haze of agony. "Remarkable specimen, indeed."

"Hmph. If he were worth my time, this array wouldn't hold him at all." The Grandmaster's dismissive tones were easy to identify, however. "But he will serve regardless. Paladin. You said you had a gift for us."

"Indeed I do, Grandmaster Kel'lyv," said the High Justiciar. "But first I would ask to speak of our boon—"

"Paladin, the undead run rampant and are getting worse. Soon, they will expand even beyond these lands. Only the power of holy fire can keep them at bay, and only the Highest Flame can provide what is needed. If you cannot provide the burnt offerings required to meet our needs, then our alliance is at an end." The Grandmaster's voice was hard as granite and deathly quiet. Despite the horrifying pain, Felix could hear the fearful swallows of every single Paladin.

The High Justiciar's brow furrowed, but the smile remained on his face. "We have provided for you at least ten thousand bodies. The last of which are being marched from the lowest layers now. Surely that is enough to—"

"The Yttin can be replaced. While the labor they represent hangs heavy in this world, dimpling the Corporeal with its importance to our lives and safety, they are but hands. Even with this supposed Seer and his small army, the scale is not balanced. We need true significance to strengthen the Flame, Paladin."

"You're not...touching my people," Felix tried to growl, but it came out more as a whisper.

"Oh? Your people are already mine. The Temple Knights are down there gathering them up as we speak." Kel'lyv didn't even bother to turn and face Felix as he said that, instead maintaining eye contact with the grizzled leader of the Paladins. "You. Give us what was promised."

Haim hesitated for only a moment, before smiling wider than before. "Of course. You are right, as always, Grandmaster." He snapped his fingers, and there was a rustling among the Paladins behind him. Quickly, an ornate case made from transparent crystal was handed to the High Justiciar. He regarded it silently. "This is it. Handed down in our order through the Ages, a piece of our history soaked in the blood of a thousand heretics and a million innocents lost to the Broken Path. A scrap of tabard from the Regalia of the Pathless Himself."

The moment Haim opened the ornate case, Felix felt everything lurch. Mana from *everywhere* surged toward the open container, condensing around it in a storm of power. The sheer weight of it was like a magnet, yanking Mana and eyes alike to its innocuous shape: a simple, fraying piece of cloth, once white and touched by the tiniest drop of bright red.

Blood, he thought. He knew what it was instantly, and the Divine Tree within his core trembled as if in a storm breeze. *That's the blood of a god.*

"This," hissed the Grandmaster. "This is worth it, after all. Yes." He took the case in hand and marveled at its contents. To Felix, the tiny scrap of cloth pulsed with so much significance that he was surprised it didn't fall out of the gray-man's hands and bore its way to the center of the planet. "With this to burn, the Flame will be the most powerful Urge on the Continent."

"As it should be," the High Justiciar remarked.

The two kept talking, marveling at the Regalia scrap, and Felix felt panic start to set in. His friends at least were mostly Journeyman Tier, so the suppression array held them but weren't crushing them to pieces. The exception was Evie, whose Body was shaking with constant tremors. He could feel her wheeze and choke, struggling to breathe. He had to get free. To get them out of this. He trembled, his legs barely able to move, but he heaved against the array with everything he could muster.

Very faintly, the ground trembled.

Only the rotund Master looked at him sharply, but scoffed and ignored him when Felix could barely breathe afterward. The Paladins weren't so quick to dismiss him, however.

"Hey! Enough strugglin'!" A Captain, his cloak adorned with the same pattern as that guy from the Caleph Pass, jabbed at Felix with his halberd, catching him in the ribs and making him fall under the increased strain. Some sort of enchantment on the blade sparked as it hit him, burning with a mote of radiant light. "Stay down, heretic!"

Shaking, Felix pushed back up again. The Captain didn't hesitate and struck again. This time, Felix stayed up, but for his trouble got a bloody gash opened in his side. Blood dribbled onto the polished floor, but Felix gave the man a desperate grin.

"You sorcerous piece of shit," the man hissed. He jabbed and sliced, cutting into Felix's arms and back and shoulders, each time drawing blood. More and more of it pooled beneath Felix. "On your face, heretic! Or I'll gut you here and now."

Felix looked up, his head quivering at the strain, and met the Paladin's gaze. He spat in his face.

"You—!" The Captain hefted his polearm again, and Felix could feel him marshaling some sort of Skill. "I said, stay—!"

The Paladin tensed his muscles and brought the weapon down with enough force to cut a keening note out of the air itself.

"Down!"

But Felix wasn't there. Instead, the weapon struck into the floor...and the tiny array of sigils Felix had inscribed in his own blood. The man's face paled, but it was too late. A mote of light Mana surged from his weapon's enchantment, catalyzing the tiny, almost worthless array. Worthless except that it had been connected to the flaring lines of the suppression...and that it had a single purpose.

Devour, Felix thought.

The floor *exploded*.

Screams echoed all around the room, each of the Masters calling on their impressive powers to protect themselves, but none of them expected to see two bloody halves of a Paladin Captain thrown at their feet.

"He stands!" one of the Masters cried out.

Chthonic Tribute!

With a powerful inhalation, the remainder of the array and *every other* piece of inscribed magic within the room was torn into Felix's channels. He grinned a bloody grin, his body scaled and teeth sharp as knives.

"Oh, I'm gonna do a whole lot more than that."

A wave of lightning and force hit the Paladins and Masters alike, hurling many from their feet. Llathyn, powerful Master of Stone and Shaper of Glories, remained standing.

This bastard thinks to contend with us?! He lifted his arms. "Reach of the Pinnacle!"

Two sets of massive, muscular arms made entirely of dark stone manifested upon Llathyn's girth. He slammed two of them down into the polished floor behind him, further weathering the strange force arrayed against them. The other pair he shot ahead, outward, their huge hands spread to grip and crush. Death came for him, but the idiot child—clad in monstrous *scales* for some reason—merely lowered his stance.

"Die, then!"

His arms struck, and the polished expanse of flooring erupted into a cloud of stone chips and dust. A concussive wave of air and force whipped all around where the brat and his friends stood, enough that the stone beneath their feet cratered slightly.

"HAH!" Llathyn crowed. He would have to pay to repair the council chambers, but the cost meant little to him. "Pathetic little Journeyman. You—eh?"

Somehow—*impossibly!*—the boy still stood. And not only stood.

He—he caught my arms...?

His stone arms were wrenched aside by sheer Strength, a feat that Llathyn's Mind boggled to see. Before he could pull them back, a searing pain shot across the Master's middle, and he doubled up in sudden pain. Llathyn blinked, too slow, and felt the blood flee his face as he beheld the too-close snarl of the beast he had mistaken for a boy. A boy who held a hooked blade that dripped with Llathyn's own blood and guts.

"H—how?" he asked, falling. Skills in his core space mustered, his passives attempting to boost his healing while others dragged at the earth Mana swirling within him. But he found his Mana seized as soon as it escaped his Gates, grabbed so viciously and turned to manacles and bars and slammed into him. Over and over again.

Darkness surged, and Llathyn still wasn't sure what had happened.

Where is he? The boy. Where—where did he—?

There was fire and searing light, then there was nothing at all.

Felix leaped from the dying corpse of the earth-attuned Master. It had been alarmingly easy to turn the man's Mana against him with Chthonic Tribute and Stone Shaping, draining him onto the edge of his Inheritor's Will. Lances of light, the Paladin's long range weapon of choice, flew at him, but they were simple to dodge. The Paladins weren't a concern, and he even noticed the High Justiciar had fled the room. It was the Masters he had to worry about.

"You think you'll survive against all of us, Veil?" the red-haired Master snarled at him. "You will burn! Here or at the feet of our patron, it does not matter!"

Flame and more flame came at him, filling the air with an inferno that seared Felix's skin. Pieces of it were redirected, turned back against the Paladins and three remaining Masters, while silver spears chased after their light-formed counterparts. His friends were up and fighting, but their movements were slow. They were all injured.

"Go! Get out of here!" Vess shouted at him.

"That's my line," Felix screamed back, dodging another torrent of fire. "I can hold them for a time, but you three need to run!"

"You idiot!" Evie said. She had coated herself in a thick layer of frost, but it was melting rapidly. "You think we'll make it? You think we'll live to see the street?"

Felix almost stumbled as her words hit him, and he glanced back at his friends. All of them were heaving and sweating, giving everything against the forces arrayed against them. But Evie was right.

They weren't getting out.

No. No, I refuse. I'm not going anywhere!

"Run you muscle-bound fool!" Atar shouted, while Alister barely blocked heaving wood and stone from shredding them to pieces. "Run! Spiritual Immolation!"

Atar's body ignited, fire manifesting above his skin and clothes and hair. It raged, a bloody orange stark against the yellow-orange of the Masters' attacks. He drew a deep breath and screamed.

"Strength Ignition!"

The fires descending on them diverted, turning instead to funnel into Atar's Body. The flames of his own making vanished, but were soon replaced by a deluge of fire. He took it all.

"Atar! You dare use my own technique against us?"

The Grandmaster's voice shook the chamber. Literally shook it. Evie, Vess, and Alister all flinched from the noise, blood running from their ears. The man walked out of the blaze of light and flames and approached them. His Spirit raged, so strong it congealed in a physical presence of pure orange flames licking across his limbs. Without a single word, the fire Mana in the air reversed direction, pulled from Atar and into the Grandmaster. All at once, the flames from all over were extinguished utterly.

The Grandmaster stood alone between Felix's friends and the Masters and Paladins. Atar groaned and collapsed, his Body and Spirit spent. Kel'lyv curled his lip in disgust.

"Pathetic now as you were before. Chasing after sigaldry instead of the purity that is fire magic. Power," he said, hand raised and igniting with a white-hot ball of flame. A miniature sun the size of a baseball pointed at Atar's heaving chest. "Power is all that you need, boy."

"No!"

Relentless Resolution!

Adamant Discord!

Chthonic Tribute!

Felix blurred forward, faster than he'd moved in his life, but the Grandmaster turned. He fired his shot directly at Felix.

It hit him like a cannonball. Unimaginable pain lanced across his chest as the flames burrowed through scales and skin and muscle and bone, turning his flesh to ash. The force of it sent him tearing through benches and stone, his Body forced through the foundations of the rotunda until suddenly, he was tumbling free across a sandy lawn.

Felix gasped, overcome. His Health had dropped fully half with that one attack. His chest pumped a river of blood from him, soaking the soil before his Sovereign of Flesh stopped the bleeding. Felix looked up and saw the hole his Body had bored through the Council Rotunda. He could almost see his friends...stretched out on the ground...

Fuck. He stood. *Gotta get them out.*

He couldn't even react when a burning comet sped out of that hole, hurling both of them up and into the darkened sky.

Cloudstep!

Felix kicked off a panel of Mana, redirecting himself as the comet released him, and flared his greatest power.

Adamant Discord.

Lightning crackled off his frame as he hung in the air, face-to-face with Grandmaster Kel'lyv. A man who was glowing like the goddamn sun.

"You intrigue me, Veil. You are far stronger than you appear, but your Temper leaves something to be desired." He chuckled. "It is a pity I cannot spend time to toy with you—I would truly love to pull you apart and see just what makes you tick. But I haven't the time. The ritual of the sacrifice must be observed in two days. So you must either join them now...or die."

"I don't die so easily," Felix said through his burnt throat and bleeding chest.

The Grandmaster merely smiled, and it was one of the scariest smiles Felix had ever seen.

"Good."

All Felix perceived was a sudden blaze of orange-white light, and he was falling. His leg—! He couldn't even scream, because the Grandmaster hit him again, and again, pieces of Felix flying in all directions. His scales offered him no protection, and only the prodigious Health regeneration of his Sovereign of Flesh kept him breathing.

Felix flared his Adamant Discord, if only to hurl him away. To run. He dropped down, arcing over the strange buildings of Ahkestria and out into the open air, off the side of the immense mesa. There, the storm surged yards away, but the Grandmaster caught him easily. The man laughed.

"The stormwall would kill you, Veil," he hissed, a shudder of pleasure in his voice. "And you promised me to make this last."

A sharp knee smashed his pelvis, followed by a cataclysmic elbow that sent Felix crashing into the outskirts of the Risen Ward. He healed, just enough to stand and fumble away, but the bastard found him again and again. He pummeled him, hit after savage hit. Strikes fueled by fire and powerful, impossible Strength. Far greater than Felix's. His bones snapped, muscles tore and were severed. His blood painted the edge of the mesa, and as he collapsed, it was only inches from the swirling, lightning filled stormwall.

Kel'lyv crouched beside him and grinned. He still shone, bright as any lightning bolt above them, but it had faded just a bit.

"I'll...kill you," Felix said. Kel'lyv only shook his head.

"You are still ignorant. Before you die, you shall know the glory and the might of those the Highest Flame anoints Her Chosen," the Grandmaster whispered into his bloodied ear. "I shall burn it into your Body, so that your Spirit and Mind will never forget it."

A-adamant Discord!

With every ounce of his Willpower and Intent he could still muster, Felix flared his Skill. Not to attack or to defend.

To run.

In a flash of light, Felix hurled himself off the edge of the mesa and into the stormwall.

Before the wild winds claimed him, Felix heard the bastard scoff.

"Too easy."

CHAPTER SEVENTY-SIX

Zara raced through the lower Wards, riding a wave of her own power across chasms and ledges as she circumvented the simple stairs and switchback trails around her. Her Mind blazed, working ahead of the problem as she advanced, chewing over what she had seen down below.

Isla's base had been violated, but not by the Urge's lackeys or the Council guards. By *Paladins*. She killed them all, of course, but not before extracting what little they knew of events. Of the sacrifice that the High Justiciar was facilitating, at the behest of the Council.

The fools. Short-sighted fools!

The Pathless' Orders did not help other nations, let alone one's reigned over by a powerful Urge. It was clear now what was happening, the rounding up of the miners and their transport to the higher layers. She hadn't yet found her sister of the Cantus, but that concern took second place to the fact that Felix and his people were meeting with the Council right at that very moment. Isla may have been in trouble, but her first priority was keeping Felix alive. No matter what.

The cloying darkness of the shadowed layers faded gradually, Ward by Ward as she ascended the City of Embers. Yet, even as Zara burst through the final stretch, her wave of Mana at her heels, it was to a curiously empty plaza. Night had descended, but it was still early evening, and the Risen Ward was a center of trade and stunning wealth. She would have expected couples and individuals out and about.

The Temples...

The night sky was lit in only that direction, where the darkened vault of the heavens was braised with red-orange light from soaring towers. Zara focused, folding her Intent into the dual stats of Perception and Affinity...and heard a multitude struggling in that direction, but far less than she imagined. Moreover, she could sense people in their homes behind locked doors and barred shutters, while a chord of fear and anxiety rippled the air.

The Yttin and other miners are being held at the Temples...and so are Evie and Vess, she confirmed with a tight grimace. Though she no longer had a Mark on any of them, the sound of their Spirits was unmistakable. *Atar and Alister are likely with them as well. But what of the rest?*

Before she could check, a streak of blinding fire cut across the stars. A man, his Body blazing, hurtled from the far edge of the city toward the low shape of the Council Rotunda.

Grandmaster Kel'lyv. Zara had buried her questing Intent under layers of concealment the moment she'd sensed the man, but watched him warily. There was little knowing the extent of the power of a Grandmaster, even if—as she suspected—this one derived the majority of his power from an Urge. *What was he doing over there?*

Quietly, and with far more exacting care, Zara sped along the shadowed streets and narrow alleys between estates. Her senses had caught several things before she'd hidden them away, first among them the danger posed to their weaker followers. She stopped, a full block away, and sucked in a tight breath.

Avet's blackened eyes.

The estate they had been held in was on lockdown. A veritable army of Temple Knights were outside the heavy gates, while every wall bristled with archers with arrows trained on the soldiers of the Fiend's Claw. Even limited, her senses could pick out Darius and Harn among all of them, just as she could tell that no one had been hurt. Yet.

The sound of boots hitting the smooth pavestones came to her only a moment later, followed swiftly by the labored breathing and tumultuous Spirit of a familiar face. Zara pressed herself against the brick wall and thanked her god for the darkness of his chorister's robes. Fiammetta had zero time to resist when the chanter flowed out of the shadows, stiletto pressed to her freckled neck.

"If you scream or otherwise alert your dogs, I will encase your soul in an ice so deep, no Urge could set you free," she whispered.

The Faun trembled, but offered no resistance as Zara walked both of them farther into the night's gloom. Zara considered her charred attire and frazzled hair, as well as the panic and guilt that sang from the girl.

"Tell me, *Disciple.* What has become of my people? Where is Veil?"

———

Drip.

Drip.

The sound was loud in his ears. Each rippling impact like a bomb going off. Felix twitched, shuddered.

Drip.

Images and memories spun behind closed eyelids. Of burning, colossal strikes and barefisted blows that broke bones and rent his organs. He stood amid the sky as a blazing star descended upon him and scorched the skin and scales from his body.

"Wake up—"

"AH!" Felix shouted, his Body surging to his feet and sending a small tidal wave of water in every direction. Everything blazed in a pain that turned his stupor into miserable awareness. He blinked, his vision hazy and unfocused for a moment, practically unable to see in the darkness. Spots of brilliant light were seared into his eyes in jagged lines and splotchy orbs. "Who—who is it? Who's th—there?"

No one answered.

Manasight!

For the first time in a long while, Felix had to consciously flare his Manasight. His core responded, sluggish and limping, but power fed into it and then up into the bundle of sensations that encompassed his Perception. It hurt, a thousand burning knives in his skull as it activated. It was a roar of jagged, incoherent sound in his ears, but his surroundings were revealed.

Earth and shadow Mana abounded, outlining craggy grey rocks and a dark chasm that extended upward for hundreds of feet, and in a jagged path many times farther forward and behind him. Around him, wisps of wood and stone were less solid and rigid, cast about as if a plane had crash landed in the area. He quickly picked out the remains of hovels and lean-tos, scraps of cloth, and the occasional abandoned pick-axe. And, most notably, the entire area was filled with knee-deep, ice-cold water.

"Water?" He moved his foot, splashing it a little.

"It came with you, Winged One," said a voice. The same voice that had spoken earlier.

"Who said that?" he asked.

A figure resolved out of the water and detritus. It was covered in blueish bandages and had eyes that glowed copper in the dark.

"A Yttin. What are you doing here?"

"I live here," the Yttin said, his voice edged by a heavy clicking noise. "There...ah, but it once was up there," the woman said, pointing back a ways. "Until you and the miracle arrived, Winged One."

"Miracle? Wait, Winged One? Why—?" Before he could finish the question, he realized wings extended from his back in a mass of bloodied feathers and torn muscles. Spots were scoured and ground away, with char edging many of the feathers, as if something had—the storm.

It flashed across his Mind, a too-perfect memory of dodged lightning and devoured earth Mana. Agony chased hot on its heels, a molten hot torment that crazed his Body, Mind, and Spirit. Pit had thrown up his own wings from Felix's back, shielding him from errant blasts and winds that cut like knives. Of desperately crashing through a wall of Mana crystals to flee the relentless, unbeatable storm. Trying to eat them, ripping them free of their hardened shells and into his core as he careened through...of so much water that even now his inner abyss seemed queasy. Felix reeled, his hands raw and pink with freshly healed skin...and his core space all but empty of Essence.

Pit? Pit are you okay? he sent. A quiet, whimpering confirmation met his senses, and Felix took a relieved breath despite the pain. *Me, too...I think. I feel...I can't say I feel great, but I'm alive.*

His Health, Stamina, and Mana were mostly full, though his Health was lagging behind around seventy percent. His Sovereign of Flesh had done what it had needed to...but based on his Essence store, he simply lacked any more fuel to keep it running. Apparently, he was stuck with his wings until he could take in some more...but the mere thought of it made his insides squirm. His Aspects were strained to the very edge of breaking, and his Body had taken the greatest abuse from that bastard of a Grandmaster. Felix touched his chest where his Garment was burnt through, and his chest was filled with patchy, too-pink skin.

A splash and clatter sounded somewhere behind him. Distant, but smaller splashes moved closer. Felix's ears pricked and he winced at the sound, but he could make out a number of figures advancing toward him.

"They're coming to rob you," the Yttin said, her voice full of fear. "Not many folks left, but these hid. They hid, and they are so hungry. They will kill you, Winged One."

There were at least six, probably twice that, but any further specificity was beyond him. It didn't matter anyway. His everything hurt, and that wasn't gonna change soon, but Felix could handle a dozen bandits. He lifted his fists, ready to fight, but the small Yttin raised her blue-wrapped hands.

"No! Please! My brother is with them!" she said. "They're scared and hungry, but they're—they're good people. Please." She practically sobbed when Felix turned his gaze back on her. "Please. So many were taken."

Blue light played off her face and chest, enough to tell him that his eyes were burning once again. "Taken by who?" he growled.

"Humans. Not the normal guards, but dressed in golden flames."

"Those fuckers," Felix said. A fissure of agony opened within his Mind, but his anger held it together with staples and super glue. He recalled exactly what the Paladins and Masters had said about Yttin and miners. "The temple took them." He heard the Yttin gasp, but he couldn't give her his attention anymore. Everything was focused on the pain. "Your brother had the right idea. Run and hide. The flame is looking to burn everyone up."

"My family was taken!"

Felix took a deep, steadying breath. Then he heard it. A sound in the distance, soft and enticing. It resonated with something deep inside of him, drawing him onward. Words tumbled from his brain to his mouth, inspired and unthinking.

"Do you know the Beastsworn tribe? Get out. Tell them that the Beast is coming. The world is gonna change and fast. Get everyone out of here. Hide away from the knights until the beast takes them all."

Felix wasn't sure if it was his bonuses to positive relations with the Yttin, but the woman didn't argue. The clicking sounds she made with her throat were fearful and awed. Without another word, she scurried off, back toward her brother.

Hopefully, that gets them moving and out of the city.

He put it out of his mind and turned back toward the sound. It shook in his chest and down his arms, and where it quivered, his Body felt...not better, but stranger.

Pit squawked.

"I don't know, man," Felix said. He took a step, fumbling through the knee-deep water. Everything felt bruised, if not worse. Inside, his gut fluid sloshed around in ways he was pretty sure weren't good for him. "But we can't go back up. That Grandmaster nearly killed us."

Then where? Pit asked.

Felix didn't answer. He only stumbled through the water, deeper into the dark.

———

Invocation is level 65!
Theurgist of the Rise is level 81!
Armored Skin is level 80!
Corrosive Strike is level 73!
Cloudstep is level 49!

The fight had been good for Skill levels, if little else. Felix brought up the notifications as he traversed the watery chasm, pressing deeper and deeper into the rocky heart of the mesa.

New Title(s)!
ERROR!
Due To Advanced Tier, Acquisition Of New Titles Less Than Rare Are Restricted!
Unbound Detected!
Recalculating...
New Titles Lost!

Despite his bone deep aches, he snorted derisively. *Of course.*

Recalculating...
New Skill!
Last Cry Of The Chthonic Host (Mythic), Level 1!
You were born of the earth and fire both, and though the darkness is home, you will not be denied the heavens. Though the

fiery hosts might hurl you down, you shall always, always rise. As your Health approaches zero, expend Essence and significance to instantly bring Health and Stamina back to full. Can be used once per month. Frequency of use increases slightly with level.

The power of that Skill doubled Felix over, sending him splashing to his knees as System power thundered through his core space. The Skill formed, a Skill almost as complex as his Transcendent Rarity ones, and just as big and bright as his Bastion of Will, despite its low level. The song of it shook him, heels to the ends of his hair, and his Aspects all failed him at once.

Like a candle in the wind, everything went out.

Time slipped away, but when the spinning darkness resolved once more into the waterlogged tunnel, Felix just laid there and let the water course over his overheated skin.

Fuck me, what kinda Skill is that? He pushed himself up on an elbow, the water barely up to his armpit, and scrubbed his face. *It looks damn useful, though. If I had that against that gray-skinned prick...I'd still be here, most likely.*

It was hard to lie to himself, sometimes.

Felix stood shakily, his Body twinging in every conceivable spot, but as he did, he noticed that the water level had decreased considerably. In fact, the sound he had been following was clearer than ever but was also now accompanied by the soft roar of a waterfall.

"Hear that, Pit? Sounds like a big drop and some wide-open space," he mumbled. Pit let out a ragged chirrup, happy at the idea of freedom but too tired to celebrate it. The tenku was entirely too large for the narrow chasm, even if he had recovered from the Grandmaster's assault.

Etheric Concordance is level 77!

Felix knew his Companion wasn't only hurt, but sour about his inability to fight against the Grandmaster. Everything in that battle had happened so fast, the two of them hadn't even had a chance to separate. And even if they had, Felix doubted it would have mattered. That fight had been a wake-up call. Maybe Felix was strong and had the stats of someone far above him, but there was a gulf of power he hadn't even approached yet.

They followed the twisty chasm, taking branching paths as the song ebbed and flowed alongside the water. Felix's Health was just shy of full, but that didn't matter for what ailed him. He limped and gasped along the uneven pathway, pushing himself despite his sudden weakness.

It'll pass. Strain just takes a bit to heal, that's all. Felix tried not to think about what was happening up above, about the sacrifice the Grandmaster and Paladins were planning. Kel'lyv said two days. Two days before the "ritual" was needed to be performed. Could he heal up before then? Even if he did, what could he do against someone so far above him?

The song flared again, encouraging him to follow it further. He knew now that it was a piece of the Grand Harmony. Zara had shown him a snippet once back in Haarwatch, and he recognized its like now. The piece was short and repetitive, as if it were a signal being broadcast across the area...or a lure. There was an Intent buried in the song, and though he couldn't parse all of it out, it amounted to: *come and find me.*

It was an intoxicating melody, and Felix found his steps speeding up the closer he came to its origin. He barely noticed the chasm end with water cascading over a lip of stone, and a narrow pathway etched by nature into the sheer cliff face. Pit chirped curiously as they half-slid down the trail, while a yawning abyss spread out to their right. Winds howled far below, as if the ground was breathing, buffeting Felix but doing little to his extraordinarily heavy Body. He plodded onward until the path opened up once more.

A far deeper ledge had been formed here, and atop it was a ramshackle cottage made of carefully stacked stones and thick, woven reeds. Felix approached it carefully, spotting a shadow moving among the yellow-orange illumination. A fire burned merrily in a wide, pot-bellied oven, and as Felix drew abreast of the door, a Yttin wearing embroidered silken robes turned in surprise.

"Oh," the Yttin clicked. Its copper eyes glowed, bright and round. "I was not expecting you at all."

CHAPTER SEVENTY-SEVEN

Felix leaned back, letting the stove warm him. The water had cooled him down enough that his overheating body had grown comfortable, but the howling wind of the chasm just outside the dilapidated hut had turned that chill into something more bone-deep. He nursed a mug of mulled wine, holding it close, and watched the owner of the hut over the chipped rim.

The Yttin, named Naos, was bustling about the hovel. He cleaned fastidiously, wiping surfaces and sweeping out stray bits of stone and dirt Felix had tracked in. His hands and the prehensile appendages upon his back were never still—they gripped the broom of bundled reeds, a well-worn rag, and carefully adjusted wall hangings from their hammered wooden pegs. The hovel was all one large chamber, with a narrow bed in the corner and rickety shelves tacked along every flat section of wall. Knick-knacks lined those shelves, polished pieces of stone, a tiny Mana crystal, and even a couple dog-eared books with cracked spines. It was a cozy and clean space, if so very clearly poor.

Embarrassingly, Felix had spent a full minute speaking with Naos before the Yttin had politely reminded him of his state of dress. Felix's Garment had burnt up across his chest and stomach and revealed a large swath of pink skin. He had also learned that his Garment could get stuck in a shape if he fixated on it too much—Felix's Mind had been lingering so much on the battle that it had stayed locked in that disheveled state, a charred and torn remnant of his fight. The moment Naos pointed it out, however, he fed enough Mana into it that a new tunic appeared almost instantly.

"So you live down here?" he asked again. "How?"

Naos didn't stop moving, but his copper eyes flashed in amusement. "Day to day, my boy. Day to day."

"All alone in the dark? Seems pretty lonely," Felix said. He took another sip of the mulled wine. The warm liquid felt good on his throat. "How far below Ahkestria are we?"

"Deeper by far than they let most go," Naos said in that amused, almost teasing tone. Clicks trilled at the edges of his words. "How did you find yourself here...Veil, was it?"

"Mhm," Felix agreed, letting a mouthful of wine give him a moment to think. His Mind was just as strained as the rest of him, but even concussed, he wasn't about to give his real name to some stranger. "The Temple Knights are rounding up the miners. I don't know why, but I'm not interested in finding out."

Deception is level 34!

"So I saw. But you're no miner, boy." Naos turned, extra appendages lifting his slight, bandage-wrapped body up and onto the bed on the far side of the hut. He folded his legs beneath him and smiled. "No miner could afford such a...curious bit of clothing."

Right. Shit. His Mind really wasn't at its best—Felix hadn't even thought of what his special magical artifact would look like to a poor Yttin. "A gift. For a job well done."

"Oh? Must have been quite the job. I've not seen such clever use of sigaldry in a long while."

Felix blinked. It was there, again. A fitful flash across the Yttin's shoulders and down the spider-like appendages on its back. He had spotted it once or twice before, but dismissed the phenomenon as a trick of the light and his tired eyes. "Naos. That is a...curious name. I feel like I've heard it before."

Felix took another long sip of his wine, and the Yttin shrugged. "A common enough name among my people."

"A hut in the deepest parts of a chasm, where few go. I think I'd go crazy from boredom," Felix said. His Mind felt a bit clearer already, and something was prodding him not to trust this man.

"I keep busy. My people, the poorest of the poor, need services I can provide, after all. Healing ointments, splinting broken limbs from rockslides and cave-ins, that sort of thing."

"It'd be easier to do that up above, wouldn't it? Where the miners live?" That was a guess on Felix's part, but it followed reason that the miners would be living at the bottom-most layers. "How would they reach you here?"

Naos smiled. It was just as unnerving as any other Yttin, all thin lips and tiny, sharp teeth. "Perhaps I too did not wish to be herded above."

Felix couldn't blame him for that. But did Naos know what was going to happen? "You're a healer...do you have any way to heal Aspects?" he asked.

"It is possible, though quite difficult," Naos said. He had begun pulling small bundles off his shelves and placing them on a cracked wooden tray. "One's Aspects are a confluence of Stats and Tempers. Each varies, person to person...unless you follow one of the guilds or temples, then they are dangerously similar." Naos pursed his lips, but that humor danced behind his eyes. "I can tell you're made of sterner stuff, Mr. Veil."

"Mm," Felix allowed, taking another long sip. "Why's that?"

"Not many can fight a Grandmaster and live."

Felix froze, cup at his lips. His cores spun, a riot blaring above his navel. "Who are you?" he asked.

"Who are you? Because I know your name is not Veil, no matter what my Analyze tells me." Naos kept moving, now pressing a root vegetable into a small bowl. "Some might consider it rude to lie to your host. Not I, of course. But some."

Felix smiled, his Mind whirling. Hesitantly, Felix reached out with his Affinity...and felt nothing from the Yttin. Nothing at all. Yet more startling than that was that neither his Spirit or Mind hurt from reaching out. His surprise wasn't unnoticed.

"Ah, you've attempted to Analyze me?" He asked, chuckling. A pestle in his hands ground the roots and a sprinkle of glittering Mana crystals. "Or was it something else? I imagine your Mind is already feeling better?"

"My—" he looked suddenly at the wine in his hands, and focused his Voracious Eye on it. It hadn't offered up any secrets before, but he'd been so turned around...yet this time, his Eye cut through a faint resistance he'd not even noticed before. "The wine."

Name: Panacea
Type: Consumable (Elixir)
Lore: Derived from potent materials, this drink was prepared by a Master of Alchemy in order to cure the ails of those at Master Tier or lower. Provides a measure of healing to all Status Conditions, wounds, curses, and limited aid to Aspects. The lower the imbiber's Tier, the greater the effect.

"You...gave me an elixir," Felix said slowly. His stomach curdled, mostly in sudden worry. The Yttin could have poisoned him just as easily. "Why didn't you tell me?"

Naos shrugged and poured a putty-like mixture out of his stone bowl. He pressed it carefully into a wide swath of cloth, spreading it evenly. "You are difficult to read, warrior. It is...curious. I did not know your motivations, or even why you fought the Grandmaster of the Desert's Fire. Only that you had and survived. Truly a tale worthy to be told."

With a few deft twists, he closed up the cloth, producing a very large poultice that he carried off the bed and toward Felix. He stood and moved as the Yttin drew closer, but Naos only placed it in a shallow tray above the stove and let it sit. "There. That just needs to warm some. Don't be so nervous, warrior. I've no need or want to hurt you. I am a healer, after all."

Felix wet his lips. The cup he set aside, which earned him a displeased cluck of the tongue from the Yttin. It had helped him, he couldn't deny that, even if there was still some strain remaining on his Mind and Spirit. Felix could hear the hum of Harmony again, and it was powerfully strong in the tiny hut...but was intensely quiet around Naos. That flash of light was there again, on Naos' body, a line at the edge of his Perception. *As if he isn't here or isn't—*

"You aren't Yttin," Felix said. Naos' amused face froze, though he couldn't tell if it was out of surprise, fear, or wariness. Naos. It had clicked, where Felix had first heard the name. "Who are you?"

Both of them stood stock still, their eyes unblinking. Yet, before Felix could open his mouth again, a bellow came from the chasm outside.

"Naos! Naos! I need your help! The Temple Knights are pushing deeper, and all your friends are running for some reason—" A huge form pushed into the room. A half-man, half-bull with sweeping horns, massive shoulders, and shaggy fur. He looked at Felix in utter shock. "W-who're you?"

Felix's stomach twisted. "Unbound," he said. "We have a lot of things to talk about."

———

Things...happened very quickly after that.

Before Felix could say anything else, the Minotaur had torn across the hut, charging at him head-first. Horns crashed into him, smashing a startled Felix off his feet and *through* the stacked-stone wall.

"Die, Paladin!" the bovine shouted.

Relentless Resolution!

The moment they cleared the wall, Felix kicked off the Minotaur's skull. He flipped backward, arcing twenty feet to land in a sliding crouch. His opponent snorted and shook his head, confused for a brief moment before finding Felix in the driving clouds of stone dust.

"How did you follow me?" he asked, and looked around. Sand and blood matted the fur along his neck and left shoulder, where his stolen Paladin armor had been broken apart. "Only I can get through the stormwall!"

"You walked through the city's protections?" Felix asked. *He's tougher than I thought.*

"You're not gonna get Naos, Paladin! Not even if there are a hundred of ya hidden around here!"

"There's only me. And I'm not a Pal—" Felix was cut off by the Minotaur suddenly appearing before him, meaty arm cocked for a wicked left jab. He dodged, stepping out of the jab's path. "Hey, that's Relentless Charge! I used to have that!"

"Wha—Shut up and fight!" the Minotaur growled. His punch missed Felix, but he turned it into a lumbering smash onto the ground beneath them, and Felix saw streams of black, green, and gold Mana burst from his fist. "Chitin Construction!"

Faster than he expected, the Minotaur whipped his hand up, now holding a massive, jagged hammer made out of overlapping plates. Felix put out his hand and caught the maul's hammer head...but the guy was also stronger than he expected. He skidded two feet backward from the blow, and his Health even took a tiny hit. His Armored Skin blunted almost all of the attack, but he still couldn't summon his scales due to lack of Essence. Yet the idea of absorbing more made the abyss within him whimper, the recent influx of water Mana having proven too much too soon.

Damn. I don't know if I can fight him off without relying on some of my more intense Skills. Felix set himself and spread his arms, only feet from the edge of the chasm. "I don't want to fight you, Michael. I'm here to help."

Me, too. Let me help, Pit sent.

Not yet, Felix replied, refocusing on the Unbound just in time to catch a complicated series of emotions crawling across his inhuman face.

"How do you know my—that name?" the Minotaur demanded. He drew himself up, steam and spittle pouring from his snout as he hefted his great maul. "Who told you it!"

"I know a lot of things," Felix said slowly. "If you'd just listen—"

"How do you *know that name*?!"

Michael wasn't listening, and he flashed forward with another Relentless Charge. Felix sighed and did the only thing he could think of: he twisted, grabbing the bull by the horns...and kicked off the ground.

Right into the chasm.

"MICHAEL!"

A horrified shout came from above, but it was lost to the howling of frigid winds and the Minotaur's fearful bellows. That maul swung wildly and thick fingers grabbed at Felix's body with relentless abandon. Felix's left hand was bashed loose, but on the hammer's return strike Felix made a single, sharp gesture.

Corrosive Strike!

The great maul burst apart, crazed by lines of sizzling acid. Michael screamed, his rage turning to fear as the dark floor of the chasm rose up to meet them both. His inhuman hands seized onto Felix's arms, wrenching him forward into a tumbling grapple, and Felix allowed it.

It made his next task way easier, after all.

Adamant Discord!

Lightning erupted beneath them into a column of blue-white light, and their fall was almost entirely arrested. Almost. They hit the rolling dunes of crimson sand like meteorites.

Felix stood almost immediately. The two of them had been thrown apart by the collision, and his eyes swiftly swept the rolling dunes for his fellow Unbound. *Fuck, did I cushion the impact enough?*

That worry was put to bed when a horned man roared up from a sea of cascading sands. His limbs were bloody, but Michael stood up seemingly without a hitch.

"Good, you didn't die," Felix said.

"I don't die so easily," Michael snapped back.

I don't appreciate the irony, universe. Felix spread his senses, feeling out the terrain of rolling dunes shaped by the ceaseless, gale-force winds around them. Cave openings dotted the stone in multiple directions, black eyes in the dim lighting, and source of the winds as well as the sands. *These caves lead...outside? Must be how he got in from the Expanse. Still, that'd require a lot of Health or maybe just a crap load of Endurance.*

Voracious Eye!

Felix raised an eyebrow as Michael clumsily slid down the dune that separated them. He was bleeding heavily now, but still working ponderously to reach Felix. "You're level 38, but you're only barely out of Apprentice Tier. You've been here a year, right?" Felix asked. "You're Unbound. Your growth should be faster than this, Michael."

And what was with that *name?*

"SHUT UP! Chitin Construction! Relentless Charge!"

Sand sprayed in all directions, and the Minotaur ascended Felix's dune, a new maul forming in his meaty hands. Yet before he could reach the summit, a dozen stone formations shot upward from below.

Stone Shaping!

Michael shattered through several of them before losing all momentum and had to break them apart with his Strength. But by the time he reached Felix's position, he was already gone.

"Now you're running? Realized your magic spells can't break my Body, huh?" Michael spun until he spotted Felix, who was another dune over. "You might be fast, but you can't hold up against my Strength and Endurance. No one can."

"Really?" Felix said. He grinned. "Show me, then."

"Nah," Michael said with a sneer. "Cuz I got magic too, noob."

The shaggy Minotaur lifted his hand, which glowed with blackened green threads before they launched outward into the sands. "Hallowed Call!"

Felix was still recovering from hearing someone say "noob" unironically when the sands exploded all around him. Six bone knights wearing broken Paladin armor rose from the sands, swords and axes in hand. He swept them with his Eye and dismissed them out of hand. He didn't even try to stop them as they scurried up the dune toward him.

"You can do more than this," Felix said. Michael's eyes widened before narrowing angrily. "I've seen it, man. You're going to need so much more to handle me."

"Fuck you! You want it all?" The Minotaur practically glowed with necrotic Mana as a thickened cord shot off toward one of the caverns. "Take it all!"

A wave of sand rolled out of the dark, a veritable tsunami of granules, and within it was a massive shape of overlapping plates. The wave surged and broke across their position, forcing Felix to use his movement Skill to evade and stay upright. As the sand settled, a huge centipede reared up into the air, easily the width of a subway train. Eyes glowed with blackened-green light as its mandibles flexed with small crashes.

"Michael. You have called us?" it boomed into the air.

"PvP time, Hallow! Enemy at twelve o'clock! Kill!"

"As you wish."

The creature—an undead Multipede according to his Eye—surged forward, the spikes and horns atop its skull slamming into Felix's dune like a falling tenement.

Relentless Resolution!

Cloudstep!

Cloudstep is level 50!
Journeyman Tier!
You Gain:
+5 AGL
+5 DEX
+5 PER

Felix skidded atop panels of crackling Mana, only just able to stay ahead of the Multipede's dangerous thrashings. Perhaps he might have survived its hit, but with his Aspects still strained and his scales unavailable, Felix wasn't interested in finding out. He had other tools, though.

Cardinal Flame!

Red-gold flames burst along the undead insect as well as the undead knights that scurried across the sands toward him. The knights froze, their bodies burning, but the Multipede shook it off. The knights writhed in pain, and so did Michael.

"Ahhh! Hallow! Stop him!"

Convergence!

Pit screeched in joy, finally free as he materialized in a flash of blinding light. Michael shouted, throwing up an arm and creating a shield of chitin, but Pit wasn't going for him. He descended on the undead knights instead, unleashing a slew of Wingblades and Frost Spears.

The knights were crushed, instantly.

"No!" Michael wailed, flinching as if he'd taken the hits. "Those took so long to—What the hell is that?" he demanded.

Felix shrugged and grinned. "Attack dog."

Michael bellowed again, and the air shook with it. Felix felt a debuff try to worm itself into his Body, but he shrugged it off just as the Multipede slammed down onto his spot again. He dove, rolling out from under the body slam and only catching one of the creature's sharpened legs across the back. Felix grunted in pain but kept moving, racing to meet the furious Minotaur raising a shield and hammer at him.

"How're you so fast?" Michael yelled, swinging the hammer for his head.

Felix ducked it easily, and jabbed his palm up into the weapon's haft. It snapped and the head flung off into the dark. "Michael." He spun out of range of a shield bash, kicking off another Cloudstep to redirect around the bull warrior. "Michael, why are you so weak?"

Felix sundered his shield with a single, unpowered strike.

"I'm not!" Abandoning his split shield, two new hammers appeared in his hands, each the size of a great sword. He swung, sending geysers of sand with each missed strike. Felix danced among the hits, barely trying.

"You're Unbound. You should be stronger," Felix said.

"You don't know anything!"

Crackling explosions and opposing shrieks filled the air behind them, and Felix could tell Michael was distracted by the battle between their friends. Whatever Hallow was to him, it was easy for Felix to see that Michael cared.

He caught the Minotaur's hammers and dug in his fingers, holding them in place. "We don't have to fight," Felix said.

Michael heaved on the weapons, but was unable to budge them from Felix's grip. "How are you so strong?"

"Do you have bad dreams, Michael?" Felix asked. "Dreams that feel real?"

Chthonic Tribute!

With a herculean effort, Felix pulled on his Skill. The hammers dissolved into smoke and were pulled into Felix's channels, burning him all the way.

Sovereign of Flesh!

Blinding agony seared across every nerve ending, but Felix forced the Skill to engage. Black scales erupted across Felix's neck and chest and arms, a midnight void in the dark chasm. His eyes blazed with blue fire.

"You..." Michael's eyes widened, and despite his bull face and grisly affect, he suddenly seemed incredibly young. "It's you."

"Like I said." Felix grimaced through the pain in his core. "I think we need to talk."

CHAPTER SEVENTY-EIGHT

The morning dawned on the Risen Ward, and already the streets were crowded. Most notably, folks gathered thickest near the Temple and Council Rotunda, where a wide platform had been erected in the night. The Matrons and Masters stood behind a minor official as they offered a proclamation. From her position across the Ward, Zara could not make out the entire speech, but it was easy enough to guess the rest of it.

They're rallying the people against us. Blaming a...someone killed a Master? Zara squeezed her eyes shut, a headache threatening just behind her eyes. *Felix. Of course. And now they're all condemned as traitors.*

"Did a Master truly die? You did not mention that before," she said aloud. Beside her, skirts rustled, and armor clinked softly.

"I was not able to see much that occurred...only that your representative was far stronger than anyone expected." Fiammetta shuddered. "He defeated one of the Masters, and though I did not see him die, I am not surprised if he had. Or rather, I am. I—that level of strength, and he is a mere political envoy? Who is your ruler, then?"

Zara didn't bother to answer that. The girl had proven herself useful after Zara interrogated her. In fact, the Chanter hadn't even had to do much except ask questions. The Faun was quick to give everything she knew. That was why Zara wasn't particularly surprised about the proclamation and what it claimed. What did alarm her, however, was the idea of this sacrifice. It was precisely the sort of thing the Hierocracy fabricated to hunt down those who did not kowtow to their little god.

Avet let me live to see the day they all burn, she thought. It was less of a prayer and more of a wishful promise to herself. *And let today be the last day these hateful fools darken this world.*

Across the square, she spotted movement atop the walls of her target.

Zara stood. "Come. A number of the Knights have already left to attend that proclamation. While the crowds and officials are distracted, now is the time to strike."

"Right," Fiammetta said. She hefted a mace in her left hand, made almost entirely of a golden alloy and etched with a number of sigils. "How are we to do this, then?"

"If you cannot recall, then I do not need you on this endeavor," Zara said dismissively. "I will rescue my people alone."

"No!" she said quickly. And then, after a breath. "No. I can do this."

"Can you? Can you kill Temple Knights? These are your brothers and sisters in arms, are they not?" Zara needled her, Affinity dialed in on her Spirit. She could hear a bevy of emotions strum through the girl's heart, but rising from them all was a sense of guilt coupled with a strident determination.

"I cannot allow the Matrons to do this horrible thing. It is not what I was taught, nor is it in the best interests of this city. I—I am sorry for my part in events, but had I an inkling of what the Masters were planning, I would have...I would have done *something*. I know it." The Faun's eyes were still red-rimmed from her confessions earlier in the night, but her gaze was unwavering now. "This sacrifice must not happen. There must be another way to save the Highest Flame."

Zara grinned and was pleased to see the Faun barely flinch from her sharp teeth.

"Then do as I say, exactly."

———

Felix drank down a third cup of Panacea wine and hesitated only a second longer before filling a fourth. As much as he didn't want to admit it, the mixture was doing wonders for his Aspects. The fire in the potbellied stove was crackling and warm as ever, but he was uneasy. After he'd convinced Michael to stop trying to kill him, the two of them had ascended a set of hidden stairs in the cliff face, until they returned to Naos' small hut. Despite their wild fight, the hut didn't show a single sign it had ever been partially collapsed.

Naos had offered both of them some space to rest and relax after their altercation, and though the Yttin seemed *immensely* curious about Felix, he restrained himself from asking any questions. Michael, for all his talk of Endurance, passed out almost immediately after laying down. The Minotaur's snores had soon filled the hut and beyond.

Felix found it difficult to trust the Yttin, but sleep had been too tempting to refuse. Pit had remained outside, too big to enter, but was more than enough to watch over him while he rested. Eventually, Felix allowed himself to drift off.

That had been hours ago. Now he sat on a poorly crafted chair and watched Naos fuss over the Minotaur's many wounds. The poultice the

Yttin had prepared before was wrapped tight against Michael's huge shoulder. Outside, Pit and that enormous Multipede sniffed curiously at one another.

"I'm fine," Michael insisted again.

"You were bleeding all over the sand, boy," Naos said acerbically. "If I am to play at being your teacher, then perhaps you should listen to me and *not* try and murder my houseguests, hmm?"

"Not even bleeding anymore," he muttered. Quietly.

"Teacher?" Felix asked.

"Oh yes. I've been tutoring willful children for many years now." Naos smiled in that unnerving way all Yttin did.

"And how many years have you worn the face of a Yttin?" It was a guess, phrasing it that way, but he'd watched those flashes of light ripple across the healer's body multiple times now. They looked like *seams*.

"You speak nonsense." Naos narrowed his copper eyes at him. "You see far too much for a young man, to speak of Unbound and faces that change. Who are you, Veil? Truly?"

Felix set down his mug, half-drained, and spread his hands. "Just a guy from Florida."

"Wait," Michael straightened, his dark green eyes wide. "Florida? That's...that's not on the Continent, right? There isn't like, a Florida full of Elves or something, right?"

The thought of that made Felix chuckle. "No. Not that I'm aware of. I'm just like you, Michael."

"You're from Earth? Holy shit." The Minotaur surged to his feet, his bullish face giddy. "Naos said there were others, but I didn't—I haven't met anyone who knew about Earth!"

"There are nine of us," Felix said, before he caught up with Michael's rushed words. "Naos said that, huh?" He stared at the Yttin, who had gone very still in the corner. "Did he also tell you we were summoned here to fight a war?"

"Be careful what you speak of, Veil. You tread on dangerous ground," Naos warned him, but Felix snorted.

"Can't exactly say that's new for me," he said, but didn't press the topic. From the way Michael was pacing and laughing, he wasn't sure how much the guy even cared.

"Naos said we got summoned, yeah yeah. Said he and some of his friends disrupted the ritual-thing and got us free. Naos is smart. Definitely min-maxed in Intelligence and Wisdom," Michael said.

"Wisdom...isn't one of the stats."

The big guy stammered and then snorted bullishly. "I uh, I meant Willpower. Same diff, right?"

"Uh. I mean, sort of," Felix allowed.

"So you are Unbound as well," Naos said, finally drawing closer to him. He moved slowly and kept his hands well away from his person, as if approaching a feral animal. "Two. Here, under my roof."

"Oh yeah, I'm definitely an Unbound," Felix said, letting his teeth show. "And you're a Chanter, aren't you?"

Naos' eyes went wide.

"How did you—what are you talking about? I am Yttin; I have lived here for centuries! Ask anyone!" He gestured to the empty level, devoid of anyone. "Well, ask anyone another time. But I am only Naos."

Felix rolled his eyes. "I already established that you're wearing a disguise. And it's not made of Mana...at least, not entirely. It's too convincing. That's Chant-made, and you're Cantus Sodalus." Felix snapped his finger. "Isla, isn't it?"

"Tch." The imperious-looking Yttin deflated and surprised Felix by pouting. "I can recognize a Chanted artifact when I see one, and that amulet is impressive indeed. You've met a member of my Order, then?"

"Zara."

Naos—Isla—laughed, the noise almost girlish and ill-fitting in his mouth. "That old bag of bones dragged herself to the desert. For what? She clearly had already found you."

"My visions...I was seeing Michael here, and he was in trouble." He looked at the Minotaur. "I came to help."

Michael huffed a long, relieved breath. "Help. And you're from Earth?" he asked again. His eyes watered, as if worried Felix would change his mind.

"Yeah. I think all of us are from Earth," Felix said.

"Wow," he said. "Wait. Why'd you call Naos something else? What is the Catan Sodapop?"

"In due time, dear boy," Naos said. "I did not get your name, child. Your real name, if you please."

Felix leaned back, scooping up the mug of wine once more. "Felix Nevarre. Nice to meet you."

Silence overtook the cramped hut, then Naos began to laugh.

———

"So I've been in the desert a while, ya know? Fightin' shit and stuff," Michael said as they stood on the outside of the hut. He patted the rough carapace of his strange companion. "Hallow helped me through a lot of it, really."

Hallow, the Multipede, nodded its truck-sized head. The spaces between its segmented chitin glowed blackened-green.

"Is Hallow your Companion?" Felix asked, stepping away from the chasm's ledge. He was unhappy to realize that, while he knew he could survive the fall, the idea of jumping into it again made his stomach decidedly queasy. *Or maybe that's just my little hungry abyss,* he mused. It was still complaining—sort of. The communication between Felix and his Hunger wasn't exactly on the level of words or even sense-impressions like with Pit. More like vague concepts.

"I am one," Hallow said. Its voice was oddly resonant, though definitely female.

"One what?" Felix asked the creature.

"Don't bother. She says that when I ask, too," Michael admitted. "Don't really know what she is, just that she's the one that, uh, fills up all the bodies I can control."

"Fills up, huh," Felix said. "In the visions I had of you, that was pretty clear. How does that work?"

"I am legion," Hallow said. Soft as it was, the voice reverberated, and Felix felt his teeth vibrate.

"Oh yeah, she says that, too," the Minotaur said with a shrug. "No clue what that means, either."

Pit was sitting nearby, golden eyes trained on the unnerving insectile length of Hallow. He kept sniffing the air and making short chirrups.

What's up, bud?

Pit shrugged. *Smells good.*

Interesting. Felix wouldn't have bet on that.

"So...did you get hit by lights, too?" Michael asked.

"What?"

"Like, when you were brought here?" He shrugged, a bit awkwardly. "I was hit by like, this huge wave of liquid light? I was in my room, playing SwordLore. Almost got to the last boss, too."

"SwordLore?" Felix's Mind reached back to the hazier memories of Earth. "That was an...MMO right? The one with all those professional guilds and stuff?"

"You never played it? What? Everyone at school played it non-stop." Michael snorted, his bull-snout twitching. "I didn't, uh, I didn't have any kinda guild or anything. More of a solo player, ya know?"

"Sure," Felix said. He'd never been a fan of online gaming, preferring to play singleplayer games or tabletop stuff. "Been a while since I played any sort of game, to be honest."

"What do you mean? We live *here* now!" Michael spread his heavily muscled arms. The guy was huge, and his reach was really impressive. "This is like every awesome game I've ever played, but a million times better!"

Felix frowned, but Michael kept talking, his gestures growing more animated as he went.

"Anyway, the light wave grabbed me an' yanked me through like space or something? I don't remember much, except landing here. South of this city, deeper in the desert. It was a nasty time." His enthusiasm waned a bit. "Real bloody at first. There's...there's lots of bad things out in the sands during the day. So, when I got the chance to pick my own Race? Hell yeah! That was amazing. So I chose my favorite. A powerful body that could win."

"Minotaur is a good choice. I imagine you get extra Strength and Endurance each level?" Felix asked.

"And Vitality. They're like, custom-made to be awesome warriors," Michael said with a wide smile. "Can't believe you stuck with Human, though."

Felix shrugged. "If you don't mind me asking, what's your Omen?"

"Oh, yeah that thing." For some reason the guy looked suddenly embarrassed. "Promise not to laugh, okay?"

"Okay?" Felix said, unsure.

"It's just...ugh. I got the Lovers Omen."

Michael looked down at the ground, as if profoundly ashamed, and Felix didn't know what to say. "Why would I laugh at that?" he asked.

"What? Because it's all about love and stuff? That's dumb," Michael said with a distinct pout in his voice. "I dunno what's out there, but I wanted like King Kickass or something. And I got some lame female MC thing? It's not fair."

"I—" Felix sighed. *This is stupid.* "What bonuses does it give you?"

With an annoyed grunt, Michael swiped his hand across the air. A blue notification window rotated into Felix's view.

Omen: The Lovers - Bonded and sealed. +2 INT, +1 VIT, +1 END

"That's pretty solid," Felix said. *'Bonded and sealed' is interesting. Is that why Michael was able to develop this Companion of his?* "Spells hit harder, a little extra Mana, and even more Stamina and Health boosts. What's not to like?"

Michael only shrugged. "I dunno."

Felix rolled his eyes and decided to keep the conversation moving. "After that, you decided to rename yourself, then?"

"Oh!" Michael's eyes regained their luster with a vengeance. "Yeah! It's cool, isn't it? Like, I wanted my old handle I had in SwordLore, but the System wouldn't let me add special characters."

"So you...picked *Beefhammer* instead?" Felix asked, trying and failing to contain a smirk.

"Bruh. I'm a big slab of beef now! Took some doing to get my hammer, but I got it! Now I kick ass all over the desert." Michael —*Beefhammer*—flexed his arms and posed. Felix couldn't help it as a laugh bubbled out of his throat. "What?"

"Just—" Felix said, shaking from restraining more laughter. "It's just Beefhammer is...it's, *hoo*, it's a great name."

"It is, isn't it?" Michael said, clearly just as proud as he was oblivious to Felix's amusement. "Though, could you stop calling me Michael? That's...that's my old name, for the old me. I'm Beefhammer now."

The guy's tone shifted so seriously, and his Spirit followed. This was important to him. Felix nodded. "I can do that, Beef."

Beef grinned. "Cool."

The door to the hut creaked open and closed, and a Human woman entered, with long limbs and piles of platinum blonde hair that tumbled from a strangely woven, metallic headpiece. She had a strong nose over dark eyebrows and eyes with an almost hawk-like intensity.

"Whoooa, who're you?" Beef asked, a conjured great maul suddenly in his hands.

"Isla, I presume," Felix said, looking at the Minotaur. "Formerly Naos." He turned back to the Chanter and inclined his head slightly. "Nice to finally meet you."

"Naos! You got boobs!" Beef said, staring in confusion at the Chanter before him. "When you said you were wearing a mask, I thought you meant like...I don't know. But you're Human? Not Yttin?"

"Yes, dear boy. I know it's confusing, but such is the nature of magic." She shrugged delicately and smirked at Felix. "Nice to meet you both, officially. Michael. Autarch Nevarre."

"Autarch," Michael said with a wondering laugh. "Man, I still can't believe you conquered a whole Territory. You're in like...endgame content already. Or at least mid-game."

Felix spotted the heavy bags at Isla's side. "What's the plan, then? Taking the fight to the Grandmaster?"

"No. That's foolish, and *I've* nothing to prove," Isla said. "I go to find my sister and help her evade this sacrifice. To help those I can."

Felix nodded at her bags. "What's with the luggage?"

"Some may heal with Skills alone, but I have always found bandages and the appropriate tools to be greatly beneficial." She held out a hand before Felix could open his mouth again. "No, you cannot come with me. You Unbound are too important, to *everything*. I cannot risk that on some petty vengeance."

"They have my *friends*, Isla. I'm not going to sit around and just wait for them to be rescued," Felix said, and he felt his eyes burn.

"Calm yourself. Autarch or not, I will force you to stay here if I have to. You cannot fight the Grandmaster as you are, and if you follow me, that is what will happen. Kel'lyv is a savvy man, and he will not miss your return." Isla's face softened with her tone. "If I go alone, I can evade all of their notice. I will be able to find and rescue your friends. I promise it."

Felix took a breath, flaring his nostrils. As much as he wanted to fight her, Isla had a point. *Would Abyssal Skein even hide me from someone at that level?* He simply didn't know.

"I—I will have to trust you, then," Felix said at last. "I don't like it, though."

"I go to aid my sister Zara. With her help, we can overcome any obstacles before us. With you here, I can trust that Michael is in good hands." She looked at the Minotaur and smiled. "He's stubborn, but you'll both be safe while you fully recover. We can settle the rest at a later date, yes?"

"Fine. Just please, make sure you bring back everyone. I gave you their names, and all of the members of my company." Felix shook his head. "I got them into this mess, and I need to see them out of it."

Isla bowed, a good bit more than Felix had for her. "I will see it done."

When she straightened, a swell of harmonious music erupted, and she vanished. Or rather, her Body was sent zooming into the dark chasm above with incredible speed. In a blink, she was gone.

"Holy shit," Beef said, clomping up next to Felix. "Naos can fly?"

"Apparently."

There was a beat while both of them looked after the spot where Isla had disappeared. Felix could still sense traces of her Mana, like a plane's contrails, but the abundance of crystalline resonance above them made it all a mess after a short distance.

"Well, this is boring." Beef clapped his hands and turned to Felix. "Wanna see a dead body?"

CHAPTER SEVENTY-NINE

The temporary estate of Representative Veil, delegate from the Territory of Nagast was silent as the grave. The gates, so wrapped in wards that they shimmered in the midday sun, were a bulwark against all any violence that might crash against it. The walls were tall, crenelated, and defensively constructed, with battlements for warriors to walk.

Yet they were empty.

"What is happening here?" Captain Jorald Malphas demanded. "Where are the gate guards?"

He had marched his Fist of Knights at double-time across the entire Ward at the Matron of Incandescence's command. Elite they may be, but a direct order from a Matron? Not even Malphas could deny those that were Chosen of the Flame, and all they were to do was escort a company of traitors to the temple. Simple and an insult to the captain's abilities. Yet when he arrived, what did he find? Guards so lazy they could not keep men at the gate!

The wardings aren't even responding to my Will! This is unacceptable! Malphas stomped his golden boot, cracking the roadway for six entire strides.

"Sir, my Lord Captain, sir."

Malphas snapped his attention toward a bowing scout. He had no idea what his name was, but it didn't matter. Scouts had a tragically short lifespan, even on controlled hunts. It wasn't even worth it to Analyze him, even if Malphas had the Skill. Which he didn't. "What?"

"Sir, there is no response from the estate, sir."

"I *know* that; why do you think we are still standing here?"

The scout blanched, but kept talking. "N—no, that is—what I mean is —! Sir, there is no response from anything. No Skill can make contact."

Malphas felt the cold worm of fear squirm in his belly. He drew his side-sword. "Men, with me. We're breaking down this gate, now!"

"Aye, sir!" his knights all cried in unison.

The captain spun around and lifted his gilt blade into the air. "Let Flame Beget Flame! Molten Strike!"

A geyser of orange Mana vapor shot upward from his sword, igniting into a baleful bonfire twice the sword's length. Malphas strode to the gate and brought it down with all of the Strength he could muster. The wards burned away while the wooden gates ashed to nothing.

Malphas pulled his still-blazing sword back up and grinned. "Men! Forwar—!"

A boot caught him in the face, crumbling his helmet and sending the captain tumbling, ass over teakettle into his Fist. Water followed, but nothing natural; instead he found himself floundering in an endless bubble of the stuff, unable to breathe or orient himself properly. Outside, crackling lightning and flashing steel burst from the sundered gates. Men and women, armored and armed to the teeth, flooded outward with death in their eyes.

Malphas screamed, releasing a stream of bubbles before realizing he was wasting his breath. He saw his Knights cut down, one-by-one then in great swaths by the traitorous force. Rage kindled in the captain, enough to fuel his heat Skill that began boiling the water Mana all around him. He poured everything he had into the Skill, earning himself two entire Skill levels yet coming no closer to freeing himself. By the time his Mana ran out, his lungs were burning in utter agony, and his eyes were flashing with blooms of random, blinding color.

He witnessed a giant of a man step forward, carrying a massive blade bigger than himself. He lifted it, and Malphas twitched...that was all he could manage to save his life. With an immense swing, the water finally burst, and Malphas was rolling wildly across the cobblestone street. He fetched up against the stone lip of a fountain, but barely noticed. The sight of his own body took up his fading attention, splayed out on the ground, headless.

How—?

"Is everyone quite finished?" Zara asked. "Darius?"

Reed straightened and flicked his oversized blade, casting a bright line of red to splatter on the ground."Yeah. I'm done here. Harn?"

"Hrm. Claw. Stealth Formation Number Two." The fully armored warrior watched as the members of the Fiend's Claw moved relatively smoothly into the proper positions. There were a few slower learners among them, but overall, Harn was impressed. All of them were dedicated to improving. "Ready to move."

"What, erm, what is to be done with the bodies?"

That question came from the Faun, a girl Harn had been very confused to see at Zara's side. Harn grunted. "Fourth Talon, put the bodies inside the courtyard. Quickly now." He glanced at the Faun and noticed she was still quite pale, watching the bleeding corpses of her former allies. "You could always stay here," he said.

Fiammetta started. "No! No, I am dedicated to...to stopping all of this. That doesn't mean I cannot wish that my...that people weren't going to die."

"It is either them or us, at this point," Zara said. The Fourth Talon hustled back out of the burnt gateway, bodies disposed of, and she clucked her tongue. "They have given us little choice."

Harn watched that blue-green Mana manifest into a shimmering, illusive door. It glowed with inner light before growing dull and seemingly solid. He even spotted bits of glowing sigils on it, like it still had wards. It was damn impressive.

And if she were there with Evie, maybe we'd be outta this situation already. Harn clenched his jaw hard enough that his teeth ached. He knew blaming Zara for this was unfair, but his gut was boiling with hate enough to spare. *Evie'd better be fine, or I'm gonna kill every Master on that Council. Don't care how strong they are.*

"I—I am most impressed that all of your people were ready and waiting for our assault," Fiammetta said to him. "To be quite honest, I had expected far more difficulty in extracting all of you from this estate."

Harn bared his teeth. "I never trust a cage. The Fiend's Claw stands ready, always."

A soft exhalation extended outward from Harn's position as each Talon took up the chant in low voices. The Disciple looked around, eyebrows drawn low in...it wasn't annoyance, but what was that word? It was a big one. *Consternation, that's it. She's consternated.*

"The Autarch would never leave us behind. We knew someone would come," Loquis said from beside them. He and his Talon, now three times the size, stood at attention. "Commander. We march when you're ready."

Harn slapped him on the back. "Good man. We move, now."

"Autarch?" Fiammetta asked.

"Perhaps later, dear," Zara said, approaching. "We must reach the Council Rotunda. Darius? We are aimed at rescuing our people, and whoever else is held within. None are to be sacrificed, you understand?"

"I will demolish their dungeon brick by brick if I have to," the Hand said, his breath heavy and scowl furious. "They have laid hands on the duke's daughter, and they'll pay for it."

"Aye. We'll see to that," Harn agreed, and he led them all down the sun-bright thoroughfares. His core rang with blow after blow on his visualized anvil, each strike propelling him onward. Faster. Faster. "We'll tear 'em apart, Reed."

"Wait. Explain this again," Felix said. "There's a monster nearby?"

"Oh yeah. Huge one, according to legends, and dead, too. Sposed to be a tomb or something where it was left. Been looking for it so I can get Hallow a new upgrade."

They were walking down the hidden staircase carved into the cliff face while Pit and Hallow flew and crawled down to the chasm floor, respectively. Felix reflected that they could have ridden their Companions, but Beef had taken off toward the stairs before he could suggest it.

"The Multipede is great, don't get me wrong. But it can't fight off everyone, and Hallow gets tired after a certain number of Bodies get lost. So even if I made an army of weak creatures, if they can get wiped off the map fast enough, Hallow is too exhausted to fight with me." Beef made a grumbling noise in his bull-like throat. "I'm strong, but magic is so much stronger. Found that out too late."

"Oh?" Felix asked as he followed behind. "How's that?"

"Well, after I made the change to this," he said, gesturing to his impressive physique. "I uh, I got a little wild. There's these mobs called Sandwolves out there, and they're nasty. Almost killed me before my Race changed, but after that, I could handle 'em. Killed a bunch, earning a whole slew of new Skills and stuff. That was a rush. But...Sandwolves travel in packs, and I nearly died a bunch of times. So I specc'd toward Vitality and Strength, leaning into my leveling bonuses. I can't exactly be mad about that, since doing that let me survive the worst of it."

"That is all very familiar, dude. I didn't arrive in a desert, but it wasn't a picnic, that's for sure," Felix said. He clapped Beef on the back—the Minotaur was a full two feet taller than him, so he managed only to hit his shoulder blade. "Survival comes first. The rest'll come later."

Beef smiled at him, looking relieved. His Spirit wobbled and calmed...though it was a little hard to make out, even for Felix. *Odd. Wonder why?*

"Well, when a huge pack of Sandwolves almost killed me, I escaped by running into one of those sandstorms. The Cursewinds, they call 'em." Beef laughed, but it was tinged with chagrin. "Nearly died in there. But when I saw that storm, close-up? I saw swirling winds and sand and dark flashing of lightning and...and it was power. *Real* power. I saw it summon corpses out of the sky to kill the Sandwolves. Even fought them myself." Beef shook his head and licked his lips. "They were strong, even the weakest ones. I barely survived. But I got out.

"That night, when everything was calm, I couldn't get that magic outta my head. I felt inspired, you know? Like how teachers talk about it in history class. I was that light bulb guy, right? I saw the thing and realized it could be so powerful and stuff. Magic. Magic was the way forward. Naos...er, Isla? Was that her name? Anyway he uh, she told me I 'kindled my Mote' or whatever at that point. She called it a 'spirit of possession' or like, what was it?" Beef snapped his thick fingers. "A wisp of undeath. But uh, nicer."

"Hallow," Felix said, putting the pieces together. "He's part of you."

"Yup. Something like that. I don't really get the whole," Beef cut himself off and waggled his fingers mysteriously. "The more complicated bits are weird. Naos tried teaching me, but I guess I'm just better at hitting things. My magic hasn't gotten much better. Each level I've gotten has just made my Body stronger. My Spirit and Mind are lagging behind, according to Naos. Isla. Fuck."

They chatted more, Beef getting more and more invested in telling Felix all of the enemies he'd fought around the desert. He'd waged a genocidal war against the Sandwolves, nearly wiping them out as they kept coming at him again and again. Some of his first faux-undead were Sandwolves, which Beef clearly relished. The guy was surprisingly blood-thirsty, but Felix couldn't exactly throw stones on that account. Anyone who chased power on the Continent was bound to get a taste for it...or else they wouldn't be around for very long at all.

The more Beef talked, the more Felix got a handle on his strange Hallow abilities. The creature that inhabited his Risen, as the System called them, seemed tied to Beef's Spirit Aspect in some way. How it split itself apart was anyone's guess, but clearly raising his Intelligence, Willpower, and Perception were key to increasing their capabilities. Not to mention Harmonic Stats, which dealt more directly with the Spirit. When he asked Beef about those, the guy hadn't a clue. Apparently Isla was keeping the cards close to her chest, for some reason.

He had met Isla, then Naos, in one of the mining layers of Ahkestria. After some Yttin told him of a city, he'd set out to find it and eventually did after a lot of searching. He'd had to muscle through the stormwall around the city to get in, but even then Beef managed it. Nearly died, but he did it. Except once he was inside, he couldn't get much higher than the lowest layers. Apparently, people need a badge of citizenship to climb the upper layers, and Beef had been refused entry on account of him not having anything except the bloody Sandwolf pelts on his frame.

"Naos showed up and helped me, giving me some healing for all the cuts I'd taken coming through the storm," Beef said. He blew air through his snout. "Taught me all sorts of things I hadn't learned out fighting in the desert."

For months, they had a mentor/student relationship. Naos would provide him with healing, and Beefhammer would fight and level and grow, each time pushing back out through the stormwall. Naos helped him temper, too, which was a revelation. Beef didn't like the direction Naos insisted on guiding him, but was told it was necessary to solidify his "foundation."

"Naos wanted me to focus on Strength and Vitality, just like I'd origi-nally planned. But I refused. I had magic, finally, and I was gonna use it. You know?"

Beef grew stronger and more capable, and slowly his magic came into its own. He even learned a few tricks from Naos, who had a weird insect theme going on, like the Chitin Construction Skill he'd used earlier. Hallow was getting stronger, a bit, securing enough Risen for him to fight against the desert's monstrosities, and things were getting better.

"Then I heard about the Tomb, and I knew I *had* to get to it. A big monster just sitting around? How strong could I get with something like that?" Beef grinned and rubbed his big hands together. "It has OP written all over it."

They reached the bottom of the stairs, and Beef led them up the first sloping dune. Felix followed behind, more than happy to listen as this strangely exuberant Minotaur rattled off his life story. Felix did notice, however, that Beef never really talked about who he was *before* he came to the Continent. They reached the top of the dune, and Beef pointed into the distance, where the darkened maws of a hundred wide caverns punctured the walls.

"Gotta go through those and get outside the city and stormwall, then we can find the Tomb," he said.

"Wait, outside the city?" Felix frowned and reflexively looked up. He obviously couldn't see through the miles of stone and darkness, but the connections to his friends and allies were there, bundled in his chest. They each gave off a faint, humming vibration. "I thought you said this monster body was close? I figured it was down here somewhere."

"Oh no. It's outside the city a ways. I was searching for the Tomb for like, weeks. That's how I got my armor," Beef said, slapping a hand against his breastplate. As Felix had noted before in his visions, it was the blood-red plate of a Paladin.

"The Paladins? In those dreams I mentioned, I saw you fighting against them a couple times," Felix said. "Why are they after this Tomb?"

Beef shrugged. "No clue. The old legends talk about it like its some king's final resting place, though Ahkestria's never had any kings according to the High Justiciar."

"Wait. You spoke to Haim?" Felix stopped walking, the slimy face of that jerk popping perfectly to mind. "How? When?"

"It was a coincidence, really. I was looking for the Tomb and found an encampment of dudes in full-on armor. And those swords? Damn, they are nice. Aside from the insect armor I can make, I'd never seen so much quality gear. I uh, well I got excited. Introduced myself right away. They were nice, too, inviting me in for food and drink, all that." Beef scratched the back of his neck. "Haim was even nice. Gave me this armor."

"Really," Felix said through his curled lip.

"Hey! I didn't know they were assholes at first! Paladins are good guys! We talked, Haim and I, for a while. All night, it felt like." Beef sighed. "I may have told them more than I should've. Like how to get into the city, so long as you can stomach the storm, about monsters around the area.

"About the Tomb."

Felix bared his teeth, immediately spreading his Perception all around them. Could the Paladins be down here now? But no, they wouldn't survive the stormwall. Beef could, and Felix had done it, but it likely took a considerable amount of protection to manage it. If they could have done it easily, the Paladins would have taken over the city already.

"I take it they were interested in the city," Felix said.

"A little. Well, more than a little, but they seemed more into the Tomb. Haim was really interested, said he'd heard of it himself. And I may or may not have told him, uh, everything about it. All the stories I'd heard, where I thought it would be." Beef recoiled from the look Felix gave him. "Hey! He was a Paladin! That's so cool! How was I to know he was a dick?"

Beef sighed. "After a while, though, the questions stopped, and Haim stopped being so friendly. Said I was a 'Lost Race,' whatever that meant, and after talking so long about myself, I may have let slip that I just...appeared in the desert one day."

"He knew you were Unbound," Felix said. "That's why they've been chasing you and knew who and what you were. You basically told them."

"Uh, yeah. It was the first time I'd heard the term. Naos didn't even use it 'til I came back. The Justiciar guy went from nice to evil in a second, having the guards come hold me down. Said I'd be coming back to his boss or whatever, and the way he said it...I just knew it wasn't good."

"How'd you get out?" Felix asked. Pit had landed nearby and was listening as well. Hallow was nowhere to be seen, though.

"Well, I never told him about my magic. Figured I'd save that to really impress him." Beef laughed, bitterly. "Good thing I did, too. None of them expected Hallow to come blasting outta the ground in Multipede form. I got out, and with my Strength put some distance between us. None of them were stronger than me alone, and that paid off. A few were really fast, though, and I...I had to kill them."

Felix only nodded. "And the Tomb? The Paladins have found it?"

"Yeah. They've been guarding it a while now, trying to get into the doors of it...I figure, together, maybe we could get past them and check it out?"

"You want to go fight an unknown number of Paladins, thwarting whatever plans they have for this Tomb, all on the off-chance it lets your friend grow stronger?" Felix asked, listing the points off on his fingers.

Beef grimaced. "Uh, yeah."

"Which tunnel are we taking?"

CHAPTER EIGHTY

<Now.>

Loquis gestured, and the Blades in his Talon crept forward. The sun was high in the sky, but that only meant the glare reflected off the Mana crystal lamps, ruining the guards' vision. The Blades struck, and the guards died, quietly.

All around the grounds, guards fell, killed by the other Talons and the commanders. Commander Harn and Reed were hulking brutes, but they moved faster than Loquis could track. The Talons moved as one, securing the path forward into the servant passages of the Council Rotunda. Most amazing of all was that there was no sound at all from all of their feet, whether that was across the lush grass or stone-lined pathways. Air Mana clung to all of them, muffling their movements at the behest of Commander Reed.

It was an astounding show of magical strength.

Once inside, Loquis and his Talon moved down the right-most hallway, following the slender figure of the defected Disciple. Asaad didn't trust her and neither did Loquis, but the Commanders did. He paced after her, keeping his breathing as even as he could make it.

Fiammetta led them deeper, while the other half of their forces took the opposite hall. Very soon, they hit a checkpoint manned by lounging guards, but Loquis' Fulmination stopped them in their tracks. Lightning, he had found, did not play nicely with others' Bodies, and all three guards fell to the ground. While they twitched, two Bones clubbed them across the skulls, and judging by the spatter of blood and viscera, they would not be standing again. Loquis tried not to care. They were the enemy, and the Commanders had given them orders.

Free everyone. Show no mercy.

The room the guards had been occupying was filled wall-to-wall with cubby holes, racks, and shelving. All of it was stacked with various pieces of contraband, as well as a few distinctive pieces of weaponry and armor. At a word from the mage, his people grabbed the necessary pieces.

To the far right of the checkpoint and between the rounded arch of skillfully carved stone was a thick, heavily locked door. Before Geir could smash it down, however, Pava skipped forward with the keys. "Work smarter, not harder, boys," she said.

Door opened, they swept down two sets of stairs and suddenly found one of the two dungeons. Fiammetta lifted her hand, and a dozen motes of yellow light kindled in her grasp. She threw them forward, the motes stopping before each cell with unerring accuracy. Loquis swallowed. Her finesse was far greater than his...and judging by how little she seemed affected by such Mana use, she had a greater Willpower as well.

"Noctis' tits, that's bright."

Evie Aren was mere feet from Loquis, leaning against the bars of her cell and dressed in nothing more than a blouse and a set of cotton trousers. Her face, however, was cut and bloodied. The mage swallowed again, this time far more nervously. "H-hello. We're here to save you."

She snorted. "About time. But what's *she* doin' here?"

Instead of answering, Loquis nodded to his Talon, and they spread out. Pava took the lead, still holding the ring of keys. She quickly unlocked Lady Aren's cell and moved down the line, Blades and Fists ready to fight any guards they might have missed.

"I am working on your side," the Disciple stated firmly. Her crimson brows were drawn low over her freckled, deer-like nose. "That terrifying woman has already pressed the repercussions of betraying you, so please do not tread over old ground."

Lady Aren blinked. "Zara's back. Good. And don't worry: I won't let you betray us, little doe."

The way Lady Aren smiled was unnerving and utterly mesmerizing. It was violence and passion all wound into the shine of teeth and ruby lips. Loquis gestured, and his men stepped forward with chain and leather armor as well as a coil of thick, dangerously spiked chain. "Um, Lady Aren, here. Your effects."

"Oho, yes," Evie hissed, her grin growing wilder. She took her weapon into her rough, calloused hands. "I've some new scores to settle. You, flame girl. Help me get my armor on."

"I—Very well."

The Faun walked into Lady Aren's cell, and Loquis quickly busied himself with duties that involved *not* peeking into those shadows. Down the corridor, dozens of people were blinking up at the motes of light, most bloodied and clutching at one another for safety. The mage stepped forward, tongue cleaving to the roof of his mouth. Most were Yttin, but not all, and far too many had the size and slenderness of children. His skin prickled, and rage swelled within his breast.

"Please, do not be afraid. We are here on behalf of the Autarch of Nagast. You will be safe," he said.

As if he'd shaken them, those closest to the mage fixed him with glowing copper eyes. The intensity of their regard was remarkable despite their diminutive size.

"The Autarch...he...he is here?" one of them said.

Loquis kept his face straight. No need to tell them they didn't know where the Fiend had gone, or whether he even lived. "He is. We've come to bring you out of here."

Murmurs passed through the Yttin, and the few captive Goblins and Orcs among them looked about in confusion.

"The Weaving shapes all," one of them whispered, but they were quickly hushed.

"We shall follow you, mage. Until the Beast comes to render our world undone."

"Uh, great." Loquis tried and failed to keep his confusion from his face.

"What's the holdup?" Lady Aren shouted from behind him. She had emerged from her cell, fully kitted out with her spiked chain looped around a shoulder. "Everyone who doesn't want to die, fall in. I'm about to carve my way out, and anyone who wants a piece of battle can join up."

She brandished her chain, drawing powerfully bright sparks from the stone.

"Or stay. Don't ruffle me none."

She strode out and up the staircase, pulling everyone after her like a lodestone.

———

They met the other Talons on their way out, but not before facing down two dozen guards. Silence was still the order of the day, and each patrol they encountered was dispatched as quickly and as quietly as possible. Despite his Talon's abilities, Lady Aren did most of the killing, with Loquis and the rest providing support. The battles were quick and brutal.

Little more than blood and mangled limbs was left in her wake.

The other team, however, seemed far more composed. Lords Atar, Alister, and Lady Dayne were joined up with them, though they also trailed a motley collection of captured civilians.

"Evie, you are covered in blood," Lady Dayne pointed out. "Was there trouble? An alarm sounded?"

"Nah, just had some fun. How about you? Get everyone free?" she asked.

"Everyone we found," Lady Zara said, striding to the fore. She, at least, had some blood spread across her dark robes. "We must move briskly. I sense greater powers in close proximity, and I would not like to see you face against them. Darius, Atar, if you would."

Commander Reed made a sweeping gesture, and the restrictive feeling of thickened air settled on Loquis' shoulders. On everyone, he could tell. A shimmer of dark power rushed out of Atar and enveloped the leadership with an extra layer of muffling while a thinner working was sent out over the Claw.

Zara caught their eyes, commanding their attention even more effectively than Evie's bloody magnetism. "We move as quickly as we can. We do not stop for fighting or bloodshed. Go. Now!"

They burst out into the Rotunda grounds with all the speed they could, but Loquis felt the strain of herding so many Untempered civilians. Had they been alone, they would have raced across the grassy paths, but now they were bogged down by the slowest child or elder. Still, they were making it. The lesser used servant gates loomed ahead, the guards subdued and bound in their little stations, and—

A shimmering screen of aquamarine light flashed above them an instant before a column of fire consumed them all. Untempered screamed and tried to scatter, but the Claw tightened up, holding them together and brandishing their various weapons. Fire and watery Mana both vanished, and three figures were suddenly standing between them and the exit.

"Master Perys and Matrons Mikaf and Lumes," Lord Atar snarled. "Get out of our way."

"You overstep yourself, V'as," a woman said. Her hair was a fiery red streaked heavily with white. The Matrons beside her were both olive-skinned with bright blonde hair, similar to Lord Atar himself. "All of you are guilty of conspiring to destroy the city, and you, mage, are a treasonous child. You will return to your cells to await your judgment."

"Or else what? You'll kill us?" The fire mage laughed and brandished a metal stave, its end glowing with crimson-streaked fire Mana. "Why are you doing this? The Highest Flame would not seek out sacrifices on Her own. I know it!"

"You know little, V'as. The Highest Flame dwindled while you were gallivanting in the Hierocracy, and nothing will save Her...nothing but what we must do." The Matrons were abruptly wreathed in sudden flames, their bodies turned to torches of horrendous heat, though their expressions never shifted. The Master conjured two long whips of flame out of the air, and spread her arms wide. "I will ask you once more. Return, or we will be forced to act."

Commander Harn caught Loquis' attention, gesturing sharply. <Formation Cradle, Burning Building,> he signed. The Half-Orc mage nodded and passed the message along to Pava and Asaad. It spread, quiet and subtle...and hopefully, it would be enough.

"I think we will not," Lady Zara said, stepping forward. How the enemy hadn't noticed her before was unclear to Loquis, but now Master Perys gaped in clear alarm.

"Another Master-Tier," she hissed.

"Far more than that, you burning cretins." The toll of an immense bell sounded from Lady Zara's position, so deep and loud it shook the ground beneath their feet. "You will not have what you desire."

<GO!>

The Talons split, each of them ushering small groups of Untempered between them as they ran. Whips of flame and screaming columns tore through the air, manifesting right above Lady Zara and meeting a shield of inscrutable blue-green power. Loquis nearly fell over from the sheer weight of impact, but he stumbled onward. He even managed to scoop up a fallen Yttin child into his arms, holding them tight as the skies above them *burned*.

"We're gonna die!" Asaad screamed.

"Shut up and run!" Osyk shouted right back. The normally collected Henaari was grim-faced as he carried two other children, while Geir thundered at the rear with six others in his arms.

Magical forces slammed into one another, the likes of which Loquis had never seen before. He had caught a glimpse of the Fiend's battle against the usurper, DuFont, but this was on an entirely different level. A Master and two High Adepts against Zara on her own...yet there was nothing Loquis could do to help. So he focused ahead, leading his Talon through the servants' gate and out onto the wide, sun-baked streets.

Only to find rank upon rank of armored Knights leveling heavy crossbows at them all.

"Shit!" The other Talons were close behind, but they wouldn't be there in time. "Fulminat—!"

Before Loquis could mobilize his Mana, each and every Knight gasped in sudden agony. Crossbows fell, several discharging into each other, before the Knights, too, fell to the perfectly smooth street. In their midst, a lone Human woman with bright blond hair and some sort of crown stood, fairly glowing with ripples of green-gold Mana.

"Where is Zara?" she asked.

———

The tunnels at the base of the chasm were far colder than elsewhere, owing perhaps to the ceaseless winds that tore down their length. The walls of the tunnels looked to have been originally natural caves, but over time had been eroded to smooth tubes of stone, with only the occasional craggy pit and textured abscess where the wind and sands could not readily reach.

It wasn't a pleasant walk, that was for sure, and had Felix been less hardy than he was, it would have torn him bloody after the first five minutes. But both Unbound were made of sterner stuff than the average person, so the worst thing to contend with was sand in his eyes and the ceaseless keening of the relentless wind. That, and his sudden misgivings.

"Karys, you available?" Felix asked.

His Inheritor's Will buzzed to life as the connection with his chancellor came to life. He could hear the words as if they were right in his ear, regardless of the noise all around them. "Of course. Just give me a minute to handle a matter."

"Uh, sure," Felix said, but the connection went dead before he finished. *What was that about?*

"Did you just say something?" Beef asked, his voice loud.

"Hm? Oh yeah. I can speak with my friend back at my Stronghold," he explained, just as loud.

Beef grinned. "Stronghold? What! That's so cool. What's that like, ruling a Territory?"

"It's not really ruling, exactly. More like—" His sword glowed with green-gold Mana. "Ah, gimme a sec."

"Sure!"

"Karys? You good now?" Felix asked, his voice much softer.

"Yes, of course, my Lord. I apologize for the delay."

"What brought that on?" he asked.

"Strife between the Henaari and Frost Giants. There is some debate over how far we should explore in the Foglands. Reclaiming the ruins of Shelim is hotly contested. Both wish to claim the accomplishment and expand your power base," the Paragon explained. "I have given my ruling, which is to refrain from exploration beyond the mountains until you return. That will only hold them for so long, I fear. Are you returning soon?"

"As soon as I can," Felix confirmed, before giving his chancellor a run down of events since they last spoke.

"Exalted Ancestors, sacrificed? It is good that you left their retrieval to this new Chanter, and better still that you have found the other Unbound."

"I'm not happy about being left behind, but I see the...necessity," Felix said. "I didn't just call you for a chat, though. What do you know of a royal tomb in Ahkestria?"

Karys paused. "A tomb? Hm. I...recall that the royal line was interred within a tomb beneath the waves, a symbolic burial, no doubt. Nothing more than that comes to mind, however."

"Alright, that's more than I had before," Felix said. "We're going to a tomb now, and I wanted to make sure it actually existed. Could be it's this royal burial ground."

"Now? I thought you were to wait? Aren't you injured?" Karys asked sharply.

"I'm fine. More or less," Felix said, brushing off his friend's concern. "Besides, the Paladins want this tomb for some reason. That's gotta mean something, right?"

"I suppose it would not do to let these vile lackeys get what they desire. Just...please, Felix. Show some caution. We Nym were not the only ones to protect our valuable spaces with traps to catch the unwary."

Felix grunted as a gritty patch of sand hit his cheek. "I'll keep it in mind. I'll reach out again soon."

"I await your orders, my Lord."

The connection cut, and the keening howl of the winds assaulted Felix's ears once again. Beef strode ahead, having gained a sizeable lead during Felix's conversation, and he flared his Relentless Resolution a bit to catch up. Moving through the gale-force gusts was far easier with the Skill active, even with Felix's incredible stats. His Body was in better condition after the Panacea he'd drunk, but it was still a wound that wouldn't quite heal.

I suppose fighting a Grandmaster has consequences, he thought. The memory of the grey-skinned bastard's smirk was galling. The easy, almost casual defeat at the hands of the Grandmaster made Felix burn. His cores spun faster within him, tossing off arcing flares of jarring melody. Pit, nestled within him for the walk, let out a commiserating cry. The best he could do now was kick some sand in the Paladins' faces, maybe even stop them from reaching this tomb.

He sped up.

The tunnels twisted and folded over themselves, but soon they had reached the outside world once more. Sand all but buried the opening, turning what was a several hundred-foot-wide cavern into a mouth perhaps a mere three dozen feet. The wind tore through that opening, filling its edges with crimson sand that was immediately eroded by its passage. Felix could see flashes of yellow lightning and twisting, burning air.

"There it is! Just have to get through that opening there, then put your head down!" Beef shouted. "It hurts a lot, but I can take the lightning for you!"

Stone Shaping!

The sands liquefied before them before collapsing into a deep tunnel that burrowed straight through the clogged cavern.

"What? You can do that?" Beef asked.

"Get in!" Felix shouted, before walking through himself. The passage he'd made was wonderfully quiet in comparison, though not particularly wide. Beef crowded the space behind him, and Hallow... "I don't know if I can fit your friend through here with me."

"Oh, Hallow is fine. The storm doesn't target him, for some reason," Beef said.

"Why?" Felix watched as Hallow burrowed into the sand as well, heading straight for the stormwall. "Because he's undead?"

"Probably not. I've seen it blast apart some of those Dustwights before. Pretty nasty."

"But it strikes out at you?" Felix asked.

"Every time. I've been hit by more burning rocks than anything else.

Even got zapped once or twice by the lightning," Beef said, almost proudly. "The lightning only hits the strongest creatures that come through. Did you know that?"

"Huh. I didn't." Felix kept walking, pushing onward through his tunnel. He kept it below the surface, at least twenty feet down, if his senses were right, but just beyond the edge, he could feel a chaotic churning. Heat and fire and earth Mana boiled through the sands as well as the air, and it was likely they'd be no safer underground than above. But at least below ground, he could provide some level of reinforcement. "Get ready to move when I say, alright?"

"Uh, sure. We're underground, though? We should be good, right?"

"Unlikely. I doubt this protective storm is that easy to fool," Felix said. "Stick close to me and we'll be fine...probably."

"I told you, I go through this all the time," Beef started, but Felix pushed his Stone Shaping forward, liquefying then hardening a path forward. Immediately, bolts of blinding, yellow lightning crashed into the tunnel, shattering it into pieces. "Holy balls!"

"Ready?" Felix asked, calling up his Stone Shaping again.

"Uh, that was a lot of lightning, Felix. I think maybe—"

"Go!"

CHAPTER EIGHTY-ONE

Lightning shattered the tunnel, again and again, forcing Felix to continually remake it. The sands rebelled, fighting his control, but he seized them with all the weight of his Will and Intent...and still only barely managed to stave off total destruction. Yellow lightning blasted into him, sizzling across his hands and arms, moving less like true electricity and more like a living creature.

"GAH!" Beef yelled, a piece of the storm's fury leaping onto him. Felix dared a glance back, only to see the man's stolen breastplate burned and corroded almost all the way through.

"Don't get too close! But stay with me!" Felix growled. "I'm gonna draw this goddamn storm's attention, then you can run!"

"You—you'll die!" The Minotaur said, tears starting to stream down his face. "You can't! I said I can take the damage, so let me take it!"

Stone Shaping!

Adamant Discord!

Felix surged the Mana in his core outward all at once: one formed a tunnel of compressed sand for as far as he could reach...and the other grabbed Beef by the chest in chains of lightning and *hurled* him down said tunnel. The guy didn't have a chance to do much else but scream in terror, before even that was cut off by the storm's renewed rampage. The tunnel fractured and collapsed all around Felix, swirling into a chaos of sinuous lightning strikes and burning winds that ripped at the loose sand around him.

"Fine! Let's do this the hard way, then!" Felix shouted and leaped straight up through the eroding sand above. "Chthonic Tribute!"

———

Beefhammer didn't know what the hell was happening.

First he was arguing with Felix, and then he was flying through the air. *Earth. Whatever.* Beef groaned as he emerged from the ground, his armor and fur streaming with rivers of cascading sand. He shook himself, spraying it in all directions, and took stock.

"This armor is busted," he said. The majority of it had been scorched to hell, and advanced corrosion had eaten away big chunks of its center. "Damn. This was the best stuff I could find. That lightning is nasty stuff."

The Paladin's armor had shrugged off some huge hits in the past, and it hadn't even held up to a few lightning bolts. Though they had felt stronger than before—he'd been hit by those bolts during crossings before, but never like that. They way they had slammed down, so many at once...like the storm wanted them dead, personally.

Beef shuddered and fumbled with the straps. The buckles of his breastplate were fused together, but that didn't matter much to him. He simply grabbed it where the armor had split and gave it a sharp yank. It resisted for a second, but the damage had been extensive, and he was very strong. The breastplate ripped in half, and he awkwardly shuffled out of it.

Thunder crashed, and Beef jerked his attention back toward the stormwall. How he'd ignored it was a mystery, as the thing was miles wide and miles high, a tornado bigger than anything he'd ever seen on TV. Dusty winds roared, and slashing rain of molten glass tore through the air, all while caustic yellow lightning spread like tree roots. Or, they should have. Instead, Beef watched as bolt after bolt struck the same place in blinding succession, the impacts so fast, so close together that the thunder hit like a machine gun.

"Felix!" he shouted, uncaring about what monsters were nearby. He could see his new friend, his *only* friend, as a lump of dark, unmoving material in the center of that furious onslaught. "Relentless Char—!"

Before the Skill could activate in his chest, the stormwall bulged then twisted, pulling inward on itself. Yellow lightning and crimson-orange sands turned to incandescent smoke as a dark, scaled figure erupted from the cyclone.

"What the hell?"

Beef watched, confused and unbelieving as Felix crashed into the sand, throwing it up in a huge wave. For all his size and weight, it knocked the Minotaur on his ass as it hit. "Oof!"

Clouds of crimson-orange dust swept over Beef, blocking the bright, blue, midday sky as he laid there. His Mind whirled, processing what he'd just seen and not quite believing. *Did he...did he disintegrate part of the stormwall?*

Abruptly, a claw, black taloned and monstrous, reached out of the dust, a helping hand that glowed faintly with crackling, yellow energies for a single heartbeat. Then that faded into the ebon scales.

"Sorry about throwing you," Felix said, and the clouds of sand settled enough for Beef to see two eyes of intense, glowing sapphire. His mouth quirked in a grin. Nervously, Beef grasped the proffered hand, almost shouting aloud as he was hauled to his feet.

"Fucking shit, you're strong!" Beef exclaimed. Felix looked at him with those inscrutable eyes, and Beef felt a flush of embarrassment at his outburst. Of course, the guy was strong.

"We should get moving. We're out in the open here, and I don't know what kinda monsters are about," Felix said.

Beef coughed, attempting to collect himself. *You're not some kid! You're a savage warrior! Remember!* Out loud, he said, "Erm. Lotta creatures in the sands. Dangerous stuff. Giant Scorpions and Glass Whiptails are the most of what's around here, though. They stopped being a challenge for me weeks ago." Beef looked at Felix, surprised to see that the scales along his arms and chest had vanished...and his torn clothing was repairing itself. "Is...is your shirt healing itself?"

"Hm? Oh, yeah. Cool, right?" The man walked up the dune with quick, easy movements. Somehow, he didn't sink into the sand at all. "Which way?"

Beef clambered after him, feeling ungainly. With every other step, he sank to the knee and had to yank his legs free, each time kicking up a wave of sand like a damn plow. "West. Toward those dark cliffs there."

"Hm."

Without another word, Felix started walking. His strange gryphon-looking Companion emerged in a flash of white light, though he didn't take to the air like Beef half-expected. He'd been excited to notice that Pit wore armor and a saddle, suggesting that Felix could ride on top of him during flight. The sheer idea of that sent Beef's imagination soaring. If he could get a flying creature and have Hallow possess it...but then, he hadn't seen a creature big enough to lift someone as heavy as Beef had become. His mood crashed faster than it had risen, and he trudged after the both of his new friends.

Dune after dune passed beneath their feet as the minutes ticked by. Felix and Pit were steady and unflappable, both of their eyes constantly sweeping the terrain for threats, and a low hum of...*something* came from them both. Beef shook his head. He was pretty sure he'd just lost too much blood. It happened sometimes, that ringing, but usually only when he was hurt bad enough. Beneath them all, Hallow rumbled through the sands. Beef got the distinct impression the spirit was unnerved by Felix, but couldn't figure out why and hadn't had a moment alone to ask.

Maybe just weirded out that either one of these guys could kill us easily, he thought. *How'd he survive that lightning? And without a scratch on him?*

Beef had spent a lot of time since meeting Naos thinking he was special. He had rapidly become way stronger than anything he came against, monster or otherwise, and his durability was off the charts. He could heal from any injury, given enough time, and his necromancy gave him an edge that hadn't been matched even by the Paladins.

But Felix fought both of us to a stand-still. He looked at the guy, a full two feet shorter and far smaller...and he didn't understand. *Is it just the level difference? He said he's level fifty-seven, and if I was that level, I'd have a lot more Strength and Endurance just from my Race. What...what does a Human get?* He gasped. *Did I pick the wrong Race?*

"Felix. Are Humans OP?" he asked.

The man was talking in a low voice to his Companion and had slowed, but he looked back over his shoulder at Beef with a raised eyebrow. "Overpowered? No, Humans are probably one of the weakest Races."

"Huh," Beef said, scratching his jaw. It had been weird at first, having a bull-face, but he'd gotten so used to it that now it just felt like *his* face. Beef barely remembered what Michael used to look like, and good riddance. "Then how are you so strong?"

"That...is complicated," Felix said. "Titles played a big role in my early days, but I get less of those now. The best boosts I've gotten are all due to Tempering, really. Most of them, anyway."

Beef frowned. He'd Tempered once, earning his new Aspects as Naos —Isla—recommended he did. It had made a world of difference...but Felix couldn't have had more than one more Temper above him. "That Strength and your Vitality, how high are they?"

Felix turned, his head tilting oddly. "Over two thousand," he said.

"W—what!"

That's impossible! Beef's Strength was barely over a thousand, and he'd poured more than was reasonable into it, plus his Race, plus all of his Titles he'd earned by surviving in the desert. But to have *two* stats a thousand points *higher?* "How?" he asked.

Felix frowned, and his eyes flashed bright sapphire again. He pointed. "Monsters. Forty-nine of them, over that dune."

The statement drove all questions out of his head like a snuffed candle. He'd done this dance too many times and knew the rules: thinking instead of fighting gets you killed. Beef whirled, his great maul manifesting in his hands. The weight of it was reassuring as he dropped into a battle stance. "Level and Type?"

"You called it. Seems like Glass Whiptails, and they're pissed off." Felix laughed, which confused Beef. "Pit? You wanted to go wild, so have at it."

The tenku next to him shrieked in obvious glee and bounded into the sky just as a horde of shimmering lizards crested the nearest dune. Purple-white vapor condensed and splashed outward, manifesting into massive icicles that shot from Pit's huge wings. The Whiptails screeched as they shattered into bloody chunks, but more surged forward, their barbed and razor-sharp tails lashing wildly.

"Hey! Save some for me!" Beef yelled.

"Not gonna send Hallow in?" Felix asked. The guy didn't seem concerned at all. Like he was...bored?

"I don't need Hallow for this," Beef said, and he forced a grin so wide his cheeks hurt. A rush of fear-propelled blood roared in his ears. "Relentless Charge!"

I'll show him something interesting, then!

———

Felix watched Pit and Beef go to town on the Glass Whiptails. The creatures were around level 30 and not much of a challenge to either of them, but the sheer amount of them proved interesting. Pit was able to keep out of most of their attacks, except for the glass shards they would launch at range, and even then, he was fast enough to dodge most and tough enough to tank the rest. If nothing else, it was some good stress relief for his Companion. He'd been forced to remain cooped up in Felix's Spirit for far too long in recent days...and Felix wasn't the only one who burned at losing to Kel'lyv.

More interesting than Pit's aerial maneuvers, however, was the Minotaur. Beefhammer waded into the fray without concern for physical harm, screaming and laughing as he swung his huge maul. He was all physical force and unstoppable motion, moving from enemy to enemy without regard for their advance. Tactics was obviously a non-concern for the Minotaur—instead, he chained activations of Relentless Charge and summoned new, chitin-shaped weaponry as old ones shattered. The guy didn't even bother to avoid the Whiptails' attacks, instead tanking every one with his powerful Body.

Strong, but reckless. No plans, just all-out assault. Felix's mouth twisted in sobering self-reflection. *Sounds like me, half a year ago.* He chuckled. *Probably more recently than that.*

The fight threatened to take a while, especially since Beef was refusing to utilize his undead friend. While the Minotaur bathed in the hot, transparent blood of the glass lizards, he flared his Stone Shaping once more. Earthen Mana poured from the Mana Gates on his feet, sinking into the sands and tracing branching lines toward the swarm. Small spikes erupted from the dunes, all at once puncturing bellies and hearts and lungs of the monsters. His Eye watched them keel over, most too overcome by pain to do more than curl up and die. A rare few screeched, once, before following suit.

It was over.

You Have Killed A Glass Whiptail (x22)!
XP Earned!

He plodded after Beef, quick Stone Shapings forming just beneath his every step. Felix's surprising density and weight were a huge benefit during battle...but in the sand, it meant he was constantly sinking. A little surreptitious shaping fixed the issue, though he kept the small stone platforms he made buried by at least a six inches of sand. The last thing he needed was for some curious Paladin to come across a set of shaped tracks leading right to him.

"Great job, Beef. Let's get a move on, though. I want to find this tomb fast," he said.

The Minotaur blinked several times, as if shaking off a fugue state. "They're...all dead? That usually takes longer."

Pit landed next to them in a shower of sand, and chirruped in fierce delight. Felix laughed. "You had some help."

Surprisingly, the Minotaur sniffled. "O—oh." He cleared his throat and turned pointedly away from Felix. "Okay. Good. We uh, we need to go this way."

Felix hadn't missed the way Beef's Spirit had trembled with complicated emotions. His heart ached in sympathy for the kid; Felix knew what Beef had gone through, after all, but at least Felix had Pit and the others for much of it. Beef had been alone, all this time, with only a hidden Chanter for support. Wordlessly, Felix followed after, Pit beside him.

The journey across the desert took longer than Felix had anticipated. The warning he'd received from the Prioress was proving true as they encountered wave after wave of monstrous beasts. Most of them were in small packs, ten or fifteen at once, but a few like the Glass Whiptails showed up en masse. Felix wasn't shy about using his Mana to fend them off, and eventually Beef was convinced to commit his spirit friend to their progress, as well. With Felix's Stone Shaping and Hallow's incredible speed and ability to travel beneath the sands, they swept the rug with almost everything they encountered.

Eventually, however, they approached where Beef had indicated the tomb was located. It was a canyon fronted by a series of dark mesas that somehow screened much of the sands from flooding the area. Instead, Felix could sense a number of spots that hummed with a familiar aria. Life, thick and fecund, was within the ravines ahead of them.

As was death.

"That's a lot of undead," Beef said slowly. Just over the lip of the nearest cliff, the two of them could make out hundreds of Dustwights milling aimlessly at the bottom of every gorge in eyesight. "Way more than I've ever fought alone."

"Good thing you're not alone," Felix said. "And I've got a plan."

CHAPTER EIGHTY-TWO

Fire washed over the grass, setting all of it alight instantly. Vess danced backward, just ahead of the flames and spun all seven of her conjured Spears in unison. Air Mana surged, flooding the fire Mana of the attack —consuming the vegetation utterly but extinguishing the flames.

Dragoon's Footwork is level 74!

They had been fighting for a half glass, and this was their second wave of Temple Knights that had come for them. Now it was only the Matron facing her and Evie. Vess couldn't understand why more Knights weren't coming, let alone more Masters.

"Is that all you have?" she said. All eight of her spears, including the one in her hand, leveled at the woman in golden robes before her. "I would have expected more from a Matron. Or is this all a simple Urge-slave can manage?"

The woman, veiled in golden lace, smirked. "You cannot see through your prejudice, warrior." The Matron raised a hand, and a collection of swirling orange-yellow orbs the size of her head manifested above her and began to spin. "I will force your eyes open."

Chains of purple-white frost shot from the earth, stabbing up and into the Matron's chest. The priestess cried out, and several orbs flickered as a blade of ice jabbed into her neck.

"Lotta talkin' when you should be fightin'," Evie said, before yelping. "Hey!"

The Ice Spike in her hand had burst into steam as one of those orbs dropped onto Evie from above. She dodged back, arm clearly burned.

"I'll show you all the power of Ahkestria!" the Matron hissed.

Power thundered from the woman, her High Adept Spirit fully unleashed. Vess and Evie both winced at the pressure, but neither of them were weak...and Evie had a Low Adept's Body. When the orbs came for her, the chain warrior was able to hurl herself aside. The Matron shattered the chains around her body and twisted after Evie.

Leaving her open to three Spears in her back.

"Seven Tribulations," Vess commanded. The Spears ripped themselves apart in a three-pronged storm of metal and air Mana. The Matron screamed as blood burst from her back, shredding her fine robes, and redirected her attention to Vess.

"You think that is enough to extinguish a Chosen of That Which Burns?" The Matron gathered herself and lifted a span off the ground, buoyed by a wavering haze of power. "We are the fuel by which She is strengthened, and in turn She strengthens us!"

Her limbs transformed into whips of incandescent fire, just as Evie's chain cut through the air. It caught and tangled the girl's strike, heating the metal to a brilliant cherry red. Evie cursed and hauled back, but her chain was trapped.

"Physical weapons against the might of the Spirit...it is a surprise you have survived so long." The veiled Matron lifted her nose at them. Across the lawn, Zara fought on her own against two others, her water countering the fire of her opponents. "Your Master will die soon, and you shall join the others upon the Pyre. There is nothing you can do to stop it.

"Perhaps," Vess allowed. Sweat poured down her face even forty strides away—the strain on her Spirit from the Matron's pressure was great, and her movements had to be exact. "Or perhaps you have not considered all the possibilities."

"Oh?" The Matron laughed, still floating above the ground and holding Evie's chain tight. The metal had turned white in spots, and Evie was cursing up a storm. More brilliant orbs manifested and aimed at Vess. "What have I not considered, child?"

"My Skill can be delayed," she said.

Understanding dawned on the Matron just as the remaining four Spears slammed into the denuded earth around her. Before she could mobilize her fire spells, they exploded.

The Matron's screams of denial turned into a gurgling wail as she fell to the scorched ground

You Have Killed A Matron Of That Which Burns!
XP Earned!

Congratulations You Have Earned A New Title!
Urge Hunter II (Rare)!
You have proven effective at finding and dispatching those that worship Urges. Destroying more of their violent kind will see increased rewards! +10 END, STR, VIT

Spear of Tribulations is level 75!
Congratulations You Have Reached Adept Tier With Spear of
Tribulations (E)!
You Gain:
+10 AGL
+10 WIL
+...

She fumbled at her waist, and brought a blue-stone flask to her lips. Mana in the air swirled around her like a storm, her Elemental Eye picking out air and fire and earth as it surged toward the flask and its contents. She drank it fast.

Legendary Essence Detected During Formation!
[Essence Draught of Atlantes (Air/Metal)]

Vess let the world around her fade and focused.

Choose A Feature:
Howl
Hammer
Harken

It was unlike the curated Essence Draughts she had always been given, but it was also absolutely singing with potency. The near-universal draught felt so in sync with her Skill that the choices were like glowing monoliths of metal and swirling winds. They spoke to her, but one spoke louder than all the others.

Congratulations!
You Have Absorbed The Essence Of [Hammer]!

"Ooh, just got a whole level from that bitch," Evie said in bright tones. "Almost worth her nearly melting my sweet baby."

Vess took several deep breaths and pushed away the thrill of a new Title and Temper, but her Spirit was literally *thrumming*.

"You alright, Vess?" Evie asked. "We've got more to kill yet."

"S'fine," she managed through clenched teeth. "Just...I Tempered part of my Spirit."

"Perfect. Now we can—"

Waves of blue-green water washed over the both of them, so fast Vess could do nothing more than yelp in alarm. It swept them up and back, over the tall walls of the Rotunda grounds...and away from the seventy-span wide fireball that was falling atop them all.

Zara stood under it, both arms upraised against the other Matron and red-haired Master.

"Zara!" Vess shouted, before she fell beyond the wall and lost sight of the Naiad completely.

All at once, the light dimmed. The sky, only seconds ago a brilliant orange, as if a second sun had descended upon the world, returned to an unassuming blue. The Mana around them both vanished, dropping them to the hard cobbles, but it was replaced by a shimmering barrier only inches from Vess' face. She stared at it, but it allowed her hand to reach through it easily, and it was only visible near the surface of the road.

What in Siva's name...?

Vess surged back to her feet and raced for the servant's gate, Evie right behind her. There they found two surprising things: the first were dozens of Knights with their eyes burned out and their faces gruesome masks of terror. One figure in dark robes had their head completely blown off, and the wounds were filled with strange, fungal growths. The second was the small squad of the Legion standing near the gate, just outside the shimmering line in the road. They were peering into the interior with confused glares, but a familiar Henaari met their eyes.

"Osyk, what is going on? Why are you still here?" She looked at the bodies. "Who did this?"

"Your Grace. The rest of the Claw has fled to safety with the freed civilians, leaving a few volunteers to wait for you all to exit the Rotunda grounds." He nodded to his squad, and for some reason, the Half-Orc mage blushed. She frowned.

"And the last? Who did this?" she asked.

"The Lady Isla did it. Ended all of the Knights, even a Master that came later," said Pava, following with a belated curtsy. "Your Grace."

Vess and Evie traded a glance, then peered into the half-open servant's gate. They saw...nothing.

It's an illusion. An obfuscation, she realized in wonder. *Far larger than Thangle could ever manage.*

Vess stepped through the shimmering golden curtain, and instantly the chaos and heat of battle enveloped her. She gasped, air driven from her lungs as she beheld a nightmare field of war.

"S—Siva's Grace," she cursed. "Such power..."

In the midst of the Rotunda grounds, Zara was standing over the struggling form of the red-haired Master. The other Matron had already fallen, though Vess could only see a lump of golden cloth where her body laid half-charred upon the earth. A woman stood beside Zara, dressed in royal purple and a silver coronet atop immaculate platinum blonde curls. Together, they raised their hands, and Vess' eyes widened.

Elemental Eye is level 69!

She stumbled backward, eyes stinging, into Evie's arms.

"What happened? What's going on in there?" Her friend asked, worriedly. "Are you okay?"

"I—I am fine. But they are finished." Vess blinked rapidly, still seeing brilliant afterimages. "We have to flee. Now. Where did everyone else go?"

"I will lead, Your Grace," Osyk said.

———

"This is the plan?" Beef asked, doubt clear in his voice. Thick, transparent blood dripped off his surviving shoulder armor and the matted fur of his bestial chest. He wrinkled his snout and wretched. Again. "It's so gross."

"Don't throw up. You'll get it all over the lizard blood," Felix said, before pausing. "Actually, that might help. Go ahead."

Beef obliged, vomiting onto the sand and himself. His head couldn't move well with all the carcasses strapped to him. They had gone around and killed more of the Glass Whiptails then cut up their corpses with Felix's enchanted butcher's knife. That kept the corpses from disintegrating into black smoke, which was the whole point. After that, he'd bled the lot of them all over the Minotaur before strapping large hunks of their bodies to his back and shoulders. The point was to create so much stink that every Dustwight for miles would gather close.

Felix grimaced. The smell really was awful, all things considered, but it was his best bet for getting the undeads' attention. And it might have another benefit, which had convinced Beef in the first place.

"Urp, uh," Beef gasped. He tried to wipe his mouth but recoiled from the sick and blood on his hands. "You're—*urp*—you're *sure* I'll get a Taunt Skill from this?"

"I mean, you haven't gotten one yet, right?" Felix began walking up the sloping outcropping they were sheltering behind. "Stress and need are great motivators for the System."

Beef rumbled a bit, but Felix didn't listen in. The guy would do it. With Endurance and a Body as tough as he had, he wouldn't be in too terrible danger...and Felix could always pull him free. One way or another.

He crested the outcropping and peered down the defile, flaring his Voracious Eye all the way. Below them, clustered near the edge of the gorge, were several hundred Dustwights just...milling around. According to Beef, somewhere in the canyons was the door to the tomb, but in order to get to it, they had to clear out all of the undead. Hence the plan.

"Alright, whenever you're ready, get running," he said after carefully navigating back to the ground.

Beef took a deep breath, gagged, and nodded. He took off, slowly at first, but with increasing speed. Like an old-timey locomotive, puffing away.

Now, Felix wasn't completely sure how the Dustwights sensed others. He was pretty certain they could see, since he'd never seen them randomly attack rocks or rustling bushes, but the most advanced of the undead had growths of bone over their faces. Just like their more powerful counterparts, the Wraiths, the bone plates would have completely eliminated their eyesight. So it was clear they used other senses too. Felix had decided to hedge their bets and make Beef seem as attractive as possible. Sight, smell...and sound.

CLANG! CLANG! CLANG!

Beef smashed two summoned hammers together. "Hey idiots! Over here! Betcha can't catch me and eat my braaaaains!"

Felix snorted, while Pit tilted his head in confusion.

They don't eat brains, his friend sent.

"I'll explain later." He climbed back up the outcropping, just in time to see the undead shift fast. Beef was at their head, running now atop a narrow ledge above the gorge, while below the horde took notice. More undead started packing in, all of them following Beef's progress. "He's reaching the halfway point. Hm. The guy's faster than I anticipated."

The ledge Felix had spotted, and Beef was now racing across, was only about a thousand feet long before it tapered off into nothing. The plan was to have Beef run along the ledge, make a ruckus and get all the attention he could, and then run back to lure as many of the undead toward the front of the gorge as they could.

Whoa, that worked well.

A veritable tide of undead were racing after him, with several attempting to scale the sides of the gorge to reach Beef's ledge. Felix waved, and thankfully the Minotaur's Perception was good enough to spot the signal. Beef immediately turned around and raced back toward their position, undead hot on his heels on the canyon's floor.

Right into Felix's trap.

Mana had been pouring from his channels for the last minute, ever since Beef had taken off, and now it coalesced above the crumbling mouth of the canyon. A storm of virulent green power, flashing with barely restrained lights. Felix flared his Affinity, sounding the last piece of the Skill and shaping his Intent to boost it fully. Beef ran, churning his heavy hooves as fast as he could, but the undead were catching up. He jumped, cracking the rocky shelf and hurling himself up and out of the canyon's entry.

Rain of Cataclysm!

The clouds above unleashed a driving deluge onto the sloping canyon mouth, and the first of the Dustwights were caught full in the face with clinging, brutal acid. Their withered flesh was no match for it, and they died nearly instantly. Those who came behind were no better, nor those after. Row after row, charge after charge, the creatures ran blindly after the Minotaur that got away. Felix killed them all.

Rain of Cataclysm is level 68!

You Have Killed A Dustwight (x544)!
XP Earned!

Your Companion Pit Has Gained 4 Levels!
He Is Now Level 68!
+40 to STR! +28 to PER! +8 to VIT! +36 to END! +12 to INT!
+24 to WIL! +64 to AGL! +68 to DEX!
+20 to AFI, RES, REI!

Pit let out a shudder, shimmering with a surge of blazing Mana as the System injected him with stats. Felix felt it, too, an echo of maddening pressure in his chest and above his navel, where Harmony and Dissonance met. His Body convulsed along with Pit's, as if every minor scratch and ache were magnified a thousandfold, and his skin wanted to just leap from his bones. Bones that felt as if they were being injected with hot lava. *I didn't even level up...why does this hurt?*

Beef collapsed on the ground. He gasped for breath, feet away and blessedly downwind. "Are we done?"

Felix clenched his jaw at the pain and shook his head. "We've barely started. The first waves are out of the way, so now we move forward. Slowly. Did you get a Taunt Skill?"

Beef raised a shaky thumbs up. "Yeah. Desperate Provocation. Uncommon rarity."

"Excellent. You'll need it soon. Let's go see this Tomb."

CHAPTER EIGHTY-THREE

Now that Beef had a Taunt Skill, things moved faster.

The Minotaur would charge ahead, use his Desperate Provocation, and snag at least a dozen enemies at once. All undead. The canyon was utterly filled with the things, as they had killed everything else, monster or otherwise. Beef would use Relentless Charge to move through them, gathering more and more before turning tail and running. It took some coordination to get it right, since he had to manage both his Stamina and his relatively small Mana pool, but he got it eventually. Beef had very good instincts for combat, though he kept goggling at Felix's spell usage like a kid in a candy store.

Rain of Cataclysm *was* pretty flashy, Felix had to admit.

Rain of Cataclysm is level 72!

Felix was pretty sure he could have cleared the entire area himself, but his Body still hadn't recovered. Frankly, he was worried at how long it was taking to heal. Even with eight cups of Isla's Panacea, there was a lingering pain through his muscles and joints. Everything had been pushed to the breaking point in his fight against the Grandmaster, and then it had been worsened when Pit leveled up. The conflict between System Harmony and Primordial Dissonance was a knife in his guts—it was made infinitely more frustrating by the fact Felix had thought he'd had a handle on all that.

But it didn't start there, did it? He'd been on the mend since facing the Primordial's influence back in the Warren. The solution, he hoped, was to Temper his last two Body Skills immediately, but that was easier said than done. Sovereign of Flesh and Relentless Resolution were the clear candidates, both teetering at level 74, but both required him to push his Body hard. Not to mention the Essence requirements for Sovereign of Flesh. *And my core space still feels stretched and swollen, ever since I ate all that water Mana in the crystals.*

Even thinking of it sent a ripple of queasiness through him, emanating from the dark abyss between his cores. Felix's Hunger had routinely eaten the overflow of Mana and Essence he absorbed through his Chthonic Tribute, but with it refusing anything else, Felix was forced to store the power within his core space. It could be utilized by his Skill, but it burned atop his Divine Tree like leaves of smoldering coals, and using it to fuel Sovereign of Flesh felt even worse than normal. And changing his skin into scales and claws had never been a joyride.

Bah. Stop worrying, he chastised himself. *Either I Temper it or I don't, and we have Paladins to investigate.*

Their rapid clearing of the canyons took remarkably little time. Thanks to Felix's store of Stamina and Mana potions, Beef was back on his feet quickly after each acid bath Felix enacted, and they kept moving. Thankfully, Beef had a fairly good idea of where the entrance was, though he'd never confirmed the exact details prior to being chased off by the Pathless' lackeys.

"We're here," Beef announced in a harsh whisper.

They peeked around the sheer orange cliffs and beheld a strange sight. Bodies. Literal tons of them were piled high around a darkened section of the canyon wall, with long iron rods pressed forcibly into the dusty earth.

"Whooooa, they created a fortification out of zombies!" Beef said, a little too excitedly. He slapped a meaty hand over his own mouth. "Sorry."

Felix didn't answer but walked boldly around the corner and into the open area just outside the undead wall. "Don't worry. No one's in there. I can't hear a single person breathing or even moving...and the Mana is overwhelmingly earth and light and shadow. Not a speck of life or necromantic energy that I can see." He walked closer to the withered corpses stacked like cordwood and rammed through with more of those crude iron bars. It stank overpoweringly like powder, dry and strangely neutral. "I think...I think this is to keep the undead away. This doesn't smell like rotting corpses, and all of them have been slashed by a butcher's blade, or something like it. Yeah."

Without another word, Felix leaped straight up, easily bounding over the barrier and landing in an empty circle of bare stone. Similar walls of other Dustwights stretched around the entire area, leaving approximately a hundred square feet left around a shadowed recess. Immediately, tendrils of shadow Mana flickered and slithered from that recess, but they fell limp before they accomplished anything of note. Seconds later, they attempted to move again with the same result. Felix peered deeper, flaring his Perception.

The darkness peeled away from his vision, picking out an absolutely mammoth door. It was heavily decorated and made of the same orange stone as the canyon, except where it was banded with gold. It was covered by and surrounded with inert sigils that were carved strangely—more similar to the Archon's invented language than modern sigaldry. The place was clearly ancient and the inert sigaldry accompanied by the tatters of Mana strands suggested that it had been protected. *Not protected enough, apparently.*

The doors were ajar, revealing a deeper darkness within.

Beside him, Beef landed with a loud *thud*. "So, someone made a fort? What for?"

"To hide the door from the undead," Felix said. "The Dustwights are attracted to *something* about the living, and these corpses are like an air purifier for the desiccated set. My real concern is why aren't there any guards? If it's the Paladins inside, then why take their entire force within?"

"Maybe it's a small group?" Beef suggested.

"Hmm." That did make sense. It was likely the largest part of their force was readying themselves to assault Ahkestria, just as he had seen weeks ago. "Then we have to assume that they're very strong. Probably upper Journeyman Tier, maybe a good few Adepts, too."

"Shit," Beef said. He flexed his hands, and his giant maul manifested in his grip. "Can you...can you fight people that strong?"

"I have," Felix said. *Whether my Body will hold out when facing a company of Adepts is another question entirely.* "We shouldn't waste more time. Pit."

His Companion had been pacing along the top of the canyon, keeping to ledges and out-of-reach roosts and providing occasional air support in the form of Frost Spears and Wingblades. At Felix's call, a dark shadow enveloped them both as the tenku flew down and alighted in the small alcove of the dead.

Fight? he asked.

Soon. First, we're going for a walk down that tunnel. Felix pointed out the door, and Pit gave an annoyed chirp.

More tunnels.

Felix grinned and scratched Pit's neck. "C'mon, Beef. Call over Hallow, and we'll get going."

"Ah, about that. I think I'll leave the Multipede out here," the Minotaur said. Felix arched an eyebrow, and Beef shrugged. "Not much use for a big sand-tunneler in some rocky tunnel, right? I'd rather have smaller summons."

Blackened-green Mana flowed from Beef's channels, spearing outward from his hands, elbows, and the base of his skull to splash into the wall of corpses.

"Hallowed Rise!" he commanded.

Dustwights began wriggling and writhing within the stacks, a full dozen of them that glowed with the same necromantic light as the Multipede. They clawed forward, one or two managing to escape the press of the walls, but the rest only flailed ineffectually. Beef cursed to himself and helped the rest of them out.

"See? Instant backup," Beef said at last. The Dustwights stood utterly still and unnerving, even if Felix knew they were being controlled by Hallow. "This was all I could grab outta the shit selection here. A lot of these are too messed up for my Skill to proc."

The guy looked so proud that Felix didn't want to tell him how creepy his new minions looked. The withered corpses infused with threads of blackened-green light had eyes that glowed like tiny torches.

"Do you have an upper limit on how many you can control at once?" Felix asked instead.

Beef shrugged. "Depends on their size, how long they've been dead, all sorts of stuff that I don't really understand. But these guys were like *made* to be Risen, ya know? Still, I'm surprised I was able to take control of this many."

"Why? I thought you said they were made for this?"

"Those Cursewinds? The tornados dump lots of these guys around the desert all the time, but I've never been able to take any of them over. Aside from being just, like, really strong, something about 'em would resist my Skill." Beef tucked his maul under an arm and rubbed his hands together in glee. "But now they're all primed for it. Hah!"

They were connected to the Primordial, so Beef couldn't take them over. Now they're not. Why? And how? Was it the butchering after death? Did that sever their link? Felix frowned at the walls of undead. The enchantment on the butcher blades were meant to stop natural deterioration for a time. Once the meat or materials were removed, they achieved a new Type, changing from monsters to monster *parts*, which was not subjected to the System's cleansing. *Guess I've never thought about why the System makes monster corpses melt away. Is it...is it about severing connections of Affinity? Why?*

Felix's Mind whirled as hundreds of thoughts flitted through his brain, considered and discarded in a handful of seconds. Ultimately, he couldn't come to any real conclusions, but it was something to consider. Perhaps to experiment with in the future when he had the time. *Someday.*

"If you're ready, then we're entering. Now," Felix said. He didn't wait for Beef's answer and strode purposefully toward the huge, open door. His Perception and Affinity stretched to their limits, Felix watched in as many directions as he could manage for any traps he might have missed. The gap was wide enough that even Pit could walk through with only a little squeezing, so they all slipped inside a darkened chamber shaped like a large diamond. Sand covered the cracked tiles and countless boot prints were pressed into it, leading down the single, tunnel-like hallway.

It was utterly dark...until it wasn't.

A flash of Mana, and the walls were abruptly illuminated with glimmering crystals set in ornate sconces. Blue, green, and golden light poured across them all, totally harmless and fully exposing them to a potential ambush. Yet Felix sensed there wasn't a single living soul within range of his senses, which was considerable.

Welcome To The Tomb Of Eternal Slumber!

Exploration is level 66!

You Have Entered A Lair!
Warning! Do Not—!
ERROR!

Protections In Place! Halt—!
ERROR!

Primordial Detected!
Lair Protections Deactivated!
Be Welcomed, Scion Of The Unseen Tide!

"Fuck me," Felix whispered.

"What the hell was all that about?" Beef asked. "What's the Unseen Tide?"

Felix didn't answer, because just then, a memory flickered into place in his head. A snippet of conversation he'd witnessed during one of his visions weeks ago. It replayed in the distinct voice of Hallow.

"They are still bound to the Tomb, Michael. You cannot take possession of them until you take the Tomb as well."

"The Dustwights. They were bound to this Tomb...and you knew it," Felix said. He turned to glare at a visibly guilty Beefhammer. "What else are you holding back?"

"I—honestly, I don't know much! The Tomb is connected to the undead, but I don't know why or even how. Hallow was the one who realized they were related, but we never told Naos. Isla. Whatever."

"Dammit, of course this is how it turns out," Felix muttered, glaring around the diamond-shaped chamber. "There's gonna be more undead further in."

"So what? So what if there's more undead in here! You just *melted* an army of them!" Beef said. "I mean, they're like trash mobs to you. What's a few more?"

Felix groaned and rubbed at his temples, while Pit only shook his head at the foolish bull. "Because if those undead are connected to this Tomb, then there is a Primordial down here. And since we just killed an army of his creatures, it probably knows we're coming."

"Uh...what's a Primordial?"

———

Over the next few minutes, Felix gave Beef a terse history on Primordials, emphasizing how dangerous they were. Even when they *weren't* controlling thousands of undead, some of which would likely give the Minotaur a run for his money in Strength and would definitely outmatch him in Agility. That had penetrated the dense necro-warrior, at least.

He had refrained from informing Beef of his Race, or exactly what the Unseen Tide happened to be.

"We're in a Lair, Beef. Keep your hands to yourself and eyes up. I don't know what to expect, but it won't be pleasant," Felix said at last.

A Lair. Karys had once told him of Lairs, but Felix was more familiar with their common variation: Domains. All Lairs started as Nests, places where monsters lived or congregated in great numbers, and once a certain threshold was reached, they evolved into a Domain and began to alter the environment around itself. How the environment was altered was highly dependent on the nature and strength of the Domain Core.

A Lair was a rare Domain evolution because it required the Domain's boundaries to remain unruptured for a great length of time and an immense amount of power in the Domain Core. Basically, the opposite of what happened back in Haarwatch. And, if Felix had to make a guess, the Primordial was the Domain Core in the Tomb, so he did not expect a leisurely trip.

The path they followed was cavernous and rough, but the floor was polished smooth and inlaid with blue-green stone. Cracks marred their surface, and stone dust and sand gathered in every crevice and corner. Alcoves dotted the length of the hall and were empty and dark, save for the rare Mana crystal. While the entrance chamber had been well lit, the tunnel was increasingly decrepit the further they walked. Rust-colored streaks covered the floor and walls in places, and somewhere water dripped in random intervals.

Then they saw the bodies.

Men and women in crimson plate armor were scattered about the tunnel, most of them severed in half as if by something very, very sharp. Fresher bloodstains slicked the tiles, and with a grimace, Felix nudged the nearest corpse with his boot. The gesture made its torso wobble, the flesh giving unpleasantly. If what he recalled from thousands of hours of procedural cop dramas were accurate, then they hadn't died that long ago.

"Traps," Beef said suddenly. When Felix shot him a questioning glance, he pointed to the walls. "The stone is cut here and here. It's really thin, but I would bet that some sort of razor-sharp blade comes out swinging when people try to pass through."

Felix flared his Manasight, but either the material that comprised the tunnel or some other hidden aspect blocked his vision. He could clearly see the thin slits in the walls, however, and after a bit more searching, he spotted even more coming up from the floor as well. *That explains why that guy looks diced instead of simply split.*

"Paladins lost quite a few people to these traps, and like I said, these people were powerful. We can't underestimate the defenses in this Lair." Felix looked at the ceiling. "Looks like we can go over it, if we're careful. But," he bit his lip. "Let me check something first."

"Hey! Don't—!" Beef reached out to him, but was too slow to stop Felix from stepping exactly where a few severed Paladin legs still stood. The bulky warrior gaped for a few seconds. "Nothing's happening."

Felix grinned, thinking on the System message he'd received when entering the Tomb. "It's about time something went my way. Seems I'm exempt from the traps here."

Primordial Detected!
Lair Protections Deactivated!
Be Welcomed, Scion Of The Unseen Tide!

Be Welcomed, indeed.

"The Paladins are close, and we can catch up. Pit, Converge if you please. Beef, to me. Close as possible." His Companion chirruped once before disappearing in a flash of light, while Felix walked back out of the traps activation area.

Beef stared at the slits on the walls and was sweating, despite the coolness of the passage. "You're sure they won't go off?" he asked.

Felix's grin turned sharp. "Pretty sure. What's life without a little risk, though?"

"Uh, a good one?" Beef said. "I'm not looking to get slap-chopped into a salad."

"Salad's good for you," Felix said, grabbing the Minotaur's arm. He hauled the guy forward despite Beef digging in his hooves. "And we're in a hurry."

CHAPTER EIGHTY-FOUR

Thankfully, Felix's gamble paid off. With Beef walking so close to him, the extremely sophisticated sequence of arrays lit with power...but ultimately didn't distinguish the Minotaur from the welcomed Primordial. Hallow was a different story: the Risen that the spirit controlled simply waltzed through the path, and the arrays didn't even flicker.

Like they're part of the Tomb, Felix realized. *There must be a lingering connection to the Lair.*

He flared his Affinity, Manasight, Oathbinding, and Cardinal Flame. The Harmonic stat and three Skills all activated in different ways, a rousing song of brass and woodwinds that faded into haunting, whispered melodies. He'd learned over the weeks that, while each of them afforded a piece of insight into the workings of the Grand Harmony, all together, they were far more powerful. Strings of light extended from every being and object in Felix's line of sight. Everything. The ground, the arrays, Beef, and Felix, and the clothes they wore. The air itself.

It was too much. Felix pulled back, lowering the vibrations of his Skills with his Affinity and tweaking his Intent. The song shifted, almost imperceptibly, and he nearly lost the Chant. Felix fumbled with it all, but grasped the bare edge of control.

Manasight is level 68!
Oathbinding is level 44!

The threads of connection faded as his concentration narrowed. Oathbinding showed him vows, willingly given or coerced, and aside from the silver threads that spun off from himself, there were none present.

Manasight traced the flows of power, and Mana was a near-physical manifestation of the Grand Harmony itself...and was omnipresent.

He turned that down, pushing away the bits that didn't matter like the air and shadows around them. Cardinal Flame was internal and external Mana control, so tweaking those swirling clouds of Mana around him was easier...though when the Mana wasn't his, it was still quite hard, no matter his Willpower and Intent scores.

Finally, Affinity was sensing the connections between all things, focused mostly on living creatures. Inanimate objects were harder to detect in many ways. Only with Adamant Discord did he have an easier time, yet that was focused on things that had a connection to himself, not those that existed with others.

Slowly, lines of flickering light manifested around the Risen undead. Thick bonds of blackened green light trailed to Beef, but thinner bonds extended off into the darkened tunnels. Somewhere deeper.

Primordial bound in some minor way. I'll keep an eye on them.

"Do I got something on my face?" Beef asked.

Felix smiled but shook his head and continued on.

On the second trap, Felix lingered again, this time studying the web of labyrinthine arrays. Like the complexities of his Seat and Seal, these appeared almost as fractals of sigaldry, too dense and complicated to be broken down by his level of Skill. While Beef stood nearby, sweating at the possibility of imminent death–this one seemed to drop vats of sizzling acid–Felix used his perfect recall to preserve as much of what he was seeing as possible.

The arrays weren't just ignoring Beef, but Felix was being given some sort of higher priority. So Beef's proximity to Felix meant the traps didn't go off, so as to prevent the "welcome" Primordial from being caught in the crossfire. That was all well and good, and made sense for a sophisti-cated security system—the real question was why? Why build the Tomb like this at all? If this was the tomb of some long-lost royal family, as Karys had suggested, then why was a Primordial—of all things—allowed to walk in, unharmed?

Answers weren't forthcoming. Trap after trap met them, many with dead Paladins scattered about their circumference. A few were no longer functional due to the walls and floor getting melted to slag. As Felix couldn't even affect the high-Tier stone with his shaping Skill, that meant there were some real powerhouses among the Paladins. It was unsur-prising if unwelcome news.

After his initial scare, Beef quickly regained his confidence as they progressed down the darkened halls. What's more, every time he found a mostly intact Paladin corpse, he would raise them as part of his horde. The growing sea of blackened-green eye-lights was haunting as it followed them, but Beef was getting more and more excited with every Risen added.

"Necromancy is OP, for real. Instant army? I mean, c'mon! Like, you're strong, but you can't be everywhere. Hallow can," Beef said proudly.

"I am legion, but I cannot be everywhere, Michael," the nearest Risen said in that echoing female voice.

"It's Beefhammer, Hallow."

"Of course, Michael."

Conversations went like that for the most part—Beef supplying both sides as they moved forward as fast as they could. The Paladins might not have been too far away, but they had an unknown lead and unknown goal. Down here, in a tomb where a Primordial clearly lurked...Felix couldn't let them do as they wished. The last Primordial he'd dealt with had caused enough trouble to ravage the Void and Haarwatch with what he now knew as its flesh curse. This new one was doing the same with its Wraiths, but how much more damage could it do if it were free to use more of its power?

I don't even know if it's locked up or restrained here, but that would track. Maybe the Nym made this place, too. Felix hadn't seen any architecture or details that would indicate the Nym's particular aesthetic, but the traps were similar, at least

Eventually, the tunnel of traps ended. There had been over thirty of them still functioning, and forty including the ones someone had turned to melted lumps of rock. All told, it was an intense introduction to a place that did not want visitors...and yet as they exited the wide mouth of the tunnel, they were greeted with a huge, spacious cavern filled with warm light.

"Holy crap," Beef said quietly. "There's a whole city here."

Felix agreed with that assessment. Filling the bottom of the miles-wide cavern was a literal city with hundreds, if not thousands of buildings spreading in all directions. The tunnel had exited perhaps fifty feet above the level of the city below, and a switchback roadway led down into the confusing warren of streets. More fascinating than that, however, was that every inch of cavern wall was filled to the brim with Mana crystals.

Huge stalactites and stalagmites of brilliantly blue, brown, and golden crystals hung from the ceilings and jutted up between towering stone buildings at least thirty feet tall. It was hard to tell the scale of them, but in some places the crystals had grown completely around structures, trapping them like flies in amber. The cavern was like the inside of a geode, except a geode that blazed with multi-hued light.

"The Mana here is...intense," Hallow observed. Pit trilled in agreement and stepped out of Felix's Spirit once again, stretching his huge wings.

Air Mana is being strangled by water and earth and life, Pit said, flexing his wings again. *Flight will be hard.*

Through the weaving streets, shimmering crystals, Felix's eyes picked up a distinct flare of orange-gold light. A combination of Mana that he'd seen many times.

Manasight is level 69!

"Paladins," he said, pointing. "I can see them making their way across the city."

"To where?" Beef asked. His eyes were as wide as his dropped jaw, still taking in the breadth of everything.

"That's what we're here to find out," Felix explained, before looking down the path. "Can't fly, so let's hustle. How fast can your Risen move, and more importantly, can they be quiet?"

"Define quiet."

Great. "Just follow me then," Felix muttered.

Abyssal Skein!

The Void crawled out of Felix's core space, slipping through his channels and Mana Gates like a cold oil. Felix flared the Skill, pushing more and more of its effect outward, extending it along the connections Felix had established with them all. His Skein slithered over their Bodies, blending them into the environment. The Void acted as a thin barrier that faded them from the Corporeal Realm entirely.

"Ugh, that feels gross," Beef complained, before blinking. "Why is everything all weird colored?"

"An effect of my...magic stealth," Felix explained. "Deal with it; it'll keep us hidden so long as you don't make too much noise." He looked up, back at the bobbing motes of Mana. Without another word, he quickly walked down the path and into the light.

―――――

Ahkestria was in an uproar.

The devastation of the Council Rotunda was hard to hide, as half the grounds were on fire and the other half was flooded by what seemed a large pond's worth of water. People were in the streets, staring at the destruction and gossiping worriedly about it all. Disciples in golden robes travelled the thoroughfares, loudly proclaiming the news like a Lord's crier, passing out trite assurances that all was well, and the criminals responsible for this act of terror were being hunted.

"...even now are patrolling your neighborhoods to keep everyone safe! Fear not! For these vile villains will be brought to justice! And should you see any that are suspicious, please report them to your nearest Temple Knight!" the Disciple hollered in an impressive single breath. "Be at ease! The Masters and Matrons are here to protect you all!"

Vess watched the man retreat down another street, starting his spiel over again. She had seen him and others doing the same all afternoon, each one intent on soothing the riled fears of the rich and powerful. Few among the gossiping masses were less than Apprentice Tier, only those wearing the garb of servants or handmaidens. They were a touch weaker than those of Pax'Vrell, but then not every Territory was as martially focused as hers.

The Masters and Matrons more than make up for their lack, Vess thought with a grimace. She still had several burns from her fight against the Knights and Matron earlier that day.

She ghosted through the streets, her Dragoon's Footwork proving its worth to avoid any eyes on the packed boulevards. Sticking to alleyways and rooftops, she swiftly made her way back to a small mansion in the heart of the merchant lords' district, where soaring walls were heavily studded with Mana crystals and gilded in loud displays of wealth. It was all pointless pageantry to Vess, who saw it as a bluff at true power, especially after learning more about the mining operations in the deeper layers.

Merchants grown fat from the efforts of others, Masters and Matrons who rule by discarding the weak as pawns and disposable sacrifices. Vess spat, something she normally found repulsive, yet couldn't restrain herself. She felt as if the foul nature of this place were seeping into her by simply walking among their self-centered nobility. Power was earned, not taken. That was the lynchpin of her father's teachings, and how he expected the people of Pax'Vrell to conduct themselves. *Not even Haarwatch was as bad as this....*

Yet as Vess slipped into the darkened grounds of a shuttered mansion, she remembered DuFont and the other Guild Elders and what they were willing to do for power. About the Archon. And even a few passing snippets of courtiers from her home, those who attempted to curry favor with her father. *The powerful chased power, and it...it matters little to many of them how they achieve it.*

The admission had the heiress clenching her jaw. She was not interested in continuing such practices, no matter their form. When she returned to Pax'Vrell, she would see that such things were stamped out.

Vess passed two guards, hidden in a dark alcove by the mansion's rear entrance. She flashed coded handsign, and they did not move as she ducked under the overgrown thicket hiding a thick, warded door. Vess slipped inside.

The Chanter Isla had established this safehouse for situations such as this. It had once belonged to a family of merchants, but they had died some years ago, and it was now handled by a trust. A trust that was solely operated by the Chanter. Vess had been impressed when they had first arrived, and that feeling only deepened when she discovered the place was large enough to hold the rescued prisoners, their allies, and feed them all for at least a few days. Now, after spending much of the afternoon scouting the city and Temple, Vess was simply happy to have a bed to rest upon. Eventually.

For now, she had to report.

"We still didn't get everyone. Some of those Knights talked. More are bein' held in the Temples. Another couple thousand," Evie was saying as Vess entered the spacious parlor room. The windows were boarded up, and two head-sized, golden Mana crystals gave off enough light to see by, but they were dim as candles. The core of their team were spread around the room: Evie, Atar, Alister, Zara, Darius, Harn, and even the Faun Fiammetta. The one addition was the slender blonde woman with a coronet atop her brow. "How're we gonna get them out?"

"I don't know that we can, or should," the blonde woman said.

"What?" Atar asked in surprise. He frowned at the Chanter. "You would leave these people to be sacrificed?"

"My priority, the concern of our Order, is to save the entire Continent. I do not care for one small city, not when lingering jeopordizes my mission," she said, her hawk-like nose lifted as if in challenge. Isla stared around the room, meeting all of their eyes without fear. "My mission lies below us. Safe, for now. I think we should retreat and leave Ahkestria to deal with its own issues."

Vess took a measured breath. Isla had told them that Felix was alive and safe—but injured. He was down in the lowest layers of the city, hidden in another safehouse with the other Unbound they had come to find. Ostensibly, their mission had been fulfilled: they had found the Minotaur and he was safe from the Paladins. But that was before they learned of the Council's strange plan and the Paladins' part in it all.

"I do not think this will end here. What the Paladins are attempting...apart from its consequences, I wonder at the why of it," Vess said. Eyes turned to her, and Evie grinned. "They do nothing without a purpose, and their aid is never free. What is the Hierocracy getting out of this? We are missing something, and before we can leave, we must find out what."

"The Hierocracy, foul as it is, is a simple beast. It wants power, and it will do whatever it can to claim it," Isla said dismissively. "I am affronted that they dared attack a sister of my Order, aghast that they intend to harm so many people, but the Choices before us are simple: Either we flee with what victory we can grasp...or we all die here in a pointless conflict, leaving two Unbound to the mercies of the Continent."

"Pointless?" Vess asked. She felt her face flushing with heat, but she didn't care. "We would be stopping an injustice perpetrated on the weak and Untempered. If our strength is not meant to serve others, to protect them, then what is the point of it?"

The Chanter scoffed. "You have a lot to learn about the world, Your Grace. Pax'Vrell is an exception to the standards of the Continent."

"Isla," Zara warned in a sharp tone.

The blonde Chanter pouted. "Fine. Then have your suicidal assault. I shall—"

"Be at our side, to provide your powerful healing," Zara smoothly interrupted. "As expected of one of our Order."

Isla only frowned and mumbled something to herself.

Zara continued, her voice a rising swell that carried the conversation along. "Thanks to our scouts, we have learned a few things about our enemy. The Paladins are holding people, operating under High Justiciar Haim and his second, Captain Boldt. They are both Masters, which is another challenge, with all the rest of the Paladins operating as Journeymen under two or three Adept officers. There are thirty Paladins, two companies, and while that is concerning, it is less than I had feared."

Harn shook his head. "Paladins ain't no joke to fight. Those idiots in the Pass posed us all a challenge, but they were the rank and file. Now, we're facing their elite. That's not a fight I want to take on without a solid plan. Anyone got one of those?"

Evie shrugged and ticked off points on her fingers. "Storm the Temple, free the prisoners, take a piss in the big fire, run."

Harn chuckled.

"I don't care who is arrayed against us. I need to know why the Highest Flame is condoning this," Atar said. Alister's arm was threaded through the fire mage's, as if both were drawing support from one another. "Why is my master—why is Kel'lyv doing this?"

"The Highest Flame, ah, she has always required to consume things to grow stronger," the Faun Disciple said. "She is That Which Burns, it is the truth of Her being. Things that have power, people mostly, have um, historically been the most able to strengthen Her. The pacts She makes with individuals supports Her through lean times, but not if they are not advancing."

"And people don't advance much in this city, I take it," Vess said.

Fiammetta nodded. "We hunt the wastes, but it is hazardous to face the Cursewinds even in a large group. What's more, the undead hurt the Flame. The few hunts that have been organized have lost people and...and a curse turned them into more undead slaves for the Cursewinds."

"The Dustborn curse." Zara said.

"Yes. You know it. Of course, you faced the undead." Fiammetta's head tilted curiously. "But none of your people perished. How?"

"Felix," Isla said, and Zara's gaze sharpened. Isla waved off the woman's icy glare. "Don't look at me like that. It's a simple enough deduction."

"Felix?" Fiammetta asked. "Who is that?" Her eyes widened. "You mean that man? That monster that conquered a Lost Territory? He's here?"

Zara gave Isla another acidic look before regaining control of the conversation. "That is neither here nor there. What is interesting is that the undead are affecting the Urge by eroding its support system. But that would hardly seem to be enough. A creature as old and as powerful as the Highest Flame subsists on more than a few pacts with mortals."

Fiammetta spread her hands as if in apology. "I truly do not know. There are a great many secrets I was not privy to—would not be, not until I become a Matron. Which is...which is not likely to happen anymore."

"Yeah, super sad. Anyway, let's keep planning." Evie snapped her fingers and pointed at Zara. "What about the Primordial? Can we use that somehow?"

"What?" Isla stood, alarm writ large across her fine features. "What Primordial? Where?"

"A Primordial is behind the undead," Atar said. He tilted his head to the side. "Didn't you know?"

"I—How? The Primordials are gone," Isla insisted. She looked to Zara. "What are they talking about?"

Zara pursed her lips in thought. "An idea that might hold merit. Vess, please give Harn and Darius the route you plotted to the Temple. Isla, Atar, Alister, and Fiammetta: come with me. The rest of you, get some rest and prepare yourselves." Zara regarded them all with her ice-blue eyes, as if she were weighing them one-by-one. "The ritual is to take place at dawn, and we will be moving well before that." Zara left, trailed by those she had named.

Vess took another slow breath before motioning Harn and Darius close.

CHAPTER EIGHTY-FIVE

Abyssal Skein is level 50!
...
Abyssal Skein is level 57!
Journeyman Tier!
You Gain:
+10 PER
+10 EVA
+10 FEL

Felix learned quickly that covering so many with his Void Skill was exhausting work. It overtaxed even his Mana regeneration after only a half hour, which slowed them all considerably. The sheer pressure of the Mana around them was the problem—the potent crystals of golden-green, orange, brown, and most predominantly a deep, oceanic blue were filling the air with so much Mana that finding the space for his own Skills to activate felt like lifting a mountain at times. The sheer presence of Mana in the air even forced him to shut down his Manasight—it was less than useless when all it showed him were blinding streams of swirling colors.

However, on the flip side, recovering his Mana was exceedingly easy. Chthonic Tribute pulled the thick streams of power from the air, and so long as he directed the power to his cores, his Mana pool was instantly refreshed. Beef was having a harder time, of course, and his relatively anemic core and Mana pool were exhausted over and over again as he raised every Paladin corpse they encountered that was even mildly intact.

The traps in the tunnel were very much present in the crystalline city, which was a bit of a blessing. While it meant Beef couldn't just wander about alone, it did mean that the Paladins were progressing far slower than they were. Again and again, Felix spotted sections of the city—streets, staircases, balconies of elaborate buildings—that had been burnt and melted apart. That was not including the traps that had obviously been damaged or otherwise invalidated by the slow creep of shimmering crystal.

After around two hours pressing through the vast city, Felix had grown tired of the delays. Thanks to the traps, Beef had grown his force from simply Dustwights to more complete dead paladins. Cut in half was a problem, but burned to death or strangled with poison? Easy. They were harder for Beef to maintain in large numbers, and Hallow wasn't able to give the Risen a great deal of finesse, both facts that added to the effort Felix had to put into his Abyssal Skein. More effort than he cared to spend, with time so precious. With a little arguing on Beef's part, Felix had convinced him to stay holed up in one of the empty mansions while he and Pit scouted ahead.

Hopefully he doesn't decide to explore by himself, Felix thought with a touch of worry. Pit warbled softly in amusement, and Felix shook his head. *Beef's a bit immature, but he's not stupid.*

The two of them stood in the shadow of a particularly sharp steeple and surveyed the way forward. This neighborhood of the city narrowed into a series of convoluted passages, stairwells, and covered walkways. Much of the strange underground city reminded Felix of the Risen Ward at the top of Ahkestria. There, under the powerful sun, the architecture brought to mind the wavy lines of heat haze, but down in the Tomb, it was more like Felix was looking at them all from underwater. The eerie cast of predominantly water-blue crystals added to the effect.

Hard to spot anyone in this place, Felix groused silently. *But I'm certain they went this way.*

Below them, something moved. A sound like metal on stone drifted from an adjacent alleyway, and Felix traded a glance with his Companion. Wrapping Abyssal Skein around himself and Pit was child's play compared to before, and without a word, they ghosted across the rooftops.

If Pit had been able to fly, they would have assessed the situation from the air, but that was not a viable option. Felix had his Adamant Discord, but it was flashy in a way that not even his Void Skill could hide his presence. And the last thing he wanted to do was let the Paladins know that someone was hunting them. Felix had been tracking two groups of Paladins ever since he spotted a brief flare of torchlight several city blocks away from himself. The first he'd found swiftly, but narrowing down the second group's location had proven remarkably difficult. The nature of the place deadened his senses as much as his Skills.

I see them, Pit sent. The tenku had advanced several roofs ahead and was staring back at Felix's location. *Four Paladins. Twelve lessers. Below you.*

They're called Squires, Felix corrected offhandedly. *And they're just as nasty as their bosses. Hold on. Let me see.*

Two stories lower, on a balcony off the building Felix stood upon, several Paladins cautiously studied the streets below them. If he focused, Felix could hear more shuffling somewhere behind them, within the building proper.

"Haven't heard back from Lorc's team," a voice said in a harsh whisper. Metal shifted, rasping faintly against itself.

"Think the traps got 'em?" someone else asked.

"Maybe. Hasn't been this late before. Traps've taken out better teams than his."

"Or it's not traps." This was the third, a new voice with a much deeper timbre.

"What?"

"I swear I saw some sorta eyes watching me earlier. I told you."

"Not this again," complained the second voice.

"What're you on about, Eifan?"

"Burnin' blue eyes were watchin' us! I saw them!" Eifan—deep voice —said, entirely too loudly.

"Shut your gob-hole!" A fourth joined the conversation, and she sounded a lot more intense than the others. Felix edged just a slight amount around the gargoyle that loomed ahead of him. Through a cleft beneath his wing, he could spot the group of them, and he flared his Voracious Eye.

All Journeyman, but that woman is an Adept. High end of Adept, too, Felix sent to his Companion. *We'll take this like the last one. Right?*

Right. Pit spread his wings and leaned back, bracing his massive body against the rough tiles beneath them. *Ready.*

Adamant Discord!

The Paladins were seeking a Primordial, and Felix *was* one—that that was all the connection he needed to manipulate the threads between them. Lightning flashed downward, crashing into all three of the Journeyman Paladins and seizing them in bands of unbreakable steel. Felix pulled upward, shattering the roofing tiles beneath his feet as their armored forms were hauled upward at breakneck speed.

"OAAAUGHH!"

Their screams were almost in unison, escalating as rapidfire blades of air slammed into their breastplates and gorgets. Pit's Wingblades were turned by the advanced armor they wore, but the sheer momentum of them was enough to buckle the metal.

"B-blue eyes!" one of them gasped.

Felix whipped his hand forward, his Inheritor's Will moving faster than their eyes could track. Heads rolled.

You Have Killed A Paladin Of The Pathless (x2)!
XP Earned!

You Have Defeated A Paladin Of The Pathless!

XP Earned!

The last he threw onto the roof behind him, unconscious but bound in crackling bands of lightning for good measure. Below them, the jangle of harness and scrape of metal on stone rose in volume. Pit squawked in warning, and Felix took two quick steps backward, right before the edge of the roof exploded in a hail of golden blades.

Hm. That looks similar to Vess' Skill. Wonder if they're related.

The Adept woman rose up atop two glowing blades, while eight others manifested around her like a halo of violence. Her eyes flickered about, taking in the dead and living. "I am Lieutenant Walphis. You have attacked the Paladins of the Pathless. Killed two of my men. I sense...power in you, and for that I will ask you once: why?"

"Huh," Felix said. "Gotta say I'm surprised. Usually you Pathless types lean into the ultra-violence pretty easily. You're willing to answer some questions?"

The woman narrowed her eyes, but nodded. "So long as they are reasonable, and no more of my people die. I would rather not fight someone as strong as you."

Felix tilted his head. She likely had a Skill like his for assessing threats, even if it was simply Analyze. "Alright. What are the Paladins in this Tomb for?"

Walphis wet her lips, but the swords did not waver. "We seek peace."

"Peace?" Felix chuckled. "That's unlikely. Peace with who? Ahkestria?"

"Who else? We seek an accord, as requested by the Grandmaster of the Paladins. Peace must be achieved and allies secured for what is coming."

Felix frowned. "And what's coming?"

"Death."

Senses deadened as they were, Felix had barely any time to react to the sudden barrage of flaming projectiles. All twelve of the Squires had crept up while their lieutenant distracted him, and they unleashed a salvo of deadly power right into his blind spot.

And it wasn't enough.

Chthonic Tribute!

The projectiles flickered and vanished, pulled into the yawning chasm of Felix's Hunger, which even snagged several of the lieutenant's golden blades. It also, unfortunately, took a huge bite out of the ambient Mana around him. His Hunger, that abyss, protested at the influx, and an *incredible* nausea settled across his guts. He worried for a brief second that it would impair him, but he muscled through it and parried the flashing blades of the lieutenant.

Frost Spears descended from a nearby roof, skewering every single Squire at once, before his Companion dropped on them with beak and claw. None survived.

"You cannot hope to stop the High Justiciar, fool!" Walphis snarled at him. "He will unite this foul city under the Hierophant, for it is the will of god!"

Felix didn't reply but parried another golden blade and backhanded the woman across her face. She tried to dodge it, but it hit like a speeding truck, slapping the woman back into a thick chimney which all but collapsed under the impact.

In a flash, Felix was there, looming over the lieutenant's sprawled form. She made to get up, and he kicked her in the chest, knocking her back down. She screamed, and golden lights flashed upward, arcing for his face.

Wild Threnody!

Arrow of Perdition!

His Inheritor's Will blazed with golden-azure light, until the hooked blade looked to be made of liquid flames. Without flourish, Felix plunged it right into Walphis' torso, just above her navel. He felt the Skill catch on something, and the golden blades collapsed into formless Mana vapor. The lieutenant's scream turned to a horrified wail.

"Not really a fan of the gods," Felix muttered.

His blade found her heart.

You Have Killed Lieutenant Walphis, A Paladin Of The Pathless!
XP Earned!

"Are you sure? He said that?" Beef asked him again. "The Paladins want to burn Ahkestria to the ground?"

Felix had returned to the Minotaur and Hallow soon after dispatching the last of the Paladins. While the lieutenant had given him some information on the Hierophant's goals—namely conquering Ahkestria—it was really the lesser Paladin who gave him gold. And all it took was a little intimidation.

"That's what this guy believed. His commanding officer seemed to think they were liberating the city for the Hierocracy. Either way, the key to their goals is inside the 'palace on the hill' as he called it," Felix said. "It should be close by and was in the opposite direction we were heading to."

"You trust his directions?" Beef asked. "What if he's sending you into a trap?"

"Oh, he definitely sent me into a trap, but he was honest about what he knew." Since his Affinity had developed, not many people could lie to him anymore, and especially not people of lesser Tempers. "But I'm expecting resistance, anyway. These Paladins don't want to be interrupted."

"And...and what happened to the guy who told you this?" Beef asked, and his Spirit quailed a little at the answer. He had been oddly unnerved when Felix had told him he'd killed a couple squads of Paladins around the city, as if the Minotaur hadn't done the same himself. "Did you, uh, did you—?"

"Kill him?" Felix shook his head. "After he finished talking, the guy tried to blow me up with a fireball. What else could I do?"

Beef didn't say anything, but his Spirit tumbled about nervously. Felix could understand, but sparing the lives of Paladins in the Pass had caused him problems that he'd lived to regret. If they'd left no survivors in Caleph Pass, would the High Justiciar have known about his team and prepared for their arrival? Would they have been able to poison the Council and Matrons against them?

Harn was right. It sucks, but he was right.

"Well, at least I've got a few more Risen for the horde," Beef said, faking a cheerful smile. "The lieutenant you, uh, defeated is really strong."

"Good." Felix and Pit had carried back a number of the intact corpses for Beef to raise, and now Hallow numbered at around thirty. It was a lot to cover with Abyssal Skein, but still doable for now. "Heads up, we're here."

The narrow streets opened up, revealing a huge structure looming over them both. Mana crystals clung to its side like rock candy, and every single one was a deep, oceanic blue. It was at least a thousand feet wide, with a tall, almost brutalist design that looked like a fortress that had been under siege for centuries. Felix's stomach twisted. He recognized the design of it, and it was like being punched in the back of the head. Underneath all of the crystalline growths and swirling clouds of near-visible ambient Mana, the "palace" before them looked identical to the one he had seen in the Labyrinth below Shelim.

"The Primordial is in there," he said. It wasn't a question, but a statement that Felix felt in his bones. "Shit. They've already broken in."

A short way across the palace's walls was a large fifty-foot gate, and its doors were ajar. Before them, spread out atop a dark stone parade ground, were thirteen Paladins. All of them were Journeyman warriors, but more concerning than that were the small silver bells every one of them held in their off-hand. Mana sparked off them sporadically, and even from a distance, Felix could make out the flash of sigaldry inscribed upon them.

"Only thirteen? That's cake. Hallow can take care of them alone," Beef said. "Maybe."

"Hold on. These Paladins were left here for a reason," Felix said. "They all have inscribed bells, and from what I can make out it has something to do with amplifying sound. If we rush in there, they sound the alarm, and the only thing we have going for us is gone."

"Mhm. Stealth tactics," Beef said, nodding. "I played an assassin for a year in SwordLore. I get it. But I'm not exactly made for stealth, even with your magic thing. How do we get in?"

"Simple. Listen to me, and don't die," Felix said.

Rime Shaping!

Forced to pit his Mana and Will against the saturated air, Rime Shaping had a distinct advantage. Water Mana was only slightly removed from ice Mana, after all. With a dull crinkling, the Paladins cursed as all thirteen bells froze solid...along with several of their hands.

Rime Shaping is level 43!

"Go!" Felix shouted. *Cardinal Flame!*

Red-gold fire bloomed around the Paladins, searing against their skin and seizing one or two, but the air was too heavily attuned to water. It quashed the effect of the flames, but it was only meant as a distraction.

"Seismic Shatter!"

A cone of earth Mana blasted outward from Beef's descending maul. The maul crushed one of the Paladins to the ground, while the waves of earth Mana bashed into six others and threw all of them backward fifteen feet. The Paladins, though, were not green warriors. Swords in hand, they advanced on Beef with calm discipline, and even the Minotaur was taken aback by the threat they posed.

Then Hallow charged them, and Felix watched as the Paladins paled at the sight of corpses in crimson armor closing on them. They held just a few more moments before a blast of blue-white lightning and swirling Wingblades descended upon them all.

The battle was over before it had begun.

You Have Killed A Paladin Of The Pathless (x13)!
XP Earned!

"Fuck yeah! Eat it, douchebags!"

"Beef!" Felix hissed. "Quiet. We made enough noise with that fight."

"Right. Sorry. Just got excited." When he thought Felix wasn't looking, the Minotaur pumped his fist in victory.

Felix sighed. "This next part is gonna be very dangerous. Not that any of this has been particularly safe. If there's a Primodial in there, chained up or not, there is a high chance we die here. Are you prepared for that?"

"But...you're crazy strong." Beef looked at him with eyes that he recognized from the Legion. Like Felix was more than he was—more than he ever could be. "You're unstoppable."

Felix grimaced. "I'm extremely stoppable. Just ask that Grandmaster."

"Just a bad match-up. Stack some heat resist, and you can take on that guy. Naos told me all about those Masters, and they don't sound like much. High-level, but scrubs are scrubs."

Felix just stared at the Minotaur for a beat. Things he'd been ignoring started to connect. "Beef. How old are you?"

"Oh." Beef didn't want to meet his eyes. "I'm, uh, I'm a teenager."

"Uh huh. What age?"

"Thirteen."

Felix pinched the bridge of his nose. *Thirteen. Jesus.* That made a lot of sense. "Look. I can't make choices for you. You can stay out here, you don't have to come in."

"I'm strong enough to face it," Beef said seriously. There was a childish bravado to the phrase that struck Felix, but the Minotaur's Spirit was crooning in a mix of fear and determination and...embarrassed...pride? "I can do this. I can help."

Pit? What do you think? he asked his Companion.

The tenku trilled in approval. *He fights. He's strong. Let him fight with us.*

Felix chewed on the inside of his cheek a moment longer, but other than tying up the Minotaur, he didn't have a good way to keep him away. "I don't like it, but it's your choice. But stick close, because I'm not gonna let you get hurt if I can help it, okay?"

From within the open gates, there came a deep, tooth-vibrating noise. It was almost sub-audible, but it made every hair on Felix's body stand on end and his cores quiver. Beef sucked in a tight breath, his face drawn with pain.

"What the hell is that?" he asked.

Felix clenched his jaw. "Dissonance. Stronger than I've felt in a while. That seals it, then." He took a deep, calming breath and captured the Minotaur's gaze. "The Primordial is in there, along with the Paladins."

Beef gave a shaky smile and hefted his great maul up onto a shoulder. "Then let's go find 'em and kick their asses."

Laughter burst through Felix's lungs, short and relieving. He shook his head, but the smile lingered. "Stick close."

CHAPTER EIGHTY-SIX

Cobb was sweating, and his back ached fiercely. It was cold in the dungeons they had been shoved into, but so many of his fellow miners had been crammed together so all the small Goblin felt was an intense, swampy heat. It was enough that some of the older folk had passed out, and even though it cost the rest of them more space, Cobb had made sure to give them room enough to lie down. At least some of them could have a little comfort before the end.

And it was an end. They all knew it because the crimson-armored brutes that prowled the halls made sure everyone knew why they were there. That they were being sent to die at the hands of the Temple of the Highest Flame.

Cobb pressed his forehead against the iron bars. They were blessedly cool, and it kept his mind away from the fire that waited for them above. Like everyone else, Cobb had been angry and terrified in turns, but it had all faded to a cold numbness. It was like some vile Sorcerer cast a curse on his heart. He felt empty.

He had been pulled from the mines by Temple Knights and dragged up to the Miner's Layer, only to find hundreds of his neighbors all crowding the streets. All of them were marched away from the mines, up and up, through layers Cobb had never been allowed to visit. Miners were beaten badly if they tried to fight or flee, until the golden Knights' side swords dripped with blood as they jabbed them all forward. Eventually, they had been shoved into the bright sunlight of the Risen Ward, and it had been all he could do not to stare at how bright, shiny, and *clean* it all looked. The buildings weren't cracked or crumbling, the paths weren't rutted or filled with filthy runoff. It was like a dream of paradise.

Then the Paladins had shown up, in their dreadful armor, taking them away from the Knights. Cobb hated the Knights, but the Paladins were worse. When those in the lead were unable to move faster than the red-plated monsters demanded, they were cut down. Simple as that, without warning or explanation. More died, until they understood.

Cobb had all but run into his packed cell.

Now he wished for his trusty pickaxe more than anything else. Two of the Paladins were pacing near the end of the corridor, doing nothing except occasionally yelling at the prisoners if they sobbed too loudly. One of them said something to the other and laughed. Watching them burned something inside of Cobb, a heat that had nothing to do with the sweaty Yttin all around him.

I'll kill all of you. Some...somehow. Cobb gritted his teeth and squeezed the bars. He was Untempered though, and all he managed was to hurt his hands. *You don't get to do this.*

The laughter suddenly cut off.

"Jord?" the other said. Cobb pressed his face to the bars, trying to see them both, but could only make out one looking around in confusion. "Jord, where'd you g—"

A blue and white spear burst through the Paladin's throat, turning his words to choked gurgles. Cobb's eyes widened, and his heart slammed in his narrow chest. "Something...something is happening!" he hissed at the others around him.

A Yttin shrugged, its bandages too loose and showing its pale skin beneath. No one else even cared to shift. Cobb gave up, pushing his face against the bars again. It was silent in the corridor, absent even the sound of booted feet.

Then a woman jumped in front of him.

"AHH!" Cobb screamed, hurling himself back from the bars...and getting slapped back into them by wall of bodies behind him.

"Damn, shut up," the Human woman said. Her face and chest were speckled with red, but that didn't detract from the wide grin on her face. She jangled a set of keys. "I'm here to save you."

Cobb and the others were ushered out into the corridor, where he quickly spotted more fallen Paladins. Blood pooled around them like crimson shadows, and that heat in his belly spread up into his limbs. His fingers tingled, and he wanted nothing more than to find his pickaxe and carve his way out.

"Hey, you. Take this." The woman who had freed them handed him a long dagger, more of a sword to the small Goblin. She passed out a few more to others. "Protect yourselves, yeah? There's a whole lot more to kill after this."

Cobb stared at the dagger and his own faint reflection, like a dark smudge on the razor-sharp blade. His thoughts boiled, jagged edges tumbling over themselves before a noise cut through the chaos in his mind.

"Evie, more coming down the central staircase," a woman with a spear said. The same spear he'd seen punch through a Paladin's throat. "Is everyone free?"

"Think so. Hey uh, you," the woman, Evie, said to Cobb. "Anyone else down here?"

Cobb looked around at the sea of Yttin, Goblins, Orcs, and Dwarves. There weren't half as many as he'd seen coming up with him from below. Cobb's mouth started before his brain could catch up. "There's more. I dunno where they are. But there's lots more."

"Noctis' tits."

"Tell us where, child," another woman said, this one with earthy, ochre skin. She was looking right at him. "Don't speak, just think it."

"We don't have time for this, Zara," Evie said.

"Go help the Heiress secure the stairwell. It shall be our point of egress," Zara said. Her ice-blue eyes bored into Cobb's. "Think, child."

Cobb did as he was asked. Not to be helpful, but because he couldn't refuse this strange lady with hair like the sea. He blinked, and around him, chaos erupted once more.

"Good, I have it," Zara said over the din of fighting. She and Cobb were the only ones left in the corridor, the rest having vanished. Too close by, a grip of Temple Knights were trying to get to the woman, but a single gesture rent their armor and flesh in a single, explosive swoop. They fell in...piles. "Let us follow after your fellows, Cobb. Shall we?"

"Uhm," he said. "Sure. Where is everyone?"

"Ahead. They are holding their own, but not for long." Cobb heard a clear, crystalline chiming and was lifted bodily by a wave of watery light.

Magic! he thought with a gasp. Cobb clutched tightly to his long dagger.

Both of them swept onward, up the central staircase.

Atar peered around the wide pillar. Knights in golden armor stood at attention only thirty strides away, their halberds gleaming in the steady light of orange Mana crystals. Beyond them, Atar knew the stairs would lead to the inner sanctum of the Temple, the heart. He tried to keep his mind off the glass flask at his waist and what lay within it, but it was a daunting task to accomplish while also sneaking like a thief. As such, his attention wandered and his battlerobes caught on a pedestal he passed.

Damnation!

A delicate sculpture of a wise woman fell, and Atar's heart stopped in his chest...only for a pair of thin hands to catch it before it hit the ground.

"Careful! The Knights all have significant investments in Perception," Fiammetta scolded him as she placed the bust back on its stand. She tossed her head, red hair flicking from her eyes. "I would have thought you'd remember that."

Atar stopped himself from snapping back in kind, but only barely. It was mostly Alister's sour face staring at the Faun's back that halted him—the beautiful ponce would have fought the Disciple on behalf of Atar's pride, and it warmed his heart. Instead, he only corrected his footing. "You...are not wrong. Either way, the lady Chanter is keeping us screened."

"Doesn't mean I like diverting all the noise you make," said Lady Isla. Her nose was perhaps too generous for her face to be called beautiful, but she was striking regardless. "An Obfuscation of this size does not come without effort. So shut your mouths and focus on your tasks."

Fiammetta made a pleased noise through her doe-like nose, and Lady Isla shot her a glare. "That goes double for turncoats."

It was very hard for Atar not to grin at that.

They had penetrated the standard defenses of the Temple, thanks to Fiammetta's instruction. As a Disciple, she was well informed on the movements and placement of their defenses. However, Knights were posted everywhere, and it would have posed a serious impediment were it not for Lady Isla's Obfuscation Chant.

As far as Atar understood, it was very similar to that Gnome Thangle's work, just on a grander scale. It kept their presence from being discovered, but the effect was active, requiring the Chanter to manually eliminate any stray sound or visual that the four of them produced. All told, i she could get them into the inner sanctum, but the Obfuscation of so many eyes meant her attention was eaten away by the spell, and the way forward was up to Atar.

"Follow me," he said. The four of them softly and carefully slipped past the guards. Atar held his breath as they did so, a habit he had quickly formed, but the Knights' attention did not waver in the slightest. He glanced at Lady Isla, who had a smug twist to her lips.

Beyond the Knights was the grand staircase leading to the juncture of the three Temples of Elemental Flame, each one covering an aspect of the Urge that they worshipped. The steps were just as Atar recalled from years prior, perfectly crafted and inlaid with a repeating flame. Gold and white marble, they matched the carvings along the grand staircase, which depicted the Scorched Expanse as it was: filled with monsters and defended only by the unrelenting fury of the Highest Flame.

Atar had complicated feelings about their plan, even if it had been his insight that had produced their only weapon. Had Felix been with them, perhaps he could have devoured the Urge—but not even that was certain. Instead, Atar had posited that if the Dustborn curse was hurting the Highest Flame, then what would happen if it were used against the Urge directly?

The problem, naturally, had been that they had no undead with them, and Felix had cleansed the curse from them all. The Lady Isla, healer that she appeared to be, provided a solution, and in order to do so, the Chanter had required everyone who had ever been afflicted by the flesh curse to gather close. A resonance of the curse remained, the faintest of traces in all that had once been touched by it. Harmless, they were told, but a curse such as that was too potent for their Aspects to forget it entirely.

"The fact that it was so faint is remarkable, truly. This Autarch is a powerful man," she had said. Atar hadn't missed the edge of naked hunger in the woman's tone. She was powerful, but that only put the mage on heightened guard.

Through a complicated spellform and the Chant, Lady Isla had somehow been able to extract the resonance of the curse from their collective Aspects. She had then placed it into a glass bottle that Zara had further infused with some other strange ability. The glass had been strengthened, and even then, it barely contained the vile, twisting curse that had poured from Isla's spellform. Now that flask sat at Atar's hip, and he hated it—the thing felt...predatory, somehow.

They crested the long staircase and approached a set of golden doors inscribed with sigils of flame and heat. Fiammetta swallowed and held up a pendant of orange crystal, which glowed with a small array. The doors flashed in sympathy, and Atar felt the wardings on them loosen moments before they opened themselves. The four of them stepped within.

"Blind gods," Alister whispered. His eyes were rounded and his mouth wide open. "Atar, this place...this is bigger than the bottom floor of the Eyrie. Twice as big, even."

"And lined with more warding arrays than I can count," Atar added.

The apex of the three Temples was here, at the Smoldering Nave. Rows upon rows of marble pews spread out in a circular formation, but the majority of the nave was occupied by inlaid flooring and ascending steps, all of which led to the focal point of the Temples. The Altar of the Highest Flame, a bronze dish wider than ten men could stretch, was supported by three pillars shaped to look like men and women in flowing robes. Atop the altar, burning away, was a tower of roaring flame.

"Bit of a show-off, I see," Lady Isla said. "Hurry up, now. We haven't much time, and that flask will not hold forever."

"What?" Fiammetta said, looking askance at the boiling contents of the bottle at Atar's hip. "You never said that before."

"No point mentioning it when it's the only option," she said with a delicate shrug. She paused, then looked at Atar expectantly. "Well? Go, boy."

Atar tightened his jaw, but let the Chanter's tone slide. She was, after all, a Master Tier like Zara. "Alister, Fiammetta, with me. We'll take this one line at a time."

Before they could drop their little present, the protections around the Altar had to be deactivated. The Faun Disciple was equipped to bypass these wardings due to her position, and that's what they relied upon at first. Fiammetta held out her orange crystal, and sigils melted out of her path, allowing them through without issue. Only when they reached the last ten feet before the Altar did her access cease being effective.

"This is as far as I am allowed to come," she said. The Faun wet her lips, and Atar could hear the faintest of noises from her Spirit. It sounded like...indecision, perhaps. "Is this truly necessary?"

"They want to sacrifice citizens of your city to it," Alister said, disgust writ large across his features. "That is vile and reprehensible and must be stopped."

Atar watched the fire dance above them, separated by such a small distance, and yet the wards were more effective than walls of orichalcum if they were to attempt to brute force their way past them. He couldn't even feel the Flame's heat, great as it was, and its light seemed dimmer somehow. *Is that a function of the wards?* he wondered. *Or is that the weakness I have been hearing about?*

Alister cleared his throat. "Atar? Are you ready?"

"Yeah. Fiammetta, I understand how you feel. I, too...well, you know. We grew up here, with all of this." Atar wrinkled his nose. "But something is different now. More than anything, I need to know why."

The Faun wouldn't meet his eye, and instead stared unblinkingly at the flickering Flame. Atar sighed. He pulled out an inscription stylus and Alister joined him, scratching lines of light into the air.

Mana flowed and twitched, turned out of alignment with each sigil they inscribed. Atar moved quickly, more fluid here than he ever had been on the field of battle. As the first ward tried to buck and split, which would have warned everyone in the Temple, he guided it back into a cage of glyphs. He fashioned an opening in the array, one that would permit the three of them to close with the next layer, and he finished it off by tying the sigaldry back into itself, uninterrupted as if they had never been there at all.

Sigaldry is level 62!

And you said sigaldry is for the weak, Atar thought with a surge of bitterness. *Master.*

The next three arrays went the same way, though the effort required increased exponentially. By the last warding, all three of them were sweating with concentration, effort, and the incredible heat given off by the Altar. Atar was unsure how long they had been at it, but with an agonizing, glacial stroke of his stylus, the way was finally opened.

Sigaldry is level 70!

A blast of intense heat hit them, knocking Alister onto his rear and pushing Atar and Fiametta back two entire strides. The pressure of their opening raged for a few moments, scorching the stone at their feet before it evened out. They stood cautiously, but aside from the remarkable heat, everything seemed calm.

"Stay here," Atar told them. "I'll approach. If anything happens...run."

"Atar," Alister said.

"No, listen to me. I have the flask, and I have the strongest resistance to fire and heat. I'm going, and you're both staying here." Atar watched Alister struggle with that decision, but he ended up pressing his lips into a thin line and nodded anyway. "Thank you."

"Don't die, Atar," Fiammetta said. Her freckled face was unreadable, but it sounded like she actually meant it.

"I won't. If I'm not around for comparison, people might actually think you're talented," Atar said, forcing a grin onto his face.

"Hmph." The Faun pursed her lips. "I take it back. Go jump in."

Atar's smile was more genuine as he turned away...but it fell apart as soon as he walked through the breach in the wards. The temperature ratcheted up another dozen degrees, and he felt the stone baking him through his leather boots. A half turn around the Altar led him to the staircase he recalled from his youth, built into the side of the bronze structure and wide enough to accommodate three grown men across each step. He mounted them quickly. At the top, he beheld the Highest Flame in all its glory.

It's...it's weaker than I have ever seen it, he thought with alarm.

The pillar of flame that they had been seeing this entire time was whisper-thin and no hotter than a candleflame. Atar lifted his hand and pressed it into the flickering orange light, only to have it pass through, unharmed. The mage's resistance was considerable, but even the smallest piece of the Highest Flame should have baked flesh from his bones. It was only in its center that the Urge burned so hot it annihilated all within.

"What happened to you?" he asked, quietly. Memories resurfaced within him, of kneeling before the Urge when he was five years old. Of his mother and father holding him up on their shoulders to see the Dance of the Seven Flames during high summer. Of when he swore his pact, and could first feel the Flame's warm regard and gentle influence on his nascent core space. Good memories, all of them, almost enough to reconsider.

Then he saw the bones.

In the deep bowl of the Altar, what Atar had at first mistaken for charred logs or monster remnants were instead the charred remains of people. More people than he could count, of all shapes and sizes.

They've been sacrificing people already? he realized in dawning horror. *For how long?*

"Why are you doing this?" he asked the Urge, hoping, dreading an answer. "What is happening in my city?"

ATAR V'AS.

Atar started. He truly hadn't expected an answer. "Highest Flame?"

RUN. HE COMES.

His eyes widened. "My master...?"

HE HUNGERS IN THE TOMB. OH, HE HUNGERS, AND ALL WILL BE CONSUMED.

"Tomb? What're you—We're here to stop that. No one else will be sacrificed here."

I MUST BURN. OR ELSE LIGHT FADES. I MUST BURN.

"I don't care. Not like this." Atar gripped the flask, unhooking it from his belt.

THE STARS AND MOONS SPEAK OF THIS. OF MY END. IT CANNOT BE, FOR LIGHT FAILS WITHOUT ME. I MUST BURN, ATAR V'AS.

PLEASE.

OH, IT HURTS. THE HUNGER CANNOT BE STOPPED, HE PROWLS TOWARD US ALL, THE BEAST AT HIS BACK. FEAR HIS TEETH.

"I'm not afraid of my old master anymore," Atar said. "He cannot have his way. Not like this."

A horn shattered the silence of the Temple. First one, then many others joined in.

"That is the high alert!" Fiammetta shouted over the roaring flames. "Atar! We must flee!"

"Go! I have to do this!"

Atar lifted the flask and reared back...only to stumble as a lash of flame slashed him across the shoulders. He screamed, and his throw fell limp. The flask fell into the flames, clattering among the bones in the Altar's basin, but it remained whole and just shy of he Urge's raging center. Unbroken.

"Burning blood and ashes!" he gasped, and a second lash hit the mage. Atar was spun around by the strike, this time to see a woman hovering above and behind him, wearing a golden veil and robes. "Matron," he hissed through clenched teeth. His back was bleeding, and his Health had dropped by an entire quarter.

"Atar V'as. Truly, it is a disappointment to see you here," the Matron said. Atar never could make out their features behind their thick veils, but the condemnation in her voice was clear. "Did you think you would succeed and, what? Explode the Urge with some alchemical concoction?"

All around the Nave, doors were thrown open, and a flood of golden-armored Knights rushed down the aisles. Atar scanned around him, picking out Fiammetta and Alister standing nearby...but of Isla he could see no sign.

"And you, Fiammetta. A Disciple, taking part in such blasphemy?" The Matron's condemnation turned to a sharp anger. "You will not escape recompense for these actions tonight."

"What you are doing is wrong," the Faun said. She was shaking, but whether that was in anger or fear, Atar couldn't tell. "Sacrificing people for power is the true blasphemy!"

"Be silent, girl."

A sudden, immense pressure slammed into all of them. Fiammetta fell with a bleating cry, and Alister cursed as he was forced to his hands and knees. Atar clutched hard to the bronze railing at his side, pushing with all his Strength against a Spiritual pressure he knew as well as the back of his hand.

"Kel'lyv," Atar gasped.

His former master appeared above them, hovering atop the waves of fire Mana that poured from the Highest Flame. The other remaining Matrons and Masters, three of the former and two of the latter, descended from the vaulted ceiling. Atar could see a number of open passages up there, where they must have come through after the warning horns sounded. Kel'lyv's gray face was tight with anger as he regarded them all.

"You shall call me Grandmaster, if I deign to let you speak at all, Atar," the man snapped. Another burst of pressure knocked Atar's grip loose, and he fell to his knees at the edge of the Altar. Kel'lyv looked to the others. "How many have escaped?"

"A great many, but we shall round them up shortly," a woman with dark hair cut short at her ears. "The others are still secure, however. We may begin when you wish, Grandmaster."

Instead of answering her, the bald mage cast his gaze all over the chamber, a sneer forming on his face. "What did the Flame say to you, Atar? I know it said something."

Gasps ripped from the Matrons, but Atar barely paid them any mind. His Body couldn't put up with the amount of pressure the man was pressing against him, and it was all he could do to breathe. "She said...that you are...a monster."

Kel'lyv scoffed. "Fool. I've known you since you were a babe in swaddling. Do not lie. I will ask only once more. What did the Flame tell you?"

I HURT. THE BINDINGS MUST HOLD!

This time, the gasps echoed among the entire crowd as the Urge's voice hit them all. Knights looked up in panic at the column of flame, and Atar heard the strangely strident call of doubt blaze through their Spirits.

Kel'lyv was not one to hesitate, however. "You see? The Flame withers while we prattle on. Matrons, bring out what worthless wretches we still have. The ritual must commence."

The Matrons all but fled to do as they were bid, rushing toward a set of doors far to Atar's right. Yet, just as they reached the golden portals, the things blew off their hinges. The Matrons batted the doors away, but were unprepared for the silver Spears that impaled one of them, while the other was suddenly trapped by chains of ice.

"What is this!?" the Grandmaster cried out. "Knights! Form upon those fools!"

From the left, another set of doors were ripped open, and a wall of jagged ice spears blasted up from the flooring. Knights fell by the dozen, and those that survived were bisected by the axes of hulking Frost Giants. Lightning crackled and shot outward, burning yet more, and the pressure against Atar loosened.

"Fiend's Claw!" Harn shouted from yet another entryway, his axes raised up and blazing with silver light. "Kill 'em all!"

CHAPTER EIGHTY-SEVEN

Entering the huge palace atop the hill was like walking into a graveyard. Utter silence enveloped them, and every scrape of boot or jangle of harness felt like an explosion of sound. Very soon after entering, Felix had all of them stop and wait while he mustered up his concentration.

Abyssal Skein!

Felix made sure to extend it over all of them, Hallow's Risen included. There were far more of those than previously, the various Paladins from the city as well as those they just defeated having joined Beef's horde. But as the gelid, oily sensation spread across their growing connections, Felix caught the edge of something. The way the Void Skill moved and flowed from his channels was very different from Skills like Adamant Discord. The latter had so much of its meaning baked into the idea of *force*, of applying leverage through connections. But Abyssal Skein was about removing, subsuming and hiding. So why would he force the power outward?

Why did he have to oppose the forces around him? The Skill called out to him to slip, to slide out of view and into obscurity, through the cracks in all things. To let yourself be swallowed by the Void. That's what the Void was, after all: a hungry, endless abyss where even System energy went to die.

Abyssal Skein is level 58!

...

Abyssal Skein is level 70!

With a roar that made his ears pop, Felix felt his Abyssal Skein slip into place across his allies. It was twisted and almost invisible even to him, but if he looked at it from the right angle, Felix could see that it hung about their shoulders like a vast cloak. At the same time, the Skill level notifications pinged across his vision, rapid-fire until the surge of growth settled in at level 70. Felix staggered, slightly unbalanced by the burst of System energy that flooded his core space.

Twelve levels all at once, he thought, a little dazed. *All because I figured out a better way to use my Skill.*

He'd once been told "greater understanding" was required to advance Skills past a certain level, but Felix had always been in such mortal danger that stress, use, and his existence as an Unbound negated those necessities. Or so he had thought. The more he thought about it, in fact, Felix realized his biggest jumps in Skill level happened when he was pressed and tried something new with his Skills. Or simply overcame bonkers odds. For him, that was sadly a regular occurrence.

"Something wrong?" Beef asked him.

Felix opened his mouth just as a tremor rippled the ground beneath their feet. That deep buzzing inhalation began again, pulling in great swathes of Mana from the air. Except this time, the tremors rumbled onward, outward, into the city. A great, stentorian crack resounded from above, and one of the gold crystalline stalactites dropped like a meteor.

"Down!" Felix shouted, grabbing Beef and throwing him to the floor just as the massive stalactite impacted the city. A blastwave of concussive heat and light and sound ripped apart buildings and narrow streets, setting off a chain reaction of other Mana crystals that burst under the pressure. Burning, freezing, cloying Mana surged everywhere, even up into the palace. The earth heaved and shook, until Felix could barely tell which way was up anymore.

Chthonic Tribute!

After several minutes, the rumbling aftershocks settled, and the tide of violent Mana receded. Felix felt full almost to bursting, and his Tribute had been only able to blunt the edge of the cataclysmic tsunami of power; the rest had been turned by the palace's—the prison's—hidden wards.

"Whoa," Beef said. His voice was strangely muted, until with a painful *pop*, Felix felt his eardrums heal. "I'm really glad I didn't stay behind now."

Felix leveraged himself to his feet, feeling oddly bloated and weathered, as if he'd spent days drinking while out in the harshest of weather. "We have to keep moving. Something new is happening, and I don't like it."

Pit squawked in agreement and gathered up a number of the Risen onto his back. There was no way for the tenku to carry everyone, not even he was that big, but it helped. They moved faster than before, prodded onward by the gnawing anxiety in Felix's gut.

They encountered more traps, but every single one was violently deactivated. The hallways were by turns narrow and broad, but almost every one was partially melted. Stone and metal pooled in cooling lumps on the floor, making the walking faintly treacherous, not to mention a number of dead Paladins. These, too, joined Beef's army, and Felix didn't protest extending his Abyssal Skein. He had a feeling they would need all the help they could get, and soon.

After crossing a wide chasm that was somehow contained in the prison palace, and past Golem defenders that had been shattered or burned straight through, they came upon a break in the path. Steps led upward in a spiraling staircase, and straight ahead was a darkened passage that showed faint signs of light at the end. Felix tried to listen for sounds, but his Perception was still oddly deadened. He looked to Beef and Pit and Hallow. "Any ideas? Up or straight?"

Up, Pit sent immediately.

"You would," Felix replied. "Beef? Hallow?"

"I will follow the choices made," Hallow said quietly.

"Uh, well, if we go up, then maybe we can get a drop on them if they're ahead at ground level. Or maybe they're up above, and so we'll run into them if we go up, and down is the better option." The Minotaur chewed at one of his too-short nails. "I—I uh don't know. In games, there'd be a clear path. Like a glowing trail or something. Here it's all just...it's real."

The last bit was said with a soft exhalation. Felix stared at the kid in the burly Minotaur's body and felt like he really saw him. "It gets easier."

Beef didn't answer, just scratched his cheek and stared at his hooves. The floor was covered with the muck his Risen were slowly leaking, which was another downside of the more freshly dead corpses. Footprints were clear, and Felix was happy they hadn't had to avoid any further patrols, or else...he sucked in a sharp breath and smacked himself on the forehead. "Of course."

Tracking!

His Perception might have been deadened, but the Skill still functioned. The area around them lit up with dozens of lights, the majority of them glowing a blackened green. A few from him, Pit, and Beef were a shimmering multi-color and all led back the way they had come. However, there were others...and all of them save for one or two led straight ahead. Through the tunnel.

Tracking is level 34!

"We go up," Felix said, before explaining what he was seeing. "I'll go first, fast. Beef, you'll follow after with the Risen. I'll keep Abyssal Skein on us for as long as I can. I want any Paladins dispatched quickly and quietly, alright?" He looked at them all and received a bevy of nods and skeletal head-bobbles. "Pit, Converge please."

Under the influence of Abyssal Skein, the flash of light as Pit disappeared was hopefully unnoticed, and after a few agonizing seconds, Felix began to move. With all the Agility he possessed, he sped up the spiraling staircase, ascending it faster than the others could manage. He reached the top, the only place the staircase opened onto a landing of any sort, and stared down a short passage into an airy, open space.

Two Paladins, just out of sight. They were close enough that he could feel them at least, but Felix had no way of knowing where the rest might be located, if there were indeed more. *Gotta make this fast.*

Slowly, flaring his Skein as hard as he could, Felix crept across the ten-foot hallway and onto a wide, railing-free balcony. He had been worried about noise for nothing, because the moment he crossed the threshold, he penetrated some sort of sensory warding. The inside of the space was a thundering storm of noise and flashing lights...and the two dozen Paladins weren't even looking at the door. They were too engrossed in the multi-colored lightning playing off an absolutely gargantuan sword that rose up out of the center of the room, extending both a bit above and well below their balcony.

Felix tore his eyes from the giant, bronze blade and did what he had to do.

Rime Shaping!
Cardinal Flame!

Rime Shaping is level 45!

Red-gold flame kindled around every single Paladin all at once, catching fully half of them in its burning grip. They froze, paralyzed while the spell's dire flame ate through their skin and muscle with abandon. All of them also felt the chill sting of frostbite as hands froze to hilts and mouths froze shut. Those who could move spun wildly, looking for the source—yet by the time they had spotted him, Felix was among them all, reaping their lives with his hooked blade.

None lived to even put up a fight.

You Have Killed A Paladin Of The Pathless (x29)!
XP Earned!

Battle done and bright lights pulsing, Pit emerged from Felix's Spirit. The two of them crept toward the edge and cautiously peered down. The sword was easily two hundred feet tall and thirty feet wide, a chipped blade with a cruciform hilt and made entirely of a golden bronze.

Voracious Eye!

Name: Skyslain's Riposte
Type: Weapon (Enchanted)
Lore: Belonging to Tch'lys Skyslain, the last King of Ahkestria, the blade was a gift from the Nymean Empress. Made of Crescian Bronze and enchanted to grow at its bearer's command, it was a symbol as much as a blade. Its last use was as an anchor,

a powerful spike to trap the deadliest of foes that had wrought an untenable ruin upon the kingdom.

Its hilt came right up to the ceiling, which was plated with yet more bronze and fitted with a familiar looking crystal. Not Mana, but Belais, which solidified this construction as something the Nym had a hand in fashioning. The purple amethyst was just as wide as the sword beneath it, and it glimmered with a deep well of light.

In fact, Felix realized that the Belais Crystal *was* part of the sword, the pommel at the end of its unnaturally huge grip. Its vast blade, meanwhile, was sunk deep into the floor far, far below. They were around fifty feet from the pommel, and so the floor was over a hundred feet down. Yet nearly half of that sword-length was covered in a bony mass of...*something.*

The Skyslain's Riposte had been driven through a creature that laid down at the base of the huge, circular chamber. The creature was a collection of scales and bones—and not just any bones, but full humanoid skeletons somehow warped and woven into one another until a greater whole had been made. It reminded Felix of the Shambling Horror he'd fought in the Haestus Temple, only far, far larger.

And it was twitching.

Voracious Eye!

ERROR!
Voracious Eye Failed.

Pit hissed, and Felix felt the same. His Eye might have failed, but the miasma of Dissonance that rolled off of it was unmistakable. This close, his Perception and Affinity felt even more stifled than before, but even so, Felix was positive their connections would burn like the sun between them. They were staring at the Primordial that was controlling the entire desert's undead, the one that was hunting him specifically. And the thing was dead itself...or perhaps undead.

Is it...aware?

There were no eyes on the creature, no face or even mouth if you discounted the thousands of humanoid skulls that composed parts of its body. It had no true shape, just a mass with tangled tendrils of bone and stretched ligaments that wrapped around the huge Skyslain's Riposte and outward to the walls around them. Like webbing or ropes, bone and scale stretched toward the distant cylindrical walls of the chamber, all of which were covered with an unbroken collection of deepest blue Mana crystals. Much like the city outside, it was like standing on the inside of a geode.

And all the way around the Primordial, a huge, wildly complex sigaldry array hovered, climbing up the crystalline walls in fractal patterns and confusing concentric circles. A cage of light was spat from each confluence of arrays, spun around the sword and Primordial with a deftness and skill Felix couldn't even grasp the edge of—the working was so far beyond him that even looking too closely at it sent jabs of pain through his Mind.

At the base, where the blade sunk into the greatest chunk of the Primordial, roughly a hundred small figures in crimson armor bustled about with odd contraptions of metal and wood. The Paladins were building something, and a number of them held up long rods that inscribed glowing lines of golden light into the air. *They're creating an array? To do what?*

Felix couldn't parse the shapes they were designing, apart from a preponderance of "light" and "wash" sigils. The rest of it was rounded and strange, not like the several types of sigaldry he'd seen in the past.

Behind him, Felix heard the approach of the others, along with Beef's bellows-like panting. "I ran...as fast as...I could. What—what did I miss?"

Felix told him in quick terms, and Beef eyed the dead Paladins around them with a distinct gleam in his eye. "Don't raise them in here. Drag them onto the stairs. There's a sensory barrier at the threshold that should hide your magic from everyone in here."

Beef did just that, turning twenty-five of the twenty-nine Paladins into his Risen. Meanwhile, Felix watched the golden array build up below him. It was a measly thing compared to the mesh of magics around the Primordial and sword, but it had a presence that Felix couldn't deny.

He also realized he was wrong: the array wasn't just being created, it was being re-created. They activated their golden sigils, and the crystalline room trembled. Tremors swept outward, roaring as they erupted further away, and power was siphoned out of the Primordial's cage...before the Paladin's array collapsed on itself. Armored men and women fell, some bleeding and others dead, only to be replaced by new figures who picked up their rods and began the process all over again.

"What was that?" Beef whispered. "Felt like being on a boat about to flip over."

Felix didn't stop staring at the dead Paladins, now being dragged away by others. "They're trying to...god, it's stupid. They're trying to weaken the cage around the Primordial. Each of those tremors is a piece of its power escaping into the world, or maybe it's just backlash from unraveling this thing."

"Why the hell would they do that? I thought you said Primordials were like, endgame big bads?" Beef brushed a lock of shaggy hair out of his eyes. "How does it benefit them?"

"I don't know," Felix admitted. "I don't understand what the Paladins are doing with sigaldry, and the cage itself is beyond me. Those lines..." Felix stared at them, the cable-thick lines of light that extended outward from the sword and beast. Many to the walls, but they all curved slightly before they impacted the crystal-lined surface, and the ones up top simply went straight up. "They're going up. But what's above us?"

Felix flared Oathbinding, Cardinal Flame, and even attempted Manasight. The world devolved into streamers of blinding light, but he pressed on through it, sorting away the flood of water Mana and focusing on the stomach-churning pillar of blackened green and orange-brown that was the Primordial itself.

Manasight is level 70!

He could feel his nose bleeding, and the pain in his Mind spiked harder than ever, but there was something Felix was missing. Strands of the Primordial were being teased away, not just by the Paladins and their strange attempts, but by the cage around it. The lines of light that went up, Felix quickly realized they carried pieces of the Primordial with it, channeling it somewhere else.

Oathbinding is level 45!
Oathbinding is level 46!

Threads of Primordial power soared upward, alongside silver cords that extended deep into Felix's chest. The Oaths of his people, of his friends, were leading in the exact same direction.

"We're under Ahkestria?" he said, the realization sending a shock of horror through him. "And this array...what was its purpose?"

Manasight is level 71!

He could recognize parts of it, now that the bulk of the cage was left behind. In the cable-thick threads, he identified tiny portions that were similar to the array he'd once designed to fight off a clutch of vile Urges. In comparison however, his Devour Array couldn't hold a candle to this masterwork of complexity. It was pulling something vital from the Primordial corpse, its Essence somehow being siphoned up and out...to the city.

In a flash of understanding, Felix knew its purpose.

Theurgist of the Rise is level 82!

"The cage is stealing the Primordial's Essence and...and it's feeding it to the Highest Flame," he said.

Hallow looked at him sharply through the eyes of a man she'd just killed. Beef, meanwhile, just scratched his head. "What?"

How long have they been doing this? It appeared the cage was feeding on the Primordial in order to keep it docile and "dead," or at least quiescent. *Like the Essence Anchor, but instead of dumping all that power into the Void, it was using it.* Or it had been, because very little Essence was being extracted now, and a great deal still lingered within the writhing mass of scales and bone.

Why? Was the array failing or something else? Either way, the Paladins are clearly trying to destroy the array. Did they know it was a chain around the Primordial's neck? Or...wait.

Below them, a new array was going up, as eighteen Paladins rapidly inscribed figures in the air with golden light. Those new sigils were forming into glyphs and connecting into a new formation that finally made a bit of sense to him. Felix parsed only that it was a redirection of some sort.

"They're trying to steal the Primordial's powers?" Felix was confused. "How does that benefit them? They can't use it, or else they'll get the flesh curse, too."

"It...it feels like strings snapping," Beef said beside him. He was holding his head in clear pain and was blinking past tears. The lowest portion of the cage stripped and broke apart even more, pieces of it replaced by new, golden light. "It's so bad. Can't you hear that? The storm, Felix. It's the storm."

Oh, shit.

The Highest Flame wasn't the only one sustained by the Primordial. She was fueling the stormwall with it, too.

CHAPTER EIGHTY-EIGHT

The battle had been joined.

Atar watched Harn hew his way through the Knights, taking down their Captains with brutal speed. The Claw was behind him, roaring defiance as they flooded into the inner sanctum. Blade met Blades, and Bones, and Fists, with the crackling charge of Arclight to back them up. Knights died by the score against the improved coordination of Claw's Talons.

The same story repeated itself from another entrance, where Darius led the second half of their forces. His air attuned Skills shielded most from the fiery retaliation of the Knights, while his Windblades cut down five or six at a time. Atar was amazed at how easily their forces cut a wedge into the Temple Knights, but soon realized it was due to the fact that many of them had been focused inward, toward the Altar. That momentary advantage had translated into nearly a hundred deaths in the span of the battle, which could have been either an hour or a handful of minutes, Atar could not tell.

Frost Giants convened against a Master, flames beating back their ice, while Vess defended a lone Zara. The spearmaiden knocked aside Knights and ran them through with the nonchalance of a butcher at work, her Spears active in multiple directions at once. Zara, meanwhile, was throwing up walls of swirling green-blue water up and around the Grandmaster, hemming him in and forcing Kel'lyv to expend himself on dismantling them one-by-one. A stalling tactic, but it gave Atar time to breathe. To fight.

Sovereign of Stars!

White-hot stars shot into the line of armored Disciples, felling one and wounding six others. His Stars burned far hotter than their lesser-rarity Skills, but fire against fire was less effective than other options. Beside him, Fiammetta wove Mana into shield after shield, blocking the other Disciples' strikes. Alister called down pillars of force, smashing aside the physical shields many of the Knights held up and battering others aside entirely. The Disciples fought back with blade and magic, all the while dragging bound figures drenched in mud and blood behind them.

Atar's team was putting up a fight, but they couldn't stop the Disciples' advance.

Two Matrons, blazing with auras of orange, blasted aside Alister and Fiammetta's magic. The two recoiled, bashing into Atar, and the Disciples pounced.

"No!" Atar shouted, just as the first Disciples made it to the lip of the Altar. Straining, the men and women hurled their captives outward...into the Highest Flame.

The bound miners screamed as they hit the mounds of smoldering ash and jagged bone below, and while their rags and hair caught fire, their flesh only cooked slowly under the weakened influence of the outer flames. A wretched, unlucky few rolled into the brighter, hotter center of the altar...and they were immediately turned to ash and smoke.

A building scream flung out of the pillar of the Highest Flame, its shape surging and flaring. Atar watched as its superheated core widened by the smallest of margins, fueled by its consumption. The scream stabbed at every single person, throwing Atar and his friends to their knees just the same as any of the Disciples or Matrons.

THE SOURCE IS TAKEN! SUNDERED! THE HUNGER HAS ARRIVED, CHOSEN! ITS TEETH APPROACH AND I—I CANNOT STOP THEM! BEWARE!

A distant, alarming creaking and crashing sounded from far off...until it halted with a choking finality. Above, the Grandmaster staggered, dropping a dozen strides from the sky while Masters and Matrons alike fell, some crashing through the pews to land, suddenly weakened. Driven to their knees, none of them continued the battle as Knights and Disciples and Claw alike all looked around in confused wonder. A burgeoning silence seized the world, a silence that none currently living in Ahkestria had ever heard before.

The silence of a still sky.

"The storm..." a Matron whispered in horror.

"The Highest lost control of the storm," said a dark-bearded Master.

"The undead will come," another Matron said. "Blessed Flame, but the undead will come for us now."

As if welling from deep below their feet, a preternatural howling filled the city. A Spirit the size of the city itself clawed upward, slamming Disciples, Knights, and Claw members to the splintering ground. Blood arced all around him, and Atar only avoided an invisible slash that split a portion of the golden Altar at his back. His head was screaming with a droning buzz, too loud and pervasive to even think. *What is this? What's happening?*

"The beast is awakening," Kel'lyv said, his eyes searching out the Altar. He rose, stuttering on burning streamers of flame. "Push those cretins in! The Flame must be strengthened, or all is lost! Where are the Paladins!?"

There was a sound at Atar's side, audible in the silence the Grandmaster tried to fill. Even the buzzing that rose from the ground and swarmed his Affinity was driven from his awareness when he caught sight of the woman standing in the flames. Her hair and face were a smoldering ruin, her body succumbing to the Altar, but she held a bundled object up to him no bigger than a Gnome.

Her bonds had burned away, but she couldn't climb the smooth, sloping sides of the Altar basin. Unthinking, Atar reached into the flames, grasping the bundle—the child—through the burning and yanking them from the offering arms of their mother. The mother fell into the ashes, her body too damaged, but the child was swaddled, and as Atar absorbed the flames with Strength Ignition...he found it alive.

"Your Fire Resistance is nicely leveled," said a voice above his shoulder.

Atar jerked in alarm, but he and the bundled child bloomed with a flush of green-gold Mana that settled his alarm. Forcibly so, but he couldn't muster the will to be concerned. The flush of life Mana spread into the Urge's flames as well, soaking into the men and women who writhed outside the savage core. Atar looked languidly up at the bright, angry eyes of Isla. She raised a finger to her lips and vanished.

Status Condition: Forged Calm removed!

Blinking back to himself, Atar held the child close as it began to whimper. The Chanter may have healed it, but they were not safe. He stood with fresh panic in his heart just in time to see the Paladins march confidently through the doors nearest his location.

"Damn it," Alister said, shaking out an arm and picking up his rapier again. His limb was covered in blood, and the sleeve was rent, but Atar could no longer see a wound. "This isn't going well."

The Paladins were all wearing great helms covering their faces, and heavy crimson cloaks hung like shrouds around their intimidating plate armor. The Disciples let them through their ranks, no more than fifty but armed to the teeth. Their leader, wearing a badge of office Atar vaguely recognized as the High Justiciar, drew up just outside the lip of the Altar...and only ten paces from their desperate stand.

Fiammetta conjured a mace and a narrow dagger in her hands, shaped from yellow heat Mana in the air. She brandished them threateningly. "Don't you come closer, murderers!"

That howl tore through again, and Atar winced at its buzzing atonality. Fear surged again, but it was a distant thing happening to someone else. Atar's focus cut through it all, his Mind whirring as he tried to figure out a solution.

Meanwhile, the Grandmaster rose higher, now blazing with a brilliant internal flame that competed with the Urge itself. "High Justiciar Haim! We need the Regalia of the Pathless now! The beast is nearly loose! Throw that cloth into the Altar, and you shall have all that you have asked for!"

"All that I have asked?" the man in the lead asked. His voice reverberated inside the helmet. "Even the right of establishing a church of the Pathless within your city?"

"Yes! Even that!" Kel'lyv said through grinding teeth. A number of Matrons shifted as if to protest, but his dark looks silenced them. "Do it now, and our deal is set in stone."

The High Justiciar reached into his cloak and pulled out a crystalline case, holding it up to catch the light. It glinted in the rising sun, casting a prism of colors out into the inner sanctum. Atar couldn't make out the man's features, but he tilted his head as if he were considering something, while another howl welled up from far below. It felt weaker now, somehow, and the buzzing in Atar's ears had dimmed to a teeth-rattling hum.

The Grandmaster growled, drawing closer to them all. "Haim! What are you doing? Complete our agreement!"

To Atar's utter amazement, the Paladin laughed. Then, with a rueful shake of his head, he opened the Regalia case...and there was nothing within. "No. I do not think I will."

Kel'lyv only stared in shock, veins across his forehead all but ready to burst while the flames at his back faded to almost nothing. Part of Atar even enjoyed the man's apoplexy, though his fears were running wild within his breast. The Paladin reached up and took off his great helm, revealing features that did not match Atar's recollection of the High Justiciar, little as he remembered.

"Captain Boldt! Where is your commanding officer?" Kel'lyv demanded. The flames returned, rallying with a vengeance as the mage grappled with this betrayal.

The captain laughed, high and sharp. "You think Lord Haim would let some heretic touch even a scrap of the true god's power? You're a fool, Kel'lyv."

The rising sun so prominently on view in the windows about them were suddenly darkened. Atar watched giant Manaships rise up around them, three in their direct vicinity and more in the distance. All of them were fitted with crimson sails emblazoned with the standard of the Paladins, and upon their decks, easily visible in the closer ships, were hundreds of armored figures armed with spears and swords blazing with golden light.

Boldt smiled, like a hungry wolf. "And your city will fall this day."

———

The Primordial howled, a terrible sound that punched through Felix's Mind like a consuming flame. Fear kindled in him before he crushed it ruthlessly. His Willpower and Call of Defiance Title were nothing to scoff at, even before a Primordial's undead influence.

Beef wasn't so lucky. The Minotaur fell to his knees, a quivering mess that tried to push as far away from the massive sword and Primordial as possible. At his side was Hallow, skeleton hands over Beef's snout, bodily restraining the massive teen with nearly every one of her Bodies. She stared helplessly at Felix in a remarkably Human gesture, but maybe he was getting signals crossed—whatever Hallow was, she wasn't Human...just as she clearly was unaffected by the Primordial's aura of fear.

That is...bad, Pit sent. Every feather and piece of fur on his body was on end, and his already bushy fox tail looked like a static-filled bottle-brush. *How do we fight them all?*

"One at a time," Felix said, keeping his voice quiet and level. The fear aura was fading, retracting almost, as Felix watched cords of its magical cage fray then snap. Each one was a gunshot burst in his Affinity, a roar of musicality overtaken by Dissonance. The noise above them stopped entirely, and Felix *knew* that the storm had fallen apart once those cords broke, and that meant Ahkestria was unguarded.

Now, all that power was lingering in the Primordial. No longer siphoned out to power storms, and only the central column connecting to the inferno far in the distance. The Paladins were working to change that, and fast.

Below them, the golden sigils had slowly overtaken the multi-hued glyphwork around the bony mass and sword. It spread outward like a shining rash, infecting the working as it rotated and the Paladins etched out sigil after sigil. Some of them had fallen, a few even had scratched their eyes out and were still howling in terror, but there were more ready to take up the inscription process.

"At least you weren't down there, Beef. Seems the Paladins got hit with a lot more of that fear aura," he said. The Minotaur had stopped trying to scream and was just lying on the ground, breathing hard as a bellows. He didn't answer except to sit up shakily. "I still don't know what the Paladins are trying to do, though. They're changing the array, redirecting the power from above...but if their goal was just to stop the stormwall, they've already achieved it."

They are not done, Pit agreed.

Beef made it to his feet, though his muscles kept twitching spasmodically. His head jerked as he leaned slightly to see below. "Sorry. The Status Condition hit me like a sack of bricks."

"Don't worry about it. Willpower helps shake off that kind of thing, but mental attacks are always a pain." Felix waved off his apologies.

"Hopefully, that's the last blast of fear, but I doubt it. Did you get a mental resistance Skill?"

"I, uh, how'd you know? Mental Resistance. That *thing* brought it up to level 10 already."

"Lucky guess," Felix said, smiling without much feeling. "You'll see it jump a few more times more, I imagine. I—"

As Felix was about to tell Beef of his own experiences, there was a flash of light below, and a series of strange, ephemeral objects appeared. High Justiciar Rahven Haim stood below, helm off and dark hair streaming in a gathering breeze. He was holding a series of golden panels, each one forged of light Mana and connected to the growing array by shimmering lines of sigaldry. The panels morphed and folded, origami-like, until they formed a bowl-like receptacle that hovered just before the man's face.

"That's Haim!" Beef hissed. "But what's *that*?"

A familiar crystalline case was pulled from the man's cloak, and even at such a distance, Felix could *feel* it pulse with potency. He gasped. "That's a piece of god-cloth," he said. "Regalia."

Beef clearly didn't understand, but Felix couldn't spare the moment to explain. The array had started making sense to his Skill, and he realized it wasn't just a redirection of energies, but a *purification*. *They're trying to steal the Primordial's Essence for themselves. To do what, though?*

With the cage array weakened and redirected, the suppression he'd been feeling had faded. Felix could feel his connections better than ever, could even sense a faint echo of emotion that rattled down their lengths. The ghost of a thousand screams shook their way to him, coming clearly from the city. They were out of time.

"This is it," Felix said. "Last chance to run, Beef."

The Minotaur snorted and stamped a hoof. He threw his head, like a true bull tossing aside an obstacle. "I...hear them. Above us. Those people need help, don't they?" Felix nodded. Beef hefted his chitin hammer and firmed up his bovine jaw. "I'm done running."

Felix felt his gut sink, but he couldn't help but respect the kid's choice. He'd learned not too long ago that choice has a power even the System wouldn't gainsay. "Alright. Pit and I will take on Haim and distract the others. You and Hallow need to disrupt those inscription circles. A good blow or blast of Mana oughta do it for them; they're only temporary. I think."

"Got it." Beef squeezed the haft of his hammer and turned to return down the spiral staircase.

Before he reached the door, Felix raised his voice. "Kick their asses...Beefhammer."

Beef grinned, a surprisingly vicious-looking thing, and Felix could feel his Spirit scream in joy and excitement as he took the stairs at a jog. Felix gave Pit a glance. "You ready?"

Pit drew himself up and rustled his wing feathers. *Always.*

Felix cracked his knuckles and stepped up to the edge of the balcony. He stared down the length of the huge sword and the vile behemoth of bones beneath them. "I'll go first, and you follow behind. Use Frost Spears to—"

Actually, Pit interrupted with a sending of fearful anticipation. *I have an idea.*

His Companion explained, and Felix slowly bared his teeth.

CHAPTER EIGHTY-NINE

Sounding his Skill but holding its activation back with his Intent and Willpower, Felix focused instead on pouring clouds of acid-green Mana from his channels. He stood at the edge of the balcony, careful to keep himself from leaning over and exposing himself, though he shouldn't have worried. The chaos below and raging forces of the Primordial's cage the Paladins were contending with had consumed all of their attention. Which meant he had time to prepare, according to Pit's plan.

Twice his Mana bottomed out as he poured more and more vapor into the air, coalescing into green thunderheads that flashed power held in abeyance. They crowded around the balcony and hilt of the Skyslain's Riposte, until he could no longer see the ground far below. At his side, Pit preened his feathers and subtly adjusted the barding around his chest, neck, and forelegs. Then he nudged Felix with a wing. *Enough, I think. Take it,* he sent.

Felix let the vapor peter out and took several deep breaths. His Mana regenerated fast, but hitting rock bottom again and again was never fun; add in the effort of activating a Skill with the Chant but refusing to let it fully engage, and it all made Felix's head swim just a little. Still, he could handle this and more.

Turning to Pit, he gripped the proffered handle of a weapon he usually kept stored with his Companion. He pulled it free and stepped closer to the edge with a grin. "I'll see you down there, bud."

He stepped out into the air.

Adamant Discord!

A crackling discharge boom through the air, so loud Felix was sure even the Paladins had heard it—but it didn't matter. Felix was rocketed downward, propelled by gravity and hurling force of his Skill so fast that the Paladins had barely looked up. He landed, booted feet-first, atop a set of armored shoulders...and crushed them into the massive crater he tore into the floor.

BOOM!

Before they could respond, Felix was up, speeding out of the crater and swinging his massive, six-foot long greatsword. The Blade of the Fang sizzled through the air, pumped full of Essence and shimmering with its own brand of sigaldry as it caught another two Paladins across the waist and chest respectively. It tore them in half.

Notifications flickered against Felix's awareness, but his eyes sought out the High Justiciar. "Haim!"

"Mr. Veil," said the older man, a frown on his face. He had moved faster than Felix's fall had accounted for, dodging easily out of the way. "You have made quite the mess, Representative."

More Paladins crowded close, their swords and halberds leveled toward Felix's throat. "You're playing with fire here, Haim," Felix said. He flexed his forearm, and blood wicked from the edge of the greatsword he held with a single hand. "I suggest you turn around and leave. Now."

The High Justiciar didn't answer him, but his frown turned into a wide smile. He gestured to his men. "Kill him."

The Paladins rushed forward, halberds thrusting and chopping at him in equal measure. Felix flared his Dexterity and Strength, rotating his Fang in a sharp, wide circle around his body. The sharpened tooth cut through every haft in an instant, before he slammed it downward through the nearest Paladin. Before the holy warrior fell into two equal pieces, Felix already pivoted, swinging his six-foot sword through one and then another Paladin.

You Have Killed A Paladin Of The Pathless (x3)!
XP Earned!

"Stop standing there and kill him!" Haim screamed.

Felix whirled and dashed, a slashing cyclone of death as he advanced on the High Justiciar. The gormless jerk retreated to the line of inscriptionists who were still scratching out golden lines of sigaldry into the air. He moved, and Paladins died, but there were *so many* of them, and the crimson-armored warriors stopped just dying. Beveled shields of conjured, golden light erupted between him and the Justiciar, while similar constructions in the form of swords and halberds slammed into his Body from all sides.

Backpedaling, Felix considered his options, his Intelligence and potent Mind firing on all cylinders. He held up the Blade of the Fang...and sunk it thirteen inches into the tiled flooring. "I was never really that good with a sword," he said, and a haze of black-grey vapor poured from his palms. They spread, solidifying into four ten-foot long coils of thick, shadowy Mana. "Whips though. I've gotten pretty good with those."

He flexed his fingers, and the four whips split into eight, then sixteen separate strands. Flicking his wrists, the whips lashed outward, each tendril grabbing a Paladin by the breastplate or neck before Felix clenched his fists and *pulled*. Every single Paladin was hauled off their feet, dragged toward Felix like they were on the losing side of a game of tug of war. More bolts of light Mana struck all around him, but Felix didn't dodge, too focused on his magic.

Shadow Whip is level 47!

Every tendril of shadow Mana flexed like a bicep, and each snagged Paladin was lifted bodily into the air...then Felix began to move.

Shadow Whip is level 48!

The warriors screamed as Felix rotated his shoulders, twisted his hips, and wielded them as the world's weirdest flail. Armored bodies crashed down into conjured shields, shattering them to pieces and knocking more Paladins aside like gruesome bowling pins.

"Fusillade Flash!" cried dozens of voices all at once. More of those elongated bolts of light coalesced and shot at Felix. He twisted and interposed the bodies of his captives for most of them, but a few still found their mark. His Body shrieked in further strain as burns burst and bled across his chest and legs. The Aspect struggled to keep up with his movements and applied stats, fraying rapidly.

I need to get closer now! he thought frantically. Then, from above, he heard a faint whistling. *Pit!*

A barrage of long, one-foot-diameter spikes of ice dropped from above, slamming into the hundreds of Paladins and outright killing several. Pit's Frost Spears, dropped from above and through the cloud of acid, were a cloudy green that soon brightened to a virulent purple-yellow as each and every one of them *exploded*.

Paladins fell back, the closest felled by shards of jagged ice, but even those thirty feet away were hit by the wash of sizzling, noxious acid. Their screams escalating, turning to wails of pain as more Frost Spears dropped, each of them exploding again with similar consequences.

Etheric Concordance is level 78!
Etheric Concordance is level 79!
Etheric Concordance is level 80!

New Sub-Feature Unlocked!
Confluence - The fastness of your bond has revealed the ability to combine certain Skills between Companions to create something new or unusual. Experiment to find out more!

Yes! Pit bugled in joy. *It worked!*

Hell yeah! Felix celebrated, spinning his homemade flail into the breach of howling Paladins. Pit had been convinced he could do such a thing, but hadn't been entirely sure what the result would be—Chimeric instinct only guided him so far, Felix supposed. With a grunt, Felix released the Shadow Whips, letting the majority of them fly forward, right into Haim's scowling face.

The High Justiciar slashed his own men out of the air, his blade swiping them easily off to the side. He was fiddling with something in his off-hand, with—

The Regalia! Felix's heartbeat sped up, but he was already running into the momentary gap of confused defenders, Blade of the Fang returned to his hand. "C'mon, Haim! Come and fight!"

"Not quite yet, Mr. Veil," said the yellow-eyed Justiciar. "I will be with you after—ah, yes. This."

Suddenly, the Paladin was limned by a slick, golden glow. It sparked to life across his entire body and weapons, like a sun was setting directly behind him...and it spread rapidly to every other Paladin around them. Felix's eyes took that in as well as the crystalline case of the Regalia, which was settled neatly into that box of golden Mana in the middle of his intrusive array. Refusing to pause, Felix surged forward.

Adamant Discord!

Lightning blasted at his back as the connections to the defeated Paladins hurled Felix forward, six-foot greatsword held like a goddamn lance. The air screamed in Felix's ears as he crossed the last twenty feet with incredible speed and hit Haim square in the chest...only to be stopped dead. Felix gaped at his weapon, the tip of which hadn't even penetrated the thin layer of golden light.

Haim laughed, and that scar across his chin stretched his smile into something vicious. "You cannot hope to defeat us, Mr. Veil. Your power cannot stand up to god's Light."

Felix wet his lips, still leaning his weight into his blade. "How about a little darkness, then?"

"What?"

"BEEF'S HERE, MOTHERFUCKERS!" came an ear-splitting roar, and from the other end of the chamber, the seven-foot Minotaur waded into battle...with a horde of Risen at his back. "PAYBACK TIME!"

"What? The Unbound!" Haim screamed.

"Eyes on me!" Felix shouted, dropping the tip of his Blade and punching forward...his fist glowing with a golden-azure haze.

Wild Threnody!

Arrow of Perdition!

His fist met the Justiciar's breastplate, and unlike his blade, it caught Haim off-guard. The jerk was thrown back from Felix's sheer Strength, but that damn light dispersed his Skills and any real damage.

"Fine, Mr. Veil. I have given you a chance for an easy surrender and death." Haim lifted his side sword and lifted it to his face in an odd salute. "Do not let it be told that the Pathless is without mercy."

———

Beef slammed his maul down, shattering the skull of a Paladin, and he laughed.

Until the guy just got back up.

"That's not fair!" he shouted and launched the Paladin back with a savage kick. "How come you're all immune to bludgeoning damage?" He flipped around his maul, where the back had several savage spikes, and struck another one to little effect. "Piercing damage, too?"

"It is the light they are wrapped within," Hallow said, calm as ever. Beside him was the biggest of the repurposed god-warriors, a man almost as big as Beefhammer himself. The spirit's Risen were spread out around them, punching with a sizable fraction of Beef's Strength. It was cutting a swath through the battle, but none of the Paladins were staying down. "It is negating any damage we inflict."

"That's cheating!" Beef growled, blocking another sizzling bolt of light Mana. It splashed against his chitin armor, ripping a hole in it that Beef couldn't easily fix, not in the midst of a fight. "What're we gonna do?"

The teen-turned-Minotaur had rushed down the spiral staircase as fast as he could, but Agility was not his strong suit. It had taken way too long, and by the time Beef and his Risen had reached the ground floor again, Felix had already started fighting. Now Pit was flying around some-where above, dropping more exploding ice, which wasn't killing anyone either, but at least kept throwing Paladins off their feet. And it distracted a number of them, who were shooting wild spears of light into green cloud after the Chimera.

And then there was Felix.

He was fighting Haim, a guy that Beef was pretty sure was a Master Tier. And not just fighting—Felix was going toe-to-toe, giving just as good as he got, even if that stupid light was protecting the Paladin. Their move-ments were a chaotic blur, especially Felix, who moved faster than Beef could even track. One second, they were both on the ground swinging their swords, and the next second, they were twenty feet away, slinging blue and gold spells at each other. More than anything, it filled Beef with a star-tling, upsetting realization. *If Felix had fought me seriously...I think I'd be dead.*

A cold shiver shook him, quickly replaced by the stabbing blade of another Paladin. The pain drove the memory from Beef's Mind, sharp-ening his focus as he backhanded the warrior. He roared in surprise and pain and hauled off on the bastard. His uppercut caught the Paladin in the chest and hurled him bodily through the air over thirty feet. The guy would have doubtlessly gotten back up, completely unharmed, except

Beef had unintentionally hit him into that whirling cage thing. The moment he hit the array, that huge, building-sized mass of bones and grossness inside shook and screeched.

The Paladin, however, was held in place as his body was squeezed dry. He tried screaming, but only managed a choking gasp, until a crumpled suit of gold limned armor fell to the ground...and the Paladin didn't get back up.

The curse thing Felix mentioned! Beef grinned and grabbed another warrior, using both hands to hurl them into the air. The same thing happened as the to the first, and Beef cackled. "Ha*hah!* Ain't much when you get a face full of curse!"

Beef advanced, and this time, the Paladins ran away.

———

Felix spun away from another strike from the High Justiciar, this one scoring a line of melted stone in the tiled flooring. Dodging was easy, but the problem was doing any sort of damage at all. Nothing Felix tried seemed to work, from magic to physical force from either of his swords. The only thing he hadn't tried was his talons, but activating Sovereign of Flesh still felt dicey. His core space was less full of Essence, having used a good chunk of it to fuel the cutting edge of his Fang, but the abyss of Hunger was still unpleasantly satiated. It didn't make sense that it would affect his Sovereign of Flesh Skill, but it caused ripples of disrupting pain throughout the ability regardless.

Haim wasn't a Grandmaster, but he was at the upper edge of Master Tier, that much was clear. He was strong and fast and tough, with Stamina and Mana pools that were likely very deep. Down so close to the cage, he found his Voracious Eye relatively nonfunctional, sadly, but the way the man was throwing Skills around made it clear he had plenty of gas left in the tank. Felix did, too, but if he couldn't remove that golden glow, the fight would never end.

"You are stronger than I anticipated, Mr. Veil," Haim said, breathing light and easy. "That Strength of yours; to have devoted so much to it and yet still remain remarkably fast and deadly with magic, it intrigues me. What is your secret?"

"Show me yours, and I'll show you mine," Felix said, circling the man warily. "How does your little shield work?"

Haim scoffed. "It is the Light of God, heretic. The Pathless Himself descended to gift unto us the knowledge of this Divine array, a tool to grant his chosen warriors protection and strength unheard of on the Continent. Even if you knew its workings, you could not stop it. You are a mortal man: worthless before the might of the Divine."

Felix only narrowed his eyes, sensing with everything he had. Suppressed as they were, his various sense Skills could only barely pick out the heavy golden threads that connected Haim—and the other Paladins —to the array...and up, toward something else far above them.

The array is clearly doing some heavy lifting, and something up above is helping. That piece of Regalia at the center of their formation is key, but every time I get close, Haim shoves me back. Felix bared his teeth as Haim threw another spear of radiance at him. It missed, but the splash damage as it burst hit and consumed another Risen far behind Felix. *Damn. Okay, destroy the center and take that cloth.*

But if he did that...how would it affect the Primordial's cage?

"Hey!"

Beef was yelling across the battle, but his huge lungs made themselves known. Felix glanced at the guy just in time to see him hurl two Paladins into the Primordial's cage. Both of them were almost instantly desiccated, and their armor crushed as if by some immense force. The cage itself flickered dangerously.

Meanwhile, Beef laughed in dark delight. "The big bone pile hurts them even through their fancy shielding!"

Haim's face went ashen before it flushed with rage. The High Justiciar kicked off the ground, shattering it beneath himself as he accelerated toward the Minotaur—only for Felix to tackle him to the ground.

"Focus on the Inscriptionists! Stop them from finishing!" Felix shouted at him and grappled with the Justiciar.

Yet the Divine shield made the bastard positively slippery, and Haim wriggled free of Felix's grasp, just far enough to shout out a command himself. "Fallen Judgement: Nightfall!"

Above them all, a flare of gold, orange, and black vapor flashed into existence...and nine massive figures manifested, each twenty feet tall and half as wide, shimmering with all the colors of a fading sunset. Golems unlike any Felix had ever seen before.

Haim kicked at Felix's clawing hands and howled. "Drop!"

CHAPTER NINETY

With an earth-shattering crash, the Nightfall Golems landed. Their vaguely humanoid, twenty-foot-tall forms were stocky and squared, and as they spread their limbs, they revealed bright, glimmering blades at the ends of their stout arms.

"Do I throw them at the bone-monster, too?" Beef shouted at Felix. Then yelped as the nearest Golem slammed a blade into the ground, exploding tiles in all directions. "AH!"

Felix shifted, intending to go help the kid, but Haim positioned himself between them. The High Justiciar grinned. "Have you perhaps considered not announcing your intentions?" Behind him, two more Nightfall Golems advanced, their precise, implacable movements enough to mow down handfuls of Risen at a time. Beef danced back, deflecting a blow with his hammer, but kept getting hemmed in by the other Paladins. "Do not kill the Unbound! We need him!"

Move, Felix!

Felix darted backward as a trio of thickened acid spikes dropped onto Haim's head and shoulders. They shattered, driving the impressive High Justiciar to stumble, before coating him in a gooey layer of sizzling acid. Yet the man stood swiftly and released a barrage of blinding bolts after the swooping Chimera. "Kill that monster, however! Now!"

Pit! Felix sent back, but his Companion was too busy dodging salvo after salvo of golden beams, spears, and bolts. He was far more agile than any of the Paladins, but Felix had no idea how long he could keep it up. There were so many Paladins still.

"Foul Chimera. I should not be surprised to see such a degenerate beast in your employ, Veil. Your profane Territory will be high on the list of problems the Triumvirate wishes eradicated." Haim burned with more of that golden light, and in Felix's dimmed senses, the threads of connection thickened substantially as he drew on the array's power. The acid vanished; even the Mana of its making was snuffed out. "Do you know how rare it is to have the Priesthood, Inquisitors, and Paladins agree on a course of action? I expect them to be marching on your wretched barrier even now."

Felix didn't believe that; there was no way he could know all that, not with him out on a mission for months. "Get a lot of communications in the middle of the desert? Last I knew, we killed all of your messenger birds in the Caleph Pass."

Haim sighed, his tone that of an aggrieved, disappointed patriarch. "Not all. How else would we know to expect your party? I said it before, but I understand that you're a simple man, Mr. Veil, so I shall repeat myself. It was unwise to leave living enemies at your back."

Mana surged around Felix, and he flared Relentless Resolution, ducking below the swipe of a Nightfall Golem that had *somehow* snuck up on him. He did not, however, dodge the second, off-hand strike. The shimmering blade cut into and through his chest and gut, burning viciously with blinding pain.

Sovereign of Flesh!

The Skill activated, barely, stitching the worst of his wound closed at the cost of a great deal of Felix's gathered Essence. Blood slicked the ground, too much, and Felix slid across it as the Golem's hand-blade chased after him. Haim's bolt of burning light hit to his right, forcing Felix around it and into the range of a second Golem. He raised both swords, his Fang and Inheritor's Will, and directly blocked the Golem's falling chop—the Crescian Bronze and Primordial tooth held, but the ground beneath Felix's feet cratered underneath the impact.

"Impressive!" Haim shouted, before sending another flurry of radiant spears at his back.

Felix slipped free of the Golem's blade, letting it crash fully to the earth and block the bulk of Haim's attack. Then Felix spun back and around, avoiding the second Golem's follow-up blow. Thankfully, the magical constructs were slower than Haim, and Felix outclassed them all. Fighting Haim had simply been a matter of avoiding the man's attacks before, but now he fought for survival. *I can't summon my scales. If another of those swords hits me, it could kill me.*

Wild Threnody!

Corrosive Strike!

Felix's shorter, hooked blade came up, deflecting the stocky arm of a Golem. The pillar of acidic Mana that imbued his weapon, however, did nothing more than splash harmlessly against its golden-limned appendage. Yet the shock of impact sent a cold flash of fire along Felix's arm and spine, splintering into a thousand fissures that drove deep into his Body. The strain he'd never healed was getting worse, and each close call and failed attack was exacerbating the problem.

Everything hurt, and his Body felt stretched thin over his bones, barely able to keep up with his stats and movements. Still, he had little choice. Felix skipped backward, an errant slash of his Fang clearing space by sending three lesser Paladins flying through the crowd. Haim walked forward calmly, still glowing, still smiling while the Nightfall Golems flanked him.

"I admit to being surprised you have not yet perished," Haim admitted. "Perhaps I should not be. You survived Kel'lyv's assault, after all. A Grandmaster. To what do you owe such remarkable fortitude?"

"I eat all my vegetables," Felix said. Sovereign of Flesh was painfully chugging away, but the Skill was less than optimal at the moment, and Felix was feeling a little lightheaded from blood loss. "A sailor once told me spinach was vital."

"Hm, a rare herb? Worth looking into," Haim said, so completely serious that Felix couldn't believe it. "When we have finished here, perhaps your little Territory will amuse me for a while."

Felix felt a hot rage wash through his Spirit, part him and part Pit. The tenku wasn't even visible in the battle, hiding still in the thinning acid cloud cover, but he heard every word. "Finished...? Do you even know what you're doing? This thing shouldn't be set free!"

"Such a small mind, Veil. We are setting nothing free, nothing but a corpse. This creature has been dead for Ages, fuel for the abominations in Ahkestria to dominate this entire Territory. Who else is responsible for the scourge of undead in the Scorched Expanse? The Holy Chosen of the Pathless has decreed that we take this fuel for ourselves, for the dark days to come."

"The Ruin," Felix said, dodging another blurring attack and another, before taking a light slash against his upper arm. He skipped back, again, keeping just ahead of the Golems. "You want a Primordial's might to fight against the Ruin!"

Haim looked at him thoughtfully. "You know entirely too much, boy. Who told you of this?"

"Oh, you know," Felix gasped, rolling backward as Haim's blade of light and heat shattered tiles in a ten-foot radius. He came back smoothly to his feet, Inheritor's Will up to parry. "Here and there. So, you get a weapon and remove the defenses of Ahkestria all at once."

"Not as stupid as you look," Haim said with a wide smile. The man didn't even seem winded. Divine boon or not, that light was *cheating*. "Drop the wall, and cut the Masters and Matrons off from their power source. Easy prey. Once they're gone, there is nothing between us and total control of the city and all of its valuable resources." He tossed up a hand, signalling the advancing Golems. They stopped and soon reversed their momentum, heading back toward the golden array.

Toward Beef.

"And now you bring us the Unbound we've searched so long for, Mr.

Veil." Haim's ever-present smile grew until Felix could count every tooth in his dumb face. "Truly, the Autarch is quite generous."

There was a flare of magic from the other side of the battle, where the Inscriptionists had resumed work. The cage weakened even further as gold crept along its spinning facets, thickening and multiplying like a rabid virus, cannibalizing the elegant forces of the cage for its own design. The glow around all of them brightened until it was almost blinding, and Paladins rushed Felix from behind Haim, screaming in defiance with swords upraised.

FELIX.

Everything stopped.

Felix froze, his arm lifted in a straight jab meant for the first approaching Paladin. The Paladins were locked into running positions, their bodies leaning dramatically toward his. Mana vapor had solidified in the air, but Felix could barely see it at all; he couldn't move, not even his eyes. More terrifying than *that*, however, was the vast...force that pressed against him. It was haggard and ancient, bloated with the passage of Ages and smelling of burning dust. It did not so much speak as it commanded the universe to *stop* and *listen*.

FELIX.
SCION OF THE UNSEEN TIDE.
SCION OF HARMONY.

Primordial? Felix asked. *You're...alive?*

The presence ignored his words but kept speaking, each word a punch to his psyche. Shapes danced in Felix's arrested vision, bright and writhing.

THE MADNESS MUST END.
I CANNOT CONTROL THE CURSE, BUT YOU CAN TERMINATE IT.
I AM DEAD.
LET ME REMAIN SO.
END IT ALL.

Space rippled, distorting and tearing viciously at the muscles in Felix's shoulders and back. Time resumed its march with a roar of sound, and Felix's frozen fist shot forward and rapped into a Paladin's skull, hurling the man back into the distance. Others moved forward as if they hadn't noticed a single hitch, but Felix turned wide eyes onto the Primordial and its cage.

It was unraveling, supplanted by more and more of the golden array. And in the center, the Primordial itself was an undulating sea of bone, ligaments, and dusty scales. It *pulsed*.

Above, Pit shrieked and flung one last burst of icy magic down upon the enemy. Spikes hit and exploded, throwing back the Paladins all around Felix, but before Pit could pull back up, Haim lifted a hand.

"Pit! Run!" Felix cried, but light blossomed too fast to counter.

A barrage of light-forged lances ripped through Pit's wings, tearing them to shreds and scattering dark blood into the sky like rain. Pit bellowed in pain and fell to the earth, hitting hard enough that he took down five Paladins under his bulk.

"PIT!"

Adamant Discord!

A burst of omnidirectional force shot outward, galvanizing the connections Felix had to the floor below and the air above. Gravity, after all, had affected him his whole life. Felix pulsed his Skill, moving even faster than before as lightning trailed behind him. He raced to Pit's side, reaching him only seconds before another barrage of light lances hit them both.

Convergence!

Pit vanished into his Spirit, and Felix took every single lance instead. The ground exploded, throwing him bodily from the earth, but not before Felix could at least sort of direct his trajectory. He hit fifteen feet away, fetching right up against the Primordial's cage...but dozens of yards away from the center of the Divine array.

Beef was fighting five of the Golems and Paladins, Hallow's Risen at his side, but their numbers were dwindling, and the Minotaur was covered in his own blood. Pit was alive, for now, but all of them weren't enough to end the fight. *Not as we are.*

"What can you hope to accomplish here, Mr. Veil?" Haim shouted over the din of battle. Nightfall Golems stomped up beside him, four of them, all for Felix. "You cannot stop the will of the Divine."

Anger welled up in Felix, bright and caustic. "People keep telling me that," he said, before slapping his hand directly onto the Primordial's array.

Chthonic Tribute!

Within his core space, the abyss recoiled in horror. More clearly than ever before, the thing within him—his Hunger—wailed. *Too Much!*

No! Felix didn't have time to be surprised. *You listen to me! Chthonic Tribute!*

Intent and Willpower burning bright, the Skill had no choice but to activate. The Primordial's cage twisted and flexed, bucking as pieces of it stretched violently toward Felix's channels.

Chthonic Tribute!

Haim screamed something, and the earth shook, but Felix couldn't spare the attention. He shoved the blade of his Intent into the array, sawing against the steel-like cables of the array's formation. Sigils flared and flashed, spreading around Felix in fractal ripples, while from across the way, threads of gold raced toward him. Oppressive, controlling heat and radiance, a potency that shined like an immutable sun, all of it speared toward Felix.

Chthonic Tribute!

He recognized it, not for its specific flavor, but its origin. It was a personal cataclysm, a judgement driven by the Will of the Divine encased in the array. By the Regalia itself.

Fuck off! Felix snarled and thrust his Willpower against the descending judgement.

The world bloomed into light all around him, and suddenly Felix was in a wild, trackless forest. Trees the size of mountains spread all around him, while leafy fronds hung so thick that the world was entirely shades of green and fecund umber. A hazy figure, bathed in golden radiance, stared at him with infinite kindness and an indomitable condemnation. It lifted a single finger, and a refutation and censure flooded out from them like a physical wall.

The Pathless. Fragment or not, it was the disapproving Will of a god.

I don't give a shit!

Title: Architect of the Rise is active!
25% Bonus To Learning All Sigaldry As Well As Creating And Maintaining Complex Arrays!

Title: Born of Will is active!
You Are Your Own Maker!

Title: Tyrant of Choice is active!
You Choose Your Own Destiny!

Title: The Call Of Defiance is active!
+25% Willpower Against The Divine!

The vague figure gasped, shock and horror tearing through it as their Wills met...and the piece of Divinity was outmatched.

"NO!" Haim howled, a sound like his soul was ripping in half.

CHTHONIC TRIBUTE!

The world pulsed, and beside him, the sigaldry of the golden array and the cage holding the Primordial was torn asunder.

Everything exploded.

The vast chamber was inundated in a roar so loud that it blew Felix's eardrums out, and he was thrown bodily across the entirety of the room. He hit the tiles hard, shattering them with every bounce and roll, until he slammed up against the crystalline wall. Dark blue fragments burst in all directions as cracks drove up from his impact point, and blood fountained from Felix's mouth. Pieces of him felt liquefied.

That..those're probably...important, he thought groggily. *Sov...Sovereign of Flesh.*

Precious little of the array's power had flowed into him, instead consuming one another explosively. What little Essence he had left he fed into his Sovereign of Flesh, speeding up his recovery. But it was slower than usual, and as he blinked wearily into the smoke and fire that dominated the battlefield, he could pick out too many Paladins still standing, that golden barrier of theirs only barely diminished. Haim himself was fine, crouched behind two remaining Nightfall Golems.

Hah..! Two...down, Felix thought, a bit woozily as his ears healed with a roaring *pop. Seven more to go.*

Behind the Justiciar, the Primordial was flexing and reaching out, its bones and ligaments twisting in a sickening sort of...rebirth? It roared, making the remaining Paladins flinch backward in fear and horror.

Then its roar was answered by the tinkling shattering of more crystal high above...and the innumerable hissing screeches of hundreds of familiar foes.

"Shit," Felix said heavily. He couldn't even stand. "Fucking Dustborn Wraiths."

CHAPTER NINETY-ONE

The Paladins came through the city like a red scourge, and nowhere was their brutal fury more concentrated than the inner sanctum of the Highest Flame. Evie dodged a glimmering bolt of light even as she came face to face with the fiery swords of the Temple Knights. She parried a blade, deftly engaging her Born Trait.

"Ah!" the Temple Knight cried out, the tip of his sword falling to the tiled floors.

Evie stabbed outward with a spike of ice, punching through the Knight's throat. "Too heavy for ya?" she asked as he gurgled out his final breaths.

You Have Killed A Temple Knight Of The Elemental Fire!
XP Earned!

"Bastards." Evie shook her hand, dislodging chunks of ice and taking in the chaotic battlefield of the inner sanctum. She had found a strange, calm bubble in the sea of death that surrounded her...though *made* was a better verb. She'd killed two dozen Knights in the last quarter glass, carving this slice of quiet out by the glinting length of her chain. Bodies filled the ground, so many, but there were always more.

Not to mention all these bulky red asses, she thought. The Paladins had dominated the southernmost portion of the sanctum, nearest the Altar, and now they spread outward like a shining, golden plague. *And are they glowing?*

Three silver blurs whipped past Evie's position, landing just beyond the press of Claw and Knights before bursting into a trio of razor-sharp cyclones. Vess followed swiftly after, moving so effortlessly across the battlefield that it looked like she was dancing. The blue and white spear in her hands thrust and spun, deflecting light bolts and burning swords with equal ease, while four more silver Spears rotated around her Body. Each one was another fighter, almost as good with the spear as Vess herself. She left behind her a bleeding swath of Temple Knights and, Evie noticed with a scowl, a Matron.

Show off.

She scanned the crowd. The noise of discharging spells and flaring Skills was deafening, not to mention the roar and bellow of warriors fighting and dying. The Legion were doing well, far as she could see; Harn and Darius had that in hand. Zara was doing her big impressive magic thing in mid-air. Evie wasn't sure where to go, or how she could help the battle resolve. Atar was near the Altar, but she'd have to wade through hundreds to get to him, and even then, she'd be stuck between those hundred Knights and an equal number of Paladins.

"Tua ratha!" a voice bellowed from only a hundred feet away. "Tua fa ralla *leskos!*"

Evie's eyes caught on Ari, the Battlelord of the Frost Giants, backed by his people and facing off against two Matrons and a clutch of Knights. Flames bathed the Battlelord, his blue skin occluded by blazing sheets of fire that poured off of the two Matrons. His warriors were no better, facing the burning weapons of the Knights with their own frozen armaments. As she watched, Ari was knocked to his knees by the combined force of the Matrons' power. His huge, icy greataxe was all that shielded him from turning to charcoal.

An unwilling sympathy welled up in Evie's heart, one that she crushed with ruthless speed...and which continued to sprout, weed-like. She *hated* the Risi for what they did. *But they saved you, dummy. Can't let that stand, right?*

Evie pulled up her chain, looping it around her chest and shoulder in an easy, well-practiced motion. A Knight ran at her from the edges of the conflict, maybe because her weapon was put up, maybe because she weighed half of everyone else. Didn't matter. A throwing dagger to his eye, and an Ice Spike to his groin ended that charge up real quick.

Just beyond the churn of battle, the Frost Giants raged, and the Temple Knights shouted in triumph.

Yeah. That's enough of that. She gathered herself and leaped into the fray.

———

Zara wove her Chant carefully, threading her Intent and Affinity through the lens of her Willpower and the Grand Harmony. It was powerful, some of the Chanter's greatest workings to date, yet they only held because the Grandmaster's attention was split between her and the Captain of the

Paladins. Even now, as the Captain glowed brighter and brighter with a strange, sourceless spell, the Grandmaster of the Desert's Fire proved himself worthy of his title.

Walls of aquamarine power manifested, Mana supercharged by the vibrations of Creation itself, and were summarily torn asunder by the sheer *weight* behind each of the Grandmaster's blows.

"He's quite a bit more advanced than the Marl King," Isla hissed at her, gesturing sharply. A series of barely audible notes cascaded from the air around her, and Zara's latest projection of force expanded and thickened. "What was his name? Lrv'a the Six-Toed?"

Zara grinned as the impetus of Kel'lyv's attacks were momentarily blunted by Isla's powerful augmentation. "Lrv'a Six-Toes, King of the Marl and Defier of Destiny."

"That's the one."

The pews they stood upon suddenly blazed, an inferno of swirling flame and choking smoke. Isla stumbled, her balance lost, but Zara snagged her thin arm. "Do not take Kel'lyv lightly."

"I'll try my best," Isla said, voice tinged with frustration and fear. "He does a good job of reminding us."

Zara wicked sweat from her forehead, and the two of them shifted positions while Isla healed both of their burns. "The Paladins are keeping him occupied, but it will not last long. That barrier of theirs is vexing even him."

"What's taking that blond mage so long?" Isla snarled. "I even went in and healed them all!"

"Clearly, the job was not completed," Zara said, thickening the barriers around them and those of her allies nearby. "We must give Atar more time."

"Vultures! All of you followers of the sniveling Pathless!" Kel'lyv raged. Cords of dense, white-hot flames wove above him in a spellform that Zara couldn't follow. The inferno swelled until Zara's barriers hissed before its heat. "To come here so brazenly, to put your filthy hands upon the foundations of my city...you will pay dearly!"

Harsh, braying laughter tore from the large, crimson-clad Captain. Fire swirled around him and four other Paladins, but none of the Grandmaster's attacks even singed their cloaks. All of it was rebuffed by that golden barrier. "You're pitiful, old, and a heretic. The Hierophant gave us a message for you: fall on your knees, kiss the hem of her regalia, or else die."

That merely made the Grandmaster blaze brighter, summoning a torrent of potency that warped the stone ten feet in all directions. His own people shied away, their robes smoking, before the fire mage blasted forward faster than ever before. Straight for the Paladins.

The Captain smirked and unsheathed his side sword. They met in a shower of orange and golden sparks as a shockwave of Mana cut through

Zara's barriers. Knights and Claw warriors were sent to the ground, some of them burnt to a crisp by light or fire.

"Isla!" Zara shouted. "Heal them!"

"Already moving," her sister said, a tremble in her Spirit. Zara pretended not to notice it at all.

She too was afraid.

———

Atar tried to dodge the Mana bolts that came his way, but his feet betrayed him. He fell, careful to fall so that the squalling child in his arms was protected, and ended up sprawled over the cooling corpse of a Disciple, fully vulnerable to a barrage of gleaming death. Until a sizzling, yellow Mana cleaver the size of a door slammed into place. The bolts were deflected, at least some. The rest merely shot into the pillar of Urge behind them.

"Invest more in Agility, Atar!" Fiammetta shouted. She screamed, and the cleaver uprooted itself before spinning off toward the Disciples headed their way. It took two fully in the chest, but the other four dispelled it with a controlled burst of their own Skills. "Get up!"

"I am!" he snapped back, rolling slowly to his feet. The child still cried, but it was a softer, more terrified sound. "It'll be okay, little one." Then he hissed in pain, feeling something pull at the base of his calf. A notification blipped across his vision.

Status Condition: Minor Injury (Lower Leg)

Damn it. Atar flipped his curly hair from his eyes. *The Disciples are drawing closer and closer...and the Paladins aren't far behind.*

The three of them were still perched atop the wide lip of the Altar basin, having divided their time between defending it and trying to rescue the civilians already cast into the Highest Flame. Despite their best efforts, none but the child in his arms had been pulled free; the angle of the basin was too steep. Pulling someone free was a surefire way to fall in themselves.

Fiammetta and Alister sent flashing ripples of their Mana across the sanctum, barely stopping despite their fast-depleting Mana pools. Shields of blue force and yellow heat sprang up and died beneath spears of light and waves of flame, while pillars and weapons forged of the same Mana tried their best to delay them all.

Still holding a terrified kid, Atar had contributed by flinging his Stars of the Sovereign into the crowd, killing a number of Disciples before they had erected potent fire shields of their own. The shields could be penetrated, but combined with their Fire Resistance, any Stars that traversed them were robbed of their killing potential. At best, Atar could give them all minor burns.

The Paladins were the worse problem. At first, Atar had been almost glad for their presence—the idiots had set upon the Disciples' rear guard with abandon, slaughtering a great many of them. But that had changed when the Pathless zealots had put their burning blades to the throats of the innocent civilians the Disciples had rounded up.

Atar had raged, throwing Stars at the red-clad warriors with all the fury and precision he could muster. Many had died, prisoner and Paladin both, before the zealots were covered in a golden glow. It was as if the sun hovered behind every single one, and it rendered Atar's efforts moot. In fact, the trio had only survived because the Paladins had been called to the increasingly wild battle to the northern side of the sanctum.

Where the Grandmaster fought, fully unleashed.

"He's going to kill us all," Alister panted. The Disciples seemed sure of it, at least, as they continued to swarm forward. "And if more people are sacrificed to the Highest Flame, I don't know if even that barrier the Paladins have will protect them."

More prisoners died by the second, and worse: a sizable chunk had been successfully hurled bodily into the Altar basin. Atar could no longer even see the flask containing the Primordial's flesh curse, but seeing how the Urge appeared to be growing in strength by the moment, he figured it was a sure bet it hadn't broken open yet.

I have to do something, he realized. He'd tried to burst the flask with his magic, but the Urge diluted any Skill Atar attempted. Alister and Fiametta tried, too, with the same result. *That flask might as well be on a moon.*

"It's relays!" Alister said, and Atar jolted in surprise.

"What?"

"The glow! They're producing it with relays, look!" Alister pointed up into the sky, through the shattered windows of the inner sanctum, where two huge galleon-class Manaships bobbed in place. "Fins of orichalcum. There and there. All of them inscribed!"

Atar squinted, his Perception just barely enough to pick out the swoop and swirl of sigils on the metal fins attached to the Manaship hulls. "Just like...just like the relay arrays we saw in the Foglands."

"Exactly," Alister gasped, reacting just in time to block another spear of flame. "Now all we have to do is destroy at least one of the Manaships, and their protection would disappear!"

"Sure! Let me get right on that!" Fiammetta grunted, hurling two stride-length cleavers made of heat Mana at a Disciple's legs. The man hopped over one, but not the other, and fell with an undignified squawk. "We can barely put a dent in this battle, let alone a warded Manaship a hundred strides in the air!"

The battle raged, and chaos reigned. The Grandmaster would not be defeated, even if the Paladins were impervious, they couldn't harm him or even wear him down...

But Atar could.

He closed his eyes and took a single, shallow breath. "Take the kid, Alister."

Alister looked at him, brows furrowed, but didn't hesitate. The bundled Human toddler was hard to dislodge, but eventually went to the former Haarwatch noble. "What? What are you trying to do? I don't know that your fire spells will much hurt these Disciples—"

"Just keep them busy, Alister."

"Atar!" The force mage lunged for Atar an instant after realizing what he was doing, but it was too late.

Atar leaped into the Altar basin.

"ATAR!"

Alister's voice was drowned out almost immediately by the unmitigated roar of the Urge's flames. Atar fell, sliding along the slicked curve of the metal basin, half blinded by the streaming fire and his own smoking battlerobes. Pain tore at him, total and vast, and it was all Atar could do to stay standing among the others huddled around him.

Keep going! Find the flask!

He forced himself up, leveraging all the Willpower and Fire Resistance he had to push past the pain. The fire was stronger now that a few had died to the Urge, but the outer areas were still weaker than the core. So long as Atar did not step into the Highest Flame's center, he could survive.

He hoped.

Ashes and bones stirred beneath his feet, each of them grey with cherry-red embers burning from within. People writhed among the ashes, most of them less than whole, despite Isla's healing. *I'm sorry I couldn't get you out. I tried. Blind gods, I tried.*

He could only stumble forward, eyes fixed on the ground, hunting for the flask. The haze of heat and thick, opaque flames were a loathsome hindrance. Each second he failed to find the flask was another second his battlerobes charred and baked, the fibers turning to a foul smoke. Atar tripped over a body he hadn't noticed, and his hands were seared when he drove them down into the ash and hot metal...and found a cool, smooth surface.

The flask! Coughing and gasping for air, Atar pulled the strengthened glass bottle, holding it before his face in dull-eyed triumph. Inside, an insidious, muddy corruption writhed. Atar's Mind was swimming, however, barely registering what to do next. Slowly, glacially slowly, Atar's dry eyes widened. Before him the wall of intense, white flames at the Urge's center pulsed and expanded. It triggered something in his thoughts, a familiar voice that galvanized his remaining nerve endings into action.

Throw it! he raged at himself. *You can't get anyone out, but you can stop this! Throw it!*

With rubber bones and muscles barely listening, Atar jerked forward. The flask pitched limply from his grasp and into the Highest Flame's center.

Light shattered.

And an abhorrent, writhing dust annihilated *everything*.

CHAPTER NINETY-TWO

"Atar." Alister took an involuntarily step backward, clutching the boy-child to his chest. The swaddled toddler squirmed and shook. "Atar, what's going on?"

The pillar of the Highest Flame, thirty stride wide and more than fifty strides tall, was now filled with a storm of whirling sand and dust. Fire flashed through it, but it was in striated bursts that glassed sections of the wheeling cyclone, and those vanished into the impenetrable surface. Yet, it didn't expand past the edge of the Altar basin.

Fiammetta gasped. "The Paladins! Look!"

All at once the golden light around the Paladins dimmed to a bare fraction of its power. Alister ran his eyes around the zealots, most of whom were pulling backward nervously, shields raised. He looked up at the Manaships...but the relay fins were still glimmering with power. *What happened?* He glanced at the Urge behind him. *The Highest Flame? No, that doesn't make any sense—*

Fiammetta gasped again, but this time it was accompanied by a wretched wail. She fell to her knees, heaving and tearing at her own breastplate. "I-I can't breathe! I can't breathe!"

Alister reached for her, but pulled back with a curse as fire undulated across her limbs. It ran outward from a point in her chest, like it was flee-ing...or being pulled from her.

Similar noises filled the strangely silent air, as Disciples and Knights all toppled and were subsumed in rising flames. A Matron in his line of sight threw her head back and screamed bloody murder as her body became a pillar of incandescent flame. The force of her sudden immolation threw back everyone within ten feet of her position, Knights and a few Disciples tumbling end over end. The battle had been driven to a horrified pause as everyone else turned to view the Altar.

"The Flame!" a voice from the sky cried out. The Grandmaster's face was even more ashen than usual as he stared at the dust-infested Altar. "The Primordial is free!"

A jagged wave of aquamarine light slammed into him, and this time, the Grandmaster was almost caught unaware. He dropped from the sky, barely able to cut through the wave with a burning blade of pure fire Mana. Steam erupted in all directions, and it was like someone had restarted time.

Battlelord Ari and his giants were recovering from the flames that had blanketed them. The Knights and Matrons they had faced were still writhing on the ground or in pillars of flickering orange power, unable to fight back. Alister saw Evie land among them, and her spiked chain did its bloody work, whipping among the Knights with imposing weight. Golden armor was crushed, and battlerobes were pierced before she flowed toward the nearest flame pillar, retracting her weapon and spinning it forward in a complex series of loops. The spiralling formation wrapped tight around the flames before sinking in and catching.

Evie screamed, activating some sort of Skill and sent herself spinning backward...yanking her chain all the while. The chain pulled free, emerging from the fire in a dark, steaming spray of pulped flesh. The pillar winked out, and the mangled remains of its occupant fell bonelessly to the ground.

At the other side, Harn and Darius led the Claw, cutting into the downed defenders without mercy. Knights died by the dozen. The Paladins faced them on the edges, but all of them held up their shields and were now steadily retreating toward the southernmost wall of the sanctum. It was clear that their protection had been weakened.

"Fall back!" Captain Boldt ordered. He had backed away from the Grandmaster who was now facing Zara directly. "To the ships!"

The Paladins had barely any time to move before the Altar gave a tremendous, groaning shriek. It rattled beneath Alister's feet, and saw the flames surge within it, and he stepped up next to Fiammetta. "Kinetic Embrace!"

Flickering plates of force Mana formed across Faun, mage, and child just as a wave of obliterating dust ripped free from the Highest Flame's confines.

"AHHHH!" Alister screamed into the wind, his shields grinding down just as fast as he could replenish them. He drank three Mana Potions, one after the other, but it proved too little. He blunted the initial gale, but the sheer immensity of the outburst tore the shields to shreds and hurled the three of them off of the Altar's lip.

Alister rolled, protecting the kid in his arms, while Fiammetta's body hit the tiles hard. Above them, a cyclone of razor sand and blazing heat formed within the sanctum, quickly filling the space. Knights, Paladins,

Claw warriors, all of them buckled under the power of the storm. Brilliant, yellow lightning formed and discharged, smashing into walls and architecture with wrathful abandon, while sheets of glass formed and shattered among the sands. They were ground to nothing by the churning winds before reheating again and again. And then the true horror showed itself.

A phantom face formed from the wind and sand, glass, and lightning. A thousand skeletal hands solidified, until a monstrous, many-eyed abomination congealed. It bellowed, releasing a buzzing cacophony that drove a spike of primal fear into Alister's brain and belly. He gaped, eyes watering.

Atar...Atar, what have you done?

———

The undead were everywhere.

Wights and Wraiths poured from the walls, filling up the huge chamber and clashing directly with the now-weakened Paladins. They maintained a piece of their strange strength and shielding, but Felix could tell it was far less. A dozen Wights pulled down a red-clad warrior as he watched, tearing into his exposed face with blunt teeth and jagged claws. But they didn't need to kill the Paladins to be effective, because the flesh curse was running rampant. Scratched and bitten flesh withered, dried of its vital fluids as the Primordial's dark Will overcame their own...and Paladin turned on Paladin.

It was an ideal scenario, had Felix not been in the thick of it.

"You did this!" Haim shouted at him, sword flashing. "Heretic!"

Felix parried the blow, driving the man's blade into the tiled floor. He was stronger than Haim, but the High Justiciar was a lot better at sword fighting, and Felix was still dazed. The Paladin's blade came back up, catching Felix in the chest and slicing him open before a burst of radiant Mana shot into him. Felix was hurled backward, again.

He kept his feet, but that was the only good news. His chest was a mess of blood and exposed muscle, and his Health had dropped below fifty percent. His Sovereign of Flesh was working to heal him, Felix was devastatingly low on Essence. And his Hunger was still revolting, refusing to pull in more. "Work, god damn it!"

Felix's head swam, still not quite healed, but he lifted his two blades. Greatsword in his left hand, hooked khopesh in his right, he set his feet as Haim raced at him, lit from within with Divine power.

"Heretic! The Pathless has spoken to me!" Haim screamed, his eyes wide as if in rapturous understanding. "You cannot be afforded to live."

The High Justiciar arrived, sword descending as a wave of dust-fueled force ripped downward, hitting them all.

Felix flared Stone Shaping, hoping to blunt or catch the sandy power that fell atop them, but all he could manage was to not get knocked aside...unlike literally everyone else. Paladins and undead, even the Golems were thrown from their feet. He looked up to the distant roof of the chamber as a dusty cyclone erupted from above. It crackled with yellow lightning and eroding bursts of sand and shattered glass that tore the crystalline walls to pieces.

And it was slowly dropping lower.

"Beef!" Felix shouted, spotting his friend. He sheathed his weapons and jogged to his side, Agility letting him speed across the battlefield faster than a damn car. The Minotaur was sprawled on the ground, bleeding heavily from...everywhere. "You're hurt."

Beef accepted Felix's hand and climbed to his feet. "This? I got lots of blood. I'll be fine! I—aargh!"

The Minotaur tripped, going back down to a knee and raising his thick hands up to his head. Sparks of blackened green Mana rippled around his temples, flashing outward along thin pathways toward his Risen warriors. They, too, had fallen, and Hallow had only gotten a few up. Now they were all shaking as if being electrocuted, their backs arching and jaws clenching so hard a few even cracked teeth.

"Michael!" Hallow shouted from the nearest Risen. Its eyes strobed, waxing and waning in strength. "Michael!"

Beef forced himself to stand, his muscles and fur quivering from the effort. "I know! Ah! That bag of bones is trying to take over my undead! That's bullshit!"

Damn it, he thought, scanning the crowd. The other undead were getting back to their feet, and so were the Paladins. The roaring storm kept slowly descending, and now it glittered with the shattered remnants of thousands of Mana crystals. *Damn it, what do we do?*

The Primordial was undulating again, throbbing almost. The bones made a huge racket as they clacked and clattered, pulling and pushing at one another, the gruesome ligaments of the creature creaking as they tightened. It held no shape, and it clung to the edges of the massive bronze sword thrust through it, but it was getting more and more lively by the second. It had asked to die, but it did not seem in a hurry to do so.

Felix blinked. Along the edge of that massive blade, pulses and odd, looping glyphs formed. From them, half-invisible lines of sigaldry had speared into the Primordial's mass like harpoons. They were flickering, tattered things, terribly damaged by the destruction Felix had wrought...but he could still see the small crystal vessel holding the Regalia. He cursed. The Paladins' array had been all but obliterated, but power was still being sucked from the Primordials not-quite-corpse. Those same lines were funneling it up, through the storm...and outward into Haim and his cronies.

I have to stop the Primordial. Kill it, like it asked. To Beef, he asked, "Can you hold out?" Before the words were fully out of his mouth, however, he felt a sharp, blazing pain in his chest. Words flitted across his Companion bond, but Felix clamped down on his Spirit, refusing to let Pit out. *No, you'll be safer in there.*

Pit seethed and pushed against him, but he couldn't overcome Felix's Willpower. *I can protect you!*

No! You're hurt already, Felix sent back. "Beef!" The Minotaur was staring upward, just now noticing the annihilating storm dropping onto their heads. Felix grabbed him by his chitin breastplate and puled him close. "Beef! Can you hold out?"

Beef shook himself, and Felix let him go. The teen-turned-muscle-bound warrior wet his lips and attempted a casual grin, but it came out wan and sickly. "Yeah. Yeah, of course. These pallys do light and fire damage, and I'm sturdy against that shit. And the undead aren't much, except those big ones." His eyes flicked upward, nervously. "That doesn't look good, though."

"It's not, and if it reaches us, we're all dead." The Paladins were regrouping and scribbling out furious lines of sigaldry, Haim at their head. "That thing is fueling that storm, and fueling the Paladins, too. I'm not gonna let that continue."

"Wait, what're you doing?" Beef asked. Hallow stood next to him, most of her Risen still quivering.

"What I do best," Felix took a breath. "Something stupid."

Cloudstep!

Felix formed a series of Mana platforms and accelerated up them, each one lasting no more than a second before shattering under the weight of his momentum.

"Holy shit, that's cool!" Beef said behind him. Felix let a burst of pride warm him, just for a second, because then he hit the shifting wall of the Primordial.

Divine sigils flared around him, bursting upward from those half-invisible tethers into the Primordial's bones. They filled with light, forming into a cage to keep Felix from moving forward...but he didn't stop. He slammed against the sigaldry, but his Body chose that moment to spasm and fail. Wounds that he'd patched shut sprang open under the divine sigils' might, his left shoulder burst and dislocated while his collarbone snapped right in half. Felix suppressed a scream of pain and frustration and fell back onto a hastily summoned Cloudstep.

Haim levitated into view, buoyed by cords of golden Mana. "You cannot stop this any longer, Mr. Veil. Or should I call you Autarch?"

Felix flared his nostrils and tamped down on his pain, pushing his Song of Absolution as hard as he could. He needed focus. The arrays blocking him were vulnerable, but they weren't Divine...merely powered by a Master of the craft. He could thwart Divine Will, at least a portion of it, but against a mortal agent? It wasn't the same. The High Justiciar was strong, a warrior that Felix could *maybe* have beaten on his best days, fully rested and healed. But, as his spasming Body reminded him, that was not *this* day.

He gripped his Blade of the Fang and pulled it from his back. The baldric and sheath that held it dissolved back into his shirt and jacket, now flapping in the intensifying winds. Lightning crashed above them, and Haim leveled his own glowing blade at Felix's throat.

"Let us end this, Felix Nevarre."

CHAPTER NINETY-THREE

Suspended within Felix's Spirit, Pit could only watch as Felix fought the red-shelled Haim. Points of light danced before Pit's eyes—access to Felix's senses—and he let out outraged squawks as bursts of light Mana broke over his Companion. Over and over again. The sigaldry around them kept Felix hemmed in, flaring with caustic radiance each time he stepped too close. Felix was hurt and bleeding, but so was Haim. The protection the Paladins held was failing.

A notification tried to pop into view, but Pit dismissed it, unread. He knew what it said, what it wanted, but it wasn't the time. He had to focus on his friend. As he watched, Felix flowed forward, flipping over a spear of blinding light, and struck hard. Haim fell back, breastplate dented and blood exploding from his mouth. Pit trilled in wrathful joy.

Haim shouted something heated and bitter, spitting more blood with each word. From below, a sunset glow manifested as a beam ripped up through Felix, throwing him off of his Cloudstep and into the sigil cage. Felix screamed, and his Spirit shook. Pit didn't hesitate.

Convergence!

A flash of blinding light forced Haim to throw up his arms, shielding his face as Pit manifested in the outside world once more. More importantly, the displacement set Pit just outside the restricting cage of golden sigils, and he dropped before either the High Justiciar or Felix could react. His damaged wings left a trail of blood and feathers, but they were enough to allow Flight to guide him down.

Straight into the Primordial.

Poisonfire!

Wingblade!

Frost Spear!

All of his offensive Skills activated one after the other as he descended like a burning comet of virulent fire. The Primordial's strange body parted before his onslaught, burning and freezing and sliced open in turns, and Pit punched down into its heart. His huge size was finally an advantage as the bone and scale fought back, claws and splintered ribs tried to tear at him. Pain lanced across his shredded wings, and lines of blood and torn skin and fur decorated those parts of himself that were not armored, but the Master-Tier barding proved its worth. Javelins of immense strength hit and left deep gouges in the metal, but it held.

Rake!

Bite!

Rake is level 73!
Bite is level 70!
Poisonfire is level 72!

He tore deeper and deeper, digging for his goal while desiccating dust tried to wither his limbs and lungs. Pit's connection to Felix staved off the worst of its effects, but the flesh curse seeped into him regardless. He felt his breath shorten, even imagined he could feel his organs clenching in distress, but he didn't care. Instead, Pit summoned all of his Mana and Stamina into furious attacks, diving farther and spreading Poisonfire with every passing moment.

Pit! Felix sent along their bond. *Get outta there!*

The tenku ignored his friend. Felix meant well, but he was overly protective. Pit knew that sometimes he must fight, even when it was dangerous, even when it drove his Companion to fear.

He kept digging until he encountered the edge of the bronze sword and changed angles. *Deeper! Must go deeper!*

Bones shattered and dust swirled, all of it attempting to close against Pit like the nightmare throat of the Maw. Then he saw it: a pulsing, fleshy sac bigger than Pit's entire body, wingspan included. It was pierced directly by the immense bronze sword, pinning it to the tiled floor, almost rooted to it by veins of throbbing, scaled flesh.

The Primordial reacted by attacking him with everything it had. Tides of bone and snapping whips of dusty ligaments thrashed into Pit, bashing him into the ground before wrapping around his broken wings. Pit shrieked in agony as the ligaments tightened, pulling at the fine bones in his wings and ripping free feathers and flesh with clawed tendrils.

Wingblade!

Frost Spear!

Poisonfire!

The green, poisonous flames along Pit's body flared up, burning at the Primordial while ice and air exploded outward, over and over.

Wingblade is level 74!

Frost Spear is level 74!

The Primordial's assault wasn't stopped, or even paused much, but it severed at least a few of the restraining tendrils. Pit struggled forward, his vision flickering as his Health dropped lower and lower. The curse was settling into him, and he felt dry and dusted, each inhalation a throatful of glass shards. But he wouldn't stop.

With the quivering edge of his beak, he reached the Primordial's core. It throbbed grotesquely, and Pit took a single, final breath. *Felix...I'll save you.*

He jabbed his sharp beak forward, stabbing into the core and accessing his ignored notifications. Buzzing Dissonance tore from the fleshy core, while within him a vibrant, wild Harmony rose as if in opposition.

Your First Evolution Is Ready!
Do You Wish To Access It?
Y/N

Yes!

Congratulations!
You Have Accessed Your First Evolution!
Path Detected!
You Walk The Path Of The Guardian Beast!
Adjusting Evolution Choices...

Bone spurs and blade-edged ligament lashes stabbed and slashed at Pit, but the worst was the Mind-numbing Dissonance that blasted outward from the Primordial's core. Pit felt his blood dry up, his muscles tear, and Poisonfire die out. It was killing him, but he refused to stop. But as the notifications began to pile up, each brought with it a burst of Harmonic potency that cut through the Dissonance, layer by layer.

Choose One Of The Following!
Wardenwing Tenku
Savageclaw Tenku
Frostspire Tenku

———

Suddenly, Beef's head was clear. He dove aside, barely dodging the overhand strike from a glowing Golem, before fixing his eyes beyond his enemies. The Primordial had stopped swelling and clawing outward, and instead was folding against itself somehow. Something was happening, but he couldn't say what, only that the Primordial's Willpower had pulled back. It was more than enough for Beef, though.

"Hallow Rise!" Beef shouted, letting loose the majority of his Mana. Blackened green lines of vapor shot out of his channels and into the nearest Dustwights around him. Their grotesque faces slackened before the dark light within their corpses was forcefully replaced by Hallow's consciousness, and their eyes shone green. "Attack!"

Close as they were, Hallow could almost read Beef's Mind, but that was unnecessary. All of his available Risen—thirty of them now—rushed forward, flowing around the Golem and engaging instead with the Paladins just beyond his reach. Inscriptionists fell, blindsided by his undead horde.

"Seismic Shatter!" Beef bellowed, and the barest thread of his Mana and thick streamers of Stamina poured outward into a conical blast. Earth Mana rioted, the tiles beneath their feet shattering, launching upward and raising a cloud of obscuring dust. The Nightfall Golem charged right through it, unharmed, but when the sunset magic of its Body smashed into Beef's position...it hit nothing but bare ground.

"Ground Pound!"

Beef soared through the air, leaping fully clear of the Golem and brandishing his great maul. He landed, maul first, atop a Paladin. Armor screeched and tore, and the man didn't get up. Beef stood just outside the pitched battle between Risen and Paladins. The Golem was turning around, but while its attacks were lightning quick, its Body wasn't.

"Make a hole!" he shouted. The Risen jerked aside, puppets on strings, shoving the Paladins aside with brute Strength, and opened a pathway to the center of their operation. A many-sided box of golden light hovered in mid-air, surrounded by flickering sigils and filled with a swirling brilliance. Beef couldn't look directly at it, so he didn't.

God I hope this works!

He reached back and, with all of his mighty Strength, hurled his maul through the air.

———

Pit! Hold on!

Pain lanced upward from far below, and it was all Felix could do to contain his fear and rage. Pit was down there, in the twisting mass of Primordial, dying slowly by ten thousand cuts. He could see his Health dropping second by second, but Felix couldn't get away from Haim, let alone the sigaldry cage that restricted his movements.

"The Pathless wants you dead," Haim said through gritted teeth. Blood poured down the man's face, a fact that pleased Felix. Less pleasing was the glowing blade that hovered inches above Felix's throat, held at bay by Felix's oversized sword. They both hung in mid-air still, Felix atop his

Cloudstep and Haim hovering among the restrictive golden glyphs. "Glory be to God, for His wisdom is unending."

"Says I'm dangerous, huh?" Felix grunted, pushing back at the High Justiciar. The muscles in his arms were cramping, the fissures in his Body growing wider with each passing second. He had a crazy amount of Strength, but his damaged Journeyman Body wouldn't let him apply the full effect of his stats. Soon, he feared that even blocking Haim's sword-play would prove impossible. "Did, unf, did he mention why?"

"The Pathless does not answer to you, heretic," Haim said, before vocalizing another Skill. A rippling edge was applied to his sword, and Felix's blade began to rattle from its effect. "You must only obey and *perish.*"

Felix's Perception tingled, stabbing at his Mind with sudden warning. Beyond Haim's shoulder, he could see Beef and his Risen fighting the Inscriptionists. Felix smiled. "You aren't curious? I mean...you're retrieving Unbound." Felix shoved hard, forcing the Paladin back by an inch or two. "I'd have thought...you'd want to bring in two Unbound."

Haim flinched, his yellow eyes widening. "Two?" he gasped, just as the world was bathed in gold.

A cataclysmic explosion rocked the Tomb, releasing not fire or force, but a blastwave of violent light. Haim screamed, the golden light resonating painfully, and Felix surged forward.

Cloudstep!

Kicking off a new platform, Felix swung as hard as he could with his Fang. Haim was sent flying backward without resistance, his Body still convulsing with that writhing light, and Felix quickly dismissed his Cloud-step. He dropped.

Pit! he sent along their bond. *I'm coming!*

Adamant Discord!

Lightning flared all around Felix as he descended faster than he'd ever moved in his life. He shoved his Blade of the Fang downward, spinning it as he accelerated. He hit the hole Pit had made in the Primordial's Body, and he ripped through the half-healed opening.

"Get out of my way!" he screamed into the beast.

The connection between him and the Primordial was one of the strongest he'd ever utilized, turning from ephemeral to waist-thick steel cable in an eyeblink. Mana discharged from the spell along that tightening connection as he pulled, sending charring blasts of blue-white lightning outward into the abomination's bone-flesh. The wild cacophony of Harmony of the outside world faded, replaced by the overwhelming noise of Dissonance as he drilled deeper. Bits of the Primordial fought back, but Felix imbued the Blade with Corrosive Strike. Where the lightning of Adamant Discord or his Strength failed, the acidic Skill sliced through weakened bone.

Then he was through.

Felix landed atop bare ground in an expanding ring of crackling lightning and riotous thunder. He scanned the area, quickly finding his friend. Pit was bound to the ground, wrapped in tendrils of leathery flesh and a cage of bone that was trying and failing to enclose him entirely. Most surprising, however, was the constant wave of System harmonics that was blasting from Pit's core, disrupting the Dissonance all around them.

He quickly attempted to pull his friend back into his Spirit, but the Convergence failed. Something was blocking it. Felix rushed to Pit's side, pushing his senses toward his friend and gathering the bare edge of the circumstances. Interference. The Primordial's core was just inches away, and Pit's attempts to Evolve...Felix swallowed, panicking for a moment before ripping a section of bone cage away from his friend. He placed his hands on his bloody back and focused.

Convergence!

The resistance was there, but with physical touch, it was easier to brute force. Pit vanished in a flash of light. The cage of bone and ligaments collapsed down, but soon moved to cover the Primordial's throbbing core instead.

Pit! he sent, but all he received in return were a strained series of chirps and trilling growls. His friend's Health was still dropping for some reason, and the struggles were becoming weaker and weaker. Notifications blipped and vanished before Felix's eyes, snippets of what Pit was seeing.

WARNING!
Primordial Detected!
Primordial Of Withering Dust Has Interrupted—

—ERROR, Evolution Interrupted By Primordial Being!
Choice Cannot Be Verified!

Shit, no. Felix's Mind raced, trying to come up with a solution. He'd been told Pit was likely on the cusp of his Evolution, but to happen now? *I have to destroy this thing's core.*

Felix stowed his giant sword and grasped the layers of bone that had crawled atop the throbbing core. With a grunt of exertion, he tore them off, piece by piece, only to have them regrow. Javelins of ribs and bindings of leathery flesh tried to jab at him, restrain his movements and kill him, but Felix hunkered low, taking blow after blow to his wide back as he focused. He went faster, cracking bone and tearing open his fingers, until the barest hint of core flesh was visible. Felix dug his fingers into the unpleasantly spongy surface, and activated his Chthonic Tribute.

Chthonic Tribute Failed.

What? Felix bared his teeth in frustration. A jagged femur jabbed him in the leg, shattering against his Armored Skin, but followed by dozens of others. *Don't do this to me! Eat the damn thing! Chthonic Tribute!*

Chthonic Tribute Failed.

His Hunger fought against him, railing at the idea of absorbing *anything* else. **CANNOT TAKE. WILL NOT.**

"You stupid—! What good are you, then?!" Felix raged. He could feel the potency of the Primordial all around him, but most of all beneath his bloody fingertips. It was far greater than the Ravager King ever was, closer to the might of the Whalemaw. Only, the Will behind the Primordial of Withering Dust was chaotic and incoherent. Felix could even feel an echo of those words it had sent to him, reverberating through the wild mess of its disgusting Body.

THE MADNESS MUST END.

I CANNOT CONTROL THE CURSE, BUT YOU CAN TERMINATE IT.

Understanding flashed through Felix like a bolt of lightning.

The flesh curse isn't letting it die, he realized. It was keeping its Body alive, viable, despite being trapped here for Ages and for wanting nothing so much as death. *But...isn't the flesh curse part of its nature? All Primordials have it, according to everyone I've spoken to. Unite the Lost might do it, but it'd drain every ounce of significance I have to do it. And that...would that kill me? Or just fuck me up real bad?*

Within the Dissonance that buzzed against his Affinity, and that resonance of its sane Will among the insanity of the flesh curse, Felix saw something else. No more than a glimmer, but with his hand atop the Primordial's core, he could trace it. Deep, deep down, he felt a familiar sort of energy. Felix's Mind leaped, darting between ideas with reckless abandon, forming a shaky hypothesis that burned brighter the longer he considered it.

That can't be right. Can it? Felix grimaced, the Primordial's attacks against him now drawing blood. *Only one way to find out.*

Manasight.

Felix screamed as his eyes burned, literally catching into blue flame as he perceived the sea of chaotic, unfathomable energies all around him. Dissonance and Harmony waged war against one another, clashing and smashing in an outsized display that reminded him of his own dual cores. In the breach, multi-colored glyphs danced among them all, ever-changing in shape and texture. Patterns folded and unfolded as images seared themselves into his eyes.

A piece of the Divine. A Primordial's corpse. Their cloaks were tossed aside, and though it was barely a fragment of their true potency, reality itself was buckling under the pressure.

Felix's eyesight burned away, blackness consuming his vision. But Manasight never relied on his eyes, despite its name. He could smell the colors of Mana, of chaos, hear the stink of rotting death and pungent floral decay of brilliant light.

The connection was there, hidden among the confluence of opposing forces, all but invisible. A blazing cable the size of continents, drawn taut between the Primordial of Withering Dust and the far distant sky. A similarity he could not deny, and a pattern that repeated itself into infinity, echoed all around them by the now-faded golden sigaldry.

A piece of the Primordial, the fragment that animated its undead Body, echoed the strains of the Regalia itself. A dire shard of the Divine, buried deep within the Primordial's being.

The flesh curse is Divine, Felix realized. *That's how the Pathless was going to absorb its power. And it's how I neutralized the curse, too...because I have a fragment of the Divine in me.*

Yet with that realization came a sudden and overwhelming terror. Sound vanished, and his vision was miraculously restored, the darkness replaced by a burned and blackened sky holding all six moons. Monstrous figures strode the heavens, chained to it by incomprehensible formations that boiled the stars. All at once, their vast gazes turned downward.

To him.

CHAPTER NINETY-FOUR

The charred earth and sky tried to crush everything that was Felix into paste, driving him to his knees and bursting blood vessels across his Body. Nightmarish figures stood in the heavens, a moon among their tangle of limbs and joints. An aura of dark power hung around them all, restrained by its unseen chains but mighty regardless. Yet Felix's Will was not so easily dominated.

Title: Born of Will is active!
You Are Your Own Maker!
Title: The Call of Defiance is active!
+25% Willpower Against The Divine!

Beneath the collective glare of the gods, even he could not force himself to his feet...but that did not mean he couldn't give them a dour stare right back.

"You should not be here, child," said a calm voice. It sounded as if it was whispered into his ear, but it radiated from the sky like a proclamation. A silver moon shimmered and burned in the dark Void. As he stared, it flickered, turning from a moon to a vast and endless bundle of woven threads. A spider at the center of its web. "You should not have seen this."

"He should not *exist*," scoffed a second voice, this one a harsh, guttural hiss. He could smell a fetid stench from its breath, for all that it spoke to him across an endless horizon. A bronze moon hung low, pock-marked and wan and...not a moon at all, but an infinite bog of boiling foulness and withered plants. "A Primordial Unbound is not allowed!"

"Primordial, Nym, *and* a touch of the Divine," chortled a deeper voice. It sounded like nothing so much as a kindly old man...and it came from nowhere at all. No moon shuddered in his strained Affinity, and there was no figurative, godly hallucination.

Who, then? Felix wondered, his Mind beginning to fray under the pressure these beings exerted. His limbs trembled, but he maintained eye contact with the barely visible figures.

"Quiet, troublemaker," said another voice. Two voices, actually, low and high overlaid atop one another while chains the size of planets rattled. "The Remnant desires this one's death."

"The Remnant can go rot." A dark moon filled with swirling darkness manifested between the others. It was hidden and then not, phasing through existence like a ghost, and at its heart hovered a blood-red crescent that was all too familiar. The voice that accompanied the ghostly moon was hard and sharp, a bared blade. "This time, at least, the Coward has the right of it. This *thing* should not be allowed to live."

"Hold thyself, Noctis!" said twin voices, pitched in fury.

Violence cascaded across the vault of cold stars, and the shape of nightmares unravelled and stretched toward him. The blackened sky writhed at the approach of endless shadow, and the blasted earth churned and ripped apart. All of everything pressed in upon him, a vice forged of reality itself to make his head and heart pop like overripe fruit.

"No no no," Felix gasped. "Not doing this!"

He had stuck his head into a hornet's nest, and he could sure as shit pull it back out again. As a *god's* Willpower neared him, he desperately engaged his own and tried to slip back. His Mind shook, and his Spirit quaked as Noctis' frigid Will bore closer, but he could feel the trick of it, the twist of Affinity that drew him into that blasted landscape. He grasped it and *heaved* backward.

Title: Voidwalker is active!
+10% Willpower And Alacrity!

The unreality of the strange, god-nightmare vanished into mercurial darkness as Felix's Willpower swelled once again under his active Titles. Felix lost his sight, but the tendrils of wild Mana still danced all around him, within him, and his fingers flexed atop the fleshy surface of the Primordial core.

"Thief!" A soul-shaking cry followed him back into the darkness, spiking into his *everything* and slamming Felix to the ground. Yet that was all it did, as he felt the claws of a foreign Will scrabble at his own...and achieve nothing. "Thief!"

The voice faded just as Voidwalker, Born of Will, and The Call of Defiance deactivated. His Willpower reduced, and a deep, abiding ache settled into his Mind and already ragged Body. He was back, blind as before, and sprawled next to the throbbing heart of an undead Primordial. In spite of his pain, his blindness, and the increasing certainty that his Body was going to fail him, Felix still rode the sharpened edge of revelation.

They were surprised. 'You should not have seen this,' they said. Felix gripped his skull with his hands, feeling the Primordial resume its deadly attacks against him and could only hunch against the onslaught. *I saw the curse. I saw the curse and saw* them. Ideas whirled through his Adept Mind, formed and discarded in the same breath, replaced by two, four, eight more. *If the flesh curse is Divine, then it's foreign to the Primordial. I can* fix *that.*

He just hoped he had the significance to spare.

The Primordial of Withering Dust seemed to glean his Intent, however, and the attacks strengthened by an order of magnitude. A porcupine of jagged ribs and broken vertebrae stabbed inward at him, closing on the strange, empty space around them like a hundred disassembled jaws.

Relentless Resolution!

He moved, flowing between sharpened bone and serrated ligaments. Felix forced himself forward, but received savage wounds to his forearms as he tried to approach the core again. Each movement he made was countered and reacted to, every conscious decision preempted and defended against. *It can sense my Intent!* he realized, ducking below the razor edge of a foot-thick femur. He grabbed at his skull again, feeling like the thing was tearing apart. *If it can read my Mind, then I can't think!*

Felix flared the Skill again, sounding its pattern with Affinity and shaping the thrust of its effects with a weary Intent. He tried with all of his might to empty his Mind, to keep his Intent as innocuous as possible, but the Primordial preempted every movement he made. A dash and strike met by an impenetrable wall of human-sized teeth, an overhand chop of his Blade of the Fang split the wall only to have shoulder blades the size of wagons fall in his way.

So he shut off his Manasight. True darkness fell, and the Primordial attacked.

Relentless Resolution!

He stopped thinking, refusing to get lost in plans of attack and defense —he simply reacted, letting the Skill sing of its own accord. How close was he to the core? He hadn't a clue, but he refused to dwell on it. Each step led to another, and another, all while weaving a net of defense with his greatsword. His Mind ratcheted into higher gear, the ache and heat of his thoughts redoubling as they diverted toward a far more dire problem.

Fiendforge!

Never forgotten, Pit's struggles ceased as Felix gripped the Chimera's Evolving core with the pincers of his power. He pressed, holding the shifting, morphing shape of his core in abeyance for a time. It would not last long, but Felix was done playing. Felix's friend was in danger, Pit's core already cracking under the strain of its aborted Evolution. *Hold on, Pit!*

Jolting to a stop, Felix became aware that he'd fallen. Pain lanced across his shins and hips, the latter pierced by rotating claws in the shifting environment...but he'd fallen atop an orb of bone. The Primordial's core.

Corrosive Strike!

Felix put his fist through the gruesome shield, striking four times in rapid succession before he was able to thrust his hand onto the pulpy flesh of its true core. He gripped it, feeling waves of Dissonance that came off it like a tsunami...as well as the stinging burn of the flesh curse. It tried, and failed, to latch onto Felix, but he paid it no mind. Pit was failing, and his Body wasn't going to last much longer. *I hope I'm right!*

His potent Willpower rushed from his channels along with what Essence he could spare. The core flashed in his hampered senses, a bright, impossibly dense construction packed with Essence and enough signifi-cance to drown a city. Focused as he was, he could feel more than ever before—*know* more. Flesh was clay, an element to be molded and shaped into what nature demanded of it. It was complex, even labyrinthine in design, but the interplay of vessels, muscles, and fatty deposits flickered across Felix's understanding. Flesh was clay.

And he was the sculptor. The Sovereign. Of his...and all others.

Sovereign of Flesh!

Title: The Call of Defiance is active!
+25% Willpower Against The Divine!

He Chanted, sounding his Skill and shaping its form before backing it all up with the might of his Willpower. It ran on Essence, however, and he had precious little from his attempts at feeding...so he seized the Essence Motes that dangled within his Divine Tree. Each brilliant Mote of light was packed to the brim with Essence, honed with Features that he could use to Temper. To lose them would put his advancement in jeopardy, and Felix's heart clenched as he sacrificed them anyway.

WARNING!
The Primordial Of Withering Dust Defies You!
You Are Entering A Battle Of Wills!

Bring it on. The scattered sea of the Primordial's consciousness focused, slowly drawing together into a force that made Felix clench his teeth to keep them from clattering. *Oh. Oh, that's not good.*

He bore down on his Skill, pushing deeper and deeper into the Primordial's heart. Mapping it, seeking the crevices and fissures that riddled all flesh whether you were mortal or Divine. Dissonance tore at him, interrupting his progress and becoming increasingly vicious as the Primordial gathered itself, but Felix opened himself up to the song that rang in his own heart.

Harmony and Dissonance gathered together into something new. The song of it, his song, pressed back the interference even as it resonated deeply with his [Cardinal Beast Core]. A dire caterwauling tore from that resonance, of a creature overcome and *furious* about it—yet Felix ignored his Hunger. That dark passenger was not important, not now. *You had your chance to help!*

Above his cores, the Divine Tree rustled. Each Mote lost from its branches seemed to drive it to greater disruptions, until the vein-like branches were trembling violently. They grasped at nothing, at everything, and the entirety of the Tree rang with a faint music that whispered across his core space. His Hunger thrashed below while his dual cores spun with greater and greater ferocity. Yet all of that could not command Felix's attention, because the flesh curse went from homicidal to frenzied rage.

Bone and scale and ligaments collapsed against him in a tide of jagged edges and restraining bands, pulling at him, trying to force Felix to lose contact with the Primordial's core. He grunted and dug in, shoving a second hand into the breach and grasping a fistful of pulpy gristle, even as a wave of revelation assaulted him. Abruptly, bone and scale and sinew all turned aside, unable to touch Felix's form let alone pierce him. Essence Motes burned, fueling his Sovereignty, and he saw it bundled in a cage of bone and shimmering, multi-hued Mana.

The origin of the flesh curse, the seed that formed the roots of the Primordial's withering undeath.

His Divine Tree shook, its song growing more insistent as Felix grasped at the bone cage. His hands burned, skin and tendons dissolving as he handled the vile thing, but the Tree within his core rang out. Cords of blue-white and red-gold light unravelled from Felix's palms before snapping tight around the cage. Willpower trembling, pushed to the edge of what he could endure, Felix reached out with his Fiendforge and clamped it tight around his cords of light.

"This is *mine!*" he declared, and his Sovereignty stood over the Primordial's heart, demanding fealty. The cage flickered and shone, trembling along with his Divine Tree, but it was under his sway. His Will. "All of it is mine."

So Felix ripped it apart.

———

The whirlwind of obliterating grime tore at him, shredding his battlerobes, and Atar was nearly thrown from his feet. Instead, he fetched up against the piling ash and bones of those who fell before him. He gasped, once, his mouth filling with soot and dust. At his feet, where the flask had shattered, his boots withered and broke apart.

The curse!

Atar kicked off his boots, shoving his feet into the burning ash with a strangled cry—but it wasn't enough. The curse had already seeped into the flesh of his heels, and veins of its dark influence crept steadily up his calf muscles. The pain was far worse than the burn of the ash and metal basin. Wherever it traveled, his skin and muscle and even his clothing withered away. His trousers unraveled, their color bleached by the curse's touch, all of it turning to stiff, crumbling dust.

ATAR.

All at once, the pain stopped, as did the horrific winds and creeping pestilence. Atar hung above the basin in a bubble of quiet, lifted bodily by flaring tendrils of pure, unadulterated flame.

I SHALL CLEANSE YOU, PACTBEARER. DESPITE YOUR TREACHERY.

Those tendrils of flame delved into him, stopping his breath and scorching his channels as they went. An awful, somehow healing pain seeped through his Body, coiling around his burning core before pushing deeper. An intense smoldering ripped at his legs, and Atar's legs below the knee caught flame. Dark corruption hissed and steamed, attempting to push beyond the delving fire, but at each turn, it was burned away. All at once, the pain vanished.

Atar gasped, lungs unlocked. He took in huge, greedy mouthfuls of air before hacking it back up. Spit-wet dust flung from his lips, and Atar glared at the plume of flame before him. The pain had vanished, but the fiery tendrils had remained within his channels, lurking as the curse tried again and again to spread. Instead, it was burned away...but never completely.

"You can't eradicate the curse?" he asked. He was still held aloft by the Urge's power, but Atar saw no reason to be polite. "Cleansing suggests you remove it completely."

The Flame twisted. Only a small piece of it stood outside the whirling maelstrom of the duststorm, and it flickered repeatedly. As if it were on the edge of extinguishing. **THE FLESH CURSE OF A PRIMORDIAL IS NO SIMPLE THING...AND YOU BROUGHT IT TO ME, ATAR. A FOOLISH CHOICE.**

"You're killing people! Did you think there weren't going to be consequences for that?" Atar demanded.

DEATH IS BUT A FACET OF LIFE. THE WEAK PERISH TO PRESERVE THE STRENGTH OF THE MIGHTY. BUT YOU HAVE BROUGHT TO ME AN ABOMINATION OF CREATION. A CURSE THAT I CANNOT END. NOT AS I AM. I NEED YOUR AID, ATAR V'AS.

Atar squinted at the Flame. "No." The flame shuddered backward, as if surprised. Atar said it again, more forcefully. "**No.**"

The tendrils within Atar's channels flared to an excruciating degree, searing him from the inside. Atar screamed.

THE STORM CANNOT BE BORNE! THAT WHICH WAS SHACKLED MUST REMAIN! YOUR ALLIES DIE EVEN AS WE SPEAK! I AM TRYING TO AID YOU!

"You're simply trying to survive," Atar gasped. "And if you do, those people will die anyway, right?"

The storm around them howled, and lightning sheathed them in a blinding shell of yellow radiance. The Flame flickered, thinning and thickening in a gale Atar couldn't feel. What he could feel, however, was when the tendrils of power pushed inward. Into his core space.

"What are you doing?" Atar demanded, and doubled over as the tendrils stabbed into the liquid fire of his core ring. Atar convulsed, the orange fire flaring until it dominated his core space. Skills flickered, their altars creaking from the force of it all, while indescribable agony lanced through Atar's being. He opened his mouth, but neither breath nor scream could escape.

THE STORM WILL RAGE, AND THE BEAST BELOW WILL AWAKEN. RIGHT NOW, THE TERROR OF HUNGER CLAWS AT ITS CAGE! THE BEAST BELOW! THEIR DIRE CHOICE HAS ALREADY BEEN MADE, AND OUR ONLY CHANCE FOR SURVIVAL IS TO WORK TOGETHER.

Atar could see nothing but dust and fire, hear nothing but the crooning voice of the Urge. His Skills frayed, their altars and flames guttering beneath the Urge's potency.

SAVE ME! SAVE ME, SO THAT THE LIGHT OF THE SKY NEVER FAILS. FOR IF IT DOES, THEN RUIN WILL BESET US ALL.

"H—how...?" Atar forced the words through shallow breaths and a cracked and bleeding throat.

IT WAS WRITTEN, IN AGES LOST TO TIME AND MEMORY. A TRUTH I GLIMPSED IN THE VAST FIRMAMENT. THE BEAST BELOW, THE TERROR, THEY SEEK TO TWIST THE FABRIC OF WHAT IS, ATAR. TO TURN ASIDE THE LIGHT OF THE SKY. ME.

IT WILL NOT HAPPEN. JOIN ME AS YOU MUST, FOR OTHERWISE, ALL IS DOOMED.

The grip of fire on his core lessened slightly. Enough to give Atar the space to breathe. The Flame waited, watching him.

"I cannot accept what you have done," Atar said.

IN THE NAME OF SURVIVAL, WE ALL DO AS WE MUST.

"No. No, you don't get to use that excuse," Atar hissed. He shook his head and lifted a trembling arm up, placing his hand just above his navel. He could feel the excruciating heat even through his flesh. "You don't get to decide who lives and who dies, Urge!"

YOU FORGET WHO GAVE YOU YOUR BLESSINGS, CHILD. WITHOUT ME, YOU WOULD NOT BE.

"Maybe, and without people like me, you'd have guttered out. No. No, I'm done here. In the words of a friend," he said, clutching at his belly. "Fuck off."

You Have Rejected The Blessings Of The Highest Flame! WARNING!

Skills Tied To the Highest Flame Will Be Sundered And Lost!
You Cannot Undo This Choice!
Continue?
Y/N

STOP! STOP, YOU FOOLISH CHILD!

"Yes! Cut Her off!" Atar spat, just as the Urge pulsed its wicked tendrils. Fire burst and surged within him, an inferno under his skin, and his voice turned to wordless torment. A scream that felt like it was tearing his lungs apart.

THE SKY MUST NOT TARNISH! IT MUST NOT!

"Shut! Up!" Atar howled.

The pain mounted as Atar's core space began to founder. Altars of flame—Skills—began to sputter and fail while orange sigaldry broke apart. The ring of flame flared one last time, spreading outward in a destructive explosion before collapsing inward.

CHAPTER NINETY-FIVE

The last Paladin inscriptionist crashed to the ground, their head nothing more than a mashed mess. A few feet away, the Primordial's nasty bones shook and pulsed, but Beef refused to look at it—the horror made him nauseated. He straightened up and rested his maul against his shoulder with a grunt. The thing was riddled with cracks, each one leaking bright lights of blackened-green light, but he could fix it. He pulled out a Mana Potion and quaffed it in one go.

"Michael! The Golems and Wraiths are coming again," Hallow announced over the increasing din. Only sixteen Risen remained, all of them the stronger Paladins, but they could not hold back all of their enemies. The Nightfall Golems and Dustborn Wraiths weren't working together, but they all wanted to rip Beef and his Risen to pieces, and that amounted to the same thing. "I cannot hold them for more than three seconds."

Chitin Construction!

One Mississippi...

His Mana mobilized, surging from his channels to forge a new set of armor around his chest and limbs. It resembled the spiked body of a large beetle, but it was stronger with every level under his belt, and the Skill had gained five in the last fifteen minutes.

Two Mississippi...

He also reforged his maul, lengthening and enlarging the spiked head until it was comically huge. He grunted and took it in two hands, the heavy weapon dropping to his waist in order for Beef to stabilize it. The glimmering, sunset-colored Golems tore through the Risen from one end, while from the other came the steel-clawed and bone-plated Wraiths. There was no screaming or shouting, only silent, eerie death.

"Hallow!" The last of the Risen, struggling to stand, went immediately stiff before collapsing. The light in their eyes snuffed out before being rekindled within Beef's chest. Blackened-green power surged around his core, igniting the room within his heart and forcing Beef to shield his inner awareness.

The enemies charged at Beef, blades and claws outstretched, and he hunched himself, feeling his muscles bulge and tighten like coiled springs.

Three Mississippi...

"Circle of Smash!" he bellowed, and unleashed a cyclonic blow.

Beef's muscles exploded into action, accelerating him from motionless to an insanely fast spin, maul fully extended. The jagged head of the weapon hit a Wraith first, fully and completely tearing them in half before continuing onward. Wraith after Wraith were less impediment than the wind itself, and power gathered behind the attack as it sped along—until it struck a Nightfall Golem, caving in its chest and knocking the magic robot onto its glowing ass.

"Hell yeah!" he shouted, before noticing that every Wraith was reassembling themselves. And the Golem simply climbed back to its feet, damaged but undeterred. "Balls."

"RAAAAAAAAAAARH!"

Without warning, every single Wraith convulsed and began to scream. Their long, iron claws tore at their bodies and faces, scoring the bone plates and shredding withered flesh. Beef gawked, unable to figure out what was happening. The Golems, both the one he'd smashed and the two behind it, halted mid-stride as their attention was turned to Beef's right...where the sea of undulating bones had gone utterly still.

"Hallow, what is go—"

Michael! Watch out!

The storm above them dropped, far faster than it had moved previously, just as a wave of obliterating force hit them all. Wraiths and Golems were ripped off their feet, and Beef was no better. He tumbled through the air, glass and lightning blasting in all directions, accosting his body with a sudden, scorching heat. Black and brown clouds ripped outward, streaked with brilliant rainbow lights as twenty-foot long bone shards shattered through his armor and shaggy fur. Blood burst from countless wounds, until he smashed back toward the razor-sharp protrusions of crystal.

Michael!

A sheath of blackened green energy swept outward from his core and covered his Body for a single, brief moment—long enough to weather an impact that would have snapped his spine. Instead, the crystal cracked and broke, falling with him into the tiled edge of the chamber.

Be safe, Michael. The sheath winked out, and so did the presence in his chest.

"Hallow!" he screamed. Until a Golem smashed right into his face.

Felix stood among nothingness and an all-encompassing light.

He blinked in confusion. Music soared around him, filling up every available space like cotton pressed against him. Harmony was a strident, triumphant crescendo that lapped through the thickened air...while Dissonance was an opposing burr, a jagged, atonal scouring that ripped the legs out of any note that tried to rise too high. It was a violent interplay, one that was echoed by the vast emptiness and cloying brilliance that yawned around and through Felix.

Ugh, that's...that feels awful, he muttered. The sound was both heard and swallowed up entirely by the forces around him. It was a confusing experience, but a chord of familiarity stretched taut through it all. It wasn't like the Divine pocket he'd wandered into, nor was it like the Void in any meaningful way. Instead, it felt like floating underwater, except he was buoyed by sound instead of liquid. *That noise. It's just like my core space.*

With a rush of clarity, the fighting of Harmony and Dissonance took on the patterns and cadences of his dual cores, ones that constantly ground against one another to produce a strange, chimeric child of the Grand Harmony. A tapestry of sound that was neither the System nor the harshness that Primordials exuded from their very pores. *It's all meshed, badly, but still. Pieces of pieces, fragments of a great whole—The Primordial! The curse!*

Sovereign of Flesh!

The Skill was already active, was in fact overclocked to the point that his core space screamed with the effort of maintaining it. Felix hovered among the warring pieces of the Primordial as he tore it apart, a bubble of power that fought against his control.

With that realization came the knowledge that his Body, only dimly felt, was failing dramatically. His Health fell like a rock, his Stamina was barely kept afloat by his regeneration, and his store of Essence was a fingernail away from obliteration. The vast sea of power was eating away at him as it disassembled and shoved through his core space, a torrent of potency that ran through him like a filter. Clouds of Essence and Mana were pulled into his channels and back out again, not a piece of them remaining behind, and he focused. If he could harvest even a piece, it would go a long way toward healing himself.

Chthonic Tribu—!

The activation twisted, halting mid-word like his airway had been constricted. The Hunger within him could not be overcome or gainsaid. It would take no more.

Why? he railed against the dark abyss. *I need it! We're going to die!*

From within him, Felix heard a guttural, almost unintelligible snarl. *Too weak. Body flawed. No. More.*

Then obstinate silence within the chaos all around him. The cacophony of light and Essence buffeted him, a storm that spread through him, pressed and strained against the resonating branches of his Divine Tree. The Primordial's Essence entered Felix, stained by the Divine, and when it emerged from his beleaguered channels, it was rendered pure. The curse itself was catching among the branches of his Tree, skimmed from the Essence like dead bugs from the top of a swimming pool.

His Fiendforge trembled, his grip on the Primordial's heart and Pit's cracking core tenuous at best. He still held tight to the flesh curse, which he dimly realized was why the Primordial's Essence was being shoved through Felix's core space at all. Sovereign of Flesh commanded with all the force of his Willpower, and its curse obeyed.

How long have I been doing this?

Time felt immaterial within the hovering, chaotic space. Was he frozen, or was his Mind whirling so fast that a single moment stretched into a thousand? The Primordial's potency raged through him faster and faster, but it felt endless. Eternal. Like a trap he'd sprung on himself. Deep inside, a piece of his core space shook, and Felix gasped.

My Bastion....?

The cords of light, of connection, that gathered in his Bastion were thrumming and twitching wildly. One in particular sang out, a shearing sound of distress as it snapped taut, like a cable nearing its breaking point.

Atar. He knew it without conscious thought or reason. *He's in trouble. Hurt.* Felix couldn't tell which, only that their connection was pulling so hard that threads of luminous light snapped and frayed. A tiny echo of Atar was feeding back into Felix, enough that he felt the mage was grasping for something. Anything. He was falling apart...and it took very little guesswork to know why that might be. *The Urge is...dying? Or is that Atar?*

Felix did the only thing he could in that moment. He grasped the echo of Atar's need, his plea for help, and shifted his Will to seize a portion of the howling, useless Essence thundering through him. Then he shoved it into their connection.

Attempting To Establish Sympathetic Link...
Tier III Link Already Established.
Essence Redirection Allowed.

The weight all around Felix shifted, and it was like a mountain lifting off his shoulders by the barest of margins. Essence and more—significance—began to flow from Felix's stolen store into the connection with Atar. Pit groaned in clear relief, the weight of it all lightening on him as well. The cord swelled, changing slowly from silver to a bright, almost blinding white, edged in bloody crimson, and Felix grinned.

Tier III Link Advanced To Tier IV!

The connection, the Link, was remade. That white-crimson light raced down its entire length, up and out of his core space, to the mage himself. Yet around him, the chaos still raged. *Pit?*

Yes. Give it to me, the tenku agreed. *I can handle it.*

The brilliant, blue-gold and black-crimson Link between them slipped into the foreground and Felix repeated the process. Essence and significance was pulled just as it left the purifying branches of his Divine Tree, and filtered down into their bond. Into Pit directly.

A shriek of pain and fury tore from his Companion's throat, but Felix couldn't let up even if he tried. The process all but tore from his control the moment Pit accepted it.

Attempting To Establish Sympathetic Link...
Tier X Link Already Established.
Greater Essence Redirection Allowed.

The weight shifted yet again, and this time, the chaos quieted. Felix did not stop, either. He snagged the Links that shone brightest from his Bastion, the threads of connection that had only grown larger with his months upon the Continent. And one that was still quite new. *Vess. Evie. Harn. Beef.* He held them up in the palm of his Will, and he asked a single question.

Do you accept this power?

The whisper of it sped down their Links like ghosts of his voice, moving faster than lightning...and returned to him just as quickly. The answer, unanimous.

Yes!

Felix gathered himself and reached, clutching all that purified power to himself, and hurled it into their vivid Links.

Attempting To Establish Sympathetic Links...
Tier III Links Already Established.
Essence Redirection Allowed.

Tier III Link Advanced To Tier IV!

Four cords, each a brilliant silver, were remade. The concentrated power of a Primordial thundered through them, racing toward his friends and transmuting their Links to a myriad of colors. He felt them all stiffen and scream, their own trials seizing their cores, but it was only a small portion of the Primordial's might. Still, it quieted the writhing maelstrom around him, though it left so much more for Felix to deal with himself. But that was fine—he had plans for the rest.

Fiendforge!

Once more, Felix split his attention. He held Pit's cracking core in one hand, and the wild energies of the disassembling Primordial in the other. With a third, shaking grip, Felix took hold of his *own* cores.

Here goes nothing. With the cleaver of his Intent, he split the conflicting, intermingling Essence and significance in half, diverting one portion to Pit...and the other to himself. His Companion's screams intensified, and Felix hesitated.

No! I can do this! Pit insisted. *I can protect you!*

Felix was forced to accept that, because the rest of the Primordial's potency slammed through his Divine Tree and into his dual cores directly. Pressure and pain assaulted him, unlike anything he had felt since the Ravager King...and so much worse. Essence roared as it burned away, absorbed by the churning spin of his dual cores.

It would have been so much easier if he'd been able to feed some of it to his Hunger, but it was an impenetrable door. Instead, he forced it all into his cores, all the gargantuan flows of the Primordial. And just like with the Ravager King, Felix rotated his cores, spinning the rings of gel-like fire in opposing directions. The Essence and significance slammed down, growing his cores at a visible rate while Felix gritted his teeth so hard he felt a tooth crack. Spinning them was hard before, but now with his Mind and Spirit split in so many directions, it was torture to maintain it all. But Felix had no choice; it was this or be consumed by the sheer ferocity of it all.

Almost...there! The moment arcing prominences started flaring off of his two cores, Felix split his Will *again*. He felt all the balls he had in the air quiver and almost topple, Fiendforge and Sovereign of Flesh and Relentless Resolution all burning bright, a hair's breadth from failing. He screamed, grappling with the flaring tendrils of power from his cores—two from each—and hurled them out into the black of his core space.

Directly into two Skills. Sovereign of Flesh and Relentless Resolution.

They were both on the cusp, driven there by revelations and a sudden understanding...he could feel them about to advance, and with the right juice—

Sovereign of Flesh is level 75!
...
Sovereign of Flesh is level 78!
Adept Tier!

Relentless Resolution is level 75!
...
Relentless Resolution is level 77!
Adept Tier!

You Gain—
You Gain—

YES! he cried, just as Pit mimicked his triumph with a screech of righteous joy. Felix's overheating Mind sensed the tenku's power pulled inward, the opposite of Felix's process, until it condensed into a bright ball of victorious, furious melody.

Congratulations!
You Have Accessed Your First—ERROR—Second/////
ERROR
Recalculating...
First Evolution Accessed!
Path Detected!
You Walk The Path Of The Guardian Beast!
Primordial Influence Detected!
Adjusting Evolution Choices...

Felix's dual cores erupted in energy, burning up into his core space like a revivifying torch. Red-gold flame and blue-white lightning chewed up the Primordial's stolen flesh and spat it out as power, rotating it and pulling it inward to strengthen him. Claimed, it flared up once, twice, then exploded outward in a shockwave of wild force.

———

Rahven Haim climbed to his feet and pressed an ungauntleted hand against his side. His armor had been ruined by the horrendous power of the dust storm, ground down to almost nothing in places and his cloak hung in tatters from his shoulders. The faintest of glows still clung to him, proof of his God's continual blessing...but the ritual had failed. *He* had failed.

Haim stared around him, uncomprehending. No one moved at all upon the battlefield, for the storm had done its work too well. He had failed, and his elite cadre of Paladins were dead to a man. None could have survived the onslaught of undead and insane heretics, and then the sheer insanity of the dead Primordial striking out against them all.

The indignity of it was almost too much to bear.

Someone moved in the distance, and Haim narrowed his yellow eyes. His Perception was excellent, even for a Master Tier, and he picked out a familiar, long-limbed shape among the swirling dust and dispersing clouds of crackling Mana. *Felix Nevarre.*

His god had spoken to him. To him! For the first time in his long career, he had heard the direct voice of the Pathless, and it had been as glorious as he had been promised. A voice like summer sun had caressed his Mind and Spirit as He had imparted a great duty upon Haim's shoulders: Felix Nevarre, this Unbound, must die.

Rahven Haim, High Justiciar of the Paladins of the Pathless was not a man who took oaths lightly. Yet he swore an Oath to kill the bastard

Autarch without a single regret. *I will do as you Will, Pathless. I will not fail you.*

"Diurnal Lance!" he called out, and a spear of pure light Mana screamed across the intervening distance. It struck like lightning, faster than even his eyes could track, and hit the Autarch square in his chest.

Felix Nevarre gasped and took a single step back, his clothing consumed in a ball of lightborn flame...yet he stood, hand to now-bare chest. Unharmed.

What? That Skill has taken down other Masters! What did he do?

The man noticed Haim, finally, and stepped forward through the burning clouds of dissipating Mana. His legs trembled, and blood dripped from his nose and hands. "I'm really getting sick of you," he muttered.

"Diurnal Lance!" Haim hurled a second spear of light at the man, this one packed with as much extra Mana as he could manage.

Felix batted it out of the air, still walking forward. "Stop that."

To his shame, Haim took a single, fearful step backward. "Monster. You're...you're a calamity. Unbound. We were told to bring your kind in, that to do so was the will of the Divine. But I will tell you this: the Pathless hates you. He has called for your destruction, Beast. Crucible of the Just!"

This time, Haim pulsed one of his greatest Skills. A column of solid light manifested above their heads, a gallows axe shaped like the armored gauntlet of his order. Looping, Divine script covered it, imbuing it with a holy power that nothing short of a Grandmaster could survive. Its radius was such that Haim was going to be caught in it, but he no longer cared.

A breathless laugh bubbled up from the Unbound, and Haim curled his lip in disbelief and disgust. *He's gone mad from fear.* "We die together then, Beast."

"Beast? Nah," Felix panted. His legs had stopped trembling. "I'm just...some guy."

Haim threw his hand down, letting the Crucible drop. At the same time, a chaotic burst of swirling lights erupted from the Unbound's form, and a horror ripped free of its embrace. Directly into Haim's chest.

"That's the Beast."

Claws savaged him, tearing through his weakened armor and withered defenses. Haim tried to rally, to throw the huge beast off of him, but a spike of vicious pain stabbed through his Mind, staggering him. Dust and flame and lightning descended onto the Justiciar, and he felt a final, scorching tear...

Then darkness.

CHAPTER NINETY-SIX

WHAT IS THIS?

The Highest Flame's tendrils flickered and vanished from his channels. Atar fell, hitting the ash hard enough for something in his knee to snap. He sprawled into the scorching soot, too consumed with pain to pull back from it all. Worst of all, the curse within his legs sped upward, no longer held at bay by the Flame's influence. It raced up his calves, knees, and lower thighs...before halting again. The screaming sands and howling lightning of the storm around him sputtered and failed, before going silent. Then, between one breath and the next, it was all gone.

THE WITHERING DUST...DEAD? HOW?

The words rolled off Atar, as senseless as the growling of a sandwolf. His pain consumed him. The curse might have vanished, but the imploding hole just above his navel was ever-present. Magma burned in his veins and channels alike, while within his core space, it was a worsening vacuum. His core was cut off from the greatest source of his strength, and it flickered, dwindling and dying as half-visible threads were shorn free of its base. He had chosen this fate, to sever his alliance with the Highest Flame, to deny Her in the throes of death.

I don't regret it! he bellowed silently. *I reject all that you are, Flame!*

Immense cracking resounded through his Body, audible to only himself. A void opened up within him, a yawning darkness beneath the sigil-carved flooring of his core space. Fire and oil spilled into the crevasse, swallowed utterly as the screams that tried to tear from Atar's chest. Blackened blood pooled on his tongue, foul and burned by raging forces inside of him—forces that would leave nothing left of Atar V'as in the end.

Alister...!

His partner was so close, beyond the ash and still-blinding heat and flames. Fire raged upward, the white-hot center of the Urge expanding by two strides, licking at his feet. So close and so far. He would never make it away from the expanding Urge, or up the slope of the basin. The last brilliant orange thread snapped, and the crumbling depths of his core widened. He was alone, cut off from his long-earned power, and unraveling from the inside out.

Yet, in his despair, another thread was revealed. A bond he'd thought undone along with his old Oath...yet which glimmered in brilliant silver around the splintering remnants of his core. It thrummed, pulsing with sounds that he almost couldn't hear, until his Affinity snagged upon it.

Do you accept this power?

Atar did not hesitate. *YES!*

Attempting To Establish Sympathetic Link...
Tier III Link Already Established.
Essence Redirection Allowed.

A swirl of System notifications crowded Atar's vision, but they were trumped by the swell of searing heat that slammed into him. That cable of silver shunted power through a huge distance and into his core space, a torrent of raw violence that ripped through him. Yet it did no damage to his injured internals, in fact the opposite. Where it met the flesh curse, it overwhelmed it with an inexorable tide, smothering it by its sheer density and weight.

Atar wheezed at the sudden cessation of pain, numbed by the whiplash of sensation, and saw his core shift in hue. Its dimming yellow-orange flame brightened, expanding to fill its basin and turning a pure white edged in bloody crimson. The fire did not stop there, but followed the glut of Essence as it crystallized around his sundered internal space, until it felt as if Atar's entire body burned with the purest of flames.

DO NOT ACCEPT THE TEMPTATION OF IT! THE TERROR OF HUNGER IS NOT TO BE TRUSTED!

Atar ignored its ranting, instead welcoming the power. If nothing else, Felix had a knack for survival. Atar wasn't about to turn down a last-minute rescue from the man.

Tier III Link Advanced To Tier IV!

The mage's core shifted, too much to follow. The thread—the Link—was now the same crimson-edged white as his core flame, and it had branched. A veritable spider's web arced between his core and the smaller basins that once filled his internal space. Where a Skill was or had been, the threads looped and spun, holding them together just the same as it held together his central Altar. That deep well of power spread, coursing across his Skills until stone and sigil reformed, pressed together and sealed together with crystalline energies.

Deep crimson sigils puckered the floor, incorporating the repairing cracks and a spreading layer of faceted crystal. Mini-altars that had been all but shattered now pressed back together, shifting positions among the network of his core space, but reformed.

WARNING!
Skills Have Become Unmoored!
WARNING!
Tier IV Link Has Changed You!
Skills And Their Effects Have Been Affected!
All Choices Have Consequences.

Agony unlike anything before blasted through Atar's Aspects. Mind, Spirit, and Body convulsed and broke apart, the spaces between filled and rearranged by threads and gleaming, unbreakable crystal.

––––––

NO NO NO. THIS CANNOT BE!
Atar's eyes opened to an obliterating storm, one that was savaging his people...but it was not the sand and lightning they had seen before, but a swirling inferno. Huge tongues of primal flame lashed outward, charring wood and stone and melting metal beneath its annihilating heat.
I CANNOT BE EXTINGUISHED! FOR YOUR SAKE, YOU MUST AID ME!
Still dazed from the roil of power within, Atar stared in mute horror as unprotected Temple Guards and legionnaires alike were instantly turned to ash. A great many of the former had already died, as most of the Legion were cradled in green-blue shields. Much closer, a cocoon of bright yellow Mana shielded Alister and Fiammetta, though the Faun was swaying on her feet.
"Stop," Atar mumbled through the ashes around him. Despite the inferno above him, here it had all gone cold. He pushed up on trembling arms and leveraged himself until he could see the writhing center of the Urge. "Stop now!"
ATAR. BETRAYER AND FORSAKEN CHILD. YOU CANNOT HOPE TO UNDERSTAND THE STAKES. The Urge's voice was loud, stabbing at him and everyone around them. Atar was numb, though, so full up on pain that a little more made little difference. **THAT WHICH HAS PRESERVED ME, THIS ENTIRE CITY, IS**

GONE! EATEN UP BY THE HUNGER AND BEAST! BUT YOU WILL ALL SERVE AS A REPLACEMENT.

"No we won't, you pompous idiot," Atar spat, his wits spooling back together. Notifications flashed at him, pushing into his awareness and tingling gut. "I won't let you."

The Urge paused, then the sheer weight of Her pressed down on the mage. Atar grunted as the air superheated and the metal basin beneath his feet turned cherry red. His Fire Resistance was not enough to protect him in the face of it all, but Atar lifted his chin to stare the Highest Flame down regardless.

FOR THE SAKE OF THIS WORLD, EVEN THE FORSAKEN WILL SERVE, ATAR V'AS. I NEED NOT PACT NOR BOND TO TURN YOU ALL TO KINDLING.

The heat drove the air from his lungs, consuming it, and Atar gritted his teeth. His eyes and skin dried out, splitting along his cheeks and forehead, but he refused to waver. He choked out a word, pressing his tongue against the roof of his mouth for enough moisture. The fire mage grasped a potion at his waist. Most of it had boiled away in the heat, and the rest was a scalding mixture that hurt as much as it healed.

The Urge twisted, her inhuman body of flames peering at him. **STILL YOU FIGHT. NOTHING YOU CAN SAY WILL CHANGE THE WAY IT MUST BE, ATAR V'AS.**

Atar shoved his hands up, straight into the brilliant white flames of the Urge's center. It scorched him, burning his skin and ligaments instantly, but he refused to let go. "Spiritual Immolation!"

ERROR!
Spiritual Immolation Has Been Affected By Your Tier IV Link!
Calculating...
Spiritual Immolation (Rare) Has Evolved Into Primal Firestorm (Epic)!
Level Has Been Maintained!

Primal Firestorm (Epic), Level 62!
An evolution of Spiritual Immolation, this turns your very flesh to primal flame for the duration, rendering yourself immune to fire damage for a brief period of time and greatly boosting the effectiveness of fire attuned Skills. Duration increases slightly per level.

Atar became elemental fire, his form held together by only his patchwork Willpower and infant Intent. The debilitating heat of the Urge was instantly negated, but the pressure of the Highest Flame did not subside. In fact, it only increased as the Urge's surprise swiftly changed to indignation.

YOU DARE ASSUME MY SHAPE! BETRAYER AND USURPER! IS THERE NO BOTTOM TO YOUR FALL?

"Try this one," Atar said, his voice somehow conveyed among his non-body. "Strength Ignition!"

ERROR!
Strength Ignition Has Been Affected By Your Tier IV Link!
Calculating...
Strength Ignition (Uncommon) Has Evolved Into Inexorable Enkindling (Legendary)!
Level Has Been Maintained!

Inexorable Enkindling (Legendary), Level 71!
An evolution of Strength Ignition, this Skill absorbs fire and heat Mana from one's surroundings with even greater fidelity. Absorbed elemental Mana vastly increases your Strength, Endurance, and Vitality, turning a powerful mage into a potent warrior for a short period of time. Exhaustion follows the deactivation of this Skill. Amount absorbed increases slightly per level, duration increases slightly per level, exhaustion decreased slightly per level.

The heat and flame—all that was entwined in Atar's incorporeal fingertips—was pulled into him. Willpower met Willpower, Urge versus Human mage. Both were injured, but Atar's crimson-edged flame burned brighter with every passing second. Potency surged along his Link with Felix, and along with it came a weight that he'd never before experienced. A vast accumulation of meaning strengthened Atar's grasp, dislodging the Urge's resistance like the fingers of a recalcitrant child. With a horrible, screaming denial, the Highest Flame was pulled into Atar's Body.

The Urge was gone, and so was her terrible firestorm.

"Atar! You're alive!" Alister shouted. Heedless of the once-burning ash and scorching basin, the force mage leaped into the Altar and rushed to his partner's side. "Your...your eyes are burning."

Atar blinked, his smile at seeing Alister—and even Fiammetta—unharmed faltered. "My eyes?"

"You look like Felix," Alister said, slowly. He shook himself. "What did you do? Where's the Urge?"

Atar opened his mouth to answer, but explosive pain split the skin at his shoulder, releasing a gout of white-hot flame. "Step back!"

Alister scrambled backward, and Atar buckled with the pain. The Urge was inside him, absorbed into his Skill...but it wasn't gone. She raged in his core, fighting with everything she had. Legendary Skill or not, he couldn't hold her. But he could make use of her.

"Crown of Ignis!"

ERROR!
Crown of Ignis Has Been Affected By Your Tier IV Link!
Calculating...
Crown of Ignis (Rare) Has Evolved Into Astrum Revelation (Legendary)!
Level Has Been Maintained!

Astrum Revelation (Legendary), Level 71!
An evolution of Crown of Ignis, this summons a mantle of burning flame that greatly enhances the potency and quantity produced by Stars of the Sovereign. Amount and potency of Stars are increased slightly per level, aggression and sense of superiority increased per level.

A seven-tined crown the size of the Altar basin manifested around Atar. From its burning white shape emerged a dozen Stars of the Sovereign, each one the size of a full-grown man and crackling with crimson-edged violence.

"Atar? What's happening?" Alister asked. He had lifted a hand against the intense heat and peered past it blearily at Atar's heat-warped form. "We have to run! There are too many!"

"Too many?" Atar scoffed. The Urge's frustrated screams were drowned out by a sneering dominance that settled atop Atar's Mind. "Let's fix that, then."

Three of the huge Stars swept outward, enormous comets of pure destruction. Temple Knights and Paladins alike were caught in the burning ruination, which left flesh, wood, and even stone aflame in its wake. Atar laughed, amused that such idiots would dare stand up to him. The Paladins had all but retreated, some of the glow about them having faded. Atar hadn't a clue why, and he didn't care. The invaders must be destroyed, no matter the cost, so that others would know never to touch his people. His city. *His.*

"Atar! Atar, stop! Aim for the Manaships!"

The voice shouting at his side was rude and inconsiderate of his betters, but it made a valid point. *Better to destroy their ships because...because why?*

"The relays! Destroy the relays!" the familiar voice prodded, screaming now.

Ah, yes! Atar lifted his hand, sending the rest of his Stars upward, shattering through the glass windows and streaking into the sky. Two Manaships, huge galleon-sized beasts, were hit from below, and the crimson-edged fire sliced into their hulls like a hot knife through butter.

The sky exploded, white flames turning to brilliant orange blooms that consumed both ships utterly. Atar laughed, head thrown back, and the scream from inside of him was squelched entirely.

None! None can resist my power!

"V'AS!"

That word was the only warning he had as a body of brilliant flame crashed into him. Atar screeched fury and drew his Astrum Revelation close. The swirling ring of power constricted on them both, containing the Grandmaster's furious assault. "You dare steal the protection of our people? You fool!"

"I dare whatever I wish!" Atar shouted, reveling in his own audacity. "Sovereign of Stars!"

Smaller Stars of white flame manifested and flew at the grey-skinned mage. The man was hurt from his fight against Zara, but he countered the Stars with contemptuous ease. "You call that power? I shall show you and your hidden ally what it means to contend with the heavens!"

A halo of terrible might surged up around the Grandmaster, and heat spread outward to begin liquefying the metal basin around them. It was potent enough to remind Atar's delirious Mind why the man truly ruled the city of Ahkestria. Atar only grinned, however, prepping his new powers to counter his fool of a master.

Nearby, that familiar voice bellowed in fear and pain, and a true piece of Atar wrenched inside of him.

Alister!

Kel'lyv surged forward, his glowing fist leading the way. Distracted for only a second, the bonuses of his Inexorable Enkindling already fading, Atar couldn't dodge in time. Bright orange flame met crimson-edged white, and blasted it apart. The strike took him full force in the chest, and the two of them hit the cherry-red metal, bringing all of it down in a mighty crash.

———

Alister stood atop a pillar of force Mana, balanced precariously atop the slagged and crumpled Altar basin. His robes were covered in soot—scorched away completely in more than one place—and his Body was little better off...but he didn't care about any of it.

C'mon, Atar. Get up.

From the center of the basin, there came a deep groaning, the sound of heated metal rapidly cooling, then clambering hands pulled at its still-soft surface, dragging up a man in tattered robes. Alister's heart fell. The man was bald and grey, and he dusted off his robes with disgust before looking up, right at Alister.

"Would that I had the time to teach you all the same lesson," the Grandmaster said, gesturing at the darkened depression he'd climbed out of. "But you do not matter. Only that *boy.*"

The Grandmaster lifted into the air, his glow greatly diminished, but his Body wasn't hurt at all. Alister didn't care.

Grand Impetus!

A blast of force Mana surged out of Alister's rapier, refined to a needle point, but the Grandmaster parried it with nothing but the edge of his bare hand. He didn't even glance at Alister, only altered his trajectory and hurtled off, through a battalion of retreating Paladins, smearing them into bloody chunks before vanishing.

"Damn you!" Alister shouted after him, then leaped down into the cratered Altar.

CHAPTER NINETY-SEVEN

Fiendforge is level 14!

...

Fiendforge is level 18!

Haim was dead. The Paladins and undead scattered. The Golems...smashed. Felix had to double check that one, but their conjured carcasses were slowly dissipating back into the atmosphere.

The Primordial was gone, and all that remained was the immense Skyslain's Riposte. Its flesh had been subsumed by his Sovereign of Flesh, torn apart and manually drawn through Felix's core like a crofter making yarn. He hadn't even known he could do that, and here he'd done that and more.

Felix stumbled, hand to his gut as a fissure of burning energy looped outward along his channels. It felt like swallowing hot ash and glass. If Pit and the others hadn't been able to share it with him, then Felix doubted he'd have lived through the experience. Even still—

He gagged, wisps of multi-hued Mana and Essence snaking out of his open mouth. They twisted and curled, too light to fall, too volatile to stay down. "Pit. Where's Beef?"

The tenku was on his side, breathing heavily in the gruesome remains of the armored Paladin. Pit's eyes were white around the edges, and his pupils were constricted to pinpricks. *I don't know. I don't—I don't feel right.*

"Your Evolution isn't complete," Felix said. He grimaced as more Essence burned free of his Mana Gates in his palms and elbows. Blue-white electricity and red-gold flame glimmered off of his limbs, leaving behind tantalizing trails of light if he moved too fast. "We're both half-baked."

His Skills had jumped up, Tempered into Adept...but it had been chaotic. Felix held back as much as he could until they'd killed Haim, and now...now he could let it go. "We gotta finish. Now, before it kills us, Pit."

How? The Choice was made, and it asks again. What else—Pit stopped his words, shuddering as caustic yellow fire and purple-white ice chased each other across his scorched barding. *What else can I do?*

Shaken and hurt, Felix didn't hesitate to press his bloody hand against Pit's heaving side. "Show me."

Notifications swirled into his vision.

Adjusting Evolution Choices...
Choose One Of The Following!
Witherheart Tenku
Scourclaw Tenku
Stormwing Tenku

"Your old choice was invalidated apparently," Felix said with a grunt. He ran his hands through the semi-real notification. He couldn't touch it, but his over-strained senses could feel a buzzing around it all. "Which one did you choose before?"

Wardenwing.

A spasm of electric heat spiraled out from his core again, and his Tempering clawed at his weary Will. "Sounds like a tank. That's what you want, dude?"

I...need to protect you. As you have protected me.

Felix grinned and pressed his forehead against Pit's neck. Lightning, ice, and fire jumped between them, scalding his neck and shoulders, but he just pressed in tighter. "Even if you turned yourself into a shield, you can't protect me from everything, bud. Choice is yours, so I'd rather you think about what *you* want."

Pit's big head dipped, his curved beak snapping in thought.

"And quick, because I can't hold Fiendforge on you forever," he added, but his laugh was choked off by more writhing power from his channels. "And I gotta finish my Temper."

Still gripping Pit's core with Fiendforge, Felix let his own notifications spill out into his awareness. They flashed, repeating what he'd seen before.

Sovereign of Flesh is level 75!
...
Sovereign of Flesh is level 78!
Adept Tier!
You Gain:
+100 STR

He'd lost the Essence Motes and Memories he'd long held onto, and not a single Mote remained. More than a little of the Primordial of Withering Dust remained in Felix—caught in the filtering branches of his Divine Tree—but it was all significance and diluted Essence adorning his Tree like cosmic leaves. With jittering hands, he ripped open Pit's saddle-bags, releasing a glut of Health Potions and a sizeable chunk of dark blue Mana crystal. He'd taken that a day or two ago, and he tossed it to the side with trembling fingers—it wasn't what he needed.

+75 AGL

There! He snagged two blue-stone decanters, both of them among the few he had that were pure and unadulterated by the extensive process Felix and Aenea had devised. He ripped free their sealed tops with his teeth and slugged them back, one after the other. They burned like grain alcohol down his throat and screamed into his channels like a multi-colored bolt of lightning.

+...
Legendary Essence Detected During Formation!
[Essence Draught of Atlantes (Pure)]

The Essence draught went hog wild inside of him, slamming through his core space like a battering ram. It slashed through his Divine Tree, pulling in its wake the purified Primordial Essence that clung like cobwebs. It soaked into his Skill, flooding it with its liquid lightning that constantly shifted in hue with every beat and burr of the Grand Harmony and Dissonance.

Broken Path and Fatebreaker Titles Found!
Adept Tier Bonus Added!
Unbound Nature Resonates With [Essence Draught of Atlantes (Pure)]!
Calculating Effects...

Choose A Feature:
Marrow - Vital Heart
Cardinal - Elder Soul
Renewal - Unyielding Flesh

Unlike previous draughts, the one made from Spirit Fruit sang with wild power. Felix's Mind shook under its influence, barely parsing out the many melodies he'd come to know: the soft Aria of the Green Wilds, the war beat of the Wild Threnody, the solemn Song of Absolution, the dire cacophony of the Coronach, and the strident tones of the Adamant Discord. All of it tumbled among a greater whole, a song that encompassed all that was and all that would be...yet still felt empty.

Into that emptiness, however, the Dissonance of his core space manifested. Not intruded or invaded, just...rose from unknown depths within the Harmony itself. A piece of the greater whole, no different than the other songs that pervaded Felix's being. Once joined, the Dissonance resonated with the entirety of him—Mind, Body, and Spirit—in a way that he'd never experienced. At best, the interplay of Dissonance and Harmony had been one of grudging coexistence, and at worst, they had torn each other to pieces. Now, something else was occurring. Something new.

Most importantly, Felix could hear the Feature that best fit his Sovereign of Flesh. Not Marrow, though a Vital Heart sounded useful; nor Renewal, though every bit of him wished to choose it. No, the only fit was the last, Cardinal. Elder Soul.

He chose.

Congratulations!
You Have Absorbed The Essence Of [Cardinal]!

The draught sank into him, soaking through the swirling pattern of his Skill. Immediately, a change overcame it, the arcing lines of the wave-like patterns becoming more convoluted as Primordial Essence was drawn inward. The entire Skill swelled, doubling in size until it rivaled his Adamant Discord for complexity, until it sang out in an entirely new voice.

A reverberation shook through his core space and channels, carrying with it the newly changed sound of his Sovereign of Flesh. Wounds all over him closed rapidly, his broken bones mending and his over-strained Body easing by the smallest degree. Lost muscle and blood replenished itself. His Body was being remade, but slowly, and Felix hadn't time to wait.

Relentless Resolution is level 75!
...
Relentless Resolution is level 77!
Adept Tier!
You Gain:
+90 AGL
+50 DEX
+...
Legendary Essence Detected During Formation!
[Essence Draught of Atlantes (Pure)]

The second Essence Draught flooded into his Skill, dragging even more of the Primordial Essence with it. The complicated interplay of melodies and atonal inconsistencies wove tighter together than ever before. Combined, a half-step out of beat, they rose again in a violent crescendo.

Broken Path and Fatebreaker Titles Found!
Adept Tier Bonus Added!
Unbound Nature Resonates With [Essence Draught of Atlantes (Pure)]!
Calculating Effects…

Choose A Feature:
Titan - Stand Tall
Obdurate - Stand Firm
Grim - Stand Apart

The thrumming din of it all pummeled Felix's senses, his Affinity most of all. Primordial Essence chased after Legendary Draught as Harmony and Dissonance swept into a wild dance all throughout his core space. Felix stood in the middle, his Fiendforge aching, burning, trembling to let go. Holding on was all he could do, all he could think of—and it was all he needed now.

He chose.

Congratulations!
You Have Absorbed The Essence Of [Obdurate]!

Fiendforge is level 19!

His Relentless Resolution shifted, soaking up the Essence Draught like parched soil. The cascading sound gathered momentum from his two Tempering Skills, until it was a storm that raged inside of Felix's chest. Lightning and fire raced outward, along his limbs in greater amounts than before, blue-white and red-gold and accompanied by a caustic, blinding pain.

"Just…Temper already," he gasped into the dirty floor. The pressure spiked inside him, magma crawling across his channels, settling into the cracks of his Body. Sovereign of Flesh hummed along, furiously patching up the damage, and his heart hammered hard enough that Felix's shoulders jumped with every beat.

A retort cracked the sky, followed by the sound of a thousand shattering windows. Felix tilted his head, just enough to see a comet of fire and brutal fury come arcing down—a man, bald and screaming, at its center.

Pit! Felix threw his body up, no matter how painful it was, and backed into his Companion. *Finish up!*

Yet, even if Felix put everything into his own Temper, the process of creating his Adept Body would knock him out. He'd seen it happen twice now. Six hours he was out, and he doubted he'd last the next six seconds. Kel'lyv neared, and the heat went from painful to unbearable.

"C'mon!" Felix screamed at himself. "Temper!"

WARNING!
Fully Tempering Into Adept Tier Requires Immense Energy!
Proceeding May Result In Death Or Worse!
Do You Wish To—

Yes yes yes! Felix shouted at the System. *Take everything! Just do it!* Convergence!

Pit vanished, and the fireball arrived.

———

Etheric Concordance is level 81!
Etheric Concordance is level 82!

Choose One Of The Following!
Witherheart Tenku
Scourclaw Tenku
Stormwing Tenku

Pit's Mind was overcome by the pressures within and without. The furious assault of flame and brutal impact that Felix was experiencing wasn't entirely felt, but it echoed across their bond with a savage ferocity that raised Pit's hackles. Yet he couldn't confront that monster outside without fixing himself first. Internally, the energies that were soaking his core were spinning faster and faster.

Choose!

Pit squawked indignantly, and focused. He knew what he wished, but...Why did Felix have to confuse him?

Choose!

The energies of his core howled, crackling off his core in arcs of fire and ice. A tempest of power that hinted at vast possibilities. Pit trilled in frustration.

What did he *want?*

Choose!

———

3 of 3 Body Essences Formed!
Tempering Has Begun!

Felix crouched beneath the Grandmaster, forearm raised as fire washed over the both of them. The pain was numbed by his Song of Absolution, but it was still awful. It chewed at him, flensing away charring flesh with razors of heat, only to have his Skill bring it back...just it was getting slower as it went on.

"Weren't you, unf, weren't you stronger before?" Felix asked as his cheeks burned and blistered.

"Strong enough for you, Veil!" Kel'lyv shouted, and booted Felix straight in the chest.

Felix tumbled backward, flipping over and over against the ground and the armored bodies of his enemies. He flared Relentless Resolution and stabbed down with his Inheritor's Will. The curved sword bit into the bodies and stone beneath them, dragging Felix to a screeching stop. He gagged, blood pouring from his mouth before the dent in his chest healed with a grisly *pop*, and he forced a bloody smile at the Grandmaster. "Touched a nerve, I think."

"What have you done with the Primordial? Where have you hidden its body?" the Grandmaster demanded.

"Hidden?" Felix asked.

Kel'lyv slashed a hand, sending an angry arc of flame at Felix. It melted a nasty swath through undead and Paladin corpses alike, and Felix leaped over it, barely. "Do not toy with me, boy! I do not know how you accomplished it, but that creature's corpse was all that stood between my city and monsters like the Hierophant! WHERE IS IT?"

"Oh *that* Primordial, right," Felix grated out. His throat felt like he'd gargled glass, but his Sovereign of Flesh was still fixing the internal bleeding that rampaged through him from that kick. "It was gone when I got here. I think Haim was taking it back to his boss."

"Blind oafs!" Kel'lyv cursed. "How? How did they do it? The cage around that thing was erected by creatures beyond our mortal scope!"

"They're Paladins," Felix said, wetting his lips and carefully standing from his crouch. "How do you think?"

"The Pathless." The Grandmaster closed his eyes briefly as blood vessels bulged in his forehead. "Those damnable fools. What have they done?"

Just keep talking, Felix pled silently. He was fueling the Tempering process with the dense, overflowing amount of Primordial Essence in his core space. His dual cores ate it up, burning the shimmering Essence without end; Felix could almost feel his Body forming inside of him, but it was too slow. Beef was down, Hallow was nowhere to be seen, and Pit was fighting to evolve. It was just him versus a Grandmaster. Again. He shook his head, shoving away the fog that kept clouding his Mind. *Stay awake! Fall asleep, and you're dead!*

Kel'lyv stepped forward and then stopped. Looked down, then back up as the flames around his body intensified once again. Even fifty feet away, Felix could feel the heat of it all. "What is this, Veil?"

He kicked something through the air, landing it within three yards of Felix's position. A severed head, still locked in a confused scream, with bright yellow eyes glazed over in death. Felix opened his mouth once, twice before speaking. "Seems like Haim bit off more than he could chew."

The comet returned. Instantly, the Grandmaster was upon Felix, arm reaching for his throat. Felix ducked his neck and dropped, sweeping his leg at the same time as he flared Corrosive Strike. The blow took the mage in the leading leg, buckling his knee, but the jerk simply started flying instead of running. They collided.

Wild Threnody!

Rime Shaping!

Felix's fist met Kel'lyv's. Ice hit fire in a hissing shower of steam, and both of them were thrown back. The sheer magical potency behind the Grandmaster shattered Felix's knuckles and one of his forearm bones, but the mage didn't get off easy. He staggered back, keeping his feet and staring aghast at the bloody gouges ripped across his gray hand. The mage's eyes were wider than Felix had ever seen them.

"Yeah," Felix said between panting breaths. His arm was twisting and setting itself slowly. It felt like someone grinding his nerves into paste. "Definitely weaker. I—"

With a wrathful roar, the Grandmaster unleashed his potent Spirit. That familiar pressure slammed down on him, attempting to crush Felix with its sheer breadth. He grunted, wounds reopening along his sides and legs, torn by the weight of it all. Then something twinged his ears. His Affinity continued to be submerged in chaotic cacophony, but a lilting note cut through. Just enough to notice.

What is—? Felix gasped as it revealed itself to him. The lilting note wove outward, around the Grandmaster like a cloak of invisible power. *It's....it's not his Spirit...it's Authority.*

And his own Authority was resonating with it. He focused with everything that wasn't furiously holding Fiendforge, or funneling Essence into his cores, or keeping Pit alive through the riotous chaos inside of Felix's Spirit. His shreds of spare Intent grasped forward, as if using a limb he'd never known existed. Felix's Authority *twisted*, shifting up sharply, and a notification appeared before them both.

Do You Wish To Challenge Grandmaster Kel'lyv For Territorial Authority?
Y/N

"Oh hell yes," Felix said, lips already curving upward.

Attention!
Territorial Lord Grandmaster Kel'lyv Has Been Challenged For His Authority!

The Challenger Is Felix Nevarre, Autarch of Nagast!

"Autarch," Kel'lyv said with a click of his tongue. The Grandmaster's Spirit vanished, its pressure pulling back inward on the mage with a pained grunt. "I should have suspected. No mere ambassador could have survived my assault. Do you truly wish this, *Nevarre*? Only death shall end this duel."

Felix wet his lips but kept his grin. It was all he could do. "Sounds like someone's afraid."

The Grandmaster's entire body fell into shadow, as if a sun was suddenly expanding behind him. A Human-shaped solar eclipse. "You'll regret that, boy."

CHAPTER NINETY-EIGHT

Begin Challenge!

Rime Shaping!

Ice flowed upward, forming into a three-foot deep rampart ahead of Felix...and the Grandmaster smashed right through it.

"You'll have to do better than that!" he said, and fire streamed from the gray mage's mouth. "Burn!"

A cone of flame erupted from the Grandmaster's face, forcing Felix to speed out of the way. His Tempering Body surged in chaotic spasms, wildly propelling Felix through the fire head first. It hurt, eating through his already tattered Garment and charring his skin and muscle to the bone, but he didn't stop. If he stopped, he'd be dead.

Supercharged bolts of fire flung after him, screaming through the air before detonating bare inches behind Felix's mad dash. His Agility was high, but the advantage in Titles, Skills, and Stats was with the gray-skinned mage. Kicks, jabs, and brutal knee strikes flew from the Grandmaster, each one coming closer and closer.

Felix threw up barriers of ice, drawing on his own Mana, but summoning ice before the towering heat of the Grandmaster was frustrating. Even with the water Mana emanating from the crystals all around them, it was like sucking mud through a straw, and a vicious headache built rapidly behind Felix's eyes. Spikes and swirling nets hurled at the mage, but he accelerated through them without regard for his own Body.

"You cannot run forever!" Kel'lyv shouted, before landing a knife-hand chop. Felix cried out, hurled off his feet by the resulting explosion. He tumbled forward, ducking into a roll and summoning a whirling blade of ice.

Rime Shaping!

The blade swung with his rotation, dragged along the ground until it popped upward into the Grandmaster's path. It was thick enough that the two seconds it took the mage to demolish gave Felix the time he needed to regain his feet. His back was charred and bloody, but it was healing slowly. It wasn't anything like the damage the guy had inflicted on him previously, even with a glancing blow. "You *are* weaker," Felix said. His eyes flicked at the bronze sword across the chamber before settling on the mage again. "Without the Primordial's might, what happened to the Highest Flame?"

Kel'lyv bared his teeth. "Be more concerned with your own hide, Autarch. If you fall here, all of your Territory becomes mine...and I will enjoy ruining all that you have made, *boy*."

Relentless Resolution!

Adamant Discord!

Mantle of the Infinite Revolution!

Lightning blasted outward, slamming Felix into the Grandmaster faster than either could blink. At the same time, his Mana surged and spun, rotating wide and fast as the air turned into a frigid storm. Ice crackled and built in a flash, forcing Kel'lyv's eyes wide in surprise.

Rime Shaping!

Wild Threnody!

Corrosive Strike!

A conjured fist of ice ripped upward, snagging around the Grandmaster's arms, just as Felix arrived foot-first.

The impact blasted ice and stone and corpses in all directions. Twenty-four hundred points of Strength hit the Grandmaster square in the chest, reinforced by ice and acid, and the gray mage was thrown back onto his ass in an arc of blood.

Felix did, too, though it was a consequence of the rampaging energies in his chest. He convulsed once before pulling himself back to his aching feet. His Body was still forming, and the addition of his Sovereign of Flesh meant his wounds were recovering faster and faster. He was pretty sure he'd broken his leg in several places with that kick, but by the time he mustered the breath to stand, it had healed over. Broken skin shivered and pulsed, bones thickening and weaving tighter than before. His Body was changing, reshaping itself into something stronger as the Essence forced his Temper.

Only, it was *devouring* his Essence supply, leaving none for him to activate his scales or claws. He had taken a ton of purified Essence from the Primordial...but so much more had been given to Pit and his friends. That decision was biting him in the ass. Thankfully, he was surrounded by the smoking corpses of the undead.

Chthonic Tribute!

Felix shoved at the Skill, forcing it to activate while the Grandmaster was down, but barely absorbed a single wisp of Essence. His Hunger refused *again*—the rejection felt like a hot poker shoved into his guts—and

Sovereign of Flesh couldn't pull on them, either. Their flesh curse had been cleansed when he'd torn apart the Primordial, after all.

Work, damn you!

MORE, his Hunger demanded incomprehensibly.

That's what I'm trying, you idiot! Agony spiked his core space, and the dark abyss became a solid wall of convulsing teeth.

The riot of pain distracted him for a dire instant, and the Grandmaster caught him fully across the face. Superheated air and an explosion of fire took him in the skull, throwing Felix down into and across the ground, skipping him like a pebble on a lake.

Before he could smash into the far wall, the Grandmaster was there, blazing hands grasping Felix by the scruff of his Garment. "You brought all of this on yourself, Felix. Remember that as you burn."

Felix screamed as the world was dyed with flames. His Garment burnt to ashes, his skin cracked and charred, and his bloody flesh boiled beneath the Grandmaster's fury. A single, mammoth punch to his sternum sent Felix reeling back into the crystalline wall. The Mana crystals cracked, but mostly they tore into his fiery flesh, too. Kel'lyv paused to breathe in deeply...and torrents of the scorching Mana around him were sucked up and into the man. He glowed as it settled into him, just like how Atar would do it, and smiled.

Wild Threnody!

Arrow of Perdition!

"You have quite the store of Mana, boy." Kel'lyv's fists shot out lazily, deflecting his attack with one hand and blasting into Felix's shoulder with the other. Felix gasped, muscles tearing, and bones snapped inside of him. "A trick that fool Atar never learned was that Strength Ignition, once Mastered, means you are no longer restricted to your own Mana pool."

The golden-azure glow of his Skill flickered and faded, floating off his fist before turning decidedly orange. It was pulled toward and into the Grandmaster's glowing Body. "Mm, yes. That is *quite* exceptional. I'll have the rest now."

Relentless Resolu—!

Before Felix could move, the Grandmaster laid into him. A flurry of brutal blows smashed into his chest and abs, cracking bones and pulping his muscles with *incredible* force. Belatedly, Felix ducked his head and lifted his arms to block, and the mage's fists shattered through his forearms. Bones snapped, blood flowed and boiled in the fiery heat, and he couldn't even manage a scream.

Felix! Pit sent as if from far, far away. Felix's Health dropped lower and lower, his regeneration overcome. He couldn't heal fast enough, and the Grandmaster didn't stop.

Last Cry Of The Chthonic Host!

Last Cry Of The Chthonic Host is level 2!

Energy flushed Felix's body, and more of his Essence and a huge chunk of significance vanished. His Health and Stamina skyrocketed, returning to full while every wound upon his body vanished.

Kel'lyv hesitated, eyes narrowing. "A healing Skill, boy?"

Felix swallowed, Mana coiling in his channels. "We've all got tricks."

Shadow Whip!

Adamant Discord!

Black shadow and blue-white lightning lashed outward, but Kel'lyv caught them both in a net of sizzling flame. Their Mana was subsumed and torn from Felix's grasp. "Tricks are useless before overwhelming strength."

This time, the Grandmaster's counter blasted him a foot into the crystalline wall. Blood burst from Felix's throat, and he felt his sternum and shoulder blades shatter. Mana crystals broke and rained down on them, but the mage didn't pay them any mind. All of his dreadful attention was fixed on killing Felix, and his titanic, pummeling strikes increased to an all-time high.

Felix's world became pain.

Sovereign of Flesh sang within him, repairing torn vessels and replenishing his blood as it ran like rivers from his chest and legs and obliterated arms. But for every bone mended and muscle reattached, another vicious hit tore them apart again. And again, until there was only heat and brutalized nerve-endings and reforming tissue.

Sovereign of Flesh is level 79!
Sovereign of Flesh is level 80!

———

Beef opened his eyes, but everything was blurry. His Health hovered just above zero, but he was *alive*. That was all that mattered.

Hallow...?

There was no answer from his friend, and Beef's throat burned. But there was no time for tears. He had to get up. His legs wouldn't work quite right, and it wasn't until he looked down that Beef realized both were mangled beneath the corpse of a Nightfall Golem. The thing was slowly dissolving into the air, but he was trapped.

And Felix was in trouble.

Beef reached down deep, grabbing a handful of his Mana and Stamina and feeding it into his newest Skill. *It's all I can do, Felix. I'm...I'm sorry.*

With a deep breath, Beef opened his mouth and shouted as loud as he could.

———

His cores ground at one another, their contact point producing the tangled interplay of Harmony and Dissonance as Primordial Essence soaked their ring-shaped flames. The song of it resounded, a presence that had spent months building up and spreading throughout his core space, not so much noise as it was a tangible occupant within his breast.

Sovereign of Flesh glowed and thrummed, vitality pumping out in exchange for the lives of his foes, a power over his flesh...and his soul. The Essence of Cardinal was there, crouched within the newly Tempered Skill, and it resonated with the chaotic song of his heart. Relentless Resolution lit as well, a stifled, vibrating fury that pealed like a collection of vast silver bells, and was quickly joined by the steady, unstoppable beat of his Song of Absolution.

Elder Soul...

Stand Firm...

Persist Beyond...

Essences of an undying will to fight, to struggle. They howled into the chaos of pain, pulling at Dissonance and Harmony both. Each beat and breath reinforced them with each other, each moment of resonance soaking deeper and deeper into the Body that was forming just as it was dying.

I!

A burning chop blasted through his elbow, until only ligaments still held it together.

Will!

Another snapped his femur, burning away a dinner-plate sized section of his thigh.

Not!

Blow after blow, shattering ribs and pulverizing organs.

Stop!

Sovereign of Flesh is level 81!
Relentless Resolution is level 78!
The Song of Absolution is level 87!

He broke, but his flesh healed. His Body Formation surged, fueled by Felix's uncommon Will, and by the wild song of his Tempered Essences. He knew, in that moment, that Aspect Formations weren't only leveling Skills and choosing a rare and powerful Essence to Temper them—they were a piece of Truth, an echo of a greater understanding that he was burning into his very bones. His was an Elder Soul, torn from a creature that had Persisted Beyond death itself, and it called upon his Body: Stand Firm.

A torrent of blinding System energy roared in the distance, a tsunami wave of power set to crash against Felix's cores. He accepted it, welcomed it, as his flesh was remade. Strike after strike, blow after punishing blow broke Felix's skin and muscle and bone...but it healed stronger each time.

Muscles became denser, bones thicker, ligaments and joints more fluid and nimble. His inner song raged, fueled by the flood of the System, and the flame of the Grandmaster's fury burned him away, only to reveal something new.

"Why won't you die!" Kel'lyv bellowed, smashing down into Felix's shoulder with two interlocked hands. Bones creaked, and the muscle split, splatting more blood into the walls. "Know your place! And! Fall!"

"Desperate Provocation!"

A shout tore across the chamber, one that echoed with a powerful reverberation that tugged at the edges of Felix's Will. The Grandmaster, however, had been more weakened than he had admitted—because Beef's sudden Taunt arrested his latest punch just inches from Felix's face, before the mage turned around completely.

"Beef! No!" Felix shouted.

"You! How dare you interfere!" Against his Will, the Grandmaster flashed across the short distance, a spinning lash of flame and earthen debris forming into a deadly whip.

Relentless Resolution!

Adamant Discord!

Felix burst forward, blood and viscera trailing behind him as the song in his chest rose to a vehement crescendo. Power boiled within him, exploding outward across his core space before rolling into and through his entire Body. Lightning crackled, thunder roared, and Felix's hand clasped around the Grandmaster's elbow.

And stopped the mage's attack, cold. Kel'lyv exclaimed in outraged surprise, and was met by Felix's speeding fist.

Congratulations!
You Have Tempered Your Body!
You Have Formed: Chthonic Ascent Body!
+75 EVA
+100 MIG
+75 VIT
+75 STR
+200 AGL
+100 DEX

The Grandmaster backpedaled, face bloodied and fire Mana sputtering all around him. He raised a hand to his broken nose in disbelief, Beef all but forgotten. "You were...you were broken. I broke you!"

Felix stood and realized he was looking down on the gray-skinned mage. He was covered in blood and shreds of discarded flesh, but he felt...amazing. With a flex of his Skill, a bit of his remaining Essence was consumed, and his skin rippled, turning to diamond-hard scales the color of midnight. Claws burst from his fingertips, and vicious spikes emerged from his knees and elbows. He bared his teeth at the mage. "You tried."

"RAAH!" Kel'lyv screamed and turned into a comet once again. He slammed, fist-first, into Felix's abs...and was stopped dead.

"Huh," Felix said. "Barely hurt."

Before the mage could react, Felix slashed upward across the Grandmaster's face. Blood arced into the air, and the man stumbled backward with a cry of pain, three claw marks ripped across his cheek and forehead, blinding him to Felix's powerful follow-up. The kick connected with an explosive boom, the sheer force of his Strength ripping dust and debris away from them in a perfect circle. Kel'lyv was hurled forty feet backward, ass over teakettle, and landed hard enough to send Paladin corpses flying in every direction.

Felix stared at his foot and then hands in disbelief. Aside from the strangeness of being newly proportioned, he felt *incredible*, as if he could run for weeks and lift a mountain on top of his head. More importantly, another part of him felt utterly refreshed, and his Aspects surged in concert. Adept Mind, Spirit, and Body moved as one as a plan formed. *The guy's getting back up already, and I can't rely on surprising him again.* He swallowed as his Mind turned over his desperate plan. *Gotta try.*

Relentless Resolution!

Felix's increased Agility had him tear forward faster than ever before. He blurred back to the huge sword, to the pile of scattered potions at its base. For a moment, he felt a tingling call from the sword itself, an urge to grab the thing...but he ignored it. Instead, he scooped up the large Mana crystal that had fallen from Pit's saddlebag, the one he'd grabbed from the Latticeways. It was the largest chunk he could see, and had the best chance of working.

"C'mon Affinity, do your thing," he muttered.

Dimly, Felix could feel the link it had to others of its kind. A frequency buzzed at the edges of perception, one that he could feel extend outward into the desert. Not just to where he'd found the thing, but farther. Not just to one place, but to a hundred, a thousand. A field of vibrating light arced outward from his little crystal, thin strands of connection that were so numerous that it was like the horizon was briefly stained with blue. Felix knew, could feel from the draw of the crystal in his hand, that there were millions of others, billions even, all an outgrowth from a single process that began Ages ago.

The Grandmaster was up already, and the heat of his wrath filled the chamber. "*Nevarre*! You die today!"

Here goes nothing. He gripped the crystal so hard he felt it creak. *Chthonic Tribute!*

His Hunger roared to life, suddenly fully willing to consume again. *FEED ME!*

Shut up and listen! Felix hurled his Intent and Will at the creature in his abyss, wrangling it along the rails of what he needed. *Listen!*

The moment his Body had formed, Felix had understood: all his Hunger needed was his Body to catch up, to grow strong enough to contain its ravenous appetite again. He'd hit the limit, but now that goal-post had been moved, and he forced his Hunger to focus upon the connections between crystals. *There! Right there! Pull!*

He drew deeply on the connections as well, adding his efforts to his Primordial Hunger's. The resonance between crystals increased, vibrating until the chamber around them began to groan under the weight of it, but Chthonic Tribute wouldn't be enough.

Unite the Lost!

Time slowed, the Grandmaster's charge barely started, but Felix couldn't enjoy it. Every ounce of his attention was suddenly captured by his Skill.

All of the significance he'd sequestered from the Primordial of Withering Dust was flung from the branches of his Divine Tree, down to the grinding press of his dual cores. It spun through them before flowing outward into Unite the Lost. A dirge sounded from the swirling patterns of the skill, a dirge that cut through and added to the chaotic song of his core before flowing outward, racing along Felix's channels and out of his palms.

Felix focused, wrapping the energies around the Mana crystal he held, the soulful melody pulsing all the while. He pressed, his Intent shaping its direction until it found the crystal's connections. Then it raced outward, expanding rapidly and expending significance all the while. Around him, the walls echoed with the dirge, staining the air blue as a mournful, haunting call shivered through everything.

This... Felix started as a vast shape flowed past. It was the size of a skyscraper, but shaped as a serpentine whale with massive fins and a rippling, spiked ridge. He recognized it in pieces, having only seen its bones before—it was a leviathan. Felix gawked in awe as two more swam in its wake, faster than any car he'd seen.

All around him was water. An ocean filled with creatures big and small, and the chamber he had been in had vanished utterly.

A Memory? Of the Primordial?

From below, a flurry of bubbles enveloped Felix, while powerful current buffeted his body as he floated. Deep down, within the dark depths was a creature of multitudinous limbs and bright, burning motes of flame around its many palms. *The Primordial of Withering Dust, in the flesh.* It fought against...something. Something vast and terrible that Felix couldn't make out. A monstrous struggle that clearly put the Primordial on the back foot. In the darkness, Felix could see it losing. Jaws tore bits of it away, until the water was so occluded with offal that he could see nothing more.

Then, from the opaque struggle, a dire, golden radiance shone through. A scream shook the water, blasting it upward in a geyser of incredible torment.

The flesh curse? Something happened there, something big that Felix couldn't see or understand. But he was thrown out of the Memory, stumbling atop the hard tiles of the chamber. He wanted to linger, to find out more, but that wasn't his task or goal. Felix focused, and felt his Unite the Lost and Chthonic Tribute near one another.

The crystals around them literally quaked, trembling in the vast chamber and elsewhere as well. The Grandmaster was speeding forward, once more a comet of violence and flame, his moment of heightened concentration at an end.

Now!

Chthonic Tribute is level 86!
Unite the Lost is level 51!

All at once, the massive collection of blue crystals in the chamber turned to liquid. A huge deluge stormed from the sky, a waterfall that roared with a powerful voice. The wall of water hit them all, smashing them into the earth before flooding the chamber completely. Felix leaped just as the water struck, rising to the top of the waves, but even then couldn't escape their reach. The Grandmaster was swept off his feet, the inferno he wore upon his shoulder snuffed out utterly.

Rime Shaping!

A thick, boat-like platform manifested beneath Felix's feet, lifting him to the top of the raging waves. A second tendril sped outward, into the depths, to grasp at his Minotaur friend. Before he could feel it connect, however, a brutal, golden light flashed into his Mind. Felix screamed as the hand of something immeasurable reached into the still-singing connections he'd established and *pushed*. The vibrations that he'd manipulated and encouraged in this huge chamber spread, pressed outward along the billions of connections all around the Expanse.

And then it unleashed them all.

"No," Felix choked, the waves surging all around him. "No! What've you done?"

Of that golden presence however, all he felt was a sense of smug vindication. Then it was gone.

———

Ahkestria shook, and Vess nearly collapsed under the weight of the wounded she carried. Buildings around them cracked and quaked, as if the entire city were being shaken by a massive hand. "What is that?" she asked.

Zara and Isla were ashen-faced and staring out into the distance as screams began to echo all around them. Clouds manifested in the blue sky, rolling and crackling with dark-bellied storms.

"Did he—?" Isla asked.

"He did. I am not sure how, but he did." Zara looked to Vess, and the heiress flinched back from the intensity of her expression. "We must go below. People are in danger."

"We're in danger! The Paladins haven't even all left yet," Evie said, pointing at the Manaships still in the air. Yet even as she did, a bolt of cerulean lightning flashed from the clouds and blasted apart one ship's engine. The craft spun chaotically before disappearing over the edge of the city. "Whoa."

Zara clenched her jaw. "The sea has returned."

———

"It comes!" screamed a bandaged Yttin, standing atop the stone-encased skull of their Warren. "The Beast, it comes!"

Clouds piled into the sky, and all around him was the ceaseless howl of the End. Of a new Beginning. A wall of water roared toward them, three hundred feet high, sweeping across the sands like absolution itself.

Klzix only laughed as it swept over him.

———

"Goddamn Pathless!" Felix shouted. He recognized the feel of its power in retrospect. "You released all of this just to get back at me? You jackass!"

The water rose and rose, now filling nearly half the chamber and showing little signs of stopping. The amount of water that had been condensed into a single Mana crystal was immense, and now all of them, everywhere had been released. An ocean's worth of water was flooding the desert, and there was nothing Felix could do about it.

Felix rose closer and closer to the surface of the chamber now, balanced atop his impromptu ice-boat. He cast about for Beef in the rising waves. Pit was safe in his Spirit, still reeling from his Evolution, but he still hadn't seen the Minotaur. He'd even lost his swords somewhere in the depths, but Felix couldn't care less about them at that moment.

"Autarch!"

At his side, the waves burst apart, turned to sudden steam as Grandmaster Kel'lyv flew up into the air. His robes were torn to shreds and waterlogged, and his aura of fire had dimmed, but he didn't hesitate to hurl everything he had. A sphere of incandescent flame ignited around the Grandmaster, evaporating the water faster than it could accumulate around him, blasting Felix and his boat backward. He smashed into the massive bronze sword, the only constant in the swirling sea, and it tingled like electricity against his skin. "You've taken *everything!* And I'll see you dead!"

The sphere of flame shot forward, coming for Felix...but he was done. Felix leaped up, grabbing at the hilt of the massive bronze blade next to him, shoving his Will and Intent at the strange weapon as he heaved with every ounce of Strength he had.

Inheritor's Will Detected!
Strength Above Threshold!
Vitality Above Threshold!
Endurance Above Threshold!
Access Granted!

A shockwave of blue-gold radiance blasted outward as the massive Crescian Bronze sword shrank. It came loose, forming to Felix's grip just as he thrust it forward. Skyslain's Riposte shifted again, draining Felix of nearly all of his Mana to burst into a hundred-foot-long spike of Crescian Bronze, a spike that stabbed straight through the Grandmaster, pinning him to the wall.

Under the ever-falling water.

He struggled, raged, but the blade would not be budged. A cataclysmic explosion of fire tore apart the water, revealing a screaming Kel'lyv to Felix for a single moment...before the explosion burst inward, and with a concussive boom, the entire wall collapsed into the water.

You Have Killed Sig'nyh Kel'lyv, Grandmaster of the Desert's Fire!
XP Earned!
Challenge Complete!

Other notifications tried to crowd him, but Felix wavered, his Body, Mind, and Spirit all suddenly and utterly exhausted. He'd foisted off the rest that was required when Tempering, burned through it with the energy of a Primordial and Willpower enough to contend with tiny gods, but now Felix tottered. The toll was due.

Pit...? Beef...?

He fell into the water, and was dragged into chill darkness.

CHAPTER NINETY-NINE

Evolution Complete!
Congratulations, Guardian Beast!

First Evolution: Primordial Stormwing!
You Gain:
+200 AGL
+100 DEX
+100 END
+75 INT
+50 WIL
Skills Have Changed!
Do You Wish To Review?

No! Pit let out a joyous screech and emerged from Felix's Spirit in a blaze of glory, ready to reveal his newer, sleeker self to his Companion...only to find himself among the dark, freezing waters of an impossibility. Water was everywhere, a blue so dark it was almost black, lit only dimly by the strobe lights of a tempest.

What happened? he sent, keeping his beak closed against the press of liquid. The water churned violently around him, and he twisted, unable to find purchase. *Felix—? Felix!*

Beside the tenku, Felix floated utterly limp. Eyes closed, mouth open, and for a horrifying second, Pit believed him dead. Their bond burned bright, however, and Felix's Health was more than half full. It was dropping fast, though, and Pit could see why as he toggled through Felix's notifications.

Status Condition: Drowning (Severe)

Felix! he sent again, hoping it'd knock him awake, but the man's Mind didn't even spark in awareness. So instead, Pit paddled forward, sweeping his wings for speed, and grasped his friend by the shoulders with his foreclaws. With every ounce of newly evolved Strength, Pit swam for the surface.

Mighty currents tore at his feathers and fur, tumbling them up and over and around in dizzying circles. Pit flapped his wings, his sleeker Body crackling with lightning summoned up from his Evolved core. Each foot up, however, he lost as those tidal forces had their way. The waters roiled, and the lightning along Pit's limbs was answered in kind in the far distance.

A storm ruled outside the waters, and he was lucky it tingled across Pit's newfound senses, because the relentless push and pull of the currents would have utterly ruined his orientation. He hadn't the bulk anymore to throw against the waves, having chosen his Evolution in part to reduce his size and amplify his speed. Agility, however, was of little help in escaping the brutal clutch of freezing waters. And he was running out of breath, despite his newfound Endurance.

Distantly, the chime of notifications slipped through Pit's bond, echoes of Felix's own. Words that made little sense filtered across Pit's eyes.

Challenge Complete!
Congratulations!
You Have Extended Your Authority, Autarch!

You Are Now Lord Of Ahkestria And The Scorched Expanse!
ERROR!
Scorched Expanse Has Undergone Fundamental Changes!
Territory Reshaped...
Recalculating...

Pit shook his head, dismissing the errant messages. They were distractions, and he was fighting to hold his breath. Pit's lungs burned, aching to suck in life-giving air, foolishly ignorant that the water around them had none to offer. He kicked and flapped and clawed upward, carrying Felix's body. A body that had been reduced to less than a quarter of his Health.

Wingblade!

ERROR!
Wingblade (U) Has Evolved Into Dawn's Advent (Epic)!

Dawn's Advent!
A glowing arc of brilliant white-green and golden energy burst from his wings, forcing itself outward and kicking Pit's body backward through

another rushing flow. Pit squawked in alarm, losing his breath in a wild stream of bubbles before snapping his beak shut again.

The dim light above them faded, turning the depths truly black. Pit jerked his head back just in time to see a writhing, twisting shape diving through the water, its many, many legs thrashing in upsetting undulations. And it was coming right for him.

Dawn's Advent!

Another arc shot out, burning through the water and leaving a trail of boiling bubbles behind. The creature moved fluidly around the attack, and the next three that Pit unleashed. The thing was *fast*, offering Pit little chance before it spun around him completely and snapped its hold close. Jaws as large as Pit's entire body grabbed them both, twisting and rolling Pit and Felix as the thing accelerated.

To the surface.

———

Beef fought against the waves, piloting his shitty, ramshackle boat. Chitin Construction had been handy in forming it, but the last time he'd built anything, it had been made out of little plastic bricks. It had required him several dozen tries to make it strong enough and buoyant enough to keep his considerable bulk afloat, and with the tumultuous waves threatening to capsize him, it took all his concentration to stay balanced atop the narrow craft. Thunder crashed above, the winds howled, and the water heaved like a rollercoaster—but he held on.

Nevertheless, when Hallow exploded from the depths with his friends in her grip, Beef wasn't ready for the sheer mass of them all. Hallow could float in the water—quite well, in fact—but she deposited Felix and Pit in a sodden heap at the base of his craft, and the boat immediately began to flip.

Chitin Construction!

Mana surged from him, manifesting more hard, lightweight material along the hull and sides to counteract their weight. After compensating for his own, Beef had something of a handle on it, it just ate up a *lot* of his reserves. When he was done, the ship was ten feet wide with long, pontoon-like skis on either side for stability. He'd seen that in a movie once, but was pleasantly surprised it had worked.

Chitin Construction is level 48!

"Be careful!" he yelled at the nightmarish Hallow. The Multipede wriggled its antennae at him in what he supposed was an apology before swimming around his expanded boat. "I'm sorry. She could've hurt you...Pit?"

A creature had stood up from the tangle of limbs, and it looked like the Chimera but only in the vaguest sense. Gone was the hulking brute twice as large as any horse, and in its place was a sleek-looking creature with lithe muscles and powerful, if soaked, wings. A black, hawk-like head tilted at him, and were it not for the luminous golden eyes, Beef would have thought another Chimera had stolen Pit's barding.

"You're...different," he said. "So much smaller. You look like a race-horse or something."

"Stop gawking and help!" Pit spat, before his own golden eyes grew large. Beef started back.

"You can talk?" Beef stared at the Chimera stupidly, his Mind stuttering at what just happened.

Pit, however, screeched. "Help him!"

Beef rushed forward, stepping carefully. With Pit out of the way, the Minotaur realized that Felix looked different now, too. Before, he'd basically looked like a muscular Human, but now he was closer to Beef's height but far more slender, with wide shoulders and a face that looked just a touch...off. Dark, midnight scales decorated his arms, coating his hands and feet. Most concernedly, however, was that he didn't seem to be breathing at all.

"Oh god, uh, uh, I can do CPR," Beef said. He'd seen it done a few times on the internet. He laced his two hands together and pressed them against chest, just below his sternum, and pressed without even budging Felix's body. "Are you kidding me?" He leaned forward, putting all his weight behind the chest compressions...and still nothing.

Frustrated, Beef stood back up and reached out a hand. A newly made great maul formed in his grip, sizzling with blackened-green Mana vapor, and he lifted the weapon straight up into the air before slamming it down as hard as he could atop Felix's chest. The blow was so strong that Felix slammed down into the deck, cracking it deeply before rebound back up in the air. Hallow coiled about them tighter, lifting the boat above the water level as Beef brought the hammer down again and again.

And again.

Until, with an awful gurgling noise, Felix spat up a geyser of water from his lungs. Coughs wracked his entire body, curling him up on himself as more and more liquid dislodged from his lungs. His eyes remained closed throughout the entire process, but he was breathing.

"His Status Condition vanished, but his Health isn't budging," Pit said. He crouched closer and nudged Felix.

"Is he gonna be okay?" Beef asked. "Hallow?"

The Multipede leaned over the craft as the waves continued to roll across them all. She opened a set of her lower legs and gently deposited two odd swords on the deck of his ship. One was a giant tooth, and the other was curved like a weird fishing hook. Interestingly enough, another weapon was in Felix's right hand, clutched so tightly his knuckles were white. A dagger made of bronze, with a purple gemstone set in the pommel. The Spirit spoke. "It is unclear. His Body is unlike any I have experienced, and his organs are...they are strange. His heart beats too fast for a Human to survive, and his skin is burning hot. I do not think it is a fever, however."

"Is he Tempering?" Beef asked. Last time he remembered getting anything close to sick was when he was forming his new Body.

"Yes," Pit confirmed. "He is an Adept now. Or will be."

Beef whistled. The guy's Strength was something else, and he could hardly imagine how he had changed, if his Body had transformed like it had. "We need to find Naos—fuck, I mean Isla. If she can't heal Felix, no one can. Hallow, can you do the thing?"

"Of course. Please hold tightly," the Spirit said before uncoiling from around them and moving toward the back of his impromptu craft. At the same time, Beef repaired the cracked hull with Chitin Construction, at least keeping the thing from immediately sinking.

"Definitely hold on, Pit," Beef said, only to see Pit already laying across Felix's body and snugging himself up against the sides of that boat. "Ah. Good. Go for it, Hallow."

Hallow undulated at the rear, her immense strength and grace driving them forward. With a near-silent whoosh of displaced water, his ship shot forward.

———

"Be prepared to move them," Isla declared, bustling between cracked tables. Her poultices were running low, but a number of the Yttin had offered to make more, and so she focused on applying the Chant. Her voice rose, echoing a glorious design she'd once dreamed of as a young girl, one that called to mind the halcyon days of youth when nothing hurt and everything lasted forever. The poultices answered in kind, glowing with a vibrant potency that immediately seeped into dire wounds.

Sixteen patients began to heal all at once, and Isla sagged from the effort. She looked at her assistant and gestured at the patients. "Get them to the resting cots."

"Of course," Vess said, manifesting her spears to quickly and efficiently cart each patient into the nearby recovery tent.

The storm had cleared, but more voices were coming closer. Among them were cries of pain and unintelligible pleas. Isla was exhausted, but she knew her role in these sort of fights. Drawing herself ramrod straight, the Chanter lifted a hand and beckoned. "Bring them in."

———

A shield of chains dropped from above, turning aside a spear of light. Hrask and Klagg gasped in relief as they met the eyes of a slender Human woman.

"Don't worry. I got this," she said, just as the shield exploded into individual strands of chain.

The Paladins shouted in alarm, light and fire blooming, but clearly none expected the chains to wrap themselves around every one of their limbs. A second shield appeared, doing the same, until all four Paladins were trussed up tighter than a pig to market.

"Tooth and Claw," the woman uttered, and the chain in her hands came to a malicious life. It coiled and lifted like a serpent, the spikes and blades along its length gleaming with silvery Mana. "You ain't escaping again."

The Goblins ran, not bothering to look back or even at one another. Anything to get away from the cruel Paladins and the vicious, cold death from that small, slender woman.

———

Atar twitched on his cot, his Aspects awash in visceral pain. Jagged marks ran across his Body, slashes of affliction that bled a dull gray through his flesh. People bustled by, sheltering from the devastating storm and hurrying to see the healer, but Alister refused to move. Dim as his consciousness was, Atar could sense him, a worried presence at his side with rags and potions at the ready. He wanted nothing more than to embrace his partner, to tell him he was fine, but exhaustion gripped Atar like a vise. He could no more walk upon the moons than sit up.

How am I still alive? The unanswered thought tore through him, again and again. Atar remembered little after summoning his Astrum Revelation, and what there was had a layer of fog over it all, as if it had happened to someone else. *What did I do?*

Alister stood up and started talking to someone in white and gold robes, and the two of them stepped a distance away from his cot. Fiammetta. She spoke of Paladins attacking again, and Atar felt rage kindle in his chest. He wanted to speak, to reach out, but he couldn't. Instead, a small white flame kindled in his vision, and not for the first time. Atar couldn't bear to move, but he could focus on it as it swirled atop his sternum.

Go away, he insisted.

you could destroy them all, it said. **paladins deserve nothing less.**

Atar gritted his teeth. *Go away!*

burning is very, very easy. please. i can show you so many things, Atar V'as.

With a titanic effort of Will, Atar shoved the flame, turning it to a burst of flickering sparks. It vanished, and true exhaustion claimed him again.

———

In the distance, perhaps a half mile away, a towering edifice loomed. Crystals gleaming orange and green-gold and white-green filled the majority of the structure, one that Beef recognized with a gasp.

"That's...that's Ahkestria," he said. "Look! The layers are visible! The crystalline sections have been blasted apart in hundreds of places..."

The storm chose that moment to break, releasing the captured glow of the midday sun. Beams rained down, sparkling across the choppy waves and absolutely glimmering atop the jewel-like City of Embers. However, that was the only pleasant thing he could make out; the city looked devastated, and huge plumes of smoke rose up from the highest layer to stain the otherwise unblemished sky.

"The Paladins attacked," Pit said from his side. His head, now closer to Beef's chest-height, tilted to the side. "But did they win?"

"Only one way to find out," Beef said and urged Hallow to push them a bit faster. The journey was putting deep cracks in the boat almost faster than he could repair them, but he was sure they could make it. "Sooner we get to the city, the sooner we find Isla. You're sure he's fine?"

"He is stable. Fine...I don't know about fine," Pit admitted. "It's been two hours, but still he sleeps and—"

A bright notification edged in gold filigree slammed into all of their vision at the exact same moment. It rang like a bell and did not stop.

Territory-Wide Announcement!
By Right Of Challenge And Fair Combat, Felix Nevarre,
Autarch of Nagast Has Claimed Authority!
All Hail, Autarch Felix Nevarre!

"Huh," Beef said, a little numb. Then his eyes bulged. "He...he's the king of Ahkestria?"

"Just get us to the city," Pit instructed before he curled up against Felix's side. The Chimera had sounded tired and angry at the same time.

Beef glanced at Felix, his arms now half-covered in those dark scales. The change was spreading.

"Hail the hero, hail the savior of the Deep, hail the hand that wakes," said a deep, melodic voice.

The Minotaur spun, maul manifesting in his grip, and found himself looking up in shock. Another, much larger ship had come upon them without a whisper of sound or warning. It looked to be made of bone and was complete with sails and everything. Standing among the craft were a number of tall, wide-chested folks wearing strange, somewhat moth-eaten garments, and upon their back twitched a number of long weapons.

There were at least twenty of them spaced evenly around the deck of their ship, but the one in the lead spread his arms as his eyes flashed a brilliant, glowing copper. "Hail the guardian, hail the Beast Who Walks The Skies, hail the claws that protect."

Pit perked up at that, looking between Felix and the newcomers. "Klz-ix?" the Chimera asked.

The leader nodded and smiled broadly, an expression of unrestrained glee. "We have come to welcome you both to the End. May we all survive the Blackened Skies."

"Uh, right," Beef said, before whispering at Pit. "They're friendly?"

Pit shrugged, then nodded. "Maybe."

"Come! Come! We have room for you all, even your hidden friend," this Klzix said, pointing at the dark water where Hallow had vanished. "We shall take you to Ahkestria!"

"We are just fine here, I think," Beef said, patting the uneven side rail he'd slapped together. Unfortunately, his chitin boat could take no more. The cracks that had spread throughout its shape finally gave way, and water started flooding the deck. Pit squawked and dragged Felix's body away from the encroaching liquid. "Oh. Shit. I guess...I guess we could bum a ride."

"As it must be," Klzix said and bared a wide, crocodile smile of sharp, white teeth. "Let us walk to the End together."

ABOUT NICOLI GONNELLA

Nicoli Gonnella spent his formative years atop a mountain, breathing deep of the world energy and expelling impurities from his soul. Also he went to school and stuff. He always wrote but now he's abandoned everything to do it full time. Readers give him strength, spirit bomb style, and there's no telling how strong he will become. This isn't even his final form.

He lives with his wife, two kids, and a corgi named Cornelius.

Connect with Nicoli Gonnella:
NicoliGonnella.com
Discord.gg/sqQvJQhY8F
Patreon.com/Necariin
RoyalRoad.com/fiction/30321/Unbound
Facebook.com/Nicoli-Gonnella-Author-347428719693359

ABOUT MOUNTAINDALE PRESS

Dakota and Danielle Krout, a husband and wife team, strive to create as well as publish excellent fantasy and science fiction novels. Self-publishing *The Divine Dungeon: Dungeon Born* in 2016 transformed their careers from Dakota's military and programming background and Danielle's Ph.D. in pharmacology to President and CEO, respectively, of a small press. Their goal is to share their success with other authors and provide captivating fiction to readers with the purpose of solidifying Mountaindale Press as the place 'Where Fantasy Transforms Reality.'

Connect with Mountaindale Press:
MountaindalePress.com
Facebook.com/MountaindalePress
Twitter.com/_Mountaindale
Instagram.com/MountaindalePress

MOUNTAINDALE PRESS TITLES
GameLit and LitRPG

The Completionist Chronicles,
The Divine Dungeon,
Full Murderhobo, and
Year of the Sword by Dakota Krout

Metier Apocalypse by Frank G. Albelo

Arcana Unlocked by Gregory Blackburn

A Touch of Power by Jay Boyce

Red Mage and
Farming Livia by Xander Boyce

Space Seasons by Dawn Chapman

Ether Collapse and
Ether Flows by Ryan DeBruyn

Dr. Druid by Maxwell Farmer

Bloodgames by Christian J. Gilliland

Unbound by Nicoli Gonnella

Threads of Fate by Michael Head

Lion's Lineage by Rohan Hublikar and Dakota Krout

Wolfman Warlock by James Hunter and Dakota Krout

Axe Druid,
Mephisto's Magic Online, and
High Table Hijinks by Christopher Johns

Skeleton in Space by Andries Louws

Dragon Core Chronicles by Lars Machmüller

Chronicles of Ethan by John L. Monk

Pixel Dust and
Necrotic Apocalypse by David Petrie

Viceroy's Pride by Cale Plamann

Henchman by Carl Stubblefield

Artorian's Archives by Dennis Vanderkerken and Dakota Krout

Vaudevillain by Alex Wolf